LORD JIM

AN AUTHORITATIVE TEXT
BACKGROUNDS
SOURCES
ESSAYS IN CRITICISM

⇛ NORTON CRITICAL EDITIONS ⇚

JOSEPH CONRAD

LORD JIM

AN AUTHORITATIVE TEXT
BACKGROUNDS
SOURCES Edited by *Norman Sherry*
ESSAYS IN CRITICISM

≫ ≪

Edited by

THOMAS MOSER

STANFORD UNIVERSITY

W · W · NORTON & COMPANY · INC · *New York*

Acknowledgement

The text of *Lord Jim* is reprinted with permission of the Trustees of
the Estate of Joseph Conrad, Doubleday and Co., Inc.,
and J. M. Dent and Sons Ltd.

COPYRIGHT © 1968 BY W. W. NORTON & COMPANY, INC.

Library of Congress Catalog Card No. 65–22077

PRINTED IN THE UNITED STATES OF AMERICA

2 3 4 5 6 7 8 9 0

Contents

Preface

Lord Jim has the rare distinction of being a masterpiece in two separate and apparently conflicting genres. It is at once an exotic adventure story of the Eastern seas in the popular tradition of Kipling and Stevenson and a complexly wrought "art novel" in the tradition of Flaubert and James.

Strong, taciturn men face the terrors of the sea; European idealists try to bring peace and civilization to the benighted heathen; a handsome young Englishman who funks it during a disaster at sea attempts to redeem himself on a remote tropical isle and briefly finds happiness in the arms of a beautiful Eurasian girl. Melodrama abounds: murder, suicide, treachery, intrigue, cowardice, bravery, romantic love, heroic sacrifice, and even a pitched battle with pirates.

At the same time *Lord Jim* explores moral and psychological questions with a subtlety and complexity unknown in novels of adventure. Moreover, it refuses finally to find clear-cut answers to difficult questions. Conrad accomplishes this with such an array of narrative techniques as had never before been employed in the English novel. Even Henry James had tended to avoid a personal narrator like Marlow and had used subordinate narrators ("reflectors") much less profusely. And no previous novelist had ever so dislocated chronological narration or so skillfully played upon the reader's responses. Partly at least this masterpiece of literary impressionism is about how hard, how ultimately impossible, it is ever to tell precisely the way events happened and, especially, what one's attitude toward those events ought properly to be.

This edition of *Lord Jim* tries to pay adequate attention to its twin aspects—romantic Eastern subject-matter and sophisticated literary method. The material in the footnotes, glossary and gazetteer, and Norman Sherry's section on sources represents the culmination of decades of work by many Conrad scholars. In a letter to the *Times Literary Supplement* in 1923 (the year before Conrad's death), Sir Frank Swettenham identified the *Patna* story with that of the *Jeddah*, abandoned in the Indian Ocean by her white officers in August 1880. Both John D. Gordan in *Joseph Conrad: The Making of a Novelist* (1940) and Jocelyn Baines in *Joseph Conrad: A Critical Biography* (1960) refer to and enlarge upon Swettenham's letter although they do not identify the particular officer who probably inspired the creation of Jim. Augustine Podmore Williams, first mate of the *Jeddah* and later employed by a ship-chandler in Singapore, has come to be widely known as the precursor of Jim through two recent books: Miss Jerry Allen's *The Sea Years of Joseph Conrad* (1965) and Norman Sherry's *Conrad's Eastern World* (1966). These books also describe in considerable detail the people and geography of Berau, the town in Eastern Borneo that probably suggested Patusan in the novel. But

Mr. Gordan actually visited the neighborhood of Berau in 1939, and he discusses the town itself in his book. Mr. Baines mentions Berau and provides a photograph. Again, although Miss Allen and Mr. Sherry explain in detail how Conrad's reading about Rajah James Brooke and about various travelers to the East Indies enriches *Lord Jim*, Mr. Gordan and Miss Florence Clemens [1] had long before opened up the subject.

Besides presenting a detailed account of the Eastern background, Mr. Sherry's special contribution, elaborated on in this Norton Critical Edition, is to suggest how intimate was Conrad's personal relationship to the story of the *Jeddah*. Conrad must first have read in London newspapers this unexampled tale of cowardly British maritime officers just after he passed his second mate's examination and just before he got his first berth as a ship's officer. Conrad would actually have seen the *Jeddah* in harbor on his first trip to Singapore in 1883, after experiencing as second mate the disastrous burning and sinking of the *Palestine*. The *Jeddah* was referred to in Singapore newspapers during Conrad's second stay in Singapore in 1885. Most striking of all, in late 1887 Conrad found himself precisely in the shoes of A. P. Williams: he served as first mate of the little steamer *Vidar* just as Williams had done in 1882. Sensing from the novels and from his life Conrad's strong tendency to sympathetic identification, we can readily imagine how he must have felt while acting in the same capacity as Williams, the first mate who had jumped from the *Jeddah*. It is unlikely that Williams' failure was far from Conrad's consciousness a few months later when, on the occasion of his first and only command, of the barque *Otago*, Conrad underwent the most desperate and exhausting test of his maritime career: being the captain of a ship becalmed for days with virtually her entire crew disabled by malaria, an experience memorably evoked in his late novel *The Shadow-Line* (1917).

If *Lord Jim* differs from ordinary adventure stories in the actuality of its materials and the author's personal involvement with those materials, the novel differs even more in the artistry of its composition. Yet *Lord Jim* was written under amazing circumstances: Conrad thought he was writing a short story of twenty to forty thousand words and instead wrote a novel of well over one hundred thousand words. More incredible still, he wrote much of that novel while it was coming out in *Blackwood's Magazine*, and therefore he could not rewrite the early portions to fit in with later developments. Not surprisingly, he heavily revised the periodical version for book publication, as Mr. Gordan long ago pointed out.

By enabling the reader to trace the process of composition, this edition tries to provide materials for a deeper understanding of Conrad's art: a transcription of the earliest manuscript fragment, "Tuan Jim: A Sketch"; a history of the novel's composition as revealed in Conrad's correspondence, especially with his publishers; and most importantly, textual notes giving every substantive change likely to have been made by Conrad after the periodical version.

Joseph Conrad would, I fear, have had, at best, mixed feelings about this edition. No doubt he would not have liked the footnotes, gazetteer, and

1. "Conrad's Favorite Bedside Book: Wallace's *Malay Archipelago*," *South* *Atlantic Quarterly*, XXXVIII (1939), 305–315.

source material, which would seem to identify the people and places and, to his mind, to deny the fictional creation. In a late, famous letter (July 14, 1923), Conrad berated Richard Curle for such identification: he begged Curle to free him of "that infernal tail of ships." [2] Of course, Conrad is right; *Lord Jim* is *his* created world, not the "real" world. (Although the *Jeddah* crossed the Bay of Bengal, the *Patna* crossed only "the bay.") For us to read *Lord Jim* as thinly disguised actuality rather than an heroic achievement of the creative imagination is simply to miss the whole book.

Nevertheless, the factual material in this edition has, I hope, two useful functions. Partly it provides information likely to have been known to a reader in 1900 but lost to us because of the evolution of place names and because of our remoteness from nineteenth-century British maritime life. Partly, too, the factual information should remind us forcibly that this impressionist novelist—disciple of James, mentor of Ford Madox Ford, friend of Galsworthy, Wells, and Gide—had been first of all a seaman, really a seaman, and for twenty years. He thus brought to his fiction an authenticity almost unprecedented in the history of the novel.

Because this edition is genuinely a labor of love, because it tries to be the best that could possibly be done,[3] it no doubt contains many and gross errors unrecognized by its complacent editor. These are not, however, the fault of the very numerous students, colleagues, and Conradians who gave unstinting assistance. My greatest debt is to three Stanford students: Betty Moore slaved on the notes and glossary; Robin Roney Hayeck and Peter Verdurman collated endlessly. I am grateful, too, to certain other students: Jane Curry, the Kenneth Lincolns, Robin Macdonald, and David Thorburn. Three colleagues read through the entire edition: Albert J. Guerard was particularly helpful on things Conradian and French; Claude M. Simpson, Jr., on sticky editorial matters; Ian P. Watt on things Conradian, maritime, and Eastern. When asked, these other Conradians gave good advice: John D. Gordan, Bruce Harkness, Kenneth B. Newall, Norman Sherry, and Donald C. Yelton. I wish also to thank Bruce Haywood of Kenyon College and Clive E. Driver of the Philip H. and A.S.W. Rosenbach Foundation. Finally, John Benedict, the Norton editor, provided patient support far more complete than I would ever have attributed to a mere "commercial" publisher.

THOMAS C. MOSER

---

2. *Conrad to a Friend,* edited by Richard Curle, Garden City, N.Y., 1928, p. 147.
3. Unfortunately, I could not collate the Rosenbach manuscript of *Lord Jim* for the textual notes. Scholars may consult but may not copy it.

The Text of

Lord Jim

A TALE

It is certain my conviction gains infinitely,
the moment another soul will believe in it.

NOVALIS.

Author's Note[1]

When this novel first appeared in book form a notion got about that I had been bolted away with. Some reviewers maintained that the work starting as a short story had got beyond the writer's control. One or two discovered internal evidence of the fact, which seemed to amuse them. They pointed out the limitations of the narrative form. They argued that no man could have been expected to talk all that time, and other men to listen so long. It was not, they said, very credible.

After thinking it over for something like sixteen years, I am not so sure about that. Men have been known, both in the tropics and in the temperate zone, to sit up half the night "swapping yarns." This, however, is but one yarn, yet with interruptions affording some measure of relief; and in regard to the listeners' endurance, the postulate must be accepted that the story *was* interesting. It is the necessary preliminary assumption. If I hadn't believed that it *was* interesting I could never have begun to write it. As to the mere physical possibility, we all know that some speeches in Parliament have taken nearer six than three hours in delivery; whereas all that part of the book which is Marlow's narrative can be read through aloud, I should say, in less than three hours. Besides—though I have kept strictly all such insignificant details out of the tale—we may presume that there must have been refreshments on that night, a glass of mineral water of some sort to help the narrator on.

But, seriously, the truth of the matter is, that my first thought was of a short story, concerned only with the pilgrim ship episode; nothing more. And that was a legitimate conception. After writing a few pages, however, I became for some reason discontented and I laid them aside for a time. I didn't take them out of the drawer till the late Mr. William Blackwood suggested I should give something again to his magazine.

It was only then that I perceived that the pilgrim ship episode was a good starting-point for a free and wandering tale; that it was an event, too, which could conceivably colour the whole "sentiment of existence" in a simple and sensitive character. But all these preliminary moods and stirrings of spirit were rather obscure at the time, and they do not appear clearer to me now after the lapse of so many years.

The few pages I had laid aside were not without their weight in the choice of subject. But the whole was rewritten deliberately. When I sat down to it I knew it would be a long book, though I

1. The epigraph comes from the *Fragmente* of Friedrich von Hardenberg (1772–1801), the German poet and theorist of romanticism whose pseudonym was Novalis.

didn't foresee that it would spread itself over thirteen numbers of "Maga."

I have been asked at times whether this was not the book of mine I liked best. I am a great foe to favouritism in public life, in private life, and even in the delicate relationship of an author to his works. As a matter of principle I will have no favourites; but I don't go so far as to feel grieved and annoyed by the preference some people give to my *Lord Jim*. I won't even say that I "fail to understand . . ." No! But once I had occasion to be puzzled and surprised.

A friend of mine returning from Italy had talked with a lady there who did not like the book. I regretted that, of course, but what surprised me was the ground of her dislike. "You know," she said, "it is all so morbid."

The pronouncement gave me food for an hour's anxious thought. Finally I arrived at the conclusion that, making due allowances for the subject itself being rather foreign to women's normal sensibilities, the lady could not have been an Italian. I wonder whether she was European at all? In any case, no Latin temperament would have perceived anything morbid in the acute consciousness of lost honour. Such a consciousness may be wrong, or it may be right, or it may be condemned as artificial; and, perhaps, my Jim is not a type of wide commonness. But I can safely assure my readers that he is not the product of coldly perverted thinking. He is not a figure of Northern Mists either. One sunny morning in the commonplace surroundings of an Eastern roadstead, I saw his form pass by—appealing—significant—under a cloud—perfectly silent. Which is as it should be. It was for me, with all the sympathy of which I was capable, to seek fit words for his meaning. He was "one of us." [1a]

J. C.

June 1917.

[1a.] After Adam ate the forbidden fruit, God said to the angels: "Behold the man is become as one of us, to know good and evil." Genesis 3:22.

Lord Jim

Chapter One

He was an inch, perhaps two, under six feet, powerfully built, and he advanced straight at you with a slight stoop of the shoulders, head forward, and a fixed from-under stare which made you think of a charging bull. His voice was deep, loud, and his manner displayed a kind of dogged self-assertion which had nothing aggressive in it. It seemed a necessity, and it was directed apparently as much at himself as at anybody else. He was spotlessly neat, apparelled in immaculate white from shoes to hat, and in the various Eastern ports where he got his living as ship-chandler's water-clerk he was very popular.

A water-clerk need not pass an examination in anything under the sun, but he must have Ability in the abstract and demonstrate it practically. His work consists in racing under sail, steam, or oars against other water-clerks for any ship about to anchor, greeting her captain cheerily, forcing upon him a card—the business card of the ship-chandler—and on his first visit on shore piloting him firmly but without ostentation to a vast, cavern-like shop which is full of things that are eaten and drunk on board ship; where you can get everything to make her seaworthy and beautiful, from a set of chain-hooks for her cable to a book of gold-leaf for the carvings of her stern; and where her commander is received like a brother by a ship-chandler he has never seen before. There is a cool parlour, easy-chairs, bottles, cigars, writing implements, a copy of harbour regulations, and a warmth of welcome that melts the salt of a three months' passage out of a seaman's heart. The connection thus begun is kept up, as long as the ship remains in harbour, by the daily visits of the water-clerk. To the captain he is faithful like a friend and attentive like a son, with the patience of Job, the unselfish devotion of a woman, and the jollity of a boon companion. Later on the bill is sent in. It is a beautiful and humane occupation. Therefore good water-clerks are scarce. When a water-clerk who possesses Ability in the abstract has also the advantage of having been brought up to the sea, he is worth to his employer a lot of money and some humouring. Jim had always good wages and as much humouring as would have bought the fidelity of a fiend. Nevertheless, with black ingratitude he would throw up the job suddenly and depart. To his employers the reasons he gave were obviously inadequate. They said "Confounded fool!" as soon as his back was turned. This was their criticism on his exquisite sensibility.

To the white men in the waterside business and to the captains of ships he was just Jim[2]—nothing more. He had, of course, another name, but he was anxious that it should not be pronounced. His incognito, which had as many holes as a sieve, was not meant to hide a personality but a fact. When the fact broke through the incognito he would leave suddenly the seaport where he happened to be at the time and go to another—generally farther east. He kept to seaports because he was a seaman in exile from the sea, and had Ability in the abstract, which is good for no other work but that of a water-clerk. He retreated in good order towards the rising sun, and the fact followed him casually but inevitably. Thus in the course of years he was known successively in Bombay, in Calcutta, in Rangoon, in Penang, in Batavia—and in each of these halting-places was just Jim the water-clerk. Afterwards, when his keen perception of the Intolerable drove him away for good from seaports and white men, even into the virgin forest, the Malays of the jungle village, where he had elected to conceal his deplorable faculty, added a word to the monosyllable of his incognito. They called him Tuan Jim: as one might say—Lord Jim.

Originally he came from a parsonage. Many commanders of fine merchant-ships come from these abodes of piety and peace. Jim's father possessed such certain knowledge of the Unknowable as made for the righteousness of people in cottages without disturbing the ease of mind of those whom an unerring Providence enables to live in mansions. The little church on a hill had the mossy greyness of a rock seen through a ragged screen of leaves. It had stood there for centuries, but the trees around probably remembered the laying of the first stone. Below, the red front of the rectory gleamed with a warm tint in the midst of grass-plots, flower-beds, and fir-trees, with an orchard at the back, a paved stable-yard to the left, and the sloping glass of greenhouses tacked along a wall of bricks. The living had belonged to the family for generations; but Jim was one of five sons, and when after a course of light holiday literature his vocation for the sea had declared itself, he was sent at once to a "training-ship for officers of the mercantile marine."[3]

He learned there a little trigonometry and how to cross top-gallant yards. He was generally liked. He had the third place in navigation and pulled stroke in the first cutter. Having a steady head with an

---

2. Probably comes from James Lingard; the early life resembles that of A. P. Williams. See "Sources."
3. Probably the *Conway*, referred to explicitly in "Youth" (1898). A Mercantile Marine School Ship for boys who intended to make the merchant service their profession, she was anchored in the estuary of the River Mersey at Liverpool, accepting her first cadets in 1859. (See John Masefield, *The Conway*, London, 1933.)

excellent physique, he was very smart aloft. His station was in the fore-top, and often from there he looked down, with the contempt of a man destined to shine in the midst of dangers, at the peaceful multitude of roofs cut in two by the brown tide of the stream, while scattered on the outskirts of the surrounding plain the factory chimneys rose perpendicular against a grimy sky, each slender like a pencil, and belching out smoke like a volcano. He could see the big ships departing, the broad-beamed ferries constantly on the move, the little boats floating far below his feet, with the hazy splendour of the sea in the distance, and the hope of a stirring life in the world of adventure.

On the lower deck in the babel of two hundred voices he would forget himself, and beforehand live in his mind the sea-life of light literature. He saw himself saving people from sinking ships, cutting away masts in a hurricane, swimming through a surf with a line; or as a lonely castaway, barefooted and half naked, walking on uncovered reefs in search of shell-fish to stave off starvation. He confronted savages on tropical shores, quelled mutinies on the high seas, and in a small boat upon the ocean kept up the hearts of despairing men —always an example of devotion to duty, and as unflinching as a hero in a book.

"Something's up. Come along."

He leaped to his feet. The boys were streaming up the ladders. Above could be heard a great scurrying about and shouting, and when he got through the hatchway he stood still—as if confounded.

It was the dusk of a winter's day. The gale had freshened since noon, stopping the traffic on the river, and now blew with the strength of a hurricane in fitful bursts that boomed like salvos of great guns firing over the ocean. The rain slanted in sheets that flicked and subsided, and between whiles Jim had threatening glimpses of the tumbling tide, the small craft jumbled and tossing along the shore, the motionless buildings in the driving mist, the broad ferry-boats pitching ponderously at anchor, the vast landing-stages heaving up and down and smothered in sprays. The next gust seemed to blow all this away. The air was full of flying water. There was a fierce purpose in the gale, a furious earnestness in the screech of the wind, in the brutal tumult of earth and sky, that seemed directed at him, and made him hold his breath in awe. He stood still. It seemed to him he was whirled around.

He was jostled. "Man the cutter!" Boys rushed past him. A coaster running in for shelter had crashed through a schooner at anchor, and one of the ship's instructors had seen the accident. A mob of boys clambered on the rails, clustered round the davits. "Collision. Just ahead of us. Mr. Symons saw it." A push made him stagger against the mizzen-mast, and he caught hold of a rope. The old training-ship chained to her moorings quivered all over, bowing

gently head to wind, and with her scanty rigging humming in a deep
bass the breathless song of her youth at sea. "Lower away!" He saw
the boat, manned, drop swiftly below the rail, and rushed after her.
He heard a splash. "Let go; clear the falls!" He leaned over. The
river alongside seethed in frothy streaks. The cutter could be seen
in the falling darkness under the spell of tide and wind, that for a
moment held her bound, and tossing abreast of the ship. A yelling
voice in her reached him faintly: "Keep stroke, you young whelps, if
you want to save anybody! Keep stroke!" And suddenly she lifted
high her bow, and, leaping with raised oars over a wave, broke the
spell cast upon her by the wind and tide.

Jim felt his shoulder gripped firmly. "Too late, youngster." The
captain of the ship laid a restraining hand on that boy, who seemed
on the point of leaping overboard, and Jim looked up with the pain
of conscious defeat in his eyes. The captain smiled sympathetically.
"Better luck next time. This will teach you to be smart."

A shrill cheer greeted the cutter. She came dancing back half full
of water, and with two exhausted men washing about on her bottom
boards. The tumult and the menace of wind and sea now appeared
very contemptible to Jim, increasing the regret of his awe at their
inefficient menace. Now he knew what to think of it. It seemed to
him he cared nothing for the gale. He could affront greater perils. He
would do so—better than anybody. Not a particle of fear was left.
Nevertheless, he brooded apart that evening while the bowman of
the cutter—a boy with a face like a girl's and big grey eyes—was the
hero of the lower deck. Eager questioners crowded round him. He
narrated: "I just saw his head bobbing, and I dashed my boat-hook
in the water. It caught in his breeches and I nearly went overboard,
as I thought I would, only old Symons let go the tiller and grabbed
my legs—the boat nearly swamped. Old Symons is a fine old chap. I
don't mind a bit him being grumpy with us. He swore at me all the
time he held my leg, but that was only his way of telling me to stick
to the boat-hook. Old Symons is awfully excitable—isn't he? No—
not the little fair chap—the other, the big one with a beard. When
we pulled him in he groaned, 'Oh, my leg! oh, my leg!' and turned
up his eyes. Fancy such a big chap fainting like a girl! Would any of
you fellows faint for a jab with a boat-hook?—I wouldn't. It went
into his leg so far." He showed the boat-hook, which he had carried
below for the purpose, and produced a sensation. "No, silly! It was
not his flesh that held him—his breeches did. Lots of blood, of
course."

Jim thought it a pitiful display of vanity. The gale had ministered
to a heroism as spurious as its own pretence of terror. He felt angry
with the brutal tumult of earth and sky for taking him unawares and
checking unfairly a generous readiness for narrow escapes. Otherwise he was rather glad he had not gone into the cutter, since a

lower achievement had served the turn. He had enlarged his knowledge more than those who had done the work. When all men flinched, then—he felt sure—he alone would know how to deal with the spurious menace of wind and seas. He knew what to think of it. Seen dispassionately, it seemed contemptible. He could detect no trace of emotion in himself, and the final effect of a staggering event was that, unnoticed and apart from the noisy crowd of boys, he exulted with fresh certitude in his avidity for adventure, and in a sense of many-sided courage.

Chapter Two

After two years of training he went to sea, and, entering the regions so well known to his imagination, found them strangely barren of adventure. He made many voyages. He knew the magic monotony of existence between sky and water: he had to bear the criticism of men, the exactions of the sea, and the prosaic severity of the daily task that gives bread—but whose only reward is in the perfect love of the work. This reward eluded him. Yet he could not go back, because there is nothing more enticing, disenchanting, and enslaving than the life at sea. Besides, his prospects were good. He was gentlemanly, steady, tractable, with a thorough knowledge of his duties; and in time, when yet very young, he became chief mate of a fine ship, without ever having been tested by those events of the sea that show in the light of day the inner worth of a man, the edge of his temper, and the fibre of his stuff; that reveal the quality of his resistance and the secret truth of his pretences, not only to others but also to himself.

Only once in all that time he had again the glimpse of the earnestness in the anger of the sea. That truth is not so often made apparent as people might think. There are many shades in the danger of adventures and gales, and it is only now and then that there appears on the face of facts a sinister violence of intention—that indefinable something which forces it upon the mind and the heart of a man, that this complication of accidents or these elemental furies are coming at him with a purpose of malice, with a strength beyond control, with an unbridled cruelty that means to tear out of him his hope and his fear, the pain of his fatigue and his longing for rest: which means to smash, to destroy, to annihilate all he has seen, known, loved, enjoyed, or hated; all that is priceless and necessary—the sunshine, the memories, the future; which means to sweep the whole precious world utterly away from his sight by the simple and appalling act of taking his life.

Jim, disabled by a falling spar at the beginning of a week of which his Scottish captain used to say afterwards, "Man! it's a pairfect meeracle to me how she lived through it!" spent many days stretched on his back, dazed, battered, hopeless, and tormented as if at the bottom of an abyss of unrest. He did not care what the end would be, and in his lucid moments overvalued his indifference. The danger, when not seen, has the imperfect vagueness of human thought. The fear grows shadowy; and Imagination, the enemy of men, the father of all terrors, unstimulated, sinks to rest in the dullness of exhausted emotion. Jim saw nothing but the disorder of his tossed cabin. He lay there battened down in the midst of a small devastation, and felt secretly glad he had not to go on deck. But now and again an uncontrollable rush of anguish would grip him bodily, make him gasp and writhe under the blankets, and then the unintelligent brutality of an existence liable to the agony of such sensations filled him with a despairing desire to escape at any cost. Then fine weather returned, and he thought no more about it.

His lameness, however, persisted, and when the ship arrived at an Eastern port [4] he had to go to the hospital. His recovery was slow, and he was left behind.

There were only two other patients in the white men's ward: the purser of a gunboat, who had broken his leg falling down a hatchway; and a kind of railway contractor from a neighbouring province, afflicted by some mysterious tropical disease, who held the doctor for an ass, and indulged in secret debaucheries of patent medicine which his Tamil servant used to smuggle in with unwearied devotion. They told each other the story of their lives, played cards a little, or, yawning and in pyjamas, lounged through the day in easy-chairs without saying a word. The hospital stood on a hill, and a gentle breeze entering through the windows, always flung wide open, brought into the bare room the softness of the sky, the languor of the earth, the bewitching breath of the Eastern waters. There were perfumes in it, suggestions of infinite repose, the gift of endless dreams. Jim looked every day over the thickets of gardens, beyond the roofs of the town, over the fronds of palms growing on the shore, at that roadstead which is a thoroughfare to the East,—at the roadstead dotted by garlanded islets, lighted by festal sunshine, its ships like toys, its brilliant activity resembling a holiday pageant, with the eternal serenity of the Eastern sky overhead and the smiling peace of the Eastern seas possessing the space as far as the horizon.

Directly he could walk without a stick, he descended into the town to look for some opportunity to get home. Nothing offered just then, and, while waiting, he associated naturally with the men of his calling in the port. These were of two kinds. Some, very few and seen there but seldom, led mysterious lives, had preserved an undefaced energy with the temper of buccaneers and the eyes of dreamers. They appeared to live in a crazy maze of plans, hopes, dangers, en-

4. Singapore. See "Sources."

terprises, ahead of civilisation, in the dark places of the sea; and their death was the only event of their fantastic existence that seemed to have a reasonable certitude of achievement. The majority were men who, like himself, thrown there by some accident, had remained as officers of country ships. They had now a horror of the home service, with its harder conditions, severer view of duty, and the hazard of stormy oceans. They were attuned to the eternal peace of Eastern sky and sea. They loved short passages, good deck-chairs, large native crews, and the distinction of being white. They shuddered at the thought of hard work, and led precariously easy lives, always on the verge of dismissal, always on the verge of engagement, serving Chinamen, Arabs, half-castes—would have served the devil himself had he made it easy enough. They talked everlastingly of turns of luck: how So-and-so got charge of a boat on the coast of China—a soft thing; how this one had an easy billet in Japan somewhere, and that one was doing well in the Siamese navy; and in all they said—in their actions, in their looks, in their persons—could be detected the soft spot, the place of decay, the determination to lounge safely through existence.

To Jim that gossiping crowd, viewed as seamen, seemed at first more unsubstantial than so many shadows. But at length he found a fascination in the sight of those men, in their appearance of doing so well on such a small allowance of danger and toil. In time, beside the original disdain there grew up slowly another sentiment; and suddenly, giving up the idea of going home, he took a berth as chief mate of the *Patna*.[5]

The *Patna* was a local steamer as old as the hills, lean like a greyhound, and eaten up with rust worse than a condemned water-tank. She was owned by a Chinaman, chartered by an Arab, and commanded by a sort of renegade New South Wales German, very anxious to curse publicly his native country, but who, apparently on the strength of Bismarck's victorious policy, brutalised all those he was not afraid of, and wore a "blood-and-iron"[6] air, combined with a purple nose and a red moustache. After she had been painted outside and whitewashed inside, eight hundred pilgrims (more or less) were driven on board of her as she lay with steam up alongside a wooden jetty.

They streamed aboard over three gangways, they streamed in urged by faith and the hope of paradise, they streamed in with a continuous tramp and shuffle of bare feet, without a word, a murmur, or

5. Name of a city in eastern India, a common brand of rice, and a ship known to Conrad. (Typically, Conrad uses the names of real ships, e.g., the *Pelion*, the *Wolverine*, and the *Sephora*, and of real ship lines, e.g., The Blue Star and The Dale.) The actual pilgrim-ship was called the *Jeddah* after Mecca's port on the Red Sea. See "Sources."

6. Epithet applied to Otto von Bismarck, first chancellor of the German empire, who said in a speech to the Prussian Diet in 1862: "Not by speechifying and counting majorities are the great questions of the time to be solved . . . but by iron and blood."

a look back; and when clear of confining rails spread on all sides over the deck, flowed forward and aft, overflowed down the yawning hatchways, filled the inner recesses of the ship—like water filling a cistern, like water flowing into crevices and crannies, like water rising silently even with the rim. Eight hundred men and women with faith and hopes, with affections and memories, they had collected there, coming from north and south and from the outskirts of the East, after treading the jungle paths, descending the rivers, coasting in praus along the shallows, crossing in small canoes from island to island, passing through suffering, meeting strange sights, beset by strange fears, upheld by one desire. They came from solitary huts in the wilderness, from populous campongs, from villages by the sea. At the call of an idea they had left their forests, their clearings, the protection of their rulers, their prosperity, their poverty, the sur- roundings of their youth and the graves of their fathers. They came covered with dust, with sweat, with grime, with rags—the strong men at the head of family parties, the lean old men pressing forward without hope of return; young boys with fearless eyes glancing curiously, shy little girls with tumbled long hair; the timid women muffled up and clasping to their breasts, wrapped in loose ends of soiled head-cloths, their sleeping babies, the unconscious pilgrims of an exacting belief.

"Look at dese cattle," said the German skipper to his new chief mate.

An Arab, the leader of that pious voyage, came last. He walked slowly aboard, handsome and grave in his white gown and large turban. A string of servants followed, loaded with his luggage; the *Patna* cast off and backed away from the wharf.

She was headed between two small islets, crossed obliquely the anchoring-ground of sailing-ships, swung through half a circle in the shadow of a hill, then ranged close to a ledge of foaming reefs. The Arab, standing up aft, recited aloud the prayer of travellers by sea. He invoked the favour of the Most High upon that journey, implored His blessing on men's toil and on the secret purposes of their hearts; the steamer pounded in the dusk the calm water of the Strait; [7] and far astern of the pilgrim ship a screw-pile lighthouse, planted by un- believers on a treacherous shoal, seemed to wink at her its eye of flame, as if in derision of her errand of faith.

She cleared the Strait, crossed the bay,[8] continued on her way through the "One-degree" passage.[9] She held on straight for the Red Sea under a serene sky, under a sky scorching and unclouded, en- veloped in a fulgor of sunshine that killed all thought, oppressed

7. The Strait of Malacca, a channel 500 miles long between the southern Malay peninsula and the island of Sumatra.
8. The Bay of Bengal.

9. The One and a Half Degree Channel; a seaway of the Indian Ocean, roughly along 1° 30′ N, between Haddummati Atoll and Suvadiva Atoll of the Maldive Islands; about 55 miles wide.

the heart, withered all impulses of strength and energy. And under the sinister splendour of that sky the sea, blue and profound, remained still, without a stir, without a ripple, without a wrinkle— viscous, stagnant, dead. The *Patna*, with a slight hiss, passed over that plain, luminous and smooth, unrolled a black ribbon of smoke across the sky, left behind her on the water a white ribbon of foam that vanished at once, like the phantom of a track drawn upon a lifeless sea by the phantom of a steamer.

Every morning the sun, as if keeping pace in his revolutions with the progress of the pilgrimage, emerged with a silent burst of light exactly at the same distance astern of the ship, caught up with her at noon, pouring the concentrated fire of his rays on the pious purposes of the men, glided past on his descent, and sank mysteriously into the sea evening after evening, preserving the same distance ahead of her advancing bows. The five whites on board lived amidships, isolated from the human cargo. The awnings covered the deck with a white roof from stem to stern, and a faint hum, a low murmur of sad voices, alone revealed the presence of a crowd of people upon the great blaze of the ocean. Such were the days, still, hot, heavy, disappearing one by one into the past, as if falling into an abyss for ever open in the wake of the ship; and the ship, lonely under a wisp of smoke, held on her steadfast way black and smouldering in a luminous immensity, as if scorched by a flame flicked at her from a heaven without pity.

The nights descended on her like a benediction.

Chapter Three

A marvellous stillness pervaded the world, and the stars, together with the serenity of their rays, seemed to shed upon the earth the assurance of everlasting security. The young moon recurved, and, shining low in the west, was like a slender shaving thrown up from a bar of gold, and the Arabian Sea, smooth and cool to the eye like a sheet of ice, extended its perfect level to the perfect circle of a dark horizon. The propeller turned without a check, as though its beat had been part of the scheme of a safe universe; and on each side of the *Patna* two deep folds of water, permanent and sombre on the unwrinkled shimmer, enclosed within their straight and diverging ridges a few white swirls of foam bursting in a low hiss, a few wavelets, a few ripples, a few undulations that, left behind, agitated the surface of the sea for an instant after the passage of the ship, subsided splashing gently, calmed down at last into the circular stillness of water and sky with the black speck of the moving hull remaining everlastingly in its centre.

Jim on the bridge was penetrated by the great certitude of unbounded safety and peace that could be read on the silent aspect of nature like the certitude of fostering love upon the placid tenderness of a mother's face. Below the roof of awnings, surrendered to the wisdom of white men and to their courage, trusting the power of their unbelief and the iron shell of their fire-ship, the pilgrims of an exacting faith slept on mats, on blankets, on bare planks, on every deck, in all the dark corners, wrapped in dyed cloths, muffled in soiled rags, with their heads resting on small bundles, with their faces pressed to bent forearms: the men, the women, the children; the old with the young, the decrepit with the lusty—all equal before sleep, death's brother.

A draught of air, fanned from forward by the speed of the ship, passed steadily through the long gloom between the high bulwarks, swept over the rows of prone bodies; a few dim flames in globe-lamps were hung short here and there under the ridge-poles, and in the blurred circles of light thrown down and trembling slightly to the unceasing vibration of the ship appeared a chin upturned, two closed eyelids, a dark hand with silver rings, a meagre limb draped in a torn covering, a head bent back, a naked foot, a throat bared and stretched as if offering itself to the knife. The well-to-do had made for their families shelters with heavy boxes and dusty mats; the poor reposed side by side with all they had on earth tied up in a rag under their heads; the lone old men slept, with drawn-up legs, upon their prayer-carpets, with their hands over their ears and one elbow on each side of the face; a father, his shoulders up and his knees under his forehead, dozed dejectedly by a boy who slept on his back with tousled hair and one arm commandingly extended; a woman covered from head to foot, like a corpse, with a piece of white sheeting, had a naked child in the hollow of each arm; the Arab's belongings, piled right aft, made a heavy mound of broken outlines, with a cargo-lamp swung above, and a great confusion of vague forms behind: gleams of paunchy brass pots, the foot-rest of a deck-chair, blades of spears, the straight scabbard of an old sword leaning against a heap of pillows, the spout of a tin coffee-pot. The patent log on the taffrail periodically rang a single tinkling stroke for every mile traversed on an errand of faith. Above the mass of sleepers a faint and patient sigh at times floated, the exhalation of a troubled dream; and short metallic clangs bursting out suddenly in the depths of the ship, the harsh scrape of a shovel, the violent slam of a furnace-door, exploded brutally, as if the men handling the mysterious things below had their breasts full of fierce anger: while the slim, high hull of the steamer went on evenly ahead, without a sway of her bare masts, cleaving continuously the great calm of the waters under the inaccessible serenity of the sky.

Jim paced athwart, and his footsteps in the vast silence were loud to his own ears, as if echoed by the watchful stars: his eyes, roaming about the line of the horizon, seemed to gaze hungrily into the unattainable, and did not see the shadow of the coming event. The only shadow on the sea was the shadow of the black smoke pouring heavily from the funnel its immense streamer, whose end was constantly dissolving in the air. Two Malays, silent and almost motionless, steered, one on each side of the wheel, whose brass rim shone fragmentarily in the oval of light thrown out by the binnacle. Now and then a hand, with black fingers alternately letting go and catching hold of revolving spokes, appeared in the illumined part; the links of wheel-chains ground heavily in the grooves of the barrel. Jim would glance at the compass, would glance around the unattainable horizon, would stretch himself till his joints cracked with a leisurely twist of the body, in the very excess of well-being; and, as if made audacious by the invincible aspect of the peace, he felt he cared for nothing that could happen to him to the end of his days. From time to time he glanced idly at a chart pegged out with four drawing-pins on a low three-legged table abaft the steering-gear case. The sheet of paper portraying the depths of the sea presented a shiny surface under the light of a bull's-eye lamp lashed to a stanchion, a surface as level and smooth as the glimmering surface of the waters. Parallel rulers with a pair of dividers reposed on it; the ship's position at last noon was marked with a small black cross, and the straight pencil-line drawn firmly as far as Perim figured the course of the ship—the path of souls towards the holy place, the promise of salvation, the reward of eternal life—while the pencil with its sharp end touching the Somali coast lay round and still like a naked ship's spar floating in the pool of a sheltered dock. "How steady she goes!" thought Jim with wonder, with something like gratitude for this high peace of sea and sky. At such times his thoughts would be full of valorous deeds: he loved these dreams and the success of his imaginary achievements. They were the best parts of life, its secret truth, its hidden reality. They had a gorgeous virility, the charm of vagueness, they passed before him with an heroic tread; they carried his soul away with them and made it drunk with the divine philtre of an unbounded confidence in itself. There was nothing he could not face. He was so pleased with the idea that he smiled, keeping perfunctorily his eyes ahead; and when he happened to glance back he saw the white streak of the wake drawn as straight by the ship's keel upon the sea as the black line drawn by the pencil upon the chart.

The ash-buckets racketed, clanking up and down the stroke-hold ventilators, and this tin-pot clatter warned him the end of his watch was near. He sighed with content, with regret as well at having to part from that serenity which fostered the adventurous freedom of his thoughts. He was a little sleepy too, and felt a pleasurable lan-

guor running through every limb as though all the blood in his body
had turned to warm milk. His skipper had come up noiselessly, in
pyjamas and with his sleeping-jacket flung wide open. Red of face,
only half awake, the left eye partly closed, the right staring stupid
and glassy, he hung his big head over the chart and scratched his
ribs sleepily. There was something obscene in the sight of his naked
flesh. His bared breast glistened soft and greasy as though he had
sweated out his fat in his sleep. He pronounced a professional remark in a voice harsh and dead, resembling the rasping sound of a
wood-file on the edge of a plank; the fold of his double chin hung
like a bag triced up close under the hinge of his jaw. Jim started, and
his answer was full of deference; but the odious and fleshy figure, as
though seen for the first time in a revealing moment, fixed itself in
his memory for ever as the incarnation of everything vile and base
that lurks in the world we love: in our own hearts we trust for our
salvation in the men that surround us, in the sights that fill our eyes,
in the sounds that fill our ears, and in the air that fills our lungs.

The thin gold shaving of the moon floating slowly downwards
had lost itself on the darkened surface of the waters, and the eternity
beyond the sky seemed to come down nearer to the earth, with the
augmented glitter of the stars, with the more profound sombreness
in the lustre of the half-transparent dome covering the flat disc of an
opaque sea. The ship moved so smoothly that her onward motion
was imperceptible to the senses of men, as though she had been a
crowded planet speeding through the dark spaces of ether behind
the swarm of suns, in the appalling and calm solitudes awaiting the
breath of future creations. "Hot is no name for it down below," said
a voice.

Jim smiled without looking round. The skipper presented an unmoved breadth of back: it was the renegade's trick to appear point-
edly unaware of your existence unless it suited his purpose to turn at
you with a devouring glare before he let loose a torrent of foamy,
abusive jargon that came like a gush from a sewer. Now he emitted
only a sulky grunt; the second engineer at the head of the bridge-
ladder, kneading with damp palms a dirty sweat-rag, unabashed,
continued the tale of his complaints. The sailors had a good time of
it up here, and what was the use of them in the world he would be
blowed if he could see. The poor devils of engineers had to get the
ship along anyhow, and they could very well do the rest too; by gosh
they—"Shut up," growled the German stolidly. "Oh yes! Shut
up—and when anything goes wrong you fly to us, don't you?" went
on the other. He was more than half cooked, he expected; but anyway, now, he did not mind how much he sinned, because these
last three days he had passed through a fine course of training for the
place where the bad boys go when they die—b'gosh, he had—besides

being made jolly well deaf by the blasted racket below. The durned, compound, surface-condensing, rotten scrap-heap rattled and banged down there like an old deck-winch, only more so; and what made him risk his life every night and day that God made amongst the refuse of a breaking-up yard flying round at fifty-seven revolutions, was more than *he* could tell. He must have been born reckless, b'gosh. He . . . "Where did you get drink?" inquired the German, very savage, but motionless in the light of the binnacle, like a clumsy effigy of a man cut out of a block of fat. Jim went on smiling at the retreating horizon; his heart was full of generous impulses, and his thought was contemplating his own superiority. "Drink!" repeated the engineer, with amiable scorn: he was hanging on with both hands to the rail, a shadowy figure with flexible legs. "Not from you, captain. You're far too mean, b'gosh. You would let a good man die sooner than give him a drop of schnapps. That's what you Germans call economy. Penny wise, pound foolish." He became sentimental. The chief had given him a four-finger nip about ten o'clock—"only one, s'elp me!"—good old chief; but as to getting the old fraud out of his bunk—a five-ton crane couldn't do it. Not it. Not to-night anyhow. He was sleeping sweetly like a little child, with a bottle of prime brandy under his pillow. From the thick throat of the commander of the *Patna* came a low rumble, on which the sound of the word *schwein* fluttered high and low like a capricious feather in a faint stir of air. He and the chief engineer had been cronies for a good few years—serving the same jovial, crafty old Chinaman, with horn-rimmed goggles and strings of red silk plaited into the venerable grey hairs of his pigtail. The quay-side opinion in the *Patna*'s home-port was that these two in the way of brazen peculation "had done together pretty well everything you can think of." Outwardly they were badly matched: one dull-eyed, malevolent, and of soft, fleshy curves; the other lean, all hollows, with a head long and bony like the head of an old horse, with sunken cheeks, with sunken temples, with an indifferent glazed glance of sunken eyes. He had been stranded out East somewhere—in Canton, in Shanghai, or perhaps in Yokohama; he probably did not care to remember himself the exact locality, nor yet the cause of his shipwreck. He had been, in mercy to his youth, kicked quietly out of his ship twenty years ago or more, and it might have been so much worse for him that the memory of the episode had in it hardly a trace of misfortune. Then, steam navigation expanding in these seas and men of his craft being scarce at first, he had "got on" after a sort. He was eager to let strangers know in a dismal mumble that he was "an old stager out here." When he moved, a skeleton seemed to sway loose in his clothes; his walk was mere wandering, and he was given to wander thus around the engine-room skylight, smoking, without relish, doctored tobacco in a brass bowl at the end of a cherrywood stem four feet long, with the imbecile gravity of a thinker evolving a system of philosophy from the hazy glimpse of a truth. He was usually anything but free with his private store of liquor; but on that night he had departed from his principles, so that his second, a weak-headed child of Wapping, what with the unexpectedness of the treat and the strength of the stuff, had become very happy, cheeky, and talkative. The fury of the New South Wales German was extreme; he puffed like an exhaust-pipe, and Jim, faintly amused by the scene, was impatient for the time when he could get below: the last ten minutes of the watch were irritating like a gun that hangs fire; those men did not belong to the world of heroic adventure; they weren't bad chaps though. Even the skipper himself . . . His gorge rose at the mass of panting flesh from which issued gurgling mutters, a cloudy trickle of filthy expressions; but he was too pleasurably languid to dislike actively this or any other thing. The quality of these men did not matter; he rubbed shoulders with them, but they could not touch him; he shared the air they breathed, but he was different. . . . Would the skipper go for the engineer? . . . The life was easy and he was too sure of himself—too sure of himself to . . . The line dividing his meditation from a surreptitious doze on his feet was thinner than a thread in a spider's web.

The second engineer was coming by easy transitions to the consideration of his finances and of his courage.

"Who's drunk? I? No, no, captain! That won't do. You ought to know by this time the chief ain't free-hearted enough to make a sparrow drunk, b'gosh. I've never been the worse for liquor in my life; the stuff ain't made yet that would make *me* drunk. I could drink liquid fire against your whisky peg for peg, b'gosh, and keep as cool as a cucumber. If I thought I was drunk I would jump overboard —do away with myself, b'gosh. I would! Straight! And I won't go off the bridge. Where do you expect me to take the air on a night like this, eh? On deck amongst that vermin down there? Likely— ain't it! And I am not afraid of anything you can do."

The German lifted two heavy fists to heaven and shook them a little without a word.

"I don't know what fear is," pursued the engineer, with the enthusiasm of sincere conviction. "I am not afraid of doing all the bloomin' work in this rotten hooker, b'gosh! And a jolly good thing for you that there are some of us about the world that aren't afraid of their lives, or where would you be—you and this old thing here with her plates like brown paper—brown paper, s'elp me? It's all very fine for you—you get a power of pieces out of her one way and another; but what about me—what do I get? A measly hundred and fifty dollars a month and find yourself. I wish to ask you respectfully

—respectfully, mind—who wouldn't chuck a dratted job like this? 'Tain't safe, s'elp me, it ain't! Only I am one of them fearless fellows. . . ."

He let go the rail and made ample gestures as if demonstrating in the air the shape and extent of his valour; his thin voice darted in prolonged squeaks upon the sea, he tiptoed back and forth for the better emphasis of utterance, and suddenly pitched down head first as though he had been clubbed from behind. He said "Damn!" as he tumbled; an instant of silence followed upon his screeching: Jim and the skipper staggered forward by common accord, and, catching themselves up, stood very stiff and still gazing, amazed, at the undisturbed level of the sea. Then they looked upwards at the stars.

What had happened? The wheezy thump of the engines went on. Had the earth been checked in her course? They could not understand; and suddenly the calm sea, the sky without a cloud, appeared formidably insecure in their immobility, as if poised on the brow of yawning destruction. The engineer rebounded vertically full length and collapsed again into a vague heap. This heap said "What's that?" in the muffled accents of profound grief. A faint noise as of thunder, of thunder infinitely remote, less than a sound, hardly more than a vibration, passed slowly, and the ship quivered in response, as if the thunder had growled deep down in the water. The eyes of the two Malays at the wheel glittered towards the white men, but their dark hands remained closed on the spokes. The sharp hull driving on its way seemed to rise a few inches in succession through its whole length, as though it had become pliable, and settled down again rigidly to its work of cleaving the smooth surface of the sea. Its quivering stopped, and the faint noise of thunder ceased all at once, as though the ship had steamed across a narrow belt of vibrating water and of humming air.

Chapter Four

A month or so afterwards, when Jim, in answer to pointed questions, tried to tell honestly the truth of this experience, he said, speaking of the ship: "She went over whatever it was as easy as a snake crawling over a stick." The illustration was good: the questions were aiming at facts, and the official inquiry was being held in the police court of an Eastern port. He stood elevated in the witness-box, with burning cheeks in a cool, lofty room: the big framework of punkahs moved gently to and fro high above his head, and from below many eyes were looking at him out of dark faces, out of white faces, out of red faces, out of faces attentive, spellbound, as if all these people sitting in orderly rows upon narrow benches had been enslaved by the fascination of his voice. It was very loud, it rang startling in his own ears, it was the only sound audible in the world, for the terribly distinct questions that extorted his answers seemed to shape themselves in anguish and pain within his breast—came to him poignant and silent like the terrible questioning of one's conscience. Outside the court the sun blazed—within was the wind of great punkahs that made you shiver, the shame that made you burn, the attentive eyes whose glance stabbed. The face of the presiding magistrate, clean-shaved and impassible, looked at him deadly pale between the red faces of the two nautical assessors.[1] The light of a broad window under the ceiling fell from above on the heads and shoulders of the three men, and they were fiercely distinct in the half-light of the big court-room where the audience seemed composed of staring shadows. They wanted facts. Facts! They demanded facts from him, as if facts could explain anything!

"After you had concluded you had collided with something floating awash, say a water-logged wreck, you were ordered by your captain to go forward and ascertain if there was any damage done. Did you think it likely from the force of the blow?" asked the assessor sitting to the left. He had a thin horseshoe beard, salient cheekbones, and with both elbows on the desk clasped his rugged hands before his face, looking at Jim with thoughtful blue eyes; the other, a heavy, scornful man, thrown back in his seat, his left arm extended full length, drummed delicately with his finger-tips on a blotting-pad: in the middle the magistrate upright in the roomy arm-chair, his head inclined slightly on the shoulder, had his arms crossed on his breast and a few flowers in a glass vase by the side of his inkstand.

"I did not," said Jim. "I was told to call no one, and to make no noise for fear of creating a panic. I thought the precaution reasonable. I took one of the lamps that were hung under the awnings and went forward. After opening the forepeak hatch I heard splashing in there. I lowered then the lamp the whole drift of its lanyard, and saw that the forepeak was more than half full of water already. I knew then there must be a big hole below the water-line." He paused.

"Yes," said the big assessor, with a dreamy smile at the blotting-pad; his fingers played incessantly, touching the paper without noise.

"I did not think of danger just then. I might have been a little startled: all this happened in such a quiet way and so very suddenly. I knew there was no other bulkhead in the ship but the collision bulkhead separating the forepeak from the forehold. I went back to tell the captain. I came upon the second engineer getting up at

---

1. Appointed to assist a judge or magistrate; especially persons with professional knowledge of the subject to be decided (as legal assessors, nautical assessors, etc.).

the foot of the bridge-ladder: he seemed dazed, and told me he thought his left arm was broken; he had slipped on the top step when getting down while I was forward. He exclaimed, 'My God! That rotten bulkhead'll give way in a minute, and the damned thing will go down under us like a lump of lead.' He pushed me away with his right arm and ran before me up the ladder, shouting as he climbed. His left arm hung by his side. I followed up in time to see the captain rush at him and knock him down flat on his back. He did not strike him again: he stood bending over him and speaking angrily but quite low. I fancy he was asking him why the devil he didn't go and stop the engines, instead of making a row about it on deck. I heard him say, 'Get up! Run! fly!' He swore also. The engineer slid down the starboard ladder and bolted round the sky-light to the engine-room companion which was on the port-side. He moaned as he ran. . . ."

He spoke slowly; he remembered swiftly and with extreme vividness; he could have reproduced like an echo the moaning of the engineer for the better information of these men who wanted facts. After his first feeling of revolt he had come round to the view that only a meticulous precision of statement would bring out the true horror behind the appalling face of things. The facts those men were so eager to know had been visible, tangible, open to the senses, occupying their place in space and time, requiring for their existence a fourteen-hundred-ton steamer and twenty-seven minutes by the watch; they made a whole that had features, shades of expression, a complicated aspect that could be remembered by the eye, and something else besides, something invisible, a directing spirit of perdition that dwelt within, like a malevolent soul in a detestable body. He was anxious to make this clear. This had not been a common affair, everything in it had been of the utmost importance, and fortunately he remembered everything. He wanted to go on talking for truth's sake, perhaps for his own sake also; and while his utterance was deliberate, his mind positively flew round and round the serried circle of facts that had surged up all about him to cut him off from the rest of his kind: it was like a creature that, finding itself imprisoned within an enclosure of high stakes, dashes round and round, distracted in the night, trying to find a weak spot, a crevice, a place to scale, some opening through which it may squeeze itself and escape. This awful activity of mind made him hesitate at times in his speech. . . .

"The captain kept on moving here and there on the bridge; he seemed calm enough, only he stumbled several times; and once as I stood speaking to him he walked right into me as though he had been stone-blind. He made no definite answer to what I had to tell. He mumbled to himself; all I heard of it were a few words that sounded like 'confounded steam!' and 'infernal steam!'—something about steam. I thought . . ."

He was becoming irrelevant; a question to the point cut short his speech, like a pang of pain, and he felt extremely discouraged and weary. He was coming to that, he was coming to that—and now, checked brutally, he had to answer by yes or no. He answered truthfully by a curt, "Yes, I did"; and fair of face, big of frame, with young, gloomy eyes, he held his shoulders upright above the box while his soul writhed within him. He was made to answer another question so much to the point and so useless, then waited again. His mouth was tastelessly dry, as though he had been eating dust, then salt and bitter as after a drink of sea-water. He wiped his damp forehead, passed his tongue over parched lips, felt a shiver run down his back. The big assessor had dropped his eyelids, and drummed on without a sound, careless and mournful; the eyes of the other above the sunburnt, clasped fingers seemed to glow with kindliness; the magistrate had swayed forward; his pale face hovered near the flowers, and then dropping sideways over the arm of his chair, he rested his temple in the palm of his hand. The wind of the punkahs eddied down on the heads, on the dark-faced natives wound about in voluminous draperies, on the Europeans sitting together very hot and in drill [2] suits that seemed to fit them as close as their skins, and holding their round pith hats on their knees; while gliding along the walls the court peons, buttoned tight in long white coats, flitted rapidly to and fro, running on bare toes, red-sashed, red turban on head, as noiseless as ghosts, and on the alert like so many retrievers.

Jim's eyes, wandering in the intervals of his answers, rested upon a white man who sat apart from the others, with his face worn and clouded, but with quiet eyes that glanced straight, interested, and clear. Jim answered another question and was tempted to cry out, "What's the good of this? What's the good?" He tapped with his foot slightly, bit his lip, and looked away over the heads. He met the eyes of the white man. The glance directed at him was not the fascinated stare of the others. It was an act of intelligent volition. Jim between two questions forgot himself so far as to find leisure for a thought. This fellow—ran the thought—looks at me as though he could see somebody or something past my shoulder. He had come across that man before—in the street perhaps. He was positive he had never spoken to him. For days, for many days, he had spoken to no one, but had held silent, incoherent, and endless converse with himself, like a prisoner alone in his cell or like a wayfarer lost in a wilderness. At present he was answering questions that did not matter though they had a purpose, but he doubted whether he would ever again speak out as long as he lived. The sound of his own

2. A strong durable cotton fabric, having a diagonal weave.

truthful statements confirmed his deliberate opinion that speech was of no use to him any longer. That man there seemed to be aware of his hopeless difficulty. Jim looked at him, then turned away resolutely, as after a final parting.

And later on, many times, in distant parts of the world, Marlow [3] showed himself willing to remember Jim, to remember him at length, in detail and audibly.

Perhaps it would be after dinner, on a verandah draped in motionless foliage and crowned with flowers, in the deep dusk speckled by fiery cigar-ends. The elongated bulk of each cane-chair harboured a silent listener. Now and then a small red glow would move abruptly, and expanding light up the fingers of a languid hand, part of a face in profound repose, or flash a crimson gleam into a pair of pensive eyes overshadowed by a fragment of an unruffled forehead; and with the very first word uttered Marlow's body, extended at rest in the seat, would become very still, as though his spirit had winged its way back into the lapse of time and were speaking through his lips from the past.

Chapter Five

"Oh yes. I attended the inquiry," he would say, "and to this day I haven't left off wondering why I went. I am willing to believe each of us has a guardian angel, if you fellows will concede to me that each of us has a familiar devil as well. I want you to own up, because I don't like to feel exceptional in any way, and I know I have him—the devil, I mean. I haven't seen him, of course, but I go upon circumstantial evidence. He is there right enough, and, being malicious, he lets me in for that kind of thing. What kind of thing, you ask? Why, the inquiry thing, the yellow-dog thing—you wouldn't think a mangy, native tyke would be allowed to trip up people in the verandah of a magistrate's court, would you?—the kind of thing that by devious, unexpected, truly diabolical ways causes me to run up against men with soft spots, with hard spots, with hidden plague spots, by Jove! and loosens their tongues at the sight of me for their infernal confidences; as though, forsooth, I had no confidences to make to myself, as though—God help me!—I didn't have enough confidential information about myself to harrow my own soul till the end of my appointed time. And what I have done to be thus favoured I want to know. I declare I am as full of my own concerns as the next man, and I have as much memory as the average pilgrim in this valley, so you see I am not particularly fit to be a receptacle of confessions. Then why? Can't tell—unless it be to

3. The narrator also of Conrad's "Youth" (1898), "Heart of Darkness" (1899), and *Chance* (1913).

make time pass away after dinner. Charley, my dear chap, your dinner was extremely good, and in consequence these men here look upon a quiet rubber as a tumultuous occupation. They wallow in your good chairs and think to themselves, 'Hang exertion. Let that Marlow talk.'

"Talk! So be it. And it's easy enough to talk of Master Jim, after a good spread, two hundred feet above the sea-level, with a box of decent cigars handy, on a blessed evening of freshness and starlight that would make the best of us forget we are only on sufferance here and got to pick our way in cross lights, watching every precious minute and every irremediable step, trusting we shall manage yet to go out decently in the end—but not so sure of it after all—and with dashed little help to expect from those we touch elbows with right and left. Of course there are men here and there to whom the whole of life is like an after-dinner hour with a cigar; easy, pleasant, empty, perhaps enlivened by some fable of strife to be forgotten before the end is told—before the end is told—even if there happens to be any end to it.

"My eyes met his for the first time at that inquiry. You must know that everybody connected in any way with the sea was there, because the affair had been notorious for days, ever since that mysterious cable message came from Aden to start us all cackling. I say mysterious, because it was so in a sense though it contained a naked fact, about as naked and ugly as a fact can well be. The whole waterside talked of nothing else. First thing in the morning as I was dressing in my state-room, I would hear through the bulkhead my Parsee Dubash jabbering about the *Patna* with the steward, while he drank a cup of tea, by favour, in the pantry. No sooner on shore I would meet some acquaintance, and the first remark would be, 'Did you ever hear of anything to beat this?' and according to his kind the man would smile cynically, or look sad, or let out a swear or two. Complete strangers would accost each other familiarly, just for the sake of easing their minds on the subject: every confounded loafer in the town came in for a harvest of drinks over this affair: you heard of it in the harbour office, at every ship-broker's, at your agent's, from whites, from natives, from half-castes, from the very boatmen squatting half naked on the stone steps as you went up—by Jove! There was some indignation, not a few jokes, and no end of discussions as to what had become of them, you know. This went on for a couple of weeks or more, and the opinion that whatever was mysterious in this affair would turn out to be tragic as well, began to prevail, when one fine morning, as I was standing in the shade by the steps of the harbour office, I perceived four men walking towards me along the quay. I wondered for a while where that queer lot had sprung from, and suddenly, I may say, I shouted to myself,

'Here they are!'

"There they were, sure enough, three of them as large as life, and one much larger of girth than any living man has a right to be, just landed with a good breakfast inside of them from an outwardbound Dale Line steamer that had come in about an hour after sunrise. There could be no mistake; I spotted the jolly skipper of the *Patna* at the first glance: the fattest man in the whole blessed tropical belt clear round that good old earth of ours. Moreover, nine months or so before, I had come across him in Samarang. His steamer was loading in the Roads, and he was abusing the tyrannical institutions of the German empire, and soaking himself in beer all day long and day after day in De Jongh's back shop, till De Jongh, who charged a guilder for every bottle without as much as the quiver of an eyelid, would beckon me aside, and, with his little leathery face all puckered up, declare confidentially, 'Business is business, but this man, captain, he make me very sick. Tfui!'

"I was looking at him from the shade. He was hurrying on a little in advance, and the sunlight beating on him brought out his bulk in a startling way. He made me think of a trained baby elephant walking on hind legs. He was extravagantly gorgeous too—got up in a soiled sleeping-suit, bright green and deep orange vertical stripes, with a pair of ragged straw slippers on his bare feet, and somebody's cast-off pith hat, very dirty and two sizes too small for him, tied up with a manilla rope-yarn on the top of his big head. You understand a man like that hasn't the ghost of a chance when it comes to borrowing clothes. Very well. On he came in hot haste, without a look right or left, passed within three feet of me, and in the innocence of his heart went on pelting upstairs in the harbour office to make his deposition, or report, or whatever you like to call it.

"It appears he addressed himself in the first instance to the principal shipping-master. Archie Ruthvel had just come in, and, as his story goes, was about to begin his arduous day by giving a dressing-down to his chief clerk. Some of you might have known him—an obliging little Portuguese half-caste with a miserably skinny neck, and always on the hop to get something from the ship-masters in the way of eatables—a piece of salt pork, a bag of biscuits, a few potatoes, or what not. One voyage, I recollect, I tipped him a live sheep out of the remnant of my sea-stock: not that I wanted him to do anything for me—he couldn't, you know—but because his child-like belief in the sacred right to perquisites quite touched my heart. It was so strong as to be almost beautiful. The race—the two races rather—and the climate . . . However, never mind. I know where I have a friend for life.

"Well, Ruthvel says he was giving him a severe lecture—on official mortality, I suppose—when he heard a kind of subdued commotion at his back, and turning his head, he saw, in his own words, something round and enormous, resembling a sixteen-hundred-weight sugar-hogshead wrapped in striped flannelette, up-ended in the middle of the large floor space in the office. He declares he was so taken aback that for quite an appreciable time he did not realise the thing was alive, and sat still wondering for what purpose and by what means that object had been transported in front of his desk. The archway from the ante-room was crowded with punkah-pullers, sweepers, police peons, the coxswain and crew of the harbour steam-launch, all craning their necks and almost climbing on each other's backs. Quite a riot. By that time the fellow had managed to tug and jerk his hat clear of his head, and advanced with slight bows at Ruthvel, who told me the sight was so discomposing that for some time he listened quite unable to make out what that apparition wanted. It spoke in a voice harsh and lugubrious but intrepid, and little by little it dawned upon Archie that this was a development of the *Patna* case. He says that as soon as he understood who it was before him he felt quite unwell—Archie is so sympathetic and easily upset—but pulled himself together and shouted, 'Stop! I can't listen to you. You must go to the Master Attendant. I can't possibly listen to you. Captain Elliot is the man you want to see. This way, this way.' He jumped up, ran round that long counter, pulled, shoved: the other let him, surprised but obedient at first, and only at the door of the private office some sort of animal instinct made him hang back and snort like a frightened bullock. 'Look here! what's up? Let go! Look here!' Archie flung open the door without knocking. 'The master of the *Patna*, sir,' he shouts. 'Go in, captain.' He saw the old man lift his head from some writing so sharp that his nose-nippers fell off, banged the door to, and fled to his desk, where he had some papers waiting for his signature: but he says the row that burst out in there was so awful that he couldn't collect his senses sufficiently to remember the spelling of his own name. Archie's the most sensitive shipping-master in the two hemispheres. He declares he felt as though he had thrown a man to a hungry lion. No doubt the noise was great. I heard it down below, and I have every reason to believe it was heard clear across the Esplanade as far as the bandstand. Old father Elliot had a great stock of words and could shout—and didn't mind who he shouted at either. He would have shouted at the Viceroy himself. As he used to tell me: 'I am as high as I can get; my pension is safe. I've a few pounds laid by, and if they don't like my notions of duty I would just as soon go home as not. I am an old man, and I have always spoken my mind. All I care for now is to see my girls married before I die.' He was a little crazy on that point. His three daughters were awfully nice, though they resembled him amazingly, and on the mornings he woke up with a gloomy view of their matrimonial prospects the office would read it in his eye and tremble, because, they said, he was sure to have somebody for breakfast. However, that morning he did not eat the renegade, but if I may be allowed to carry on the metaphor, chewed him up very small, so to speak, and—ah! ejected him again.

"Thus in a very few moments I saw his monstrous bulk descend in haste and stand still on the outer steps. He had stopped close to me for the purpose of profound meditation: his large purple cheeks quivered. He was biting his thumb, and after a while noticed me with a sidelong vexed look. The other three chaps that had landed with him made a little group waiting at some distance. There was a sallow-faced, mean little chap with his arm in a sling, and a long individual in a blue flannel coat, as dry as a chip and no stouter than a broomstick, with drooping grey moustaches, who looked about him with an air of jaunty imbecility. The third was an upstanding, broad-shouldered youth, with his hands in his pockets, turning his back on the other two who appeared to be talking together earnestly. He stared across the empty Esplanade. A ramshackle gharry, all dust and venetian blinds, pulled up short opposite the group, and the driver, throwing up his right foot over his knee, gave himself up to the critical examination of his toes. The young chap, making no movement, not even stirring his head, just stared into the sunshine. This was my first view of Jim. He looked as unconcerned and unapproachable as only the young can look. There he stood, clean-limbed, clean-faced, firm on his feet, as promising a boy as the sun ever shone on; and, looking at him, knowing all he knew and a little more too, I was as angry as though I had detected him trying to get something out of me by false pretences. He had no business to look so sound. I thought to myself—well, if this sort can go wrong like that . . . and I felt as though I could fling down my hat and dance on it from sheer mortification, as I once saw the skipper of an Italian barque do because his duffer of a mate got into a mess with his anchors when making a flying moor in a roadstead full of ships. I asked myself, seeing him there apparently so much at ease —is he silly? is he callous? He seemed ready to start whistling a tune. And note, I did not care a rap about the behaviour of the other two. Their persons somehow fitted the tale that was public property, and was going to be the subject of an official inquiry. 'That old mad rogue upstairs called me a hound,' said the captain of the *Patna*. I can't tell whether he recognised me—I rather think he did; but at any rate our glances met. He glared—I smiled; hound was the very mildest epithet that had reached me through the open window. 'Did he?' I said from some strange inability to hold my tongue. He nodded, bit his thumb again, swore under his breath: then lifting his head and looking at me with sullen and passionate impudence—'Bah! the Pacific is big, my friendt. You damned Englishmen can do your worst; I know where there's plenty room for a man like me: I am well aguaindt in Apia, in Honolulu, in . . .' He paused reflectively, while without effort I could depict to myself the sort of people he was 'aguaindt' with in those places. I won't make a secret of it that I had been 'aguaindt' with not a few of that sort myself. There are times when a man must act as though life were equally sweet in any company. I've known such a time, and, what's more, I shan't now pretend to pull a long face over my necessity, because a good many of that bad company from want of moral—moral—what shall I say?—posture, or from some other equally profound cause, were twice as instructive and twenty times more amusing than the usual respectable thief of commerce you fellows ask to sit at your table without any real necessity—from habit, from cowardice, from good-nature, from a hundred sneaking and inadequate reasons.

" 'You Englishmen are all rogues,' went on my patriotic Flensborg or Stettin Australian. I really don't recollect now what decent little port on the shores of the Baltic was defiled by being the nest of that precious bird. 'What are you to shout? Eh? You tell me? You no better than other people, and that old rogue he make Gottam fuss with me.' His thick carcass trembled on its legs that were like a pair of pillars; it trembled from head to foot. 'That's what you English always make—make a tam' fuss—for any little thing, because I was not born in your tam' country. Take away my certificate. Take it. I don't want the certificate. A man like me don't want your verfluchte [4] certificate. I shpit on it.' He spat. 'I vill an Amerigan citizen begome,' he cried, fretting and fuming and shuffling his feet as if to free his ankles from some invisible and mysterious grasp that would not let him get away from that spot. He made himself so warm that the top of his bullet head positively smoked. Nothing mysterious prevented me from going away: curiosity is the most obvious of sentiments, and it held me there to see the effect of a full information upon that young fellow who, hands in pockets, and turning his back upon the sidewalk, gazed across the grass-plots of the Esplanade at the yellow portico of the Malabar Hotel with the air of a man about to go for a walk as soon as his friend is ready. That's how he looked, and it was odious. I waited to see him overwhelmed, confounded, pierced through and through, squirming like an impaled beetle—and I was half afraid to see it too—if you understand what I mean. Nothing more awful than to watch a man who has been found out, not in a crime but in a more than criminal weakness. The commonest sort of fortitude prevents us from becoming criminals in a legal sense; it is from weakness unknown, but perhaps

4. Confounded, damned.

suspected, as in some parts of the world you suspect a deadly snake in every bush—from weakness that may lie hidden, watched or unwatched, prayed against or manfully scorned, repressed or maybe ignored more than half a lifetime, not one of us is safe. We are snared into doing things for which we get called names, and things for which we get hanged, and yet the spirit may well survive—survive the condemnations, survive the halter, by Jove! And there are things —they look small enough sometimes too—by which some of us are totally and completely undone. I watched the youngster there. I liked his appearance; I knew his appearance; he came from the right place; he was one of us. He stood there for all the parentage of his kind, for men and women by no means clever or amusing, but whose very existence is based upon honest faith, and upon the instinct of courage. I don't mean military courage, or civil courage, or any special kind of courage. I mean just that inborn ability to look temptations straight in the face—a readiness unintellectual enough, goodness knows, but without pose—a power of resistance, don't you see, ungracious if you like, but priceless—an unthinking and blessed stiffness before the outward and inward terrors, before the might of nature, and the seductive corruption of men—backed by a faith invulnerable to the strength of facts, to the contagion of example, to the solicitation of ideas. Hang ideas! They are tramps, vagabonds, knocking at the back door of your mind, each taking a little of your substance, each carrying away some crumb of that belief in a few simple notions you must cling to if you want to live decently and would like to die easy!

"This has nothing to do with Jim, directly; only he was outwardly so typical of that good, stupid kind we like to feel marching right and left of us in life, of the kind that is not disturbed by the vagaries of intelligence and the perversions of—of nerves, let us say. He was the kind of fellow you would, on the strength of his looks, leave in charge of the deck—figuratively and professionally speaking. I say I would, and I ought to know. Haven't I turned out youngsters enough in my time, for the service of the Red Rag, to the craft of the sea, to the craft whose whole secret could be expressed in one short sentence, and yet must be driven afresh every day into young heads till it becomes the component part of every waking thought—till it is present in every dream of their young sleep? The sea has been good to me, but when I remember all these boys that passed through my hands, some grown up now and some drowned by this time, but all good stuff for the sea, I don't think I have done badly by it either. Were I to go home to-morrow, I bet that before two days passed over my head some sunburnt young chief mate would overtake me at some dock gateway or other, and a fresh, deep voice speaking above my hat would ask: 'Don't you remember me, sir? Why! little So-and-so. Such and such a ship. It was my first voyage.' And I would remember a bewildered little shaver, no higher than the back of this chair, with a mother and perhaps a big sister on the quay, very quiet but too upset to wave their handkerchiefs at the ship that glides out gently between the pier-heads; or perhaps some decent, middle-aged father who had come early with his boy to see him off, and stays all the morning because he is interested in the windlass apparently, and stays too long, and has got to scramble ashore at last with no time at all to say good-bye. The mud pilot on the poop sings out to me in a drawl, 'Hold her with the check line for a moment, Mister Mate. There's a gentleman wants to get shore. . . . Up with you, sir. Nearly got carried off to Talcahuano, didn't you? Now's your time; easy does it. . . . All right. Slack away again forward there.' The tugs, smoking like the pit of perdition, get hold and churn the old river into fury; the gentleman ashore is dusting his knees—the benevolent steward has shied his umbrella after him. All very proper. He has offered his bit of sacrifice to the sea, and now he may go home pretending he thinks nothing of it; and the little willing victim will be very seasick before next morning. By and by, when he has learned all the little mysteries and the one great secret of the craft, he shall be fit to live or die as the sea may decree; and the man who had taken a hand in this fool game, in which the sea wins every toss, will be pleased to have his back slapped by a heavy young hand, and to hear a cheery sea-puppy voice: 'Do you remember me, sir? The little So-and-so.'

"I tell you this is good; it tells you that once in your life at least you had gone the right way to work. I have been thus slapped, and I have winced, for the slap was heavy, and I have glowed all day long and gone to bed feeling less lonely in the world by virtue of that hearty thump. Don't I remember the little So-and-so's! I tell you I ought to know the right kind of looks. I would have trusted the deck to that youngster on the strength of a single glance, and gone to sleep with both eyes—and, by Jove!—it wouldn't have been safe. There are depths of horror in that thought. He looked as genuine as a new sovereign,[5] but there was some infernal alloy in his metal. How much? The least thing—the least drop of something rare and accursed; the least drop!—but he made you—standing there with his don't-care-hang air—he made you wonder whether perchance he were nothing more rare than brass.

"I couldn't believe it. I tell you I wanted to see him squirm for the honour of the craft. The other two no-account chaps spotted their captain, and began to move slowly towards us. They chatted together as they strolled, and I did not care any more than if they

5. A British gold coin worth one pound.

had not been visible to the naked eye. They grinned at each other
—might have been exchanging jokes, for all I know. I saw that
with one of them it was the case of a broken arm; and as to the
long individual with grey moustaches he was the chief engineer,
and in various ways a pretty notorious personality. They were no-
bodies. They approached. The skipper gazed in an inanimate way
between his feet: he seemed to be swollen to an unnatural size by
some awful disease, by the mysterious action of an unknown
poison. He lifted his head, saw the two before him waiting, opened
his mouth with an extraordinary, sneering contortion of his puffed
face—to speak to them, I suppose—and then a thought seemed to
strike him. His thick, purplish lips came together without a sound,
he went off in a resolute waddle to the gharry and began to jerk at
the door-handle with such a blind brutality of impatience that I
expected to see the whole concern overturned on its side, pony and
all. The driver, shaken out of his meditation over the sole of his
foot, displayed at once all the signs of intense terror, and held
with both hands, looking round from his box at this vast carcass
forcing its way into his conveyance. The little machine shook and
rocked tumultuously, and the crimson nape of that lowered neck,
the size of those straining thighs, the immense heaving of that
dingy, striped green-and-orange back, the whole burrowing effort
of that gaudy and sordid mass troubled one's sense of probability
with a droll and fearsome effect, like one of those grotesque and
distinct visions that scare and fascinate one in a fever. He disappeared. I half expected the roof to split in two, the little box on
wheels to burst open in the manner of a ripe cotton-pod—but it
only sank with a click of flattened springs, and suddenly one venetian blind rattled down. His shoulders reappeared, jammed in the
small opening; his head hung out, distended and tossing like a
captive balloon, perspiring, furious, spluttering. He reached for
the gharry-wallah with vicious flourishes of a fist as dumpy and
red as a lump of raw meat. He roared at him to be off, to go
on. Where? Into the Pacific, perhaps. The driver lashed; the pony
snorted, reared once, and darted off at a gallop. Where? To Apia?
To Honolulu? He had 6000 miles of tropical belt to disport himself in, and I did not hear the precise address. A snorting pony
snatched him into 'ewigkeit'[6] in the twinkling of an eye, and I
never saw him again; and, what's more, I don't know of anybody that ever had a glimpse of him after he departed from my
knowledge sitting inside a ramshackle little gharry that fled round
the corner in a white smother of dust. He departed, disappeared,
vanished, absconded; and absurdly enough it looked as though he
had taken that gharry with him, for never again did I come

6. Eternity.

across a sorrel pony with a slit ear and a lackadaisical Tamil driver afflicted by a sore foot. The Pacific is indeed big; but whether he found a place for a display of his talents in it or not, the fact remains he had flown into space like a witch on a broomstick. The little chap with his arm in a sling started to run after the carriage, bleating, 'Captain! I say, Captain! I sa-a-ay!'—but after a few steps stopped short, hung his head, and walked back slowly. At the sharp rattle of the wheels the young fellow spun round where he stood. He made no other movement, no gesture, no sign, and remained facing in the new direction after the gharry had swung out of sight.

"All this happened in much less time than it takes to tell, since I am trying to interpret for you into slow speech the instantaneous effect of visual impressions. Next moment the half-caste clerk, sent by Archie to look a little after the poor castaways of the *Patna*, came upon the scene. He ran out eager and bareheaded, looking right and left, and very full of his mission. It was doomed to be a failure as far as the principal person was concerned, but he approached the others with fussy importance, and, almost immediately, found himself involved in a violent altercation with the chap that carried his arm in a sling and who turned out to be extremely anxious for a row. He wasn't going to be ordered about —'not he, b'gosh.' He wouldn't be terrified with a pack of lies by a cocky, half-bred little quill-driver. He was not going to be bullied by 'no object of that sort,' if the story were true 'ever so!' He bawled his wish, his desire, his determination to go to bed. 'If you weren't a God-forsaken Portuguee,' I heard him yell, 'you would know that the hospital is the right place for me.' He pushed the fist of his sound arm under the other's nose; a crowd began to collect; the half-caste, flustered, but doing his best to appear dignified, tried to explain his intentions. I went away without waiting to see the end.

"But it so happened that I had a man in the hospital at the time, and going there to see about him the day before the opening of the inquiry, I saw in the white men's ward that little chap tossing on his back, with his arm in splints, and quite light-headed. To my great surprise the other one, the long individual with drooping white moustaches, had also found his way there. I remembered I had seen him slinking away during the quarrel, in a half prance, half shuffle, and trying very hard not to look scared. He was no stranger to the port, it seems, and in his distress was able to make tracks straight for Mariani's billiard-room and grog-shop near the bazaar. That unspeakable vagabond, Mariani, who had known the man and had ministered to his vices in one or two other places, kissed the ground, in a manner of speaking, before him, and

shut him up with a supply of bottles in an upstairs room of his infamous hovel. It appears he was under some hazy apprehension as to
his personal safety, and wished to be concealed. However, Mariani
told me a long time after (when he came on board one day to dun
my steward for the price of some cigars) that he would have done
more for him without asking any questions, from gratitude for some
unholy favour received very many years ago—as far as I could make
out. He thumped twice his brawny chest, rolled enormous black-and-
white eyes glistening with tears: 'Antonio never forget—Antonio
never forget!' What was the precise nature of the immoral obligation
I never learned, but be it what it may, he had every facility given
him to remain under lock and key, with a chair, a table, a mat-
tress in a corner, and a litter of fallen plaster on the floor, in an
irrational state of funk, and keeping up his pecker [7] with such
tonics as Mariani dispensed. This lasted till the evening of the
third day, when, after letting out a few horrible screams, he found
himself compelled to seek safety in flight from a legion of centi-
pedes. He burst the door open, made one leap for dear life down
the crazy little stairway, landed bodily on Mariani's stomach,
picked himself up, and bolted like a rabbit into the streets. The
police plucked him off a garbage-heap in the early morning. At
first he had a notion they were carrying him off to be hanged, and
fought for liberty like a hero, but when I sat down by his bed he
had been very quiet for two days. His lean bronzed head, with
white moustaches, looked fine and calm on the pillow, like the
head of a war-worn soldier with a child-like soul, had it not
been for a hint of spectral alarm that lurked in the blank glitter
of his glance, resembling a nondescript form of a terror crouching
silently behind a pane of glass. He was so extremely calm, that
I began to indulge in the eccentric hope of hearing something explanatory of the famous affair from his point of view. Why I longed
to go grubbing into the deplorable details of an occurrence which,
after all, concerned me no more than as a member of an obscure
body of men held together by a community of inglorious toil and by
fidelity to a certain standard of conduct, I can't explain. You may
call it an unhealthy curiosity if you like; but I have a distinct
notion I wished to find something. Perhaps, unconsciously, I hoped
I would find that something, some profound and redeeming cause,
some merciful explanation, some convincing shadow of an excuse.
I see well enough now that I hoped for the impossible—for the
laying of what is the most obstinate ghost of man's creation, of the
uneasy doubt uprising like a mist, secret and gnawing like a worm,
and more chilling than the certitude of death—the doubt of the
sovereign power enthroned in a fixed standard of conduct. It is

7. Beak, nose; here British slang phrase similar to "keep your chin up."

the hardest thing to stumble against; it is the thing that breeds
yelling panics and good, little, quiet villainies; it's the true shadow
of calamity. Did I believe in a miracle? And why did I desire it so
ardently? Was it for my own sake that I wished to find some
shadow of an excuse for that young fellow, whom I had never seen
before, but whose appearance alone added a touch of personal
concern to the thoughts suggested by the knowledge of his weakness
—made it a thing of mystery and terror—like a hint of a destructive fate ready for us all whose youth—in its day—had resembled his youth? I fear that such was the secret motive of my
prying. I was, and no mistake, looking for a miracle. The only
thing that at this distance of time strikes me as miraculous is the
extent of my imbecility. I positively hoped to obtain from that
battered and shady invalid some exorcism against the ghost of
doubt. I must have been pretty desperate too, for, without loss of
time, after a few indifferent and friendly sentences which he
answered with languid readiness, just as any decent sick man would
do, I produced the word *Patna* wrapped up in a delicate question
as in a wisp of floss silk. I was delicate selfishly; I did not want to
startle him; I had no solicitude for him; I was not furious with
him and sorry for him: his experience was of no importance; his
redemption would have had no point for me. He had grown old in
minor iniquities, and could no longer inspire aversion or pity. He
repeated *Patna?* interrogatively, seemed to make a short effort of
memory, and said, 'Quite right. I am an old stager out here. I
saw her go down.' I made ready to vent my indignation at such a
stupid lie, when he added smoothly, 'She was full of reptiles.'

"This made me pause. What did he mean? The unsteady phantom of terror behind his glassy eyes seemed to stand still and look
into mine wistfully. 'They turned me out of my bunk in the middle watch to look at her sinking,' he pursued in a reflective tone.
His voice sounded alarmingly strong all at once. I was sorry for
my folly. There was no snowy-winged coif of a nursing sister to
be seen flitting in the perspective of the ward; but away in the
middle of a long row of empty iron bedsteads an accident case
from some ship in the Roads sat up brown and gaunt with a white
bandage set rakishly on the forehead. Suddenly my interesting
invalid shot out an arm thin like a tentacle and clawed my shoulder.
'Only my eyes were good enough to see. I am famous for my eyesight. That's why they called me, I expect. None of them was
quick enough to see her go, but they saw that she was gone right
enough, and sang out together—like this.' . . . A wolfish howl
searched the very recesses of my soul. 'Oh, make 'im dry up!'
whined the accident case irritably. 'You don't believe me, I suppose,' went on the other, with an air of ineffable conceit. 'I tell
you there are no such eyes as mine this side of the Persian

Gulf. Look under the bed.'

"Of course I stooped instantly. I defy anybody not to have done so. 'What can you see?' he asked. 'Nothing,' I said, feeling awfully ashamed of myself. He scrutinised my face with wild and withering contempt. 'Just so,' he said; 'but if I were to look I could see—there's no eyes like mine, I tell you.' Again he clawed, pulling at me downwards in his eagerness to relieve himself by a confidential communication. 'Millions of pink toads. There's no eyes like mine. Millions of pink toads. It's worse than seeing a ship sink. I could look at sinking ships and smoke my pipe all day long. Why don't they give me back my pipe? I would get a smoke while I watched these toads. The ship was full of them. They've got to be watched, you know.' He winked facetiously. The perspiration dripped on him off my head; my drill coat clung to my wet back: the afternoon breeze swept impetuously over the row of bedsteads, the stiff folds of curtains stirred perpendicularly, rattling on brass rods, the covers of empty beds blew about noiselessly near the bare floor all along the line, and I shivered to the very marrow. The soft wind of the tropics played in that naked ward as bleak as a winter's gale in an old barn at home. 'Don't you let him start his hollering, mister,' hailed from afar the accident case in a distressed, angry shout that came ringing between the walls like a quavering call down a tunnel. The clawing hand hauled at my shoulder; he leered at me knowingly. 'The ship was full of them, you know, and we had to clear out on the strict Q.T.,' he whispered with extreme rapidity. 'All pink. All pink—as big as mastiffs, with an eye on the top of the head and claws all round their ugly mouths. Ough! Ough!' Quick jerks as of galvanic shocks disclosed under the flat coverlet the outlines of meagre and agitated legs; he let go my shoulder and reached after something in the air; his body trembled tensely like a released harp-string; and while I looked down, the spectral horror in him broke through his glassy gaze. Instantly his face of an old soldier, with its noble and calm outlines, became decomposed before my eyes by the corruption of stealthy cunning, of an abominable caution and of desperate fear. He restrained a cry—'Ssh! what are they doing now down there?' he asked, pointing to the floor with fantastic precautions of voice and gesture, whose meaning, borne upon my mind in a lurid flash, made me very sick of my cleverness. 'They are all asleep,' I answered, watching him narrowly. That was it. That's what he wanted to hear; these were the exact words that could calm him. He drew a long breath. 'Ssh! Quiet, steady. I am an old stager out here. I know them brutes. Bash in the head of the first that stirs. There's too many of them, and she won't swim more than ten minutes.' He panted again. 'Hurry up,' he yelled suddenly; and went on in a steady scream: 'They are all awake—millions of them. They are trampling on me! Wait! Oh, wait! I'll smash them in heaps like flies. Wait for me! Help! H-e-elp!' An interminable and sustained howl completed my discomfiture. I saw in the distance the accident case raise deplorably both his hands to his bandaged head; a dresser,[8] aproned to the chin, showed himself in the vista of the ward, as if seen in the small end of a telescope. I confessed myself fairly routed, and without more ado, stepping out through one of the long windows, escaped into the outside gallery. The howl pursued me like a vengeance. I turned into a deserted landing, and suddenly all became very still and quiet around me, and I descended the bare and shiny staircase in a silence that enabled me to compose my distracted thoughts. Down below I met one of the resident surgeons who was crossing the courtyard and stopped me. 'Been to see your man, Captain? I think we may let him go to-morrow. These fools have no notion of taking care of themselves, though. I say, we've got the chief engineer of that pilgrim ship here. A curious case. D.T.'s of the worst kind. He has been drinking hard in that Greek's or Italian's grog-shop for three days. What can you expect? Four bottles of that kind of brandy a day, I am told. Wonderful, if true. Sheeted with boiler-iron inside, I should think. The head, ah! the head, of course, gone, but the curious part is there's some sort of method in his raving. I am trying to find out. Most unusual —that thread of logic in such a delirium. Traditionally he ought to see snakes, but he doesn't. Good old tradition's at a discount nowadays. Eh? His—er—visions are batrachian.[9] Ha! ha! No, seriously, I never remember being so interested in a case of jim-jams [1] before. He ought to be dead, don't you know, after such a festive experiment. Oh! he is a tough object. Four-and-twenty years of the tropics, too. You ought really to take a peep at him. Noble-looking old boozer. Most extraordinary man I ever met—medically, of course. Won't you?'

"I had been all along exhibiting the usual polite signs of interest, but now assuming an air of regret I murmured of want of time, and shook hands in a hurry. 'I say,' he cried after me; 'he can't attend that inquiry. Is his evidence material, you think?'

" 'Not in the least,' I called back from the gateway."

Chapter Six

"The authorities were evidently of the same opinion. The inquiry was not adjourned. It was held on the appointed day to satisfy the law, and it was well attended because of its human interest, no

---

8. One that serves as a doctor's assistant, especially in the dressing of wounds.

9. An order of Amphibia comprising the frogs, toads, and tree toads.
1. Slang for *delirium tremens*.

doubt. There was no incertitude as to facts—as to the one material fact, I mean. How the *Patna* came by her hurt it was impossible to find out; the court did not expect to find out; and in the whole audience there was not a man who cared. Yet, as I've told you, all the sailors in the port attended, and the waterside business was fully represented. Whether they knew it or not, the interest that drew them there was purely psychological—the expectation of some essential disclosure as to the strength, the power, the horror, of human emotions. Naturally nothing of the kind could be disclosed. The examination of the only man able and willing to face it was beating futilely round the well-known fact, and the play of questions upon it was as instructive as the tapping with a hammer on an iron box, were the object to find out what's inside. However, an official inquiry could not be any other thing. Its object was not the fundamental why, but the superficial how, of this affair.

"The young chap could have told them, and, though that very thing was the thing that interested the audience, the questions put to him necessarily led him away from what to me, for instance, would have been the only truth worth knowing. You can't expect the constituted authorities to inquire into the state of a man's soul—or is it only of his liver? Their business was to come down upon the consequences, and frankly, a casual police magistrate and two nautical assessors are not much good for anything else. I don't mean to imply these fellows were stupid. The magistrate was very patient. One of the assessors was a sailing-ship skipper with a reddish beard, and of a pious disposition. Brierly was the other. Big Brierly. Some of you must have heard of Big Brierly—the captain of the crack ship of the Blue Star line. That's the man.

"He seemed consumedly bored by the honour thrust upon him. He had never in his life made a mistake, never had an accident, never a mishap, never a check in his steady rise, and he seemed to be one of those lucky fellows who know nothing of indecision, much less of self-mistrust. At thirty-two he had one of the best commands going in the Eastern trade—and, what's more, he thought a lot of what he had. There was nothing like it in the world, and I suppose if you had asked him point-blank he would have confessed that in his opinion there was not such another commander. The choice had fallen upon the right man. The rest of mankind that did not command the sixteen-knot steel steamer *Ossa* were rather poor creatures. He had saved lives at sea, had rescued ships in distress, had a gold chronometer presented to him by the underwriters, and a pair of binoculars with a suitable inscription from some foreign Government, in commemoration of these services. He was acutely aware of his merits and of his rewards. I liked him well enough, though some I know—meek, friendly men at that—couldn't stand him at any price. I haven't the slightest doubt he considered himself vastly my superior—indeed, had you been Emperor of East and West, you could not have ignored your inferiority in his presence—but I couldn't get up any real sentiment of offence. He did not despise me for anything I could help, for anything I was—don't you know? I was a negligible quantity simply because I was not *the* fortunate man of the earth, not Montague Brierly in command of the *Ossa*, not the owner of an inscribed gold chronometer and of silver-mounted binoculars testifying to the excellence of my seamanship and to my indomitable pluck; not possessed of an acute sense of my merits and of my rewards, besides the love and worship of a black retriever, the most wonderful of its kind—for never was such a man loved thus by such a dog. No doubt, to have all this forced upon you was exasperating enough; but when I reflected that I was associated in these fatal disadvantages with twelve hundred millions of other more or less human beings, I found I could bear my share of his good-natured and contemptuous pity for the sake of something indefinite and attractive in the man. I have never defined to myself this attraction, but there were moments when I envied him. The sting of life could do no more to his complacent soul than the scratch of a pin to the smooth face of a rock. This was enviable. As I looked at him flanking on one side the unassuming pale-faced magistrate who presided at the inquiry, his self-satisfaction presented to me and to the world a surface as hard as granite. He committed suicide very soon after.

"No wonder Jim's case bored him, and while I thought with something akin to fear of the immensity of his contempt for the young man under examination, he was probably holding silent inquiry into his own case. The verdict must have been of unmitigated guilt, and he took the secret of the evidence with him in that leap into the sea. If I understand anything of men, the matter was no doubt of the gravest import, one of those trifles that awaken ideas—start into life some thought with which a man unused to such a companionship finds it impossible to live. I am in a position to know that it wasn't money, and it wasn't drink, and it wasn't woman. He jumped overboard at sea barely a week after the end of the inquiry, and less than three days after leaving port on his outward passage; as though on that exact spot in the midst of waters he had suddenly perceived the gates of the other world flung open wide for his reception.

"Yet it was not a sudden impulse. His grey-headed mate, a first-rate sailor and a nice old chap with strangers, but in his relations with his commander the surliest chief officer I've ever seen, would tell the story with tears in his eyes. It appears that when he came on deck in the morning Brierly had been writing in the chart-room. 'It was ten minutes to four,' he said, 'and the middle watch was not relieved yet, of course. He heard my voice on the bridge speaking to the second mate, and called me in. I was loath to go, and that's the truth, Captain Marlow—I couldn't stand poor Captain Brierly, I tell you with shame; we never know what a man is made of. He had been promoted over too many heads, not counting my own, and he had a damnable trick of making you feel small, nothing but by the way he said "Good morning." I never addressed him, sir, but on matters of duty, and then it was as much as I could do to keep a civil tongue in my head.' (He flattered himself there. I often wondered how Brierly could put up with his manners for more than half a voyage.) 'I've a wife and children,' he went on, 'and I had been ten years in the Company, always expecting the next command—more fool I. Says he, just like this: "Come in here, Mr. Jones," in that swagger voice of his—"come in here, Mr. Jones." In I went. "We'll lay down her position," says he, stooping over the chart, a pair of dividers in hand. By the standing orders, the officer going off duty would have done that at the end of his watch. However, I said nothing, and looked on while he marked off the ship's position with a tiny cross and wrote the date and the time. I can see him this moment writing his neat figures: seventeen, eight, four A.M. The year would be written in red ink at the top of the chart. He never used his charts more than a year, Captain Brierly didn't. I've the chart now. When he had done he stands looking down at the mark he had made and smiling to himself, then looks up at me. "Thirty-two miles more as she goes," says he, "and then we shall be clear, and you may alter the course twenty degrees to the southward."

" 'We were passing to the north of the Hector Bank that voyage. I said, "All right, sir," wondering what he was fussing about, since I had to call him before altering the course anyhow. Just then eight bells were struck: we came out on the bridge, and the second mate before going off mentions in the usual way, "Seventy-one on the log." Captain Brierly looks at the compass and then all round. It was dark and clear, and all the stars were out as plain as on a frosty night in high latitudes. Suddenly he says with a sort of a little sigh: "I am going aft, and shall set the log at zero for you myself, so that there can be no mistake. Thirty-two miles more on this course and then you are safe. Let's see—the correction on the log is six per cent. additive; say, then, thirty by the dial to run, and you may come twenty degrees to starboard at once. No use losing any distance—is there?" I had never heard him talk so much at a stretch, and to no purpose as it seemed to me. I said nothing. He went down the ladder, and the dog, that was always at his heels whenever he moved, night or day, followed, sliding nose first, after him. I heard his boot-heels tap, tap on the after-deck, then he stopped and spoke to the dog—"Go back, Rover. On the bridge, boy! Go on—get." Then he calls out to me from the dark, "Shut that dog up in the chart-room, Mr. Jones—will you?"

" 'This was the last time I heard his voice, Captain Marlow. These are the last words he spoke in the hearing of any living human being, sir.' At this point the old chap's voice got quite unsteady. 'He was afraid the poor brute would jump after him, don't you see?' he pursued with a quaver. 'Yes, Captain Marlow. He set the log for me; he—would you believe it?—he put a drop of oil in it too. There was the oil-feeder where he left it near by. The boatswain's mate got the hose along aft to wash down at half-past five; by and by he knocks off and runs up on the bridge—"Will you please come aft, Mr. Jones," he says. "There's a funny thing. I don't like to touch it." It was Captain Brierly's gold chronometer watch carefully hung under the rail by its chain.

" 'As soon as my eyes fell on it something struck me, and I knew, sir. My legs got soft under me. It was as if I had seen him go over; and I could tell how far behind he was left too. The taffrail-log marked eighteen miles and three-quarters, and four iron belaying-pins were missing round the mainmast. Put them in his pockets to help him down, I suppose; but, Lord! what's four iron pins to a powerful man like Captain Brierly. Maybe his confidence in himself was just shook a bit at the last. That's the only sign of fluster he gave in his whole life, I should think; but I am ready to answer for him, that once over he did not try to swim a stroke, the same as he would have had pluck enough to keep up all day long on the bare chance had he fallen overboard accidentally. Yes, sir. He was second to none—if he said so himself, as I heard him once. He had written two letters in the middle watch, one to the Company and the other to me. He gave me a lot of instructions as to the passage —I had been in the trade before he was out of his time—and no end of hints as to my conduct with our people in Shanghai, so that I should keep the command of the *Ossa*. He wrote like a father would to a favourite son, Captain Marlow, and I was five-and-twenty years his senior and had tasted salt water before he was fairly breeched. In his letter to the owners—it was left open for me to see —he said that he had always done his duty by them—up to that moment—and even now he was not betraying their confidence, since he was leaving the ship to as competent a seaman as could be found—meaning me, sir, meaning me! He told them that if the last act of his life didn't take away all his credit with them, they would give weight to my faithful service and to his warm recommendation, when about to fill the vacancy made by his death. And much more like this, sir. I couldn't believe my eyes. It made me feel queer all over,' went on the old chap in great perturbation, and squashing something in the corner of his eye with the end of a thumb as broad as a spatula. 'You would think, sir, he had jumped overboard only to give an unlucky man a last show to get on. What with the shock of him going in this awful rash way, and thinking myself a made man by that chance, I was nearly off my chump for a week. But no fear. The captain of the *Pelion* was shifted into the *Ossa*—came aboard in Shanghai—a little popinjay, in a grey check suit, with his hair parted in the middle. "Aw—I am—aw— your new captain, Mister—Mister—aw—Jones." He was drowned in scent—fairly stunk with it, Captain Marlow. I dare say it was the look I gave him that made him stammer. He mumbled something about my natural disappointment—I had better know at once that his chief officer got the promotion to the *Pelion*—he had nothing to do with it, of course—supposed the office knew best—sorry. . . . Says I, "Don't you mind old Jones, sir; damn his soul, he's used to it." I could see directly I had shocked his delicate ear, and while we sat at our first tiffin [2] together he began to find fault in a nasty manner with this and that in the ship. I never heard such a voice out of a Punch and Judy show. I set my teeth hard, and glued my eyes to my plate, and held my peace as long as I could; but at last I had to say something. Up he jumps tiptoeing, ruffling all his pretty plumes, like a little fighting-cock. "You'll find you have a different person to deal with than the late Captain Brierly." "I've found it," says I, very glum, but pretending to be mighty busy with my steak. "You are an old ruffian, Mister—aw—Jones; and what's more, you are known for an old ruffian in the employ," he squeaks at me. The damned bottle-washers stood about listening with their mouths stretched from ear to ear. "I may be a hard case," answers I, "but I ain't so far gone as to put up with the sight of you sitting in Captain Brierly's chair." With that I lay down my knife and fork. "You would like to sit in it yourself—that's where the shoe pinches," he sneers. I left the saloon, got my rags together, and was on the quay with all my dunnage about my feet before the stevedores had turned to again. Yes. Adrift—on shore—after ten years' service—and with a poor woman and four children six thousand miles off depending on my half-pay for every mouthful they ate. Yes, sir! I chucked it rather than hear Captain Brierly abused. He left me his night-glasses—here they are; and he wished me to take care of the dog—here he is. Hallo, Rover, poor boy. Where's the captain, Rover?' The dog looked up at us with mournful, yellow eyes, gave

2. Usual Anglo-Indian word for a meal; normally, for a light midday meal.

one desolate bark, and crept under the table.

"All this was taking place, more than two years afterwards, on board that nautical ruin the *Fire-Queen* this Jones had got charge of—quite by a funny accident, too—from Matherson—mad Matherson they generally called him—the same who used to hang out in Haï-phong, you know, before the occupation days. The old chap snuffled on:

" 'Ay, sir, Captain Brierly will be remembered here, if there's no other place on earth. I wrote fully to his father, and did not get a word in reply—neither Thank you, nor Go to the devil!—nothing! Perhaps they did not want to know.'

"The sight of that watery-eyed old Jones mopping his bald head with a red cotton handkerchief, the sorrowing yelp of the dog, the squalor of that fly-blown cuddy which was the only shrine of his memory, threw a veil of inexpressibly mean pathos over Brierly's remembered figure, the posthumous revenge of fate for that belief in his own splendour which had almost cheated his life of its legitimate terrors. Almost! Perhaps wholly. Who can tell what flattering view he had induced himself to take of his own suicide?

" 'Why did he commit the rash act, Captain Marlow—can you think?' asked Jones, pressing his palms together. 'Why? It beats me! Why?' He slapped his low and wrinkled forehead. 'If he had been poor and old and in debt—and never a show—or else mad. But he wasn't of the kind that goes mad, not he. You trust me. What a mate don't know about his skipper isn't worth knowing. Young, healthy, well off, no cares. . . . I sit here sometimes thinking, thinking, till my head fairly begins to buzz. There was some reason.'

" 'You may depend on it, Captain Jones,' said I, 'it wasn't anything that would have disturbed much either of us two,' I said; and then, as if a light had been flashed into the muddle of his brain, poor old Jones found a last word of amazing profundity. He blew his nose, nodding at me dolefully: 'Ay, ay! neither you nor I, sir, had ever thought so much of ourselves.'

"Of course the recollection of my last conversation with Brierly is tinged with the knowledge of his end that followed so close upon it. I spoke with him for the last time during the progress of the inquiry. It was after the first adjournment, and he came up with me in the street. He was in a state of irritation, which I noticed with surprise, his usual behaviour when he condescended to converse being perfectly cool, with a trace of amused tolerance, as if the existence of his interlocutor had been a rather good joke. 'They caught me for that inquiry, you see,' he began, and for a while enlarged complainingly upon the inconveniences of daily attendance in court. 'And goodness knows how long it will last. Three days, I suppose.'

I heard him out in silence; in my then opinion it was a way as good as another of putting on side. 'What's the use of it? It is the stupidest set-out [3] you can imagine,' he pursued hotly. I remarked that there was no option. He interrupted me with a sort of pent-up violence. 'I feel like a fool all the time.' I looked up at him. This was going very far—for Brierly—when talking of Brierly. He stopped short, and seizing the lapel of my coat, gave it a slight tug. 'Why are we tormenting that young chap?' he asked. This question chimed in so well to the tolling of a certain thought of mine that, with the image of the absconding renegade in my eye, I answered at once, 'Hanged if I know, unless it be that he lets you.' I was astonished to see him fall into line, so to speak, with that utterance, which ought to have been tolerably cryptic. He said angrily, 'Why, yes. Can't he see that wretched skipper of his has cleared out? What does he expect to happen? Nothing can save him. He's done for.' We walked on in silence a few steps. 'Why eat all that dirt?' he exclaimed, with an oriental energy of expression—about the only sort of energy you can find a trace of east of the fiftieth meridian. I wondered greatly at the direction of his thoughts, but now I strongly suspect it was strictly in character: at bottom poor Brierly must have been thinking of himself. I pointed out to him that the skipper of the *Patna* was known to have feathered his nest pretty well, and could procure almost anywhere the means of getting away. With Jim it was otherwise: the Government was keeping him in the Sailors' Home for the time being, and probably he hadn't a penny in his pocket to bless himself with. It costs some money to run away. 'Does it? Not always,' he said, with a bitter laugh, and to some further remark of mine—'Well, then, let him creep twenty feet underground and stay there! By heavens! *I* would.' I don't know why his tone provoked me, and I said, 'There is a kind of courage in facing it out as he does, knowing very well that if he went away nobody would trouble to run after him.' 'Courage be hanged!' growled Brierly. 'That sort of courage is of no use to keep a man straight, and I don't care a snap for such courage. If you were to say it was a kind of cowardice now—of softness. I tell you what, I will put up two hundred rupees if you put up another hundred and undertake to make the beggar clear out early to-morrow morning. The fellow's a gentleman if he ain't fit to be touched—he will understand. He must! This infernal publicity is too shocking: there he sits while all these confounded natives, serangs, lascars, quartermasters, are giving evidence that's enough to burn a man to ashes with shame. This is abominable. Why, Marlow, don't you think, don't you feel, that this is abominable? Don't you now—come—as a seaman? If he went away all this would stop at once.'

3. A to-do or fuss.

Brierly said these words with a most unusual animation, and made as if to reach after his pocket-book. I restrained him, and declared coldly that the cowardice of these four men did not seem to me a matter of such great importance. 'And you call yourself a seaman, I suppose?' he pronounced angrily. I said that's what I called myself, and I hoped I was too. He heard me out, and made a gesture with his big arm that seemed to deprive me of my individuality, to push me away into the crowd. 'The worst of it,' he said, 'is that all you fellows have no sense of dignity; you don't think enough of what you are supposed to be.'

"We had been walking slowly meantime, and now stopped opposite the harbour office, in sight of the very spot from which the immense captain of the *Patna* had vanished as utterly as a tiny feather blown away in a hurricane. I smiled. Brierly went on: 'This is a disgrace. We've got all kinds amongst us—some anointed scoundrels in the lot; but, hang it, we must preserve professional decency or we become no better than so many tinkers going about loose. We are trusted. Do you understand?—trusted! Frankly, I don't care a snap for all the pilgrims that ever came out of Asia, but a decent man would not have behaved like this to a full cargo of old rags in bales. We aren't an organised body of men, and the only thing that holds us together is just the name for that kind of decency. Such an affair destroys one's confidence. A man may go pretty near through his whole sea-life without any call to show a stiff upper lip. But when the call comes . . . Aha! . . . If I . . .'

"He broke off, and in a changed tone, 'I'll give you two hundred rupees now, Marlow, and you just talk to that chap. Confound him! I wish he had never come out here. Fact is, I rather think some of my people know his. The old man's a parson, and I remember now I met him once when staying with my cousin in Essex last year. If I am not mistaken, the old chap seemed rather to fancy his sailor son. Horrible. I can't do it myself—but you . . .'

"Thus, apropos of Jim, I had a glimpse of the real Brierly a few days before he committed his reality and his sham together to the keeping of the sea. Of course I declined to meddle. The tone of this last 'but you' (poor Brierly couldn't help it), that seemed to imply I was no more noticeable than an insect, caused me to look at the proposal with indignation, and on account of that provocation, or for some other reason, I became positive in my mind that the inquiry was a severe punishment to that Jim, and that his facing it—practically of his own free will—was a redeeming feature in his abominable case. I hadn't been so sure of it before. Brierly went off in a huff. At the time his state of mind was more of a mystery to me than it is now.

"Next day, coming into court late, I sat by myself. Of course I could not forget the conversation I had with Brierly, and now I had them both under my eyes. The demeanour of one suggested gloomy impudence and of the other a contemptuous boredom; yet one attitude might not have been truer than the other, and I was aware that one was not true. Brierly was not bored—he was exasperated; and if so, then Jim might not have been impudent. According to my theory he was not. I imagined he was hopeless. Then it was that our glances met. They met, and the look he gave me was discouraging of any intention I might have had to speak to him. Upon either hypothesis—insolence or despair—I felt I could be of no use to him. This was the second day of the proceedings. Very soon after that exchange of glances the inquiry was adjourned again to the next day. The white men began to troop out at once. Jim had been told to stand down some time before, and was able to leave amongst the first. I saw his broad shoulders and his head outlined in the light of the door, and while I made my way slowly out talking with some one—some stranger who had addressed me casually—I could see him from within the court-room resting both elbows on the balustrade of the verandah and turning his back on the small stream of people trickling down the few steps. There was a murmur of voices and a shuffle of boots.

"The next case was that of assault and battery committed upon a money-lender, I believe; and the defendant—a venerable villager with a straight white beard—sat on a mat just outside the door with his sons, daughters, sons-in-law, their wives, and, I should think, half the population of his village besides, squatting or standing around him. A slim, dark woman, with part of her back and one black shoulder bared, and with a thin gold ring in her nose, suddenly began to talk in a high-pitched, shrewish tone. The man with me instinctively looked up at her. We were then just through the door, passing behind Jim's burly back.

"Whether those villagers had brought the yellow dog with them, I don't know. Anyhow, a dog was there, weaving himself in and out amongst people's legs in that mute, stealthy way native dogs have, and my companion stumbled over him. The dog leaped away without a sound; the man, raising his voice a little, said with a slow laugh, 'Look at that wretched cur,' and directly afterwards we became separated by a lot of people pushing in. I stood back for a moment against the wall while the stranger managed to get down the steps and disappeared. I saw Jim spin round. He made a step forward and barred my way. We were alone; he glared at me with an air of stubborn resolution. I became aware I was being held up, so to speak, as if in a wood. The verandah was empty by then, the noise and movement in court had ceased: a great silence fell upon the building, in which, somewhere far within, an oriental voice began to whine abjectly. The dog, in the very act of trying to sneak in at the door, sat down hurriedly to hunt for fleas.

" 'Did you speak to me?' asked Jim very low, and bending forward, not so much towards me but at me, if you know what I mean. I said 'No' at once. Something in the sound of that quiet tone of his warned me to be on my defence. I watched him. It was very much like a meeting in a wood, only more uncertain in its issue, since he could possibly want neither my money nor my life—nothing that I could simply give up or defend with a clear conscience. 'You say you didn't,' he said, very sombre. 'But I heard.' 'Some mistake,' I protested, utterly at a loss, and never taking my eyes off him. To watch his face was like watching a darkening sky before a clap of thunder, shade upon shade imperceptibly coming on, the gloom growing mysteriously intense in the calm of maturing violence.

" 'As far as I know, I haven't opened my lips in your hearing,' I affirmed with perfect truth. I was getting a little angry, too, at the absurdity of this encounter. It strikes me now I have never in my life been so near a beating—I mean it literally; a beating with fists. I suppose I had some hazy prescience of that eventuality being in the air. Not that he was actively threatening me. On the contrary, he was strangely passive—don't you know?—but he was lowering, and, though not exceptionally big, he looked generally fit to demolish a wall. The most reassuring symptom I noticed was a kind of slow and ponderous hesitation, which I took as a tribute to the evident sincerity of my manner and of my tone. We faced each other. In the court the assault case was proceeding. I caught the words: 'Well—buffalo—stick—in the greatness of my fear. . . .'

" 'What did you mean by staring at me all the morning?' said Jim at last. He looked up and looked down again. 'Did you expect us all to sit with downcast eyes out of regard for your susceptibilities?' I retorted sharply. I was not going to submit meekly to any of his nonsense. He raised his eyes again, and this time continued to look me straight in the face. 'No. That's all right,' he pronounced, with an air of deliberating with himself upon the truth of this statement—'that's all right. I am going through with that. Only'—and there he spoke a little faster—'I won't let any man call me names outside this court. There was a fellow with you. You spoke to him—oh yes—I know; 'tis all very fine. You spoke to him, but you meant me to hear. . . .'

"I assured him he was under some extraordinary delusion. I had no conception how it came about. 'You thought I would be afraid to resent this,' he said, with just a faint tinge of bitterness. I was interested enough to discern the slightest shades of expression, but I was not in the least enlightened; yet I don't know what in these words, or perhaps just the intonation of that phrase, induced me suddenly to make all possible allowances for him. I ceased to be annoyed at my unexpected predicament. It was some mistake on his part; he was blundering, and I had an intuition that the blunder was of an odious, of an unfortunate nature. I was anxious to end this scene on grounds of decency, just as one is anxious to cut short some unprovoked and abominable confidence. The funniest part was, that in the midst of all these considerations of the higher order I was conscious of a certain trepidation as to the possibility—nay, likelihood—of this encounter ending in some disreputable brawl which could not possibly be explained, and would make me ridiculous. I did not hanker after a three days' celebrity as the man who got a black eye or something of the sort from the mate of the *Patna*. He, in all probability, did not care what he did, or at any rate would be fully justified in his own eyes. It took no magician to see he was amazingly angry about something, for all his quiet and even torpid demeanour. I don't deny I was extremely desirous to pacify him at all costs, had I only known what to do. But I didn't know, as you may well imagine. It was blackness without a single gleam. We confronted each other in silence. He hung fire for about fifteen seconds, then made a step nearer, and I made ready to ward off a blow, though I don't think I moved a muscle. 'If you were as big as two men and as strong as six,' he said very softly, 'I would tell you what I think of you. You . . .' 'Stop!' I exclaimed. This checked him for a second. 'Before you tell me what you think of me,' I went on quickly, 'will you kindly tell me what it is I've said or done?' During the pause that ensued he surveyed me with indignation, while I made supernatural efforts of memory, in which I was hindered by the oriental voice within the court-room expostulating with impassioned volubility against a charge of falsehood. Then we spoke almost together. 'I will soon show you I am not,' he said, in a tone suggestive of a crisis. 'I declare I don't know,' I protested earnestly at the same time. He tried to crush me by the scorn of his glance. 'Now that you see I am not afraid you try to crawl out of it,' he said. 'Who's a cur now—hey?' Then, at last, I understood.

"He had been scanning my features as though looking for a place where he would plant his fist. 'I will allow no man,' . . . he mumbled threateningly. It was, indeed, a hideous mistake; he had given himself away utterly. I can't give you an idea how shocked I was. I suppose he saw some reflection of my feelings in my face, because his expression changed just a little. 'Good God!' I stammered, 'you don't think I . . .' 'But I am sure I've heard,' he persisted, raising his voice for the first time since the beginning of this deplorable scene. Then with a shade of disdain he added, 'It wasn't you, then? Very well; I'll find the other.' 'Don't be a fool,' I cried in exasperation; 'it wasn't that at all.' 'I've heard,' he said again, with an unshaken and sombre perseverance.

"There may be those who could have laughed at his pertinacity. I didn't. Oh, I didn't! There had never been a man so mercilessly shown up by his own natural impulse. A single word had stripped him of his discretion—of that discretion which is more necessary to the decencies of our inner being than clothing is to the decorum of our body. 'Don't be a fool,' I repeated. 'But the other man said it, you don't deny that?' he pronounced distinctly, and looking in my face without flinching. 'No, I don't deny,' said I, returning his gaze. At last his eyes followed downwards the direction of my pointing finger. He appeared at first uncomprehending, then confounded, and at last amazed and scared as though a dog had been a monster and he had never seen a dog before. 'Nobody dreamt of insulting you,' I said.

"He contemplated the wretched animal, that moved no more than an effigy: it sat with ears pricked and its sharp muzzle pointed into the doorway, and suddenly snapped at a fly like a piece of mechanism.

"I looked at him. The red of his fair, sunburnt complexion deepened suddenly under the down of his cheeks, invaded his forehead, spread to the roots of his curly hair. His ears became intensely crimson, and even the clear blue of his eyes was darkened many shades by the rush of blood to his head. His lips pouted a little, trembling as though he had been on the point of bursting into tears. I perceived he was incapable of pronouncing a word from the excess of his humiliation. From disappointment too—who knows? Perhaps he looked forward to that hammering he was going to give me for rehabilitation, for appeasement? Who can tell what relief he expected from this chance of a row? He was naive enough to expect anything; but he had given himself away for nothing in this case. He had been frank with himself—let alone with me—in the wild hope of arriving in that way at some effective refutation, and the stars had been ironically unpropitious. He made an inarticulate noise in his throat like a man imperfectly stunned by a blow on the head. It was pitiful.

"I didn't catch up again with him till well outside the gate. I had even to trot a bit at the last, but when, out of breath at his elbow, I taxed him with running away, he said, 'Never!' and at once turned at bay. I explained I never meant to say he was running away from *me*. 'From no man—from not a single man on earth,' he affirmed with a stubborn mien. I forebore to point out the one obvious exception which would hold good for the bravest of us; I thought he would find out by himself very soon. He looked at me patiently while I was thinking of something to say, but I could find nothing on the spur of the moment, and he began to walk on. I kept up, and, anxious not to lose him, I said hurriedly that I couldn't think of leaving him under a false impression of my—of my—I stammered. The stupidity of the phrase appalled me while I was trying to finish it, but the power of sentences has nothing to do with their sense or the logic of their construction. My idiotic mumble seemed to please him. He cut it short by saying, with courteous placidity that argued an immense power of self-control or else a wonderful elasticity of spirits—'Altogether my mistake.' I marvelled greatly at this expression: he might have been alluding to some trifling occurrence. Hadn't he understood its deplorable meaning? 'You may well forgive me,' he continued; and went on a little moodily, 'All these staring people in court seemed such fools that—that it might have been as I supposed.'

"This opened suddenly a new view of him to my wonder. I looked at him curiously, and met his unabashed and impenetrable eyes. 'I can't put up with this kind of thing,' he said very simply, 'and I don't mean to. In court it's different; I've got to stand that—and I can do it too.'

"I don't pretend I understood him. The views he let me have of himself were like those glimpses through the shifting rents in a thick fog—bits of vivid and vanishing detail, giving no connected idea of the general aspect of a country. They fed one's curiosity without satisfying it; they were no good for purposes of orientation. Upon the whole he was misleading. That's how I summed him up to myself after he left me late in the evening. I had been staying at the Malabar House for a few days, and on my pressing invitation he dined with me there."

Chapter Seven

"An outward-bound mail-boat had come in that afternoon, and the big dining-room of the hotel was more than half full of people with a-hundred-pounds-round-the-world tickets in their pockets. There were married couples looking domesticated and bored with each other in the midst of their travels; there were small parties and large parties, and lone individuals dining solemnly or feasting boisterously, but all thinking, conversing, joking, or scowling as was their wont at home; and just as intelligently receptive of new impressions as their trunks upstairs. Henceforth they would be labelled as having passed through this and that place, and so would be their luggage. They would cherish this distinction of their persons, and preserve the gummed tickets on their portmanteaux as documentary evidence, as the only permanent trace of their improving enterprise. The dark-faced servants tripped without noise over the vast and polished floor; now and then a girl's laugh would be heard, as innocent and empty as her mind, or, in a sudden hush of crockery, a few words in an affected drawl from some wit embroidering for the benefit of a grinning tableful the last funny story of shipboard scandal. Two nomadic old maids, dressed up to kill, worked acrimoniously through the bill of fare, whispering to each other with faded lips, wooden-faced and bizarre, like two sumptuous scarecrows. A little wine opened Jim's heart and loosened his tongue. His appetite was good, too, I noticed. He seemed to have buried somewhere the opening episode of our acquaintance. It was like a thing of which there would be no more question in this world. And all the time I had before me these blue, boyish eyes looking straight into mine, this young face, these capable shoulders, the open, bronzed forehead with a white line under the roots of clustering fair hair, this appearance appealing at sight to all my sympathies: this frank aspect, the artless smile, the youthful seriousness. He was of the right sort; he was one of us. He talked soberly, with a sort of composed unreserve, and with a quiet bearing that might have been the outcome of manly self-control, of impudence, of callousness, of a colossal unconsciousness, of a gigantic deception. Who can tell? From our tone we might have been discussing a third person, a football match, last year's weather. My mind floated in a sea of conjectures till the turn of the conversation enabled me, without being offensive, to remark that, upon the whole, this inquiry must have been pretty trying to him. He darted his arm across the tablecloth, and clutching my hand by the side of my plate, glared fixedly. I *was* startled. 'It must be awfully hard,' I stammered, confused by this display of speechless feeling. 'It is—hell,' he burst out in a muffled voice.

"This movement and these words caused two well-groomed male globe-trotters at a neighbouring table to look up in alarm from their iced pudding. I rose, and we passed into the front gallery for coffee and cigars.

"On little octagon tables candles burned in glass globes; clumps of stiff-leaved plants separated sets of cosy wicker chairs; and between the pairs of columns, whose reddish shafts caught in a long row the sheen from the tall windows, the night, glittering and sombre, seemed to hang like a splendid drapery. The riding lights of ships winked afar like setting stars, and the hills across the roadstead resembled rounded black masses of arrested thunder-clouds.

" 'I couldn't clear out,' Jim began. 'The skipper did—that's all very well for him. I couldn't, and I wouldn't. They all got out of it in one way or another, but it wouldn't do for me.'

"I listened with concentrated attention, not daring to stir in my chair; I wanted to know—and to this day I don't know, I can only guess. He would be confident and depressed all in the same breath, as if some conviction of innate blamelessness had checked the truth writhing within him at every turn. He began by saying, in the tone in which a man would admit his inability to jump a twenty-foot wall, that he could never go home now; and this declaration recalled to my mind what Brierly had said, 'that the old parson in Essex seemed to fancy his sailor son not a little.'

"I can't tell you whether Jim knew he was especially 'fancied,' but the tone of his references to 'my Dad' was calculated to give me a notion that the good old rural dean was about the finest man that ever had been worried by the cares of a large family since the beginning of the world. This, though never stated, was implied with an anxiety that there should be no mistake about it, which was really very true and charming, but added a poignant sense of lives far off to the other elements of the story. 'He has seen it all in the home papers by this time,' said Jim. 'I can never face the poor old chap.' I did not dare to lift my eyes at this till I heard him add, 'I could never explain. He wouldn't understand.' Then I looked up. He was smoking reflectively, and after a moment, rousing himself, began to talk again. He discovered at once a desire that I should not confound him with his partners in—in crime, let us call it. He was not one of them; he was altogether of another sort. I gave no sign of dissent. I had no intention, for the sake of barren truth, to rob him of the smallest particle of any saving grace that would come in his way. I didn't know how much of it he believed himself. I didn't know what he was playing up to—if he was playing up to anything at all—and I suspect he did not know either; for it is my belief no man ever understands quite his own artful dodges to escape from the grim shadow of self-knowledge. I made no sound all the time he was wondering what he had better do after 'that stupid inquiry was over.'

"Apparently he shared Brierly's contemptuous opinion of these proceedings ordained by law. He would not know where to turn, he confessed, clearly thinking aloud rather than talking to me. Certificate gone, career broken, no money to get away, no work that he could obtain as far as he could see. At home he could perhaps get something; but it meant going to his people for help, and that he would not do. He saw nothing for it but ship before the mast—could get perhaps a quartermaster's billet in some steamer. Would do for a quartermaster. . . . 'Do you think you would?' I asked pitilessly. He jumped up, and going to the stone balustrade looked out into the night. In a moment he was back, towering above my chair, with his youthful face clouded yet by the pain of a conquered emotion. He had understood very well I did not doubt his ability to steer a ship. In a voice that quavered a bit he asked me why did I say that? I had been 'no end kind' to him. I had not even laughed at him when—here he began to mumble—'that mistake, you know —made a confounded ass of myself.' I broke in by saying rather warmly that for me such a mistake was not a matter to laugh at. He sat down and drank deliberately some coffee, emptying the small cup to the last drop. 'That does not mean I admit for a moment the cap fitted,' he declared distinctly. 'No?' I said. 'No,' he affirmed, with quiet decision. 'Do you know what *you* would have done? Do you? And you don't think yourself' . . . he gulped something . . . 'you don't think yourself a—a—cur?'

"And with this—upon my honour!—he looked up at me inquisitively. It was a question, it appears—a *bona fide* [4] question! However, he didn't wait for an answer. Before I could recover he went on, with his eyes straight before him, as if reading off something written on the body of the night. 'It is all in being ready. I wasn't; not—not then. I don't want to excuse myself; but I would like to explain—I would like somebody to understand—somebody —one person at least! You! Why not you?'

"It was solemn, and a little ridiculous, too, as they always are, those struggles of an individual trying to save from the fire his idea of what his moral identity should be, this precious notion of a convention, only one of the rules of the game, nothing more, but all the same so terribly effective by its assumption of unlimited power over natural instincts, by the awful penalties of its failure. He began his story quietly enough. On board that Dale Line steamer that had picked up these four floating in a boat upon the discreet sunset glow of the sea, they had been after the first day looked askance upon. The fat skipper told some story, the others had been silent, and at first it had been accepted. You don't cross-examine poor castaways you had the good luck to save, if not from cruel death, then at least from cruel suffering. Afterwards, with time to think it over, it might have struck the officers of the *Avondale* that there was 'something fishy' in the affair; but of course they would keep their doubts to themselves. They had picked up the captain, the mate, and two engineers of the steamer *Patna* sunk at sea, and that, very properly, was enough for them. I did not ask Jim about the nature of his feelings during the ten days he spent on board. From the way he narrated that part I was at liberty to infer he was partly stunned by the discovery he had made—the discovery about himself —and no doubt was at work trying to explain it away to the only man who was capable of appreciating all its tremendous magnitude. You must understand he did not try to minimise its importance. Of that I am sure; and therein lies his distinction. As to what sensations he experienced when he got ashore and heard the unforeseen conclusion of the tale in which he had taken such a pitiful part, he told me

4. Made in good faith. (Latin.)

nothing of them, and it is difficult to imagine. I wonder whether he felt the ground cut from under his feet? I wonder? But no doubt he managed to get a fresh foothold very soon. He was ashore a whole fortnight waiting in the Sailors' Home, and as there were six or seven men staying there at the time, I had heard of him a little. Their languid opinion seemed to be that in addition to his other shortcomings, he was a sulky brute. He had passed these days on the verandah, buried in a long chair, and coming out of his place of sepulture only at meal-times or late at night, when he wandered on the quays all by himself, detached from his surroundings, irresolute and silent, like a ghost without a home to haunt. 'I don't think I've spoken three words to a living soul in all that time,' he said, making me very sorry for him; and directly he added, 'One of these fellows would have been sure to blurt out something I had made up my mind not to put up with, and I didn't want a row. No! Not then. I was too—too . . . I had no heart for it.' 'So that bulkhead held out after all,' I remarked cheerfully. 'Yes,' he murmured, 'it held. And yet I swear to you I felt it bulge under my hand.' 'It's extraordinary what strains old iron will stand sometimes,' I said. Thrown back in his seat, his legs stiffly out and arms hanging down, he nodded slightly several times. You could not conceive a sadder spectacle. Suddenly he lifted his head; he sat up; he slapped his thigh. 'Ah! what a chance missed! My God! what a chance missed!' he blazed out; but the ring of the last 'missed' resembled a cry wrung out by pain.

"He was silent again with a still, far-away look of fierce yearning after that missed distinction, with his nostrils for an instant dilated, sniffing the intoxicating breath of that wasted opportunity. If you think I was either surprised or shocked you do me an injustice in more ways than one! Ah, he was an imaginative beggar! He would give himself away; he would give himself up. I could see in his glance darted into the night all his inner being carried on, projected headlong into the fanciful realm of recklessly heroic aspirations. He had no leisure to regret what he had lost, he was so wholly and naturally concerned for what he had failed to obtain. He was very far away from me who watched him across three feet of space. With every instant he was penetrating deeper into the impossible world of romantic achievements. He got to the heart of it at last! A strange look of beatitude overspread his features, his eyes sparkled in the light of the candle burning between us; he positively smiled! He had penetrated to the very heart—to the very heart. It was an ecstatic smile that your faces —or mine either—will never wear, my dear boys. I whisked him back by saying, 'If you had stuck to the ship, you mean!'

"He turned upon me, his eyes suddenly amazed and full of pain, with a bewildered, startled, suffering face, as though he had tumbled down from a star. Neither you nor I will ever look like this on any man. He shuddered profoundly, as if a cold finger-tip had touched his heart. Last of all he sighed.

"I was not in a merciful mood. He provoked one by his contradictory indiscretions. 'It is unfortunate you didn't know beforehand!' I said with every unkind intention; but the perfidious shaft fell harmless—dropped at his feet like a spent arrow, as it were, and he did not think of picking it up. Perhaps he had not even seen it. Presently, lolling at ease, he said, 'Dash it all! I tell you it bulged. I was holding up my lamp along the angle-iron in the lower deck when a flake of rust as big as the palm of my hand fell off the plate, all of itself.' He passed his hand over his forehead. 'The thing stirred and jumped off like something alive while I was looking at it.' 'That made you feel pretty bad,' I observed casually. 'Do you suppose,' he said, 'that I was thinking of myself, with a hundred and sixty people at my back, all fast asleep in that fore-'tween-deck alone—and more of them aft; more on the deck—sleeping—knowing nothing about it—three times as many as there were boats for, even if there had been time? I expected to see the iron open out as I stood there and the rush of water going over them as they lay. . . . What could I do—what?'

"I can easily picture him to myself in the peopled gloom of the cavernous place, with the light of the bulk-lamp falling on a small portion of the bulkhead that had the weight of the ocean on the other side, and the breathing of unconscious sleepers in his ears. I can see him glaring at the iron, startled by the falling rust, over-burdened by the knowledge of an imminent death. This, I gathered, was the second time he had been sent forward by that skipper of his, who, I rather think, wanted to keep him away from the bridge. He told me that his first impulse was to shout and straightway make all those people leap out of sleep into terror; but such an overwhelming sense of his helplessness came over him that he was not able to produce a sound. This is, I suppose, what people mean by the tongue cleaving to the roof of the mouth. 'Too dry,' was the concise expression he used in reference to this state. Without a sound, then, he scrambled out on deck through the number one hatch. A wind-sail rigged down there swung against him accidentally, and he remembered that the light touch of the canvas on his face nearly knocked him off the hatchway ladder.

"He confessed that his knees wobbled a good deal as he stood on the foredeck looking at another sleeping crowd. The engines having been stopped by that time, the steam was blowing off. Its deep rumble made the whole night vibrate like a bass string. The ship trembled to it.

"He saw here and there a head lifted off a mat, a vague form uprise in sitting posture, listen sleepily for a moment, sink down again into the billowy confusion of boxes, steam-winches, ventilators. He was aware all these people did not know enough to take intelligent notice of that strange noise. The ship of iron, the men with white faces, all the sights, all the sounds, everything on board to that ignorant and pious multitude was strange alike, and as trustworthy as it would for ever remain incomprehensible. It occurred to him that the fact was fortunate. The idea of it was simply terrible.

"You must remember he believed, as any other man would have done in his place, that the ship would go down at any moment; the bulging, rust-eaten plates that kept back the ocean, fatally must give way, all at once like an undermined dam, and let in a sudden and overwhelming flood. He stood still looking at these recumbent bodies, a doomed man aware of his fate, surveying the silent company of the dead. They *were* dead! Nothing could save them! There were boats enough for half of them perhaps, but there was no time. No time! No time! It did not seem worth while to open his lips, to stir hand or foot. Before he could shout three words, or make three steps, he would be floundering in a sea whitened awfully by the desperate struggles of human beings, clamorous with the distress of cries for help. There was no help. He imagined what would happen perfectly; he went through it all motionless by the hatchway with the lamp in his hand—he went through it to the very last harrowing detail. I think he went through it again while he was telling me these things he could not tell the court.

" 'I saw as clearly as I see you now that there was nothing I could do. It seemed to take all life out of my limbs. I thought I might just as well stand where I was and wait. I did not think I had many seconds . . .' Suddenly the steam ceased blowing off. The noise, he remarked, had been distracting, but the silence at once became intolerably oppressive.

" 'I thought I would choke before I got drowned,' he said.

"He protested he did not think of saving himself. The only distinct thought formed, vanishing, and re-forming in his brain, was: eight hundred people and seven boats; eight hundred people and seven boats.

" 'Somebody was speaking aloud inside my head,' he said a little wildly. 'Eight hundred people and seven boats—and no time! Just think of it.' He leaned towards me across the little table, and I tried to avoid his stare. 'Do you think I was afraid of death?' he asked in a voice very fierce and low. He brought down his open hand with a bang that made the coffee-cups dance. 'I am ready to swear I was not—I was not. . . . By God—no!' He hitched himself upright and crossed his arms; his chin fell on his breast.

"The soft clashes of crockery reached us faintly through the high windows. There was a burst of voices, and several men came out in high good-humour into the gallery. They were exchanging jocular reminiscences of the donkeys in Cairo. A pale, anxious youth stepping softly on long legs was being chaffed by a strutting and rubicund globe-trotter about his purchases in the bazaar. 'No, really—do you think I've been done to that extent?' he inquired, very earnest and deliberate. The band moved away, dropping into chairs as they went; matches flared, illuminating for a second faces without the ghost of an expression and the flat glaze of white shirt-fronts; the hum of many conversations animated with the ardour of feasting sounded to me absurd and infinitely remote.

" 'Some of the crew were sleeping on the number one hatch within reach of my arm,' began Jim again.

"You must know they kept Kalashee watch in that ship, all hands sleeping through the night, and only the reliefs of quartermasters and look-out men being called. He was tempted to grip and shake the shoulder of the nearest lascar, but he didn't. Something held his arms down along his sides. He was not afraid—oh no! only he just couldn't—that's all. He was not afraid of death perhaps, but I'll tell you what, he was afraid of the emergency. His confounded imagination had evoked for him all the horrors of panic, the trampling rush, the pitiful screams, boats swamped—all the appalling incidents of a disaster at sea he had ever heard of. He might have been resigned to die, but I suspect he wanted to die without added terrors, quietly, in a sort of peaceful trance. A certain readiness to perish is not so very rare, but it is seldom that you meet men whose souls, steeled in the impenetrable armour of resolution, are ready to fight a losing battle to the last; the desire of peace waxes stronger as hope declines, till at last it conquers the very desire of life. Which of us here has not observed this, or maybe experienced something of that feeling in his own person—this extreme weariness of emotions, the vanity of effort, the yearning for rest? Those striving with unreasonable forces know it well—the shipwrecked castaways in boats, wanderers lost in a desert, men battling against the unthinking might of nature, or the stupid brutality of crowds."

Chapter Eight

"How long he stood stock-still by the hatch expecting every moment to feel the ship dip under his feet and the rush of water to take him at the back and toss him like a chip, I cannot say. Not very long—two minutes perhaps. A couple of men he could not make out began to converse drowsily, and also, he could not tell where, he detected a curious noise of shuffling feet. Above these faint sounds there was that awful stillness preceding a catastrophe, that trying silence of the moment before the crash; then it came into his head that perhaps he would have time to rush along and cut all the lanyards of the gripes, so that the boats would float off as the ship went down.

"The *Patna* had a long bridge, and all the boats were up there, four on one side and three on the other—the smallest of them on the port side and nearly abreast of the steering-gear. He assured me, with evident anxiety to be believed, that he had been most careful to keep them ready for instant service. He knew his duty. I dare say he was a good enough mate as far as that went. 'I always believed in being prepared for the worst,' he commented, staring anxiously in my face. I nodded my approval of the sound principle, averting my eyes before the subtle unsoundness of the man.

"He started unsteadily to run. He had to step over legs, avoid stumbling against the heads. Suddenly some one caught hold of his coat from below, and a distressed voice spoke under his elbow. The light of the lamp he carried in his right hand fell upon an upturned dark face whose eyes entreated him together with the voice. He had picked up enough of the language to understand the word water, repeated several times in a tone of insistence, of prayer, almost of despair. He gave a jerk to get away, and felt an arm embrace his leg.

" 'The beggar clung to me like a drowning man,' he said impressively. 'Water, water! What water did he mean? What did he know? As calmly as I could I ordered him to let go. He was stopping me, time was pressing, other men began to stir; I wanted time—time to cut the boats adrift. He got hold of my hand now, and I felt that he would begin to shout. It flashed upon me it was enough to start a panic, and I hauled off with my free arm and slung the lamp in his face. The glass jingled, the light went out, but the blow made him let go, and I ran off—I wanted to get at the boats; I wanted to get at the boats. He leaped after me from behind. I turned on him. He would not keep quiet; he tried to shout; I had half throttled him before I made out what he wanted. He wanted some water—water to drink; they were on strict allowance, you know, and he had with him a young boy I had noticed several times. His child was sick—and thirsty. He had caught sight of me as I passed by, and was begging for a little water. That's all. We were under the bridge, in the dark. He kept on snatching at my wrists; there was no getting rid of him. I dashed into my berth, grabbed my water-bottle, and thrust it into his hands. He vanished. I didn't find out till then how much I was in want of a drink myself.' He leaned on one elbow with a hand over his eyes.

"I felt a creepy sensation all down my backbone; there was something peculiar in all this. The fingers of the hand that shaded his brow trembled slightly. He broke the short silence.

" 'These things happen only once to a man and . . . Ah, well! When I got on the bridge at last the beggars were getting one of the boats off the chocks. A boat! I was running up the ladder when a heavy blow fell on my shoulder, just missing my head. It didn't stop me, and the chief engineer—they had got him out of his bunk by then—raised the boat-stretcher again. Somehow I had no mind to be surprised at anything. All this seemed natural—and awful—and awful. I dodged that miserable maniac, lifted him off the deck as though he had been a little child, and he started whispering in my arms: "Don't! don't! I thought you were one of them niggers." I flung him away; he skidded along the bridge and knocked the legs from under the little chap—the second. The skipper, busy about the boat, looked round, and came at me head down, growling like a wild beast. I flinched no more than a stone. I was as solid standing there as this,' he tapped lightly with his knuckles the wall beside his chair. 'It was as though I had heard it all, seen it all, gone through it all twenty times already. I wasn't afraid of them. I drew back my fist and he stopped short, muttering:

" ' "Ah! it's you. Lend a hand quick."

" 'That's what he said. Quick! As if anybody could be quick enough. "Aren't you going to do something?" I asked. "Yes. Clear out," he snarled over his shoulder.

" 'I don't think I understood then what he meant. The other two had picked themselves up by that time, and they rushed together to the boat. They tramped, they wheezed, they shoved, they cursed the boat, the ship, each other—cursed me. All in mutters. I didn't move, I didn't speak. I watched the slant of the ship. She was as still as if landed on the blocks in a dry dock—only she was like this.' He held up his hand, palm under, the tips of the fingers inclined downwards. 'Like this,' he repeated. 'I could see the line of the horizon before me, as clear as a bell, above her stem-head; I could see the water far off there black and sparkling, and still— still as a pond, deadly still, more still than ever sea was before— more still than I could bear to look at. Have you watched a ship floating head down, checked in sinking by a sheet of old iron too rotten to stand being shored up? Have you? Oh yes, shored up? I thought of that—I thought of every mortal thing; but can you shore up a bulkhead in five minutes—or in fifty for that matter?

Where was I going to get men that would go down below? And the timber—the timber! Would you have had the courage to swing the maul for the first blow if you had seen that bulkhead? Don't say you would: you had not seen it; nobody would. Hang it —to do a thing like that you must believe there is a chance, one in a thousand, at least, some ghost of a chance; and you would not have believed. Nobody would have believed. You think me a cur for standing there, but what would you have done? What! You can't tell—nobody can tell. One must have time to turn round. What would you have me do? Where was the kindness in making crazy with fright all those people I could not save single-handed—that nothing could save? Look here! As true as I sit on this chair before you . . .'

"He drew quick breaths at every few words and shot quick glances at my face, as though in his anguish he were watchful of the effect. He was not speaking to me, he was only speaking before me, in a dispute with an invisible personality, an antagonistic and inseparable partner of his existence—another possessor of his soul. These were issues beyond the competency of a court of inquiry: it was a subtle and momentous quarrel as to the true essence of life, and did not want a judge. He wanted an ally, a helper, an accomplice. I felt the risk I ran of being circumvented, blinded, decoyed, bullied, perhaps, into taking a definite part in a dispute impossible of decision if one had to be fair to all the phantoms in possession—to the reputable that had its claims and to the dis-reputable that had its exigencies. I can't explain to you who haven't seen him and who hear his words only at second hand the mixed nature of my feelings. It seemed to me I was being made to comprehend the Inconceivable—and I know of nothing to compare with the discomfort of such a sensation. I was made to look at the convention that lurks in all truth and on the essential sincerity of falsehood. He appealed to all sides at once—to the side turned perpetually to the light of day, and to that side of us which, like the other hemisphere of the moon, exists stealthily in perpetual darkness, with only a fearful ashy light falling at times on the edge. He swayed me. I own to it, I own up. The occasion was obscure, insignificant—what you will: a lost youngster, one in a million—but then he was one of us; an incident as completely devoid of importance as the flooding of an ant-heap, and yet the mystery of his attitude got hold of me as though he had been an individual in the forefront of his kind, as if the obscure truth involved were momentous enough to affect mankind's conception of itself. . . ."

Marlow paused to put new life into his expiring cheroot, seemed to forget all about the story, and abruptly began again.

"My fault of course. One has no business really to get interested. It's a weakness of mine. His was of another kind. My weakness consists in not having a discriminating eye for the incidental—for the externals—no eye for the hod [5] of the rag-picker or the fine linen of the next man. Next man—that's it. I have met so many men," he pursued, with momentary sadness—"met them, too, with a certain—certain—impact, let us say; like this fellow, for instance—and in each case all I could see was merely the human being. A confounded democratic quality of vision which may be better than total blindness, but has been of no advantage to me, I can assure you. Men expect one to take into account their fine linen. But I never could get up any enthusiasm about these things. Oh! it's a failing; it's a failing; and then comes a soft evening; a lot of men too indolent for whist—and a story. . . ."

He paused again to wait for an encouraging remark perhaps, but nobody spoke; only the host, as if reluctantly performing a duty, murmured:

"You are so subtle, Marlow."

"Who? I?" said Marlow in a low voice. "Oh no! But *he* was; and try as I may for the success of this yarn, I am missing innumerable shades—they were so fine, so difficult to render in colourless words. Because he complicated matters by being so simple, too—the simplest poor devil! . . . By Jove! he was amazing. There he sat telling me that just as I saw him before my eyes he wouldn't be afraid to face anything—and believing in it, too. I tell you it was fabulously innocent and it was enormous, enormous! I watched him covertly, just as though I had suspected him of an intention to take a jolly good rise out of me.[6] He was confident that, on the square, 'on the square, mind!' there was nothing he couldn't meet. Ever since he had been 'so high'—'quite a little chap,' he had been preparing himself for all the difficulties that can beset one on land and water. He confessed proudly to this kind of foresight. He had been elaborating dangers and defences, expecting the worst, rehearsing his best. He must have led a most exalted existence. Can you fancy it? A succession of adventures, so much glory, such a victorious progress! and the deep sense of his sagacity crowning every day of his inner life. He forgot himself; his eyes shone; and with every word my heart, searched by the light of his absurdity, was growing heavier in my breast. I had no mind to laugh, and lest I should smile I made for myself a stolid face. He gave signs of irritation.

" 'It is always the unexpected that happens,' I said in a propitiatory tone. My obtuseness provoked him into a contemptuous 'Pshaw!' I suppose he meant that the unexpected couldn't touch

---

5. Possibly from hodden, a coarse cloth of undyed wool.

6. Outwit or make a person the subject of a jest.

him; nothing less than the unconceivable itself could get over his perfect state of preparation. He had been taken unawares—and he whispered to himself a malediction upon the waters and the firmament, upon the ship, upon the men. Everything had betrayed him! He had been tricked into that sort of high-minded resignation which prevented him lifting as much as his little finger, while these others who had a very clear perception of the actual necessity were tumbling against each other and sweating desperately over that boat business. Something had gone wrong there at the last moment. It appears that in their flurry they had contrived in some mysterious way to get the sliding bolt of the foremost boat-chock jammed tight, and forthwith had gone out of the remnants of their minds over the deadly nature of that accident. It must have been a pretty sight, the fierce industry of these beggars toiling on a motionless ship that floated quietly in the silence of a world asleep, fighting against time for the freeing of that boat, grovelling on all-fours, standing up in despair, tugging, pushing, snarling at each other venomously, ready to kill, ready to weep, and only kept from flying at each other's throats by the fear of death that stood silent behind them like an inflexible and cold-eyed taskmaster. Oh yes! It must have been a pretty sight. He saw it all, he could talk about it with scorn and bitterness; he had a minute knowledge of it by means of some sixth sense, I conclude, because he swore to me he had remained apart without a glance at them and at the boat—without one single glance. And I believe him. I should think he was too busy watching the threatening slant of the ship, the suspended menace discovered in the midst of the most perfect security—fascinated by the sword hanging by a hair over his imaginative head.

"Nothing in the world moved before his eyes, and he could depict to himself without hindrance the sudden swing upwards of the dark skyline, the sudden tilt up of the vast plain of the sea, the swift still rise, the brutal fling, the grasp of the abyss, the struggle without hope, the starlight closing over his head for ever like the vault of a tomb—the revolt of his young life—the black end. He could! By Jove! who couldn't? And you must remember he was a finished artist in that peculiar way, he was a gifted poor devil with the faculty of swift and forestalling vision. The sights it showed him had turned him into cold stone from the soles of his feet to the nape of his neck; but there was a hot dance of thoughts in his head, a dance of lame, blind, mute thoughts—a whirl of awful cripples. Didn't I tell you he confessed himself before me as though I had the power to bind and to loose? [7] He burrowed deep, deep, in the hope of my absolution, which would have been

---

7. Cf. Jesus' words to Peter: "And I will give unto thee the keys of the kingdom of heaven: and whatsoever thou shalt bind on earth shall be bound in heaven: and whatsoever thou shalt loose on earth shall be loosed in heaven." (Matthew 16:17–19.)

of no good to him. This was one of those cases which no solemn deception can palliate, which no man can help; where his very Maker seems to abandon a sinner to his own devices.

"He stood on the starboard side of the bridge, as far as he could get from the struggle for the boat, which went on with the agitation of madness and the stealthiness of a conspiracy. The two Malays had meantime remained holding to the wheel. Just picture to yourselves the actors in that, thank God! unique episode of the sea, four beside themselves with fierce and secret exertions, and three looking on in complete immobility, above the awnings covering the profound ignorance of hundreds of human beings, with their weariness, with their dreams, with their hopes, arrested, held by an invisible hand on the brink of annihilation. For that they were so, makes no doubt to me: given the state of the ship, this was the deadliest possible description of accident that could happen. These beggars by the boat had every reason to go distracted with funk. Frankly, had I been there I would not have given as much as a counterfeit farthing for the ship's chance to keep above water to the end of each successive second. And still she floated! These sleeping pilgrims were destined to accomplish their whole pilgrimage to the bitterness of some other end. It was as if the Omnipotence whose mercy they confessed had needed their humble testimony on earth for a while longer, and had looked down to make a sign, 'Thou shalt not!' to the ocean. Their escape would trouble me as a prodigiously inexplicable event, did I not know how tough old iron can be—as tough sometimes as the spirit of some men we meet now and then, worn to a shadow and breasting the weight of life. Not the least wonder of these twenty minutes, to my mind, is the behaviour of the two helmsmen. They were amongst the native batch of all sorts brought over from Aden to give evidence at the inquiry. One of them, labouring under intense bashfulness, was very young, and with his smooth, yellow, cheery countenance looked even younger than he was. I remember perfectly Brierly asking him, through the interpreter, what he thought of it at the time, and the interpreter, after a short colloquy, turning to the court with an important air:

" 'He says he thought nothing.'

"The other, with patient, blinking eyes, a blue cotton handkerchief, faded with much washing, bound with a smart twist over a lot of grey wisps, his face shrunk into grim hollows, his brown skin made darker by a mesh of wrinkles, explained that he had a knowledge of some evil thing befalling the ship, but there had been no order; he could not remember an order; why should he leave the helm? To some further questions he jerked back his spare shoulders, and declared it never came into his mind then

that the white men were about to leave the ship through fear of
death. He did not believe it now. There might have been secret
reasons. He wagged his old chin knowingly. Aha! secret reasons.
He was a man of great experience, and he wanted *that* white
Tuan to know—he turned towards Brierly, who didn't raise his
head—that he had acquired a knowledge of many things by serving white men on the sea for a great number of years—and,
suddenly, with shaky excitement he poured upon our spellbound
attention a lot of queer-sounding names, names of dead-and-gone
skippers, names of forgotten country ships, names of familiar and
distorted sound, as if the hand of dumb time had been at work
on them for ages. They stopped him at last. A silence fell upon
the court—a silence that remained unbroken for at least a minute,
and passed gently into a deep murmur. This episode was *the* sensation of the second day's proceedings—affecting all the audience, affecting everybody except Jim, who was sitting moodily at the end
of the first bench, and never looked up at this extraordinary and
damning witness that seemed possessed of some mysterious theory
of defence.

"So these two lascars stuck to the helm of that ship without steerage-way, where death would have found them if such had been
their destiny. The whites did not give them half a glance, had
probably forgotten their existence. Assuredly Jim did not remember it. He remembered he could do nothing; he could do nothing,
now he was alone. There was nothing to do but to sink with the
ship. No use making a disturbance about it. Was there? He waited
upstanding, without a sound, stiffened in the idea of some sort
of heroic discretion. The first engineer ran cautiously across the
bridge to tug at his sleeve.

" 'Come and help! For God's sake, come and help!'

"He ran back to the boat on the points of his toes, and returned
directly to worry at his sleeve, begging and cursing at the same
time.

" 'I believe he would have kissed my hands,' said Jim savagely,
'and, next moment he starts foaming and whispering in my face,
"If I had the time I would like to crack your skull for you." I
pushed him away. Suddenly he caught hold of me round the neck.
Damn him! I hit him. I hit out without looking. "Won't you save
your own life—you infernal coward?" he sobs. Coward! He called
me an infernal coward! Ha! ha! ha! ha! He called me—ha! ha!
ha! . . .'

"He had thrown himself back and was shaking with laughter. I
had never in my life heard anything so bitter as that noise. It
fell like a blight on all the merriment about donkeys, pyramids,
bazaars, or what not. Along the whole dim length of the gallery the

voices dropped, the pale blotches of faces turned our way with one accord, and the silence became so profound that the clear tinkle of a teaspoon falling on the tessellated floor of the verandah rang out like a tiny and silvery scream.

" 'You mustn't laugh like this, with all these people about,' I remonstrated. 'It isn't nice for them, you know.'

"He gave no sign of having heard at first, but after a while, with a stare that, missing me altogether, seemed to probe the heart of some awful vision, he muttered carelessly: 'Oh! they'll think I am drunk.'

"And after that you would have thought from his appearance he would never make a sound again. But—no fear! He could no more stop telling now than he could have stopped living by the mere exertion of his will."

Chapter Nine

" 'I was saying to myself, "Sink—curse you! Sink!" ' These were the words with which he began again. He wanted it over. He was severely left alone, and he formulated in his head this address to the ship in a tone of imprecation, while at the same time he enjoyed the privilege of witnessing scenes—as far as I can judge—of low comedy. They were still at that bolt. The skipper was ordering. 'Get under and try to lift'; and the others naturally shirked. You understand that to be squeezed flat under the keel of a boat wasn't a desirable position to be caught in if the ship went down suddenly. 'Why don't you—you the strongest?' whined the little engineer. 'Gott-for-dam! I am too thick,' spluttered the skipper in despair. It was funny enough to make angels weep. They stood idle for a moment, and suddenly the chief engineer rushed again at Jim.

" 'Come and help, man! Are you mad to throw your only chance away? Come and help, man! Man! Look there—look!'

"And at last Jim looked astern where the other pointed with maniacal insistence. He saw a silent black squall which had eaten up already one-third of the sky. You know how these squalls come up there about that time of the year. First you see a darkening of the horizon—no more; then a cloud rises opaque like a wall. A straight edge of vapour lined with sickly, whitish gleams flies up from the south-west, swallowing the stars in whole constellations; its shadow flies over the waters, and confounds sea and sky into one abyss of obscurity. And all is still. No thunder, no wind, no sound; not a flicker of lightning. Then in the tenebrous immensity a livid arch appears; a swell or two like undulations of the very darkness run past, and suddenly, wind and rain strike together with a peculiar impetuosity as if they had burst through something solid. Such a

cloud had come up while they weren't looking. They had just noticed it, and were perfectly justified in surmising that if in absolute
stillness there was some chance for the ship to keep afloat a few
minutes longer, the least disturbance of the sea would make an end
of her instantly. Her first nod to the swell that precedes the burst of
such a squall would be also her last, would become a plunge, would,
so to speak, be prolonged into a long dive, down, down to the bottom. Hence these new capers of their fright, these new antics in
which they displayed their extreme aversion to die.

" 'It was black, black,' pursued Jim, with moody steadiness. 'It
had sneaked upon us from behind. The infernal thing! I suppose
there had been at the back of my head some hope yet. I don't
know. But that was all over anyhow. It maddened me to see myself
caught like this. I was angry, as though I had been trapped. I *was*
trapped! The night was hot, too, I remember. Not a breath of air.'

"He remembered so well that, gasping in the chair, he seemed to
sweat and choke before my eyes. No doubt it maddened him; it
knocked him over afresh—in a manner of speaking—but it made
him also remember that important purpose which had sent him
rushing on that bridge only to slip clean out of his mind. He had intended to cut the life-boats clear of the ship. He whipped out his
knife and went to work slashing as though he had seen nothing, had
heard nothing, had known of no one on board. They thought him
hopelessly wrong-headed and crazy, but dared not protest noisily
against this useless loss of time. When he had done he returned to
the very same spot from which he had started. The chief was there,
ready with a clutch at him to whisper close to his head, scathingly, as
though he wanted to bite his ear:

" 'You silly fool! do you think you'll get the ghost of a show
when all that lot of brutes is in the water? Why, they will batter
your head for you from these boats.'

"He wrung his hands, ignored, at Jim's elbow. The skipper kept
up a nervous shuffle in one place and mumbled, 'Hammer! hammer! Mein Gott! Get a hammer.'

"The little engineer whimpered like a child, but broken arm and
all, he turned out the least craven of the lot as it seems, and, actually, mustered enough pluck to run an errand to the engine-room.
No trifle, it must be owned in fairness to him. Jim told me he
darted desperate looks like a cornered man, gave one low wail, and
dashed off. He was back instantly clambering, hammer in hand, and
without a pause flung himself at the bolt. The others gave up Jim
at once and ran off to assist. He heard the tap, tap of the hammer,
the sound of the released chock falling over. The boat was clear.
Only then he turned to look—only then. But he kept his distance—
he kept his distance. He wanted me to know he had kept his dis-

tance; that there was nothing in common between him and these men—who had the hammer. Nothing whatever. It is more than probable he thought himself cut off from them by a space that could not be traversed, by an obstacle that could not be overcome, by a chasm without bottom. He was as far as he could get from them —the whole breadth of the ship.

"His feet were glued to that remote spot and his eyes to their indistinct group bowed together and swaying strangely in the common torment of fear. A hand-lamp lashed to a stanchion above a little table rigged up on the bridge—the *Patna* had no chart-room amidships—threw a light on their labouring shoulders, on their arched and bobbing backs. They pushed at the bow of the boat; they pushed out into the night; they pushed, and would no more look back at him. They had given him up as if indeed he had been too far, too hopelessly separated from themselves, to be worth an appealing word, a glance, or a sign. They had no leisure to look back upon his passive heroism, to feel the sting of his abstention. The boat was heavy; they pushed at the bow with no breath to spare for an encouraging word: but the turmoil of terror that had scattered their self-control like chaff before the wind, converted their desperate exertions into a bit of fooling, upon my word fit for knockabout clowns in a farce. They pushed with their hands, with their heads, they pushed for dear life with all the weight of their bodies, they pushed with all the might of their souls—only no sooner had they succeeded in canting the stem clear of the davit than they would leave off like one man and start a wild scramble into her. As a natural consequence the boat would swing in abruptly, driving them back, helpless and jostling against each other. They would stand nonplussed for a while, exchanging in fierce whispers all the infamous names they could call to mind, and go at it again. Three times this occurred. He described it to me with morose thoughtfulness. He hadn't lost a single movement of that comic business. 'I loathed them. I hated them. I had to look at all that,' he said without emphasis, turning upon me a sombrely watchful glance. 'Was ever there any one so shamefully tried?'

"He took his head in his hands for a moment, like a man driven to distraction by some unspeakable outrage. These were things he could not explain to the court—and not even to me; but I would have been little fitted for the reception of his confidences had I not been able at times to understand the pauses between the words. In this assault upon his fortitude there was the jeering intention of a spiteful and vile vengeance; there was an element of burlesque in his ordeal—a degradation of funny grimaces in the approach of death or dishonour.

"He related facts which I have not forgotten, but at this distance of time I couldn't recall his very words: I only remember that he managed wonderfully to convey the brooding rancour of his mind into the bare recital of events. Twice, he told me, he shut his eyes in the certitude that the end was upon him already, and twice he had to open them again. Each time he noted the darkening of the great stillness. The shadow of the silent cloud had fallen upon the ship from the zenith, and seemed to have extinguished every sound of her teeming life. He could no longer hear the voices under the awnings. He told me that each time he closed his eyes a flash of thought showed him that crowd of bodies, laid out for death, as plain as daylight. When he opened them, it was to see the dim struggle of four men fighting like mad with a stubborn boat. 'They would fall back before it time after time, stand swearing at each other, and suddenly make another rush in a bunch. . . . Enough to make you die laughing,' he commented with downcast eyes; then raising them for a moment to my face with a dismal smile, 'I ought to have a merry life of it, by God! for I shall see that funny sight a good many times yet before I die.' His eyes fell again. 'See and hear. . . . See and hear,' he repeated twice, at long intervals, filled by vacant staring.

"He roused himself.

" 'I made up my mind to keep my eyes shut,' he said, 'and I couldn't. I couldn't, and I don't care who knows it. Let them go through that kind of thing before they talk. Just let them—and do better—that's all. The second time my eyelids flew open and my mouth too. I had felt the ship move. She just dipped her bows—and lifted them gently—and slow! everlastingly slow; and ever so little. She hadn't done that much for days. The cloud had raced ahead, and this first swell seemed to travel upon a sea of lead. There was no life in that stir. It managed, though, to knock over something in my head. What would you have done? You are sure of yourself—aren't you? What would you do if you felt now—this minute—the house here move, just move a little under your chair? Leap! By heavens! you would take one spring from where you sit and land in that clump of bushes yonder.'

"He flung his arm out at the night beyond the stone balustrade. I held my peace. He looked at me very steadily, very severe. There could be no mistake: I was being bullied now, and it behoved me to make no sign lest by a gesture or a word I should be drawn into a fatal admission about myself which would have had some bearing on the case. I was not disposed to take any risk of that sort. Don't forget I had him before me, and really he was too much like one of us not to be dangerous. But if you want to know, I don't mind telling you that I did, with a rapid glance, estimate the distance to the mass of denser blackness in the middle of the grass-plot before the verandah. He exaggerated. I would have landed short by several feet—and that's the only thing of which I am fairly certain.

"The last moment had come, as he thought, and he did not move. His feet remained glued to the planks if his thoughts were knocking about loose in his head. It was at this moment, too, that he saw one of the men around the boat step backwards suddenly, clutch at the air with raised arms, totter and collapse. He didn't exactly fall, he only slid gently into a sitting posture, all hunched up and with his shoulders propped against the side of the engine-room skylight. 'That was the donkey-man. A haggard, white-faced chap with a ragged moustache. Acted third engineer,' he explained.

" 'Dead?' I said. We had heard something of that in court.

" 'So they say,' he pronounced with sombre indifference. 'Of course I never knew. Weak heart. The man had been complaining of being out of sorts for some time before. Excitement. Over-exertion. Devil only knows. Ha! ha! ha! It was easy to see he did not want to die either. Droll, isn't it? May I be shot if he hadn't been fooled into killing himself! Fooled—neither more nor less. Fooled into it, by heavens! just as I . . . Ah! If he had only kept still; if he had only told them to go to the devil when they came to rush him out of his bunk because the ship was sinking! If he had only stood by with his hands in his pockets and called them names!'

"He got up, shook his fist, glared at me, and sat down.

" 'A chance missed, eh?' I murmured.

" 'Why don't you laugh?' he said. 'A joke hatched in hell. Weak heart! . . . I wish sometimes mine had been.'

"This irritated me. 'Do you?' I exclaimed with deep-rooted irony. 'Yes! Can't *you* understand?' he cried. 'I don't know what more you could wish for,' I said angrily. He gave me an utterly uncomprehending glance. This shaft had also gone wide of the mark, and he was not the man to bother about stray arrows. Upon my word, he was too unsuspecting; he was not fair game. I was glad that my missile had been thrown away—that he had not even heard the twang of the bow.

"Of course he could not know at the time the man was dead. The next minute—his last on board—was crowded with a tumult of events and sensations which beat about him like the sea upon a rock. I use the simile advisedly, because from his relation I am forced to bèlieve he had preserved through it all a strange illusion of passiveness, as though he had not acted but had suffered himself to be handled by the infernal powers who had selected him for the victim of their practical joke. The first thing that came to him was the grinding surge of the heavy davits swinging out at last—a jar which seemed to enter his body from the deck through the soles of his feet, and travel up his spine to the crown of his head. Then, the

squall being very near now, another and a heavier swell lifted the
passive hull in a threatening heave that checked his breath, while
his brain and his heart together were pierced as with daggers by
panic-stricken screams. 'Let go! For God's sake, let go! Let go! She's
going.' Following upon that the boat-falls ripped through the
blocks, and a lot of men began to talk in startled tones under the
awnings. 'When these beggars did break out, their yelps were
enough to wake the dead,' he said. Next after the splashing shock of
the boat literally dropped in the water, came the hollow noises of
stamping and tumbling in her, mingled with confused shouts: 'Unhook! Unhook! Shove! Unhook! Shove for your life! Here's the
squall down on us. . . .' He heard, high above his head, the faint
muttering of the wind; he heard below his feet a cry of pain. A lost
voice alongside started cursing a swivel hook. The ship began to
buzz fore and aft like a disturbed hive, and, as quietly as he was
telling me all this—because just then he was very quiet in attitude,
in face, in voice—he went on to say without the slightest warning as
it were, 'I stumbled over his legs.'

"This was the first I heard of his having moved at all. I could not
restrain a grunt of surprise. Something had started him off at last,
but of the exact moment, of the cause that tore him out of his immobility, he knew no more than the uprooted tree knows of the
wind that laid it low. All this had come to him: the sounds, the
sights, the legs of the dead man—by Jove! The infernal joke was
being crammed devilishly down his throat, but—look you—he was
not going to admit of any sort of swallowing motion in his gullet. It's
extraordinary how he could cast upon you the spirit of his illusion.
I listened as if to a tale of black magic at work upon a corpse.

" 'He went over sideways, very gently, and this is the last thing I
remember seeing on board,' he continued. 'I did not care what he
did. It looked as though he were picking himself up: I thought he
was picking himself up, of course: I expected him to bolt past me
over the rail and drop into the boat after the others. I could hear
them knocking about, down there, and a voice as if crying up a shaft
called out "George!" Then three voices together raised a yell. They
came to me separately: one bleated, another screamed, one howled.
Ough!'

"He shivered a little, and I beheld him rise slowly as if a steady
hand from above had been pulling him out of the chair by his hair.
Up, slowly—to his full height, and when his knees had locked stiff
the hand let him go, and he swayed a little on his feet. There was a
suggestion of awful stillness in his face, in his movements, in his very
voice when he said, 'They shouted'—and involuntarily I pricked up
my ears for the ghost of that shout that would be heard directly
through the false effect of silence. 'There were eight hundred

people in that ship,' he said, impaling me to the back of my seat with an awful blank stare. 'Eight hundred living people, and they were yelling after the one dead man to come down and be saved! "Jump, George! Jump! Oh, jump!" I stood by with my hand on the davit. I was very quiet. It had come over pitch-dark. You could see neither sky nor sea. I heard the boat alongside go bump, bump, and not another sound down there for a while, but the ship under me was full of talking noises. Suddenly the skipper howled, "Mein Gott! The squall! The squall! Shove off!" With the first hiss of rain, and the first gust of wind, they screamed, "Jump, George! We'll catch you! Jump!" The ship began a slow plunge; the rain swept over her like a broken sea; my cap flew off my head; my breath was driven back into my throat. I heard as if I had been on the top of a tower another wild screech, "Geo-o-o-orge! Oh, jump!" She was going down, down, head first under me. . . .'

"He raised his hand deliberately to his face, and made picking motions with his fingers as though he had been bothered with cobwebs, and afterwards he looked into the open palm for quite half a second before he blurted out:

" 'I had jumped . . .' he checked himself, averted his gaze . . . 'it seems,' he added.

"His clear blue eyes turned to me with a piteous stare, and looking at him standing before me, dumbfounded and hurt, I was oppressed by a sad sense of resigned wisdom, mingled with the amused and profound pity of an old man helpless before a childish disaster.

" 'Looks like it,' I muttered.

" 'I knew nothing about it till I looked up,' he explained hastily. And that's possible, too. You had to listen to him as you would to a small boy in trouble. He didn't know. It had happened somehow. It would never happen again. He had landed partly on somebody and fallen across a thwart. He felt as though all his ribs on his left side must be broken; then he rolled over, and saw vaguely the ship he had deserted uprising above him, with the red side-light glowing large in the rain like a fire on the brow of a hill seen through a mist. 'She seemed higher than a wall; she loomed like a cliff over the boat. . . . I wish I could die,' he cried. 'There was no going back. It was as if I had jumped into a well—into an everlasting deep hole. . . .' "

Chapter Ten

"He locked his fingers together and tore them apart. Nothing could be more true: he had indeed jumped into an everlasting deep hole. He had tumbled from a height he could never scale again. By that time the boat had gone driving forward past the bows. It was too dark just then for them to see each other, and, moreover, they were blinded and half drowned with rain. He told me it was like being swept by a flood through a cavern. They turned their backs to the squall; the skipper, it seems, got an oar over the stern to keep the boat before it, and for two or three minutes the end of the world had come through a deluge in a pitchy blackness. The sea hissed 'like twenty thousand kettles.' That's his simile, not mine. I fancy there was not much wind after the first gust; and he himself had admitted at the inquiry that the sea never got up that night to any extent. He crouched down in the bows and stole a furtive glance back. He saw just one yellow gleam of the masthead light high up and blurred like a last star ready to dissolve. 'It terrified me to see it still there,' he said. That's what he said. What terrified him was the thought that the drowning was not over yet. No doubt he wanted to be done with that abomination as quickly as possible. Nobody in the boat made a sound. In the dark she seemed to fly, but of course she could not have had much way. Then the shower swept ahead, and the great, distracting, hissing noise followed the rain into distance and died out. There was nothing to be heard then but the slight wash about the boat's sides. Somebody's teeth were chattering violently. A hand touched his back. A faint voice said, 'You there?' Another cried out shakily, 'She's gone!' and they all stood up together to look astern. They saw no lights. All was black. A thin, cold drizzle was driving into their faces. The boat lurched slightly. The teeth chattered faster, stopped, and began again twice before the man could master his shiver sufficiently to say, 'Ju-ju-st in ti-ti-me. . . . Brrrr.' He recognised the voice of the chief engineer saying surlily, 'I saw her go down. I happened to turn my head.' The wind had dropped almost completely.

"They watched in the dark with their heads half turned to windward as if expecting to hear cries. At first he was thankful the night had covered up the scene before his eyes, and then to know of it and yet to have seen and heard nothing appeared somehow the culminating point of an awful misfortune. 'Strange, isn't it?' he murmured, interrupting himself in his disjointed narrative.

"It did not seem so strange to me. He must have had an unconscious conviction that the reality could not be half as bad, not half as anguishing, appalling, and vengeful as the created terror of his imagination. I believe that, in this first moment, his heart was wrung with all the suffering, that his soul knew the accumulated savour of all the fear, all the horror, all the despair of eight hundred human beings pounced upon in the night by a sudden and violent death, else why should he have said, 'It seemed to me that I must jump out of that accursed boat and swim back to see—half a mile—

more—any distance—to the very spot . . .'? Why this impulse? Do
you see the significance? Why back to the very spot? Why not drown
alongside—if he meant drowning? Why back to the very spot, to
see—as if his imagination had to be soothed by the assurance that
all was over before death could bring relief? I defy any one of you
to offer another explanation. It was one of those bizarre and exciting
glimpses through the fog. It was an extraordinary disclosure. He let
it out as the most natural thing one could say. He fought down that
impulse and then he became conscious of the silence. He mentioned
this to me. A silence of the sea, of the sky, merged into one indefinite immensity still as death around these saved, palpitating
lives. 'You might have heard a pin drop in the boat,' he said with a
queer contraction of his lips, like a man trying to master his sensibilities while relating some extremely moving fact. A silence! God alone,
who had willed him as he was, knows what he made of it in his
heart. 'I didn't think any spot on earth could be so still,' he said.
'You couldn't distinguish the sea from the sky; there was nothing
to see and nothing to hear. Not a glimmer, not a shape, not a sound.
You could have believed that every bit of dry land had gone to the
bottom; that every man on earth but I and these beggars in the boat
had got drowned.' He leaned over the table with his knuckles
propped amongst coffee-cups, liqueur-glasses, cigar-ends. 'I seemed to
believe it. Everything was gone and—all was over . . .' he fetched a
deep sigh . . . 'with me.' "

Marlow sat up abruptly and flung away his cheroot with force. It
made a darting red trail like a toy rocket fired through the drapery of
creepers. Nobody stirred.

"Hey, what do you think of it?" he cried with sudden animation.
"Wasn't he true to himself, wasn't he? His saved life was over for
want of ground under his feet, for want of sights for his eyes, for
want of voices in his ears. Annihilation—hey! And all the time it
was only a clouded sky, a sea that did not break, the air that did not
stir. Only a night; only a silence.

"It lasted for a while, and then they were suddenly and unani-
mously moved to make a noise over their escape. 'I knew from the
first she would go.' 'Not a minute too soon.' 'A narrow squeak,
b'gosh!' He said nothing, but the breeze that had dropped came
back, a gentle draught freshened steadily, and the sea joined its
murmuring voice to this talkative reaction succeeding the dumb
moments of awe. She was gone! She was gone! Not a doubt of it.
Nobody could have helped. They repeated the same words over and
over again as though they couldn't stop themselves. Never doubted
she would go. The lights were gone. No mistake. The lights were
gone. Couldn't expect anything else. She had to go. . . . He noticed that they talked as though they had left behind them nothing

but an empty ship. They concluded she would not have been long when she once started. It seemed to cause them some sort of satisfaction. They assured each other that she couldn't have been long about it—'Just shot down like a flat-iron.' The chief engineer declared that the masthead light at the moment of sinking seemed to drop 'like a lighted match you throw down.' At this the second laughed hysterically. 'I am g-g-glad, I am gla-a-a-d.' His teeth went on 'like an electric rattle,' said Jim, 'and all at once he began to cry. He wept and blubbered like a child, catching his breath and sobbing, "Oh dear! oh dear! oh dear!" He would be quiet for a while and start suddenly, "Oh, my poor arm! oh, my poor a-a-arm!" I felt I could knock him down. Some of them sat in the stern-sheets. I could just make out their shapes. Voices came to me, mumble, mumble, grunt, grunt. All this seemed very hard to bear. I was cold, too. And I could do nothing. I thought that if I moved I would have to go over the side and . . .'

"His hand groped stealthily, came in contact with a liqueur-glass, and was withdrawn suddenly as if it had touched a red-hot coal. I pushed the bottle slightly. 'Won't you have some more?' I asked. He looked at me angrily. 'Don't you think I can tell you what there is to tell without screwing myself up?' [8] he asked. The squad of globe-trotters had gone to bed. We were alone but for a vague white form erect in the shadow, that, being looked at, cringed forward, hesitated, backed away silently. It was getting late, but I did not hurry my guest.

"In the midst of his forlorn state he heard his companions begin to abuse some one. 'What kept you from jumping, you lunatic?' said a scolding voice. The chief engineer left the stern-sheets, and could be heard clambering forward as if with hostile intentions against 'the greatest idiot that ever was.' The skipper shouted with rasping effort offensive epithets from where he sat at the oar. He lifted his head at that uproar, and heard the name 'George,' while a hand in the dark struck him on the breast. 'What have you got to say for yourself, you fool?' queried somebody, with a sort of virtuous fury. 'They were after me,' he said. 'They were abusing me—abusing me . . . by the name of George.'

"He paused to stare, tried to smile, turned his eyes away and went on. 'That little second puts his head right under my nose, "Why, it's that blasted mate!" "What!" howls the skipper from the other end of the boat. "No!" shrieks the chief. And he, too, stooped to look at my face.'

"The wind had left the boat suddenly. The rain began to fall again, and the soft, uninterrupted, a little mysterious sound with which the sea receives a shower arose on all sides in the night. 'They were too taken aback to say anything more at first,' he narrated

8. Getting intoxicated; a synoynm of "tight," the metaphor being the same.

steadily, 'and what could I have to say to them?' He faltered for a moment, and made an effort to go on. 'They called me horrible names.' His voice, sinking to a whisper, now and then would leap up suddenly, hardened by the passion of scorn, as though he had been talking of secret abominations. 'Never mind what they called me,' he said grimly. 'I could hear hate in their voices. A good thing, too. They could not forgive me for being in that boat. They hated it. It made them mad. . . .' He laughed short. . . . 'But it kept me from—look! I was sitting with my arms crossed, on the gunwale. . . .' He perched himself smartly on the edge of the table and crossed his arms. . . . 'Like this—see? One little tilt backwards and I would have been gone—after the others. One little tilt—the least bit—the least bit.' He frowned, and tapping his forehead with the tip of his middle finger, 'It was there all the time,' he said impressively. 'All the time—that notion. And the rain—cold, thick, cold as melted snow—colder—on my thin cotton clothes—I'll never be so cold again in my life, I know. And the sky was black, too—all black. Not a star, not a light anywhere. Nothing outside that confounded boat and those two yapping before me like a couple of mean mongrels at a tree'd thief. Yap! yap! "What you doing here? You're a fine sort! Too much of a bloomin' gentleman to put your hand to it. Come out of your trance, did you? To sneak in? Did you?" Yap! yap! "You ain't fit to live!" Yap! yap! Two of them together trying to out-bark each other. The other would bay from the stern through the rain—couldn't see him—couldn't make it out—some of his filthy jargon. Yap! yap! Bow-ow-ow-ow-ow! Yap! yap! It was sweet to hear them; it kept me alive, I tell you. It saved my life. At it they went, as if trying to drive me overboard with the noise! . . . "I wonder you had pluck enough to jump. You ain't wanted here. If I had known who it was, I would have tipped you over—you skunk! What have you done with the other? Where did you get the pluck to jump—you coward? What's to prevent us three from firing you overboard?" . . . They were out of breath; the shower passed away upon the sea. Then nothing. There was nothing round the boat, not even a sound. Wanted to see me overboard, did they? Upon my soul! I think they would have had their wish if they had only kept quiet. Fire me overboard! Would they? "Try," I said. "I would for twopence." "Too good for you," they screeched together. It was so dark that it was only when one or the other of them moved that I was quite sure of seeing him. By heavens, I only wish they had tried!'

"I couldn't help exclaiming, 'What an extraordinary affair!'

" 'Not bad—eh?' he said, as if in some sort astounded. 'They pretended to think I had done away with that donkey-man for some reason or other. Why should I? And how the devil was I to know? Didn't I get somehow into that boat? into that boat—I . . .' The muscles round his lips contracted into an unconscious grimace that tore through the mask of his usual expression— something violent, short-lived, and illuminating like a twist of lightning that admits the eye for an instant into the secret convo- lutions of a cloud. 'I did. I was plainly there with them—wasn't I? Isn't it awful a man should be driven to do a thing like that— and be responsible? What did I know about their George they were howling after? I remembered I had seen him curled up on the deck. "Murdering coward!" the chief kept on calling me. He didn't seem able to remember any other two words. I didn't care, only his noise began to worry me. "Shut up," I said. At that he collected himself for a confounded screech. "You killed him! You killed him!" "No," I shouted, "but I will kill you directly." I jumped up, and he fell backwards over a thwart with an awful loud thump. I don't know why. Too dark. Tried to step back, I suppose. I stood still facing aft, and the wretched little second be- gan to whine, "You ain't going to hit a chap with a broken arm— and you call yourself a gentleman, too." I heard a heavy tramp— one—two—and wheezy grunting. The other beast was coming at me, clattering his oar over the stern. I saw him moving, big, big —as you see a man in a mist, in a dream. "Come on," I cried. I would have tumbled him over like a bale of shakings. He stopped, muttering to himself, and went back. Perhaps he had heard the wind. I didn't. It was the last heavy gust we had. He went back to his oar. I was sorry. I would have tried to—to . . .'

"He opened and closed his curved fingers, and his hands had an eager and cruel flutter. 'Steady, steady,' I murmured.

" 'Eh? What? I am not excited,' he remonstrated awfully hurt, and with a convulsive jerk of his elbow knocked over the cognac bottle. I started forward, scraping my chair. He bounced off the table as if a mine had been exploded behind his back, and half turned before he alighted, crouching on his feet to show me a startled pair of eyes and a face white about the nostrils. A look of intense annoyance succeeded. 'Awfully sorry. How clumsy of me!' he mumbled very vexed, while the pungent odour of spilt alcohol enveloped us suddenly with an atmosphere of a low drinking-bout in the cool, pure darkness of the night. The lights had been put out in the dining-hall; our candle glimmered solitary in the long gallery, and the columns had turned black from pediment to capital. On the vivid stars the high corner of the Harbour Office stood out distinct across the Esplanade, as though the sombre pile had glided nearer to see and hear.

"He assumed an air of indifference.

" 'I dare say I am less calm now than I was then. I was ready for anything. These were trifles. . . .'

" 'You had a lively time of it in that boat,' I remarked.

" 'I was ready,' he repeated. 'After the ship's lights had gone, anything might have happened in that boat—anything in the world —and the world no wiser. I felt this, and I was pleased. It was just dark enough, too. We were like men walled up quick in a roomy grave. No concern with anything on earth. Nobody to pass an opinion. Nothing mattered.' For the third time during this conversation he laughed harshly, but there was no one about to suspect him of being only drunk. 'No fear, no law, no sounds, no eyes—not even our own, till—till sunrise at least.'

"I was struck by the suggestive truth of his words. There is something peculiar in a small boat upon the wide sea. Over the lives borne from under the shadow of death there seems to fall the shadow of madness. When your ship fails you, your whole world seems to fail you; the world that made you, restrained you, took care of you. It is as if the souls of men floating on an abyss and in touch with immensity had been set free for any excess of heroism, absurdity, or abomination. Of course, as with belief, thought, love, hate, conviction, or even the visual aspect of material things, there are as many shipwrecks as there are men, and in this one there was something abject which made the isolation more complete—there was a villainy of circumstances that cut these men off more completely from the rest of mankind, whose ideal of conduct had never undergone the trial of a fiendish and appalling joke. They were exasperated with him for being a half-hearted shirker: he focused on them his hatred of the whole thing; he would have liked to take a signal revenge for the abhorrent opportunity they had put in his way. Trust a boat on the high seas to bring out the Irrational that lurks at the bottom of every thought, sentiment, sensation, emotion. It was part of the burlesque meanness pervading that particular disaster at sea that they did not come to blows. It was all threats, all a terribly effective feint, a sham from beginning to end, planned by the tremendous disdain of the Dark Powers whose real terrors, always on the verge of triumph, are perpetually foiled by the steadfastness of men. I asked, after waiting for a while, 'Well, what happened?' A futile question. I knew too much already to hope for the grace of a single uplifting touch, for the favour of hinted madness, of shadowed horror. 'Nothing,' he said. 'I meant business, but they meant noise only. Nothing happened.'

"And the rising sun found him just as he had jumped up first in the bows of the boat. What a persistence of readiness! He had been holding the tiller in his hand, too, all the night. They had dropped the rudder overboard while attempting to ship it, and I suppose the tiller got kicked forward somehow while they were rushing up and down that boat trying to do all sorts of things at once so as to get clear of the side. It was a long, heavy piece of hard wood, and apparently he had been clutching it for six hours or so. If you don't call that being ready! Can you imagine him, silent and on his feet half the night, his face to the gusts of rain, staring at sombre forms, watchful of vague movements, straining his ears to catch rare, low murmurs in the stern-sheets! Firmness of courage or effort of fear? What do you think? And the endurance is undeniable, too. Six hours more or less on the defensive; six hours of alert immobility while the boat drove slowly or floated arrested, according to the caprice of the wind; while the sea, calmed, slept at last; while the clouds passed above his head; while the sky from an immensity lustreless and black, diminished to a sombre and lustrous vault, scintillated with a greater brilliance, faded to the east, paled at the zenith; while the dark shapes blotting the low stars astern got outlines, relief; became shoulders, heads, faces, features,—confronted him with dreary stares, had dishevelled hair, torn clothes, blinked red eyelids at the white dawn. 'They looked as though they had been knocking about drunk in gutters for a week,' he described graphically; and then he muttered something about the sunrise being of a kind that foretells a calm day. You know that sailor habit of referring to the weather in every connection. And on my side his few mumbled words were enough to make me see the lower limb of the sun clearing the line of the horizon, the tremble of a vast ripple running over all the visible expanse of the sea, as if the waters had shuddered, giving birth to the globe of light, while the last puff of the breeze would stir the air in a sigh of relief.

" 'They sat in the stern shoulder to shoulder, with the skipper in the middle, like three dirty owls, and stared at me,' I heard him say with an intention of hate that distilled a corrosive virtue [9] into the commonplace words like a drop of powerful poison falling into a glass of water; but my thoughts dwelt upon that sunrise. I could imagine under the pellucid emptiness of the sky these four men imprisoned in the solitude of the sea, the lonely sun, regardless of the speck of life, ascending the clear curve of the heaven as if to gaze ardently from a greater height at his own splendour reflected in the still ocean. 'They called out to me from aft,' said Jim, 'as though we had been chums together. I heard them. They were begging me to be sensible and drop that "blooming piece of wood." Why *would* I carry on so? They hadn't done me any harm—had they? There had been no harm. . . . No

9. An active quality or power whether of physical or of moral nature.

harm!'

"His face crimsoned as though he could not get rid of the air in his lungs.

" 'No harm!' he burst out. 'I leave it to you. You can understand. Can't you? You see it—don't you? No harm! Good God! What more could they have done? Oh yes, I know very well—I jumped. Certainly. I jumped! I told you I jumped; but I tell you they were too much for any man. It was their doing as plainly as if they had reached up with a boat-hook and pulled me over. Can't you see it? You must see it. Come. Speak—straight out.'

"His uneasy eyes fastened upon mine, questioned, begged, challenged, entreated. For the life of me I couldn't help murmuring, 'You've been tried.' 'More than is fair,' he caught up swiftly. 'I wasn't given half a chance—with a gang like that. And now they were friendly—oh, so damnably friendly! Chums, shipmates. All in the same boat. Make the best of it. They hadn't meant anything. They didn't care a hang for George. George had gone back to his berth for something at the last moment and got caught. The man was a manifest fool. Very sad, of course. . . . Their eyes looked at me; their lips moved; they wagged their heads at the other end of the boat—three of them; they beckoned—to me. Why not? Hadn't I jumped? I said nothing. There are no words for the sort of things I wanted to say. If I had opened my lips just then I would have simply howled like an animal. I was asking myself when I would wake up. They urged me aloud to come aft and hear quietly what the skipper had to say. We were sure to be picked up before the evening—right in the track of all the Canal[1] traffic; there was smoke to the north-west now.

" 'It gave me an awful shock to see this faint, faint blur, this low trail of brown mist through which you could see the boundary of sea and sky. I called out to them that I could hear very well where I was. The skipper started swearing, as hoarse as a crow. He wasn't going to talk at the top of his voice for *my* accommodation. "Are you afraid they will hear you on shore?" I asked. He glared as if he would have liked to claw me to pieces. The chief engineer advised him to humour me. He said I wasn't right in my head yet. The other rose astern, like a thick pillar of flesh—and talked—talked. . . .'

"Jim remained thoughtful. 'Well?' I said. 'What did I care what story they agreed to make up?' he cried recklessly. 'They could tell what they jolly well liked. It was their business. I knew the story. Nothing they could make people believe could alter it for me. I let him talk, argue—talk, argue. He went on and on and

---

1. Suez Canal, joining the Mediterranean with the Gulf of Suez and thus with the Red Sea and the Orient.

on. Suddenly I felt my legs give way under me. I was sick, tired
—tired to death. I let fall the tiller, turned my back on them, and
sat down on the foremost thwart. I had enough. They called to me
to know if I understood—wasn't it true, every word of it?
It was true, by God! after their fashion. I did not turn my head.
I heard them palavering together. "The silly ass won't say anything." "Oh, he understands well enough." "Let him be; he will
be all right." "What can he do?" What could I do? Weren't we
all in the same boat? I tried to be deaf. The smoke had disappeared
to the northward. It was a dead calm. They had a drink from the
water-breaker, and I drank, too. Afterwards they made a great
business of spreading the boat-sail over the gunwales. Would I keep
a look out? They crept under, out of my sight, thank God! I felt
weary, weary, done up, as if I hadn't had one hour's sleep since
the day I was born. I couldn't see the water for the glitter of the
sunshine. From time to time one of them would creep out, stand
up to take a look all round, and get under again. I could hear spells
of snoring below the sail. Some of them could sleep. One of them
at least. I couldn't! All was light, light, and the boat seemed to be
falling through it. Now and then I would feel quite surprised to find
myself sitting on a thwart. . . .'

"He began to walk with measured steps to and fro before my
chair, one hand in his trousers pocket, his head bent thoughtfully,
and his right arm at long intervals raised for a gesture that seemed
to put out of his way an invisible intruder.

"'I suppose you think I was going mad,' he began in a changed
tone. 'And well you may, if you remember I had lost my cap. The
sun crept all the way from east to west over my bare head, but that
day I could not come to any harm, I suppose. The sun could not
make me mad. . . .' His right arm put aside the idea of madness.
. . . 'Neither could it kill me. . . .' Again his arm repulsed
a shadow. . . . '*That* rested with me.'

"'Did it?' I said, inexpressibly amazed at this new turn, and I
looked at him with the same sort of feeling I might be fairly
conceived to experience had he, after spinning round on his heel,
presented an altogether new face.

"'I didn't get brain fever, I did not drop dead either,' he went
on. 'I didn't bother myself at all about the sun over my head.
I was thinking as coolly as any man that ever sat thinking in the
shade. That greasy beast of a skipper poked his big cropped head
from under the canvas and screwed his fishy eyes up at me.
"Donnerwetter! [2] you will die," he growled, and drew in like a
turtle. I had seen him. I had heard him. He didn't interrupt me. I
was thinking just then that I wouldn't.'

2. Exclamation; literally, "thunderweather."

"He tried to sound my thought with an attentive glance dropped on me in passing. 'Do you mean to say you had been deliberating with yourself whether you would die?' I asked in as impenetrable a tone as I could command. He nodded without stopping. 'Yes, it had come to that as I sat there alone,' he said. He passed on a few steps to the imaginary end of his beat, and when he flung round to come back both his hands were thrust deep into his pockets. He stopped short in front of my chair and looked down. 'Don't you believe it?' he inquired with tense curiosity. I was moved to make a solemn declaration of my readiness to believe implicitly anything he thought fit to tell me."

Chapter Eleven

"He heard me out with his head on one side, and I had another glimpse through a rent in the mist in which he moved and had his being. The dim candle spluttered within the ball of glass, and that was all I had to see him by; at his back was the dark night with the clear stars, whose distant glitter disposed in retreating planes lured the eye into the depths of a greater darkness; and yet a mysterious light seemed to show me his boyish head, as if in that moment the youth within him had, for a second, glowed and expired. 'You are an awful good sort to listen like this,' he said. 'It does me good. You don't know what it is to me. You don't . . .' Words seemed to fail him. It was a distinct glimpse. He was a youngster of the sort you like to see about you; of the sort you like to imagine yourself to have been; of the sort whose appearance claims the fellowship of these illusions you had thought gone out, extinct, cold, and which, as if rekindled at the approach of another flame, give a flutter deep, deep down somewhere, give a flutter of light . . . of heat! . . . Yes; I had a glimpse of him then . . . and it was not the last of that kind. . . . 'You don't know what it is for a fellow in my position to be believed—make a clean breast of it to an elder man. It is so difficult—so awfully unfair—so hard to understand.'

"The mists were closing again. I don't know how old I appeared to him—and how much wise. Not half as old as I felt just then; not half as uselessly wise as I knew myself to be. Surely in no other craft as in that of the sea do the hearts of those already launched to sink or swim go out so much to the youth on the brink, looking with shining eyes upon that glitter of the vast surface which is only a reflection of his own glances full of fire. There is such magnificent vagueness in the expectations that had driven each of us to sea, such a glorious indefiniteness, such a beautiful greed of adventures that are their own and only reward. What we get—well, we won't talk of that; but can one of us restrain a smile? In no other kind of life is the illusion more wide of reality— in no other is the beginning *all* illusion—the disenchantment more swift—the subjugation more complete. Hadn't we all commenced with the same desire, ended with the same knowledge, carried the memory of the same cherished glamour through the sordid days of imprecation? What wonder that when some heavy prod gets home the bond is found to be close; that besides the fellowship of the craft there is felt the strength of a wider feeling —the feeling that binds a man to a child. He was there before me, believing that age and wisdom can find a remedy against the pain of truth, giving me a glimpse of himself as a young fellow in a scrape that is the very devil of a scrape, the sort of scrape greybeards wag at solemnly while they hide a smile. And he had been deliberating upon death—confound him! He had found *that* to meditate about because he thought he had saved his life, while all its glamour had gone with the ship in the night. What more natural! It was tragic enough and funny enough in all conscience to call aloud for compassion, and in what was I better than the rest of us to refuse him my pity? And even as I looked at him the mists rolled into the rent, and his voice spoke:

" 'I was so lost, you know. It was the sort of thing one does not expect to happen to one. It was not like a fight, for instance.'

" 'It was not,' I admitted. He appeared changed, as if he had suddenly matured.

" 'One couldn't be sure,' he muttered.

" 'Ah! You were not sure,' I said, and was placated by the sound of a faint sigh that passed between us like the flight of a bird in the night.

" 'Well, I wasn't,' he said courageously. 'It was something like that wretched story they made up. It was not a lie—but it wasn't truth all the same. It was something. . . . One knows a downright lie. There was not the thickness of a sheet of paper between the right and wrong of this affair.'

" 'How much more did you want?' I asked; but I think I spoke so low that he did not catch what I said. He had advanced his argument as though life had been a network of paths separated by chasms. His voice sounded reasonable.

" 'Suppose I had not—I mean to say, suppose I had stuck to the ship? Well. How much longer? Say a minute—half a minute. Come. In thirty seconds, as it seemed certain then, I would have been overboard; and do you think I would not have laid hold of the first thing that came in my way—oar, life-buoy, grating—anything? Wouldn't you?'

" 'And be saved,' I interjected.

" 'I would have meant to be,' he retorted. 'And that's more than I meant when I' . . . he shivered as if about to swallow some nauseous drug . . . 'jumped,' he pronounced with a convulsive effort, whose stress, as if propagated by the waves of the air, made my body stir a little in the chair. He fixed me with lowering eyes. 'Don't you believe me?' he cried. 'I swear! . . . Confound it! You got me here to talk, and . . . You must! . . . You said you would believe.' 'Of course I do,' I protested in a matter-of-fact tone which produced a calming effect. 'Forgive me,' he said. 'Of course I wouldn't have talked to you about all this if you had not been a gentleman. I ought to have known . . . I am—I am—a gentleman, too . . .' 'Yes, yes,' I said hastily. He was looking me squarely in the face and withdrew his gaze slowly. 'Now you understand why I didn't after all . . . didn't go out in that way. I wasn't going to be frightened at what I had done. And, anyhow, if I had stuck to the ship I would have done my best to be saved. Men have been known to float for hours—in the open sea—and be picked up not much the worse for it. I might have lasted it out better than many others. There's nothing the matter with *my* heart.' He withdrew his right fist from his pocket, and the blow he struck on his chest resounded like a muffled detonation in the night.

" 'No,' I said. He meditated, with his legs slightly apart and his chin sunk. 'A hair's-breadth,' he muttered. 'Not the breadth of a hair between this and that. And at the time . . .'

" 'It is difficult to see a hair at midnight,' I put in, a little viciously, I fear. Don't you see what I mean by the solidarity of the craft? I was aggrieved against him, as though he had cheated me—me!—of a splendid opportunity to keep up the illusion of my beginnings, as though he had robbed our common life of the last spark of its glamour. 'And so you cleared out—at once.'

" 'Jumped,' he corrected me incisively. 'Jumped—mind!' he repeated, and I wondered at the evident but obscure intention. 'Well, yes! Perhaps I could not see then. But I had plenty of time and any amount of light in that boat. And I could think, too. Nobody would know, of course, but this did not make it any easier for me. You've got to believe that, too. I did not want all this talk. . . . No . . . Yes . . . I won't lie . . . I wanted it: it is the very thing I wanted—there. Do you think you or anybody could have made me if I . . . I am—I am not afraid to tell. And I wasn't afraid to think either. I looked it in the face. I wasn't going to run away. At first—at night, if it hadn't been for those fellows I might have . . . No! by heavens! I was not going to give them that satisfaction. They had done enough. They made up a story, and believed it for all I know. But I knew the truth, and I would live it down

—alone, with myself. I wasn't going to give in to such a beastly unfair thing. What did it prove after all? I was confoundedly cut up. Sick of life—to tell you the truth; but what would have been the good to shirk it—in—in—that way? That was not the way. I believe—I believe it would have—it would have ended—nothing.'

"He had been walking up and down, but with the last word he turned short at me.

" 'What do *you* believe?' he asked with violence. A pause ensued, and suddenly I felt myself overcome by a profound and hopeless fatigue, as though his voice had startled me out of a dream of wandering through empty spaces whose immensity had harrassed my soul and exhausted my body.

" ' . . . Would have ended nothing,' he muttered over me obstinately, after a little while. 'No! the proper thing was to face it out—alone—for myself—wait for another chance—find out . . .' "

Chapter Twelve

"All around everything was still as far as the ear could reach. The mist of his feelings shifted between us, as if disturbed by his struggles, and in the rifts of the immaterial veil he would appear to my staring eyes distinct of form and pregnant with vague appeal like a symbolic figure in a picture. The chill air of the night seemed to lie on my limbs as heavy as a slab of marble.

" 'I see,' I murmured, more to prove to myself that I could break my state of numbness than for any other reason.

" 'The *Avondale* picked us up just before sunset,' he remarked moodily. 'Steamed right straight for us. We had only to sit and wait.'

"After a long interval, he said, 'They told their story.' And again there was that oppressive silence. 'Then only I knew what it was I had made up my mind to,' he added.

" 'You said nothing,' I whispered.

" 'What could I say?' he asked, in the same low tone. . . . 'Shock slight. Stopped the ship. Ascertained the damage. Took measures to get the boats out without creating a panic. As the first boat was lowered ship went down in a squall. Sank like lead. . . . What could be more clear' . . . he hung his head . . . 'and more awful?' His lips quivered while he looked straight into my eyes. 'I had jumped—hadn't I?' he asked, dismayed. 'That's what I had to live down. The story didn't matter.' . . . He clasped his hands for an instant, glanced right and left into the gloom: 'It was like cheating the dead,' he stammered.

" 'And there were no dead,' I said.

"He went away from me at this. That is the only way I can describe it. In a moment I saw his back close to the balustrade. He stood there for some time, as if admiring the purity and the peace of the night. Some flowering shrub in the garden below spread its powerful scent through the damp air. He returned to me with hasty steps.

" 'And that did not matter,' he said, as stubbornly as you please.

" 'Perhaps not,' I admitted. I began to have a notion he was too much for me. After all, what did I know?

" 'Dead or not dead, I could not get clear,' he said. 'I had to live; hadn't I?'

" 'Well, yes—if you take it in that way,' I mumbled.

" 'I was glad, of course,' he threw out carelessly, with his mind fixed on something else. 'The exposure,' he pronounced slowly, and lifted his head. 'Do you know what was my first thought when I heard? I was relieved. I was relieved to learn that those shouts—did I tell you I had heard shouts? No? Well, I did. Shouts for help . . . blown along with the drizzle. Imagination, I suppose. And yet I can hardly . . . How stupid. . . . The others did not. I asked them afterwards. They all said No. No? And I was hearing them even then! I might have known—but I didn't think—I only listened. Very faint screams—day after day. Then that little half-caste chap here came up and spoke to me. "The *Patna* . . . French gunboat . . . towed successfully to Aden . . . Investigation . . . Marine Office . . . Sailors' Home . . . arrangements made for your board and lodging!" I walked along with him, and I enjoyed the silence. So there had been no shouting. Imagination. I had to believe him. I could hear nothing any more. I wonder how long I could have stood it. It was getting worse, too . . . I mean—louder.'

"He fell into thought.

" 'And I had heard nothing! Well—so be it. But the lights! The lights did go! We did not see them. They were not there. If they had been, I would have swam back—I would have gone back and shouted alongside—I would have begged them to take me on board. . . . I would have had my chance. . . . You doubt me? . . . How do you know how I felt? . . . What right have you to doubt? . . . I very nearly did it as it was—do you understand?' His voice fell. 'There was not a glimmer—not a glimmer,' he protested mournfully. 'Don't you understand that if there had been, you would not have seen me here? You see me—and you doubt.'

"I shook my head negatively. This question of the lights being lost sight of when the boat could not have been more than a quarter of a mile from the ship was a matter for much discussion. Jim stuck to it that there was nothing to be seen after the first shower had cleared away; and the others had affirmed the same thing to the officers of the *Avondale*. Of course people shook their heads and smiled. One old skipper who sat near me in court tickled my ear with his white beard to murmur, 'Of course they would lie.' As a matter of fact nobody lied; not even the chief engineer with his story of the masthead light dropping like a match you throw down. Not consciously, at least. A man with his liver in such a state might very well have seen a floating spark in the corner of his eye when stealing a hurried glance over his shoulder. They had seen no light of any sort though they were well within range, and they could only explain this in one way: the ship had gone down. It was obvious and comforting. The foreseen fact coming so swiftly had justified their haste. No wonder they did not cast about for any other explanation. Yet the true one was very simple, and as soon as Brierly suggested it the court ceased to bother about the question. If you remember, the ship had been stopped, and was lying with her head on the course steered through the night, with her stern canted high and her bows brought low down in the water through the filling of the fore-compartment. Being thus out of trim, when the squall struck her a little on the quarter, she swung head to wind as sharply as though she had been at anchor. By this change in her position all her lights were in a very few moments shut off from the boat to leeward. It may very well be that, had they been seen, they would have had the effect of a mute appeal—that their glimmer lost in the darkness of the cloud would have had the mysterious power of the human glance that can awaken the feelings of remorse and pity. It would have said, 'I am here—still here' . . . and what more can the eye of the most forsaken of human beings say? But she turned her back on them as if in disdain of their fate: she had swung round, burdened, to glare stubbornly at the new danger of the open sea which she so strangely survived to end her days in a breaking-up yard, as if it had been her recorded fate to die obscurely under the blows of many hammers. What were the various ends their destiny provided for the pilgrims I am unable to say; but the immediate future brought, at about nine o'clock next morning, a French gunboat homeward bound from Réunion. The report of her commander was public property. He had swept a little out of his course to ascertain what was the matter with that steamer floating dangerously by the head upon a still and hazy sea. There was an ensign, union down, flying at her main gaff (the serang had the sense to make a signal of distress at daylight); but the cooks were preparing the food in the cooking-boxes forward as usual. The decks were packed as close as a sheep-pen: there were people perched all along the rails, jammed on the bridge in a solid mass; hundreds of eyes stared, and not a sound was heard when the gunboat ranged abreast, as if all that multitude of lips had been sealed by a spell.

"The Frenchman hailed, could get no intelligible reply, and after ascertaining through his binoculars that the crowd on deck did not look plague-stricken, decided to send a boat. Two officers came on board, listened to the serang, tried to talk with the Arab, couldn't make head or tail of it: but of course the nature of the emergency was obvious enough. They were also very much struck by discovering a white man, dead and curled up peacefully on the bridge. '*Fort intrigués par ce cadavre,*' [3] as I was informed a long time after by an elderly French lieutenant whom I came across one afternoon in Sydney, by the merest chance, in a sort of café, and who remembered the affair perfectly. Indeed this affair, I may notice in passing, had an extraordinary power of defying the shortness of memories and the length of time: it seemed to live, with a sort of uncanny vitality, in the minds of men, on the tips of their tongues. I've had the questionable pleasure of meeting it often, years afterwards, thousands of miles away, emerging from the remotest possible talk, coming to the surface of the most distant allusions. Has it not turned up to-night between us? And I am the only seaman here. I am the only one to whom it is memory. And yet it has made its way out! But if two men who, unknown to each other, knew of this affair met accidentally on any spot of this earth, the thing would pop up between them as sure as fate, before they parted. I had never seen that Frenchman before, and at the end of an hour we had done with each other for life: he did not seem particularly talkative either; he was a quiet, massive chap in a creased uniform sitting drowsily over a tumbler half full of some dark liquid. His shoulder-straps were a bit tarnished, his clean-shaved cheeks were large and sallow; he looked like a man who would be given to taking snuff—don't you know? I won't say he did; but the habit would have fitted that kind of man. It all began by his handing me a number of *Home News*, which I didn't want, across the marble table. I said, 'Merci.' We exchanged a few apparently innocent remarks, and suddenly, before I knew how it had come about, we were in the midst of it, and he was telling me how much they had been 'intrigued by that corpse.' It turned out he had been one of the boarding officers.

"In the establishment where we sat one could get a variety of foreign drinks which were kept for the visiting naval officers, and he took a sip of the dark, medical-looking stuff, which probably was nothing more nasty than *cassis à l'eau*, [4] and glancing with one eye into the tumbler, shook his head slightly. '*Impossible de comprendre—vous concevez,*' he said, with a curious mixture of unconcern and thoughtfulness. I could very easily conceive how impossible it had been for them to understand. Nobody in the gunboat knew enough English to get hold of the story as told by the serang. There

3. Much intrigued by that corpse.   4. Black-currant cordial and water.

was a good deal of noise, too, round the two officers. 'They crowded upon us. There was a circle round that dead man (*autour de ce mort*),' he described. 'One had to attend to the most pressing. These people were beginning to agitate themselves—*Parbleu!* [5] A mob like that—don't you see?' he interjected with philosophic indulgence. As to the bulkhead, he had advised his commander that the safest thing was to leave it alone, it was so villainous to look at. They got two hawsers on board promptly (*en toute hâte*) and took the *Patna* in tow—stern foremost at that—which, under the circumstances, was not so foolish, since the rudder was too much out of the water to be of any great use for steering, and this manœuvre eased the strain on the bulkhead, whose state, he expounded with stolid glibness, demanded the greatest care (*éxigeait les plus grands ménagements*). I could not help thinking that my new acquaintance must have had a voice in most of these arrangements: he looked a reliable officer, no longer very active, and he was seamanlike, too, in a way, though as he sat there, with his thick fingers clasped lightly on his stomach, he reminded you of one of those snuffy, quiet village priests, into whose ears are poured the sins, the sufferings, the remorse of peasant generations, on whose faces the placid and simple expression is like a veil thrown over the mystery of pain and distress. He ought to have had a threadbare black *soutane* [6] buttoned smoothly up to his ample chin, instead of a frock-coat with shoulder-straps and brass buttons. His broad bosom heaved regularly while he went on telling me that it had been the very devil of a job, as doubtless (*sans doute*) I could figure to myself in my quality of a seaman (*en votre qualité de marin*). At the end of the period he inclined his body slightly towards me, and, pursing his shaved lips, allowed the air to escape with a gentle hiss. 'Luckily,' he continued, 'the sea was level like this table, and there was no more wind than there is here. . . .' The place struck me as indeed intolerably stuffy, and very hot; my face burned as though I had been young enough to be embarrassed and blushing. They had directed their course, he pursued, to the nearest English port '*naturellement*,' [7] where their responsibility ceased '*Dieu merci*. . . .' [8] He blew out his flat cheeks a little. . . . 'Because, mind you (*notez bien*), all the time of towing we had two quartermasters stationed with axes by the hawsers, to cut us clear of our tow in case she . . .' He fluttered downwards his heavy eyelids, making his meaning as plain as possible. . . . 'What would you? One does what one can (*on fait ce qu'on peut*),' and for a moment he managed to invest his ponderous immobility with an air of resignation. 'Two quarter-

---

5. Mild oath.
6. The style of cassock worn by Roman Catholic priests.

7. Naturally.
8. Thank God.

masters—thirty hours—always there. Two!' he repeated, lifting up his right hand a little, and exhibiting two fingers. This was absolutely the first gesture I saw him make. It gave me the opportunity to 'note' a starred scar on the back of his hand—effect of a gunshot clearly; and, as if my sight had been made more acute by this discovery, I perceived also the seam of an old wound, beginning a little below the temple and going out of sight under the short grey hair at the side of his head—the graze of a spear or the cut of a sabre. He clasped his hands on his stomach again. 'I remained on board that—that—my memory is going (*s'en va*). Ah! *Patt-nà. C'est bien ça.*[9] *Patt-nà. Merci.* It is droll how one forgets. I stayed on that ship thirty hours. . . .'

" 'You did!' I exclaimed. Still gazing at his hands, he pursed his lips a little, but this time made no hissing sound. 'It was judged proper,' he said, lifting his eyebrows dispassionately, 'that one of the officers should remain to keep an eye open (*pour ouvrir l'œil*)' . . . he sighed idly . . . 'and for communicating by signals with the towing ship—do you see?—and so on. For the rest, it was my opinion, too. We made our boats ready to drop over—and I also on that ship took measures. . . . *Enfin!* [1] One has done one's possible. It was a delicate position. Thirty hours! They prepared me some food. As for the wine—go and whistle for it—not a drop.' In some extraordinary way, without any marked change in his inert attitude and in the placid expression of his face, he managed to convey the idea of profound disgust. 'I—you know—when it comes to eating without my glass of wine—I am nowhere.'

"I was afraid he would enlarge upon the grievance, for though he didn't stir a limb or twitch a feature, he made one aware how much he was irritated by the recollection. But he seemed to forget all about it. They delivered their charge to the 'port authorities,' as he expressed it. He was struck by the calmness with which it had been received. 'One might have thought they had such a droll find (*drôle de trouvaille*) brought them every day. You are extraordinary—you others,' he commented, with his back propped against the wall, and looking himself as incapable of an emotional display as a sack of meal. There happened to be a man-of-war and an Indian Marine steamer in the harbour at the time, and he did not conceal his admiration of the efficient manner in which the boats of these two ships cleared the *Patna* of her passengers. Indeed his torpid demeanour concealed nothing: it had that mysterious, almost miraculous, power of producing striking effects by means impossible of detection, which is the last word of the highest art. 'Twenty-five minutes—watch in hand—twenty-five, no more. . . .' He unclasped and clasped again his fingers without removing his hands

9. That's it exactly.   1. Untranslatable. Suggests shift in thinking.

from his stomach, and made it infinitely more effective than if he had thrown up his arms to heaven in amazement. . . . 'All that lot (*tout ce monde*) on shore—with their little affairs—nobody left but a guard of seamen (*marins de l' Etat*) and that interesting corpse (*cet intéressant cadavre*). Twenty-five minutes. . . .' With downcast eyes and his head tilted slightly on one side he seemed to roll knowingly on his tongue the savour of a smart bit of work. He persuaded one without any further demonstration that his approval was eminently worth having, and resuming his hardly interrupted immobility he went on to inform me that, being under orders to make the best of their way to Toulon, they left in two hours' time, 'so that (*de sorte que*) there are many things in this incident of my life (*dans cet épisode de ma vie*) which have remained obscure.' "

Chapter Thirteen

"After these words, and without a change of attitude, he, so to speak, submitted himself passively to a state of silence. I kept him company; and suddenly, but not abruptly, as if the appointed time had arrived for his moderate and husky voice to come out of his immobility, he pronounced, '*Mon Dieu*! how the time passes!' Nothing could have been more commonplace than this remark; but its utterance coincided for me with a moment of vision. It's extraordinary how we go through life with eyes half shut, with dull ears, with dormant thoughts. Perhaps it's just as well; and it may be that it is this very dullness that makes life to the incalculable majority so supportable and so welcome. Nevertheless, there can be but few of us who had never known one of these rare moments of awakening when we see, hear, understand ever so much—everything—in a flash—before we fall back again into our agreeable somnolence. I raised my eyes when he spoke, and I saw him as though I had never seen him before. I saw his chin sunk on his breast, the clumsy folds of his coat, his clasped hands, his motionless pose, so curiously suggestive of his having been simply left there. Time had passed indeed: it had overtaken him and gone ahead. It had left him hopelessly behind with a few poor gifts: the iron-grey hair, the heavy fatigue of the tanned face, two scars, a pair of tarnished shoulder-straps; one of those steady, reliable men who are the raw material of great reputations, one of those uncounted lives that are buried without drums and trumpets under the foundations of monumental successes. 'I am now third lieutenant of the *Victorieuse*' (she was the flagship of the French Pacific squadron at the time), he said, detaching his shoulders from the wall a couple of inches to introduce himself. I bowed slightly on my side of the

table, and told him I commanded a merchant vessel at present
anchored in Rushcutters' Bay. He had 'remarked' her—a pretty
little craft. He was very civil about it in his impassive way. I even
fancy he went the length of tilting his head in compliment as he
repeated, breathing visibly the while, 'Ah, yes. A little craft
painted black—very pretty—very pretty (*très coquet*).' After a time
he twisted his body slowly to face the glass door on our right. 'A
dull town (*triste ville*),' he observed, staring into the street. It was
a brilliant day; a southerly buster was raging, and we could see the
passers-by, men and women, buffeted by the wind on the sidewalks,
the sunlit fronts of the houses across the road blurred by the tall
whirls of dust. 'I descended on shore,' he said, 'to stretch my legs a
little, but . . .' He didn't finish, and sank into the depths of his
repose. 'Pray—tell me,' he began, coming up ponderously, 'what
was there at the bottom of this affair—precisely (*au juste*)? It is
curious. That dead man, for instance—and so on.'

" 'There were living men too,' I said; 'much more curious.'

" 'No doubt, no doubt,' he agreed half audibly; then, as if after
mature consideration, murmured, 'Evidently.' I made no difficulty
in communicating to him what had interested me most in this
affair. It seemed as though he had a right to know: hadn't he spent
thirty hours on board the *Patna*—had he not taken the succession,
so to speak, had he not done 'his possible'? He listened to me,
looking more priestlike than ever, and with what—probably on
account of his downcast eyes—had the appearance of devout con-
centration. Once or twice he elevated his eyebrows (but without
raising his eyelids), as one would say, 'The devil!' Once he calmly
exclaimed, 'Ah, bah!' under his breath, and when I had finished he
pursed his lips in a deliberate way and emitted a sort of sorrowful
whistle.

"In any one else it might have been an evidence of boredom, a
sign of indifference; but he, in his occult way, managed to make
his immobility appear profoundly responsive, and as full of valuable
thoughts as an egg is of meat. What he said at last was nothing more
than a 'Very interesting,' pronounced politely, and not much above
a whisper. Before I got over my disappointment he added, but as if
speaking to himself, 'That's it. That *is* it.' His chin seemed to sink
lower on his breast, his body to weigh heavier on his seat. I was
about to ask him what he meant, when a sort of preparatory
tremor passed over his whole person, as a faint ripple may be seen
upon stagnant water even before the wind is felt. 'And so that poor
young man ran away along with the others,' he said with grave
tranquillity.

"I don't know what made me smile: it is the only genuine smile
of mine I can remember in connection with Jim's affair. But some-

how this simple statement of the matter sounded funny in French. . . . '*S'est enfui avec les autres*,' had said the lieutenant. And suddenly I began to admire the discrimination of the man. He had made out the point at once: he did get hold of the only thing I cared about. I felt as though I were taking professional opinion on the case. His imperturbable and mature calmness was that of an expert in possession of the facts, and to whom one's perplexities are mere child's-play. 'Ah! The young, the young,' he said indulgently. 'And after all, one does not die of it.' 'Die of what?' I asked swiftly. 'Of being afraid.' He elucidated his meaning and sipped his drink.

"I perceived that the three last fingers of his wounded hand were stiff and could not move independently of each other, so that he took up his tumbler with an ungainly clutch. 'One is always afraid. One may talk, but . . .' He put down the glass awkwardly. . . . 'The fear, the fear—look you—it is always there. . . .' He touched his breast near a brass button on the very spot where Jim had given a thump to his own when protesting that there was nothing the matter with his heart. I suppose I made some sign of dissent, because he insisted, 'Yes! yes! One talks, one talks; this is all very fine; but at the end of the reckoning one is no cleverer than the next man—and no more brave. Brave! This is always to be seen. I have rolled my hump (*roulé ma bosse*),' he said, using the slang expression with imperturbable seriousness, 'in all parts of the world; I have known brave men—famous ones! *Allez!* . . .' He drank carelessly. . . . 'Brave—you conceive—in the Service—one has got to be—the trade demands it (*le métier veux ça*). Is it not so?' he appealed to me reasonably. '*Eh bien!* Each of them—I say each of them, if he were an honest man—*bien entendu*[2]—would confess that there is a point—there is a point—for the best of us—there is somewhere a point when you let go everything (*vous lachez tout*). And you have got to live with that truth—do you see? Given a certain combination of circumstances, fear is sure to come. Abominable funk (*un trac épouvantable*). And even for those who do not believe this truth there is fear all the same—the fear of themselves. Absolutely so. Trust me. Yes. Yes. . . . At my age one knows what one is talking about—*que diable!*[3] . . .' He had delivered himself of all this as immovably as though he had been the mouthpiece of abstract wisdom, but at this point he heightened the effect of detachment by beginning to twirl his thumbs slowly. 'It's evident—*parbleu!*' he continued; 'for, make up your mind as much as you like, even a simple headache or a fit of indigestion (*un dérangement d'estomac*) is enough to . . . Take me, for instance—I have made my proofs. *Eh bien!* I, who am speaking to you, once . . .'

"He drained his glass and returned to his twirling. 'No, no; one

---

2. Of course; understood.   3. What the devil!

does not die of it,' he pronounced finally, and when I found he did not mean to proceed with the personal anecdote, I was extremely disappointed; the more so as it was not the sort of story, you know, one could very well press him for. I sat silent, and he too, as if nothing could please him better. Even his thumbs were still now. Suddenly his lips began to move. 'That is so,' he resumed placidly. 'Man is born a coward (*L'homme est né poltron*). It is a difficulty —*parbleu!* It would be too easy otherwise. But habit—habit— necessity—do you see?—the eye of others—*voilà*. One puts up with it. And then the example of others who are no better than yourself, and yet make good countenance. . . .'

"His voice ceased.

" 'That young man—you will observe—had none of these inducements—at least at the moment,' I remarked.

"He raised his eyebrows forgivingly: 'I don't say; I don't say. The young man in question might have had the best dispositions—the best dispositions,' he repeated, wheezing a little.

" 'I am glad to see you taking a lenient view,' I said. 'His own feeling in the matter was—ah!—hopeful, and . . .'

"The shuffle of his feet under the table interrupted me. He drew up his heavy eyelids. Drew up, I say—no other expression can describe the steady deliberation of the act—and at last was disclosed completely to me. I was confronted by two narrow grey circlets, like two tiny steel rings around the profound blackness of the pupils. The sharp glance, coming from that massive body, gave a notion of extreme efficiency, like a razor-edge on a battle-axe. 'Pardon,' he said punctiliously. His right hand went up, and he swayed forward. 'Allow me . . . I contended that one may get on knowing very well that one's courage does not come of itself (*ne vient pas tout seul*). There's nothing much in that to get upset about. One truth the more ought not to make life impossible. . . . But the honour— the honour, monsieur! . . . The honour . . . that is real—that is! And what life may be worth when' . . . he got on his feet with a ponderous impetuosity, as a startled ox might scramble up from the grass . . . 'when the honour is gone—*ah ça! par exemple*⁴—I can offer no opinion. I can offer no opinion—because —monsieur—I know nothing of it.'

"I had risen, too, and, trying to throw infinite politeness into our attitudes, we faced each other mutely, like two china dogs on a mantlepiece. Hang the fellow! he had pricked the bubble. The blight of futility that lies in wait for men's speeches had fallen upon our conversation, and made it a thing of empty sounds. 'Very well,' I said, with a disconcerted smile, 'but couldn't it reduce itself to not being found out?' He made as if to retort readily, but when

4. Expression of surprise.

he spoke he had changed his mind. 'This, monsieur, is too fine for me—much above me—I don't think about it.' He bowed heavily over his cap, which he held before him by the peak, between the thumb and the forefinger of his wounded hand. I bowed, too. We bowed together: we scraped our feet at each other with much ceremony, while a dirty specimen of a waiter looked on critically, as though he had paid for the performance. 'Serviteur,' said the Frenchman. Another scrape. 'Monsieur' . . . 'Monsieur. . . .' The glass door swung behind his burly back. I saw the southerly buster get hold of him and drive him down wind with his hand to his head, his shoulders braced, and the tails of his coat blown hard against his legs.

"I sat down again alone and discouraged—discouraged about Jim's case. If you wonder that after more than three years it had preserved its actuality, you must know that I had seen him only very lately. I had come straight from Samarang, where I had loaded a cargo for Sydney: an utterly uninteresting bit of business,—what Charley here would call one of my rational transactions,—and in Samarang I had seen something of Jim. He was then working for De Jongh, on my recommendation. Water-clerk. 'My representative afloat,' as De Jongh called him. You can't imagine a mode of life more barren of consolation, less capable of being invested with a spark of glamour—unless it be the business of an insurance canvasser. Little Bob Stanton—Charley here knew him well—had gone through that experience. The same who got drowned afterwards trying to save a lady's-maid in the *Sephora* disaster. A case of collision on a hazy morning off the Spanish coast, you may remember. All the passengers had been packed tidily into the boats and shoved clear of the ship when Bob sheered alongside again and scrambled back on deck to fetch that girl. How she had been left behind I can't make out; anyhow, she had gone completely crazy —wouldn't leave the ship—held to the rail like grim death. The wrestling-match could be seen plainly from the boats; but poor Bob was the shortest chief mate in the merchant service, and the woman stood five feet ten in her shoes and was as strong as a horse, I've been told. So it went on, pull devil, pull baker,[5] the wretched girl screaming all the time, and Bob letting out a yell now and then to warn his boat to keep well clear of the ship. One of the hands told me, hiding a smile at the recollection, 'It was for all the world, sir, like a naughty youngster fighting with his mother.' The same old chap said that 'At the last we could see that Mr. Stanton had given up hauling at the gal, and just stood by looking at her, watchful-like. We thought afterwards he must 'ave been reckoning that, maybe, the rush of water would tear her away from the rail

5. Proverbial expression implying a contest of varying fortunes.

by and by and give him a show to save her. We daren't come alongside for our life; and after a bit the old ship went down all on a
sudden with a lurch to starboard—plop. The suck in was something awful. We never saw anything alive or dead come up.' Poor
Bob's spell of shore-life had been one of the complications of a love
affair, I believe. He fondly hoped he had done with the sea for ever,
and made sure he had got hold of all the bliss on earth, but it came
to canvassing in the end. Some cousin of his in Liverpool put him
up to it. He used to tell us his experiences in that line. He made us
laugh till we cried, and, not altogether displeased at the effect,
undersized and bearded to the waist like a gnome, he would tiptoe
amongst us and say, 'It's all very well for you beggars to laugh, but
my immortal soul was shrivelled down to the size of a parched pea
after a week of that work.' I don't know how Jim's soul accommodated itself to the new conditions of his life—I was kept too busy
in getting him something to do that would keep body and soul
together—but I am pretty certain his adventurous fancy was suffering all the pangs of starvation. It had certainly nothing to feed upon
in this new calling. It was distressing to see him at it, though he
tackled it with a stubborn serenity for which I must give him full
credit. I kept my eye on his shabby plodding with a sort of notion
that it was a punishment for the heroics of his fancy—an expiation
for his craving after more glamour than he could carry. He had
loved too well to imagine himself a glorious racehorse, and now he
was condemned to toil without honour like a costermonger's[6]
donkey. He did it very well. He shut himself in, put his head down,
said never a word. Very well; very well indeed—except for certain
fantastic and violent outbreaks, on the deplorable occasions when
the irrepressible *Patna* case cropped up. Unfortunately, that scandal
of the Eastern seas would not die out. And this is the reason why I
could never feel I had done with Jim for good.

"I sat thinking of him after the French lieutenant had left, not,
however, in connection with De Jongh's cool and gloomy backshop,
where we had hurriedly shaken hands not very long ago, but as I
had seen him years before in the last flickers of the candle, alone
with me in the long gallery of the Malabar House, with the chill
and the darkness of the night at his back. The respectable sword of
his country's law was suspended over his head. To-morrow—or was
it to-day? (midnight had slipped by long before we parted)—the
marble-faced police magistrate, after distributing fines and terms
of imprisonment in the assault-and-battery case, would take up
the awful weapon and smite his bowed neck. Our communion in
the night was uncommonly like a last vigil with a condemned man.
He was guilty, too. He was guilty—as I had told myself repeatedly,

6. Street vendor.

guilty and done for; nevertheless, I wished to spare him the mere detail of a formal execution. I don't pretend to explain the reasons of my desire—I don't think I could; but if you haven't got a sort of notion by this time, then I must have been very obscure in my narrative, or you too sleepy to seize upon the sense of my words. I don't defend my morality. There was no morality in the impulse which induced me to lay before him Brierly's plan of evasion—I may call it—in all its primitive simplicity. There were the rupees—absolutely ready in my pocket and very much at his service. Oh! a loan; a loan, of course—and if an introduction to a man (in Rangoon) who could put some work in his way . . . Why! with the greatest pleasure. I had pen, ink, and paper in my room on the first floor. And even while I was speaking I was impatient to begin the letter: day, month, year, 2.30 a.m. . . . for the sake of our old friendship I ask you to put some work in the way of Mr. James So-and-so, in whom, etc. etc. . . . I was even ready to write in that strain about him. If he had not enlisted my sympathies he had done better for himself—he had gone to the very fount and origin of that sentiment, he had reached the secret sensibility of my egoism. I am concealing nothing from you, because were I to do so my action would appear more unintelligible than any man's action has the right to be, and—in the second place—to-morrow you will forget my sincerity along with the other lessons of the past. In this transaction, to speak grossly and precisely, I was the irreproachable man; but the subtle intentions of my immorality were defeated by the moral simplicity of the criminal. No doubt he was selfish, too, but his selfishness had a higher origin, a more lofty aim. I discovered that, say what I would, he was eager to go through the ceremony of execution; and I didn't say much, for I felt that in argument his youth would tell against me heavily: he believed where I had already ceased to doubt. There was something fine in the wildness of his unexpressed, hardly formulated hope. 'Clear out! Couldn't think of it,' he said, with a shake of the head. 'I make you an offer for which I neither demand nor expect any sort of gratitude,' I said; 'you shall repay the money when convenient, and . . .' 'Awfully good of you,' he muttered, without looking up. I watched him narrowly: the future must have appeared horribly uncertain to him; but he did not falter, as though indeed there had been nothing wrong with his heart. I felt angry—not for the first time that night. 'The whole wretched business,' I said, 'is bitter enough, I should think, for a man of your kind. . . .' 'It is, it is,' he whispered twice, with his eyes fixed on the floor. It was heart-rending. He towered above the light, and I could see the down on his cheek, the colour mantling warm under the smooth skin of his face. Believe me or not, I say it was outrageously heart-rending. It provoked me to brutality. 'Yes,' I said; 'and allow me to confess that I am totally unable to imagine what advantage you can expect from this licking of the dregs.' 'Advantage!' he murmured out of his stillness. 'I am dashed if I do,' I said, enraged. 'I've been trying to tell you all there is in it,' he went on slowly, as if meditating something unanswerable. 'But after all, it is *my* trouble.' I opened my mouth to retort, and discovered suddenly that I'd lost all confidence in myself; and it was as if he, too, had given me up, for he mumbled like a man thinking half aloud. 'Went away . . . went into hospitals. . . . Not one of them would face it. . . . They . . .' He moved his hand slightly to imply disdain. 'But I've got to get over this thing, and I mustn't shirk any of it or . . . I won't shirk any of it.' He was silent. He gazed as though he had been haunted. His unconscious face reflected the passing expressions of scorn, of despair, of resolution—reflected them in turn, as a magic mirror would reflect the gliding passage of unearthly shapes. He lived surrounded by deceitful ghosts, by austere shades. 'Oh, nonsense, my dear fellow!' I began. He had a movement of impatience. 'You don't seem to understand,' he said incisively; then looking at me without a wink, 'I may have jumped, but I don't run away.' 'I meant no offence,' I said; and added stupidly, 'Better men than you have found it expedient to run, at times.' He coloured all over, while in my confusion I half choked myself with my own tongue. 'Perhaps so,' he said at last; 'I am not good enough; I can't afford it. I am bound to fight this thing down—I am fighting it *now*.' I got out of my chair and felt stiff all over. The silence was embarrassing, and to put an end to it I imagined nothing better but to remark, 'I had no idea it was so late,' in an airy tone. . . . 'I dare say you have had enough of this,' he said brusquely: 'and to tell you the truth'—he began to look round for his hat—'so have I.'

"Well! he had refused this unique offer. He had struck aside my helping hand; he was ready to go now, and beyond the balustrade the night seemed to wait for him very still, as though he had been marked down for its prey. I heard his voice. 'Ah! here it is.' He had found his hat. For a few seconds we hung in the wind. 'What will you do after—after? . . .' I asked very low. 'Go to the dogs as likely as not,' he answered in a gruff mutter. I had recovered my wits in a measure, and judged best to take it lightly. 'Pray remember,' I said, 'that I should like very much to see you again before you go.' 'I don't know what's to prevent you. The damned thing won't make me invisible,' he said with intense bitterness,—'no such luck.' And then at the moment of taking leave he treated me to a ghastly muddle of dubious stammers and movements, to an awful display of hesitations. God forgive him—me! He had taken it into his fanciful head that I was likely to make some difficulty as to shaking hands.

It was too awful for words. I believe I shouted suddenly at him as you would bellow to a man you saw about to walk over a cliff; I remember our voices being raised, the appearance of a miserable grin on his face, a crushing clutch on my hand, a nervous laugh. The candle spluttered out, and the thing was over at last, with a groan that floated up to me in the dark. He got himself away somehow. The night swallowed his form. He was a horrible bungler. Horrible. I heard the quick crunch-crunch of the gravel under his boots. He was running. Absolutely running, with nowhere to go to. And he was not yet four-and-twenty."

Chapter Fourteen

"I slept little, hurried over my breakfast, and after a slight hesitation gave up my early morning visit to my ship. It was really very wrong of me, because, though my chief mate was an excellent man all round, he was the victim of such black imaginings that if he did not get a letter from his wife at the expected time he would go quite distracted with rage and jealousy, lose all grip on the work, quarrel with all hands, and either weep in his cabin or develop such a ferocity of temper as all but drove the crew to the verge of mutiny. The thing had always seemed inexplicable to me: they had been married thirteen years; I had a glimpse of her once, and, honestly, I couldn't conceive a man abandoned enough to plunge into sin for the sake of such an unattractive person. I don't know whether I have not done wrong by refraining from putting that view before poor Selvin: the man made a little hell on earth for himself, and I also suffered indirectly, but some sort of, no doubt, false delicacy prevented me. The marital relations of seamen would make an interesting subject, and I could tell you instances. . . . However, this is not the place, nor the time, and we are concerned with Jim— who was unmarried. If his imaginative conscience or his pride; if all the extravagant ghosts and austere shades that were the disastrous familiars[7] of his youth would not let him run away from the block, I, who of course can't be suspected of such familiars, was irresistibly impelled to go and see his head roll off. I wended my way towards the court. I didn't hope to be very much impressed or edified, or interested or even frightened—though, as long as there is any life before one, a jolly good fright now and then is a salutary discipline. But neither did I expect to be so awfully depressed. The bitterness of his punishment was in its chill and mean atmosphere. The real significance of crime is in its being a breach of faith with the community of mankind, and from that point of view he was no mean traitor, but his execution was a hole-and-corner affair. There

7. Intimate associate; also communicating spirit.

was no high scaffolding, no scarlet cloth (did they have scarlet cloth on Tower Hill? [8] They should have had), no awe-stricken multitude to be horrified at his guilt and be moved to tears at his fate—no air of sombre retribution. There was, as I walked along, the clear sunshine, a brilliance too passionate to be consoling, the streets full of jumbled bits of colour like a damaged kaleidoscope: yellow, green, blue, dazzling white, the brown nudity of an undraped shoulder, a bullock-cart with a red canopy, a company of native infantry in a drab body with dark heads marching in dusty laced boots, a native policeman in a sombre uniform of scanty cut and belted in patent leather, who looked up at me with orientally pitiful eyes as though his migrating spirit were suffering exceedingly from that unforeseen—what d'ye call 'em?—avatar—incarnation. Under the shade of a lonely tree in the courtyard, the villagers connected with the assault case sat in a picturesque group, looking like a chromolithograph of a camp in a book of Eastern travel. One missed the obligatory thread of smoke in the foreground and the pack-animals grazing. A blank yellow wall rose behind overtopping the tree, reflecting the glare. The court-room was sombre, seemed more vast. High up in the dim space the punkahs were swaying short to and fro, to and fro. Here and there a draped figure, dwarfed by the bare walls, remained without stirring amongst the rows of empty benches, as if absorbed in pious meditation. The plaintiff, who had been beaten,—an obese, chocolate-coloured man with shaved head, one fat breast bare and a bright yellow caste-mark above the bridge of his nose,—sat in pompous immobility: only his eyes glittered, rolling in the gloom, and the nostrils dilated and collapsed violently as he breathed. Brierly dropped into his seat looking done up, as though he had spent the night in sprinting on a cinder-track. The pious sailing-ship skipper appeared excited and made uneasy movements, as if restraining with difficulty an impulse to stand up and exhort us earnestly to prayer and repentance. The head of the magistrate, delicately pale under the neatly arranged hair, resembled the head of a hopeless invalid after he had been washed and brushed and propped up in bed. He moved aside the vase of flowers—a bunch of purple with a few pink blossoms on long stalks—and seizing in both hands a long sheet of bluish paper, ran his eye over it, propped his forearms on the edge of the desk, and began to read aloud in an even, distinct, and careless voice.

"By Jove! For all my foolishness about scaffolds and heads rolling off—I assure you it was infinitely worse than a beheading. A heavy sense of finality brooded over all this, unrelieved by the hope of rest and safety following the fall of the axe. These proceedings had

8. Site of the Tower of London, ancient fortress on the east side of the city of London, famous as a prison and place of execution.

all the cold vengefulness of a death-sentence, had all the cruelty of a sentence of exile. This is how I looked at it that morning—and even now I seem to see an undeniable vestige of truth in that exaggerated view of a common occurrence. You may imagine how strongly I felt this at the time. Perhaps it is for that reason that I could not bring myself to admit the finality. The thing was always with me, I was always eager to take opinion on it, as though it had not been practically settled: individual opinion—international opinion—by Jove! That Frenchman's, for instance. His own country's pronouncement was uttered in the passionless and definite phraseology a machine would use, if machines could speak. The head of the magistrate was half hidden by the paper, his brow was like alabaster.

"There were several questions before the court. The first as to whether the ship was in every respect fit and seaworthy for the voyage. The court found she was not. The next point, I remember, was, whether up to the time of the accident the ship had been navigated with proper and seamanlike care. They said Yes to that, goodness knows why, and then they declared that there was no evidence to show the exact cause of the accident. A floating derelict probably. I myself remember that a Norwegian barque bound out with a cargo of pitch-pine had been given up as missing about that time, and it was just the sort of craft that would capsize in a squall and float bottom up for months—a kind of maritime ghoul on the prowl to kill ships in the dark. Such wandering corpses are common enough in the North Atlantic, which is haunted by all the terrors of the sea—fogs, icebergs, dead ships bent upon mischief, and long, sinister gales that fasten upon one like a vampire till all the strength and the spirit and even hope are gone, and one feels like the empty shell of a man. But there—in those seas—the incident was rare enough to resemble a special arrangement of a malevolent providence, which, unless it had for its object the killing of a donkeyman and the bringing of worse than death upon Jim, appeared an utterly aimless piece of devilry. This view occurring to me took off my attention. For a time I was aware of the magistrate's voice as a sound merely; but in a moment it shaped itself into distinct words . . . 'in utter disregard of their plain duty,' it said. The next sentence escaped me somehow, and then . . . 'abandoning in the moment of danger the lives and property confided to their charge' . . . went on the voice evenly, and stopped. A pair of eyes under the white forehead shot darkly a glance above the edge of the paper. I looked for Jim hurriedly, as though I had expected him to disappear. He was very still—but he was there. He sat pink and fair and extremely attentive. 'Therefore . . .' began the voice emphatically. He stared with parted lips, hanging upon the words of the man behind the desk. These came out into the stillness wafted on the wind made by the punkahs, and I, watching for their effect upon him, caught only the fragments of official language. . . . 'The Court . . . Gustav So-and-so . . . master . . . native of Germany . . . James So-and-so . . . mate . . . certificates cancelled.' A silence fell. The magistrate had dropped the paper, and leaning sideways on the arm of his chair, began to talk with Brierly easily. People started to move out; others were pushing in, and I also made for the door. Outside I stood still, and when Jim passed me on his way to the gate, I caught at his arm and detained him. The look he gave discomposed me, as though I had been responsible for his state: he looked at me as if I had been the embodied evil of life. 'It's all over,' I stammered. 'Yes,' he said thickly. 'And now let no man . . .' He jerked his arm out of my grasp. I watched his back as he went away. It was a long street, and he remained in sight for some time. He walked rather slow, and straddling his legs a little, as if he had found it difficult to keep a straight line. Just before I lost him I fancied he staggered a bit.

" 'Man overboard,' said a deep voice behind me. Turning round, I saw a fellow I knew slightly, a West Australian; Chester[9] was his name. He, too, had been looking after Jim. He was a man with an immense girth of chest, a rugged, clean-shaved face of mahogany colour, and two blunt tufts of iron-grey, thick wiry hairs on his upper lip. He had been pearler, wrecker, trader, whaler, too, I believe; in his own words—anything and everything a man may be at sea, but a pirate. The Pacific, north and south, was his proper hunting-ground; but he had wandered so far afield looking for a cheap steamer to buy. Lately he had discovered—so he said—a guano[1] island somewhere, but its approaches were dangerous, and the anchorage, such as it was, could not be considered safe, to say the least of it. 'As good as a gold-mine,' he would exclaim. 'Right bang in the middle of the Walpole Reefs, and if it's true enough that you can get no holding-ground anywhere in less than forty fathom, then what of that? There are the hurricanes, too. But it's a first-rate thing. As good as a gold-mine—better! Yet there's not a fool of them that will see it. I can't get a skipper or a shipowner to go near the place. So I made up my mind to cart the blessed stuff myself. . . .' This was what he required a steamer for, and I knew he was just then negotiating enthusiastically with a Parsee firm for an old, brig-rigged, sea-anachronism of ninety horse-power. We had met and spoken together several times. He looked knowingly after

9. Chester and Robinson were sailors well known in Conrad's day who sailed in Australian waters.

1. The manure of sea birds, found especially on certain islands of the Pacific and used as fertilizer.

Jim. 'Takes it to heart?' he asked scornfully. 'Very much,' I said.
'Then he's no good,' he opined. 'What's all the to-do about? A bit
of ass's skin. That never yet made a man. You must see things
exactly as they are—if you don't, you may just as well give in at
once. You will never do anything in this world. Look at me. I made
it a practice never to take anything to heart.' 'Yes,' I said, 'you see
things as they are.' 'I wish I could see my partner coming along,
that's what I wish to see,' he said. 'Know my partner? Old Robinson. Yes; *the* Robinson. Don't *you* know? The notorious Robinson. The man who smuggled more opium and bagged more seals in
his time than any loose Johnny now alive. They say he used to
board the sealing-schooners up Alaska way when the fog was so
thick that the Lord God, He alone, could tell one man from another. Holy-Terror Robinson. That's the man. He is with me in that
guano thing. The best chance he ever came across in his life.' He
put his lips to my ear. 'Cannibal?—well, they used to give him the
name years and years ago. You remember the story? A shipwreck
on the west side of Stewart Island; that's right; seven of them got
ashore, and it seems they did not get on very well together. Some
men are too cantankerous for anything—don't know how to make
the best of a bad job—don't see things as they are—as they *are*, my
boy! And then what's the consequence? Obvious! Trouble, trouble;
as likely as not a knock on the head; and serve 'em right, too. That
sort is the most useful when it's dead. The story goes that a boat
of Her Majesty's ship *Wolverine* found him kneeling on the kelp,
naked as the day he was born, and chanting some psalm-tune or
other; light snow was falling at the time. He waited till the boat
was an oar's length from the shore, and then up and away. They
chased him for an hour up and down the boulders, till a marine
flung a stone that took him behind the ear providentially and
knocked him senseless. Alone? Of course. But that's like that tale
of sealing-schooners; the Lord God knows the right and the wrong
of that story. The cutter did not investigate much. They wrapped
him in a boat-cloak and took him off as quick as they could, with a
dark night coming on, the weather threatening, and the ship firing
recall guns every five minutes. Three weeks afterwards he was as
well as ever. He didn't allow any fuss that was made on shore to
upset him; he just shut his lips tight, and let people screech. It was
bad enough to have lost his ship, and all he was worth besides,
without paying attention to the hard names they called him. That's
the man for me.' He lifted his arm for a signal to some one down
the street. 'He's got a little money, so I had to let him into my
thing. Had to! It would have been sinful to throw away such a find,
and I was cleaned out myself. It cut me to the quick, but I could
see the matter just as it was, and if I *must* share—thinks I—with

any man, then give me Robinson. I left him at breakfast in the
hotel to come to court, because I've an idea. . . . Ah! Good
morning, Captain Robinson. . . . Friend of mine, Captain Robinson.'

"An emaciated patriarch in a suit of white drill, a solah topi with
a green-lined rim on a head trembling with age, joined us after
crossing the street in a trotting shuffle, and stood propped with
both hands on the handle of an umbrella. A white beard with amber
streaks hung lumpily down to his waist. He blinked his creased
eyelids at me in a bewildered way. 'How do you do? how do you
do?' he piped amiably, and tottered. 'A little deaf,' said Chester
aside. 'Did you drag him over six thousand miles to get a cheap
steamer?' I asked. 'I would have taken him twice round the world
as soon as look at him,' said Chester with immense energy. 'The
steamer will be the making of us, my lad. Is it my fault that every
skipper and shipowner in the whole of blessed Australasia turns out
a blamed fool? Once I talked for three hours to a man in Auckland.
"Send a ship," I said, "send a ship. I'll give you half of the first
cargo for yourself, free gratis for nothing—just to make a good
start." Says he, "I wouldn't do it if there was no other place on
earth to send a ship to." Perfect ass, of course. Rocks, currents, no
anchorage, sheer cliff to lay to, no insurance company would take the
risk, didn't see how he could get loaded under three years. Ass! I
nearly went on my knees to him. "But look at the thing as it is," says
I. "Damn rocks and hurricanes. Look at it as it is. There's guano
there Queensland sugar-planters would fight for—fight for on the
quay, I tell you. . . ." What can you do with a fool? . . . "That's one
of your little jokes, Chester," he says. . . . Joke! I could have wept.
Ask Captain Robinson here. . . . And there was another shipowning
fellow—a fat chap in a white waistcoat in Wellington, who seemed
to think I was up to some swindle or other. "I don't know what sort
of fool you're looking for," he says, "but I am busy just now. Good
morning." I longed to take him in my two hands and smash him
through the window of his own office. But I didn't. I was as mild as
a curate. "Think of it," says I. "Do think it over. I'll call to-morrow."
He grunted something about being "out all day." On the stairs I felt
ready to beat my head against the wall from vexation. Captain Robinson here can tell you. It was awful to think of all that lovely stuff
lying waste under the sun—stuff that would send the sugar-cane
shooting sky-high. The making of Queensland! The making of
Queensland! And in Brisbane, where I went to have a last try, they
gave me the name of a lunatic. Idiots! The only sensible man I
came across was the cabman who drove me about. A broken-down
swell he was, I fancy. Hey! Captain Robinson? You remember I told
you about my cabby in Brisbane—dont you? The chap had a won-

derful eye for things. He saw it all in a jiffy. It was a real pleasure to talk with him. One evening after a devil of a day amongst ship-owners I felt so bad that, says I, "I must get drunk. Come along; I must get drunk, or I'll go mad." "I am your man," he says; "go ahead." I don't know what I would have done without him. Hey! Captain Robinson.'

"He poked the ribs of his partner. 'He! he! he!' laughed the Ancient, looked aimlessly down the street, then peered at me doubtfully with sad, dim pupils. . . . 'He! he! he!' . . . He leaned heavier on the umbrella, and dropped his gaze on the ground. I needn't tell you I had tried to get away several times, but Chester had foiled every attempt by simply catching hold of my coat. 'One min-ute. I've a notion.' 'What's your infernal notion?' I exploded at last. 'If you think I am going in with you . . .' 'No, no, my boy. Too late, if you wanted ever so much. We've got a steamer.' 'You've got the ghost of a steamer,' I said. 'Good enough for a start—there's no superior nonsense about us. Is there, Captain Robinson?' 'No! no! no!' croaked the old man without lifting his eyes, and the senile tremble of his head became almost fierce with determination. 'I understand you know that young chap,' said Chester, with a nod at the street from which Jim had disappeared long ago. 'He's been having grub with you in the Malabar last night—so I was told.'

"I said that was true, and after remarking that he, too, liked to live well and in style, only that, for the present, he had to be saving of every penny—'none too many for the business! Isn't that so, Captain Robinson?'—he squared his shoulders and stroked his dumpy moustache, while the notorious Robinson, coughing at his side, clung more than ever to the handle of the umbrella, and seemed ready to subside passively into a heap of old bones. 'You see, the old chap has all the money,' whispered Chester confiden-tially. 'I've been cleaned out trying to engineer the dratted thing. But wait a bit, wait a bit. The good time is coming. . . .' He seemed suddenly astonished at the signs of impatience I gave. 'Oh, crakee!' [2] he cried; 'I am telling you of the biggest thing that ever was, and you . . .' 'I have an appointment,' I pleaded mildly. 'What of that?' he asked with genuine surprise; 'let it wait.' 'That's exactly what I am doing now,' I remarked; 'hadn't you better tell me what it is you want?' 'Buy twenty hotels like that,' he growled to him-self; 'and every joker boarding in them, too—twenty times over.' He lifted his head smartly. 'I want that young chap.' 'I don't under-stand,' I said. 'He's no good, is he?' said Chester crisply. 'I know nothing about it,' I protested. 'Why, you told me yourself he was taking it to heart,' argued Chester. 'Well, in my opinion a chap

---

2. Originally an oath (Christ), but by this time merely a jocular slang exclama-tion of surprise, admiration, etc.

who . . . Anyhow, he can't be much good; but then you see I am on the look out for somebody, and I've just got a thing that will suit him. I'll give him a job on my island.' He nodded significantly. 'I'm going to dump forty coolies there—if I've got to steal 'em. Somebody must work the stuff. Oh! I mean to act square: wooden shed, corrugated-iron roof—I know a man in Hobart who will take my bill at six months for the materials. I do. Honour bright. Then there's the water-supply. I'll have to fly round and get somebody to trust me for half a dozen second-hand iron tanks. Catch rain-water, hey? Let him take charge. Make him supreme boss over the coolies. Good idea, isn't it? What do you say?' 'There are whole years when not a drop of rain falls on Walpole,' I said, too amazed to laugh. He bit his lip and seemed bothered. 'Oh, well, I will fix up something for them—or land a supply. Hang it all! That's not the question.'

"I said nothing. I had a rapid vision of Jim perched on a shadowless rock, up to his knees in guano, with the screams of sea-birds in his ears, the incandescent ball of the sun above his head; the empty sky and the empty ocean all a-quiver, simmering together in the heat as far as the eye could reach. 'I wouldn't advise my worst enemy . . .' I began. 'What's the matter with you?' cried Chester; 'I mean to give him a good screw[3]—that is, as soon as the thing is set going, of course. It's as easy as falling off a log. Simply nothing to do; two six-shooters in his belt. . . . Surely he wouldn't be afraid of anything forty coolies could do—with two six-shooters and he the only armed man, too! It's much better than it looks. I want you to help me to talk him over.' 'No!' I shouted. Old Robinson lifted his bleared eyes dismally for a moment, Chester looked at me with infinite contempt. 'So you wouldn't advise him?' he uttered slowly. 'Certainly not,' I answered, as indignant as though he had requested me to help murder somebody; 'moreover, I am sure he wouldn't. He is badly cut up, but he isn't mad as far as I know.' 'He is no earthly good for anything,' Chester mused aloud. 'He would just have done for me. If you only could see a thing as it is, you would see it's the very thing for him. And besides . . . Why! it's the most splendid, sure chance . . .' He got angry suddenly. 'I must have a man. There! . . .' He stamped his foot and smiled unpleasantly. 'Anyhow, I could guarantee the island wouldn't sink under him— and I believe he is a bit particular on that point.' 'Good morning,' I said curtly. He looked at me as though I had been an incomprehensible fool. . . . 'Must be moving, Captain Robinson,' he yelled suddenly into the old man's ear. 'These Parsee Johnnies are

3. Salary, wages. The metaphor implies the employer's attempts to lower the rate, or the employee's efforts to force higher payment, of the salary, which has to be screwed out.

waiting for us to clinch the bargain.' He took his partner under the arm with a firm grip, swung him round, and, unexpectedly, leered at me over his shoulder. 'I was trying to do him a kindness,' he asserted, with an air and tone that made my blood boil. 'Thank you you for nothing—in his name,' I rejoined. 'Oh, you are devilish smart!' he sneered; 'but you are like the rest of them. Too much in the clouds. See what *you* will do with him.' 'I don't know that I want to do anything with him.' 'Don't you?' he spluttered; his grey moustache bristled with anger, and by his side the notorious Robinson, propped on the umbrella, stood with his back to me, as patient and still as a worn-out cab-horse. 'I haven't found a guano island,' I said. 'It's my belief you wouldn't know one if you were led right up to it by the hand,' he riposted[4] quickly; 'and in this world you've got to see a thing first, before you can make use of it. Got to see it through and through at that, neither more nor less.' 'And get others to see it, too,' I insinuated, with a glance at the bowed back by his side. Chester snorted at me. 'His eyes are right enough—don't you worry. He ain't a puppy.' 'Oh dear, no!' I said. 'Come along, Captain Robinson,' he shouted, with a sort of bullying deference under the rim of the old man's hat; the Holy Terror gave a submissive little jump. The ghost of a steamer was waiting for them, Fortune on that fair isle! They made a curious pair of Argonauts.[5] Chester strode on leisurely, well set up, portly, and of conquering mien; the other, long, wasted, drooping, and hooked to his arm, shuffled his withered shanks with desperate haste."

Chapter Fifteen

"I did not start in search of Jim at once, only because I had really an appointment which I could not neglect. Then, as ill-luck would have it, in my agent's office I was fastened upon by a fellow fresh from Madagascar with a little scheme for a wonderful piece of business. It had something to do with cattle and cartridges and a Prince Ravonalo something; but the pivot of the whole affair was the stupidity of some admiral—Admiral Pierre, I think. Everything turned on that, and the chap couldn't find words strong enough to express his confidence. He had globular eyes starting out of his head with a fishy glitter, bumps on his forehead, and wore his long hair brushed back without a parting. He had a favourite phrase which he kept on repeating triumphantly, 'The minimum of risk with the maximum of profit is my motto. What?' He made my head ache, spoiled my tiffin, but got his own out of me all right; and soon as

4. Delivered a verbal counterthrust; made a telling retort.
5. The mythical Greek heroes who ac- companied Jason on board the ship *Argo* to Colchis to recover the Golden Fleece.

I had shaken him off, I made straight for the waterside. I caught sight of Jim leaning over the parapet of the quay. Three native boatmen quarrelling over five annas were making an awful row at his elbow. He didn't hear me come up, but spun round as if the slight contact of my finger had released a catch. 'I was looking,' he stammered. I don't remember what I said, not much anyhow, but he made no difficulty in following me to the hotel.

"He followed me as manageable as a little child, with an obedient air, with no sort of manifestation, rather as though he had been waiting for me there to come along and carry him off. I need not have been so surprised as I was at his tractability. On all the round earth, which to some seems so big and that others affect to consider as rather smaller than a mustard-seed, he had no place where he could—what shall I say?—where he could withdraw. That's it! Withdraw—be alone with his loneliness. He walked by my side very calm, glancing here and there, and once turned his head to look after a Sidiboy fireman in a cutaway coat and yellowish trousers, whose black face had silky gleams like a lump of anthracite coal. I doubt, however, whether he saw anything, or even remained all the time aware of my companionship, because if I had not edged him to the left here, or pulled him to the right there, I believe he would have gone straight before him in any direction till stopped by a wall or some other obstacle. I steered him into my bedroom, and sat down at once to write letters. This was the only place in the world (unless, perhaps, the Walpole Reef—but that was not so handy) where he could have it out with himself without being bothered by the rest of the universe. The damned thing—as he had expressed it—had not made him invisible, but I behaved exactly as though he were. No sooner in my chair I bent over my writing-desk like a medieval scribe, and, but for the movement of the hand holding the pen, remained anxiously quiet. I can't say I was frightened; but I certainly kept as still as if there had been something dangerous in the room, that at the first hint of a movement on my part would be provoked to pounce upon me. There was not much in the room —you know how these bedrooms are—a sort of four-poster bedstead under a mosquito-net, two or three chairs, the table I was writing at, a bare floor. A glass door opened on an upstairs verandah, and he stood with his face to it, having a hard time with all possible privacy. Dusk fell; I lit a candle with the greatest economy of movement and as much prudence as though it were an illegal proceeding. There is no doubt that he had a very hard time of it, and so had I, even to the point, I must own, of wishing him to the devil, or on Walpole Reef at least. It occurred to me once or twice that, after all, Chester was, perhaps, the man to deal effectively with such a disaster. That strange idealist had found a practical use for it at once—unerringly, as it were. It was enough to make one suspect that, maybe, he really could see the true aspect of things that appeared mysterious or utterly hopeless to less imaginative persons. I wrote and wrote; I liquidated all the arrears of my correspondence, and then went on writing to people who had no reason whatever to expect from me a gossipy letter about nothing at all. At times I stole a sidelong glance. He was rooted to the spot, but convulsive shudders ran down his back; his shoulders would heave suddenly. He was fighting, he was fighting—mostly for his breath, as it seemed. The massive shadows, cast all one way from the straight flame of the candle, seemed possessed of gloomy consciousness; the immobility of the furniture had to my furtive eye an air of attention. I was becoming fanciful in the midst of my industrious scribbling; and though, when the scratching of my pen stopped for a moment, there was complete silence and stillness in the room, I suffered from that profound disturbance and confusion of thought which is caused by a violent and menacing uproar—of a heavy gale at sea, for instance. Some of you may know what I mean: that mingled anxiety, distress, and irritation with a sort of craven feeling creeping in—not pleasant to acknowledge, but which gives a quite special merit to one's endurance. I don't claim any merit for standing the stress of Jim's emotions; I could take refuge in the letters; I could have written to strangers if necessary. Suddenly, as I was taking up a fresh sheet of notepaper, I heard a low sound, the first sound that, since we had been shut up together, had come to my ears in the dim stillness of the room. I remained with my head down, with my hand arrested. Those who have kept vigil by a sick-bed have heard such faint sounds in the stillness of the night-watches, sounds wrung from a racked body, from a weary soul. He pushed the glass door with such force that all the panes rang: he stepped out, and I held my breath, straining my ears without knowing what else I expected to hear. He was really taking too much to heart an empty formality which to Chester's rigorous criticism seemed unworthy the notice of a man who could see things as they were. An empty formality; a piece of parchment. Well, well. As to the inaccessible guano deposit, that was another story altogether. One could intelligibly break one's heart over that. A feeble burst of many voices mingled with the tinkle of silver and glass floated up from the dining-room below; through the open door the outer edge of the light from my candle fell on his back faintly; beyond all was black; he stood on the brink of a vast obscurity, like a lonely figure by the shore of a sombre and hopeless ocean. There was the Walpole Reef in it—to be sure—a speck in the dark void, a straw for the drowning man. My compassion for him took the shape of the thought that I wouldn't have liked his people to see him at that moment. I found it trying myself. His back was no longer shaken by his gasps; he stood straight as an arrow, faintly visible and still; and the meaning of this stillness sank to the bottom of my soul like lead into the water, and made it so heavy that for a second I wished heartily that the only course left open for me was to pay for his funeral. Even the law had done with him. To bury him would have been such an easy kindness! It would have been so much in accordance with the wisdom of life, which consists in putting out of sight all the reminders of our folly, of our weakness, of our mortality; all that makes against our efficiency—the memory of our failures, the hints of our undying fears, the bodies of our dead friends. Perhaps he did take it too much to heart. And if so, then— Chester's offer . . . At this point I took up a fresh sheet and began to write resolutely. There was nothing but myself between him and the dark ocean. I had a sense of responsibility. If I spoke, would that motionless and suffering youth leap into the obscurity— clutch at the straw? I found out how difficult it may be sometimes to make a sound. There is a weird power in a spoken word. And why the devil not? I was asking myself persistently while I drove on with my writing. All at once, on the blank page, under the very point of the pen, the two figures of Chester and his antique partner, very distinct and complete, would dodge into view with stride and gestures, as if reproduced in the field of some optical toy. I would watch them for a while. No! They were too phantasmal and extravagant to enter into any one's fate. And a word carries far—very far—deals destruction through time as the bullets go flying through space. I said nothing; and he, out there with his back to the light, as if bound and gagged by all the invisible foes of man, made no stir and made no sound."

Chapter Sixteen

"The time was coming when I should see him loved, trusted, admired, with a legend of strength and prowess forming round his name as though he had been the stuff of a hero. It's true—I assure you; as true as I'm sitting here talking about him in vain. He, on his side, had that faculty of beholding at a hint the face of his desire and the shape of his dream, without which the earth would know no lover and no adventurer. He captured much honour and an Arcadian happiness (I won't say anything about innocence) in the bush, and it was as good to him as the honour and the Arcadian happiness of the streets to another man. Felicity, felicity— how shall I say it?—is quaffed out of a golden cup in every latitude: the flavour is with you—with you alone, and you can make it as intoxicating as you please. He was of the sort that would drink deep, as you may guess from what went before. I found him, if not exactly intoxicated, then at least flushed with the elixir at his lips. He had not obtained it at once. There had been, as you know, a period of probation amongst infernal ship-chandlers, during which he had suffered and I had worried about—about—my trust—you may call it. I don't know that I am completely reassured now, after beholding him in all his brilliance. That was my last view of him—in a strong light, dominating, and yet in complete accord with his surroundings—with the life of the forests and with the life of men. I own that I was impressed, but I must admit to myself that after all this is not the lasting impression. He was protected by his isolation, alone of his own superior kind, in close touch with Nature, that keeps faith on such easy terms with her lovers. But I cannot fix before my eye the image of his safety. I shall always remember him as seen through the open door of my room, taking, perhaps, too much to heart the mere consequences of his failure. I am pleased, of course, that some good—and even some splendour—came out of my endeavours; but at times it seems to me it would have been better for my peace of mind if I had not stood between him and Chester's confoundedly generous offer. I wonder what his exuberant imagination would have made of Walpole islet—that most hopelessly forsaken crumb of dry land on the face of the waters! It is not likely I would ever have heard, for I must tell you that Chester, after calling at some Australian port to patch up his brig-rigged sea-anachronism, steamed out into the Pacific with a crew of twenty-two hands all told, and the only news having a possible bearing upon the mystery of his fate was the news of a hurricane which is supposed to have swept in its course over the Walpole shoals, a month or so afterwards. Not a vestige of the Argonauts ever turned up; not a sound came out of the waste. Finis! The Pacific is the most discreet of live, hot-tempered oceans: the chilly Antarctic can keep a secret, too, but more in the manner of a grave.

"And there is a sense of blessed finality in such discretion, which is what we all more or less sincerely are ready to admit—for what else is it that makes the idea of death supportable? End! Finis! the potent word that exorcises from the house of life the haunting shadow of fate. This is what—notwithstanding the testimony of my eyes and his own earnest assurances—I miss when I look back upon Jim's success. While there's life there is hope, truly; but there is fear, too. I don't mean to say that I regret my action, nor will I pretend that I can't sleep o' nights in consequence; still, the idea obtrudes itself that he made so much of his disgrace while it is the guilt alone that matters. He was not—if I may say so—clear to me. He was not clear. And there is a suspicion he was not clear to himself either. There were his fine sensibilities, his fine feelings, his

fine longings—a sort of sublimated, idealised selfishness. He was—
if you allow me to say so—very fine; very fine—and very unfortunate. A little coarser nature would not have borne the strain; it
would have had to come to terms with itself—with a sigh, with a
grunt, or even with a guffaw; a still coarser one would have remained
invulnerably ignorant and completely uninteresting.

"But he was too interesting or too unfortunate to be thrown to
the dogs, or even to Chester. I felt this while I sat with my face
over the paper and he fought and gasped, struggling for his breath
in that terrible stealthy way, in my room; I felt it when he rushed
out on the verandah as if to fling himself over—and didn't; I felt
it more and more all the time he remained outside, faintly lighted
on the background of night, as if standing on the shore of a sombre
and hopeless sea.

"An abrupt, heavy rumble made me lift my head. The noise
seemed to roll away, and suddenly a searching and violent glare fell
on the blind face of the night. The sustained and dazzling
flickers seemed to last for an unconscionable time. The growl of
the thunder increased steadily while I looked at him, distinct and
black, planted solidly upon the shore of a sea of light. At the
moment of greatest brilliance the darkness leaped back with a
culminating crash, and he vanished before my dazzled eyes as
utterly as though he had been blown to atoms. A blustering sigh
passed; furious hands seemed to tear at the shrubs, shake the tops of
the trees below, slam doors, break window-panes, all along the
front of the building. He stepped in, closing the door behind him,
and found me bending over the table: my sudden anxiety as to
what he would say was very great, and akin to a fright. 'May I have
a cigarette?' he asked. I gave a push to the box without raising my
head. 'I want—want—tobacco,' he muttered. I became extremely
buoyant. 'Just a moment,' I grunted pleasantly. He took a few steps
here and there. 'That's over,' I heard him say. A single distant clap
of thunder came from the sea like a gun of distress. 'The monsoon
breaks up early this year,' he remarked, conversationally, somewhere behind me. This encouraged me to turn around, which I
did as soon as I had finished addressing the last envelope. He was
smoking greedily in the middle of the room, and though he heard
the stir I made, he remained with his back to me for a time.

" 'Come—I carried it off pretty well,' he said, wheeling suddenly.
'Something's paid off—not much. I wonder what's to come?' His
face did not show any emotion, only it appeared a little darkened
and swollen, as though he had been holding his breath. He smiled
reluctantly as it were, and went on while I gazed up at him mutely.
. . . 'Thank you, though—your room—jolly convenient—for a
chap—badly hipped.[6] . . .' The rain pattered and swished in the

6. Melancholy, bored, depressed; originally, suffering from hypochondria.

garden; a water-pipe (it must have had a hole in it) performed just outside the window a parody of blubbering woe with funny sobs and gurgling lamentations, interrupted by jerky spasms of silence. . . . 'A bit of shelter,' he mumbled, and ceased.

"A flash of faded lightning darted in through the black framework of the windows and ebbed out without any noise. I was thinking how I had best approach him (I did not want to be flung off again) when he gave a little laugh. 'No better than a vagabond now' . . . the end of the cigarette smouldered between his fingers . . . 'without a single—single,' he pronounced slowly; 'and yet . . .' He paused; the rain fell with redoubled violence. 'Some day one's bound to come upon some sort of chance to get it all back again. Must!' he whispered distinctly, glaring at my boots.

"I did not even know what it was he wished so much to regain, what it was he had so terribly missed. It might have been so much that it was impossible to say. A piece of ass's skin, according to Chester. . . . He looked up at me inquisitively. 'Perhaps. If life's long enough,' I muttered through my teeth with unreasonable animosity. 'Don't reckon too much on it.'

" 'Jove! I feel as if nothing could ever touch me,' he said in a tone of sombre conviction. 'If this business couldn't knock me over, then there's no fear of there being not enough time to—climb out, and . . .' He looked upwards.

"It struck me that it is from such as he that the great army of waifs and strays is recruited, the army that marches down, down into all the gutters of the earth. As soon as he left my room, that 'bit of shelter,' he would take his place in the ranks, and begin the journey towards the bottomless pit. I at least had no illusions; but it was I, too, who a moment ago had been so sure of the power of words, and now was afraid to speak, in the same way one dares not move for fear of losing a slippery hold. It is when we try to grapple with another man's intimate need that we perceive how incomprehensible, wavering, and misty are the beings that share with us the sight of the stars and the warmth of the sun. It is as if loneliness were a hard and absolute condition of existence; the envelope of flesh and blood on which our eyes are fixed melts before the outstretched hand, and there remains only the capricious, inconsolable, and elusive spirit that no eye can follow, no hand can grasp. It was the fear of losing him that kept me silent, for it was borne upon me suddenly and with unaccountable force that should I let him slip away into the darkness I would never forgive myself.

" 'Well. Thanks—once more. You've been—er—uncommonly— really there's no word to . . . Uncommonly! I don't know why, I am sure. I am afraid I don't feel as grateful as I would if the whole thing hadn't been so brutally sprung on me. Because at bottom . . . you, yourself . . .' He stuttered.

" 'Possibly,' I struck in. He frowned.

" 'All the same, one is responsible.' He watched me like a hawk.

" 'And that's true, too,' I said.

" 'Well. I've gone with it to the end, and I don't intend to let any man cast it in my teeth without—without—resenting.' He clenched his fist.

" 'There's yourself,' I said with a smile—mirthless enough, God knows—but he looked at me menacingly. 'That's my business,' he said. An air of indomitable resolution came and went upon his face like a vain and passing shadow. Next moment he looked a dear, good boy in trouble, as before. He flung away the cigarette. 'Goodbye,' he said, with the sudden haste of a man who had lingered too long in view of a pressing bit of work waiting for him; and then for a second or so he made not the slightest movement. The downpour fell with the heavy, uninterrupted rush of a sweeping flood, with a sound of unchecked, overwhelming fury that called to one's mind the images of collapsing bridges, of uprooted trees, of undermined mountains. No man could breast the colossal and headlong stream that seemed to break and swirl against the dim stillness in which we were precariously sheltered as if on an island. The perforated pipe gurgled, choked, spat, and splashed in odious ridicule of a swimmer fighting for his life. 'It is raining,' I remonstrated, 'and I . . .' 'Rain or shine,' he began brusquely, checked himself, and walked to the window. 'Perfect deluge,' he muttered after a while: he leaned his forehead on the glass. 'It's dark, too.'

" 'Yes, it is very dark,' I said.

"He pivoted on his heels, crossed the room, and had actually opened the door leading into the corridor before I leaped up from my chair. 'Wait,' I cried, 'I want you to . . .' 'I can't dine with you again to-night,' he flung at me, with one leg out of the room already. 'I haven't the slightest intention of asking you,' I shouted. At this he drew back his foot, but remained mistrustfully in the very doorway. I lost no time in entreating him earnestly not to be absurd; to come in and shut the door."

Chapter Seventeen

"He came in at last; but I believe it was mostly the rain that did it; it was falling just then with a devastating violence which quieted down gradually while we talked. His manner was very sober and set; his bearing was that of a naturally taciturn man possessed by an idea. My talk was of the material aspect of his position; it had the sole aim of saving him from the degradation, ruin, and despair that out there close so swiftly upon a friendless, homeless man; I pleaded with him to accept my help; I argued reasonably: and every time I looked up at that absorbed, smooth face, so grave and youthful, I had a disturbing sense of being no help but rather an obstacle to some mysterious, inexplicable, impalpable striving of his wounded spirit.

" 'I suppose you intend to eat and drink and to sleep under shelter in the usual way,' I remember saying with irritation. 'You say you won't touch the money that is due to you. . . .' He came as near as his sort can to making a gesture of horror. (There were three weeks and five days' pay owing him as mate of the *Patna*.) 'Well, that's too little to matter anyhow; but what will you do to-morrow? Where will you turn? You must live . . .' 'That isn't the thing,' was the comment that escaped him under his breath. I ignored it, and went on combating what I assumed to be the scruples of an exaggerated delicacy. 'On every conceivable ground,' I concluded, 'you must let me help you.' 'You can't,' he said very simply and gently, and holding fast to some deep idea which I could detect shimmering like a pool of water in the dark, but which I despaired of ever approaching near enough to fathom. I surveyed his well-proportioned bulk. 'At any rate,' I said, 'I am able to help what I can see of you. I don't pretend to do more.' He shook his head sceptically without looking at me. I got very warm. 'But I can,' I insisted. 'I can do even more. I *am* doing more. I am trusting you . . .' 'The money . . .' he began. 'Upon my word, you deserve being told to go to the devil,' I cried, forcing the note of indignation. He was startled, smiled, and I pressed my attack home. 'It isn't a question of money at all. You are too superficial,' I said (and at the same time I was thinking to myself: Well, here goes! And perhaps he is after all). 'Look at the letter I want you to take. I am writing to a man of whom I've never asked a favour, and I am writing about you in terms that one only ventures to use when speaking of an intimate friend. I make myself unreservedly responsible for you. That's what I am doing. And really, if you will only reflect a little what that means . . .'

"He lifted his head. The rain had passed away; only the waterpipe went on shedding tears with an absurd drip, drip outside the window. It was very quiet in the room, whose shadows huddled together in corners, away from the still flame of the candle flaring upright in the shape of a dagger; his face after a while seemed suffused by a reflection of a soft light as if the dawn had broken already.

" 'Jove!' he gasped out. 'It is noble of you!'

"Had he suddenly put out his tongue at me in derision, I could not have felt more humiliated. I thought to myself—Serve me right for a sneaking humbug. . . . His eyes shone straight into my face, but I perceived it was not a mocking brightness. All at once he sprang into jerky agitation, like one of those flat wooden figures that are worked by a string. His arms went up, then came down with a slap. He became another man altogether. 'And I had never seen,' he shouted; then suddenly bit his lip and frowned. 'What a bally[7] ass I've been,' he said very slow in an awed tone. . . . 'You are a brick!' he cried next in a muffled voice. He snatched my hand as though he had just then seen it for the first time, and dropped it at once. 'Why! this is what I—you—I . . .' he stammered, and then with a return of his old stolid, I may say mulish, manner he began heavily, 'I would be a brute now if I . . .' and then his voice seemed to break. 'That's all right,' I said. I was almost alarmed by this display of feeling, through which pierced a strange elation. I had pulled the string accidentally, as it were; I did not fully understand the working of the toy. 'I must go now,' he said. 'Jove! You *have* helped me. Can't sit still. The very thing . . .' He looked at me with puzzled admiration. 'The very thing . . .'

"Of course it was the thing. It was ten to one that I had saved him from starvation—of that peculiar sort that is almost invariably associated with drink. This was all. I had not a single illusion on that score, but looking at him, I allowed myself to wonder at the nature of the one he had, within the last three minutes, so evidently taken into his bosom. I had forced into his hand the means to carry on decently the serious business of life, to get food, drink, and shelter of the customary kind while his wounded spirit, like a bird with a broken wing, might hop and flutter into some hole to die quietly of inanition there. This is what I had thrust upon him: a definitely small thing; and—behold!—by the manner of its reception it loomed in the dim light of the candle like a big, indistinct, perhaps a dangerous shadow. 'You don't mind me not saying anything appropriate,' he burst out. 'There isn't anything one could say. Last night already you had done me no end of good. Listening to me—you know. I give you my word I've thought more than once the top of my head would fly off . . .' He darted—positively darted— here and there, rammed his hands into his pockets, jerked them out again, flung his cap on his head. I had no idea it was in him to be so airily brisk. I thought of a dry leaf imprisoned in an eddy of wind, while a mysterious apprehension, a load of indefinite doubt, weighed me down in my chair. He stood stock-still, as if struck motionless by a discovery. 'You have given me confidence,' he declared soberly. 'Oh! for God's sake, my dear fellow—don't!' I entreated, as though he had hurt me. 'All right. I'll shut up now and henceforth. Can't prevent me thinking, though. . . . Never mind! . . . I'll show yet . . .' He went to the door in a hurry, paused with his head down, and came back, stepping deliberately. 'I always thought that if a fellow could

7. Schoolboy slang equivalent of "damn"; originally a euphemism for bloody.

begin with a clean slate . . . And now you . . . in a measure . . . yes . . . clean slate.' I waved my hand, and he marched out without looking back; the sound of his footfalls died out gradually behind the closed door—the unhesitating tread of a man walking in broad daylight.

"But as to me, left alone with the solitary candle, I remained strangely unenlightened. I was no longer young enough to behold at every turn the magnificence that besets our insignificant footsteps in good and in evil. I smiled to think that, after all, it was yet he, of us two, who had the light. And I felt sad. A clean slate, did he say? As if the initial word of each our destiny were not graven in imperishable characters upon the face of a rock!"

Chapter Eighteen

"Six months afterwards my friend (he was a cynical, more than middle-aged bachelor, with a reputation for eccentricity, and owned a rice-mill) wrote to me, and judging, from the warmth of my recommendation, that I would like to hear, enlarged a little upon Jim's perfections. These were apparently of a quiet and effective sort. 'Not having been able so far to find more in my heart than a resigned toleration for any individual of my kind, I have lived till now alone in a house that even in this steaming climate could be considered as too big for one man. I have had him to live with me for some time past. It seems I haven't made a mistake.' It seemed to me on reading this letter that my friend had found in his heart more than tolerance for Jim—that there were the beginnings of active liking. Of course he stated his grounds in a characteristic way. For one thing, Jim kept his freshness in the climate. Had he been a girl—my friend wrote—one could have said he was blooming—blooming modestly—like a violet, not like some of these blatant tropical flowers. He had been in the house for six weeks, and had not as yet attempted to slap him on the back, or address him as 'old boy,' or try to make him feel a superannuated fossil. He had nothing of the exasperating young man's chatter. He was good-tempered, had not much to say for himself, was not clever by any means, thank goodness—wrote my friend. It appeared, however, that Jim was clever enough to be quietly appreciative of his wit, while, on the other hand, he amused him by his naiveness. 'The dew is yet on him, and since I had the bright idea of giving him a room in the house and having him at meals I feel less withered myself. The other day he took it into his head to cross the room with no other purpose but to open a door for me; and I felt more in touch with mankind that I had been for years. Ridiculous, isn't it? Of course I guess there is something—some awful little scrape—

which you know all about—but if I am sure that it is terribly heinous, I fancy one could manage to forgive it. For my part, I declare I am unable to imagine him guilty of anything much worse than robbing an orchard. Is *it* much worse? Perhaps you ought to have told me; but it is such a long time since we both turned saints that you may have forgotten we, too, had sinned in our time? It may be that some day I shall have to ask you, and then I shall expect to be told. I don't care to question him myself till I have some idea what it is. Moreover, it's too soon as yet. Let him open the door a few times more for me. . . .' Thus my friend. I was trebly pleased—at Jim's shaping so well, at the tone of the letter, at my own cleverness. Evidently I had known what I was doing. I had read characters aright, and so on. And what if something unexpected and wonderful were to come of it? That evening, reposing in a deck-chair under the shade of my own poop awning (it was in Hong-Kong harbour), I laid on Jim's behalf the first stone of a castle in Spain.

"I made a trip to the northward, and when I returned I found another letter from my friend waiting for me. It was the first envelope I tore open. 'There are no spoons missing, as far as I know,' ran the first line; 'I haven't been interested enough to inquire. He is gone, leaving on the breakfast-table a formal little note of apology, which is either silly or heartless. Probably both—and it's all one to me. Allow me to say, lest you should have some more mysterious young men in reserve, that I have shut up shop, definitely and for ever. This is the last eccentricity I shall be guilty of. Do not imagine for a moment that I care a hang; but he is very much regretted at tennis-parties, and for my own sake I've told a plausible lie at the club. . . .' I flung the letter aside and started looking through the batch on my table, till I came upon Jim's handwriting. Would you believe it? One chance in a hundred! But it is always that hundredth chance! That little second engineer of the *Patna* had turned up in a more or less destitute state, and got a temporary job of looking after the machinery of the mill. 'I couldn't stand the familiarity of the little beast,' Jim wrote from a seaport seven hundred miles south of the place where he should have been in clover. 'I am now for the time with Egström & Blake,[8] ship-chandlers, as their— well—runner, to call the thing by its right name. For reference I gave them your name, which they know, of course, and if you could write a word in my favour it would be a permanent employment.' I was utterly crushed under the ruins of my castle, but of course I wrote as desired. Before the end of the year my new charter took

8. Perhaps the Singapore ship-chand- lers, McAlister & Co., housed in the same building with Emmerson's Tiffin- Rooms, where ships' officers and traders like Captain William Lingard congre- gated. (See "Sources.")

me that way, and I had an opportunity of seeing him.

"He was still with Egström & Blake, and we met in what they called 'our parlour' opening out of the store. He had that moment come in from boarding a ship, and confronted me head down, ready for a tussle. 'What have you got to say for yourself?' I began as soon as we had shaken hands. 'What I wrote you—nothing more,' he said stubbornly. 'Did the fellow blab—or what?' I asked. He looked up at me with a troubled smile. 'Oh no! He didn't. He made it a kind of confidential business between us. He was most damnably mysterious whenever I came over to the mill; he would wink at me in a respectful manner—as much as to say, "We know what we know." Infernally fawning and familiar—and that sort of thing.' He threw himself into a chair and stared down his legs. 'One day we happened to be alone, and the fellow had the cheek to say, "Well, Mr. James"—I was called Mr. James there as if I had been the son—"here we are together once more. This is better than the old ship—ain't it? . . ." Wasn't it appalling, eh? I looked at him, and he put on a knowing air. "Don't you be uneasy, sir," he says. "I know a gentleman when I see one, and I know how a gentleman feels. I hope, though, you will be keeping me on this job. I had a hard time of it, too, along of that rotten old *Patna* racket." Jove! It was awful. I don't know what I should have said or done if I had not just then heard Mr. Denver calling me in the passage. It was tiffin-time, and we walked together across the yard and through the garden to the bungalow. He began to chaff me in his kindly way . . . I believe he liked me . . .'

"Jim was silent for a while.

"'I know he liked me. That's what made it so hard. Such a splendid man! That morning he slipped his hand under my arm. . . . He, too, was familiar with me.' He burst into a short laugh, and dropped his chin on his breast. 'Pah! When I remembered how that mean little beast had been talking to me,' he began suddenly in a vibrating voice, 'I couldn't bear to think of myself . . . I suppose you know . . .' I nodded. . . . 'More like a father,' he cried; his voice sank. 'I would have had to tell him. I couldn't let it go on—could I?' 'Well?' I murmured, after waiting a while. 'I preferred to go,' he said slowly; 'this thing must be buried.'

"We could hear in the shop Blake upbraiding Egström in an abusive, strained voice. They had been associated for many years, and every day from the moment the doors were opened to the last minute before closing, Blake, a little man with sleek, jetty hair and unhappy, beady eyes, could be heard rowing his partner incessantly with a sort of scathing and plaintive fury. The sound of that everlasting scolding was part of the place like the other fixtures; even strangers would very soon come to disregard it completely, unless it be perhaps to mutter 'Nuisance,' or to get up suddenly and shut the door of the 'parlour.' Egström himself, a raw-boned, heavy Scandinavian, with a busy manner and immense blonde whiskers, went on directing his people, checking parcels, making out bills or writing letters at a stand-up desk in the shop, and comported hii.iself in that clatter exactly as though he had been stone-deaf. Now and again he would emit a bothered perfunctory 'Sssh,' which neither produced nor was expected to produce the slightest effect. 'They are very decent to me here,' said Jim. 'Blake's a little cad, but Egström's all right.' He stood up quickly, and walking with measured steps to a tripod telescope standing in the window and pointed at the roadstead, he applied his eye to it. 'There's that ship which has been becalmed outside all the morning has got a breeze now and is coming in,' he remarked patiently; 'I must go and board.' We shook hands in silence, and he turned to go. 'Jim!' I cried. He looked round with his hand on the lock. 'You-you have thrown away something like a fortune.' He came back to me all the way from the door. 'Such a splendid old chap,' he said. 'How could I? How could I?' His lips twitched. '*Here* it does not matter.' 'Oh! you—you——' I began, and had to cast about for a suitable word, but before I became aware that there was no name that would just do, he was gone. I heard outside Egström's deep, gentle voice saying cheerily, 'That's the *Sarah* W. *Granger*, Jimmy. You must manage to be first aboard'; and directly Blake struck in, screaming after the manner of an outraged cockatoo, 'Tell the captain we've got some of his mail here. That'll fetch him. D'ye hear, Mister What's-your-name?' And there was Jim answering Egström with something boyish in his tone. 'All right. I'll make a race of it.' He seemed to take refuge in the boat-sailing part of that sorry business.

"I did not see him again that trip, but on my next (I had a six months' charter) I went up to the store. Ten yards away from the door Blake's scolding met my ears, and when I came in he gave me a glance of utter wretchedness; Egström, all smiles, advanced, extending a large, bony hand. 'Glad to see you, captain. . . . Sssh. . . . Been thinking you were about due back here. What did you say, sir? . . . Sssh. . . . Oh! him! He has left us. Come into the parlour. . . .' After the slam of the door Blake's strained voice became faint, as the voice of one scolding desperately in a wilderness. . . .'Put us to a great inconvenience, too. Used us badly— I must say . . .' 'Where's he gone to? Do you know?' I asked. 'No. It's no use asking either,' said Egström, standing bewhiskered and obliging before me with his arms hanging down his sides clumsily and a thin silver watch-chain looped very low on a rucked-up [9] blue

9. Drawn or worked into wrinkles or creases; puckered.

serge waistcoat. 'A man like that don't go anywhere in particular.' I was too concerned at the news to ask for the explanation of that pronouncement, and he went on. 'He left—let's see—the very day a steamer with returning pilgrims from the Red Sea put in here with two blades of her propeller gone. Three weeks ago now.' 'Wasn't there something said about the *Patna* case?' I asked, fearing the worst. He gave a start, and looked at me as if I had been a sorcerer. 'Why, yes! How do you know? Some of them were talking about it here. There was a captain or two, the manager of Vanlo's engineering shop at the harbour, two or three others, and myself. Jim was in here, too, having a sandwich and a glass of beer; when we were busy—you see, captain—there's no time for a proper tiffin. He was standing by this table eating sandwiches, and the rest of us were round the telescope watching that steamer come in; and by and by Vanlo's manager began to talk about the chief of the *Patna*; he had done some repairs for him once, and from that he went on to tell us what an old ruin she was, and the money that had been made out of her. He came to mention her last voyage, and then we all struck in. Some said one thing and some another—not much—what you or any other man might say; and there was some laughing. Captain O'Brien of the *Sarah W. Granger*, a large, noisy old man with a stick—he was sitting listening to us, in this armchair here—he let drive suddenly with his stick at the floor, and roars out, "Skunks! . . ." Made us all jump. Vanlo's manager winks at us and asks, "What's the matter, Captain O'Brien?" "Matter! matter!" the old man began to shout; "what are you Injuns laughing at? It's no laughing matter. It's a disgrace to human natur'—that's what it is. I would despise being seen in the same room with one of those men. Yes, sir!" He seemed to catch my eye like, and I had to speak out of civility. "Skunks!" says I, "of course, Captain O'Brien, and I wouldn't care to have them here myself, so you're quite safe in this room, Captain O'Brien. Have a little something cool to drink." "Dam' your drink, Egström," says he, with a twinkle in his eye; "when I want a drink I will shout for it. I am going to quit. It stinks here now." At this all the others burst out laughing, and out they go after the old man. And then, sir, that blasted Jim he puts down the sandwich he had in his hand and walks round the table to me; there was his glass of beer poured out quite full. "I am off," he says—just like this. "It isn't half-past one yet," says I; "you might snatch a smoke first." I thought he meant it was time for him to go down to his work. When I understood what he was up to, my arms fell—so! Can't get a man like that every day, you know, sir; a regular devil for sailing a boat; ready to go out miles to sea to meet ships in any sort of weather. More than once a captain would come in here full of it, and the first thing he would say would be, "That's a reckless sort of a lunatic you've got for water-clerk, Egström. I was feeling my way in at daylight under short canvas when there comes flying out of the mist right under my forefoot a boat half under water, sprays going over the masthead, two frightened niggers on the bottom boards, a yelling fiend at the tiller. Hey! hey! Ship ahoy! ahoy! Captain! Hey! hey! Egström & Blake's man first to speak to you! Hey! hey! Egström & Blake! Hallo! hey! whoop! Kick the niggers—out reefs—a squall on at the time—shoots ahead whooping and yelling to me to make sail and he would give me a lead in—more like a demon than a man. Never saw a boat handled like that in all my life. Couldn't have been drunk—was he? Such a quiet, soft-spoken chap, too—blush like a girl when he came on board. . . . " I tell you, Captain Marlow, nobody had a chance against us with a strange ship when Jim was out. The other ship-chandlers just kept their old customers, and . . .'

"Egström appeared overcome with emotion.

" 'Why, sir—it seemed as though he wouldn't mind going a hundred miles out to sea in an old shoe to nab a ship for the firm. If the business had been his own and all to make yet, he couldn't have done more in that way. And now . . . all at once . . . like this! Thinks I to myself: "Oho! a rise in the screw—that's the trouble—is it? All right," says I, "no need of all that fuss with me, Jimmy. Just mention your figure. Anything in reason." He looks at me as if he wanted to swallow something that stuck in his throat. "I can't stop with you." "What's that blooming joke?" I asks. He shakes his head, and I could see in his eye he was as good as gone already, sir. So I turned to him and slanged him till all was blue. "What is it you're running away from?" I asks. "Who has been getting at you? What scared you? You haven't as much sense as a rat; they don't clear out from a good ship. Where do you expect to get a better berth?—you this and you that." I made him look sick, I can tell you. "This business ain't going to sink," says I. He gave a big jump. "Good-bye," he says, nodding at me like a lord; "you ain't half a bad chap, Egström. I give you my word that if you knew my reasons you wouldn't care to keep me." "That's the biggest lie you ever told in your life," says I; "I know my own mind." He made me so mad that I had to laugh. "Can't you really stop long enough to drink this glass of beer here, you funny beggar, you?" I don't know what came over him; he didn't seem able to find the door; something comical, I can tell you, captain. I drank the beer myself. "Well, if you're in such a hurry, here's luck to you in your own drink," says I; "only, you mark my words, if you keep up this game you'll very soon find that the earth ain't big enough to hold you—that's all." He gave me one black look and out he rushed with a face fit to scare little children.'

"Egström snorted bitterly, and combed one auburn whisker with knotty fingers. 'Haven't been able to get a man that was any good since. It's nothing but worry, worry, worry in business. And where might you have come across him, captain, if it's fair to ask?'

" 'He was the mate of the *Patna* that voyage,' I said, feeling that I owed some explanation. For a time Egström remained very still, with his fingers plunged in the hair at the side of his face, and then exploded. 'And who the devil cares about that?' 'I dare say no one . . .' I began. 'And what the devil is he—anyhow—for to go on like this?' He stuffed suddenly his left whisker into his mouth and stood amazed. 'Jee!' he exclaimed, 'I told him the earth wouldn't be big enough to hold his caper.' "

Chapter Nineteen

"I have told you these two episodes at length to show his manner of dealing with himself under the new conditions of his life. There were many others of the sort, more than I could count on the fingers of my two hands.

"They were all equally tinged by a high-minded absurdity of intention which made their futility profound and touching. To fling away your daily bread so as to get your hands free for a grapple with a ghost may be an act of prosaic heroism. Men had done it before (though we who have lived know full well that it is not the haunted soul but the hungry body that makes an outcast), and men who had eaten and meant to eat every day had applauded the creditable folly. He was indeed unfortunate, for all his recklessness could not carry him out from under the shadow. There was always a doubt of his courage. The truth seems to be that it is impossible to lay the ghost of a fact. You can face it or shirk it—and I have come across a man or two who could wink at their familiar shades. Obviously Jim was not of the winking sort; but what I could never make up my mind about was whether his line of conduct amounted to shirking his ghost or to facing him out.

"I strained my mental eyesight only to discover that, as with the complexion of all our actions, the shade of difference was so delicate that it was impossible to say. It might have been flight and it might have been a mode of combat. To the common mind he became known as a rolling stone, because this was the funniest part; he did after a time become perfectly known, and even notorious, within the circle of his wanderings (which had a diameter of, say, three thousand miles), in the same way as an eccentric character is known to a whole countryside. For instance, in Bankok, where he found employment with Yucker Brothers,[1] charterers and teak merchants, it was almost pathetic to see him go about in sunshine hugging his secret,

1. Jucker, Sigg and Co. were teak merchants in Bankok. (See Norman Sherry, *Conrad's Eastern World*, Cambridge, 1966, p. 238.)

which was known to the very up-country logs on the river. Schomberg,[2] the keeper of the hotel where he boarded, a hirsute Alsatian of manly bearing and an irrepressible retailer of all the scandalous gossip of the place, would, with both elbows on the table, impart an adorned version of the story to any guest who cared to imbibe knowledge along with the more costly liquors. 'And, mind you, the nicest fellow you could meet,' would be his generous conclusion; 'quite superior.' It says a lot for the casual crowd that frequented Schomberg's establishment that Jim managed to hang out in Bankok for a whole six months. I remarked that people, perfect strangers, took to him as one takes to a nice child. His manner was reserved, but it was as though his personal appearance, his hair, his eyes, his smile, made friends for him wherever he went. And, of course, he was no fool. I heard Siegmund Yucker (native of Switzerland), a gentle creature ravaged by a cruel dyspepsia, and so frightfully lame that his head swung through a quarter of a circle at every step he took, declare appreciatively that for one so young he was 'of great gabasidy,' as though it had been a mere question of cubic contents. 'Why not send him up country?' I suggested anxiously. (Yucker Brothers had concessions and teak forests in the interior.) 'If he has capacity, as you say, he will soon get hold of the work. And physically he is very fit. His health is always excellent.' 'Ach! It's a great ting in dis goundry to be vree vrom tispep-shia,' sighed poor Yucker enviously, casting a stealthy glance at the pit of his ruined stomach. I left him drumming pensively on his desk and muttering, 'Es ist ein idee. Es ist ein idee.' Unfortunately, that very evening an unpleasant affair took place in the hotel.

"I don't know that I blame Jim very much, but it was a truly regrettable incident. It belonged to the lamentable species of bar-room scuffles, and the other party to it was a cross-eyed Dane of sorts whose visiting-card recited, under his misbegotten name: first lieutenant in the Royal Siamese Navy. The fellow, of course, was utterly hopeless at billiards, but did not like to be beaten, I suppose. He had had enough to drink to turn nasty after the sixth game, and make some scornful remark at Jim's expense. Most of the people there didn't hear what was said, and those who had heard seemed to have had all precise recollection scared out of them by the appalling nature of the consequences that immediately ensued. It was very lucky for the Dane that he could swim, because the room opened on a verandah and the Menam flowed below very wide and black. A boat-load of Chinamen, bound, as likely as not, on some thieving expedition, fished out the officer of the King of Siam, and

2. Plays an important role in "Falk" (1903) and *Victory* (1915). His hotel was probably suggested by the smaller of two European hotels in Bangkok, the Universal, owned and managed by Schumaker and Ulrich. The name Schomberg, however, belongs to a Singapore broker. (See Sherry, pp. 239 ff.)

Jim turned up at about midnight on board my ship without a hat. 'Everybody in the room seemed to know,' he said, gasping yet from the contest, as it were. He was rather sorry, on general principles, for what had happened, though in this case there had been, he said, 'no option.' But what dismayed him was to find the nature of his burden as well known to everybody as though he had gone about all that time carrying it on his shoulders. Naturally after this he couldn't remain in the place. He was universally condemned for the brutal violence, so unbecoming a man in his delicate position; some maintained he had been disgracefully drunk at the time; others criticised his want of tact. Even Schomberg was very much annoyed. 'He is a very nice young man,' he said, argumentatively, to me, 'but the lieutenant is a first-rate fellow, too. He dines every night at my *table d'hôte,*³ you know. And there's a billiard-cue broken. I can't allow that. First thing this morning I went over with my apologies to the lieutenant, and I think I've made it all right for myself; but only think, captain, if everybody started such games! Why, the man might have been drowned! And here I can't run out into the next street and buy a new cue. I've got to write to Europe for them. No, no! A temper like that won't do! . . .' He was extremely sore on the subject.

"This was the worst incident of all in his—his retreat. Nobody could deplore it more than myself; for if, as somebody said hearing him mentioned, 'Oh yes! I know. He has knocked about a good deal out here,' yet he had somehow avoided being battered and chipped in the process. This last affair, however, made me seriously uneasy, because if his exquisite sensibilities were to go the length of involving him in pot-house shindies,⁴ he would lose his name of an inoffensive, if aggravating, fool, and acquire that of a common loafer. For all my confidence in him I could not help reflecting that in such cases from the name to the thing itself is but a step. I suppose you will understand that by that time I could not think of washing my hands of him. I took him away from Bankok in my ship, and we had a longish passage. It was pitiful to see how he shrank within himself. A seaman, even if a mere passenger, takes an interest in a ship, and looks at the sea-life around him with the critical enjoyment of a painter, for instance, looking at another man's work. In every sense of the expression he is 'on deck'; but my Jim, for the most part, skulked down below as though he had been a stowaway. He infected me so that I avoided speaking on professional matters, such as would suggest themselves naturally to two sailors during a passage. For whole days we did not exchange a word; I felt extremely unwilling to give orders to my officers in his presence. Often, when alone with

3. French phrase denoting a common table for guests at a hotel or restaurant. The meal there is customarily paid for at a set rate.
4. Rows, fracases in low taverns.

him on deck or in the cabin, we didn't know what to do with our eyes.

"I placed him with De Jongh, as you know, glad enough to dispose of him in any way, yet persuaded that his position was now growing intolerable. He had lost some of that elasticity which had enabled him to rebound back into his uncompromising position after every overthrow. One day, coming ashore, I saw him standing on the quay; the water of the roadstead and the sea in the offing made one smooth ascending plane, and the outermost ships at anchor seemed to ride motionless in the sky. He was waiting for his boat, which was being loaded at our feet with packages of small stores for some vessel ready to leave. After exchanging greetings, we remained silent—side by side. 'Jove!' he said suddenly, 'this is killing work.'

"He smiled at me; I must say he generally could manage a smile. I made no reply. I knew very well he was not alluding to his duties; he had an easy time of it with De Jongh. Nevertheless, as soon as he had spoken I became completely convinced that the work was killing. I did not even look at him. 'Would you like,' said I, 'to leave this part of the world altogether; try California or the West Coast? I'll see what I can do . . .' He interrupted me a little scornfully. 'What difference would it make? . . .' I felt at once convinced that he was right. It would make no difference; it was not relief he wanted; I seemed to perceive dimly that what he wanted, what he was, as it were, waiting for, was something not easy to define—something in the nature of an opportunity. I had given him many opportunities, but they had been merely opportunities to earn his bread. Yet what more could any man do? The position struck me as hopeless, and poor Brierly's saying recurred to me, 'Let him creep twenty feet underground and stay there.' Better that, I thought, than this waiting above ground for the impossible. Yet one could not be sure even of that. There and then, before his boat was three oars' lengths away from the quay, I had made up my mind to go and consult Stein in the evening.

"This Stein was a wealthy and respected merchant. His 'house' (because it was a house, Stein & Co., and there was some sort of partner who, as Stein said, 'looked after the Moluccas') had a large inter-island business, with a lot of trading posts established in the most out-of-the-way places for collecting the produce. His wealth and his respectability were not exactly the reasons why I was anxious to seek his advice. I desired to confide my difficulty to him because he was one of the most trustworthy men I had ever known. The gentle light of a simple, unwearied, as it were, and intelligent good-nature illumined his long, hairless face. It had deep, downward folds, and was pale as of a man who had always led a sedentary life—which was indeed very far from being the case. His hair was thin, and brushed back from a massive and lofty forehead. One fancied that at twenty he must have looked very much like what he was now at threescore. It was a student's face; only the eyebrows, nearly all white, thick and bushy, together with the resolute, searching glance that came from under them, were not in accord with his, I may say, learned appearance. He was tall and loose-jointed; his slight stoop, together with an innocent smile, made him appear benevolently ready to lend you his ear; his long arms with pale, big hands had rare, deliberate gestures of a pointing out, demonstrating kind. I speak of him at length, because under this exterior, and in conjunction with an upright and indulgent nature, this man possessed an intrepidity of spirit and a physical courage that could have been called reckless had it not been like a natural function of the body—say good digestion, for instance—completely unconscious of itself. It is sometimes said of a man that he carries his life in his hand. Such a saying would have been inadequate if applied to him; during the early part of his existence in the East he had been playing ball with it. All this was in the past, but I knew the story of his life and the origin of his fortune. He was also a naturalist of some distinction, or perhaps I should say a learned collector. Entomology was his special study. His collection of *Buprestidæ* and *Longicorns*—beetles all—horrible miniature monsters, looking malevolent in death and immobility, and his cabinet of butterflies, beautiful and hovering under the glass of cases on lifeless wings, had spread his fame far over the earth. The name of this merchant, adventurer, sometime adviser of a Malay sultan (to whom he never alluded otherwise than as 'my poor Mohammed Bonso' [5]), had, on account of a few bushels of dead insects, become known to learned persons in Europe, who could have had no conception, and certainly would not have cared to know anything, of his life or character. I, who knew, considered him an eminently suitable person to receive my confidences about Jim's difficulties as well as my own."

Chapter Twenty

"Late in the evening I entered his study, after traversing an imposing but empty dining-room very dimly lit. The house was silent. I was preceded by an elderly, grim Javanese servant in a sort of livery of white jacket and yellow sarong, who, after throwing the door open, exclaimed low, 'O master!' and stepping aside, vanished in a mysterious way as though he had been a ghost only momentarily

5. The name comes from *Memoirs of a Malayan Family*, transcribed by W.   Marsden, London, 1830. (See Sherry, p. 140.)

embodied for that particular service. Stein turned round with the chair, and in the same movement his spectacles seemed to get pushed up on his forehead. He welcomed me in his quiet and humorous voice. Only one corner of the vast room, the corner in which stood his writing-desk, was strongly lighted by a shaded reading-lamp, and the rest of the spacious apartment melted into shapeless gloom like a cavern. Narrow shelves filled with dark boxes of uniform shape and colour ran round the walls, not from floor to ceiling, but in a sombre belt about four feet broad—catacombs of beetles. Wooden tablets were hung above at irregular intervals. The light reached one of them, and the word *Coleoptera* written in gold letters glittered mysteriously upon a vast dimness. The glass cases containing the collection of butterflies were ranged in three long rows upon slender-legged little tables. One of these cases had been removed from its place and stood on the desk, which was bestrewn with oblong slips of paper blackened with minute handwriting.

" 'So you see me—so,' he said. His hand hovered over the case where a butterfly in solitary grandeur spread out dark bronze wings, seven inches or more across, with exquisite white veinings and a gorgeous border of yellow spots. 'Only one specimen like this they have in *your* London, and then—no more. To my small native town this my collection I shall bequeath. Something of me. The best.'

"He bent forward in the chair and gazed intently, his chin over the front of the case. I stood at his back. 'Marvellous,' he whispered, and seemed to forget my presence. His history was curious. He had been born in Bavaria, and when a youth of twenty-two had taken an active part in the revolutionary movement of 1848.[6] Heavily compromised, he managed to make his escape, and at first found refuge with a poor republican watchmaker in Trieste. From there he made his way to Tripoli with a stock of cheap watches to hawk about,— not a very great opening truly, but it turned out lucky enough, because it was there he came upon a Dutch traveller—a rather famous man, I believe, but I don't remember his name. It was that naturalist who, engaging him as a sort of assistant, took him to the East. They travelled in the Archipelago[7] together and separately, collecting insects and birds, for four years or more. Then the naturalist went home, and Stein, having no home to go to, remained with an old trader[8] he had come across in his journeys in the in-

6. A series of revolutions throughout Europe, variously motivated. In Germany the dominant motives were constitutional and nationalist.

7. The Malay Archipelago, the largest group of islands in the world, including Sumatra, Borneo, Java, Celebes, New Guinea, the Moluccas, and the Philippines.

8. Probably Francis James Secretan, a Singapore merchant, whose ships traded throughout the Dutch East Indies. When Secretan died in 1864, his trading interests devolved upon Captain William Lingard, a hero of Conrad's who appears as Captain Tom Lingard in *Almayer's Folly*, (1895), *An Outcast of the Islands* (1896), and *The Rescue* (1920). (See Sherry, pp. 90 ff.)

terior of Celebes—if Celebes may be said to have an interior. This old Scotsman, the only white man allowed to reside in the country at the time, was a privileged friend of the chief ruler of Wajo States, who was a woman. I often heard Stein relate how that chap, who was slightly paralysed on one side, had introduced him to the native court a short time before another stroke carried him off. He was a heavy man with a patriarchal white beard, and of imposing stature. He came into the council-hall where all the rajahs, pangerans, and head-men were assembled, with the queen, a fat, wrinkled woman (very free in her speech, Stein said), reclining on a high couch under a canopy. He dragged his leg, thumping with his stick, and grasped Stein's arm, leading him right up to the couch. 'Look, queen, and you rajahs, this is my son,' he proclaimed in a stentorian voice. 'I have traded with your fathers, and when I die he shall trade with you and your sons.'

"By means of this simple formality Stein inherited the Scotsman's privileged position and all his stock-in-trade, together with a fortified house on the banks of the only navigable river in the country. Shortly afterwards the old queen, who was so free in her speech, died, and the country became disturbed by various pretenders to the throne. Stein joined the party of a younger son, the one of whom thirty years later he never spoke otherwise but as 'my poor Mohammed Bonso.' They both became the heroes of innumerable exploits; they had wonderful adventures, and once stood a siege in the Scotsman's house for a month, with only a score of followers against a whole army. I believe the natives talk of that war to this day. Meantime, it seems, Stein never failed to annex on his own account every butterfly or beetle he could lay hands on. After some eight years of war, negotiations, false truces, sudden outbreaks, reconciliation, treachery, and so on, and just as peace seemed at last permanently established, his 'poor Mohammed Bonso' was assassinated at the gate of his own royal residence while dismounting in the highest spirits on his return from a successful deer-hunt. This event rendered Stein's position extremely insecure, but he would have stayed perhaps had it not been that a short time afterwards he lost Mohammed's sister ('my dear wife the princess,' he used to say solemnly), by whom he had had a daughter—mother and child both dying within three days of each other from some infectious fever. He left the country, which this cruel loss had made unbearable to him. Thus ended the first and adventurous part of his existence. What followed was so different that, but for the reality of sorrow which remained with him, this strange part must have resembled a dream. He had a little money; he started life afresh, and in the course of years acquired a considerable fortune. At first he had travelled a good deal amongst the islands, but age had stolen upon him, and of late he seldom left his spacious house three miles out of town, with an extensive garden, and surrounded by stables, offices, and bamboo cottages for his servants and dependants, of whom he had many. He drove in his buggy every morning to town, where he had an office with white and Chinese clerks. He owned a small fleet of schooners and native craft, and dealt in island produce on a large scale. For the rest he lived solitary, but not misanthropic, with his books and his collection, classing and arranging specimens, corresponding with entomologists in Europe, writing up a descriptive catalogue of his treasures. Such was the history of the man whom I had come to consult upon Jim's case without any definite hope. Simply to hear what he would have to say would have been a relief. I was very anxious, but I respected the intense, almost passionate absorption with which he looked at a butterfly, as though on the bronze sheen of these frail wings, in the white tracings, in the gorgeous markings, he could see other things, an image of something as perishable and defying destruction as these delicate and lifeless tissues displaying a splendour unmarred by death.

" 'Marvellous!' he repeated, looking up at me. 'Look! The beauty —but that is nothing—look at the accuracy, the harmony. And so fragile! And so strong! And so exact! This is Nature—the balance of colossal forces. Every star is so—and every blade of grass stands so—and the mighty Kosmos in perfect equilibrium produces—this. This wonder; this masterpiece of Nature—the great artist.'

" 'Never heard an entomologist go on like this,' I observed cheerfully. 'Masterpiece! And what of man?'

" 'Man is amazing, but he is not a masterpiece,' he said, keeping his eyes fixed on the glass case. 'Perhaps the artist was a little mad. Eh? What do you think? Sometimes it seems to me that man is come where he is not wanted, where there is no place for him; for if not, why should he want all the place? Why should he run about here and there making a great noise about himself, talking about the stars, disturbing the blades of grass? . . .'

" 'Catching butterflies,' I chimed in.

"He smiled, threw himself back in his chair, and stretched his legs. 'Sit down,' he said. 'I captured this rare specimen myself one very fine morning. And I had a very big emotion. You don't know what it is for a collector to capture such a rare specimen. You can't know.'

"I smiled at my ease in a rocking-chair. His eyes seemed to look far beyond the wall at which they stared; and he narrated how, one night, a messenger arrived from his 'poor Mohammed,' requiring his presence at the 'residenz'—as he called it—which was distant some nine or ten miles by a bridle-path over a cultivated plain, with patches of forest here and there. Early in the morning he started from his fortified house, after embracing his little Emma, and leaving the 'princess,' his wife, in command. He described how she came with him as far as the gate, walking with one hand on the neck of his horse; she had on a white jacket, gold pins in her hair, and a brown leather belt over her left shoulder with a revolver in it. 'She talked as women will talk,' he said, 'telling me to be careful, and to try to get back before dark, and what a great wickedness it was for me to go alone. We were at war, and the country was not safe; my men were putting up bullet-proof shutters to the house and loading their rifles, and she begged me to have no fear for her. She could defend the house against anybody till I returned. And I laughed with pleasure a little. I liked to see her so brave and young and strong. I, too, was young then. At the gate she caught hold of my hand and gave it one squeeze and fell back. I made my horse stand still outside till I heard the bars of the gate put up behind me. There was a great enemy of mine, a great noble—and a great rascal, too—roaming with a band in the neighbourhood. I cantered for four or five miles; there had been rain in the night, but the mists had gone up, up—and the face of the earth was clean; it lay smiling to me, so fresh and innocent—like a little child. Suddenly somebody fires a volley—twenty shots at least it seemed to me. I hear bullets sing in my ears, and my hat jumps to the back of my head. It was a little intrigue, you understand. They got my poor Mohammed to send for me and then laid that ambush. I see it all in a minute, and I think—— This wants a little management. My pony snort, jump, and stand, and I fall slowly forward with my head on his mane. He begins to walk, and with one eye I could see over his neck a faint cloud of smoke hanging in front of a clump of bamboos to my left. I think—— Aha! my friends, why you not wait long enough before you shoot? This is not yet *gelungen*.[9] Oh no! I get hold of my revolver with my right hand—quiet—quiet. After all, there were only seven of these rascals. They get up from the grass and start running with their sarongs tucked up, waving spears above their heads, and yelling to each other to look out and catch the horse, because I was dead. I let them come as close as the door here, and then bang, bang, bang—take aim each time, too. One more shot I fire at a man's back, but I miss. Too far already. And then I sit alone on my horse with the clean earth smiling at me, and there are the bodies of three men lying on the ground. One was curled up like a dog, another on his back had an arm over his eyes as if to keep off the sun, and the third man he draws up his leg very slowly and makes it with one kick straight again. I watch him very carefully from my horse, but there is no more—*bleibt ganz ruhig*—keep still, so.

9. Successful.

And as I looked at his face for some sign of life I observed something like a faint shadow pass over his forehead. It was the shadow of this butterfly. Look at the form of the wing. This species fly high with a strong flight. I raised my eyes and I saw him fluttering away. I think—— Can it be possible? And then I lost him. I dismounted and went on very slow, leading my horse and holding my revolver with one hand and my eyes darting up and down and right and left, everywhere! At last I saw him sitting on a small heap of dirt ten feet away. At once my heart began to beat quick. I let go my horse, keep my revolver in one hand, and with the other snatch my soft felt hat off my head. One step. Steady. Another step. Flop! I got him! When I got up I shook like a leaf with excitement, and when I opened these beautiful wings and made sure what a rare and so extraordinary perfect specimen I had, my head went round and my legs became so weak with emotion that I had to sit on the ground. I had greatly desired to possess myself of a specimen of that species when collecting for the professor. I took long journeys and underwent great privations; I had dreamed of him in my sleep, and here suddenly I had him in my fingers—for myself! In the words of the poet' (he pronounced it 'boet') :

> ' "So halt' ich's endlich denn in meinen Händen,
> Und nenn' es in gewissem Sinne mein." ' [1]

He gave to the last word the emphasis of a suddenly lowered voice, and withdrew his eyes slowly from my face. He began to charge a long-stemmed pipe busily and in silence, then, pausing with his thumb on the orifice of the bowl, looked again at me significantly.

" 'Yes, my good friend. On that day I had nothing to desire; I had greatly annoyed my principal enemy; I was young, strong; I had friendship; I had the love' (he said 'lof') 'of woman, a child I had, to make my heart very full—and even what I had once dreamed in my sleep had come into my hand, too!'

"He struck a match, which flared violently. His thoughtful, placid face twitched once.

" 'Friend, wife, child,' he said slowly, gazing at the small flame —'phoo!' The match was blown out. He sighed and turned again to the glass case. The frail and beautiful wings quivered faintly, as if his breath had for an instant called back to life that gorgeous object of his dreams.

" 'The work,' he began suddenly, pointing to the scattered slips,

1. "I hold it, then, at length within my hands,/And in a certain sense can call it mine." (Goethe, *Torquato Tasso*, I, iii, 393–394, from the translation by Anna Swanwick, 1882.)

and in his usual gentle and cheery tone, 'is making great progress.
I have been this rare specimen describing. . . . Na! And what is
your good news?'

" 'To tell you the truth, Stein,' I said, with an effort that surprised me, 'I came here to describe a specimen. . . .'

" 'Butterfly?' he asked, with an unbelieving and humorous eagerness.

" 'Nothing so perfect,' I answered, feeling suddenly dispirited
with all sorts of doubts. 'A man!'

" 'Ach so!' he murmured, and his smiling countenance, turned
to me, became grave. Then after looking at me for a while he said
slowly, 'Well—I am a man, too.'

"Here you have him as he was; he knew how to be so generously encouraging as to make a scrupulous man hesitate on the
brink of confidence; but if I did hesitate it was not for long.

"He heard me out, sitting with crossed legs. Sometimes his
head would disappear completely in a great eruption of smoke,
and a sympathetic growl would come out from the cloud. When
I finished he uncrossed his legs, laid down his pipe, leaned forward towards me earnestly with his elbows on the arms of his
chair, the tips of his fingers together.

" 'I understand very well. He is romantic.'

"He had diagnosed the case for me, and at first I was quite
startled to find how simple it was; and indeed our conference resembled so much a medical consultation—Stein, of learned aspect, sitting in an arm-chair before his desk; I, anxious, in another,
facing him, but a little to one side—that it seemed natural to
ask:

" 'What's good for it?'

"He lifted up a long forefinger.

" 'There is only one remedy! One thing alone can us from being
ourselves cure!' The finger came down on the desk with a
smart rap. The case which he had made to look so simple before
became if possible still simpler—and altogether hopeless. There
was a pause. 'Yes,' said I, 'strictly speaking, the question is not
how to get cured, but how to live.'

"He approved with his head, a little sadly as it seemed. '*Ja! ja!*
In general, adapting the words of your great poet: That is the
question. . . .' He went on nodding sympathetically. . . . 'How
to be! *Ach!* How to be.'

"He stood up, with the tips of his fingers resting on the desk.

" 'We want in so many different ways to be,' he began again.
'This magnificent butterfly finds a little heap of dirt and sits still
on it; but man he will never on his heap of mud keep still. He
want to be so, and again he want to be so. . . .' He moved his

hand up, then down. . . . 'He wants to be a saint, and he wants to be a devil—and every time he shuts his eyes he sees himself as a very fine fellow—so fine as he can never be. . . . In a dream. . . .'

"He lowered the glass lid, the automatic lock clicked sharply, and taking up the case in both hands he bore it religiously away to its place, passing out of the bright circle of the lamp into the ring of fainter light—into shapeless dusk at last. It had an odd effect—as if these few steps had carried him out of this concrete and perplexed world. His tall form, as though robbed of its substance, hovered noiselessly over invisible things with stooping and indefinite movements; his voice, heard in that remoteness where he could be glimpsed mysteriously busy with immaterial cares, was no longer incisive, seemed to roll voluminous and grave—mellowed by distance.

" 'And because you not always can keep your eyes shut there comes the real trouble—the heart pain—the world pain. I tell you, my friend, it is not good for you to find you cannot make your dream come true, for the reason that you not strong enough are, or not clever enough. *Ja!* . . . And all the time you are such a fine fellow, too! *Wie? Was? Gott im Himmel!* [2] How can that be? Ha! ha! ha!'

"The shadow prowling amongst the graves of butterflies laughed boisterously.

" 'Yes! Very funny this terrible thing is. A man that is born falls into a dream like a man who falls into the sea. If he tries to climb out into the air as inexperienced people endeavour to do, he drowns—*nicht war?* [3] . . . No! I tell you! The way is to the destructive element submit yourself, and with the exertions of your hands and feet in the water make the deep, deep sea keep you up. So you ask me—how to be?'

"His voice leaped up extraordinarily strong, as though away there in the dusk he had been inspired by some whisper of knowledge. 'I will tell you! For that, too, there is only one way.'

"With a hasty swish-swish of his slippers he loomed up in the ring of faint light, and suddenly appeared in the bright circle of the lamp. His extended hand aimed at my breast like a pistol; his deep-set eyes seemed to pierce through me, but his twitching lips uttered no word, and the austere exaltation of a certitude seen in the dusk vanished from his face. The hand that had been pointing at my breast fell, and by and by, coming a step nearer, he laid it gently on my shoulder. There were things, he said mournfully, that perhaps could never be told, only he had lived so much alone that sometimes he forgot—he forgot. The light had destroyed the assurance which had inspired him in the distant shadows. He sat down and, with both elbows on the desk, rubbed his forehead. 'And yet it is true—it is true. In the destructive element immerse. . . .' He spoke in a subdued tone, without looking at me, one hand on each side of his face. 'That was the way. To follow the dream, and again to follow the dream—and so —*ewig*[4]—*usque ad finem.*[5] . . .' The whisper of his conviction seemed to open before me a vast and uncertain expanse, as of a crepuscular horizon on a plain at dawn—or was it, perchance, at the coming of the night? One had not the courage to decide; but it was a charming and deceptive light, throwing the impalpable poesy of its dimness over pitfalls—over graves. His life had begun in sacrifice, in enthusiasm for generous ideas; he had traveled very far, on various ways, on strange paths, and whatever he followed it had been without faltering, and therefore without shame and without regret. In so far he was right. That was the way, no doubt. Yet for all that, the great plain on which men wander amongst graves and pitfalls remained very desolate under the impalpable poesy of its crepuscular light, overshadowed in the centre, circled with a bright edge as if surrounded by an abyss full of flames. When at last I broke the silence it was to express the opinion that no one could be more romantic than himself.

"He shook his head slowly, and afterwards looked at me with a patient and inquiring glance. It was a shame, he said. There we were sitting and talking like two boys, instead of putting our heads together to find something practical—a practical remedy—for the evil—for the great evil—he repeated, with a humorous and indulgent smile. For all that, our talk did not grow more practical. We avoided pronouncing Jim's name as though we had tried to keep flesh and blood out of our discussion, or he were nothing but an erring spirit, a suffering and nameless shade. 'Na!' said Stein, rising. 'To-night you sleep here, and in the morning we shall do something practical—practical. . . .' He lit a two-branched candlestick and led the way. We passed through empty, dark rooms, escorted by gleams from the lights Stein carried. They glided along the waxed floors, sweeping here and there over the polished surface of a table, leaped upon a fragmentary curve of a piece of furniture, or flashed perpendicularly in and out of dis-

4. Forever.
5. Until the end. A proverbial Latin phrase found several times in the Vulgate Bible, as in the following passage: "For we are made partakers of Christ, if we hold the beginning of our confidence steadfast unto the end." (Hebrews 3:14.) See also the November 9, 1891 letter to Conrad from his uncle and guardian, Thaddeus Bobrowski: "I have gone through a lot, I have suffered my own fate and the fate of my family and my Nation, and perhaps just because of these sufferings and disappointments I have developed in myself this calm outlook on the problem of life, whose motto, I venture to say, was, is, and will be 'usque ad finem.'" *(Conrad's Polish Background*, ed. Zdzislaw Najder, New York, 1964, p. 155.)

tant mirrors, while the forms of two men and the flicker of two flames could be seen for a moment stealing silently across the depths of a crystalline void. He walked slowly a pace in advance with stooping courtesy; there was a profound, as it were a listening, quietude on his face; the long, flaxen locks mixed with white threads were scattered thinly upon his slightly bowed neck.

" 'He is romantic—romantic,' he repeated. 'And that is very bad —very bad. . . . Very good, too,' he added. 'But *is he?*' I queried.

" '*Gewiss*,' [6] he said, and stood still holding up the candelabrum, but without looking at me. 'Evident! What is it that by inward pain makes him know himself? What is it that for you and me makes him—exist?'

"At that moment it was difficult to believe in Jim's existence— starting from a country parsonage, blurred by crowds of men as by clouds of dust, silenced by the clashing claims of life and death in a material world—but his imperishable reality came to me with a convincing, with an irresistible force! I saw it vividly, as though in our progress through the lofty, silent rooms amongst fleeting gleams of light and the sudden revelations of human figures stealing with flickering flames within unfathomable and pellucid depths, we had approached nearer to absolute Truth, which, like Beauty itself, floats elusive, obscure, half submerged, in the silent, still waters of mystery. 'Perhaps he is,' I admitted with a slight laugh, whose unexpectedly loud reverberation made me lower my voice directly; 'but I am sure you are.' With his head dropping on his breast and the light held high he began to walk again. 'Well—I exist, too,' he said.

"He preceded me. My eyes followed his movements, but what I did see was not the head of the firm, the welcome guest at afternoon receptions, the correspondent of learned societies, the entertainer of stray naturalists; I saw only the reality of his destiny, which he had known how to follow with unfaltering footsteps, that life begun in humble surroundings, rich in generous enthusiasms, in friendship, love, war—in all the exalted elements of romance. At the door of my room he faced me. 'Yes,' I said, as though carrying on a discussion, 'and amongst other things you dreamed foolishly of a certain butterfly; but when one fine morning your dream came in your way you did not let the splendid opportunity escape. Did you? Whereas he . . .' Stein lifted his hand. 'And do you know how many opportunities I let escape; how many dreams I had lost that had come in my way?' He shook his head regretfully. 'It seemed to me that some would have been very fine—if I had made them come true. Do you know how many? Perhaps I myself don't know.' 'Whether his were fine or not,' I

6. Of course.

said, 'he knows of one which he certainly did not catch.' 'Everybody knows of one or two like that,' said Stein; 'and that is the trouble—the great trouble. . . .'

"He shook hands on the threshold, peered into my room under his raised arm. 'Sleep well. And to-morrow we must do something practical—practical. . . .'

"Though his own room was beyond mine, I saw him return the way he came. He was going back to his butterflies."

Chapter Twenty-One

"I don't suppose any of you have ever heard of Patusan?" [7] Marlow resumed, after a silence occupied in the careful lighting of a cigar. "It does not matter; there's many a heavenly body in the lot crowding upon us of a night that mankind had never heard of, it being outside the sphere of its activities and of no earthly importance to anybody but to the astronomers who are paid to talk learnedly about its composition, weight, path—the irregularities of its conduct, the aberrations of its light—a sort of scientific scandal-mongering. Thus with Patusan. It was referred to knowingly in the inner government circles in Batavia, especially as to its irregularities and aberrations, and it was known by name to some few, very few, in the mercantile world. Nobody, however, had been there, and I suspect no one desired to go there in person—just as an astronomer, I should fancy, would strongly object to being transported into a distant heavenly body, where, parted from his earthly emoluments, he would be bewildered by the view of an unfamiliar heavens. However, neither heavenly bodies nor astronomers have anything to do with Patusan. It was Jim who went there. I only meant you to understand that had Stein arranged to send him into a star of the fifth magnitude the change could not have been greater. He left his earthly failings behind him and what sort of reputation he had, and there was a totally new set of conditions for his imaginative faculty to work upon. Entirely new, entirely remarkable. And he got hold of them in a remarkable way.

"Stein was the man who knew more about Patusan than anybody else. More than was known in the government circles, I suspect. I have no doubt he had been there, either in his butterfly-hunting days or later on, when he tried in his incorrigible way to season

7. Conrad was thinking of an area in Dutch East Borneo named Berau for the river running through it (also called the Pantai). The native settlement of Berau is now called Tandjong Redeb and lies some thirty-four miles up the river from the Celebes Sea. He probably took the name Patusan from an account of the destruction of a large pirate stronghold by that name in Sarawak, North Borneo, in Captain the Hon. Henry Keppel's *Expedition to Borneo*, London, 1846, II, 76–92.

with a pinch of romance the fattening dishes of his commercial kitchen. There were very few places in the Archipelago he had not seen in the original dusk of their being, before light (and even electric light) had been carried into them for the sake of better morality and—and—well—the greater profit, too. It was at breakfast of the morning following our talk about Jim that he mentioned the place, after I had quoted poor Brierly's remark: 'Let him creep twenty feet underground and stay there.' He looked up at me with interested attention, as though I had been a rare insect. 'This could be done, too,' he remarked, sipping his coffee. 'Bury him in some sort,' I explained. 'One doesn't like to do it, of course, but it would be the best thing, seeing what he is.' 'Yes; he is young,' Stein mused. 'The youngest human being now in existence,' I affirmed. '*Schön*.[8] There's Patusan,' he went on in the same tone. . . . 'And the woman is dead now,' he added incomprehensibly.

"Of course I don't know that story; I can only guess that once before Patusan had been used as a grave for some sin, transgression, or misfortune. It is imposible to suspect Stein. The only woman that had ever existed for him was the Malay girl he called 'My wife the princess,' or, more rarely in moments of expansion, 'the mother of my Emma.' Who was the woman he had mentioned in connection with Patusan I can't say; but from his allusions I understand she had been an educated and very good-looking Dutch-Malay girl, with a tragic or perhaps only a pitiful history, whose most painful part no doubt was her marriage with a Malacca Portuguese who had been clerk in some commercial house in the Dutch colonies. I gathered from Stein that this man was an unsatisfactory person in more ways than one, all being more or less indefinite and offensive. It was solely for his wife's sake that Stein had appointed him manager of Stein & Co.'s trading post in Patusan; but commercially the arrangement was not a success, at any rate for the firm, and now the woman had died, Stein was disposed to try another agent there. The Portuguese, whose name was Cornelius, considered himself a very deserving but ill-used person, entitled by his abilities to a better position. This man Jim would have to relieve. 'But I don't think he will go away from the place,' remarked Stein. 'That has nothing to do with me. It was only for the sake of the woman that I . . . But as I think there is a daughter left, I shall let him, if he likes to stay, keep the old house.'

"Patusan is a remote district of a native-ruled state, and the chief settlement bears the same name. At a point on the river about forty miles from the sea, where the first houses come into

8. Fine.

view, there can be seen rising above the level of the forest the summits of two steep hills very close together, and separated by what
looks like a deep fissure, the cleavage of some mighty stroke. As
a matter of fact, the valley between is nothing but a narrow ravine;
the appearance from the settlement is of one irregularly conical
hill split in two, and with the two halves leaning slightly apart.
On the third day after the full, the moon, as seen from the open
space in front of Jim's house (he had a very fine house in the
native style when I visited him), rose exactly behind these hills, its
diffused light at first throwing the two masses into intensely black
relief, and then the nearly perfect disc, glowing ruddily, appeared, gliding upwards between the sides of the chasm, till it
floated away above the summits, as if escaping from a yawning grave
in gentle triumph. 'Wonderful effect,' said Jim by my side. 'Worth
seeing. Is it not?'

"And this question was put with a note of personal pride that
made me smile, as though he had had a hand in regulating that
unique spectacle. He had regulated so many things in Patusan—
things that would have appeared as much beyond his control as
the motions of the moon and the stars.

"It was inconceivable. That was the distinctive quality of the
part into which Stein and I had tumbled him unwittingly, with
no other notion than to get him out of the way; out of his own
way, be it understood. That was our main purpose, though, I own,
I might have had another motive which had influenced me a little.
I was about to go home for a time; and it may be I desired, more
than I was aware of myself, to dispose of him—to dispose of him,
you understand—before I left. I was going home, and he had
come to me from there, with his miserable trouble and his shadowy claim, like a man panting under a burden in a mist. I cannot
say I had ever seen him distinctly—not even to this day, after
I had my last view of him; but it seemed to me that the less I understood the more I was bound to him in the name of that doubt
which is the inseparable part of our knowledge. I did not know
so much more about myself. And then, I repeat, I was going home
—to that home distant enough for all its hearthstones to be like
one hearthstone, by which the humblest of us has the right to sit.
We wander in our thousands over the face of the earth, the illustrious and the obscure, earning beyond the seas our fame, our
money, or only a crust of bread; but it seems to me that for each
of us going home must be like going to render an account. We
return to face our superiors, our kindred, our friends—those whom
we obey, and those whom we love; but even they who have neither,
the most free, lonely, irresponsible and bereft of ties,—even those

for whom home holds no dear face, no familiar voice,—even they have to meet the spirit that dwells within the land, under its sky, in its air, in its valleys, and on its rises, in its fields, in its waters and its trees—a mute friend, judge, and inspirer. Say what you like, to get its joy, to breathe its peace, to face its truth, one must return with a clear consciousness. All this may seem to you sheer sentimentalism; and indeed very few of us have the will or the capacity to look consciously under the surface of familiar emotions. There are the girls we love, the men we look up to, the tenderness, the friendships, the opportunities, the pleasures! But the fact remains that you must touch your reward with clean hands, lest it turn to dead leaves, to thorns, in your grasp. I think it is the lonely, without a fireside or an affection they may call their own, those who return not to a dwelling but to the land itself, to meet its disembodied, eternal, and unchangeable spirit —it is those who understand best its severity, its saving power, the grace of its secular right to our fidelity, to our obedience. Yes! few of us understand, but we all feel it though, and I say *all* without exception, because those who do not feel do not count. Each blade of grass has its spot on earth whence it draws its life, its strength; and so is man rooted to the land from which he draws his faith together with his life. I don't know how much Jim understood; but I know he felt, he felt confusedly but powerfully, the demand of some such truth or some such illusion—I don't care how you call it, there is so little difference, and the difference means so little. The thing is that in virtue of his feeling he mattered. He would never go home now. Not he. Never. Had he been capable of picturesque manifestations he would have shuddered at the thought and made you shudder too. But he was not of that sort, though he was expressive enough in his way. Before the idea of going home he would grow desperately stiff and immovable, with lowered chin and pouted lips, and with those candid blue eyes of his glowering darkly under a frown, as if before something unbearable, as if before something revolting. There was imagination in that hard skull of his, over which the thick clustering hair fitted like a cap. As to me, I have no imagination (I would be more certain about him to-day if I had), and I do not mean to imply that I figured to myself the spirit of the land uprising above the white cliffs of Dover, to ask me what I—returning with no bones broken, so to speak—had done with my very young brother. I could not make such a mistake. I knew very well he was of those about whom there is no inquiry; I had seen better men go out, disappear, vanish utterly, without provoking a sound of curiosity or sorrow. The spirit of the land, as becomes the ruler of great enterprises, is careless of innumerable lives. Woe to the stragglers! We exist only in so far as we hang together. He had strag-

gled in a way; he had not hung on; but he was aware of it with
an intensity that made him touching, just as a man's more intense
life makes his death more touching than the death of a tree. I happened to be handy, and I happened to be touched. That's all there
is to it. I was concerned as to the way he would go out. It would
have hurt me if, for instance, he had taken to drink. The earth is
so small that I was afraid of, some day, being waylaid by a blear-
eyed, swollen-faced, besmirched loafer, with no soles to his canvas
shoes, and with a flutter of rags about the elbows, who, on the
strength of old acquaintance, would ask for a loan of five dollars.
You know the awful jaunty bearing of these scarecrows coming to
you from a decent past, the rasping, careless voice, the half-
averted, impudent glances—those meetings more trying to a man
who believes in the solidarity of our lives than the sight of an im-
penitent death-bed to a priest. That, to tell you the truth, was
the only danger I could see for him and for me; but I also mistrusted my want of imagination. It might even come to something
worse; in some way it was beyond my powers of fancy to foresee. He
wouldn't let me forget how imaginative he was, and your imaginative people swing farther in any direction, as if given a longer
scope of cable in the uneasy anchorage of life. They do. They take
to drink, too. It may be I was belittling him by such a fear. How
could I tell? Even Stein could say no more than that he was romantic. I only knew he was one of us. And what business had he
to be romantic? I am telling you so much about my own instinctive
feelings and bemused reflections because there remains so little to be told of him. He existed for me, and after all it is only
through me that he exists for you. I've led him out by the hand;
I have paraded him before you. Were my commonplace fears unjust? I won't say—not even now. You may be able to tell better,
since the proverb has it that the onlookers see most of the game.
At any rate, they were superfluous. He did not go out, not at
all; on the contrary, he came on wonderfully, came on straight as
a die and in excellent form, which showed that he could stay as
well as spurt. I ought to be delighted, for it is a victory in which
I had taken my part; but I am not so pleased as I would have expected to be. I ask myself whether his rush had really carried
him out of that mist in which he loomed interesting if not very
big, with floating outlines—a straggler yearning inconsolably for
his humble place in the ranks. And besides, the last word is not
said—probably shall never be said. Are not our lives too short for
that full utterance which through all our stammerings is of course
our only and abiding intention? I have given up expecting those
last words, whose ring, if they could only be pronounced, would
shake both heaven and earth. There is never time to say our last

word—the last word of our love, of our desire, faith, remorse, submission, revolt. The heaven and the earth must not be shaken, I suppose—at least, not by us who know so many truths about either. My last words about Jim shall be few. I affirm he had achieved greatness; but the thing would be dwarfed in the telling, or rather in the hearing. Frankly, it is not my words that I mistrust, but your minds. I could be eloquent were I not afraid you fellows had starved your imaginations to feed your bodies. I do not mean to be offensive; it is respectable to have no illusions—and safe —and profitable—and dull. Yet you, too, in your time must have known the intensity of life, that light of glamour created in the shock of trifles, as amazing as the glow of sparks struck from a cold stone—and as short-lived, alas!"

Chapter Twenty-Two

"The conquest of love, honour, men's confidence—the pride of it, the power of it, are fit materials for an heroic tale; only our minds are struck by the externals of such a success, and to Jim's successes there were no externals. Thirty miles of forest shut it off from the sight of an indifferent world, and the noise of the white surf along the coast overpowered the voice of fame. The stream of civilisation, as if divided on a headland a hundred miles north of Patusan, branches east and south-east, leaving its plains and valleys, its old trees and its old mankind, neglected and isolated, such as an insignificant and crumbling islet between the two branches of a mighty, devouring stream. You find the name of the country pretty often in collections of old voyages. The seventeenth-century traders went there for pepper, because the passion for pepper seemed to burn like a flame of love in the breast of Dutch and English adventurers about the time of James the First. Where wouldn't they go for pepper! For a bag of pepper they would cut each other's throats without hesitation, and would forswear their souls, of which they were so careful otherwise: the bizarre obstinacy of that desire made them defy death in a thousand shapes—the unknown seas, the loathsome and strange diseases; wounds, captivity, hunger, pestilence, and despair. It made them great! By heavens! it made them heroic; and it made them pathetic, too, in their craving for trade with the inflexible death levying its toll on young and old. It seems impossible to believe that mere greed could hold men to such a steadfastness of purpose, to such a blind persistence in endeavour and sacrifice. And indeed those who adventured their persons and lives risked all they had for a slender reward. They left their bones to lie bleaching on distant shores, so that wealth might flow to the living at home. To us, their less tried successors, they appear magnified, not as agents of trade but as instruments of a recorded destiny, pushing out into the unknown in obedience to an inward voice, to an impulse beating in the blood, to a dream of the future. They were wonderful; and it must be owned they were ready for the wonderful. They recorded it complacently in their sufferings, in the aspect of the seas, in the customs of strange nations, in the glory of splendid rulers.

"In Patusan they had found lots of pepper, and had been impressed by the magnificence and the wisdom of the Sultan; but somehow, after a century of chequered intercourse, the country seems to drop gradually out of the trade. Perhaps the pepper had given out. Be it as it may, nobody cares for it now; the glory has departed, the Sultan is an imbecile youth with two thumbs on his left hand and an uncertain and beggarly revenue extorted from a miserable population and stolen from him by his many uncles.

"This of course I have from Stein. He gave me their names and a short sketch of life and character of each. He was as full of information about native states as an official report, but infinitely more amusing. He *had* to know. He traded in so many, and in some districts—as in Patusan, for instance—his firm was the only one to have an agency by special permit from the Dutch authorities. The Government trusted his discretion, and it was understood that he took all the risks. The men he employed understood that, too, but he made it worth their while apparently. He was perfectly frank with me over the breakfast-table in the morning. As far as he was aware (the last news was thirteen months old, he stated precisely), utter insecurity for life and property was the normal condition. There were in Patusan antagonistic forces,[9] and one of them was Rajah Allang,[1] the worst of the Sultan's uncles, the governor of the river, who did the extorting and the stealing, and ground down to the point of extinction the country-born Malays, who, utterly defenceless, had not even the resource of emigrating—'For indeed,' as Stein remarked, 'where could they go, and how could they get away?' No doubt they did not even desire to get away. The world

9. According to Jerry Allen (*The Sea Years of Joseph Conrad*, New York, 1965, pp. 187–240) the history of Berau is roughly as follows: By the beginning of the nineteenth century when records were first kept, Berau had long been under the control of Malay Moslems who had subdued the native, pagan, forest-Dyaks. After a protracted civil war, the district of Sambaliung became an independent sultanate in 1844, the remainder becoming the sultanate of Gunung Tabur. Sporadically, these two sultanates, facing each other across the river, continued to wage war.

In 1882, when the sultan of Gunung Tabur died, his son being too young to rule, his father's first cousin, Hadji Adji Kuning, became regent. By 1887 when Conrad stopped several times in Berau, the regent was levying exorbitant duty on all exports, mistreating the native population, and fomenting new trouble with the sultan of Sambaliung.
1. The name comes from Major Fred McNair's *Perak and the Malays*, London, 1878. The names of Doramin and Tamb' Itam ("black messenger") come from the same source. (See Jocelyn Baines, *Joseph Conrad*, New York, 1960, p. 254 and Sherry, pp. 148, 167.)

(which is circumscribed by lofty impassable mountains) has been given into the hand of the high-born, and *this* Rajah they knew: he was of their own royal house. I had the pleasure of meeting the gentleman later on. He was a dirty, little, used-up old man with evil eyes and a weak mouth, who swallowed an opium pill every two hours, and in defiance of common decency wore his hair uncovered and falling in wild, stringy locks about his wizened, grimy face. When giving audience he would clamber upon a sort of narrow stage erected in a hall like a ruinous barn with a rotten bamboo floor, through the cracks of which you could see, twelve or fifteen feet below, the heaps of refuse and garbage of all kinds lying under the house. That is where and how he received us when, accompanied by Jim, I paid him a visit of ceremony. There were about forty people in the room, and perhaps three times as many in the great courtyard below. There was constant movement, coming and going, pushing and murmuring, at our backs. A few youths in gay silks glared from the distance; the majority, slaves and humble dependants, were half naked, in ragged sarongs, dirty with ashes and mud-stains. I had never seen Jim look so grave, so self-possessed, in an impenetrable, impressive way. In the midst of these dark-faced men, his stalwart figure in white apparel, the gleaming clusters of his fair hair, seemed to catch all the sunshine that trickled through the cracks in the closed shutters of that dim hall, with its walls of mats and a roof of thatch. He appeared like a creature not only of another kind but of another essence. Had they not seen him come up in a canoe they might have thought he had descended upon them from the clouds. He did, however, come in a crazy dug-out, sitting (very still and with his knees together, for fear of overturning the thing) —sitting on a tin box—which I had lent him—nursing on his lap a revolver of the Navy pattern—presented by me on parting—which, through an interposition of Providence, or through some wrong-headed notion, that was just like him, or else from sheer instinc-tive sagacity, he had decided to carry unloaded. That's how he ascended the Patusan river. Nothing could have been more prosaic and more unsafe, more extravagantly casual, more lonely. Strange, this fatality that would cast the complexion of a flight upon all his acts, of impulsive, unreflecting desertion—of a jump into the un-known.

"It is precisely the casualness of it that strikes me most. Neither Stein nor I had a clear conception of what might be on the other side when we, metaphorically speaking, took him up and hove him over the wall with scant ceremony. At the moment I merely wished to achieve his disappearance. Stein characteristically enough had a sentimental motive. He had a notion of paying off (in kind, I sup-pose) the old debt he had never forgotten. Indeed he had been all his life especially friendly to anybody from the British Isles. His late benefactor, it is true, was a Scot—even to the length of being called Alexander M'Neil—and Jim came from a long way south of the Tweed; [2] but at the distance of six or seven thousand miles Great Britain, though never diminished, looks foreshortened enough even to its own children to rob such details of their importance. Stein was excusable, and his hinted intentions were so generous that I begged him most earnestly to keep them secret for a time. I felt that no consideration of personal advantage should be allowed to influence Jim; that not even the risk of such influence should be run. We had to deal with another sort of reality. He wanted a refuge, and refuge at the cost of danger should be offered him—nothing more.

"Upon every other point I was perfectly frank with him, and I even (as I believed at the time) exaggerated the danger of the undertaking. As a matter of fact I did not do it justice; his first day in Patusan was nearly his last—would have been his last if he had not been so reckless or so hard on himself and had condescended to load that revolver. I remember, as I unfolded our precious scheme for his retreat, how his stubborn but weary resignation was gradually replaced by surprise, interest, wonder, and by boyish eagerness. This was a chance he had been dreaming of. He couldn't think how he merited that I . . . He would be shot if he could see to what he owed . . . And it was Stein, Stein the merchant, who . . . but of course it was me he had to . . . I cut him short. He was not articulate, and his gratitude caused me inexplicable pain. I told him that if he owed this chance to any one especially, it was to an old Scot of whom he had never heard, who had died many years ago, of whom little was remembered besides a roaring voice and a rough sort of honesty. There was really no one to receive his thanks. Stein was passing on to a young man the help he had received in his own young days, and I had done no more than to mention his name. Upon this he coloured, and, twisting a bit of paper in his fingers, he remarked bashfully that I had always trusted him.

"I admitted that such was the case, and added after a pause that I wished he had been able to follow my example. 'You think I don't?' he asked uneasily, and remarked in a mutter that one had to get some sort of show first; then brightening up, and in a loud voice he protested he would give me no occasion to regret my confidence, which—which . . .

" 'Do not misapprehend,' I interrupted. 'It is not in your power to make me regret anything.' There would be no regrets; but if there were, it would be altogether my own affair: on the other hand, I wished him to understand clearly that this arrangement, this—this—experiment, was his own doing; he was responsible for it and

2. A river forming part of the border between Scotland and England.

no one else. 'Why? Why,' he stammered, 'this is the very thing that I . . .' I begged him not to be dense, and he looked more puzzled than ever. He was in a fair way to make life intolerable to himself. . . . 'Do you think so?' he asked, disturbed; but in a moment added confidently, 'I was going on, though. Was I not?' It was impossible to be angry with him: I could not help a smile, and told him that in the old days people who went on like this were on the way of becoming hermits in a wilderness. 'Hermits be hanged!' he commented with engaging impulsiveness. Of course he didn't mind a wilderness. . . . 'I was glad of it,' I said. That was where he would be going to. He would find it lively enough, I ventured to promise. 'Yes, yes,' he said keenly. He had shown a desire, I continued inflexibly, to go out and shut the door after him. . . . 'Did I?' he interrupted in a strange access of gloom that seemed to envelop him from head to foot like the shadow of a passing cloud. He was wonderfully expressive after all. Wonderfully! 'Did I?' he repeated bitterly. 'You can't say I made much noise about it. And I can keep it up, too—only, confound it! you show me a door. . . .' 'Very well. Pass on,' I struck in. I could make him a solemn promise that it would be shut behind him with a vengeance. His fate, whatever it was, would be ignored, because the country, for all its rotten state, was not judged ripe for interference. Once he got in, it would be for the outside world as though he had never existed. He would have nothing but the soles of his two feet to stand upon, and he would have first to find his ground at that. 'Never existed—that's it, by Jove!' he murmured to himself. His eyes, fastened upon my lips, sparkled. If he had thoroughly understood the conditions, I concluded, he had better jump into the first gharry he could see and drive on to Stein's house for his final instructions. He flung out of the room before I had fairly finished speaking."

Chapter Twenty-Three

"He did not return till next morning. He had been kept to dinner and for the night. There never had been such a wonderful man as Mr. Stein. He had in his pocket a letter for Cornelius ('the Johnnie who's going to get the sack,' he explained, with a momentary drop in his elation), and he exhibited with glee a silver ring, such as natives use, worn down very thin and showing faint traces of chasing.

"This was his introduction to an old chap called Doramin—one of the principal men out there—a big pot—who had been Mr. Stein's friend in that country where he had all these adventures. Mr. Stein called him 'war-comrade.' War-comrade was good. Wasn't it? And didn't Mr. Stein speak English wonderfully well? Said he had learned it in Celebes—of all places! That was awfully funny. Was it not? He did speak with an accent—a twang—did I notice? That chap Doramin had given him the ring. They had exchanged presents when they parted for the last time. Sort of promising eternal friendship. He called it fine—did I not? They had to make a dash for dear life out of the country when that Mohammed—Mohammed—What's-his-name had been killed. I knew the story, of course. Seemed a beastly shame, didn't it? . . .

"He ran on like this, forgetting his plate, with a knife and fork in hand (he had found me at tiffin), slightly flushed, and with his eyes darkened many shades, which was with him a sign of excitement. The ring was a sort of credential—('It's like something you read of in books,' he threw in appreciatively)—and Doramin would do his best for him. Mr. Stein had been the means of saving that chap's life on some occasion; purely by accident, Mr. Stein had said, but he —Jim—had his own opinion about that. Mr. Stein was just the man to look out for such accidents. No matter. Accident or purpose, this would serve his turn immensely. Hoped to goodness the jolly old beggar had not gone off the hooks [3] meantime. Mr. Stein could not tell. There had been no news for more than a year; they were kicking up no end of an all-fired row amongst themselves, and the river was closed. Jolly awkward, this; but, no fear; he would manage to find a crack to get in.

"He impressed, almost frightened me with his elated rattle. He was voluble like a youngster on the eve of a long holiday with a prospect of delightful scrapes, and such an attitude of mind in a grown man and in this connection had in it something phenomenal, a little mad, dangerous, unsafe. I was on the point of entreating him to take things seriously when he dropped his knife and fork (he had begun eating, or rather swallowing food, as it were, unconsciously), and began a search all round his plate. The ring! The ring! Where the devil . . . Ah! Here it was. . . . He closed his big hand on it, and tried all his pockets one after another. Jove! wouldn't do to lose the thing. He meditated gravely over his fist. Had it? Would hang the bally affair round his neck! And he proceeded to do this immediately, producing a string (which looked like a bit of a cotton shoe-lace) for the purpose. There! That would do the trick! It would be the deuce if . . . He seemed to catch sight of my face for the first time, and it steadied him a little. I probably didn't realise, he said with a naive gravity, how much importance he attached to that token. It meant a friend; and it is a good thing to have a friend. He knew something about that. He nodded at me expressively, but before my disclaiming gesture he leaned his head on his hand and for a while sat silent, playing thoughtfully with the breadcrumbs on the

3. Lost his reason.

cloth. . . . 'Slam the door!—that was jolly well put,' he cried, and jumping up, began to pace the room, reminding me by the set of the shoulders, the turn of his head, the headlong and uneven stride, of that night when he had paced thus, confessing, explaining—what you will—but, in the last instance, living—living before me, under his own little cloud, with all his unconscious subtlety which could draw consolation from the very source of sorrow. It was the same mood, the same and different, like a fickle companion that to-day guiding you on the true path, with the same eyes, the same step, the same impulse, to-morrow will lead you hopelessly astray. His tread was assured, his straying, darkened eyes seemed to search the room for something. One of his footfalls somehow sounded louder than the other—the fault of his boots probably—and gave a curious impression of an invisible halt in his gait. One of his hands was rammed deep into his trousers pocket, the other waved suddenly above his head. 'Slam the door!' he shouted. 'I've been waiting for that. I'll show yet . . . I'll . . . I'm ready for any confounded thing. . . . I've been dreaming of it . . . Jove! Get out of this. Jove! This is luck at last. . . . You wait. I'll . . .'

"He tossed his head fearlessly, and I confess that for the first and last time in our acquaintance I perceived myself unexpectedly to be thoroughly sick of him. Why these vapourings? He was stumping about the room flourishing his arm absurdly, and now and then feeling on his breast for the ring under his clothes. Where was the sense of such exaltation in a man appointed to be a trading-clerk, and in a place where there was no trade—at that? Why hurl defiance at the universe? This was not a proper frame of mind to approach any undertaking; an improper frame of mind not only for him, I said, but for any man. He stood still over me. Did I think so? he asked, by no means subdued, and with a smile in which I seemed to detect suddenly something insolent. But then I am twenty years his senior. Youth *is* insolent; it is its right—its necessity; it has got to assert itself, and all assertion in this world of doubts is a defiance, is an insolence. He went off into a far corner, and coming back, he, figuratively speaking, turned to rend me. I spoke like that because I—even I, who had been no end kind to him—even I remembered—remembered—against him—what—what had happened. And what about others—the—the—world? Where's the wonder he wanted to get out, meant to get out, meant to stay out —by heavens! And I talked about proper frames of mind!

"'It is not I or the world who remember,' I shouted. 'It is you—you, who remember.'

"He did not flinch, and went on with heat, 'Forget everything, everybody, everybody. . . .' His voice fell. . . . 'But you,' he added.

" 'Yes—me, too—if it would help,' I said, also in a low tone. After this we remained silent and languid for a time, as if exhausted. Then he began again, composedly, and told me that Mr. Stein had instructed him to wait for a month or so, to see whether it was possible for him to remain, before he began building a new house for himself, so as to avoid 'vain expense.' He did make use of funny expressions—Stein did. 'Vain expense' was good. . . . Remain? Why! of course. He would hang on. Let him only get in—that's all; he would answer for it he would remain. Never get out. It was easy enough to remain.

" 'Don't be foolhardy,' I said, rendered uneasy by his threatening tone. 'If you only live long enough you will want to come back.'

" 'Come back to what?' he asked absently, with his eyes fixed upon the face of a clock on the wall.

"I was silent for a while. 'Is it to be never, then?' I said. 'Never,' he repeated dreamily, without looking at me, and then flew into sudden activity. 'Jove! Two o'clock, and I sail at four!'

"It was true. A brigantine of Stein's was leaving for the westward that afternoon, and he had been instructed to take his passage in her, only no orders to delay the sailing had been given. I suppose Stein forgot. He made a rush to get his things while I went aboard my ship, where he promised to call on his way to the outer roadstead. He turned up accordingly in a great hurry and with a small leather valise in his hand. This wouldn't do, and I offered him an old tin trunk of mine supposed to be water-tight, or at least damp-tight. He effected the transfer by the simple process of shooting out the contents of his valise as you would empty a sack of wheat. I saw three books in the tumble; two small, in dark covers, and a thick green-and-gold volume—a half-crown complete Shakespeare. 'You read this?' I asked. 'Yes. Best thing to cheer up a fellow,' he said hastily. I was struck by this appreciation, but there was no time for Shakespearean talk. A heavy revolver and two small boxes of cartridges were lying on the cuddy-table. 'Pray take this,' I said. 'It may help you to remain.' No sooner were these words out of my mouth than I perceived what grim meaning they could bear. 'May help you to get in,' I corrected myself remorsefully. He, however, was not troubled by obscure meanings; he thanked me effusively and bolted out, calling good-bye over his shoulder. I heard his voice through the ship's side urging his boatmen to give way, and looking out of the stern-port I saw the boat rounding under the counter. He sat in her leaning forward, exciting his men with voice and gestures; and as he had kept the revolver in his hand and seemed to be presenting it at their heads, I shall never forget the scared faces of the four Javanese, and the frantic swing of their stroke which snatched that vision from under my eyes. Then turning away, the first thing I saw were the two boxes of cartridges on the cuddy-table. He had forgotten to take them.

"I ordered my gig manned at once; but Jim's rowers, under the impression that their lives hung on a thread while they had that madman in the boat, made such excellent time that before I had traversed half the distance between the two vessels I caught sight of him clambering over the rail, and of his box being passed up. All the brigantine's canvas was loose, her mainsail was set, and the windlass was just beginning to clink as I stepped upon her deck: her master, a dapper little half-caste of forty or so, in a blue flannel suit, with lively eyes, his round face the colour of lemon-peel, and with a thin little black moustache drooping on each side of his thick, dark lips, came forward smirking. He turned out, notwithstanding his self-satisfied and cheery exterior, to be of a careworn temperament. In answer to a remark of mine (while Jim had gone below for a moment) he said, 'Oh yes. Patusan.' He was going to carry the gentleman to the mouth of the river, but would 'never ascend.' His flowing English seemed to be derived from a dictionary compiled by a lunatic. Had Mr. Stein desired him to 'ascend,' he would have 'reverentially'—(I think he wanted to say respectfully —but devil only knows)—'reverentially made objects for the safety of properties.' If disregarded, he would have presented 'resignation to quit.' Twelve months ago he had made his last voyage there, and though Mr. Cornelius 'propitiated many offertories' to Mr. Rajah Allang and the 'principal populations,' on conditions which made the trade 'a snare and ashes in the mouth,' yet his ship had been fired upon from the woods by 'irresponsive parties' all the way down the river; which causing his crew 'from exposure to limb to remain silent in hidings,' the brigantine was nearly stranded on a sandbank at the bar, where she 'would have been perishable beyond the act of man.' The angry disgust at the recollection, the pride of his fluency, to which he turned an attentive ear, struggled for the possession of his broad, simple face. He scowled and beamed at me, and watched with satisfaction the undeniable effect of his phraseology. Dark frowns ran swiftly over the placid sea, and the brigantine, with her fore-topsail to the mast and her main-boom amidships, seemed bewildered amongst the cat's-paws. He told me further, gnashing his teeth, that the Rajah was a 'laughable hyæna' (can't imagine how he got hold of hyænas); while somebody else was many times falser than the 'weapons of a crocodile.' Keeping one eye on the movements of his crew forward, he let loose his volubility—comparing the place to a 'cage of beasts made ravenous by long impenitence.' I fancy he meant impunity. He had no intention, he cried, to 'exhibit himself to be made attached purposefully to robbery.' The long-drawn wails, giving the time for the pull of the men catting the anchor, came to an end, and he lowered his voice. 'Plenty too much enough of Patusan,' he concluded with energy.

"I heard afterwards he had been so indiscreet as to get himself tied up by the neck with a rattan halter to a post planted in the middle of a mud-hole before the Rajah's house. He spent the best part of a day and a whole night in that unwholesome situation, but there is every reason to believe the thing had been meant as a sort of joke. He brooded for a while over that horrid memory, I suppose, and then addressed in a quarrelsome tone the man coming aft to the helm. When he turned to me again it was to speak judicially, without passion. He would take the gentleman to the mouth of the river at Batu Kring (Patusan town 'being situated internally,' he remarked, 'thirty miles'). But in his eyes, he continued—a tone of bored, weary conviction replacing his previous voluble delivery— the gentleman was already 'in the similitude of a corpse.' 'What? What do you say?' I asked. He assumed a startlingly ferocious demeanour, and imitated to perfection the act of stabbing from behind. 'Already like the body of one deported,' he explained, with the insufferably conceited air of his kind after what they imagine a display of cleverness. Behind him I perceived Jim smiling silently at me, and with a raised hand checking the exclamation on my lips.

"Then, while the half-caste, bursting with importance, shouted his orders, while the yards swung creaking and the heavy boom came surging over, Jim and I, alone as it were to leeward of the mainsail, clasped each other's hands and exchanged the last hurried words. My heart was freed from that dull resentment which had existed side by side with interest in his fate. The absurd chatter of the half-caste had given more reality to the miserable dangers of his path than Stein's careful statements. On that occasion the sort of formality that had been always present in our intercourse vanished from our speech; I believe I called him 'dear boy,' and he tacked on the words 'old man' to some half-uttered expression of gratitude, as though his risk set off against my years had made us more equal in age and in feeling. There was a moment of real and profound intimacy, unexpected and short-lived like a glimpse of some everlasting, of some saving truth. He exerted himself to soothe me as though he had been the more mature of the two. 'All right, all right,' he said rapidly, and with feeling. 'I promise to take care of myself. Yes; I won't take any risks. Not a single blessed risk. Of course not. I mean to hang out. Don't you worry. Jove! I feel as if nothing could touch me. Why! this is luck from the word Go. I wouldn't spoil such a magnificent chance! . . .' A magnificent chance! Well, it *was* magnificent, but chances are what men make them, and how was I to know? As he had said, even I—even I remembered—his—his misfortunes against him. It was true. And the best thing for him was to go.

"My gig had dropped in the wake of the brigantine, and I saw him aft detached upon the light of the westering sun, raising his cap high above his head. I heard an indistinct shout, 'You—shall—hear—of—me.' Of me, or from me, I don't know which. I think it must have been *of* me. My eyes were too dazzled by the glitter of the sea below his feet to see him clearly; I am fated never to see him clearly; but I can assure you no man could have appeared less 'in the similitude of a corpse,' as that half-caste croaker had put it. I could see the little wretch's face, the shape and colour of a ripe pumpkin, poked out somewhere under Jim's elbow. He, too, raised his arm as if for a downward thrust. *Absit omen.*" [4]

Chapter Twenty-Four

"The coast of Patusan (I saw it nearly two years afterwards) is straight and sombre, and faces a misty ocean. Red trails are seen like cataracts of rust streaming under the dark green foliage of brushes and creepers clothing the low cliffs. Swampy plains open out at the mouth of rivers, with a view of jagged blue peaks beyond the vast forests. In the offing a chain of islands, dark, crumbling shapes, stand out in the everlasting sunlit haze like the remnants of a wall breached by the sea.

"There is a village of fisher-folk at the mouth of the Batu Kring branch of the estuary.[5] The river, which had been closed so long, was open then, and Stein's little schooner, in which I had my passage, worked her way up in three tides without being exposed to a fusillade from 'irresponsive parties.' Such a state of affairs belonged already to ancient history, if I could believe the elderly head-man of the fishing village, who came on board to act as a sort of pilot. He talked to me (the second white man he had ever seen) with confidence, and most of his talk was about the first white man he had ever seen. He called him Tuan Jim, and the tone of his references was made remarkable by a strange mixture of familiarity and awe. They, in the village, were under that lord's special protection, which showed that Jim bore no grudge. If he had warned me that I would hear of him it was perfectly true. I was hearing of him. There was already a story that the tide had turned two hours before its time to help him on his journey up the river. The talkative old man himself had steered the canoe and had marvelled at the phenomenon. Moreover, all the glory was in his family. His son and his son-in-law had paddled; but they were

---

4. Evil omens aside. A proverbial Latin saying.
5. Navigation maps show a Batu Point at the mouth of the Berau River. In Malay, batu means rock, and kring means dry.

only youths without experience, who did not notice the speed of the canoe till he pointed out to them the amazing fact.

"Jim's coming to that fishing village was a blessing; but to them, as to many of us, the blessing came heralded by terrors. So many generations had been released since the last white man had visited the river that the very tradition had been lost. The appearance of the being that descended upon them and demanded inflexibly to be taken up to Patusan was discomposing; his insistence was alarming; his generosity more than suspicious. It was an unheard-of request. There was no precedent. What would the Rajah say to this? What would he do to them? The best part of the night was spent in consultation; but the immediate risk from the anger of that strange man seemed so great that at last a cranky dug-out was got ready. The women shrieked with grief as it put off. A fearless old hag cursed the stranger.

"He sat in it, as I've told you, on his tin box, nursing the unloaded revolver on his lap. He sat with precaution—than which there is nothing more fatiguing—and thus entered the land he was destined to fill with the fame of his virtues, from the blue peaks inland to the white ribbon of surf on the coast. At the first bend he lost sight of the sea with its labouring waves for ever rising, sinking, and vanishing to rise again—the very image of struggling mankind—and faced the immovable forests rooted deep in the soil, soaring towards the sunshine, everlasting in the shadowy might of their tradition, like life itself. And his opportunity sat veiled by his side like an Eastern bride waiting to be uncovered by the hand of the master. He, too, was the heir of a shadowy and mighty tradition! He told me, however, that he had never in his life felt so depressed and tired as in that canoe. All the movement he dared to allow himself was to reach, as it were by stealth, after the shell of half a cocoanut floating between his shoes, and bale some of the water out with a carefully restrained action. He discovered how hard the lid of a block-tin case was to sit upon. He had heroic health; but several times during that journey he experienced fits of giddiness, and between whiles he speculated hazily as to the size of the blister the sun was raising on his back. For amusement he tried by looking ahead to decide whether the muddy object he saw lying on the water's edge was a log of wood or an alligator. Only very soon he had to give that up. No fun in it. Always alligator. One of them flopped into the river and all but capsized the canoe. But this excitement was over directly. Then in a long, empty ˙reach he was very grateful to a troop of monkeys who came right down on the bank and made an insulting hullabaloo on his passage. Such was the way in which he was approaching greatness as genuine as any man ever achieved. Principally, he longed for sunset; and meantime his three paddlers were preparing to put into execution their plan of delivering him up to the Rajah.

" 'I suppose I must have been stupid with fatigue, or perhaps I did doze off for a time,' he said. The first thing he knew was his canoe coming to the bank. He became instantaneously aware of the forest having been left behind, of the first houses being visible higher up, of a stockade on his left, and of his boatmen leaping out together upon a low point of land and taking to their heels. Instinctively he leaped out after them. At first he thought himself deserted for some inconceivable reason, but he heard excited shouts, a gate swung open, and a lot of people poured out, making towards him. At the same time a boat full of armed men appeared on the river and came alongside his empty canoe, thus shutting off his retreat.

" 'I was too startled to be quite cool—don't you know?— and if that revolver had been loaded I would have shot somebody —perhaps two, three bodies, and that would have been the end of me. But it wasn't. . . .' 'Why not?' I asked. 'Well, I couldn't fight the whole population, and I wasn't coming to them as if I were afraid of my life,' he said, with just a faint hint of his stubborn sulkiness in the glance he gave me. I refrained from pointing out to him that they could not have known the chambers were actually empty. He had to satisfy himself in his own way. . . . 'Anyhow it wasn't,' he repeated good-humouredly, 'and so I just stood still and asked them what was the matter. That seemed to strike them dumb. I saw some of these thieves going off with my box. That long-legged old scoundrel Kassim (I'll show him to you to-morrow) ran out fussing to me about the Rajah wanting to see me. I said, "All right." I, too, wanted to see the Rajah, and I simply walked in through the gate and—and—here I am.' He laughed, and then with unexpected emphasis, 'And do you know what's the best in it?' he asked. 'I'll tell you. It's the knowledge that had I been wiped out it is this place that would have been the loser.'

"He spoke thus to me before his house on that evening I've mentioned—after we had watched the moon float away above the chasm between the hills like an ascending spirit out of a grave; its sheen descended, cold and pale, like the ghost of dead sunlight. There is something haunting in the light of the moon; it has all the dispassionateness of a disembodied soul, and something of its inconceivable mystery. It is to our sunshine, which—say what you like—is all we have to live by, what the echo is to the sound: misleading and confusing whether the note be mocking or sad. It robs all forms of matter—which, after all, is our domain—of their substance, and gives a sinister reality to shadows alone. And the shadows were very real around us, but Jim by my side looked very stalwart, as though nothing—not even the occult power of moonlight—could rob him of his reality in my eyes. Perhaps, indeed, nothing could touch him since he had survived the assault of the dark powers. All was silent, all was still; even on the river the moonbeams slept as on a pool. It was the moment of high water, a moment of immobility that accentuated the utter isolation of this lost corner of the earth. The houses crowding along the wide, shining sweep without ripple or glitter, stepping into the water in a line of jostling, vague, grey, silvery forms mingled with black masses of shadow, were like a spectral herd of shapeless creatures pressing forward to drink in a spectral and lifeless stream. Here and there a red gleam twinkled within the bamboo walls, warm, like a living spark, significant of human affections, of shelter, of repose.

"He confessed to me that he often watched these tiny warm gleams go out one by one, that he loved to see people go to sleep under his eyes, confident in the security of to-morrow. 'Peaceful here, eh?' he asked. He was not eloquent, but there was a deep meaning in the words that followed. 'Look at these houses; there's not one where I am not trusted. Jove! I told you I would hang on. Ask any man, woman, or child . . .' He paused. 'Well, I am all right anyhow.'

"I observed quickly that he had found that out in the end. I had been sure of it, I added. He shook his head. 'Were you?' He pressed my arm lightly above the elbow. 'Well, then—you were right.'

"There was elation and pride, there was awe almost, in that low exclamation. 'Jove!' he cried, 'only think what it is to me.' Again he pressed my arm. 'And you asked me whether I thought of leaving. Good God! I! want to leave! Especially now after what you told me of Mr. Stein's . . . Leave! Why! That's what I was afraid of. It would have been—it would have been harder than dying. No—on my word. Don't laugh. I must feel—every day, every time I open my eyes—that I am trusted—that nobody has a right— don't you know? Leave! For where? What for? To get what?'

"I had told him (indeed it was the main object of my visit) that it was Stein's intention to present him at once with the house and the stock of trading goods, on certain easy conditions which would make the transaction perfectly regular and valid. He began to snort and plunge at first. 'Confound your delicacy!' I shouted. 'It isn't Stein at all. It's giving you what you had made for yourself. And in any case keep your remarks for M'Neil— when you meet him in the other world. I hope it won't happen soon. . . .' He had to give in to my arguments, because all his conquests, the trust, the fame, the friendships, the love—all these things that made him master had made him a captive, too. He looked with an owner's eye at the peace of the evening, at the river, at the houses, at the everlasting life of the forests, at the life of the old mankind, at the secrets of the land, at the pride of his own heart; but it was they that possessed him and made him their own to the innermost thought, to the slightest stir of blood, to his last breath.

"It was something to be proud of. I, too, was proud—for him, if not so certain of the fabulous value of the bargain. It was wonderful. It was not so much of his fearlessness that I thought. It is strange how little account I took of it: as if it had been something too conventional to be at the root of the matter. No. I was more struck by the other gifts he had displayed. He had proved his grasp of the unfamiliar situation, his intellectual alertness in that field of thought. There was his readiness, too! Amazing. And all this had come to him in a manner like keen scent to a well-bred hound. He was not eloquent, but there was a dignity in this constitutional reticence, there was a high seriousness in his stammerings. He had still his old trick of stubborn blushing. Now and then, though, a word, a sentence, would escape him that showed how deeply, how solemnly, he felt about that work which had given him the certitude of rehabilitation. That is why he seemed to love the land and the people with a sort of fierce egoism, with a contemptuous tenderness."

Chapter Twenty-Five

" 'This is where I was prisoner for three days,' he murmured to me (it was on the occasion of our visit to the Rajah), while we were making our way slowly through a kind of awestruck riot of dependants across Tunku Allang's courtyard. 'Filthy place, isn't it? And I couldn't get anything to eat either, unless I made a row about it, and then it was only a small plate of rice and a fried fish not much bigger than a stickleback—confound them! Jove! I've been hungry prowling inside this stinking enclosure with some of these vagabonds shoving their mugs right under my nose. I had given up that famous revolver of yours at the first demand. Glad to get rid of the bally thing. Looked like a fool walking about with an empty shooting-iron in my hand.' At that moment we came into the presence, and he became unflinchingly grave and complimentary with his late captor. Oh! magnificent! I want to laugh when I think of it. But I was impressed, too. The old disreputable Tunku Allang could not help showing his fear (he was no hero, for all the tales of his hot youth he was fond of telling); and at the same time there was a wistful confidence in his manner towards his late prisoner. Note! Even where he would be most hated he was still trusted. Jim—as far as I could follow the conversation—was improving the occasion by the delivery of a lecture. Some poor villagers had been waylaid and robbed while on their way to Doramin's house with a few pieces of gum or beeswax which they wished to exchange for rice. 'It was Doramin who was a thief,' burst out the Rajah. A shaking fury seemed to enter that old, frail body. He writhed weirdly on his mat, gesticulating with his hands and feet, tossing the tangled strings of his mop—an impotent incarnation of rage. There were staring eyes and dropping jaws all around us. Jim began to speak. Resolutely, coolly, and for some time he enlarged upon the text that no man should be prevented from getting his food and his children's food honestly. The other sat like a tailor at his board, one palm on each knee, his head low, and fixing Jim through the grey hair that fell over his very eyes. When Jim had done there was a great stillness. Nobody seemed to breathe even; no one made a sound till the old Rajah sighed faintly, and looking up, with a toss of his head, said quickly, 'You hear, my people! No more of these little games.' This decree was received in profound silence. A rather heavy man, evidently in a position of confidence, with intelligent eyes, a bony, broad, very dark face, and a cheerily officious manner (I learned later on he was the executioner), presented to us two cups of coffee on a brass tray, which he took from the hands of an inferior attendant. 'You needn't drink,' muttered Jim very rapidly. I didn't perceive the meaning at first, and only looked at him. He took a good sip and sat composedly, holding the saucer in his left hand. In a moment I felt excessively annoyed. 'Why the devil,' I whispered, smiling at him amiably, 'do you expose me to such a stupid risk?' I drank, of course, there was nothing for it, while he gave no sign, and almost immediately afterwards we took our leave. While we were going down the courtyard to our boat, escorted by the intelligent and cheery executioner, Jim said he was very sorry. It was the barest chance, of course. Personally he thought nothing of poison. The remotest chance. He was—he assured me—considered to be infinitely more useful than dangerous, and so . . . 'But the Rajah is afraid of you abominably. Anybody can see that,' I argued, with, I own, a certain peevishness, and all the time watching anxiously for the first twist of some sort of ghastly colic. I was awfully disgusted. 'If I am to do any good here and preserve my position,' he said, taking his seat by my side in the boat, 'I must stand the risk: I take it once every month, at least. Many people trust me to do that—for them. Afraid of me! That's just it. Most likely he is afraid of me because I am not afraid of his coffee.' Then showing me a place on the north front of the stockade where the pointed tops of several stakes were broken, 'This is where I leaped over on my third day in Patusan. They haven't put new stakes there yet. Good leap, eh?' A moment later we passed the mouth of a muddy creek. 'This is my second leap. I had a bit of a run and took this one flying, but fell short. Thought I would leave my skin there. Lost my shoes struggling. And all the time I was thinking to myself how beastly it would be to get a jab with a bally long spear while sticking in the mud like this. I remember how sick I felt wriggling in that slime. I mean really sick—as if I had bitten something rotten.'

"That's how it was—and the opportunity ran by his side, leaped over the gap, floundered in the mud . . . still veiled. The unexpectedness of his coming was the only thing, you understand, that saved him from being at once dispatched with krisses and flung into the river. They had him, but it was like getting hold of an apparition, a wraith, a portent. What did it mean? What to do with it? Was it too late to conciliate him? Hadn't he better be killed without more delay? But what would happen then? Wretched old Allang went nearly mad with apprehension and through the difficulty of making up his mind. Several times the council was broken up, and the advisers made a break helter-skelter for the door and out on to the verandah. One—it is said—even jumped down to the ground—fifteen feet, I should judge—and broke his leg. The royal governor of Patusan had bizarre mannerisms, and one of them was to introduce boastful rhapsodies into every arduous discussion, when, getting gradually excited, he would end by flying off his perch with a kriss in his hand. But, barring such interruptions, the deliberations upon Jim's fate went on night and day.

"Meanwhile he wandered about the courtyard, shunned by some, glared at by others, but watched by all, and practically at the mercy of the first casual ragamuffin with a chopper, in there. He took possession of a small tumble-down shed to sleep in; the effluvia of filth and rotten matter incommoded him greatly: it seems he had not lost his appetite though, because—he told me—he had been hungry all the blessed time. Now and again 'some fussy ass' deputed from the council-room would come out running to him, and in honeyed tones would administer amazing interrogatories: 'Were the Dutch coming to take the country? Would the white man like to go back down the river? What was the object of coming to such a miserable country? The Rajah wanted to know whether the white man could repair a watch?' They did actually bring out to him a nickel clock of New England make, and out of sheer unbearable boredom he busied himself in trying to get the alarum to work. It was apparently when thus occupied in his shed that the true perception of his extreme peril dawned upon him. He dropped the thing—he says—'like a hot potato,' and walked out hastily, without the slightest idea of what he would, or indeed could, do. He only knew that the position was intolerable. He strolled aimlessly beyond a sort of ramshackle little granary on posts, and his eyes fell on the broken stakes of the palisade; and then—he says—at once, without any mental process as it were, without any stir of emotion, he set about his escape as if executing a plan matured for a month. He walked off carelessly to give himself a good run, and when he faced about there was some dignitary, with two spearmen in attendance, close at his elbow ready with a question. He started off 'from under his very nose,' went over 'like a bird,' and landed on the other side with a fall that jarred all his bones and seemed to split his head. He picked himself up instantly. He never thought of anything at the time; all he could remember—he said—was a great yell; the first houses of Patusan were before him four hundred yards away; he saw the creek, and as it were mechanically put on more pace. The earth seemed fairly to fly backwards under his feet. He took off from the last dry spot, felt himself flying through the air, felt himself, without any shock, planted upright in an extremely soft and sticky mudbank. It was only when he tried to move his legs and found he couldn't that, in his own words, 'he came to himself.' He began to think of the 'bally long spears.' As a matter of fact, considering that the people inside the stockade had to run to the gate, then get down to the landing-place, get into boats, and pull round a point of land, he had more advance than he imagined. Besides, it being low water, the creek was without water—you couldn't call it dry—and practically he was safe for a time from everything but a very long shot perhaps. The higher firm ground was about six feet in front of him. 'I thought I would have to die there all the same,' he said. He reached and grabbed desperately with his hands, and only succeeded in gathering a horrible cold, shiny heap of slime against his breast—up to his very chin. It seemed to him he was burying himself alive, and then he struck out madly, scattering the mud with his fists. It fell on his head, on his face, over his eyes, into his mouth. He told me that he remembered suddenly the courtyard, as you remember a place where you had been very happy years ago. He longed—so he said—to be back there again, mending the clock. Mending the clock—that was the idea. He made efforts, tremendous sobbing, gasping efforts, efforts that seemed to burst his eyeballs in their sockets and make him blind, and culminating into one mighty supreme effort in the darkness to crack the earth asunder, to throw it off his limbs—and he felt himself creeping feebly up the bank. He lay full length on the firm ground and saw the light, the sky. Then as a sort of happy thought the notion came to him that he would go to sleep. He will have it that he *did* actually go to sleep; that he slept—perhaps for a minute, perhaps for twenty seconds, or only for one second, but he recollects distinctly the violent convulsive start of awakening. He remained lying still for a while, and then he arose muddy from head to foot and stood there, thinking he was alone of his kind for hundreds of miles, alone, with no help, no sympathy, no pity to expect from any one, like a hunted animal. The first houses were not more than twenty yards from him; and it was the desperate screaming of a frightened woman trying to carry off a child that started him again. He pelted straight on in his socks, beplastered with filth out of all semblance to a human being. He traversed more than half the length of the settlement. The nimbler women fled right and left, the slower men just dropped whatever they had in their hands, and remained petrified with dropping jaws. He was a flying terror. He says he noticed the little children trying to run for life, falling on their little stomachs and kicking. He swerved between two houses up a slope, clambered in desperation over a barricade of felled trees (there wasn't a week without some fight in Patusan at that time), burst through a fence into a maize-patch, where a scared boy flung a stick at him, blundered upon a path, and ran all at once into the arms of several startled men. He just had breath enough to gasp out, 'Doramin! Doramin!' He remembers being half carried, half rushed to the top of the slope, and in a vast enclosure with palms and fruit trees being run up to a large man sitting massively in a chair in the midst of the greatest possible commotion and excitement. He fumbled in mud and clothes to produce the ring, and, finding himself suddenly on his back, wondered who had knocked him down. They had simply let him go—don't you know?—but he couldn't stand. At the foot of the slope random shots were fired, and above the roofs of the settlement there rose a dull roar of amazement. But he was safe. Doramin's people were barricading the gate and pouring water down his throat; Doramin's old wife, full of business and commiseration, was issuing shrill orders to her girls. 'The old woman,' he said softly, 'made a to-do over me as if I had been her own son. They put me into an immense bed—her state bed—and she ran in and out wiping her eyes to give me pats on the back. I must have been a pitiful object. I just lay there like a log for I don't know how long.'

"He seemed to have a great liking for Doramin's old wife. She on her side had taken a motherly fancy to him. She had a round, nut-brown, soft face, all fine wrinkles, large, bright red lips (she chewed betel assiduously), and screwed-up, winking, benevolent eyes. She was constantly in movement, scolding busily and ordering unceasingly a troop of young women with clear brown faces and big grave eyes, her daughters, her servants, her slave-girls. You know how it is in these households: it's generally impossible to tell the difference. She was very spare, and even her ample outer garment, fastened in front with jewelled clasps, had somehow a skimpy effect. Her dark, bare feet were thrust into yellow straw slippers of Chinese make. I have seen her myself flitting about with her extremely thick, long, grey hair falling about her shoulders. She uttered homely, shrewd sayings, was of noble birth, and was eccentric and arbitrary. In the afternoon she would sit in a very roomy arm-chair, opposite her husband, gazing steadily through a wide opening in the wall which gave an extensive view of the settlement and the river.

"She invariably tucked up her feet under her, but old Doramin sat squarely, sat imposingly as a mountain sits on a plain. He was only of the *nakhoda* or merchant class, but the respect shown to him and the dignity of his bearing were very striking. He was the chief of the second power in Patusan. The immigrants from Celebes (about sixty families that, with dependants and so on, could muster some two hundred men 'wearing the kriss') had elected him years ago for their head. The men of that race are intelligent, enterprising, revengeful, but with a more frank courage than the other Malays, and restless under oppression. They formed the party opposed to the Rajah. Of course the quarrels were for trade. This was the primary cause of faction fights, of the sudden outbreaks that would fill this or that part of the settlement with smoke, flame, the noise of shots and shrieks. Villages were burnt, men were dragged into the Rajah's stockade to be killed or tortured for the crime of trading with anybody else but himself. Only a day or two before Jim's arrival several heads of households in the very fishing village that was afterwards taken under his especial protection had been driven over the cliffs by a party of the Rajah's spearmen, on suspicion of having been collecting edible birds' nests for a Celebes trader. Rajah Allang pretended to be the only trader in his country, and the penalty for the breach of the monopoly was death; but his idea of trading was indistinguishable from the commonest forms of robbery. His cruelty and rapacity had no other bounds than his cowardice, and he was afraid of the organised power of the Celebes men, only—till Jim came—he was not afraid enough to keep quiet. He struck at them through his subjects, and thought himself pathetically in the right. The situation was complicated by a wandering stranger, an Arab half-breed, who, I believe, on purely religious grounds, had incited the tribes in the interior (the bush-folk, as Jim himself called them) to rise, and had established himself in a fortified camp on the summit of one of the twin hills. He hung over the town of Patusan like a hawk over a poultry-yard, but he devastated the open country. Whole villages, deserted, rotted on their blackened posts over the banks of clear streams, dropping piecemeal into the water the grass of their walls, the leaves of their roofs, with a curious effect of natural decay as if they had been a form of vegetation stricken by a blight at its very root. The two parties in Patusan were not sure which one this partisan most desired to plunder. The Rajah intrigued with him feebly. Some of the Bugis settlers, weary with endless insecurity, were half inclined to call him in. The younger spirits amongst them, chafing, advised to 'get Sherif Ali with his wild men and drive the Rajah Allang out of the country.' Doramin restrained them with difficulty. He was growing old, and, though his influence had not diminished, the situation was getting beyond him. This was the state of affairs when Jim, bolting from the Rajah's stockade, appeared before the chief of the Bugis, produced the ring, and was received, in a manner of speaking, into the heart of the community."

Chapter Twenty-Six

"Doramin was one of the most remarkable men of his race I had ever seen. His bulk for a Malay was immense, but he did not look merely fat; he looked imposing, monumental. This motionless body, clad in rich stuffs, coloured silks, gold embroideries; this huge head, enfolded in a red-and-gold headkerchief; the flat, big, round face, wrinkled, furrowed, with two semicircular heavy folds starting on each side of wide, fierce nostrils, and enclosing a thick-lipped mouth; the throat like a bull; the vast corrugated brow overhanging the staring proud eyes—made a whole that, once seen, can never be forgotten. His impassive repose (he seldom stirred a limb when once he sat down) was like a display of dignity. He was never known to raise his voice. It was a hoarse and powerful murmur, slightly veiled as if heard from a distance. When he walked, two short, sturdy young fellows, naked to the waist, in white sarongs and with black skull-caps on the backs of their heads, sustained his elbows; they would ease him down and stand behind his chair till he wanted to rise, when he would turn his head slowly, as if with difficulty, to the right and to the left, and then they would catch him under his armpits and help him up. For all that, there was nothing of a cripple about him: on the contrary, all his ponderous movements were like manifestations of a mighty, deliberate force. It was generally believed he consulted his wife as to public affairs; but nobody, as far as I know, had ever heard them exchange a single word. When they sat in state by the wide opening it was in silence. They could see below them in the declining light the vast expanse of the forest country, a dark, sleeping sea of sombre green undulating as far as the violet and purple range of mountains; the shining sinuosity of the river like an immense letter S of beaten silver; the brown ribbon of houses following the sweep of both banks, overtopped by the twin hills uprising above the nearer tree-tops. They were wonderfully contrasted: she, light, delicate, spare, quick, a little witch-like, with a touch of motherly fussiness in her repose; he, facing her, immense and heavy, like a figure of a man roughly fashioned of stone, with something magnanimous and ruthless in his immobility. The son of these old people was a most distinguished youth.

"They had him late in life. Perhaps he was not really so young as he looked. Four or five-and-twenty is not so young when a man is already father of a family at eighteen. When he entered the large room, lined and carpeted with fine mats, and with a high ceiling of white sheeting, where the couple sat in state surrounded by a most deferential retinue, he would make his way straight to Doramin, to kiss his hand—which the other abandoned to him majestically— and then would step across to stand by his mother's chair. I suppose I may say they idolised him, but I never caught them giving him an overt glance. Those, it is true, were public functions. The room was generally thronged. The solemn formality of greetings and leave-takings, the profound respect expressed in gestures, on the faces, in the low whispers, is simply indescribable. 'It's well worth seeing,' Jim had assured me while we were crossing the river, on our way back. 'They are like people in a book, aren't they?' he said triumphantly. 'And Dain Waris [6]—their son—is the best friend (barring you) I ever had. What Mr. Stein would call a good "war-comrade." I was in luck. Jove! I was in luck when I tumbled amongst them at my last gasp.' He meditated with bowed head, then rousing himself he added:

"'Of course I didn't go to sleep over it, but . . .' He paused again. 'It seemed to come to me,' he murmured. 'All at once I saw what I had to do . . .'

"There was no doubt that it had come to him; and it had come through the war, too, as is natural, since this power that came to him was the power to make peace. It is in this sense alone that might so often *is* right. You must not think he had seen his way at once. When he arrived the Bugis community was in a most critical position. 'They were all afraid,' he said to me—'each man afraid for himself; while I could see as plain as possible that they must do something at once, if they did not want to go under one after another, what between the Rajah and that vagabond Sherif.' But to see that was nothing. When he got his idea he had to drive it into reluctant minds, through the bulwarks of fear, of selfishness. He drove it

6. Malay word for heir.

in at last. And that was nothing. He had to devise the means. He devised them—an audacious plan; and his task was only half done. He had to inspire with his own confidence a lot of people who had hidden and absurd reasons to hang back; he had to conciliate imbecile jealousies, and argue away all sorts of senseless mistrusts. Without the weight of Doramin's authority, and his son's fiery enthusiasm, he would have failed. Dain Waris, the distinguished youth, was the first to believe in him; theirs was one of those strange, profound, rare friendships between brown and white, in which the very difference of race seems to draw two human beings closer by some mystic element of sympathy. Of Dain Waris, his own people said with pride that he knew how to fight like a white man. This was true; he had that sort of courage—the courage in the open, I may say—but he had also a European mind. You meet them sometimes like that, and are surprised to discover unexpectedly a familiar turn of thought, an unobscured vision, a tenacity of purpose, a touch of altruism. Of small stature, but admirably well proportioned, Dain Waris had a proud carriage, a polished, easy bearing, a temperament like a clear flame. His dusky face, with big black eyes, was in action expressive, and in repose thoughtful. He was of a silent disposition; a firm glance, an ironic smile, a courteous deliberation of manner seemed to hint at great reserves of intelligence and power. Such beings open to the Western eye, so often concerned with mere surfaces, the hidden possibilities of races and lands over which hangs the mystery of unrecorded ages. He not only trusted Jim, he understood him, I firmly believe. I speak of him because he had captivated me. His—if I may say so —his caustic placidity, and, at the same time, his intelligent sympathy with Jim's aspirations, appealed to me. I seemed to behold the very origin of friendship. If Jim took the lead, the other had captivated his leader. In fact, Jim the leader was a captive in every sense. The land, the people, the friendship, the love, were like the jealous guardians of his body. Every day added a link to the fetters of that strange freedom. I felt convinced of it, as from day to day I learned more of the story.

"The story! Haven't I heard the story? I've heard it on the march, in camp (he made me scour the country after invisible game); I've listened to a good part of it on one of the twin summits, after climbing the last hundred feet or so on my hands and knees. Our escort (we had volunteer followers from village to village) had camped meantime on a bit of level ground half-way up the slope, and in the still, breathless evening the smell of wood-smoke reached our nostrils from below with the penetrating delicacy of some choice scent. Voices also ascended, wonderful in their distinct and immaterial clearness. Jim sat on the trunk of a felled tree, and pulling out his pipe began to smoke. A new growth of grass and bushes was springing up; there were traces of an earthwork under a mass of thorny twigs. 'It all started from here,' he said, after a long and meditative silence. On the other hill, two hundred yards across a sombre precipice, I saw a line of high blackened stakes, showing here and there ruinously—the remnants of Sherif Ali's impregnable camp.

"But it had been taken, though. That had been his idea. He had mounted Doramin's old ordnance on the top of that hill; two rusty iron 7-pounders, a lot of small brass cannon—currency cannon. But if the brass guns represent wealth, they can also, when crammed recklessly to the muzzle, send a solid shot to some little distance. The thing was to get them up there. He showed me where he had fastened the cables, explained how he had improvised a rude capstan out of a hollowed log turning upon a pointed stake, indicated with the bowl of his pipe the outline of the earthwork. The last hundred feet of the ascent had been the most difficult. He had made himself responsible for success on his own head. He had induced the war party to work hard all night. Big fires lighted at intervals blazed all down the slope, 'but up here,' he explained, 'the hoisting gang had to fly around in the dark.' From the top he saw men moving on the hillside like ants at work. He himself on that night had kept on rushing down and climbing up like a squirrel, directing, encouraging, watching all along the line. Old Doramin had himself carried up the hill in his arm-chair. They put him down on the level place upon the slope, and he sat there in the light of one of the big fires—'amazing old chap—real old chieftain,' said Jim, 'with his little, fierce eyes—a pair of immense flintlock pistols on his knees. Magnificent things, ebony, silver-mounted, with beautiful locks and a calibre like an old blunderbuss. A present from Stein, it seems—in exchange for that ring, you know. Used to belong to good old M'Neil. God only knows how *he* came by them. There he sat, moving neither hand nor foot, a flame of dry brushwood behind him, and lots of people rushing about, shouting and pulling round him—the most solemn, imposing old chap you can imagine. *He* wouldn't have had much chance if Sherif Ali had let his infernal crew loose at us and stampeded my lot. Eh? Anyhow, he had come up there to die if anything went wrong. No mistake! Jove! It thrilled me to see him there—like a rock. But the Sherif must have thought us mad, and never troubled to come and see how we got on. Nobody believed it could be done. Why! I think the very chaps who pulled and shoved and sweated over it did not believe it could be done! Upon my word I don't think they did. . . .'

"He stood erect, the smouldering brierwood in his clutch, with a smile on his lips and a sparkle in his boyish eyes. I sat on the stump of a tree at his feet, and below us stretched the land, the great expanse of the forests, sombre under the sunshine, rolling like a sea, with glints of winding rivers, the grey spots of villages, and here and there a clearing, like an islet of light amongst the dark waves of continuous tree-tops. A brooding gloom lay over this vast and monotonous landscape; the light fell on it as if into an abyss. The land devoured the sunshine; only far off, along the coast, the empty ocean, smooth and polished within the faint haze, seemed to rise up to the sky in a wall of steel.

"And there I was with him, high in the sunshine on the top of that historic hill of his. He dominated the forest, the secular gloom, the old mankind. He was like a figure set up on a pedestal, to represent in his persistent youth the power, and perhaps the virtues, of races that never grow old, that have emerged from the gloom. I don't know why he should always have appeared to me symbolic. Perhaps this is the real cause of my interest in his fate. I don't know whether it was exactly fair to him to remember the incident which had given a new direction to his life, but at that very moment I remembered very distinctly. It was like a shadow in the light."

Chapter Twenty-Seven

"Already the legend had gifted him with supernatural powers. Yes, it was said, there had been many ropes cunningly disposed, and a strange contrivance that turned by the efforts of many men, and each gun went up tearing slowly through the bushes, like a wild pig rooting its way in the undergrowth, but . . . and the wisest shook their heads. There was something occult in all this, no doubt; for what is the strength of ropes and of men's arms? There is a rebellious soul in things which must be overcome by powerful charms and incantations. Thus old Sura—a very respectable householder of Patusan—with whom I had a quiet chat one evening. However, Sura was a professional sorcerer also, who attended all the rice sowings and reapings for miles around for the purpose of subduing the stubborn souls of things. This occupation he seemed to think a most arduous one, and perhaps the souls of things are more stubborn than the souls of men. As to the simple folk of outlying villages, they believed and said (as the most natural thing in the world) that Jim had carried the guns up the hill on his back—two at a time.

"This would make Jim stamp his foot in vexation and exclaim with an exasperated little laugh, 'What can you do with such silly beggars? They will sit up half the night talking bally rot, and the greater the lie the more they seem to like it.' You could trace the subtle influence of his surroundings in this irritation. It was part of his captivity. The earnestness of his denials was amusing, and at last I said, 'My dear fellow, you don't suppose *I* believe this.' He looked at me quite startled. 'Well, no! I suppose not,' he said, and burst into a Homeric peal of laughter. 'Well, anyhow the guns were there, and went off together at sunrise. Jove! You should have seen the splinters fly,' he cried. By his side Dain Waris, listening with a quiet smile, dropped his eyelids and shuffled his feet a little. It appears that the success in mounting the guns had given Jim's people such a feeling of confidence that he ventured to leave the battery under charge of two elderly Bugis who had seen some fighting in their day, and went to join Dain Waris and the storming party who were concealed in the ravine. In the small hours they began creeping up, and when two-thirds of the way up, lay in the wet grass waiting for the appearance of the sun, which was the agreed signal. He told me with what impatient, anguishing emotion he watched the swift coming of the dawn; how, heated with the work and the climbing, he felt the cold dew chilling his very bones; how afraid he was he would begin to shiver and shake like a leaf before the time came for the advance. 'It was the slowest half-hour in my life,' he declared. Gradually the silent stockade came out on the sky above him. Men scattered all down the slope were crouching amongst the dark stones and dripping bushes. Dain Waris was lying flattened by his side. 'We looked at each other,' Jim said, resting a gentle hand on his friend's shoulder. 'He smiled at me as cheery as you please, and I dared not stir my lips for fear I would break out into a shivering fit. 'Pon my word, it's true! I had been streaming with perspiration when we took cover—so you may imagine . . .' He declared, and I believe him, that he had no fears as to the result. He was only anxious as to his ability to repress these shivers. He didn't bother about the result. He was bound to get to the top of that hill and stay there, whatever might happen. There could be no going back for him. Those people had trusted him implicitly. Him alone! His bare word. . . .

"I remember how, at this point, he paused with his eyes fixed upon me. 'As far as he knew, they never had an occasion to regret it yet,' he said. 'Never. He hoped to God they never would. Meantime—worse luck!—they had got into the habit of taking his word for anything and everything. I could have no idea! Why, only the other day an old fool he had never seen in his life came from some village miles away to find out if he should divorce his wife. Fact. Solemn word. That's the sort of thing. . . . He wouldn't have believed it. Would I? Squatted on the verandah chewing betel-nut, sighing and spitting all over the place for more than an hour, and as glum as an undertaker before he came out with that dashed conundrum. That's the kind of thing that isn't so funny as it looks. What was a fellow to say?—Good wife?—Yes. Good wife—old though. Started a confounded long story about some brass pots. Been living together for fifteen years—twenty years—could not tell. A long, long time. Good wife. Beat her a little—not much—just a little, when she was young. Had to—for the sake of his honour. Suddenly in her old age she goes and lends three brass pots to her sister's son's wife, and begins to abuse him every day in a loud voice. His enemies jeered at him; his face was utterly blackened. Pots totally lost. Awfully cut up about it. Impossible to fathom a story like that; told him to go home, and promised to come along myself and settle it all. It's all very well to grin, but it was the dashedest nuisance! A day's journey through the forest, another day lost in coaxing a lot of silly villagers to get at the rights of the affair. There was the making of a sanguinary shindy in the thing. Every bally idiot took sides with one family or the other, and one half of the village was ready to go for the other half with anything that came handy. Honour bright! No joke! . . . Instead of attending to their bally crops. Got him the infernal pots back, of course—and pacified all hands. No trouble to settle it. Of course not. Could settle the deadliest quarrel in the country by crooking his little finger. The trouble was to get at the truth of anything. Was not sure to this day whether he had been fair to all parties. It worried him. And the talk! Jove! There didn't seem to be any head or tail to it. Rather storm a twenty-foot-high old stockade any day. Much! Child's play to that other job. Wouldn't take so long either. Well, yes; a funny set out, upon the whole—the fool looked old enough to be his grandfather. But from another point of view it was no joke. His word decided everything —ever since the smashing of Sherif Ali. An awful responsibility,' he repeated. 'No, really—joking apart, had it been three lives instead of three rotten brass pots it would have been the same. . . .'

"Thus he illustrated the moral effect of his victory in war. It was in truth immense. It had led him from strife to peace, and through death into the innermost life of the people; but the gloom of the land spread out under the sunshine preserved its appearance of inscrutable, of secular repose. The sound of his fresh young voice— it's extraordinary how very few signs of wear he showed—floated lightly, and passed away over the unchanged face of the forests like the sound of the big guns on that cold, dewy morning when he had no other concern on earth but the proper control of the chills in his body. With the first slant of sunrays along these immovable tree-tops the summit of one hill wreathed itself, with heavy reports, in white clouds of smoke, and the other burst into an amazing noise of yells, war-cries, shouts of anger, of surprise, of dismay. Jim and Dain Waris were the first to lay their hands on the stakes. The popular story has it that Jim with a touch of one finger had thrown down the gate. He was, of course, anxious to disclaim this achievement. The whole stockade—he would insist on explaining to you—was a poor affair (Sherif Ali trusted mainly to the inaccessible position); and, anyway, the thing had been already knocked to pieces and only hung together by a miracle. He put his shoulder to it like a little fool and went in head over heels. Jove! If it hadn't been for Dain Waris, a pock-marked, tattooed vagabond would have pinned him with his spear to a balk of timber like one of Stein's beetles. The third man in, it seems, had been Tamb' Itam, Jim's own servant. This was a Malay from the north, a stranger who had wandered into Patusan, and had been forcibly detained by Rajah Allang as paddler of one of the state boats. He had made a bolt of it at the first opportunity, and finding a precarious refuge (but very little to eat) amongst the Bugis settlers, had attached himself to Jim's person. His complexion was very dark, his face flat, his eyes prominent and injected with bile. There was something excessive, almost fanatical, in his devotion to his 'white lord.' He was inseparable from Jim like a morose shadow. On state occasions he would tread on his master's heels, one hand on the haft of his kriss, keeping the common people at a distance by his truculent, brooding glances. Jim had made him the head-man of his establishment, and all Patusan respected and courted him as a person of much influence. At the taking of the stockade he had distinguished himself greatly by the methodical ferocity of his fighting. The storming party had come on so quick —Jim said—that notwithstanding the panic of the garrison, there was a 'hot five minutes hand-to-hand inside that stockade, till some bally ass set fire to the shelters of boughs and dry grass, and we all had to clear out for dear life.'

"The rout, it seems, had been complete. Doramin, waiting immovably in his chair on the hillside, with the smoke of the guns spreading slowly above his big head, received the news with a deep grunt. When informed that his son was safe and leading the pursuit, he, without another sound, made a mighty effort to rise; his attendants hurried to his help, and, held up reverently, he shuffled with great dignity into a bit of shade where he laid himself down to sleep, covered entirely with a piece of white sheeting. In Patusan the excitement was intense. Jim told me that from the hill, turning his back on the stockade with its embers, black ashes, and half-consumed corpses, he could see time after time the open spaces between the houses on both sides of the stream fill suddenly with a seething rush of people and get empty in a moment. His ears caught feebly from below the tremendous din of gongs and drums; the wild shouts of the crowd reached him in bursts of faint roaring. A lot of streamers made a flutter as of little white, red, yellow birds amongst the brown ridges of roofs. 'You must have enjoyed it,' I murmured, feeling the stir of sympathetic emotion.

" 'It was . . . it was immense! Immense!' he cried aloud, flinging his arms open. The sudden movement startled me as though I had seen him bare the secrets of his breast to the sunshine, to the brooding forests, to the steely sea. Below us the town reposed in easy curves upon the banks of a stream whose current seemed to sleep. 'Immense!' he repeated for a third time, speaking in a whisper, for himself alone.

"Immense! No doubt it was immense; the seal of success upon his words, the conquered ground for the soles of his feet, the blind trust of men, the belief in himself snatched from the fire, the solitude of his achievement. All this, as I've warned you, gets dwarfed in the telling. I can't with mere words convey to you the impression of his total and utter isolation. I know, of course, he was in every sense alone of his kind there, but the unsuspected qualities of his nature had brought him in such close touch with his surroundings that this isolation seemed only the effect of his power. His loneliness added to his stature. There was nothing within sight to compare him with, as though he had been one of those exceptional men who can be only measured by the greatness of their fame; and his fame, remember, was the greatest thing around for many a day's journey. You would have to paddle, pole, or track a long, weary way through the jungle before you passed beyond the reach of its voice. Its voice was not the trumpeting of the disreputable goddess we all know—not blatant—not brazen. It took its tone from the stillness and gloom of the land without a past, where his word was the one truth of every passing day. It shared something of the nature of that silence through which it accompanied you into unexplored depths, heard continuously by your side, penetrating, far-reaching—tinged with wonder and mystery on the lips of whispering men."

Chapter Twenty-Eight

"The defeated Sherif Ali fled the country without making another stand, and when the miserable, hunted villagers began to crawl out of the jungle back to their rotting houses, it was Jim who, in consultation with Dain Waris, appointed the head-men. Thus he became the virtual ruler of the land. As to old Tunku Allang, his fears at first had known no bounds. It is said that at the intelligence of the successful storming of the hill he flung himself, face down, on the bamboo floor of his audience-hall, and lay motionless for a whole night and a whole day, uttering stifled sounds of such an appalling nature that no man dared approach his prostrate form nearer than a spear's length. Already he could see himself driven ignominiously out of Patusan, wandering abandoned, stripped, without opium, without his women, without followers, a fair game for the first comer to kill. After Sherif Ali his turn would come, and who could resist an attack led by such a devil? And indeed he owed his life and such authority as he still possessed at the time of my visit to Jim's idea of what was fair alone. The Bugis had been extremely anxious to pay off old scores, and the impassive old Doramin cherished the hope of yet seeing his son ruler of Patusan. During one of our interviews he deliberately allowed me to get a glimpse of this secret ambition. Nothing could be finer in its way than the dignified wariness of his approaches. He himself—he began by declaring—had used his strength in his young days, but now he had grown old and tired. . . . With his imposing bulk and haughty little eyes darting sagacious, inquisitive glances, he reminded one irresistibly of a cunning old elephant; the slow rise and fall of his vast breast went on powerful and regular, like the heave of a calm sea. He, too, as he protested, had an unbounded confidence in Tuan Jim's wisdom. If he could only obtain a promise! One word would be enough! . . . His breathing silences, the low rumblings of his voice, recalled the last efforts of a spent thunderstorm.

"I tried to put the subject aside. It was difficult, for there could be no question that Jim had the power; in his new sphere there did not seem to be anything that was not his to hold or to give. But that, I repeat, was nothing in comparison with the notion, which occurred to me, while I listened with a show of attention, that he seemed to have come very near at last to mastering his fate. Doramin was anxious about the future of the country, and I was struck by the turn he gave to the argument. The land remains where God had put it; but white men—he said—they come to us and in a little while they go. They go away. Those they leave behind do not know when to look for their return. They go to their own land, to their people, and so this white man, too, would. . . . I don't know what induced me to commit myself at this point by a vigorous 'No, no.' The whole extent of this indiscretion became apparent when Doramin, turning full upon me his face, whose expression, fixed in rugged, deep folds, remained unalterable, like a huge brown mask, said that this was good news indeed, reflectively; and then wanted to know why.

"His little, motherly witch of a wife sat on my other hand, with her head covered and her feet tucked up, gazing through the great shutter-hole. I could only see a straying lock of grey hair, a high cheek-bone, the slight masticating motion of the sharp chin. Without removing her eyes from the vast prospect of forests stretching as far as the hills, she asked me in a pitying voice why was it that he so young had wandered from his home, coming so far, through so many dangers? Had he no household there, no kinsmen in his own country? Had he no old mother, who would always remember his face? . . .

"I was completely unprepared for this. I could only mutter and shake my head vaguely. Afterwards I am perfectly aware I cut a very poor figure trying to extricate myself out of this difficulty. From that moment, however, the old *nakhoda* became taciturn. He was not very pleased, I fear, and evidently I had given him food for thought. Strangely enough, on the evening of that very day (which was my last in Patusan) I was once more confronted with the same question, with the unanswerable why of Jim's fate. And this brings me to the story of his love.

"I suppose you think it is a story that you can imagine for yourselves. We have heard so many such stories, and the majority of us don't believe them to be stories of love at all. For the most part we look upon them as stories of opportunities: episodes of passion at best, or perhaps only of youth and temptation, doomed to forgetfulness in the end, even if they pass through the reality of tenderness and regret. This view mostly is right, and perhaps is this case, too.

. . .Yet I don't know. To tell this story is by no means so easy as it should be—were the ordinary standpoint adequate. Apparently it is a story very much like the others: for me, however, there is visible in its background the melancholy figure of a woman, the shadow of a cruel wisdom buried in a lonely grave, looking on wistfully, helplessly, with sealed lips. The grave itself, as I came upon it during an early morning stroll, was a rather shapeless brown mound, with an inlaid neat border of white lumps of coral at the base, and enclosed within a circular fence made of split saplings, with the bark left on. A garland of leaves and flowers was woven about the heads of the slender posts—and the flowers were fresh.

"Thus, whether the shadow is of my imagination or not, I can at all events point out the significant fact of an unforgotten grave. When I tell you besides that Jim with his own hands had worked at the rustic fence, you will perceive directly the difference, the individual side of the story. There is in his espousal of memory and affection belonging to another human being something characteristic of his seriousness. He had a conscience, and it was a romantic conscience. Through her whole life the wife of the unspeakable Cornelius had no other companion, confidante, and friend but her daughter. How the poor woman had come to marry the awful Malacca Portuguese—after the separation from the father of her girl—and how that separation had been brought about, whether by death, which can be sometimes merciful, or by the merciless pressure of conventions, is a mystery to me. From the little which Stein (who knew so many stories) had let drop in my hearing, I am convinced that she was no ordinary woman. Her own father had been a white; a high official; one of the brilliantly endowed men who are not dull enough to nurse a success, and whose careers so often end under a cloud. I suppose she, too, must have lacked the saving dullness—and her career ended in Patusan. Our common fate . . . for where is the man—I mean a real sentient man—who does not remember vaguely having been deserted in the fullness of possession by some one or something more precious than life? . . . our common fate fastens upon the women with a peculiar cruelty. It does not punish like a master, but inflicts lingering torment, as if to gratify a secret, unappeasable spite. One would think that, appointed to rule on earth, it seeks to revenge itself upon the beings that come nearest to rising above the trammels of earthly caution; for it is only women who manage to put at times into their love an element just palpable enough to give one a fright—an extra-terrestrial touch. I ask myself with wonder—how the world can look to them—whether it has the shape and substance *we* know, the air *we* breathe! Sometimes I fancy it must be a region of unreasonable sublimities seething with the excitement of their adventurous souls, lighted by the glory of all possible risks and renunciations. However, I suspect there are very few women in the world, though of course I am aware of the multitudes of mankind and of the equality of sexes—in point of numbers, that is. But I am sure that the mother was as much of a woman as the daughter seemed to be. I cannot help picturing to myself these two, at first the young woman and the child, then the old woman and the young girl, the awful sameness and the swift passage of time, the barrier of forest, the solitude and the turmoil round these two lonely lives, and every word spoken between them penetrated with sad meaning. There must have been confidences, not so much of fact, I suppose, as of innermost feelings—regrets—fears—warnings, no doubt: warnings that the younger did not fully understand till the elder was dead—and Jim came along. Then I am sure she understood much—not everything—the fear mostly, it seems. Jim called her by a word that means precious, in the sense of a precious gem—jewel. Pretty, isn't it? But he was capable of anything. He was equal to his fortune, as he—after all—must have been equal to his misfortune. Jewel he called her; and he would say this as he might have said 'Jane,' don't you know?—with a marital, homelike, peaceful effect. I heard the name for the first time ten minutes after I had landed in his courtyard, when, after nearly shaking my arm off, he darted up the steps and began to make a joyous, boyish disturbance at the door under the heavy eaves. 'Jewel! O Jewel! Quick! Here's a friend come,' . . . and suddenly peering at me in the dim verandah, he mumbled earnestly, 'You know—this—no confounded nonsense about it—can't tell you how much I owe to her—and so—you understand—I—exactly as if . . .'

His hurried, anxious whispers were cut short by the flitting of a white form within the house, a faint exclamation, and a childlike but energetic little face with delicate features and a profound, attentive glance peeped out of the inner gloom, like a bird out of the recess of a nest. I was struck by the name, of course; but it was not till later on that I connected it with an astonishing rumour that had met me on my journey, at a little place on the coast about 230 miles south of Patusan River. Stein's schooner, in which I had my passage, put in there, to collect some produce, and going ashore, I found to my great surprise that the wretched locality could boast of a third-class deputy-assistant resident, a big, fat, greasy, blinking fellow of mixed descent, with turned-out, shiny lips. I found him lying extended on his back in a cane chair, odiously unbuttoned, with a large green leaf of some sort on the top of his steaming head, and another in his hand which he used lazily as a fan. . . . Going to Patusan? Oh yes. Stein's Trading Company. He knew. Had a permission? No business of his. It was not so bad there now, he remarked negligently, and, he went on drawling, 'There's some sort of white vagabond has got in there, I hear. . . . Eh? What you say? Friend of yours? So! . . . Then it was true there was one of these *verdamte*—What was he up to? Found his way in, the rascal. Eh? I had not been sure. Patusan—they cut throats there—no business of ours.' He interrupted himself to groan. 'Phoo! Almighty! The heat! The heat! Well, then, there might be something in the story, too, after all, and . . .' He shut one of his beastly glassy eyes (the eyelid went on quivering) while he leered at me atrociously with the other. 'Look here,' says he mysteriously, 'if—do you understand?—if he has really got hold of something fairly good—none of your bits of green glass—understand?—I am a Government official—you tell the rascal . . . Eh? What? Friend of yours?' . . . He continued wallowing calmly in the chair. . . . 'You said so; that's just it; and I am pleased to give you the hint. I suppose you, too, would like to get something out of it? Don't interrupt. You just tell him I've heard the tale, but to my Government I have made no report. Not yet. See? Why make a report? Eh? Tell him to come to me if they let him get alive out of the country. He had better look out for himself. Eh? I promise to ask no questions. On the quiet—you understand? You, too—you shall get something from me. Small commission for the trouble. Don't interrupt. I am a Government official, and make no report. That's business. Understand? I know some good people that will buy anything worth having, and can give him more money than the scoundrel ever saw in his life. I know his sort.' He fixed me steadfastly with both his eyes open, while I stood over him utterly amazed, and asking myself whether he was mad or drunk. He perspired, puffed, moaning feebly, and scratching himself with such horrible composure that I could not bear the sight long enough to find out. Next day, talking casually with the people of the little native court of the place, I discovered that a story was travelling slowly down the coast about a mysterious white man in Patusan who had got hold of an extraordinary gem —namely, an emerald of an enormous size, and altogether priceless. The emerald seems to appeal more to the Eastern imagination than any other precious stone. The white man had obtained it, I was told, partly by the exercise of his wonderful strength and partly by cunning, from the ruler of a distant country, whence he had fled instantly, arriving in Patusan in utmost distress, but frightening the people by his extreme ferocity, which nothing seemed able to subdue. Most of my informants were of the opinion that the stone was probably unlucky—like the famous stone of the Sultan of Succadana, which in the old times had brought wars and untold calamities upon that country. Perhaps it was the same stone—one couldn't say. Indeed the story of a fabulously large emerald is as old as the arrival of the first white men in the Archipelago; and the belief in it is so persistent that less than forty years ago there had been an official Dutch inquiry into the truth of it. Such a jewel— it was explained to me by the old fellow from whom I heard most of this amazing Jim-myth—a sort of scribe to the wretched little Rajah of the place—such a jewel, he said, cocking his poor purblind eyes up at me (he was sitting on the cabin floor out of respect), is best preserved by being concealed about the person of a woman. Yet it is not every woman that would do. She must be young—he sighed deeply—and insensible to the seductions of love. He shook his head sceptically. But such a woman seemed to be actually in existence. He had been told of a tall girl, whom the white man treated with great respect and care, and who never went forth from the house unattended. People said the white man could be seen with her almost any day; they walked side by side, openly, he holding her arm under his—pressed to his side—thus— in a most extraordinary way. This might be a lie, he conceded, for it was indeed a strange thing for any one to do: on the other hand, there could be no doubt she wore the white man's jewel concealed upon her bosom."

Chapter Twenty-Nine

"This was the theory of Jim's marital evening walks. I made a third on more than one occasion, unpleasantly aware every time of Cornelius, who nursed the aggrieved sense of his legal paternity, slinking in the neighbourhood with that peculiar twist of his mouth as if he were perpetually on the point of gnashing his teeth. But do you notice how, three hundred miles beyond the end of telegraph cables and mail-boat lines, the haggard utilitarian lies of our civilisation wither and die, to be replaced by pure exercises of imagination, that have the futility, often the charm, and sometimes the deep hidden truthfulness, of works of art? Romance had singled Jim for its own—and that was the true part of the story, which otherwise was all wrong. He did not hide his jewel. In fact, he was extremely proud of it.

"It comes to me now that I had, on the whole, seen very little of her. What I remember best is the even, olive pallor of her complexion, and the intense blue-black gleams of her hair, flowing abundantly from under a small crimson cap she wore far back on her shapely head. Her movements were free, assured, and she blushed a dusky red. While Jim and I were talking, she would come and go with rapid glances at us, leaving on her passage an impression of grace and charm and a distinct suggestion of watchfulness. Her manner presented a curious combination of shyness and audacity. Every pretty smile was succeeded swiftly by a look of silent, repressed anxiety, as if put to flight by the recollection of some abiding danger. At times she would sit down with us and, with her soft cheek dimpled by the knuckles of her little hand, she would listen to our talk; her big clear eyes would remain fastened on our lips, as though each pronounced word had a visible shape. Her mother had taught her to read and write; she had learned a good bit of English from Jim, and she spoke it most amusingly, with his own clipping, boyish intonation. Her tenderness hovered over him like a flutter of wings. She lived so completely in his contemplation that she had acquired something of his outward aspect, something that recalled him in her movements, in the way she stretched her arm, turned her head, directed her glances. Her vigilant affection had an intensity that made it almost perceptible to the senses; it seemed actually to exist in the ambient matter of space, to envelop him like a peculiar fragrance, to dwell in the sunshine like a tremulous, subdued, and impassioned note. I suppose you think that I, too, am romantic, but it is a mistake. I am relating to you the sober impressions of a bit of youth, of a strange, uneasy romance that had come in my way. I observed with interest the work of his—well—good fortune. He was jealously loved, but why she should be jealous, and of what, I could not tell. The land, the people, the forests were her accomplices, guarding him with vigilant accord, with an air of seclusion, of mystery, of invincible possession. There was no appeal, as it were; he was imprisoned within the very freedom of his power, and she, though ready to make a footstool of her head for his feet, guarded her conquest inflexibly—as though he were hard to keep.

The very Tamb' Itam, marching on our journeys upon the heels of his white lord, with his head thrown back, truculent and be-weaponed like a janissary,[7] with kriss, chopper, and lance (besides carrying Jim's gun); even Tamb' Itam allowed himself to put on the airs of uncompromising guardianship, like a surly, devoted jailer ready to lay down his life for his captive. On the evenings when we sat up late, his silent, indistinct form would pass and repass under the verandah, with noiseless footsteps, or lifting my head I would unexpectedly make him out standing rigidly erect in the shadow. As a general rule he would vanish after a time, without a sound; but when we rose he would spring up close to us as if from the ground, ready for any orders Jim might wish to give. The girl, too, I believe, never went to sleep till we had separated for the night. More than once I saw her and Jim through the window of my room come out together quietly and lean on the rough balustrade—two white forms very close, his arm about her waist, her head on his shoulder. Their soft murmurs reached me, penetrating, tender, with a calm, sad note in the stillness of the night, like a self-communion of one being carried on in two tones. Later on, tossing on my bed under the mosquito-net, I was sure to hear slight creakings, faint breathing, a throat cleared cautiously—and I would know that Tamb' Itam was still on the prowl. Though he had (by the favour of the white lord) a house in the compound, had 'taken wife,' and had lately been blessed with a child, I believe that, during my stay at all events, he slept on the verandah every night. It was very difficult to make this faithful and grim retainer talk. Even Jim himself was answered in jerky, short sentences, under protest as it were. Talking, he seemed to imply, was no business of his. The longest speech I heard him volunteer was one morning when, suddenly extending his hand towards the courtyard, he pointed at Cornelius and said, 'Here comes the Nazarene.' I don't think he was addressing me, though I stood at his side; his object seemed rather to awaken the indignant attention of the universe. Some muttered allusions, which followed, to dogs and the smell of roast meat, struck me as singularly felicitous. The courtyard, a large square space, was one torrid blaze of sunshine, and, bathed in intense light, Cornelius was creeping across in full view with an inexpressible effect of stealthiness, of dark and secret slinking. He reminded one of everything that is unsavoury. His slow, laborious walk resembled the creeping of a repulsive beetle, the legs alone moving with horrid industry while the body glided evenly. I suppose he made straight enough for the place where he wanted to get to, but his progress with one shoulder carried forward seemed oblique. He was often seen circling slowly amongst the sheds, as if following a scent; passing before the veran-

7. A soldier (originally a slave) in the Turkish sultan's guard.

dah with upward, stealthy glances; disappearing without haste round the corner of some hut. That he seemed free of the place demonstrated Jim's absurd carelessness or else his infinite disdain, for Cornelius had played a very dubious part (to say the least of it) in a certain episode which might have ended fatally for Jim. As a matter of fact, it had redounded to his glory. But everything redounded to his glory; and it was the irony of his good fortune that he, who had been too careful of it once, seemed to bear a charmed life.

"You must know he had left Doramin's place very soon after his arrival—much too soon, in fact, for his safety, and of course a long time before the war. In this he was actuated by a sense of duty; he had to look after Stein's business, he said. Hadn't he? To that end, with an utter disregard of his personal safety, he crossed the river and took up his quarters with Cornelius. How the latter had managed to exist through the troubled times I can't say. As Stein's agent, after all, he must have had Doramin's protection in a measure; and in one way or another he had managed to wriggle through all the deadly complications, while I have no doubt that his conduct, whatever line he was forced to take, was marked by that abjectness which was like the stamp of the man. That was his characteristic; he was fundamentally and outwardly abject, as other men are markedly of a generous, distinguished, or venerable appearance. It was the element of his nature which permeated all his acts and passions and emotions; he raged abjectly, smiled abjectly, was abjectly sad; his civilities and his indignations were alike abject. I am sure his love would have been the most abject of sentiments— but can one imagine a loathsome insect in love? And his loathsomeness, too, was abject, so that a simply disgusting person would have appeared noble by his side. He has his place neither in the background nor in the foreground of the story; he is simply seen skulking on its outskirts, enigmatical and unclean, tainting the fragrance of its youth and of its naiveness.

"His position in any case could not have been other than extremely miserable, yet it may very well be that he found some advantages in it. Jim told me he had been received at first with an abject display of the most amicable sentiments. 'The fellow apparently couldn't contain himself for joy,' said Jim with disgust. 'He flew at me every morning to shake both my hands—confound him!—but I could never tell whether there would be any breakfast. If I got three meals in two days I considered myself jolly lucky, and he made me sign a chit for ten dollars every week. Said he was sure Mr. Stein did not mean him to keep me for nothing. Well—he kept me on nothing as near as possible. Put it down to the unsettled state of the country, and made as if to tear his hair out, begging my pardon twenty times a day, so that I had at last to entreat him not to worry. It made me sick. Half the roof of his house had fallen in, and the whole place had a mangy look, with wisps of dry grass sticking out and the corners of broken mats flapping on every wall. He did his best to make out that Mr. Stein owed him money on the last three years' trading, but his books were all torn, and some were missing. He tried to hint it was his late wife's fault. Disgusting scoundrel! At last I had to forbid him to mention his late wife at all. It made Jewel cry. I couldn't discover what became of all the trade goods; there was nothing in the store but rats, having a high old time amongst a litter of brown paper and old sacking. I was assured on every hand that he had a lot of money buried somewhere, but of course could get nothing out of him. It was the most miserable existence I led there in that wretched house. I tried to do my duty by Stein, but I had also other matters to think of. When I escaped to Doramin old Tunku Allang got frightened and returned all my things. It was done in a roundabout way, and with no end of mystery, through a Chinaman who keeps a small shop here; but as soon as I left the Bugis quarter and went to live with Cornelius it began to be said openly that the Rajah had made up his mind to have me killed before long. Pleasant, wasn't it? And I couldn't see what there was to prevent him if he really *had* made up his mind. The worst of it was, I couldn't help feeling I wasn't doing any good either for Stein or for myself. Oh, it was beastly—the whole six weeks of it.' "

Chapter Thirty

"He told me further that he didn't know what made him hang on —but of course we may guess. He sympathised deeply with the defenceless girl, at the mercy of that 'mean, cowardly scoundrel.' It appears Cornelius led her an awful life, stopping only short of actual ill-usage, for which he had not the pluck, I suppose. He insisted upon her calling him father—'and with respect, too—with respect,' he would scream, shaking a little yellow fist in her face. 'I am a respectable man, and what are you? Tell me—what are you? You think I am going to bring up somebody else's child and not to be treated with respect? You ought to be glad I let you. Come—say Yes, father. . . . No? . . . You wait a bit.' Thereupon he would begin to abuse the dead woman, till the girl would run off with her hands to her head. He pursued her, dashing in and out and round the house and amongst the sheds, would drive her into some corner, where she would fall on her knees stopping her ears, and then he would stand at a distance and declaim filthy denunciations at her back for half an hour at a stretch. 'Your mother was a devil, a deceitful devil—and you, too, are a devil,' he would shriek in a final outburst, pick up a bit of dry earth or a handful of mud (there was plenty of mud around the house), and fling it into her hair. Sometimes, though, she would hold out full of scorn, confronting him in silence, her face sombre and contracted, and only now and then uttering a word or two that would make the other jump and writhe with the sting. Jim told me these scenes were terrible. It was indeed a strange thing to come upon in a wilderness. The endlessness of such a subtly cruel situation was appalling—if you think of it. The respectable Cornelius (Inchi 'Nelyus the Malays called him, with a grimace that meant many things) was a much-disappointed man. I don't know what he had expected would be done for him in consideration of his marriage; but evidently the liberty to steal, and embezzle, and appropriate to himself for many years and in any way that suited him best the goods of Stein's Trading Company (Stein kept the supply up unfalteringly as long as he could get his skippers to take it there) did not seem to him a fair equivalent for the sacrifice of his honourable name. Jim would have enjoyed exceedingly thrashing Cornelius within an inch of his life; on the other hand, the scenes were of so painful a character, so abominable, that his impulse would be to get out of earshot, in order to spare the girl's feelings. They left her agitated, speechless, clutching her bosom now and then with a stony, desperate face, and then Jim would lounge up and say unhappily, 'Now—come—really—what's the use—you must try to eat a bit,' or give some such mark of sympathy. Cornelius would keep on slinking through the doorways, across the verandah and back again, as mute as a fish, and with malevolent, mistrustful, underhand glances. 'I can stop his game,' Jim said to her once. 'Just say the word.' And do you know what she answered? She said—Jim told me impressively—that if she had not been sure he was intensely wretched himself, she would have found the courage to kill him with her own hands. 'Just fancy that! The poor devil of a girl, almost a child, being driven to talk like that!' he exclaimed in horror. It seemed impossible to save her not only from that mean rascal but even from herself! It wasn't that he pitied her so much, he affirmed; it was more than pity; it was as if he had something on his conscience, while that life went on. To leave the house would have appeared a base desertion. He had understood at last that there was nothing to expect from a longer stay, neither accounts nor money, nor truth of any sort, but he stayed on, exasperating Cornelius to the verge, I won't say of insanity, but almost of courage. Meantime he felt all sorts of dangers gathering obscurely about him. Doramin had sent over twice a trusty servant to tell him seriously that he could do nothing for his safety unless he would recross the river again and live amongst the Bugis as at first. People of every condition used to call, often in the dead of night, in order to disclose to him plots for his assassination. He was to be poisoned. He was to be stabbed in the bath-house. Arrangements were being made to have him shot from a boat on the river. Each of these informants professed himself to be his very good friend. It was enough—he told me—to spoil a fellow's rest for ever. Something of the kind was extremely possible—nay, probable—but the lying warnings gave him only the sense of deadly scheming going on all around him, on all sides, in the dark. Nothing more calculated to shake the best of nerve. Finally, one night, Cornelius himself, with a great apparatus of alarm and secrecy, unfolded in solemn, wheedling tones a little plan wherein for one hundred dollars—or even for eighty; let's say eighty—he, Cornelius, would procure a trustworthy man to smuggle Jim out of the river, all safe. There was nothing else for it now—if Jim cared a pin for his life. What's eighty dollars? A trifle. An insignificant sum. While he, Cornelius, who had to remain behind, was absolutely courting death by his proof of devotion to Mr. Stein's young friend. The sight of his abject grimacing was—Jim told me—very hard to bear: he clutched at his hair, beat his breast, rocked himself to and fro with his hands pressed to his stomach, and actually pretended to shed tears. 'Your blood be on your own head,' he squeaked at last, and rushed out. It is a curious question how far Cornelius was sincere in that performance. Jim confessed to me that he did not sleep a wink after the fellow had gone. He lay on his back on a thin mat spread over the bamboo flooring, trying idly to make out the bare rafters, and listening to the rustlings in the torn thatch. A star suddenly twinkled through a hole in the roof. His brain was in a whirl; but, nevertheless, it was on that very night that he matured his plan for overcoming Sherif Ali. It had been the thought of all the moments he could spare from the hopeless investigation into Stein's affairs, but the notion—he says—came to him then all at once. He could see, as it were, the guns mounted on the top of the hill. He got very hot and excited lying there; sleep was out of the question more than ever. He jumped up, and went out barefooted on the verandah. Walking silently, he came upon the girl, motionless against the wall, as if on the watch. In his then state of mind it did not surprise him to see her up, nor yet to hear her ask in an anxious whisper where Cornelius could be. He simply said he did not know. She moaned a little, and peered into the campong. Everything was very quiet. He was possessed by his new idea, and so full of it that he could not help telling the girl all about it at once. She listened, clapped her hands lightly, whispered softly her admiration, but was evidently on the alert all the time. It seems he had been used to make a confidante of her all along—and that she on her part could and did give him a lot of useful hints as to Patusan affairs there is no doubt. He assured me more than once that he had never found himself the worse for her advice. At any rate, he was proceeding to explain his plan fully to her there and then, when she pressed his arm once, and vanished from his side. Then Cornelius appeared from somewhere, and, perceiving Jim, ducked sideways, as though he had been shot at, and afterwards stood very still in the dusk. At last he came forward prudently, like a suspicious cat. 'There were some fishermen there—with fish,' he said in a shaky voice. 'To sell fish—you understand. . . .' It must have been then two o'clock in the morning—a likely time for anybody to hawk fish about!

"Jim, however, let the statement pass, and did not give it a single thought. Other matters occupied his mind, and besides, he had neither seen nor heard anything. He contented himself by saying, 'Oh!' absently, got a drink of water out of a pitcher standing there, and leaving Cornelius a prey to some inexplicable emotion— that made him embrace with both arms the worm-eaten rail of the verandah as if his legs had failed—went in again and lay down on his mat to think. By and by he heard stealthy footsteps. They stopped. A voice whispered tremulously through the wall, 'Are you asleep?' 'No! What is it?' he answered briskly, and there was an abrupt movement outside, and then all was still, as if the whisperer had been startled. Extremely annoyed at this, Jim came out impetuously, and Cornelius with a faint shriek fled along the verandah as far as the steps, where he hung on to the broken banister. Very puzzled, Jim called out to him from the distance to know what the devil he meant. 'Have you given your consideration to what I spoke to you about?' asked Cornelius, pronouncing the words with difficulty, like a man in the cold fit of a fever. 'No!' shouted Jim in a passion. 'I have not, and I don't intend to. I am going to live here, in Patusan.' 'You shall d-d-die h-h-here,' answered Cornelius, still shaking violently, and in a sort of expiring voice. The whole performance was so absurd and provoking that Jim didn't know whether he ought to be amused or angry. 'Not till I have seen you tucked away, you bet,' he called out, exasperated, yet ready to laugh. Half seriously (being excited with his own thoughts, you know) he went on shouting, 'Nothing can touch me! You can do your damnedest.' Somehow the shadowy Cornelius far off there seemed to be the hateful embodiment of all the annoyances and difficulties he had found in his path. He let himself go—his nerves had been overwrought for days—and called him many pretty names—swindler, liar, sorry rascal: in fact, carried on in an extraordinary way. He admits he passed all bounds, that he was quite beside himself—defied all Patusan to scare him away— declared he would make them all dance to his own tune yet, and so on, in a menacing, boasting strain. Perfectly bombastic and ridiculous, he said. His ears burned at the bare recollection. Must have been off his chump in some way. . . . The girl, who was sitting with us, nodded her little head at me quickly, frowned faintly, and said, 'I heard him,' with childlike solemnity. He laughed and blushed. What stopped him at last, he said, was the silence, the completely deathlike silence, of the indistinct figure far over there, that seemed to hang collapsed, doubled over the rail in a weird immobility. He came to his senses, and ceasing suddenly, wondered greatly at himself. He watched for a while. Not a stir, not a sound. 'Exactly as if the chap had died while I had been making all that noise,' he said. He was so ashamed of himself that he went indoors in a hurry without another word, and flung himself down again. The row seemed to have done him good, though, because he went to sleep for the rest of the night like a baby. Hadn't slept like that for weeks. 'But *I* didn't sleep,' struck in the girl, one elbow on the table and nursing her cheek. 'I watched.' Her big eyes flashed, rolling a little, and then she fixed them on my face intently."

Chapter Thirty-One

"You may imagine with what interest I listened. All these details were perceived to have some significance twenty-four hours later. In the morning Cornelius made no allusion to the events of the night. 'I suppose you will come back to my poor house,' he muttered surlily, slinking up just as Jim was entering the canoe to go over to Doramin's campong. Jim only nodded, without looking at him. 'You find it good fun, no doubt,' muttered the other in a sour tone. Jim spent the day with the old *nakhoda*, preaching the necessity of vigorous action to the principal men of the Bugis community, who had been summoned for a big talk. He remembered with pleasure how very eloquent and persuasive he had been. 'I managed to put some backbone into them that time, and no mistake,' he said. Sherif Ali's last raid had swept the outskirts of the settlement, and some women belonging to the town had been carried off to the stockade. Sheriff Ali's emissaries had been seen in the market-place the day before, strutting about haughtily in white cloaks, and boasting of the Rajah's friendship for their master. One of them stood forward in the shade of a tree, and, leaning on the long barrel of a rifle, exhorted the people to prayer and repentance, advising them to kill all the strangers in their midst, some of whom, he said, were infidels and others even worse—children of Satan in the guise of Moslems. It was reported that several of the Rajah's people amongst the listeners had loudly expressed their approbation. The terror amongst the common people was intense. Jim, immensely pleased with his day's work, crossed the river again before sunset.

"As he had got the Bugis irretrievably committed to action, and had made himself responsible for success on his own head, he was so elated that in the lightness of his heart he absolutely tried to be civil with Cornelius. But Cornelius became wildly jovial in response, and it was almost more than he could stand, he says, to hear his little squeaks of false laughter, to see him wriggle and blink, and suddenly catch hold of his chin and crouch low over the table with a distracted stare. The girl did not show herself, and Jim retired early. When he rose to say good-night, Cornelius jumped up, knocking his chair over, and ducked out of sight as if to pick up something he had dropped. His good-night came huskily from under the table. Jim was amazed to see him emerge with a dropping jaw, and staring, stupidly frightened eyes. He clutched the edge of the table. 'What's the matter? Are you unwell?' asked Jim. 'Yes, yes, yes. A great colic in my stomach,' says the other; and it is Jim's opinion that it was perfectly true. If so, it was, in view of his contemplated action, an abject sign of a still imperfect callousness for which he must be given all due credit.

"Be it as it may, Jim's slumbers were disturbed by a dream of heavens like brass resounding with a great voice, which called upon him to Awake! Awake! so loud that, notwithstanding his desperate determination to sleep on, he did wake up in reality. The glare of a red spluttering conflagration going on in mid-air fell on his eyes. Coils of black, thick smoke curved round the head of some apparition, some unearthly being, all in white, with a severe, drawn, anxious face. After a second or so he recognised the girl. She was holding a dammar torch at arm's-length aloft, and in a persistent, urgent monotone she was repeating, 'Get up! Get up! Get up!'

"Suddenly he leaped to his feet; at once she put into his hand a revolver, his own revolver, which had been hanging on a nail, but loaded this time. He gripped it in silence, bewildered, blinking in the light. He wondered what he could do for her.

"She asked rapidly and very low, 'Can you face four men with this?' He laughed while narrating this part at the recollection of his polite alacrity. It seems he made a great display of it, 'Certainly—of course—certainly—command me.' He was not properly awake, and had a notion of being very civil in these extraordinary circumstances, of showing his unquestioning, devoted readiness. She left the room, and he followed her; in the passage they disturbed an old hag who did the casual cooking of the household, though she was so decrepit as to be hardly able to understand human speech. She got up and hobbled behind them, mumbling toothlessly. On the verandah a hammock of sailcloth, belonging to Cornelius, swayed lightly to the touch of Jim's elbow. It was empty.

"The Patusan establishment, like all the posts of Stein's Trading Company, had originally consisted of four buildings. Two of them were represented by two heaps of sticks, broken bamboos, rotten thatch, over which the four corner-posts of hardwood leaned sadly at different angles: the principal storeroom, however, stood yet, facing the agent's house. It was an oblong hut, built of mud and clay; it had at one end a wide door of stout planking, which so far had not come off the hinges, and in one of the side walls there was a square aperture, a sort of window, with three wooden bars. Before descending the few steps the girl turned her face over her shoulder and said quickly, 'You were to be set upon while you slept.' Jim tells me he experienced a sense of deception. It was the old story. He was weary of these attempts upon his life. He had had his fill of these alarms. He was sick of them. He assured me he was angry with the girl for deceiving him. He had followed her under the impression that it was she who wanted his help, and now he had half a mind to turn on his heel and go back in disgust. 'Do you know,' he commented profoundly, 'I rather think I was not quite myself for whole weeks on end about that time.' 'Oh yes. You were though,' I couldn't help contradicting.

"But she moved on swiftly, and he followed her into the courtyard. All its fences had fallen in a long time ago; the neighbours' buffaloes would pace in the morning across the open space, snorting profoundly, without haste; the very jungle was invading it already. Jim and the girl stopped in the rank grass. The light in which they stood made a dense blackness all round, and only above their heads there was an opulent glitter of stars. He told me it was a beautiful night— quite cool, with a little stir of breeze from the river. It seems he noticed its friendly beauty. Remember this is a love story I am telling you now. A lovely night seemed to breathe on them a soft caress. The flame of the torch streamed now and then with a fluttering noise like a flag, and for a time this was the only sound. 'They are in the storeroom waiting,' whispered the girl; 'they are waiting for the signal.' 'Who's to give it?' he asked. She shook the torch, which blazed up after a shower of sparks. 'Only you have been sleeping so restlessly,' she continued in a murmur; 'I watched your sleep, too.' 'You!' he exclaimed, craning his neck to look about him. 'You think I watched on this night only!' she said, with a sort of despairing indignation.

"He says it was as if he had received a blow on the chest. He gasped. He thought he had been an awful brute somehow, and he felt remorseful, touched, happy, elated. This, let me remind you again, is a love story; you can see it by the imbecility, not a repulsive imbecility, the exalted imbecility of these proceedings, this station in torchlight, as if they had come there on purpose to have it out for the edification of concealed murderers. If Sherif Ali's emissaries had been possessed—as Jim remarked—of a pennyworth of spunk, this was the time to make a rush. His heart was thumping—not with fear —but he seemed to hear the grass rustle, and he stepped smartly out of the light. Something dark, imperfectly seen, flitted rapidly out of sight. He called out in a strong voice, 'Cornelius! O Cornelius!' A profound silence succeeded: his voice did not seem to have carried twenty feet. Again the girl was by his side. 'Fly!' she said. The old woman was coming up; her broken figure hovered in crippled little jumps on the edge of the light; they heard her mumbling, and a light, moaning sigh. 'Fly!' repeated the girl excitedly. 'They are frightened now—this light—the voices. They know you are awake now—they know you are big, strong, fearless . . .' 'If I am all that,' he began; but she interrupted him: 'Yes—to-night! But what of to-morrow night? Of the next night? Of the night after—of all the many, many nights? Can I be always watching?' A sobbing catch of her breath affected him beyond the power of words.

"He told me that he had never felt so small, so powerless—and as to courage, what was the good of it? he thought. He was so helpless that even flight seemed of no use; and though she kept on whispering, 'Go to Doramin! go to Doramin!' with feverish insistence, he realised that for him there was no refuge from that loneliness which centupled all his dangers except—in her. 'I thought,' he said to me, 'that if I went away from her it would be the end of everything somehow.' Only as they couldn't stop there for ever in the middle of that court-yard, he made up his mind to go and look into the storehouse. He let her follow him without thinking of any protest, as if they had been indissolubly united. 'I am fearless—am I?' he muttered through his teeth. She restrained his arm. 'Wait till you hear my voice,' she said, and, torch in hand, ran lightly round the corner. He remained alone in the darkness, his face to the door; not a sound, not a breath came from the other side. The old hag let out a dreary groan some-where behind his back. He heard a high-pitched, almost screaming call from the girl. 'Now! Push!' He pushed violently; the door swung with a creak and a clatter, disclosing to his intense astonishment the low, dungeon-like interior illuminated by a lurid, wavering glare. A turmoil of smoke eddied down upon an empty wooden crate in the middle of the floor, a litter of rags and straw tried to soar, but only stirred feebly in the draught. She had thrust the light through the bars of the window. He saw her bare round arm extended and rigid, holding up the torch with the steadiness of an iron bracket. A con-ical ragged heap of old mats cumbered a distant corner almost to the ceiling, and that was all.

"He explained to me that he was bitterly disappointed at this. His fortitude had been tried by so many warnings, he had been for weeks surrounded by so many hints of danger, that he wanted the relief of some reality, of something tangible that he could meet. 'It would have cleared the air for a couple of hours at least, if you know what I mean,' he said to me. 'Jove! I had been living for days with a stone on my chest.' Now at last he had thought he would get hold of something, and—nothing! Not a trace, not a sign of anybody. He had raised his weapon as the door flew open, but now his arm fell. 'Fire! Defend yourself,' the girl outside cried in an agonising voice. She, being in the dark and with her arm thrust in to the shoulder through the small hole, couldn't see what was going on, and she dared not withdraw the torch now to run round. 'There's nobody here!' yelled Jim contemptuously; but his impulse to burst into a resentful, exasperated laugh died without a sound: he had perceived in the very act of turning away that he was exchanging glances with a pair of eyes in the heap of mats. He saw a shifting gleam of whites. 'Come out!' he cried in a fury, a little doubtful, and a dark-faced head, a head without a body, shaped itself in the rubbish— a strangely detached head, that looked at him with a steady scowl. Next moment the whole mound stirred, and with a low grunt a man emerged swiftly, and bounded towards Jim. Behind him the mats as it were jumped and flew, his right arm was raised with a crooked elbow, and the dull blade of a kriss protruded from his fist held off, a little above his head. A cloth wound tight round his loins seemed dazzlingly white on his bronze skin; his naked body glistened as if wet.

"Jim noted all this. He told me he was experiencing a feeling of unutterable relief, of vengeful elation. He held his shot, he says, deliberately. He held it for the tenth part of a second, for three strides of the man—an unconscionable time. He held it for the pleasure of saying to himself, That's a dead man! He was absolutely positive and certain. He let him come on because it did not matter. A dead man, anyhow. He noticed the dilated nostrils, the wide eyes, the intent, eager stillness of the face, and then he fired.

"The explosion in that confined space was stunning. He stepped back a pace. He saw the man jerk his head up, fling his arms forward, and drop the kriss. He ascertained afterwards that he had shot him through the mouth, a little upwards, the bullet coming out high at the back of the skull. With the impetus of his rush the man drove straight on, his face suddenly gaping disfigured, with his hands open before him gropingly, as though blinded, and landed with terrific violence on his forehead, just short of Jim's bare toes. Jim says he didn't lose the smallest detail of all this. He found himself calm, appeased, without rancour, without uneasiness, as if the death of that man had atoned for everything. The place was getting very full of sooty smoke from the torch, in which the unswaying flame burned blood-red without a flicker. He walked in resolutely, striding over the dead body, and covered with his revolver another naked figure outlined vaguely at the other end. As he was about to pull the trigger, the man threw away with force a short, heavy spear, and squatted submissively on his hams, his back to the wall and his clasped hands between his legs. 'You want your life?' Jim said. The other made no sound. 'How many more of you?' asked Jim again. 'Two more, Tuan,' said the man very softly, looking with big, fascinated eyes into the muzzle of the revolver. Accordingly, two more crawled from under the mats, holding out ostentatiously their empty hands."

Chapter Thirty-Two

"Jim took up an advantageous position and shepherded them out in a bunch through the doorway: all that time the torch had remained vertical in the grip of a little hand, without so much as a tremble. The three men obeyed him, perfectly mute, moving automatically. He ranged them in a row. 'Link arms!' he ordered. They did so. 'The first who withdraws his arms or turns his head is a dead man,' he said. 'March!' They stepped out together rigidly; he followed, and at the side the girl, in a trailing white gown, her black hair falling as low as her waist, bore the light. Erect and swaying, she seemed to glide without touching the earth; the only sound was the silky swish and rustle of the long grass. 'Stop!' cried Jim.

"The river-bank was steep; a great freshness ascended, the light fell on the edge of smooth, dark water frothing without a ripple; right and left the shapes of the houses ran together below the sharp outlines of the roofs. 'Take my greetings to Sherif Ali—till I come myself,' said Jim. Not one head of the three budged. 'Jump!' he thundered. The three splashes made one splash, a shower flew up, black heads bobbed convulsively, and disappeared; but a great blowing and spluttering went on, growing faint, for they were diving industriously, in great fear of a parting shot. Jim turned to the girl, who had been a silent and attentive observer. His heart seemed suddenly to grow too big for his breast and choke him in the hollow of his throat. This probably made him speechless for so long, and after returning his gaze, she flung the burning torch with a wide sweep of the arm into the river. The ruddy, fiery glare, taking a long flight through the night, sank with a vicious hiss, and the calm, soft starlight descended upon them, unchecked.

"He did not tell me what it was he said when at last he recovered his voice. I don't suppose he could be very eloquent. The world was still, the night breathed on them, one of those nights that seem created for the sheltering of tenderness, and there are moments when our souls, as if freed from their dark envelope, glow with an exquisite sensibility that makes certain silences more lucid than speeches. As to the girl, he told me, 'She broke down a bit. Excitement—don't you know. Reaction. Deucedly tired she must have been—and all that kind of thing. And—and—hang it all—she was fond of me, don't you see. . . . I, too . . . didn't know, of course . . . never entered my head. . . .'

"Then he got up and began to walk about in some agitation. 'I—I love her dearly. More than I can tell. Of course one cannot tell. You take a different view of your actions when you come to understand, when you are *made* to understand every day that your existence is necessary—you see, absolutely necessary—to another person. I am made to feel that. Wonderful! But only try to think what her life has been. It is too extravagantly awful! Isn't it? And me finding her here like this—as you may go out for a stroll and come suddenly upon somebody drowning in a lonely, dark place. Jove! No time to lose. Well, it is a trust, too . . . I believe I am equal to it. . . .'

"I must tell you the girl had left us to ourselves some time before. He slapped his chest. 'Yes! I feel that, but I believe I am equal to all my luck!' He had the gift of finding a special meaning in everything that happened to him. This was the view he took of his love affair; it was idyllic, a little solemn, and also true, since his belief had all the unshakable seriousness of youth. Some time after, on another occasion, he said to me, 'I've been only two years here, and now, upon my word, I can't conceive being able to live anywhere else. The very thought of the world outside is enough to give me a fright; because, don't you see,' he continued, with downcast eyes watching the action of his boot busied in squashing thoroughly a tiny bit of dried mud (we were strolling on the riverbank)—'because I have not forgotten why I came here. Not yet!'

"I refrained from looking at him, but I think I heard a short sigh; we took a turn or two in silence. 'Upon my soul and conscience,' he began again, 'if such a thing can be forgotten, then I think I have a right to dismiss it from my mind. Ask any man here' . . . his voice changed. 'Is it not strange,' he went on in a gentle, almost yearning tone, 'that all these people, all these people who would do anything for me, can never be made to understand? Never! If you disbelieve me I could not call them up. It seems hard, somehow. I am stupid, am I not? What more can I want? If you ask them who is brave—who is true—who is just—who is it they would trust with their lives?—they would say, Tuan Jim. And yet they can never know the real, real truth. . . .'

"That's what he said to me on my last day with him. I did not let a murmur escape me: I felt he was going to say more, and come no nearer to the root of the matter. The sun, whose concentrated glare dwarfs the earth into a restless mote of dust, had sunk behind the forest, and the diffused light from an opal sky seemed to cast upon a world without shadows and without brilliance the illusion of a calm and pensive greatness. I don't know why, listening to him, I should have noted so distinctly the gradual darkening of the river, of the air; the irresistible slow work of the night settling silently on all the visible forms, effacing the outlines, burying the shapes deeper and deeper, like a steady fall of impalpable black dust.

" 'Jove!' he began abruptly, 'there are days when a fellow is too absurd for anything; only I know I can tell you what I like. I talk about being done with it—with the bally thing at the back of my head. . . . Forgetting . . . Hang me if I know! I can think of it quietly. After all, what has it proved? Nothing. I suppose you don't think so. . . .'

"I made a protesting murmur.

" 'No matter,' he said. 'I am satisfied . . . nearly. I've got to look only at the face of the first man that comes along to regain my confidence. They can't be made to understand what is going on in me. What of that? Come! I haven't done so badly.'

" 'Not so badly,' I said.

" 'But all the same, you wouldn't like to have me aboard your own ship—hey?'

" 'Confound you!' I cried. 'Stop this.'

" 'Aha! You see,' he cried, crowing, as it were, over me placidly. 'Only,' he went on, 'you just try to tell this to any of them here. They would think you a fool, a liar, or worse. And so I can stand it. I've done a thing or two for them, but this is what they have done for me.'

" 'My dear chap,' I cried, 'you shall always remain for them an insoluble mystery.' Thereupon we were silent.

" 'Mystery,' he repeated, before looking up. 'Well, then let me always remain here.'

"After the sun had set, the darkness seemed to drive upon us, borne in every faint puff of the breeze. In the middle of a hedged path I saw the arrested, gaunt, watchful, and apparently one-legged silhouette of Tamb' Itam; and across the dusky space my eye detected something white moving to and fro behind the supports of the roof. As soon as Jim, with Tamb' Itam at his heels, had started upon his evening rounds, I went up to the house alone, and, unexpectedly, found myself waylaid by the girl, who had been clearly waiting for this opportunity.

"It is hard to tell you what it was precisely she wanted to wrest from me. Obviously it would be something very simple—the simplest impossibility in the world; as, for instance, the exact description of the form of a cloud. She wanted an assurance, a statement, a promise, an explanation—I don't know how to call it: the thing has no name. It was dark under the projecting roof, and all I could see were the flowing lines of her gown, the pale, small oval of her face, with the white flash of her teeth, and, turned towards me, the big, sombre orbits of her eyes, where there seemed to be a faint stir, such as you may fancy you can detect when you plunge your gaze to the bottom of an immensely deep well. What is it that moves there? you ask yourself. Is it a blind monster or only a lost gleam from the universe? It occurred to me—don't laugh—that all things being dissimilar, she was more inscrutable in her childish ignorance than the Sphinx propounding childish riddles to wayfarers. She had been carried off to Patusan before her eyes were open. She had grown up there; she had seen nothing, she had known nothing, she had no conception of anything. I ask myself whether she were sure that anything else existed. What notions she may have formed of the outside world is to me inconceivable; all that she knew of its inhabitants were a betrayed woman and a sinister pantaloon.[8] Her lover also came to her from there, gifted with irresistible seductions; but what would become of her if he should return to these inconceivable regions that seemed always to claim back their own? Her mother had warned her of this with tears, before she died. . . .

"She had caught hold of my arm firmly, and as soon as I had stopped she had withdrawn her hand in haste. She was audacious and shrinking. She feared nothing, but she was checked by the profound incertitude and the extreme strangeness—a brave person groping in the dark. I belonged to this Unknown that might claim Jim for its own at any moment. I was, as it were, in the secret of its nature and of its intentions—the confidant of a threatening mystery—armed with its power, perhaps! I believe she supposed I could with a word whisk Jim away out of her very arms; it is my sober conviction she went through agonies of apprehension during my long talks with Jim; through a real and intolerable anguish that might have conceivably driven her into plotting my murder, had the fierceness of her soul been equal to the tremendous situation it had created. This is my impression, and it is all I can give you: the whole thing dawned gradually upon me, and as it got clearer and clearer I was overwhelmed by a slow, incredulous amazement. She made me believe her; but there is no word that on my lips could render the effect of the headlong and vehement whisper, of the soft, passionate tones, of the sudden breathless pause and the appealing movement of the white arms extended swiftly. They fell; the ghostly figure swayed like a slender tree in the wind, the pale oval of the face drooped; it was impossible to distinguish her features, the darkness of the eyes was unfathomable; two wide

8. A pantomime character, a buffoon, usually a vicious old dotard, the butt and accomplice of the clown.

sleeves uprose in the dark like unfolding wings, and she stood silent, holding her head in her hands."

Chapter Thirty-Three

"I was immensely touched: her youth, her ignorance, her pretty beauty, which had the simple charm and the delicate vigour of a wild flower, her pathetic pleading, her helplessness, appealed to me with almost the strength of her own unreasonable and natural fear. She feared the unknown as we all do, and her ignorance made the unknown infinitely vast. I stood for it, for myself, for you fellows, for all the world that neither cared for Jim nor needed him in the least. I would have been ready enough to answer for the indifference of the teeming earth but for the reflection that he, too, belonged to this mysterious unknown of her fears, and that, however much I stood for, I did not stand for him. This made me hesitate. A murmur of hopeless pain unsealed my lips. I began by protesting that I at least had come with no intention to take Jim away.

"Why did I come, then? After a slight movement she was as still as a marble statue in the night. I tried to explain briefly: friendship, business; if I had any wish in the matter it was rather to see him stay. . . . 'They always leave us,' she murmured. The breath of sad wisdom from the grave which her piety wreathed with flowers seemed to pass in a faint sigh. . . . Nothing, I said, could separate Jim from her.

"It is my firm conviction now; it was my conviction at the time; it was the only possible conclusion from the facts of the case. It was not made more certain by her whispering in a tone in which one speaks to oneself, 'He swore this to me.' 'Did you ask him?' I said.

"She made a step nearer. 'No. Never!' She had asked him only to go away. It was that night on the river-bank, after he had killed the man—after she had flung the torch in the water because he was looking at her so. There was too much light, and the danger was over then—for a little time—for a little time. He said then he would not abandon her to Cornelius. She had insisted. She wanted him to leave her. He said that he could not—that it was impossible. He trembled while he said this. She had felt him tremble. . . . One does not require much imagination to see the scene, almost to hear their whispers. She was afraid for him, too. I believe that then she saw in him only a predestined victim of dangers which she understood better than himself. Though by nothing but his mere presence he had mastered her heart, had filled all her thoughts, and had possessed himself of all her affections, she underestimated his chances of success. It is obvious that at about that time everybody was inclined to underestimate his chances. Strictly speaking, he didn't seem to have any. I know this was Cornelius's view. He confessed that much to me in extenuation of the shady part he had played in Sherif Ali's plot to do away with the infidel. Even Sherif Ali himself, as it seems certain now, had nothing but contempt for the white man. Jim was to be murdered mainly on religious gounds, I believe. A simple act of piety (and so far infinitely meritorious), but otherwise without much importance. In the last part of this opinion Cornelius concurred. 'Honourable sir,' he argued abjectly on the only occasion he managed to have me to himself—'honourable sir, how was I to know? Who was he? What could he do to make people believe him? What did Mr. Stein mean sending a boy like that to talk big to an old servant? I was ready to save him for eighty dollars. Only eighty dollars. Why didn't the fool go? Was I to get stabbed myself for the sake of a stranger?' He grovelled in spirit before me, with his body doubled up insinuatingly and his hands hovering about my knees, as though he were ready to embrace my legs. 'What's eighty dollars? An insignificant sum to give to a defenceless old man ruined for life by a deceased she-devil.' Here he wept. But I anticipate. I didn't that night chance upon Cornelius till I had had it out with the girl.

"She was unselfish when she urged Jim to leave her, and even to leave the country. It was his danger that was foremost in her thoughts—even if she wanted to save herself, too—perhaps unconsciously: but then look at the warning she had, look at the lesson that could be drawn from every moment of the recently ended life in which all her memories were centred. She fell at his feet—she told me so—there by the river, in the discreet light of stars which showed nothing except great masses of silent shadows, indefinite open spaces, and trembling faintly upon the broad stream made it appear as wide as the sea. He had lifted her up. He lifted her up, and then she would struggle no more. Of course not. Strong arms, a tender voice, a stalwart shoulder to rest her poor, lonely little head upon. The need—the infinite need—of all this for the aching heart, for the bewildered mind;—the promptings of youth—the necessity of the moment. What would you have? One understands —unless one is incapable of understanding anything under the sun. And so she was content to be lifted up—and held. 'You know —Jove! this is serious—no nonsense in it!' as Jim had whispered hurriedly with a troubled, concerned face on the threshold of his house. I don't know so much about nonsense, but there was nothing light-hearted in their romance: they came together under the shadow of a life's disaster, like knight and maiden meeting to exchange vows amongst haunted ruins. The starlight was good enough for that story, a light so faint and remote that it cannot resolve shadows into shapes, and show the other shore of a stream. I did look upon the stream that night and from the very place; it rolled silent and as black as Styx: [9] the next day I went away, but I am not likely to forget what it was she wanted to be saved from when she entreated him to leave her while there was time. She told me what it was, calmed—she was now too passionately interested for mere excitement—in a voice as quiet in the obscurity as her white half-lost figure. She told me, 'I didn't want to die weeping.' I thought I had not heard aright.

" 'You did not want to die weeping?' I repeated after her. 'Like my mother,' she added readily. The outlines of her white shape did not stir in the least. 'My mother had wept bitterly before she died,' she explained. An inconceivable calmness seemed to have risen from the ground around us, imperceptibly, like the still rise of a flood in the night, obliterating the familiar landmarks of emotions. There came upon me, as though I had felt myself losing my footing in the midst of waters, a sudden dread, the dread of the unknown depths. She went on explaining that, during the last moments, being alone with her mother, she had to leave the side of the couch to go and set her back against the door, in order to keep Cornelius out. He desired to get in, and kept on drumming with both fists, only desisting now and again to shout huskily, 'Let me in! Let me in! Let me in!' In a far corner upon a few mats the moribund woman, already speechless and unable to lift her arm, rolled her head over, and with a feeble movement of her hand seemed to command —'No! No!' and the obedient daughter, setting her shoulders with all her strength against the door, was looking on. 'The tears fell from her eyes—and then she died,' concluded the girl in an imperturbable monotone, which more than anything else, more than the white statuesque immobility of her person, more than mere words could do, troubled my mind profoundly with the passive, irremediable horror of the scene. It had the power to drive me out of my conception of existence, out of that shelter each of us makes for himself to creep under in moments of danger, as a tortoise withdraws within its shell. For a moment I had a view of a world that seemed to wear a vast and dismal aspect of disorder, while, in truth, thanks to our unwearied efforts, it is as sunny an arrangement of small conveniences as the mind of man can conceive. But still—it was only a moment: I went back into my shell directly. One *must*—don't you know?—though I seemed to have lost all my words in the chaos of dark thoughts I had contemplated for a second or two beyond the pale. These came back, too, very soon, for words also belong to the sheltering conception of light and order which is our refuge. I had them ready at my disposal before she

9. A river of Hades.

whispered softly, 'He swore he would never leave me, when we stood there alone! He swore to me!' . . . 'And is it possible that you—you!—do not believe him?' I asked, sincerely reproachful, genuinely shocked. Why couldn't she believe? Wherefore this craving for incertitude, this clinging to fear, as if incertitude and fear had been the safeguards of her love. It was monstrous. She should have made for herself a shelter of inexpugnable peace out of that honest affection. She had not the knowledge—not the skill perhaps. The night had come on apace; it had grown pitch-dark where we were, so that without stirring she had faded like the intangible form of a wistful and perverse spirit. And suddenly I heard her quiet whisper again, 'Other men had sworn the same thing.' It was like a meditative comment on some thoughts full of sadness, of awe. And she added, still lower if possible, 'My father did.' She paused the time to draw an inaudible breath. 'Her father, too. . . .' These were the things she knew! At once I said, 'Ah! but he is not like that.' This, it seemed, she did not intend to dispute; but after a time the strange, still whisper wandering dreamily in the air stole into my ears. 'Why is he different? Is he better? Is he . . .' 'Upon my word of honour,' I broke in, 'I believe he is.' We subdued our tones to a mysterious pitch. Amongst the huts of Jim's workmen (they were mostly liberated slaves from the Sherif's stockade) somebody started a shrill, drawling song. Across the river a big fire (at Doramin's, I think) made a glowing ball, completely isolated in the night. 'Is he more true?' she murmured. 'Yes,' I said. 'More true than any other man?' she repeated in lingering accents. 'Nobody here,' I said, 'would dream of doubting his word—nobody would dare—except you.'

"I think she made a movement at this. 'More brave?' she went on in a changed tone. 'Fear will never drive him away from you,' I said a little nervously. The song stopped short on a shrill note, and was succeeded by several voices talking in the distance. Jim's voice, too. I was struck by her silence. 'What has he been telling you? He has been telling you something?' I asked. There was no answer. 'What is it he told you?' I insisted.

" 'Do you think I can tell you? How am I to know? How am I to understand?' she cried at last. There was a stir. I believe she was wringing her hands. 'There is something he can never forget.'

" 'So much the better for you,' I said gloomily.

" 'What is it? What is it?' She put an extraordinary force of appeal into her supplicating tone. 'He says he had been afraid. How can I believe this? Am I a mad woman to believe this? You all remember something! You all go back to it. What is it? You tell me! What is this thing? Is it alive?—is it dead? I hate it. It is cruel. Has it got a face and a voice—this calamity? Will he see it?—will he hear it. In his sleep perhaps when he cannot see me—and then arise and go. Ah! I shall never forgive him. My mother had forgiven —but I, never! Will it be a sign—a call?'

"It was a wonderful experience. She mistrusted his very slumbers—and she seemed to think I could tell her why! Thus a poor mortal seduced by the charm of an apparition might have tried to wring from another ghost the tremendous secret of the claim the other world holds over a disembodied soul astray amongst the passions of this earth. The very ground on which I stood seemed to melt under my feet. And it was so simple, too; but if the spirits evoked by our fears and our unrest have ever to vouch for each other's constancy before the forlorn magicians that we are, then I— I alone of us dwellers in the flesh—have shuddered in the hopeless chill of such a task. A sign, a call! How telling in its expression was her ignorance! A few words! How she came to know them, how she came to pronounce them, I can't imagine. Women find their inspiration in the stress of moments that for us are merely awful, absurd, or futile. To discover that she had a voice at all was enough to strike awe into the heart. Had a spurned stone cried out in pain it could not have appeared a greater and more pitiful miracle. These few sounds wandering in the dark had made their two benighted lives tragic to my mind. It was impossible to make her understand. I chafed silently at my impotence. And Jim, too—poor devil! Who would need him? Who would remember him? He had what he wanted. His very existence probably had been forgotten by this time. They had mastered their fates. They were tragic.

"Her immobility before me was clearly expectant, and my part was to speak for my brother from the realm of forgetful shades. I was deeply moved at my responsibility and at her distress. I would have given anything for the power to soothe her frail soul, tormenting itself in its invincible ignorance like a small bird beating about the cruel wires of a cage. Nothing easier than to say, Have no fear! Nothing more difficult. How does one kill fear, I wonder? How do you shoot a spectre through the heart, slash off its spectral head, take it by its spectral throat? It is an enterprise you rush into while you dream, and are glad to make your escape with wet hair and every limb shaking. The bullet is not run, the blade not forged, the man not born; even the winged words of truth drop at your feet like lumps of lead. You require for such a desperate encounter an enchanted and poisoned shaft dipped in a lie too subtle to be found on earth. An enterprise for a dream, my masters!

"I began my exorcism with a heavy heart, with a sort of sullen anger in it, too. Jim's voice, suddenly raised with a stern intonation, carried across the courtyard, reproving the carelessness of some dumb sinner by the riverside. Nothing—I said, speaking in a distinct murmur—there could be nothing in that unknown world she fancied so eager to rob her of her happiness, there was nothing, neither living nor dead, there was no face, no voice, no power, that could tear Jim from her side. I drew breath, and she whispered softly, 'He told me so.' 'He told you the truth,' I said. 'Nothing,' she sighed out, and abruptly turned upon me with a barely audible intensity of tone: 'Why did you come to us from out there? He speaks of you too often. You make me afraid. Do you—do you want him?' A sort of stealthy fierceness had crept into our hurried mutters. 'I shall never come again,' I said bitterly. 'And I don't want him. No one wants him.' 'No one,' she repeated in a tone of doubt. 'No one,' I affirmed, feeling myself swayed by some strange excitement. 'You think him strong, wise, courageous, great—why not believe him to be true, too? I shall go to-morrow—and that is the end. You shall never be troubled by a voice from there again. This world you don't know is too big to miss him. You understand? Too big. You've got his heart in your hand. You must feel that. You must know that.' 'Yes, I know that,' she breathed out, hard and still, as a statue might whisper.

"I felt I had done nothing. And what is it that I had wished to do? I am not sure now. At the time I was animated by an inexplicable ardour, as if before some great and necessary task—the influence of the moment upon my mental and emotional state. There are in all our lives such moments, such influences, coming from the outside, as it were, irresistible, incomprehensible—as if brought about by the mysterious conjunctions of the planets. She owned, as I had put it to her, his heart. She had that and everything else—if she could only believe it. What I had to tell her was that in the whole world there was no one who ever would need his heart, his mind, his hand. It was a common fate, and yet it seemed an awful thing to say of any man. She listened without a word, and her stillness now was like the protest of an invincible unbelief. What need she care for the world beyond the forests? I asked. From all the multitudes that peopled the vastness of that unknown there would come, I assured her, as long as he lived, neither a call nor a sign for him. Never. I was carried away. Never! Never! I remember with wonder the sort of dogged fierceness I displayed. I had the illusion of having got the spectre by the throat at last. Indeed the whole real thing has left behind the detailed and amazing impression of a dream. Why should she fear? She knew him to be strong, true, wise, brave. He was all that. Certainly. He was more. He was great —invincible—and the world did not want him, it had forgotten him, it would not even know him.

"I stopped; the silence over Patusan was profound, and the feeble, dry sound of a paddle striking the side of a canoe somewhere in the middle of the river seemed to make it infinite. 'Why?' she murmured. I felt that sort of rage one feels during a hard tussle. The spectre was trying to slip out of my grasp. 'Why?' she repeated louder; 'tell me!' And as I remained confounded, she stamped with her foot like a spoilt child. 'Why? Speak.' 'You want to know?' I asked in a fury. 'Yes!' she cried. 'Because he is not good enough,' I said brutally. During the moment's pause I noticed the fire on the other shore blaze up, dilating the circle of its glow like an amazed stare, and contract suddenly to a red pin-point. I only knew how close to me she had been when I felt the clutch of her fingers on my forearm. Without raising her voice, she threw into it an infinity of scathing contempt, bitterness, and despair.

" 'This is the very thing he said. . . . You lie!'

"The last two words she cried at me in the native dialect. 'Hear me out!' I entreated. She caught her breath tremulously, flung my arm away. 'Nobody, nobody is good enough,' I began with the greatest earnestness. I could hear the sobbing labour of her breath frightfully quickened. I hung my head. What was the use? Footsteps were approaching; I slipped away without another word. . . .''

Chapter Thirty-Four

Marlow swung his legs out, got up quickly, and staggered a little, as though he had been set down after a rush through space. He leaned his back against the balustrade and faced a disordered array of long cane chairs. The bodies prone in them seemed startled out of their torpor by his movement. One or two sat up as if alarmed; here and there a cigar glowed yet; Marlow looked at them all with the eyes of a man returning from the excessive remoteness of a dream. A throat was cleared; a calm voice encouraged negligently, "Well."

"Nothing," said Marlow with a slight start. "He had told her—that's all. She did not believe him—nothing more. As to myself, I do not know whether it be just, proper, decent for me to rejoice or to be sorry. For my part, I cannot say what I believed—indeed I don't know to this day, and never shall probably. But what did the poor devil believe himself? Truth shall prevail—don't you know, *Magna est veritas et*[1] . . . Yes, when it gets a chance. There is a law, no doubt—and likewise a law regulates your luck in the throwing of dice. It is not Justice the servant of men, but accident, hazard, Fortune—the ally of patient Time—that holds an even and scrupulous balance. Both of us had said the very same thing. Did we both speak the truth—or one of us did—or neither? . . .''

---

1. From the Vulgate Bible: "Magna est veritas et praevalet." (III Esdras 4:41.) The King James translation is: "Great is truth, and mighty above all things."

Marlow paused, crossed his arms on his breast, and in a changed tone:

"She said we lied. Poor soul! Well—let's leave it to Chance, whose ally is Time, that cannot be hurried, and whose enemy is Death, that will not wait. I had retreated—a little cowed, I must own. I had tried a fall with fear itself and got thrown—of course. I had only succeeded in adding to her anguish the hint of some mysterious collusion, of an inexplicable and incomprehensible conspiracy to keep her for ever in the dark. And it had come easily, naturally, unavoidably, by his act, by her own act! It was as though I had been shown the working of the implacable destiny of which we are the victims—and the tools. It was appalling to think of the girl whom I had left standing there motionless; Jim's footsteps had a fateful sound as he tramped by, without seeing me, in his heavy laced boots. 'What? No lights!' he said in a loud, surprised voice. 'What are you doing in the dark—you two?' Next moment he caught sight of her, I suppose. 'Hallo, girl!' he cried cheerily. 'Hallo, boy!' she answered at once, with amazing pluck.

"This was their usual greeting to each other, and the bit of swagger she would put into her rather high but sweet voice was very droll, pretty, and childlike. It delighted Jim greatly. This was the last occasion on which I heard them exchange this familiar hail, and it struck a chill into my heart. There was the high, sweet voice, the pretty effort, the swagger; but it all seemed to die out prematurely, and the playful call sounded like a moan. It was too confoundedly awful. 'What have you done with Marlow?' Jim was asking; and then, 'Gone down—has he? Funny I didn't meet him. . . . You there, Marlow?'

"I didn't answer. I wasn't going in—not yet at any rate. I really couldn't. While he was calling me I was engaged in making my escape through a little gate leading out upon a stretch of newly cleared ground. No; I couldn't face them yet. I walked hastily with lowered head along a trodden path. The ground rose gently, the few big trees had been felled, the undergrowth had been cut down and the grass fired. He had a mind to try a coffee-plantation there. The big hill, rearing its double summit coal-black in the clear, yellow glow of the rising moon, seemed to cast its shadow upon the ground prepared for that experiment. He was going to try ever so many experiments; I had admired his energy, his enterprise, and his shrewdness. Nothing on earth seemed less real now than his plans, his energy, and his enthusiasm; and raising my eyes, I saw part of the moon glittering through the bushes at the bottom of the chasm. For a moment it looked as though the smooth disc, falling from its place in the sky upon the earth, had rolled to the bottom of that precipice; its ascending movement was like a leisurely rebound; it disengaged itself from the tangle of twigs; the bare, contorted limb of some tree, growing on the slope, made a black crack right across its face. It threw its level rays afar as if from a cavern, and in this mournful eclipse-like light the stumps of felled trees uprose very dark, the heavy shadows fell at my feet on all sides, my own moving shadow, and across my path the shadow of the solitary grave perpetually garlanded with flowers. In the darkened moonlight the interlaced blossoms took on shapes foreign to one's memory and colours indefinable to the eye, as though they had been special flowers gathered by no man, grown not in this world, and destined for the use of the dead alone. Their powerful scent hung in the warm air, making it thick and heavy like the fumes of incense. The lumps of white coral shone round the dark mound like a chaplet of bleached skulls, and everything around was so quiet that when I stood still all sound and all movements in the world seemed to come to an end.

"It was a great peace, as if the earth had been one grave, and for a time I stood there thinking mostly of the living who, buried in remote places out of the knowledge of mankind, still are fated to share in its tragic or grotesque miseries. In its noble struggles, too —who knows? The human heart is vast enough to contain all the world. It is valiant crough to bear the burden, but where is the courage that would cast it off?

"I suppose I must have fallen into a sentimental mood; I only know that I stood there long enough for the sense of utter solitude to get hold of me so completely that all I had lately seen, all I had heard, and the very human speech itself, seemed to have passed away out of existence, living only for a while longer in my memory, as though I had been the last of mankind. It was a strange and melancholy illusion, evolved half consciously like all our illusions, which I suspect only to be visions of remote, unattainable truth, seen dimly. This was, indeed, one of the lost, forgotten, unknown places of the earth; I had looked under its obscure surface; and I felt that when to-morrow I had left it for ever, it would slip out of existence, to live only in my memory till I myself passed into oblivion. I have that feeling about me now; perhaps it is that feeling which has incited me to tell you the story, to try to hand over to you, as it were, its very existence, its reality—the truth disclosed in a moment of illusion.

"Cornelius broke upon it. He bolted out, vermin-like, from the long grass growing in a depression of the ground. I believe his house was rotting somewhere near by, though I've never seen it, not having been far enough in that direction. He ran towards me upon the path; his feet, shod in dirty white shoes, twinkled on the dark earth; he pulled himself up, and began to whine and cringe under a tall, stove-pipe hat. His dried-up little carcass was swallowed up, totally lost, in a suit of black broadcloth. That was his costume for holidays and ceremonies, and it reminded me that this was the fourth Sunday I had spent in Patusan. All the time of my stay I had been vaguely aware of his desire to confide in me, if he only could get me all to himself. He hung about with an eager, craving look on his sour, yellow little face; but his timidity had kept him back as much as my natural reluctance to have anything to do with such an unsavoury creature. He would have succeeded, nevertheless, had he not been so ready to slink off as soon as you looked at him. He would slink off before Jim's severe gaze, before my own, which I tried to make indifferent, even before Tamb' Itam's surly, superior glance. He was perpetually slinking away; whenever seen he was seen moving off deviously, his face over his shoulder, with either a mistrustful snarl or a woe-begone, piteous, mute aspect; but no assumed expression could conceal this innate, irremediable abjectness of his nature, any more than an arrangement of clothing can conceal some monstrous deformity of the body.

"I don't know whether it was the demoralisation of my utter defeat in my encounter with a spectre of fear less than an hour ago, but I let him capture me without even a show of resistance. I was doomed to be the recipient of confidences, and to be confronted with unanswerable questions. It was trying; but the contempt, the unreasoned contempt, the man's appearance provoked, made it easier to bear. He couldn't possibly matter. Nothing mattered, since I had made up my mind that Jim, for whom alone I cared, had at last mastered his fate. He had told me he was satisfied . . . nearly. This is going further than most of us dare. I—who have the right to think myself good enough—dare not. Neither does any of you here, I suppose? . . ."

Marlow paused, as if expecting an answer. Nobody spoke.

"Quite right," he began again. "Let no soul know, since the truth can be wrung out of us only by some cruel, little, awful catastrophe. But he is one of us, and he could say he was satisfied . . . nearly. Just fancy this! Nearly satisfied. One could almost envy him his catastrophe. Nearly satisfied. After this nothing could matter. It did not matter who suspected him, who trusted him, who loved him, who hated him—especially as it was Cornelius who hated him.

"Yet after all, this was a kind of recognition. You shall judge of a man by his foes as well as by his friends, and this enemy of Jim was such as no decent man would be ashamed to own, without, however, making too much of him. This was the view Jim took, and in which I shared; but Jim disregarded him on general grounds. 'My dear

Marlow,' he said, 'I feel that if I go straight nothing can touch me. Indeed I do. Now you have been long enough here to have a good look round—and, frankly, don't you think I am pretty safe? It all depends upon me, and, by Jove! I have lots of confidence in myself. The worst thing he could do would be to kill me, I suppose. I don't think for a moment he would. He couldn't, you know—not if I were myself to hand him a loaded rifle for the purpose, and then turn my back on him. That's the sort of thing he is. And suppose he would—suppose he could? Well—what of that? I didn't come here flying for my life—did I? I came here to set my back against the wall, and I am going to stay here . . .'

" 'Till you are *quite* satisfied,' I struck in.

"We were sitting at the time under the roof in the stern of the boat; twenty paddles flashed like one, ten on a side, striking the water with a single splash, while behind our backs Tamb' Itam dipped silently right and left, and stared right down the river, attentive to keep the long canoe in the greatest strength of the current. Jim bowed his head, and our last talk seemd to flicker out for good. He was seeing me off as far as the mouth of the river. The schooner had left the day before, working down and drifting on the ebb, while I had prolonged my stay overnight. And now he was seeing me off.

"Jim had been a little angry with me for mentioning Cornelius at all. I had not, in truth, said much. The man was too insignificant to be dangerous, though he was as full of hate as he could hold. He had called me 'honourable sir' at every second sentence, and had whined at my elbow as he followed me from the grave of his 'late wife' to the gate of Jim's compound. He declared himself the most unhappy of men, a victim, crushed like a worm; he entreated me to look at him. I wouldn't turn my head to do so; but I could see out of the corner of my eye his obsequious shadow gliding after mine, while the moon, suspended on our right hand, seemed to gloat serenely upon the spectacle. He tried to explain—as I've told you—his share in the events of the memorable night. It was a matter of expediency. How could he know who was going to get the upper hand? 'I would have saved him, honourable sir! I would have saved him for eighty dollars,' he protested in dulcet tones, keeping a pace behind me. 'He has saved himself,' I said, 'and he has forgiven you.' I heard a sort of tittering, and turned upon him; at once he appeared ready to take to his heels. 'What are you laughing at?' I asked, standing still. 'Don't be deceived, honourable sir!' he shrieked, seemingly losing all control over his feelings. 'He save himself! He knows nothing, honourable sir—nothing whatever. Who is he? What does he want here—the big thief? What does he want here? He throws dust into everybody's eyes; he throws dust into your eyes, honourable sir; but he can't throw dust into my eyes. He is a big fool, honourable sir.' I laughed contemptuously, and, turning on my heel, began to walk on again. He ran up to my elbow and whispered forcibly, 'He's no more than a little child here—like a little child—a little child.' Of course I didn't take the slightest notice, and seeing the time pressed, because we were approaching the bamboo fence that glittered over the blackened ground of the clearing, he came to the point. He commenced by being abjectly lachrymose. His great misfortunes had affected his head. He hoped I would kindly forget what nothing but his troubles made him say. He didn't mean anything by it; only the honourable sir did not know what it was to be ruined, broken down, trampled upon. After this introduction he approached the matter near his heart, but in such a rambling, ejaculatory, craven fashion, that for a long time I couldn't make out what he was driving at. He wanted me to intercede with Jim in his favour. It seemed, too, to be some sort of money affair. I heard time and again the words, 'Moderate provision—suitable present.' He seemed to be claiming value for something, and he even went the length of saying with some warmth that life was not worth having if a man were to be robbed of everything. I did not breathe a word, of course, but neither did I stop my ears. The gist of the affair, which became clear to me gradually, was in this, that he regarded himself as entitled to some money in exchange for the girl. He had brought her up. Somebody else's child. Great trouble and pains—old man now—suitable present. If the honourable sir would say a word. . . . I stood still to look at him with curiosity, and fearful lest I should think him extortionate, I suppose, he hastily brought himself to make a concession. In consideration of a 'suitable present' given at once, he would, he declared, be willing to undertake the charge of the girl, 'without any other provision—when the time came for the gentleman to go home.' His little yellow face, all crumpled as though it had been squeezed together, expressed the most anxious, eager avarice. His voice whined coaxingly, 'No more trouble—natural guardian—a sum of money. . . .'

"I stood there and marvelled. That kind of thing, with him, was evidently a vocation. I discovered suddenly in his cringing attitude a sort of assurance, as though he had been all his life dealing in certitudes. He must have thought I was dispassionately considering his proposal, because he became as sweet as honey. 'Every gentleman made a provision when the time came to go home,' he began insinuatingly. I slammed the little gate. 'In this case, Mr. Cornelius,' I said, 'the time will never come.' He took a few seconds to gather this in. 'What!' he fairly squealed. 'Why,' I continued from my side of the gate, 'haven't you heard him say so himself? He will never

go home.' 'Oh, this is too much!' he shouted. He would not address
me as 'honoured sir' any more. He was very still for a time, and
then without a trace of humility began very low: 'Never go—ah! He
—he—he comes here devil knows from where—comes here—devil
knows why—to trample on me till I die—ah—trample' (he stamped
softly with both feet), 'trample like this—nobody knows why—till
I die. . . .' His voice became quite extinct; he was bothered by a
little cough; he came up close to the fence and told me, dropping
into a confidential and piteous tone, that he would *not* be trampled
upon. 'Patience—patience,' he muttered, striking his breast. I had
done laughing at him, but unexpectedly he treated me to a wild,
cracked burst of it. 'Ha! ha! ha! We shall see! We shall see! What!
Steal from me! Steal from me everything! Everything! Everything!'
His head drooped on one shoulder, his hands were hanging before
him lightly clasped. One would have thought he had cherished the
girl with surpassing love, that his spirit had been crushed and his
heart broken by the most cruel of spoliations. Suddenly he lifted
his head and shot out an infamous word. 'Like her mother—she is
like her deceitful mother. Exactly. In her face, too. In her face.
The devil!' He leaned his forehead against the fence, and in that
position uttered threats and horrible blasphemies in Portuguese in
very weak ejaculations, mingled with miserable plaints and groans,
coming out with a heave of the shoulders as though he had been
overtaken by a deadly fit of sickness. It was an inexpressibly grotesque and vile performance, and I hastened away. He tried to
shout something after me. Some disparagement of Jim, I believe
—not too loud though, we were too near the house. All I heard
distinctly was, 'No more than a little child—a little child.' "

Chapter Thirty-Five

"But next morning, at the first bend of the river shutting off the
houses of Patusan, all this dropped out of my sight bodily, with
its colour, its design, and its meaning, like a picture created by
fancy on a canvas, upon which, after long contemplation, you turn
your back for the last time. It remains in the memory motionless,
unfaded, with its life arrested, in an unchanging light. There are the
ambitions, the fears, the hate, the hopes, and they remain in my
mind just as I had seen them—intense and as if for ever suspended
in their expression. I had turned away from the picture and was
going back to the world where events move, men change, light
flickers, life flows in a clear stream, no matter whether over mud or
over stones. I wasn't going to dive into it; I would have enough
to do to keep my head above the surface. But as to what I was leaving behind, I cannot imagine any alteration. The immense and mag-

nanimous Doramin and his little motherly witch of a wife, gazing together upon the land and nursing secretly their dreams of parental
ambition; Tunku Allang, wizened and greatly perplexed; Dain
Waris, intelligent and brave, with his faith in Jim, with his firm
glance and his ironic friendliness; the girl, absorbed in her frightened, suspicious adoration; Tamb' Itam, surly and faithful; Cornelius, leaning his forehead against the fence under the moonlight
—I am certain of them. They exist as if under an enchanter's
wand. But the figure round which all these are grouped—that one
lives, and I am not certain of him. No magician's wand can immo-
bilise him under my eyes. He is one of us.

"Jim, as I've told you, accompanied me on the first stage of my
journey back to the world he had renounced, and the way at times
seemed to lead through the very heart of untouched wilderness.
The empty reaches sparkled under the high sun; between the high
walls of vegetation the heat drowsed upon the water, and the boat,
impelled vigorously, cut her way through the air that seemed to
have settled dense and warm under the shelter of lofty trees.

"The shadow of the impending separation had already put an
immense space between us, and when we spoke it was with an
effort, as if to force our low voices across a vast and increasing distance. The boat fairly flew; we sweltered side by side in the
stagnant, superheated air; the smell of mud, of marsh, the primeval
smell of fecund earth, seemed to sting our faces; till suddenly at a
bend it was as if a great hand far away had lifted a heavy curtain, had
flung open an immense portal. The light itself seemed to stir, the
sky above our heads widened, a far-off murmur reached our ears, a
freshness enveloped us, filled our lungs, quickened our thoughts,
our blood, our regrets—and, straight ahead, the forests sank down
against the dark blue ridge of the sea.

"I breathed deeply, I revelled in the vastness of the opened
horizon, in the different atmosphere that seemed to vibrate with a
toil of life, with the energy of an impeccable world. This sky and
this sea were open to me. The girl was right—there was a sign, a call
in them—something to which I responded with every fibre of my
being. I let my eyes roam through space, like a man released from
bonds who stretches his cramped limbs, runs, leaps, responds to the
inspiring elation of freedom. 'This is glorious!' I cried, and then I
looked at the sinner by my side. He sat with his head sunk on his
breast and said 'Yes,' without raising his eyes, as if afraid to see writ
large on the clear sky of the offing the reproach of his romantic
conscience.

"I remember the smallest details of that afternoon. We landed
on a bit of white beach. It was backed by a low cliff wooded on the
brow, draped in creepers to the very foot. Below us the plain of the

sea, of a serene and intense blue, stretched with a slight upward tilt to the thread-like horizon drawn at the height of our eyes. Great waves of glitter blew lightly along the pitted dark surface, as swift as feathers chased by the breeze. A chain of islands sat broken and massive facing the wide estuary, displayed in a sheet of pale, glassy water reflecting faithfully the contour of the shore. High in the colourless sunshine a solitary bird, all black, hovered, dropping and soaring above the same spot with a slight rocking motion of the wings. A ragged, sooty bunch of flimsy mat hovels was perched over its own inverted image upon a crooked multitude of high piles the colour of ebony. A tiny black canoe put off from amongst them with two tiny men, all black, who toiled exceedingly, striking down at the pale water: and the canoe seemed to slide painfully on a mirror. This bunch of miserable hovels was the fishing village that boasted of the white lord's especial protection, and the two men crossing over were the old head-man and his son-in-law. They landed and walked up to us on the white sand, lean, dark brown as if dried in smoke, with ashy patches on the skin of their naked shoulders and breasts. Their heads were bound in dirty but carefully folded handkerchiefs, and the old man began at once to state a complaint, voluble, stretching a lank arm, screwing up at Jim his old, bleared eyes confidently. The Rajah's people would not leave them alone; there had been some trouble about a lot of turtles' eggs his people had collected on the islets there—and leaning at arm's-length upon his paddle, he pointed with a brown, skinny hand over the sea. Jim listened for a time without looking up, and at last told him gently to wait. He would hear him by and by. They withdrew obediently to some little distance, and sat on their heels, with their paddles lying before them on the sand; the silvery gleams in their eyes followed our movements patiently; and the immensity of the outspread sea, the stillness of the coast, passing north and south beyond the limits of my vision, made up one colossal Presence watching us four dwarfs isolated on a strip of glistening sand.

" 'The trouble is,' remarked Jim moodily, 'that for generations these beggars of fishermen in that village there had been considered as the Rajah's personal slaves—and the old rip can't get it into his head that . . .'

"He paused. 'That you have changed all that,' I said.

" 'Yes. I've changed all that,' he muttered in a gloomy voice.

" 'You have had your opportunity,' I pursued.

" 'Have I?' he said. 'Well, yes. I suppose so. Yes. I have got back my confidence in myself—a good name—yet sometimes I wish . . . No! I shall hold what I've got. Can't expect anything more.' He flung his arm out towards the sea. 'Not out there anyhow.' He stamped his foot upon the sand. 'This is my limit, because nothing less will do.'

"We continued pacing the beach. 'Yes, I've changed all that,' he went on, with a sidelong glance at the two patient, squatting fishermen; 'but only try to think what it would be if I went away. Jove! can't you see it? Hell loose. No! To-morrow I shall go and take my chance of drinking that silly old Tunku Allang's coffee, and I shall make no end of fuss over these rotten turtles' eggs. No. I can't say—enough. Never. I must go on, go on for ever holding up my end, to feel sure that nothing can touch me. I must stick to their belief in me to feel safe and to—to' . . . he cast about for a word, seemed to look for it on the sea . . . 'to keep in touch with' . . . his voice sank suddenly to a murmur . . . 'with those whom, perhaps, I shall never see any more. With—with—you, for instance.'

"I was profoundly humbled by his words. 'For God's sake,' I said, 'don't set me up, my dear fellow; just look to yourself.' I felt a gratitude, an affection, for that straggler whose eyes had singled me out, keeping my place in the ranks of an insignificant multitude. How little that was to boast of, after all! I turned my burning face away; under the low sun, glowing, darkened and crimson, like an ember snatched from the fire, the sea lay outspread, offering all its immense stillness to the approach of the fiery orb. Twice he was going to speak, but checked himself; at last, as if he had found a formula:

" 'I shall be faithful,' he said quietly. 'I shall be faithful,' he repeated, without looking at me, but for the first time letting his eyes wander upon the waters, whose blueness had changed to a gloomy purple under the fires of sunset. Ah! he was romantic, romantic. I recalled some words of Stein's. . . . 'In the destructive element immerse! . . . To follow the dream, and again to follow the dream—and so—always—*usque ad finem* . . .' He was romantic, but none the less true. Who could tell what forms, what visions, what faces, what forgiveness he could see in the glow of the west! . . . A small boat, leaving the schooner, moved slowly, with a regular beat of two oars, towards the sandbank to take me off. 'And then there's Jewel,' he said, out of the great silence of earth, sky, and sea, which had mastered my very thoughts so that his voice made me start. 'There's Jewel.' 'Yes,' I murmured. 'I need not tell you what she is to me,' he pursued. 'You've seen. In time she will come to understand . . .' 'I hope so,' I interrupted. 'She trusts me, too,' he mused, and then changed his tone. 'When shall we meet next, I wonder?' he said.

" 'Never—unless you come out,' I answered, avoiding his glance. He didn't seem to be surprised; he kept very quiet for a while.

" 'Good-bye, then,' he said, after a pause. 'Perhaps it's just as well.'

"We shook hands, and I walked to the boat, which waited with her nose on the beach. The schooner, her mainsail set and jib-sheet to windward, curveted on the purple sea; there was a rosy tinge on her sails. 'Will you be going home again soon?' asked Jim, just as I swung my leg over the gunwale. 'In a year or so if I live,' I said. The forefoot grated on the sand, the boat floated, the wet oars flashed and dipped once, twice. Jim, at the water's edge, raised his voice. 'Tell them . . .' he began. I signed to the men to cease rowing, and waited in wonder. Tell who? The half-submerged sun faced him; I could see its red gleam in his eyes that looked dumbly at me. . . . 'No—nothing,' he said, and with a slight wave of his hand motioned the boat away. I did not look again at the shore till I had clambered on board the schooner.

"By that time the sun had set. The twilight lay over the east, and the coast, turned black, extended infinitely its sombre wall that seemed the very stronghold of the night; the western horizon was one great blaze of gold and crimson in which a big detached cloud floated dark and still, casting a slaty shadow on the water beneath, and I saw Jim on the beach watching the schooner fall off and gather headway.

"The two half-naked fishermen had arisen as soon as I had gone; they were no doubt pouring the plaint of their trifling, miserable, oppressed lives into the ears of the white lord, and no doubt he was listening to it, making it his own, for was it not a part of his luck —the luck 'from the word Go'—the luck to which he had assured me he was so completely equal? They, too, I should think, were in luck, and I was sure their pertinacity would be equal to it. Their dark-skinned bodies vanished on the dark background long before I had lost sight of their protector. He was white from head to foot, and remained persistently visible with the stronghold of the night at his back, the sea at his feet, the opportunity by his side—still veiled. What do you say? Was it still veiled? I don't know. For me that white figure in the stillness of coast and sea seemed to stand at the heart of a vast enigma. The twilight was ebbing fast from the sky above his head, the strip of sand had sunk already under his feet, he himself appeared no bigger than a child—then only a speck, a tiny white speck, that seemed to catch all the light left in a darkened world. . . . And, suddenly, I lost him. . . ."

Chapter Thirty-Six

With these words Marlow had ended his narrative, and his audience had broken up forthwith, under his abstract, pensive gaze. Men drifted off the verandah in pairs or alone without loss of time, without offering a remark, as if the last image of that incom-

plete story, its incompleteness itself, and the very tone of the
speaker, had made discussion vain and comment impossible. Each
of them seemed to carry away his own impression, to carry it away
with him like a secret; but there was only one man of all these
listeners who was ever to hear the last word of the story. It came
to him at home, more than two years later, and it came contained
in a thick packet addressed in Marlow's upright and angular
handwriting.

The privileged man opened the packet, looked in, then, laying
it down, went to the window. His rooms were in the highest flat of a
lofty building, and his glance could travel afar beyond the clear panes
of glass, as though he were looking out of the lantern of a lighthouse. The slopes of the roofs glistened, the dark, broken ridges
succeeded each other without end like sombre, uncrested waves,
and from the depths of the town under his feet ascended a confused
and unceasing mutter. The spires of churches, numerous, scattered
haphazard, uprose like beacons on a maze of shoals without a
channel; the driving rain mingled with the falling dusk of a
winter's evening; and the booming of a big clock on a tower, striking the hour, rolled past in voluminous, austere bursts of sound,
with a shrill, vibrating cry at the core. He drew the heavy curtains.

The light of his shaded reading-lamp slept like a sheltered pool,
his footfalls made no sound on the carpet, his wandering days were
over. No more horizons as boundless as hope, no more twilights
within the forests as solemn as temples, in the hot quest of the
Ever-undiscovered Country over the hill, across the stream, beyond the wave. The hour was striking! No more! No more!—but the
opened packet under the lamp brought back the sounds, the visions,
the very savour of the past—a multitude of fading faces, a tumult
of low voices, dying away upon the shores of distant seas under a
passionate and unconsoling sunshine. He sighed and sat down to
read.

At first he saw three distinct enclosures. A good many pages
closely blackened and pinned together; a loose square sheet of
greyish paper with a few words traced in a handwriting he had
never seen before, and an explanatory letter from Marlow. From
this last fell another letter, yellowed by time and frayed on the folds.
He picked it up and, laying it aside, turned to Marlow's message,
ran swiftly over the opening lines, and, checking himself, thereafter
read on deliberately, like one approaching with slow feet and
alert eyes the glimpse of an undiscovered country.

". . . I don't suppose you've forgotten," went on the letter.
"You alone have showed an interest in him that survived the telling
of his story, though I remember well you would not admit he had
mastered his fate. You prophesied for him the disaster of weariness

and of disgust with acquired honour, with the self-appointed task, with the love sprung from pity and youth. You had said you knew so well 'that kind of thing,' its illusory satisfaction, its unavoidable deception. You said also—I call to mind—that 'giving your life up to them' (*them* meaning all of mankind with skins brown, yellow, or black in colour) 'was like selling your soul to a brute.' You contended that 'that kind of thing' was only endurable and enduring when based on a firm conviction in the truth of ideas racially our own, in whose name are established the order, the morality of an ethical progress. 'We want its strength at our backs,' you had said. 'We want a belief in its necessity and its justice, to make a worthy and conscious sacrifice of our lives. Without it the sacrifice is only forgetfulness, the way of offering is no better than the way to perdition.' In other words, you maintained that we must fight in the ranks or our lives can't count. Possibly! You ought to know—be it said without malice—you who have rushed into one or two places single-handed and came out cleverly, without singeing your wings. The point, however, is that of all mankind Jim had no dealings but with himself, and the question is whether at the last he had not confessed to a faith mightier than the laws of order and progress.

"I affirm nothing. Perhaps you may pronounce—after you've read. There is much truth—after all—in the common expression 'under a cloud.' It is impossible to see him clearly—especially as it is through the eyes of others that we take our last look at him. I have no hesitation in imparting to you all I know of the last episode that, as he used to say, had 'come to him.' One wonders whether this was perhaps that supreme opportunity, that last and satisfying test for which I had always suspected him to be waiting, before he could frame a message to the impeccable world. You remember that when I was leaving him for the last time he had asked whether I would be going home soon, and suddenly cried after me, 'Tell them . . .' I had waited—curious I'll own, and hopeful, too—only to hear him shout, 'No—nothing.' That was all then—and there will be nothing more; there will be no message, unless such as each of us can interpret for himself from the language of facts, that are so often more enigmatic than the craftiest arrangement of words. He made, it is true, one more attempt to deliver himself; but that, too, failed, as you may perceive if you look at the sheet of greyish foolscap[2] enclosed here. He had tried to write; do you notice the commonplace hand? It is headed 'The Fort, Patusan.' I suppose he had carried out his intention of making out of his house a place of defence. It was an excellent plan: a deep

---

2. Common term for sheets of legal-sized paper, so called from the watermark of a fool's cap and bells used by old papermakers.

ditch, an earth wall topped by a palisade, and at the angles guns mounted on platforms to sweep each side of the square. Doramin had agreed to furnish him the guns; and so each man of his party would know there was a place of safety, upon which every faithful partisan could rally in case of some sudden danger. All this showed his judicious foresight, his faith in the future. What he called 'my own people'—the liberated captives of the Sherif—were to make a distinct quarter of Patusan, with their huts and little plots of ground under the walls of the stronghold. Within he would be an invincible host in himself. 'The Fort, Patusan.' No date, as you observe. What is a number and a name to a day of days? It is also impossible to say whom he had in his mind when he seized the pen: Stein—myself—the world at large—or was this only the aimless, startled cry of a solitary man confronted by his fate? 'An awful thing has happened,' he wrote before he flung the pen down for the first time; look at the ink blot resembling the head of an arrow under these words. After a while he had tried again, scrawling heavily, as if with a hand of lead, another line. 'I must now at once . . .' The pen had spluttered, and that time he gave it up. There's nothing more; he had seen a broad gulf that neither eye nor voice could span. I can understand this. He was overwhelmed by the inexplicable; he was overwhelmed by his own personality—the gift of that destiny which he had done his best to master.

"I send you also an old letter—a very old letter. It was found carefully preserved in his writing-case. It is from his father, and by the date you can see he must have received it a few days before he joined the *Patna*. Thus it must be the last letter he ever had from home. He had treasured it all these years. The good old parson fancied his sailor son. I've looked in at a sentence here and there. There is nothing in it except just affection. He tells his 'dear James' that the last long letter from him was very 'honest and entertaining.' He would not have him 'judge men harshly or hastily.' There are four pages of it, easy morality and family news. Tom had 'taken orders.' Carrie's husband had 'money losses.' The old chap goes on equably trusting Providence and the established order of the universe, but alive to its small dangers and its small mercies. One can almost see him, grey-haired and serene in the inviolable shelter of his book-lined, faded, and comfortable study, where for forty years he had conscientiously gone over and over again the round of his little thoughts about faith and virtue, about the conduct of life and the only proper manner of dying; where he had written so many sermons, where he sits talking to his boy, over there, on the other side of the earth. But what of the distance? Virtue is one all over the world, and there is only one faith, one conceivable conduct of life, one manner of dying. He hopes his 'dear James' will never forget that 'who once gives way to temptation, in the very instant hazards his total depravity and everlasting ruin. Therefore resolve fixedly never, through any possible motives, to do anything which you believe to be wrong.' There is also some news of a favourite dog; and a pony, 'which all you boys used to ride,' had gone blind from old age and had to be shot. The old chap invokes Heaven's blessing; the mother and all the girls then at home send their love. . . . No, there is nothing much in that yellow, frayed letter fluttering out of his cherishing grasp after so many years. It was never answered, but who can say what converse he may have held with all these placid, colourless forms of men and women peopling that quiet corner of the world as free of danger or strife as a tomb, and breathing equably the air of undisturbed rectitude. It seems amazing that he should belong to it, he to whom so many things 'had come.' Nothing ever came to them; they would never be taken unawares, and never be called upon to grapple with fate. Here they all are, evoked by the mild gossip of the father, all these brothers and sisters, bone of his bone and flesh of his flesh,[3] gazing with clear, unconscious eyes, while I seem to see him, returned at last, no longer a mere white speck at the heart of an immense mystery, but of full stature, standing disregarded amongst their untroubled shapes, with a stern and romantic aspect, but always mute, dark— under a cloud.

"The story of the last events you will find in the few pages enclosed here. You must admit that it is romantic beyond the wildest dreams of his boyhood, and yet there is to my mind a sort of profound and terrifying logic in it, as if it were our imagination alone that could set loose upon us the might of an overwhelming destiny. The imprudence of our thoughts recoils upon our heads; who toys with the sword shall perish by the sword.[3a] This astounding adventure, of which the most astounding part is that it is true, comes on as an unavoidable consequence. Something of the sort had to happen. You repeat this to yourself while you marvel that such a thing could happen in the year of grace [4] before last. But it has happened—and there is no disputing its logic.

"I put it down here for you as though I had been an eye-witness. My information was fragmentary, but I've fitted the pieces together, and there is enough of them to make an intelligible picture. I wonder how he would have related it himself. He has confided so much in me that at times it seems as though he must come in presently and tell the story in his own words, in his careless yet feeling voice, with his off-hand manner, a little puzzled, a little bothered, a little hurt, but now and then by a word or a phrase

3. Bone of my bones, and flesh of my flesh. (Genesis 2:23.)
3a. Cf. Jesus' words: "All they that take the sword shall perish with the sword." (Matthew 26:52.)
4. Any year of the Christian Era.

giving one of these glimpses of his very own self that were never any good for purposes of orientation. It's difficult to believe he will never come. I shall never hear his voice again, nor shall I see his smooth tan-and-pink face with a white line on the forehead, and the youthful eyes darkened by excitement to a profound, unfathomable blue."

Chapter Thirty-Seven

"It all begins with a remarkable exploit of a man called Brown, who stole with complete success a Spanish schooner out of a small bay near Zamboanga. Till I discovered the fellow my information was incomplete, but most unexpectedly I did come upon him a few hours before he gave up his arrogant ghost. Fortunately, he was willing and able to talk between the choking fits of asthma, and his racked body writhed with malicious exultation at the bare thought of Jim. He exulted thus at the idea that he had 'paid out the stuck-up beggar after all.' He gloated over his action. I had to bear the sunken glare of his fierce, crow-footed eyes if I wanted to know; and so I bore it, reflecting how much certain forms of evil are akin to madness, derived from intense egoism, inflamed by resistance, tearing the soul to pieces, and giving factitious vigour to the body. The story also reveals unsuspected depths of cunning in the wretched Cornelius, whose abject and intense hate acts like a subtle inspiration, pointing out an unerring way towards revenge.

" 'I could see directly I set my eyes on him what sort of a fool he was,' gasped the dying Brown. 'He a man! Hell! He was a hollow sham. As if he couldn't have said straight out, "Hands off my plunder!" blast him! That would have been like a man! Rot his superior soul! He had me there—but he hadn't devil enough in him to make an end of me. Not he! A thing like that letting me off as if I wasn't worth a kick! . . .' Brown struggled desperately for breath. . . . 'Fraud. . . . Letting me off. . . . And so I did make an end of him after all. . . .' He choked again. . . . 'I expect this thing'll kill me, but I shall die easy now. You . . . you hear . . . I don't know your name—I would give you a five-pound note if— if I had it—for the news—or my name's not Brown. . . .' He grinned horribly. . . . 'Gentleman Brown.'

"He said all these things in profound gasps, staring at me with his yellow eyes out of a long, ravaged, brown face; he jerked his left arm; a pepper-and-salt matted beard hung almost into his lap; a dirty, ragged blanket covered his legs. I had found him out in Bankok through that busybody Schomberg, the hotel-keeper, who had, confidentially, directed me where to look. It appears that a sort of loafing, fuddled vagabond—a white man living amongst

the natives with a Siamese woman—had considered it a great privilege to give a shelter to the last days of the famous Gentleman
Brown. While he was talking to me in the wretched hovel, and,
as it were, fighting for every minute of his life, the Siamese woman,
with big, bare legs and a stupid, coarse face, sat in a dark corner
chewing betel stolidly. Now and then she would get up for the
purpose of shooing a chicken away from the door. The whole hut
shook when she walked. An ugly, yellow child, naked and pot-bel-
lied like a little heathen god, stood at the foot of the couch, finger
in mouth, lost in a profound and calm contemplation of the dying
man.

"He talked feverishly; but in the middle of a word, perhaps, an
invisible hand would take him by the throat, and he would look
at me dumbly with an expression of doubt and anguish. He seemed
to fear that I would get tired of waiting and go away, leaving him
with his tale untold, with his exultation unexpressed. He died during the night, I believe, but by that time I had nothing more to
learn.

"So much as to Brown, for the present.

"Eight months before this, coming in to Samarang, I went as
usual to see Stein. On the garden side of the house a Malay on the
verandah greeted me shyly, and I remembered that I had seen him
in Patusan, in Jim's house, amongst other Bugis men who used to
come in the evening to talk interminably over their war reminiscences and to discuss State affairs. Jim had pointed him out to me
once as a respectable petty trader owning a small sea-going native
craft, who had showed himself 'one of the best at the taking of the
stockade.' I was not very surprised to see him, since any Patusan
trader venturing as far as Samarang would naturally find his way
to Stein's house. I returned his greeting and passed on. At the
door of Stein's room I came upon another Malay in whom I recognised Tamb' Itam.

"I asked him at once what he was doing there; it occurred to me
that Jim might have come on a visit. I own I was pleased and excited at the thought. Tamb' Itam looked as if he did not know
what to say. 'Is Tuan Jim inside?' I asked impatiently. 'No,' he
mumbled, hanging his head for a moment; and then with sudden
earnestness, 'He would not fight. He would not fight,' he repeated
twice. As he seemed unable to say anything else, I pushed him
aside and went in.

"Stein, tall and stooping, stood alone in the middle of the room
between the rows of butterfly cases. 'Ach! is it you, my friend?' he
said sadly, peering through his glasses. A drab sack-coat of alpaca
hung, unbuttoned, down to his knees. He had a Panama hat on his
head, and there were deep furrows on his pale cheeks. 'What's the

matter now?' I asked nervously. 'There's Tamb' Itam there. . . .'
'Come and see the girl. Come and see the girl. She is here,' he said,
with a half-hearted show of activity. I tried to detain him, but
with gentle obstinacy he would take no notice of my eager questions. 'She is here, she is here,' he repeated, in great perturbation.
'They came here two days ago. An old man like me, a stranger—
sehen sie[5]—cannot do much. . . . Come this way. . . . Young hearts
are unforgiving. . . .' I could see he was in utmost distress. . . .
'The strength of life in them, the cruel strength of life. . . .' He
mumbled, leading me round the house; I followed him, lost in dismal and angry conjectures. At the door of the drawing-room he
barred my way. 'He loved her very much?' he said interrogatively;
and I only nodded, feeling so bitterly disappointed that I would
not trust myself to speak. 'Very frightful,' he murmured. 'She
can't understand me. I am only a strange old man. Perhaps you . . .
she knows you. Talk to her. We can't leave it like this. Tell her to
forgive him. It was very frightful.' 'No doubt,' I said, exasperated
at being in the dark; 'but have *you* forgiven him?' He looked at
me queerly. 'You shall hear,' he said, and, opening the door, absolutely pushed me in.

"You know Stein's big house and the two immense reception-
rooms, uninhabited and uninhabitable, clean, full of solitude and
of shining things that look as if never beheld by the eye of man?
They are cool on the hottest days, and you enter them as you
would a scrubbed cave underground. I passed through one, and
in the other I saw the girl sitting at the end of a big mahogany
table, on which she rested her head, the face hidden in her arms.
The waxed floor reflected her dimly as though it had been a sheet
of frozen water. The rattan screens were down, and through the
strange, greenish gloom made by the foliage of the trees outside a
strong wind blew in gusts, swaying the long draperies of windows
and doorways. Her white figure seemed shaped in snow; the pen-
dent crystals of a great chandelier clicked above her head like glittering icicles. She looked up and watched my approach. I was
chilled as if these vast apartments had been the cold abode of
despair.

"She recognised me at once, and as soon as I had stopped looking down at her: 'He has left me,' she said quietly; 'you always
leave us—for your own ends.' Her face was set. All the heat of
life seemed withdrawn within some inaccessible spot in her breast.
'It would have been easy to die with him,' she went on, and made
a slight, weary gesture as if giving up the incomprehensible. 'He
would not! It was like a blindness—and yet it was I who was speaking to him; it was I who stood before his eyes; it was at me that

5. You see.

he looked all the time! Ah! you are hard, treacherous, without truth, without compassion. What makes you so wicked? Or is it that you are all mad?'

"I took her hand; it did not respond, and when I dropped it, it hung down to the floor. That indifference, more awful than tears, cries, and reproaches, seemed to defy time and consolation. You felt that nothing you could say would reach the seat of the still and benumbing pain.

"Stein had said, 'You shall hear.' I did hear. I heard it all, listening with amazement, with awe, to the tones of her inflexible weariness. She could not grasp the real sense of what she was telling me, and her resentment filled me with pity for her—for him, too. I stood rooted to the spot after she had finished. Leaning on her arm, she stared with hard eyes, and the wind passed in gusts, the crystals kept on clicking in the greenish gloom. She went on whispering to herself: 'And yet he was looking at me! He could see my face, hear my voice, hear my grief! When I used to sit at his feet, with my cheek against his knee and his hand on my head, the curse of cruelty and madness was already within him, waiting for the day. The day came! . . . and before the sun had set he could not see me any more—he was made blind and deaf and without pity, as you all are. He shall have no tears from me. Never, never. Not one tear. I will not! He went away from me as if I had been worse than death. He fled as if driven by some accursed thing he had heard or seen in his sleep. . . .'

"Her steady eyes seemed to strain after the shape of a man torn out of her arms by the strength of a dream. She made no sign to my silent bow. I was glad to escape.

"I saw her once again, the same afternoon. On leaving her I had gone in search of Stein, whom I could not find indoors; and I wandered out, pursued by distressful thoughts, into the gardens, those famous gardens of Stein, in which you can find every plant and tree of tropical lowlands. I followed the course of the canalised stream and sat for a long time on a shaded bench near the ornamental pond, where some waterfowl with clipped wings were diving and splashing noisily. The branches of casuarina trees behind me swayed lightly, incessantly, reminding me of the soughing of fir trees at home.

"This mournful and restless sound was a fit accompaniment to my meditations. She had said he had been driven away from her by a dream,—and there was no answer one could make her—there seemed to be no forgiveness for such a transgression. And yet is not mankind itself, pushing on its blind way, driven by a dream of its greatness and its power upon the dark paths of excessive cruelty and of excessive devotion? And what is the pursuit of truth, after all?

"When I rose to get back to the house I caught sight of Stein's drab coat through a gap in the foliage, and very soon at a turn of the path I came upon him walking with the girl. Her little hand rested on his forearm, and under the broad, flat rim of his Panama hat he bent over her, grey-haired, paternal, with compassionate and chivalrous deference. I stood aside, but they stopped, facing me. His gaze was bent on the ground at his feet; the girl, erect and slight on his arm, stared sombrely beyond my shoulder with black, clear, motionless eyes. '*Schrecklich*,' he murmured. 'Terrible! Terrible! What can one do?' He seemed to be appealing to me, but her youth, the length of the days suspended over her head, appealed to me more; and suddenly, even as I realised that nothing could be said, I found myself pleading his cause for her sake. 'You must forgive him,' I concluded, and my own voice seemed to me muffled, lost in an irresponsive deaf immensity. 'We all want to be forgiven,' I added after a while.

" 'What have I done?' she asked with her lips only.

" 'You always mistrusted him,' I said.

" 'He was like the others,' she pronounced slowly.

" 'Not like the others,' I protested; but she continued evenly, without any feeling:

" 'He was false.' And suddenly Stein broke in. 'No! no! no! My poor child! . . .' He patted her hand lying passively on his sleeve. 'No! no! Not false! True! true! true!' He tried to look into her stony face. 'You don't understand. Ach! Why you do not understand? . . . Terrible,' he said to me. 'Some day she *shall* understand.'

" 'Will *you* explain?' I asked, looking hard at him. They moved on.

"I watched them. Her gown trailed on the path, her black hair fell loose. She walked upright and light by the side of the tall man, whose long, shapeless coat hung in perpendicular folds from the stooping shoulders, whose feet moved slowly. They disappeared beyond that spinney (you may remember) where sixteen different kinds of bamboo grow together, all distinguishable to the learned eye. For my part, I was fascinated by the exquisite grace and beauty of that fluted grove, crowned with pointed leaves and feathery heads, the lightness, the vigour, the charm as distinct as a voice of that unperplexed, luxuriating life. I remember staying to look at it for a long time, as one would linger within reach of a consoling whisper. The sky was pearly grey. It was one of those overcast days so rare in the tropics, in which memories crowd upon one—memories of other shores, of other faces.

"I drove back to town the same afternoon, taking with me Tamb' Itam and the other Malay, in whose sea-going craft they had escaped in the bewilderment, fear, and gloom of the disaster. The shock of it seemed to have changed their natures. It had turned her passion into stone, and it made the surly, taciturn Tamb' Itam almost loquacious. His surliness, too, was subdued into puzzled humility, as though he had seen the failure of a potent charm in a supreme moment. The Bugis trader, a shy, hesitating man, was very clear in the little he had to say. Both were evidently overawed by a sense of deep, inexpressible wonder, by the touch of an inscrutable mystery."

There with Marlow's signature the letter proper ended. The privileged reader screwed up his lamp, and solitary above the billowy roofs of the town, like a lighthouse-keeper above the sea, he turned to the pages of the story.

Chapter Thirty-Eight

"It all begins, as I've told you, with the man called Brown," ran the opening sentence of Marlow's narrative. "You who have knocked about the Western Pacific must have heard of him. He was the show ruffian on the Australian coast—not that he was often to be seen there, but because he was always trotted out in the stories of lawless life a visitor from home is treated to; and the mildest of these stories which were told about him from Cape York to Eden Bay was more than enough to hang a man if told in the right place. They never failed to let you know, too, that he was supposed to be the son of a baronet. Be it as it may, it is certain he had deserted from a home ship in the early gold-digging days, and in a few years became talked about as the terror of this or that group of islands in Polynesia. He would kidnap natives, he would strip some lonely white trader to the very pyjamas he stood in, and after he had robbed the poor devil, he would as likely as not invite him to fight a duel with shot-guns on the beach—which would have been fair enough as these things go, if the other man hadn't been by that time already half dead with fright. Brown was a latter-day buccaneer, sorry enough, like his more celebrated prototypes; but what distinguished him from his contemporary brother ruffians, like Bully Hayes or the mellifluous Pease,[6] or that perfumed, Dundreary-whiskered,[7] dandified scoundrel known as Dirty Dick, was the arrogant temper of his misdeeds and a vehement scorn for mankind at large and for his victims in particular. The others were merely vulgar and greedy brutes, but he seemed moved by some complex intention. He would rob a man as if only to demonstrate

6. Capt. William Henry Hayes of Cleveland, Ohio, and Lt. George Pease, briefly of the United States Navy, were notorious South Sea adventurers and pirates who both met violent deaths in the 1870's.
7. Long flowing side-whiskers separated by shaven chin.

his poor opinion of the creature, and he would bring to the shooting or maiming of some quiet, unoffending stranger a savage and vengeful earnestness fit to terrify the most reckless of desperadoes. In the days of his greatest glory he owned an armed barque, manned by a mixed crew of Kanakas and runaway whalers, and boasted, I don't know with what truth, of being financed on the quiet by a most respectable firm of copra merchants. Later on he ran off—it was reported—with the wife of a missionary, a very young girl from Clapham [8] way, who had married the mild, flat-footed fellow in a moment of enthusiasm, and suddenly transplanted to Melanesia, lost her bearings somehow. It was a dark story. She was ill at the time he carried her off, and died on board his ship. It is said—as the most wonderful part of the tale—that over her body he gave way to an outburst of sombre and violent grief. His luck left him, too, very soon after. He lost his ship on some rocks off Malaita, and disappeared for a time as though he had gone down with her. He is heard of next at Nuka-Hiva, where he bought an old French schooner out of Government service. What creditable enterprise he might have had in view when he made that purchase I can't say, but it is evident that what with High Commissioners, consuls, men-of-war, and international control, the South Seas were getting too hot to hold gentlemen of his kidney. Clearly he must have shifted the scene of his operations farther west, because a year later he plays an incredibly audacious, but not a very profitable, part in a serio-comic business in Manila Bay, in which a peculating governor and an absconding treasurer are the principal figures; thereafter he seems to have hung around the Philippines in his rotten schoooner, battling with an adverse fortune, till at last, running his appointed course, he sails into Jim's history, a blind accomplice of the Dark Powers.

"His tale goes that when a Spanish patrol cutter captured him he was simply trying to run a few guns for the insurgents. If so, then I can't understand what he was doing off the south coast of Mindanao. My belief, however, is that he was blackmailing the native villages along the coast. The principal thing is that the cutter, throwing a guard on board, made him sail in company towards Zamboanga. On the way, for some reason or other, both vessels had to call at one of these new Spanish settlements—which never came to anything in the end—where there was not only a civil official in charge on shore, but a good stout coasting schooner lying at anchor in the little bay; and this craft, in every way much better than his own, Brown made up his mind to steal.

"He was down on his luck—as he told me himself. The world he had bullied for twenty years with fierce, aggressive disdain had

8. Residential district of London, south of the Thames.

yielded him nothing in the way of material advantage except a small bag of silver dollars, which was concealed in his cabin so that 'the devil himself couldn't smell it out.' And that was all—absolutely all. He was tired of his life, and not afraid of death. But this man, who would stake his existence on a whim with a bitter and jeering recklessness, stood in mortal fear of imprisonment. He had an unreasoning cold-sweat, nerve-shaking, blood-to-water-turning sort of horror at the bare possibility of being locked up—the sort of terror a superstitious man would feel at the thought of being embraced by a spectre. Therefore the civil official who came on board to make a preliminary investigation into the capture, investigated arduously all day long, and only went ashore after dark, muffled up in a cloak, and taking great care not to let Brown's little all clink in its bag. Afterwards, being a man of his word, he contrived (the very next evening, I believe) to send off the Government cutter on some urgent bit of special service. As her commander could not spare a prize crew, he contented himself by taking away before he left all the sails of Brown's schooner to the very last rag, and took good care to tow his two boats on to the beach a couple of miles off.

"But in Brown's crew there was a Solomon Islander, kidnapped in his youth and devoted to Brown, who was the best man of the whole gang. That fellow swam off to the coaster—five hundred yards or so—with the end of a warp made up of all the running gear unrove for the purpose. The water was smooth, and the bay dark, 'like the inside of a cow,' as Brown described it. The Solomon Islander clambered over the bulwarks with the end of the rope in his teeth. The crew of the coaster—all Tagals—were ashore having a jollification in the native village. The two ship-keepers left on board woke up suddenly and saw the devil. It had glittering eyes, and leaped quick as lightning about the deck. They fell on their knees, paralysed with fear, crossing themselves and mumbling prayers. With a long knife he found in the caboose the Solomon Islander, without interrupting their orisons, stabbed first one, then the other; with the same knife he set to sawing patiently at the coir cable till suddenly it parted under the blade with a splash. Then in the silence of the bay he let out a cautious shout, and Brown's gang, who meantime had been peering and straining their hopeful ears in the darkness, began to pull gently at their end of the warp. In less than five minutes the two schooners came together with a slight shock and a creak of spars.

"Brown's crowd transferred themselves without losing an instant, taking with them their firearms and a large supply of ammunition. They were sixteen in all: two runaway blue-jackets, a lanky deserter from a Yankee man-of-war, a couple of simple, blond

Scandinavians, a mulatto of sorts, one bland Chinaman who cooked —and the rest of the nondescript spawn of the South Seas. None of them cared; Brown bent them to his will, and Brown, indifferent to gallows, was running away from the spectre of a Spanish prison. He didn't give them the time to tranship enough provisions; the weather was calm, the air was charged with dew, and when they cast off the ropes and set sail to a faint off-shore draught there was no flutter in the damp canvas; their old schooner seemed to detach itself gently from the stolen craft and slip away silently, together with the black mass of the coast, into the night.

"They got clear away. Brown related to me in detail their passage down the Straits of Macassar. It is a harrowing and desperate story. They were short of food and water; they boarded several native craft and got a little from each. With a stolen ship Brown did not dare to put into any port, of course. He had no money to buy anything, no papers to show, and no lie plausible enough to get him out again. An Arab barque, under the Dutch flag, surprised one night at anchor off Poulo Laut, yielded a little dirty rice, a bunch of bananas, and a cask of water; three days of squally, misty weather from the north-east shot the schooner across the Java Sea. The yellow, muddy waves drenched that collection of hungry ruffians. They sighted mail-boats moving on their appointed routes; passed well-found [9] home ships with rusty iron sides anchored in the shallow sea waiting for a change of weather or the turn of the tide; an English gunboat, white and trim, with two slim masts, crossed their bows one day in the distance; and on another occasion a Dutch corvette, black and heavily sparred, loomed upon their quarter, steaming dead slow in the mist. They slipped through unseen or disregarded, a wan, sallow-faced band of utter outcasts, enraged with hunger and hunted by fear. Brown's idea was to make for Madagascar, where he expected, on grounds not altogether illusory, to sell the schooner in Tamatave, and no questions asked, or perhaps obtain some more or less forged papers for her. Yet before he could face the long passage across the Indian Ocean food was wanted—water, too.

"Perhaps he had heard of Patusan—or perhaps he just only happened to see the name written in small letters on the chart—probably that of a largish village up a river in a native state, perfectly defenceless, far from the beaten tracks of the sea and from the ends of submarine cables. He had done that kind of thing before—in the way of business—and this now was an absolute necessity, a question of life and death—or rather of liberty. Of liberty! He was sure to get provisions—bullocks—rice—sweet-potatoes. The sorry gang licked their chops. A cargo of produce for the schooner perhaps

9. Well provided.

could be extorted—and, who knows?—some real ringing coined money! Some of these chiefs and village head-men can be made to part freely. He told me he would have roasted their toes rather than be baulked. I believe him. His men believed him too. They didn't cheer aloud, being a dumb pack, but made ready wolfishly.

"Luck served him as to weather. A few days of calm would have brought unmentionable horrors on board that schooner, but with the help of land and sea breezes, in less than a week after clearing the Sunda Straits, he anchored off the Batu Kring mouth within a pistol-shot of the fishing village.

"Fourteen of them packed into the schooner's long-boat (which was big, having been used for cargo-work) and started up the river, while two remained in charge of the schooner with food enough to keep starvation off for ten days. The tide and wind helped, and early one afternoon the big white boat under a ragged sail shouldered its way before the sea breeze into Patusan Reach, manned by fourteen assorted scarecrows glaring hungrily ahead, and fingering the breech-blocks of cheap rifles. Brown calculated upon the terrifying surprise of his appearance. They sailed in with the last of the flood; the Rajah's stockade gave no sign; the first houses on both sides of the stream seemed deserted. A few canoes were seen up the reach in full flight. Brown was astonished at the size of the place. A profound silence reigned. The wind dropped between the houses; two oars were got out and the boat held on upstream, the idea being to effect a lodgment in the centre of the town before the inhabitants could think of resistance.

"It seems, however, that the head-man of the fishing village at Batu Kring had managed to send off a timely warning. When the long-boat came abreast of the mosque (which Doramin had built: a structure with gables and roof finials of carved coral) the open space before it was full of people. A shout went up, and was followed by a clash of gongs all up the river. From a point above two little brass six-pounders were discharged, and the round-shot came skipping down the empty reach, spirting glittering jets of water in the sunshine. In front of the mosque a shouting lot of men began firing in volleys that whipped athwart the current of the river; an irregular, rolling fusillade was opened on the boat from both banks, and Brown's men replied with a wild, rapid fire. The oars had been got in.

"The turn of the tide at high water comes on very quickly in that river, and the boat in midstream, nearly hidden in smoke, began to drift back stern foremost. Along both shores the smoke thickened also, lying below the roofs in a level streak as you may see a long cloud cutting the slope of a mountain. A tumult of war-cries, the vibrating clang of gongs, the deep snoring of drums,

yells of rage, crashes of volley-firing, made an awful din, in which
Brown sat confounded but steady at the tiller, working himself into
a fury of hate and rage against those people who dared to defend
themselves. Two of his men had been wounded, and he saw his
retreat cut off below the town by some boats that had put off from
Tunku Allang's stockade. There were six of them, full of men.
While he was thus beset he perceived the entrance of the narrow
creek (the same which Jim had jumped at low water). It was then
brim-full. Steering the long-boat in, they landed, and, to make a
long story short, they established themselves on a little knoll about
900 yards from the stockade, which, in fact, they commanded from
that position. The slopes of the knoll were bare, but there were a
few trees on the summit. They went to work cutting these down
for a breastwork, and were fairly entrenched before dark; meantime the Rajah's boats remained in the river with curious neutrality.
When the sun set, the glare of many brushwood blazes lighted on
the river-front, and between the double line of houses on the land
side threw into black relief the roofs, the groups of slender palms,
the heavy clumps of fruit trees. Brown ordered the grass round
his position to be fired; a low ring of thin flames under the slow,
ascending smoke wriggled rapidly down the slopes of the knoll;
here and there a dry bush caught with a tall, vicious roar. The conflagration made a clear zone of fire for the rifles of the small party,
and expired smouldering on the edge of the forests and along the
muddy bank of the creek. A strip of jungle luxuriating in a damp
hollow between the knoll and the Rajah's stockade stopped it on
that side with a great crackling and detonations of bursting bamboo stems. The sky was sombre, velvety, and swarming with stars.
The blackened ground smoked quietly with low creeping wisps, till
a little breeze came on and blew everything away. Brown expected
an attack to be delivered as soon as the tide had flowed enough
again to enable the war-boats which had cut off his retreat to enter
the creek. At any rate he was sure there would be an attempt to
carry off his long-boat, which lay below the hill, a dark high lump
on the feeble sheen of a wet mud-flat. But no move of any sort was
made by the boats in the river. Over the stockade and the Rajah's
buildings Brown saw their lights on the water. They seemed to be
anchored across the stream. Other lights afloat were moving in the
reach, crossing and recrossing from side to side. There were also
lights twinkling motionless upon the long walls of houses up the
reach, as far as the bend, and more still beyond, others isolated
inland. The loom of the big fires disclosed buildings, roofs, black
piles as far as he could see. It was an immense place. The fourteen
desperate invaders lying flat behind the felled trees raised their
chins to look over at the stir of that town that seemed to extend

up-river for miles and swarm with thousands of angry men. They did not speak to each other. Now and then they would hear a loud yell, or a single shot rang out, fired very far somewhere. But round their position everything was still, dark, silent. They seemed to be forgotten, as if the excitement keeping awake all the population had nothing to do with them, as if they had been dead already."

Chapter Thirty-Nine

"All the events of that night have a great importance, since they brought about a situation which remained unchanged till Jim's return. Jim had been away in the interior for more than a week, and it was Dain Waris who had directed the first repulse. That brave and intelligent youth ('who knew how to fight after the manner of white men') wished to settle the business off-hand, but his people were too much for him. He had not Jim's racial prestige and the reputation of invincible, supernatural power. He was not the visible, tangible incarnation of unfailing truth and of unfailing victory. Beloved, trusted, and admired as he was, he was still one of *them*, while Jim was one of *us*. Moreover, the white man, a tower of strength in himself, was invulnerable, while Dain Waris could be killed. Those unexpressed thoughts guided the opinions of the chief men of the town, who elected to assemble in Jim's fort for deliberation upon the emergency, as if expecting to find wisdom and courage in the dwelling of the absent white man. The shooting of Brown's ruffians was so far good, or lucky, that there had been half a dozen casualties amongst the defenders. The wounded were lying on the verandah tended by their women-folk. The women and children from the lower part of the town had been sent into the fort at the first alarm. There Jewel was in command, very efficient and high-spirited, obeyed by Jim's 'own people,' who, quitting in a body their little settlement under the stockade, had gone in to form the garrison. The refugees crowded round her; and through the whole affair, to the very disastrous last, she showed an extraordinary martial ardour. It was to her that Dain Waris had gone at once at the first intelligence of danger, for you must know that Jim was the only one in Patusan who possessed a store of gunpowder. Stein, with whom he had kept up intimate relations by letters, had obtained from the Dutch Government a special authorisation to export five hundred kegs of it to Patusan. The powder-magazine was a small hut of rough logs covered entirely with earth, and in Jim's absence the girl had the key. In the council, held at eleven o'clock in the evening in Jim's dining-room, she backed up Waris's advice for immediate and vigorous action. I am told that she stood up by the side of Jim's empty chair at the head of the long table and made a warlike impassioned speech, which for the moment extorted murmurs of approbation from the assembled head-men. Old Doramin, who had not showed himself outside his own gate for more than a year, had been brought across with great difficulty. He was, of course, the chief man there. The temper of the council was very unforgiving, and the old man's word would have been decisive; but it is my opinion that, well aware of his son's fiery courage, he dared not pronounce the word. More dilatory counsels prevailed. A certain Haji Saman pointed out at great length that 'these tyrannical and ferocious men had delivered themselves to a certain death in any case. They would stand fast on their hill and starve, or they would try to regain their boat and be shot from ambushes across the creek, or they would break and fly into the forest and perish singly there.' He argued that by the use of proper stratagems these evil-minded strangers could be destroyed without the risk of a battle, and his words had a great weight, especially with the Patusan men proper. What unsettled the minds of the townfolk was the failure of the Rajah's boats to act at the decisive moment. It was the diplomatic Kassim who represented the Rajah at the council. He spoke very little, listened smilingly, very friendly and impenetrable. During the sitting messengers kept arriving every few minutes almost, with reports of the invaders' proceedings. Wild and exaggerated rumours were flying: there was a large ship at the mouth of the river with big guns and many more men—some white, others with black skins and of blood-thirsty appearance. They were coming with many more boats to exterminate every living thing. A sense of near, incomprehensible danger affected the common people. At one moment there was a panic in the courtyard amongst the women; shrieking; a rush; children crying—Haji Saman went out to quiet them. Then a fort sentry fired at something moving on the river, and nearly killed a villager bringing in his women-folk in a canoe together with the best of his domestic utensils and a dozen fowls. This caused more confusion. Meantime the palaver inside Jim's house went on in the presence of the girl. Doramin sat fierce-faced, heavy, looking at the speakers in turn, and breathing slow like a bull. He didn't speak till the last, after Kassim had declared that the Rajah's boats would be called in because the men were required to defend his master's stockade. Dain Waris in his father's presence would offer no opinion, though the girl entreated him in Jim's name to speak out. She offered him Jim's own men in her anxiety to have these intruders driven out at once. He only shook his head, after a glance or two at Doramin. Finally, when the council broke up it had been decided that the houses nearest the creek should be strongly occupied to obtain the command of the enemy's boat. The boat itself was not to be interfered with openly, so that the robbers on the hill should be tempted to embark, when a well-directed fire would kill most of them, no doubt. To cut off the escape of those who might survive, and to prevent more of them coming up, Dain Waris was ordered by Doramin to take an armed party of Bugis down the river to a certain spot ten miles below Patusan, and there form a camp on the shore and blockade the stream with the canoes. I don't believe for a moment that Doramin feared the arrival of fresh forces. My opinion is, that his conduct was guided solely by his wish to keep his son out of harm's way. To prevent a rush being made into the town the construction of a stockade was to be commenced at daylight at the end of the street on the left bank. The old *nakhoda* declared his intention to command there himself. A distribution of powder, bullets, and percussion caps was made immediately under the girl's supervision. Several messengers were to be dispatched in different directions after Jim, whose exact whereabouts were unknown. These men started at dawn, but before that time Kassim had managed to open communications with the besieged Brown.

"That accomplished diplomatist and confidant of the Rajah, on leaving the fort to go back to his master, took into his boat Cornelius, whom he found slinking mutely amongst the people in the courtyard. Kassim had a little plan of his own and wanted him for an interpreter. Thus it came about that towards morning Brown, reflecting upon the desperate nature of his position, heard from the marshy overgrown hollow an amicable, quavering, strained voice crying—in English—for permission to come up, under a promise of personal safety and on a very important errand. He was overjoyed. If he was spoken to he was no longer a hunted wild beast. These friendly sounds took off at once the awful stress of vigilant watchfulness as of so many blind men not knowing whence the death-blow might come. He pretended a great reluctance. The voice declared itself 'a white man—a poor, ruined, old man who had been living here for years.' A mist, wet and chilly, lay on the slopes of the hill, and after some more shouting from one to the other, Brown called out, 'Come on, then, but alone, mind!' As a matter of fact—he told me, writhing with rage at the recollection of his helplessness—it made no difference. They couldn't see more than a few yards before them, and no treachery could make their position worse. By and by Cornelius, in his week-day attire of a ragged dirty shirt and pants, barefooted, with a broken-rimmed pith hat on his head, was made out vaguely, sidling up to the defences, hesitating, stopping to listen in a peering posture. 'Come along! You are safe,' yelled Brown, while his men stared. All their hopes of life became suddenly centred in that dilapidated, mean newcomer, who in profound silence clambered clumsily over a felled tree-trunk, and shivering, with his sour, mistrustful face, looked about at the knot of bearded, anxious, sleepless desperadoes.

"Half an hour's confidential talk with Cornelius opened Brown's eyes as to the home affairs of Patusan. He was on the alert at once. There were possibilities, immense possibilities; but before he would talk over Cornelius's proposals he demanded that some food should be sent up as a guarantee of good faith. Cornelius went off, creeping sluggishly down the hill on the side of the Rajah's palace, and after some delay a few of Tunku Allang's men came up, bringing a scanty supply of rice, chillies, and dried fish. This was immeasurably better than nothing. Later on Cornelius returned accompanying Kassim, who stepped out with an air of perfect good-humoured trustfulness, in sandals and muffled up from neck to ankles in dark-blue sheeting. He shook hands with Brown discreetly, and the three drew aside for a conference. Brown's men, recovering their confidence, were slapping each other on the back, and cast knowing glances at their captain while they busied themselves with preparations for cooking.

"Kassim disliked Doramin and his Bugis very much, but he hated the new order of things still more. It had occurred to him that these whites, together with the Rajah's followers, could attack and defeat the Bugis before Jim's return. Then, he reasoned, general defection of the townsfolk was sure to follow, and the reign of the white man who protected poor people would be over. Afterwards the new allies could be dealt with. They would have no friends. The fellow was perfectly able to perceive the difference of character, and had seen enough of white men to know that these newcomers were outcasts, men without country. Brown preserved a stern and inscrutable demeanour. When he first heard Cornelius's voice demanding admittance, it brought merely the hope of a loophole for escape. In less than an hour other thoughts were seething in his head. Urged by an extreme necessity, he had come there to steal food, a few tons of rubber or gum maybe, perhaps a handful of dollars, and had found himself enmeshed by deadly dangers. Now in consequence of these overtures from Kassim he began to think of stealing the whole country. Some confounded fellow had apparently accomplished something of the kind—single-handed at that. Couldn't have done it very well though. Perhaps they could work together—squeeze everything dry and then go out quietly. In the course of his negotiations with Kassim he became aware that he was supposed to have a big ship with plenty of men outside. Kassim begged him earnestly to have this big ship with his many guns and men brought up the river without delay for the Rajah's service. Brown professed himself willing, and on this basis the negotiation was carried on with mutual distrust. Three times in the course of the morning the courteous and active Kassim went down to consult the Rajah and came up busily with his long stride. Brown, while bargaining, had a sort of grim enjoyment in thinking of his wretched schooner with nothing but a heap of dirt in her hold, that stood for an armed ship, and a Chinaman and a lame ex-beachcomber of Levuka on board, who represented all his many men. In the afternoon he obtained further doles of food, a promise of some money, and a supply of mats for his men to make shelters for themselves. They lay down and snored, protected from the burning sunshine; but Brown, sitting fully exposed on one of the felled trees, feasted his eyes upon the view of the town and the river. There was much loot here. Cornelius, who had made himself at home in the camp, talked at his elbow, pointing out the localities, imparting advice, giving his own version of Jim's character, and commenting in his own fashion upon the events of the last three years. Brown, who, apparently indifferent and gazing away, listened with attention to every word, could not make out clearly what sort of man this Jim could be. 'What's his name? Jim! Jim! That's not enough for a man's name.' 'They call him,' said Cornelius, scornfully, 'Tuan Jim here. As you may say Lord Jim.' 'What is he? Where does he come from?' inquired Brown. 'What sort of man is he? Is he an Englishman?' 'Yes, yes, he's an Englishman. I am an Englishman, too. From Malacca. He is a fool. All you have to do is to kill him and then you are king here. Everything belongs to him,' explained Cornelius. 'It strikes me he may be made to share with somebody before very long,' commented Brown half aloud. 'No, no. The proper way is to kill him the first chance you get, and then you can do what you like,' Cornelius would insist earnestly. 'I have lived for many years here, and I am giving you a friend's advice.'

"In such converse and in gloating over the view of Patusan, which he had determined in his mind should become his prey, Brown whiled away most of the afternoon, his men, meantime, resting. On that day Dain Waris's fleet of canoes stole one by one under the shore farthest from the creek, and went down to close the river against his retreat. Of this Brown was not aware, and Kassim, who came up the knoll an hour before sunset, took good care not to enlighten him. He wanted the white man's ship to come up the river, and this news, he feared, would be discouraging. He was very pressing with Brown to send the 'order,' offering at the same time a trusty messenger, who for greater secrecy (as he explained) would make his way by land to the mouth of the river and deliver the 'order' on board. After some reflection Brown judged it expedient to tear a page out of his pocket-book, on which he simply wrote, 'We are getting on. Big job. Detain the man.' The stolid youth selected by Kassim for that service performed it faithfully, and was rewarded by being suddenly tipped, head first, into the schooner's empty hold by the ex-beachcomber and the Chinaman, who thereupon hastened to put on the hatches. What became of him afterwards Brown did not say."

Chapter Forty

"Brown's object was to gain time by fooling with Kassim's diplomacy. For doing a real stroke of business he could not help thinking the white man was the person to work with. He could not imagine such a chap (who must be confoundedly clever after all to get hold of the natives like that) refusing a help that would do away with the necessity for slow, cautious, risky cheating, that imposed itself as the only possible line of conduct for a single-handed man. He, Brown, would offer him the power. No man could hesitate. Everything was in coming to a clear understanding. Of course they would share. The idea of there being a fort—all ready to his hand—a real fort, with artillery (he knew this from Cornelius), excited him. Let him only once get in and . . . He would impose modest conditions. Not too low, though. The man was no fool, it seemed. They would work like brothers till . . . till the time came for a quarrel and a shot that would settle all accounts. With grim impatience of plunder he wished himself to be talking with the man now. The land already seemed to be his to tear to pieces, squeeze, and throw away. Meantime Kassim had to be fooled for the sake of food first—and for a second string. But the principal thing was to get something to eat from day to day. Besides, he was not averse to begin fighting on that Rajah's account, and teach a lesson to those people who had received him with shots. The lust of battle was upon him.

"I am sorry that I can't give you this part of the story, which of course I have mainly from Brown, in Brown's own words. There was in the broken, violent speech of that man, unveiling before me his thoughts with the very hand of Death upon his throat, an undisguised ruthlessness of purpose, a strange vengeful attitude towards his own past, and a blind belief in the righteousness of his will against all mankind, something of that feeling which could induce the leader of a horde of wandering cut-throats to call himself proudly the Scourge of God.[1] No doubt the natural senseless ferocity which is the basis of such a character was exasperated by failure, ill-luck, and the recent privations, as well as by the desperate position in which he found himself; but what was most remarkable of all was this, that while he planned treacherous alliances, had already settled in his own mind the fate of the white man, and intrigued in an overbearing, off-hand manner with Kassim, one could perceive that what he had really desired, almost in spite of himself, was to play havoc

1. Name given to Attila, king of the Huns.

with that jungle town which had defied him, to see it strewn over with corpses and enveloped in flames. Listening to his pitiless, panting voice, I could imagine how he must have looked at it from the hillock, peopling it with images of murder and rapine. The part nearest to the creek wore an abandoned aspect, though as a matter of fact every house concealed a few armed men on the alert. Suddenly beyond the stretch of waste ground, interspersed with small patches of low dense bush, excavations, heaps of rubbish, with trodden paths between, a man, solitary, and looking very small, strolled out into the deserted opening of the street between the shut-up, dark, lifeless buildings at the end. Perhaps one of the inhabitants, who had fled to the other bank of the river, coming back for some object of domestic use. Evidently he supposed himself quite safe at that distance from the hill on the other side of the creek. A light stockade, set up hastily, was just round the turn of the street, full of his friends. He moved leisurely. Brown saw him, and instantly called to his side the Yankee deserter, who acted as a sort of second in command. This lanky, loose-jointed fellow came forward, wooden-faced, trailing his rifle lazily. When he understood what was wanted from him a homicidal and conceited smile uncovered his teeth, making two deep folds down his sallow, leathery cheeks. He prided himself on being a dead shot. He dropped on one knee, and taking aim from a steady rest through the unlopped branches of a felled tree, fired, and at once stood up to look. The man, far away, turned his head to the report, made another step forward, seemed to hesitate, and abruptly got down on his hands and knees. In the silence that fell upon the sharp crack of the rifle, the dead shot, keeping his eyes fixed upon the quarry, guessed that 'this there coon's health would never be a source of anxiety to his friends any more.' The man's limbs were seen to move rapidly under his body in an endeavour to run on all-fours. In that empty space arose a multitudinous shout of dismay and surprise. The man sank flat, face down, and moved no more. 'That showed them what we could do,' said Brown to me. 'Struck the fear of sudden death into them. That was what we wanted. They were two hundred to one, and this gave them something to think over for the night. Not one of them had an idea of such a long shot before. That beggar belonging to the Rajah scooted downhill with his eyes hanging out of his head.'

"As he was telling me this he tried with a shaking hand to wipe the thin foam on his blue lips. 'Two hundred to one. Two hundred to one . . . strike terror . . . terror, terror, I tell you. . . .' His own eyes were starting out of their sockets. He fell back, clawing the air with skinny fingers, sat up again, bowed and hairy, glared at me sideways like some man-beast of folklore, with open mouth in his miserable and awful agony before he got his speech back after that fit. There are sights one never forgets.

"Furthermore, to draw the enemy's fire and locate such parties as might have been hiding in the bushes along the creek, Brown ordered the Solomon Islander to go down to the boat and bring an oar, as you send a spaniel after a stick into the water. This failed, and the fellow came back without a single shot having been fired at him from anywhere. 'There's nobody,' opined some of the men. It is 'onnatural,' remarked the Yankee. Kassim had gone, by that time, very much impressed, pleased, too, and also uneasy. Pursuing his tortuous policy, he had dispatched a message to Dain Waris warning him to look out for the white men's ship, which, he had had information, was about to come up the river. He minimised its strength and exhorted him to oppose its passage. This double-dealing answered his purpose, which was to keep the Bugis forces divided and to weaken them by fighting. On the other hand, he had in the course of that day sent word to the assembled Bugis chiefs in town, assuring them that he was trying to induce the invaders to retire; his messages to the fort asked earnestly for powder for the Rajah's men. It was a long time since Tunku Allang had had ammunition for the score or so of old muskets rusting in their arm-racks in the audience-hall. The open intercourse between the hill and the palace unsettled all the minds. It was already time for men to take sides, it began to be said. There would soon be much bloodshed, and thereafter great trouble for many people. The social fabric of orderly, peaceful life, when every man was sure of to-morrow, the edifice raised by Jim's hands, seemed on that evening ready to collapse into a ruin reeking with blood. The poorer folk were already taking to the bush or flying up the river. A good many of the upper class judged it necessary to go and pay their court to the Rajah. The Rajah's youths jostled them rudely. Old Tunku Allang, almost out of his mind with fear and indecision, either kept a sullen silence or abused them violently for daring to come with empty hands: they departed very much frightened; only old Doramin kept his countrymen together and pursued his tactics inflexibly. Enthroned in a big chair behind the improvised stockade, he issued his orders in a deep veiled rumble, unmoved, like a deaf man, in the flying rumours.

"Dusk fell, hiding first the body of the dead man, which had been left lying with arms outstretched as if nailed to the ground, and then the revolving sphere of the night rolled smoothly over Patusan and came to a rest, showering the glitter of countless worlds upon the earth. Again, in the exposed part of the town big fires blazed along the only street, revealing from distance to distance upon their glares the falling straight lines of roofs, the fragments of wattled walls jumbled in confusion, here and there a whole hut elevated in the glow upon the vertical black stripes of a group of high piles;

and all this line of dwellings, revealed in patches by the swaying flames, seemed to flicker tortuously away up-river into the gloom at the heart of the land. A great silence, in which the looms of successive fires played without noise, extended into the darkness at the foot of the hill; but the other bank of the river, all dark save for a solitary bonfire at the river-front before the fort, sent out into the air an increasing tremor that might have been the stamping of a multitude of feet, the hum of many voices, or the fall of an immensely distant waterfall. It was then, Brown confessed to me, while, turning his back on his men, he sat looking at it all, that notwithstanding his disdain, his ruthless faith in himself, a feeling came over him that at last he had run his head against a stone wall. Had his boat been afloat at the time, he believed he would have tried to steal away, taking his chances of a long chase down the river and of starvation at sea. It was very doubtful whether he would have succeeded in getting away. However, he didn't try this. For another moment he had a passing thought of trying to rush the town, but he perceived very well that in the end he would find himself in the lighted street, where they would be shot down like dogs from the houses. They were two hundred to one—he thought, while his men, huddling round two heaps of smouldering embers, munched the last of the bananas and roasted the few yams they owed to Kassim's diplomacy. Cornelius sat amongst them dozing sulkily.

"Then one of the whites remembered that some tobacco had been left in the boat, and, encouraged by the impunity of the Solomon Islander, said he would go to fetch it. At this all the others shook off their despondency. Brown applied to, said, 'Go, and be d—d to you,' scornfully. He didn't think there was any danger in going to the creek in the dark. The man threw a leg over the tree-trunk and disappeared. A moment later he was heard clambering into the boat and then clambering out. 'I've got it,' he cried. A flash and a report at the very foot of the hill followed. 'I am hit,' yelled the man. 'Look out, look out—I am hit,' and instantly all the rifles went off. The hill squirted fire and noise into the night like a little volcano, and when Brown and the Yankee with curses and cuffs stopped the panic-stricken firing, a profound, weary groan floated up from the creek, succeeded by a plaint whose heart-rending sadness was like some poison turning the blood cold in the veins. Then a strong voice pronounced several distinct incomprehensible words somewhere beyond the creek. 'Let no one fire,' shouted Brown. 'What does it mean?' . . . 'Do you hear on the hill? Do you hear? Do you hear?' repeated the voice three times. Cornelius translated, and then prompted the answer. 'Speak,' cried Brown, 'we hear.' Then the voice, declaiming in the sonorous inflated tone of a herald, and shifting continually on the edge of the vague waste-land, proclaimed that between the men of the Bugis nation living in Patusan and the white men on the hill and those with them, there would be no faith, no compassion, no speech, no peace. A bush rustled; a haphazard volley rang out. 'Dam' foolishness,' muttered the Yankee, vexedly grounding the butt. Cornelius translated. The wounded man below the hill, after crying out twice, 'Take me up! take me up!' went on complaining in moans. While he had kept on the blackened earth of the slope and afterwards crouching in the boat, he had been safe enough. It seems that in his joy at finding tobacco he forgot himself and jumped out on her off-side, as it were. The white boat, lying high and dry, showed him up; the creek was no more than seven yards wide in that place, and there happened to be a man crouching in the bush on the other bank.

"He was a Bugis of Tondano only lately come to Patusan, and a relation of the man shot in the afternoon. That famous long shot had indeed appalled the beholders. The man in utter security had been struck down, in full view of his friends, dropping with a joke on his lips, and they seemed to see in the act an atrocity which had stirred a bitter rage. That relation of his, Si-Lapa by name, was then with Doramin in the stockade only a few feet away. You who know these chaps must admit that the fellow showed an unusual pluck by volunteering to carry the message, alone, in the dark. Creeping across the open ground, he had deviated to the left and found himself opposite the boat. He was startled when Brown's man shouted. He came to a sitting position with his gun to his shoulder, and when the other jumped out, exposing himself, he pulled the trigger and lodged three jagged slugs point-blank into the poor wretch's stomach. Then, lying flat on his face, he gave himself up for dead, while a thin hail of lead chopped and swished the bushes close on his right hand; afterwards he delivered his speech shouting, bent double, dodging all the time in cover. With the last word he leaped sideways, lay close for a while, and afterwards got back to the houses unharmed, having achieved on that night such a renown as his children will not willingly allow to die.

"And on the hill the forlorn band let the two little heaps of embers go out under their bowed heads. They sat dejected on the ground with compressed lips and downcast eyes, listening to their comrade below. He was a strong man and died hard, with moans now loud, now sinking to a strange confidential note of pain. Sometimes he shrieked, and again, after a period of silence, he could be heard muttering deliriously a long and unintelligible complaint. Never for a moment did he cease.

" 'What's the good?' Brown had said unmoved once, seeing the Yankee, who had been swearing under his breath, prepare to go down. 'That's so,' assented the deserter, reluctantly desisting. 'There's no encouragement for wounded men here. Only his noise is calculated to make all the others think too much of the hereafter, cap'n.' 'Water!' cried the wounded man in an extraordinarily clear vigorous voice, and then went off moaning feebly. 'Ay, water. Water will do it,' muttered the other to himself resignedly. 'Plenty by and by. The tide is flowing.'

"At last the tide flowed, silencing the plaint and the cries of pain, and the dawn was near when Brown, sitting with his chin in the palm of his hand before Patusan, as one might stare at the unscalable side of a mountain, heard the brief ringing bark of a brass six-pounder far away in town somewhere. 'What's this?' he asked of Cornelius, who hung about him. Cornelius listened. A muffled roaring shout rolled down-river over the town; a big drum began to throb, and others responded, pulsating and droning. Tiny scattered lights began to twinkle in the dark half of the town, while the part lighted by the loom of fires hummed with a deep and prolonged murmur. 'He has come,' said Cornelius. 'What? Already? Are you sure?' Brown asked. 'Yes! yes! Sure. Listen to the noise.' 'What are they making that row about?' pursued Brown. 'For joy,' snorted Cornelius; 'he is a very great man, but all the same, he knows no more than a child, and so they make a great noise to please him, because they know no better.' 'Look here,' said Brown, 'how is one to get at him?' 'He shall come to talk to you,' Cornelius declared. 'What do you mean? Come down here strolling as it were?' Cornelius nodded vigorously in the dark. 'Yes. He will come straight here and talk to you. He is just like a fool. You shall see what a fool he is.' Brown was incredulous. 'You shall see; you shall see,' repeated Cornelius. 'He is not afraid—not afraid of anything. He will come and order you to leave his people alone. Everybody must leave his people alone. He is like a little child. He will come to you straight.' Alas! he knew Jim well—that 'mean little skunk,' as Brown called him to me. 'Yes, certainly,' he pursued with ardour, 'and then, captain, you tell that tall man with a gun to shoot him. Just you kill him, and you will frighten everybody so much that you can do anything you like with them afterwards—get what you like —go away when you like. Ha! ha! ha! Fine. . . .' He almost danced with impatience and eagerness; and Brown, looking over his shoulder at him, could see, shown up by the pitiless dawn, his men drenched with a dew, sitting amongst the cold ashes and the litter of the camp, haggard, cowed, and in rags."

Chapter Forty-One

"To the very last moment, till the full day came upon them with a spring, the fires on the west bank blazed bright and clear; and then Brown saw in a knot of coloured figures motionless between the advanced houses a man in European clothes, in a helmet, all white.

'That's him; look! look!' Cornelius said excitedly. All Brown's men had sprung up and crowded at his back with lustreless eyes. The group of vivid colours and dark faces with the white figure in the midst were observing the knoll. Brown could see naked arms being raised to shade the eyes and other brown arms pointing. What should he do? He looked around, and the forests that faced him on all sides walled the cock-pit of an unequal contest. He looked once more at his men. A contempt, a weariness, the desire of life, the wish to try for one more chance—for some other grave—struggled in his breast. From the outline the figure presented it seemed to him that the white man there, backed up by all the power of the land, was examining his position through binoculars. Brown jumped up on the log, throwing his arms up, the palms outwards. The coloured group closed round the white man, and fell back twice before he got clear of them, walking slowly alone. Brown remained standing on the log till Jim, appearing and disappearing between the patches of thorny scrub, had nearly reached the creek; then Brown jumped off and went down to meet him on his side.

"They met, I should think, not very far from the place, perhaps on the very spot, where Jim took the second desperate leap of his life—the leap that landed him into the life of Patusan, into the trust, the love, the confidence of the people. They faced each other across the creek, and with steady eyes tried to understand each other before they opened their lips. Their antagonism must have been expressed in their glances; I know that Brown hated Jim at first sight. Whatever hopes he might have had vanished at once. This was not the man he had expected to see. He hated him for this—and in a checked flannel shirt with sleeves cut off at the elbows, grey bearded, with a sunken, sun-blackened face—he cursed in his heart the other's youth and assurance, his clear eyes and his untroubled bearing. That fellow had got in a long way before him! He did not look like a man who would be willing to give anything for assistance. He had all the advantages on his side—possession, security, power; he was on the side of an overwhelming force! He was not hungry and desperate, and he did not seem in the least afraid. And there was something in the very neatness of Jim's clothes, from the white helmet to the canvas leggings and the pipe-clayed [2] shoes, which in Brown's sombre irritated eyes seemed to belong to things he had in the very shaping of his life contemned and flouted.

" 'Who are you?' asked Jim at last, speaking in his usual voice. 'My name's Brown,' answered the other loudly; 'Captain Brown. What's yours?' and Jim after a little pause went on quietly, as if he had not heard: 'What made you come here?' 'You want to know,' said Brown bitterly. 'It's easy to tell. Hunger. And what made you?'

2. Whitened with a certain clay, used also for making pipes.

" 'The fellow started at this,' said Brown, relating to me the opening of this strange conversation between those two men, separated
only by the muddy bed of a creek, but standing on the opposite
poles of that conception of life which includes all mankind—'The
fellow started at this and got very red in the face. Too big to be
questioned, I suppose. I told him that if he looked upon me as a
dead man with whom you may take liberties, he himself was not a
whit better off really. I had a fellow up there who had a bead drawn
on him all the time, and only waited for a sign from me. There was
nothing to be shocked at in this. He had come down of his own
freewill. "Let us agree," said I, "that we are both dead men, and let
us talk on that basis, as equals. We are all equal before death," I
said. I admitted I was there like a rat in a trap, but we had been
driven to it, and even a trapped rat can give a bite. He caught me
up in a moment. "Not if you don't go near the trap till the rat is
dead." I told him that sort of game was good enough for these native friends of his, but I would have thought him too white to serve
even a rat so. Yes, I had wanted to talk with him. Not to beg for my
life, though. My fellows were—well—what they were—men like
himself, anyhow. All we wanted from him was to come on in the
devil's name and have it out. "God d—n it," said I, while he stood
there as still as a wooden post, "you don't want to come out here
every day with your glasses to count how many of us are left on our
feet. Come. Either bring your infernal crowd along or let us go out
and starve in the open sea, by God! You have been white once, for
all your tall talk of this being your own people and you being one
with them. Are you? And what the devil do you get for it; what is
it you've found here that is so d—d precious? Hey? You don't want
us to come down here perhaps—do you? You are two hundred to
one. You don't want us to come down into the open. Ah! I promise
you we shall give you some sport before you've done. You talk about
me making a cowardly set upon unoffending people. What's that to
me that they are unoffending, when I am starving for next to no
offence? But I am not a coward. Don't you be one. Bring them
along or, by all the fiends, we shall yet manage to send half your
unoffending town to heaven with us in smoke!" '

"He was terrible—relating this to me—this tortured skeleton of
a man drawn up together with his face over his knees, upon a miserable bed in that wretched hovel, and lifting his head to look at me
with malignant triumph.

" 'That's what I told him—I knew what to say,' he began again,
feebly at first, but working himself up with incredible speed into a
fiery utterance of his scorn. 'We aren't going into the forest to wander like a string of living skeletons dropping one after another for
ants to go to work upon us before we are fairly dead. Oh no! . . .

"You don't deserve a better fate," he said. "And what do you deserve," I shouted at him, "you that I find skulking here with your mouth full of your responsibility, of innocent lives, of your infernal duty? What do you know more of me than I know of you? I came here for food. D'ye hear?—food to fill our bellies. And what did *you* come for? What did you ask for when you came here? We don't ask you for anything but to give us a fight or a clear road to go back whence we came. . . ." "I would fight with you now," says he, pulling at his little moustache. "And I would let you shoot me, and welcome," I said. "This is as good a jumping-off place for me as another. I am sick of my infernal luck. But it would be too easy. There are my men in the same boat—and, by God, I am not the sort to jump out of trouble and leave them in a d—d lurch," I said. He stood thinking for a while and then wanted to know what I had done ("out there," he says, tossing his head down-stream) to be hazed about so. "Have we met to tell each other the story of our lives?" I asked him. "Suppose you begin. No? Well, I am sure I don't want to hear. Keep it to yourself. I know it is no better than mine. I've lived—and so did you though you talk as if you were one of those people that should have wings so as to go about without touching the dirty earth. Well—it is dirty. I haven't got any wings. I am here because I was afraid once in my life. Want to know what of? Of a prison. That scares me, and you may know it—if it's any good to you. I won't ask you what scared you into this infernal hole, where you seem to have found pretty pickings. That's your luck and this is mine—the privilege to beg for the favour of being shot quickly, or else kicked out to go free and starve in my own way." . . .'

"His debilitated body shook with an exultation so vehement, so assured, and so malicious that it seemed to have driven off the death waiting for him in that hut. The corpse of his mad self-love uprose from rags and destitution as from the dark horrors of a tomb. It is impossible to say how much he lied to Jim then, how much he lied to me now—and to himself always. Vanity plays lurid tricks with our memory, and the truth of every passion wants some pretence to make it live. Standing at the gate of the other world in the guise of a beggar, he had slapped this world's face, he had spat on it, he had thrown upon it an immensity of scorn and revolt at the bottom of his misdeeds. He had overcome them all—men, women, savages, traders, ruffians, missionaries—and Jim—'that beefy-faced beggar.' I did not begrudge him this triumph *in articulo mortis*,[3] this almost posthumous illusion of having trampled all the earth under his feet. While he was boasting to me, in his sordid and repulsive agony, I couldn't help thinking of the chuckling talk relating to the

3. At the point of death. (Latin.)

time of his greatest splendour when, during a year or more, Gentle-man Brown's ship was to be seen, for many days on end, hovering off an islet befringed with green upon azure, with the dark dot of the mission-house on a white beach; while Gentleman Brown, ashore, was casting his spells over a romantic girl for whom Melanesia had been too much, and giving hopes of a remarkable conversion to her husband. The poor man, some time or other, had been heard to express the intention of winning 'Captain Brown to a better way of life.' . . . 'Bag Gentleman Brown for Glory'—as a leery-eyed loafer expressed it once—'just to let them see up above what a Western Pacific trading skipper looks like.' And this was the man, too, who had run off with a dying woman, and had shed tears over her body. 'Carried on like a big baby,' his then mate was never tired of telling, 'and where the fun came in may I be kicked to death by diseased Kanakas if *I* know. Why, gents! she was too far gone when he brought her aboard to know him; she just lay there on her back in his bunk staring at the beam with awful shining eyes—and then she died. Dam' bad sort of fever, I guess. . . .' I remembered all these stories while, wiping his matted lump of a beard with a livid hand, he was telling me from his noisome couch how he got round, got in, got home, on that confounded, immaculate, don't-you-touch-me sort of fellow. He admitted that he couldn't be scared, but there was a way, 'as broad as a turnpike, to get in and shake his twopenny soul around and inside out and upside down—by God!' "

Chapter Forty-Two

"I don't think he could do more than perhaps look upon that straight path. He seemed to have been puzzled by what he saw, for he interrupted himself in his narrative more than once to exclaim, 'He nearly slipped from me there. I could not make him out. Who was he?' And after glaring at me wildly he would go on, jubilating and sneering. To me the conversation of these two across the creek appears now as the deadliest kind of duel on which Fate looked on with her cold-eyed knowledge of the end. No, he didn't turn Jim's soul inside out, but I am much mistaken if the spirit so utterly out of his reach had not been made to taste to the full the bitterness of that contest. These were the emissaries with whom the world he had renounced was pursuing him in his retreat—white men from 'out there' where he did not think himself good enough to live. This was all that came to him—a menace, a shock, a danger to his work. I suppose it is this sad, half-resentful, half-resigned feeling, piercing through the few words Jim said now and then, that puzzled Brown so much in the reading of his character. Some great men owe most of their greatness to the ability of detecting in those they destine for their tools the exact quality of strength that matters for their work, and Brown, as though he had been really great, had a satanic gift of finding out the best and the weakest spot in his victims. He admitted to me that Jim wasn't of the sort that can be got over by truckling, and accordingly he took care to show himself as a man confronting without dismay ill-luck, censure, and disaster. The smuggling of a few guns was no great crime, he pointed out. As to coming to Patusan, who had the right to say he hadn't come to beg? The infernal people here let loose at him from both banks without staying to ask questions. He made the point brazenly, for, in truth, Dain Waris's energetic action had prevented the greatest calamities; because Brown told me distinctly that, perceiving the size of the place, he had resolved instantly in his mind that as soon as he had gained a footing he would set fire right and left, and begin by shooting down everything living in sight, in order to cow and terrify the population. The disproportion of forces was so great that this was the only way giving him the slightest chance of attaining his ends—he argued in a fit of coughing. But he didn't tell Jim this. As to the hardships and starvation they had gone through, these had been very real; it was enough to look at his band. He made, at the sound of a shrill whistle, all his men appear standing in a row on the logs in full view, so that Jim could see them. For the killing of the man, it had been done—well, it had—but was not this war, bloody war—in a corner? and the fellow had been killed cleanly, shot through the chest, not like that poor devil of his lying now in the creek. They had to listen to him dying for six hours, with his entrails torn with slugs. At any rate this was a life for a life. . . . And all this was said with the weariness, with the recklessness of a man spurred on and on by ill-luck till he cares not where he runs. When he asked Jim, with a sort of brusque despairing frankness, whether he himself—straight now—didn't understand that when 'it came to saving one's life in the dark, one didn't care who else went—three, thirty, three hundred people'—it was as if a demon had been whispering advice in his ear. 'I made him wince,' boasted Brown to me. 'He very soon left off coming the righteous over me. He just stood there with nothing to say, and looking as black as thunder—not at me—on the ground.' He asked Jim whether he had nothing fishy in his life to remember that he was so damnedly hard upon a man trying to get out of a deadly hole by the first means that came to hand—and so on, and so on. And there ran through the rough talk a vein of subtle reference to their common blood, an assumption of common experience; a sickening suggestion of common guilt, of secret knowledge that was like a bond of their minds and of their hearts.

"At last Brown threw himself down full length and watched Jim

out of the corners of his eyes. Jim on his side of the creek stood
thinking and switching his leg. The houses in view were silent, as if
a pestilence had swept them clean of every breath of life; but many
invisible eyes were turned, from within, upon the two men with
the creek between them, a stranded white boat, and the body of the
third man half sunk in the mud. On the river canoes were moving
again, for Patusan was recovering its belief in the stability of earthly
institutions since the return of the white lord. The right bank, the
platforms of the houses, the rafts moored along the shores, even the
roofs of bathing-huts, were covered with people that, far away out of
earshot and almost out of sight, were straining their eyes towards
the knoll beyond the Rajah's stockade. Within the wide irregular
ring of forests broken in two places by the sheen of the river there
was a silence. 'Will you promise to leave the coast?' Jim asked.
Brown lifted and let fall his hand, giving everything up as it were—
accepting the inevitable. 'And surrender your arms?' Jim went on.
Brown sat up and glared across. 'Surrender our arms! Not till you
come to take them out of our stiff hands. You think I am gone crazy
with funk? Oh no! That and the rags I stand in is all I have got in
the world, besides a few more breechloaders on board; and I expect
to sell the lot in Madagascar, if I ever get so far—begging my way
from ship to ship.'

"Jim said nothing to this. At last, throwing away the switch he
held in his hand, he said, as if speaking to himself, 'I don't know
whether I have the power.' . . . 'You don't know! And you wanted
me just now to give up my arms! That's good, too,' cried Brown.
'Suppose they say one thing to you, and do the other thing to me.'
He calmed down markedly. 'I dare say you have the power, or
what's the meaning of all this talk?' he continued. 'What did you
come down here for? To pass the time of day?'

" 'Very well,' said Jim, lifting his head suddenly after a long silence. 'You shall have a clear road or else a clear fight.' He turned on
his heel and walked away.

"Brown got up at once, but he did not go up the hill till he had
seen Jim disappear between the first houses. He never set his eyes
on him again. On his way back he met Cornelius slouching down
with his head between his shoulders. He stopped before Brown.
'Why didn't you kill him?' he demanded in a sour, discontented
voice. 'Because I could do better than that,' Brown said with an
amused smile. 'Never! never!' protested Cornelius with energy.
'Couldn't. I have lived here for many years.' Brown looked up at
him curiously. There were many sides to the life of that place in
arms against him; things he would never find out. Cornelius slunk
past dejectedly in the direction of the river. He was now leaving his
new friends; he accepted the disappointing course of events with a

sulky obstinacy which seemed to draw more together his little yel-low old face; and as he went down he glanced askant here and there, never giving up his fixed idea.

"Henceforth events move fast without a check, flowing from the very hearts of men like a stream from a dark source, and we see Jim amongst them, mostly through Tamb' Itam's eyes. The girl's eyes had watched him, too, but her life is too much entwined with his: there is her passion, her wonder, her anger, and, above all, her fear and her unforgiving love. Of the faithful servant, uncomprehending as the rest of them, it is the fidelity alone that comes into play; a fidelity and a belief in his lord so strong that even amazement is subdued to a sort of saddened acceptance of a mysterious failure. He has eyes only for one figure, and through all the mazes of bewilder-ment he preserves his air of guardianship, of obedience, of care.

"His master came back from his talk with the white men, walking slowly towards the stockade in the street. Everybody was rejoiced to see him return, for while he was away every man had been afraid not only of him being killed, but also of what would come after. Jim went into one of the houses, where old Doramin had retired, and re-mained alone for a long time with the head of the Bugis settlers. No doubt he discussed the course to follow with him then, but no man was present at the conversation. Only Tamb' Itam, keeping as close to the door as he could, heard his master say, 'Yes. I shall let all the people know that such is my wish; but I spoke to you, O Doramin, before all the others, and alone; for you know my heart as well as I know yours and its greatest desire. And you know well also that I have no thought but for the people's good.' Then his master, lifting the sheeting in the doorway, went out, and he, Tamb' Itam, had a glimpse of old Doramin within, sitting in the chair with his hands on his knees, and looking between his feet. Afterwards he followed his master to the fort, where all the principal Bugis and Patusan inhabitants had been summoned for a talk. Tamb' Itam himself hoped there would be some fighting. 'What was it but the taking of another hill?' he exclaimed regretfully. However, in the town many hoped that the rapacious strangers would be induced, by the sight of so many brave men making ready to fight, to go away. It would be a good thing if they went away. Since Jim's arrival had been made known before daylight by the gun fired from the fort and the beating of the big drum there, the fear that had hung over Patusan had broken and subsided like a wave on a rock, leaving the seething foam of excitement, curiosity, and endless speculation. Half of the population had been ousted out of their homes for purposes of defence, and were living in the street on the left side of the river, crowding round the fort, and in momentary expectation of seeing their abandoned dwellings on the threatened bank burst into flames.

The general anxiety was to see the matter settled quickly. Food, through Jewel's care, had been served out to the refugees. Nobody knew what their white man would do. Some remarked that it was worse than in Sherif Ali's war. Then many people did not care; now everybody had something to lose. The movements of canoes passing to and fro between the two parts of the town were watched with interest. A couple of Bugis war-boats lay anchored in the middle of the stream to protect the river, and a thread of smoke stood at the bow of each; the men in them were cooking their midday rice when Jim, after his interviews with Brown and Doramin, crossed the river and entered by the water-gate of his fort. The people inside crowded round him so that he could hardly make his way to the house. They had not seen him before, because on his arrival during the night he had only exchanged a few words with the girl, who had come down to the landing-stage for the purpose, and had then gone on at once to join the chiefs and the fighting men on the other bank. People shouted greetings after him. One old woman raised a laugh by pushing her way to the front madly and enjoining him in a scolding voice to see to it that her two sons, who were with Doramin, did not come to harm at the hands of the robbers. Several of the bystanders tried to pull her away, but she struggled and cried, 'Let me go. What is this, O Muslims? This laughter is unseemly. Are they not cruel, bloodthirsty robbers bent on killing?' 'Let her be,' said Jim, and as a silence fell suddenly, he said slowly, 'Everybody shall be safe.' He entered the house before the great sigh, and the loud murmurs of satisfaction, had died out.

"There's no doubt his mind was made up that Brown should have his way clear back to the sea. His fate, revolted, was forcing his hand. He had for the first time to affirm his will in the face of out-spoken opposition. 'There was much talk, and at first my master was silent,' Tamb' Itam said. 'Darkness came, and then I lit the candles on the long table. The chiefs sat on each side, and the lady remained by my master's right hand.'

"When he began to speak, the unaccustomed difficulty seemed only to fix his resolve more immovably. The white men were now waiting for his answer on the hill. Their chief had spoken to him in the language of his own people, making clear many things difficult to explain in any other speech. They were erring men whom suffering had made blind to right and wrong. It is true that lives had been lost already, but why lose more? He declared to his hearers, the assembled heads of the people, that their welfare was his welfare, their losses his losses, their mourning his mourning. He looked round at the grave listening faces and told them to remember that they had fought and worked side by side. They knew his courage. . . . Here a murmur interrupted him . . . And that he had never deceived them. For many years they had dwelt together. He loved the land and the people living in it with a very great love. He was ready to answer with his life for any harm that should come to them if the white men with beards were allowed to retire. They were evil-doers, but their destiny had been evil, too. Had he ever advised them ill? Had his words ever brought suffering to the people? he asked. He believed that it would be best to let these whites and their followers go with their lives. It would be a small gift. 'I whom you have tried and found always true ask you to let them go.' He turned to Doramin. The old *nakhoda* made no movement. 'Then,' said Jim, 'call in Dain Waris, your son, my friend, for in this business I shall not lead.' "

Chapter Forty-Three

"Tamb' Itam behind his chair was thunderstruck. The declaration produced an immense sensation. 'Let them go because this is best in my knowledge, which has never deceived you,' Jim insisted. There was a silence. In the darkness of the courtyard could be heard the subdued whispering, shuffling noise of many people. Doramin raised his heavy head and said that there was no more reading of hearts than touching the sky with the hand, but—he consented. The others gave their opinion in turn. 'It is best,' 'Let them go,' and so on. But most of them simply said that they 'believed Tuan Jim.'

"In this simple form of assent to his will lies the whole gist of the situation; their creed, his truth; and the testimony to that faithfulness which made him in his own eyes the equal of the impeccable men who never fall out of the ranks. Stein's words, 'Romantic!—Romantic!' seem to ring over those distances that will never give him up now to a world indifferent to his failings and his virtues, and to that ardent and clinging affection that refuses him the dole of tears in the bewilderment of a great grief and of eternal separation. From the moment the sheer truthfulness of his last three years of life carries the day against the ignorance, the fear, and the anger of men, he appears no longer to me as I saw him last—a white speck catching all the dim light left upon a sombre coast and the darkened sea—but greater and more pitiful in the loneliness of his soul, that remains even for her who loved him best a cruel and insoluble mystery.

"It is evident that he did not mistrust Brown; there was no reason to doubt the story, whose truth seemed warranted by the rough frankness, by a sort of virile sincerity in accepting the morality and the consequences of his acts. But Jim did not know the almost inconceivable egotism of the man which made him, when resisted and foiled in his will, mad with the indignant and revengeful rage of a thwarted autocrat. But if Jim did not mistrust Brown, he was evidently anxious that some misunderstanding should not occur, ending perhaps in collision and bloodshed. It was for this reason that directly the Malay chiefs had gone he asked Jewel to get him something to eat, as he was going out of the fort to take command in the town. On her remonstrating against this on the score of his fatigue, he said that something might happen for which he would never forgive himself. 'I am responsible for every life in the land,' he said. He was moody at first; she served him with her own hands, taking the plates and dishes (of the dinner-service presented him by Stein) from Tamb' Itam. He brightened up after a while; told her she would be again in command of the fort for another night. 'There's no sleep for us, old girl,' he said, 'while our people are in danger.' Later on he said jokingly that she was the best man of them all. 'If you and Dain Waris had done what you wanted, not one of these poor devils would be alive to-day.' 'Are they very bad?' she asked, leaning over his chair. 'Men act badly sometimes without being much worse than others,' he said after some hesitation.

"Tamb' Itam followed his master to the landing-stage outside the fort. The night was clear, but without a moon, and the middle of the river was dark, while the water under each bank reflected the light of many fires 'as on a night of Ramadan,' [4] Tamb' Itam said. War-boats drifted silently in the dark lane or, anchored, floated motionless with a loud ripple. That night there was much paddling in a canoe and walking at his master's heels for Tamb' Itam: up and down the street they tramped, where the fires were burning, inland on the outskirts of the town where small parties of men kept guard in the fields. Tuan Jim gave his orders and was obeyed. Last of all, they went to the Rajah's stockade, which a detachment of Jim's people manned on that night. The old Rajah had fled early in the morning with most of his women to a small house he had near a jungle village on a tributary stream. Kassim, left behind, had attended the council with his air of diligent activity to explain away the diplomacy of the day before. He was considerably cold-shouldered, but managed to preserve his smiling, quiet alertness, and professed himself highly delighted when Jim told him sternly that he proposed to occupy the stockade on that night with his own men. After the council broke up he was heard outside accosting this and that departing chief, and speaking in a loud, gratified tone of the Rajah's property being protected in the Rajah's absence.

4. In the Mohammedan year, the ninth month, on each day of which, from dawn to sunset, strict fasting is practiced, and all activities are reduced; those who can afford it turn night into day.

"About ten or so Jim's men marched in. The stockade commanded the mouth of the creek, and Jim meant to remain there till Brown had passed below. A small fire was lit on the flat, grassy point outside the wall of stakes, and Tamb' Itam placed a little folding-stool for his master. Jim told him to try and sleep. Tamb' Itam got a mat and lay down a little way off; but he could not sleep, though he knew he had to go on an important journey before the night was out. His master walked to and fro before the fire with bowed head and his hands behind his back. His face was sad. Whenever his master approached him Tamb' Itam pretended to sleep, not wishing his master to know he had been watched. At last his master stood still, looking down on him as he lay, and said softly, 'It is time.'

"Tamb' Itam arose directly and made his preparations. His mission was to go down the river, preceding Brown's boat by an hour or more, to tell Dain Waris finally and formally that the whites were to be allowed to pass out unmolested. Jim would not trust anybody else with that service. Before starting, Tamb' Itam, more as a matter of form (since his position about Jim made him perfectly known), asked for a token. 'Because, Tuan,' he said, 'the message is important, and these are thy very words I carry.' His master first put his hand into one pocket, then into another, and finally took off his forefinger Stein's silver ring, which he habitually wore, and gave it to Tamb' Itam. When Tamb' Itam left on his mission, Brown's camp on the knoll was dark but for a single small glow shining through the branches of one of the trees the white men had cut down.

"Early in the evening Brown had received from Jim a folded piece of paper on which was written, 'You get the clear road. Start as soon as your boat floats on the morning tide. Let your men be careful. The bushes on both sides of the creek and the stockade at the mouth are full of well-armed men. You would have no chance, but I don't believe you want bloodshed.' Brown read it, tore the paper into small pieces, and, turning to Cornelius, who had brought it, said jeeringly, 'Good-bye, my excellent friend.' Cornelius had been in the fort, and had been sneaking around Jim's house during the afternoon. Jim chose him to carry the note because he could speak English, was known to Brown, and was not likely to be shot by some nervous mistake of one of the men as a Malay, approaching in the dusk, perhaps might have been.

"Cornelius didn't go away after delivering the paper. Brown was sitting up over a tiny fire; all the others were lying down. 'I could tell you something you would like to know,' Cornelius mumbled crossly. Brown paid no attention. 'You did not kill him,' went on the other, 'and what do you get for it? You might have had money from the Rajah, besides the loot of all the Bugis houses, and now you get nothing.' 'You had better clear out from here,' growled Brown, without even looking at him. But Cornelius let himself drop by his side and began to whisper very fast, touching his elbow from time to time. What he had to say made Brown sit up at first, with a curse. He had simply informed him of Dain Waris's armed party down the river. At first Brown saw himself completely sold and betrayed, but a moment's reflection convinced him that there could be no treachery intended. He said nothing, and after a while Cornelius remarked, in a tone of complete indifference, that there was another way out of the river which he knew very well. 'A good thing to know, too,' said Brown, pricking up his ears; and Cornelius began to talk of what went on in town and repeated all that had been said in council, gossiping in an even undertone at Brown's ear as you talk amongst sleeping men you do not wish to wake. 'He thinks he has made me harmless, does he?' mumbled Brown very low. . . . 'Yes. He is a fool. A little child. He came here and robbed me,' droned on Cornelius, 'and he made all the people believe him. But if something happened that they did not believe him any more, where would he be? And the Bugis Dain who is waiting for you down the river there, captain, is the very man who chased you up here when you first came.' Brown observed nonchalantly that it would be just as well to avoid him, and with the same detached, musing air Cornelius declared himself acquainted with a back-water broad enough to take Brown's boat past Waris's camp. 'You will have to be quiet,' he said, as an afterthought, 'for in one place we pass close behind his camp. Very close. They are camped ashore with their boats hauled up.' 'Oh, we know how to be as quiet as mice; never fear,' said Brown. Cornelius stipulated that in case he were to pilot Brown out, his canoe should be towed. 'I'll have to get back quick,' he explained.

"It was two hours before the dawn when word was passed to the stockade from outlying watchers that the white robbers were coming down to their boat. In a very short time every armed man from one end of Patusan to the other was on the alert, yet the banks of the river remained so silent that but for the fires burning with sudden blurred flares the town might have been asleep as if in peacetime. A heavy mist lay very low on the water making a sort of illusive grey light that showed nothing. When Brown's long-boat glided out of the creek into the river, Jim was standing on the low point of land before the Rajah's stockade—on the very spot where for the first time he put his foot on Patusan shore. A shadow loomed up, moving in the greyness, solitary, very bulky, and yet constantly eluding the eye. A murmur of low talking came out of it. Brown at the tiller heard Jim speak calmly: 'A clear road. You had better trust to the current while the fog lasts; but this will lift presently.' 'Yes, presently we shall see clear,' replied Brown.

"The thirty or forty men standing with muskets at ready outside the stockade held their breath. The Bugis owner of the prau, whom I saw on Stein's verandah, and who was amongst them, told me that the boat, shaving the low point close, seemed for a moment to grow big and hang over it like a mountain. 'If you think it worth your while to wait a day outside,' called out Jim, 'I'll try to send you down something—bullock, some yams—what I can.' The shadow went on moving. 'Yes. Do,' said a voice, blank and muffled out of the fog. Not one of the many attentive listeners understood what the words meant; and then Brown and his men in their boat floated away, fading spectrally without the slightest sound.

"Thus Brown, invisible in the mist, goes out of Patusan elbow to elbow with Cornelius in the stern-sheets of the long-boat. 'Perhaps you shall get a small bullock,' said Cornelius. 'Oh yes. Bullock. Yam. You'll get it if *he* said so. He always speaks the truth. He stole everything I had. I suppose you like a small bullock better than the loot of many houses.' 'I would advise you to hold your tongue, or somebody here may fling you overboard into this damned fog,' said Brown. The boat seemed to be standing still; nothing could be seen, not even the river alongside, only the water-dust flew and trickled, condensed, down their beards and faces. It was weird, Brown told me. Every individual man of them felt as though he were adrift alone in a boat, haunted by an almost imperceptible suspicion of sighing, muttering ghosts. 'Throw me out, would you? But I would know where I was,' mumbled Cornelius surlily. 'I've lived many years here.' 'Not long enough to see through a fog like this,' Brown said, lolling back with his arm swinging to and fro on the useless tiller. 'Yes. Long enough for that,' snarled Cornelius. 'That's very useful,' commented Brown. 'Am I to believe you could find that backway you spoke of blindfold, like this?' Cornelius grunted. 'Are you too tired to row?' he asked after a silence. 'No, by God!' shouted Brown suddenly. 'Out with your oars there.' There was a great knocking in the fog, which after a while settled into a regular grind of invisible sweeps against invisible thole-pins. Otherwise nothing was changed, and but for the slight splash of a dipped blade it was like rowing a balloon car [5] in a cloud, said Brown. Thereafter Cornelius did not open his lips except to ask querulously for somebody to bale out his canoe, which was towing behind the long-boat. Gradually the fog whitened, and became luminous ahead. To the left Brown saw a darkness as though he had been looking at the back of the departing night. All at once a big bough covered with leaves appeared above his head, and ends of twigs, dripping and still, curved slenderly close alongside. Cornelius, without a word, took the tiller from his hand."

5. The earliest balloonists carried oars and tried to propel their balloons by rowing.

Chapter Forty-Four

"I don't think they spoke together again. The boat entered a narrow by-channel, where it was pushed by the oar-blades set into crumbling banks, and there was a gloom as if enormous black wings had been outspread above the mist that filled its depth to the summits of the trees. The branches overhead showered big drops through the gloomy fog. At a mutter frm Cornelius, Brown ordered his men to load. 'I'll give you a chance to get even with them before we're done, you dismal cripples, you,' he said to his gang. 'Mind you don't throw it away—you hounds.' Low growls answered that speech. Cornelius showed much fussy concern for the safety of his canoe.

"Meantime Tamb' Itam had reached the end of his journey. The fog had delayed him a little, but he had paddled steadily, keeping in touch with the south bank. By and by daylight came like a glow in a ground glass globe. The shores made on each side of the river a dark smudge, in which one could detect hints of columnar forms and shadows of twisted branches high up. The mist was still thick on the water, but a good watch was being kept, for as Tamb' Itam approached the camp the figures of two men emerged out of the white vapour, and voices spoke to him boisterously. He answered, and presently a canoe lay alongside, and he exchanged news with the paddlers. All was well. The trouble was over. Then the men in the canoe let go their grip on the side of his dug-out and incontinently fell out of sight. He pursued his way till he heard voices coming to him quietly over the water, and saw, under the now lifting, swirling mist, the glow of many little fires burning on a sandy stretch, backed by lofty thin timber and bushes. There again a look-out was kept, for he was challenged. He shouted his name as the two last sweeps of his paddle ran his canoe up on the strand. It was a big camp. Men crouched in many knots under a subdued murmur of early morning talk. Many thin threads of smoke curled slowly on the white mist. Little shelters, elevated above the ground, had been built for the chiefs. Muskets were stacked in small pyramids, and long spears were stuck singly into the sand near the fires.

"Tamb' Itam, assuming an air of importance, demanded to be led to Dain Waris. He found the friend of his white lord lying on a raised couch made of bamboo, and sheltered by a sort of shed of sticks covered with mats. Dain Waris was awake, and a bright fire was burning before his sleeping-place, which resembled a rude shrine. The only son of Nakhoda Doramin answered his greeting kindly. Tamb' Itam began by handing him the ring which vouched for the truth of the messenger's words. Dain Waris, reclining on his elbow, bade him speak and tell all the news. Beginning with the consecrated formula, 'The news is good,' Tamb' Itam delivered Jim's own words. The white men, departing with the consent of all the chiefs, were to be allowed to pass down the river. In answer to a question or two Tamb' Itam then reported the proceedings of the last council. Dain Waris listened attentively to the end, toying with the ring which ultimately he slipped on the forefinger of his right hand. After hearing all he had to say he dismissed Tamb' Itam to have food and rest. Orders for the return in the afternoon were given immediately. Afterwards Dain Waris lay down again, open-eyed, while his personal attendants were preparing his food at the fire, by which Tamb' Itam also sat talking to the men who lounged up to hear the latest intelligence from the town. The sun was eating up the mist. A good watch was kept upon the reach of the main stream where the boat of the whites was expected to appear every moment.

"It was then that Brown took his revenge upon the world which, after twenty years of contemptuous and reckless bullying, refused him the tribute of a common robber's success. It was an act of cold-blooded ferocity, and it consoled him on his deathbed like a memory of an indomitable defiance. Stealthily he landed his men on the other side of the island opposite to the Bugis camp, and led them across. After a short but quite silent scuffle, Cornelius, who had tried to slink away at the moment of landing, resigned himself to show the way where the undergrowth was most sparse. Brown held both his skinny hands together behind his back in the grip of one vast fist, and now and then impelled him forward with a fierce push. Cornelius remained as mute as a fish, abject but faithful to his purpose, whose accomplishment loomed before him dimly. At the edge of the patch of forest Brown's men spread themselves out in cover and waited. The camp was plain from end to end before their eyes, and no one looked their way. Nobody ever dreamed that the white men could have any knowledge of the narrow channel at the back of the island. When he judged the moment come, Brown yelled, 'Let them have it,' and fourteen shots rang out like one.

"Tamb' Itam told me the surprise was so great that, except for those who fell dead or wounded, not a soul of them moved for quite an appreciable time after the first discharge. Then a man screamed, and after that scream a great yell of amazement and fear went up from all the throats. A blind panic drove these men in a surging swaying mob to and fro along the shore like a herd of cattle afraid of the water. Some few jumped into the river then, but most of them did so only after the last discharge. Three times Brown's men fired into the ruck,[6] Brown, the only one in view, cursing and yelling, 'Aim low! aim low!'

"Tamb' Itam says that, as for him, he understood at the first volley what had happened. Though untouched he fell down and lay as if dead, but with his eyes open. At the sound of the first shots Dain Waris, reclining on the couch, jumped up and ran out upon the open shore, just in time to receive a bullet in his forehead at the second discharge. Tamb' Itam saw him fling his arms wide open before he fell. Then, he says, a great fear came upon him—not before. The white men retired as they had come—unseen.

"Thus Brown balanced his account with the evil fortune. Notice that even in this awful outbreak there is a superiority as of a man who carries right—the abstract thing—within the envelope of his common desires. It was not a vulgar and treacherous massacre; it was a lesson, a retribution—a demonstration of some obscure and awful attribute of our nature which, I am afraid, is not so very far under the surface as we like to think.

"Afterwards the whites depart unseen by Tamb' Itam, and seem to vanish from before men's eyes altogether; and the schooner, too, vanishes after the manner of stolen goods. But a story is told of a white long-boat picked up a month later in the Indian Ocean by a cargo steamer. Two parched, yellow, glassy-eyed, whispering skeletons in her recognised the authority of a third, who declared that his name was Brown. His schooner, he reported, bound south with a cargo of Java sugar, had sprung a bad leak and sank under his feet. He and his companions were the survivors of a crew of six. The two died on board the steamer which rescued them. Brown lived to be seen by me, and I can testify that he had played his part to the last.

"It seems, however, that in going away they had neglected to cast off Cornelius's canoe. Cornelius himself Brown had let go at the beginning of the shooting, with a kick for a parting benediction. Tamb' Itam, after arising from amongst the dead, saw the Nazarene running up and down the shore amongst the corpses and the expiring fires. He uttered little cries. Suddenly he rushed to the water, and made frantic efforts to get one of the Bugis boats into the water. 'Afterwards, till he had seen me,' related Tamb' Itam, 'he stood looking at the heavy canoe and scratching his head.' 'What became of him?' I asked. Tamb' Itam, staring at me, made an expressive gesture with his right arm. 'Twice I struck, Tuan,' he said. 'When he beheld me approaching he cast himself violently on the ground and made a great outcry, kicking. He screeched like a frightened hen till he felt the point; then he was still, and lay staring at me while his life went out of his eyes.'

6. Crowd.

"This done, Tamb' Itam did not tarry. He understood the importance of being the first with the awful news at the fort. There were, of course, many survivors of Dain Waris's party; but in the extremity of panic some had swum across the river, others had bolted into the bush. The fact is that they did not know really who struck that blow—whether more white robbers were not coming, whether they had not already got hold of the whole land. They imagined themselves to be the victims of a vast treachery, and utterly doomed to destruction. It is said that some small parties did not come in till three days afterwards. However, a few tried to make their way back to Patusan at once, and one of the canoes that were patrolling the river that morning was in sight of the camp at the very moment of the attack. It is true that at first the men in her leaped overboard and swam to the opposite bank, but afterwards they returned to their boat and started fearfully upstream. Of these Tamb' Itam had an hour's advance."

Chapter Forty-Five

"When Tamb' Itam, paddling madly, came into the town-reach, the women, thronging the platforms before the houses, were looking out for the return of Dain Waris's little fleet of boats. The town had a festive air; here and there men, still with spears or guns in their hands, could be seen moving or standing on the shore in groups. Chinamen's shops had been opened early; but the market-place was empty, and a sentry, still posted at the corner of the fort, made out Tamb' Itam, and shouted to those within. The gate was wide open. Tamb' Itam jumped ashore and ran in headlong. The first person he met was the girl coming down from the house.

"Tamb' Itam, disordered, panting, with trembling lips and wild eyes, stood for a time before her as if a sudden spell had been laid on him. Then he broke out very quickly: 'They have killed Dain Waris and many more.' She clapped her hands, and her first words were, 'Shut the gates.' Most of the fortmen had gone back to their houses, but Tamb' Itam hurried on the few who remained for their turn of duty within. The girl stood in the middle of the courtyard while the others ran about. 'Doramin,' she cried despairingly, as Tamb' Itam passed her. Next time he went by he answered her thought rapidly. 'Yes. But we have all the powder in Patusan.' She caught him by the arm, and, pointing at the house, 'Call him out,' she whispered, trembling.

"Tamb' Itam ran up the steps. His master was sleeping. 'It is I, Tamb' Itam,' he cried at the door, 'with tidings that cannot wait.' He saw Jim turn over on the pillow and open his eyes, and he burst out at once. 'This, Tuan, is a day of evil, an accursed day.' His master raised himself on his elbow to listen—just as Dain Waris had done. And then Tamb' Itam began his tale, trying to relate the story in order, calling Dain Waris Panglima, and saying: 'The Panglima then called out to the chief of his own boatmen, "Give Tamb' Itam something to eat" '—when his master put his feet to the ground and looked at him with such a discomposed face that the words remained in his throat.

" 'Speak out,' said Jim. 'Is he dead?' 'May you live long,' cried Tamb' Itam. 'It was a most cruel treachery. He ran out at the first shots and fell. . . .' His master walked to the window and with his fist struck at the shutter. The room was made light; and then in a steady voice, but speaking fast, he began to give him orders to assemble a fleet of boats for immediate pursuit, go to this man, to the other—send messengers; and as he talked he sat down on the bed, stooping to lace his boots hurriedly, and suddenly looked up. 'Why do you stand here?' he asked very red-faced. 'Waste no time.' Tamb' Itam did not move. 'Forgive me, Tuan, but . . . but,' he began to stammer. 'What?' cried his master aloud, looking terrible, leaning forward with his hands gripping the edge of the bed. 'It is not safe for thy servant to go out amongst the people,' said Tamb' Itam, after hesitating a moment.

"Then Jim understood. He had retreated from one world, for a small matter of an impulsive jump, and now the other, the work of his own hands, had fallen in ruins upon his head. It was not safe for his servant to go out amongst his own people! I believe that in that very moment he had decided to defy the disaster in the only way it occurred to him such a disaster could be defied; but all I know is that, without a word, he came out of his room and sat before the long table, at the head of which he was accustomed to regulate the affairs of his world, proclaiming daily the truth that surely lived in his heart. The dark powers should not rob him twice of his peace. He sat like a stone figure. Tamb' Itam, deferential, hinted at preparations for defence. The girl he loved came in and spoke to him, but he made a sign with his hand, and she was awed by the dumb appeal for silence in it. She went out on the verandah and sat on the threshold, as if to guard him with her body from dangers outside.

"What thoughts passed through his head—what memories? Who can tell? Everything was gone, and he who had been once unfaithful to his trust had lost again all men's confidence. It was then, I believe, he tried to write—to somebody—and gave it up. Loneliness was closing on him. People had trusted him with their lives —only for that; and yet they could never, as he had said, never be made to understand him. Those without did not hear him make a sound. Later, towards the evening, he came to the door and called for Tamb' Itam. 'Well?' he asked. 'There is much weeping. Much anger, too,' said Tamb' Itam. Jim looked up at him. 'You know,' he murmured. 'Yes, Tuan,' said Tamb' Itam. 'Thy servant does know, and the gates are closed. We shall have to fight.' 'Fight! What for?' he asked. 'For our lives.' 'I have no life,' he said. Tamb' Itam heard a cry from the girl at the door. 'Who knows?' said Tamb' Itam. 'By audacity and cunning we may even escape. There is much fear in men's hearts, too.' He went out, thinking vaguely of boats and of open sea, leaving Jim and the girl together.

"I haven't the heart to set down here such glimpses as she had given me of the hour or more she passed in there wrestling with him for the possession of her happiness. Whether he had any hope—what he expected, what he imagined—it is impossible to say. He was inflexible, and with the growing loneliness of his obstinacy his spirit seemed to rise above the ruins of his existence. She cried 'Fight!' into his ear. She could not understand. There was nothing to fight for. He was going to prove his power in another way and conquer the fatal destiny itself. He came out into the courtyard, and behind him, with streaming hair, wild of face, breathless, she staggered out and leaned on the side of the doorway. 'Open the gates,' he ordered. Afterwards, turning to those of his men who were inside, he gave them leave to depart to their homes. 'For how long, Tuan?' asked one of them timidly. 'For all life,' he said, in a sombre tone.

"A hush had fallen upon the town after the outburst of wailing and lamentation that had swept over the river, like a gust of wind from the opened abode of sorrow. But rumours flew in whispers, filling the hearts with consternation and horrible doubts. The robbers were coming back, bringing many others with them, in a great ship, and there would be no refuge in the land for any one. A sense of utter insecurity as during an earthquake pervaded the minds of men, who whispered their suspicions, looking at each other as if in the presence of some awful portent.

"The sun was sinking towards the forests when Dain Waris's body was brought into Doramin's campong. Four men carried it in, covered decently with a white sheet which the old mother had sent out down to the gate to meet her son on his return. They laid him at Doramin's feet, and the old man sat still for a long time, one hand on each knee, looking down. The fronds of palms swayed gently, and the foliage of fruit trees stirred above his head. Every single man of his people was there, fully armed, when the old *nakhoda* at last raised his eyes. He moved them slowly over the crowd, as if seeking for a missing face. Again his chin sank on his breast.

The whispers of many men mingled with the slight rustling of the leaves.

"The Malay who had brought Tamb' Itam and the girl to Samarang was there, too. 'Not so angry as many,' he said to me, but struck with a great awe and wonder at the 'suddenness of men's fate, which hangs over their heads like a cloud charged with thunder.' He told me that when Dain Waris's body was uncovered at a sign of Doramin's, he whom they often called the white lord's friend was disclosed lying unchanged with his eyelids a little open as if about to wake. Doramin leaned forward a little more, like one looking for something fallen on the ground. His eyes searched the body from its feet to its head, for the wound maybe. It was in the forehead and small; and there was no word spoken while one of the bystanders, stooping, took off the silver ring from the cold stiff hand. In silence he held it up before Doramin. A murmur of dismay and horror ran through the crowd at the sight of that familiar token. The old *nakhoda* stared at it, and suddenly let out one great fierce cry, deep from the chest, a roar of pain and fury, as mighty as the bellow of a wounded bull, bringing great fear into men's hearts, by the magnitude of his anger and his sorrow that could be plainly discerned without words. There was a great stillness afterwards for a space, while the body was being borne aside by four men. They laid it down under a tree, and on the instant, with one long shriek, all the women of the household began to wail together; they mourned with shrill cries; the sun was setting, and in the intervals of screamed lamentations the high sing-song voices of two old men intoning the Koran chanted alone.

"About this time Jim, leaning on a gun-carriage, looked at the river, and turned his back on the house; and the girl, in the doorway, panting as if she had run herself to a standstill, was looking at him across the yard. Tamb' Itam stood not far from his master, waiting patiently for what might happen. All at once Jim, who seemed to be lost in quiet thought, turned to him and said, 'Time to finish this.'

"'Tuan?' said Tamb' Itam, advancing with alacrity. He did not know what his master meant, but as soon as Jim made a movement the girl started, too, and walked down into the open space. It seems that no one else of the people of the house was in sight. She tottered slightly, and about half-way down called out to Jim, who had apparently resumed his peaceful contemplation of the river. He turned round, setting his back against the gun. 'Will you fight?' she cried. 'There is nothing to fight for,' he said; 'nothing is lost.' Saying this he made a step towards her. 'Will you fly?' she cried again. 'There is no escape,' he said, stopping short, and she stood still also, silent, devouring him with her eyes. 'And you shall go?'

she said slowly. He bent his head. 'Ah!' she exclaimed, peering at him as it were, 'you are mad or false. Do you remember the night I prayed you to leave me, and you said that you could not? That it was impossible! Impossible! Do you remember you said you would never leave me? Why? I asked you for no promise. You promised unasked—remember.' 'Enough, poor girl,' he said. 'I should not be worth having.'

"Tamb' Itam said that while they were talking she would laugh loud and senselessly like one under the visitation of God. His master put his hands to his head. He was fully dressed as for every day, but without a hat. She stopped laughing suddenly. 'For the last time,' she cried menacingly, 'will you defend yourself?' 'Nothing can touch me,' he said in a last flicker of superb egoism. Tamb' Itam saw her lean forward where she stood, open her arms, and run at him swiftly. She flung herself upon his breast and clasped him round the neck.

" 'Ah! but I shall hold thee thus,' she cried. . . . 'Thou art mine!'

"She sobbed on his shoulder. The sky over Patusan was blood-red, immense, streaming like an open vein. An enormous sun nestled crimson amongst the tree-tops, and the forest below had a black and forbidding face.

"Tamb' Itam tells me that on that evening the aspect of the heavens was angry and frightful. I may well believe it, for I know that on that very day a cyclone passed within sixty miles of the coast, though there was hardly more than a languid stir of air in the place.

"Suddenly Tamb' Itam saw Jim catch her arms, trying to unclasp her hands. She hung on them with her head fallen back; her hair touched the ground. 'Come here!' his master called, and Tamb' Itam helped to ease her down. It was difficult to separate her fingers. Jim, bending over her, looked earnestly upon her face, and all at once ran to the landing-stage. Tamb' Itam followed him, but turning his head, he saw that she had struggled up to her feet. She ran after them a few steps, then fell down heavily on her knees. 'Tuan! Tuan!' called Tamb' Itam, 'look back'; but Jim was already in a canoe, standing up paddle in hand. He did not look back. Tamb' Itam had just time to scramble in after him when the canoe floated clear. The girl was then on her knees, with clasped hands, at the water-gate. She remained thus for a time in a supplicating attitude before she sprang up. 'You are false!' she screamed out after Jim. 'Forgive me,' he cried. 'Never! Never!' she called back.

"Tamb' Itam took the paddle from Jim's hands, it being unseemly that he should sit while his lord paddled. When they

reached the other shore his master forbade him to come any farther; but Tamb' Itam did follow him at a distance, walking up the
slope to Doramin's campong.

"It was beginning to grow dark. Torches twinkled here and there.
Those they met seemed awestruck, and stood aside hastily to let
Jim pass. The wailing of women came from above. The courtyard was full of armed Bugis with their followers, and of Patusan
people.

"I do not know what this gathering really meant. Were these
preparations for war, or for vengeance, or to repulse a threatened
invasion? Many days elapsed before the people had ceased to look
out, quaking, for the return of the white men with long beards
and in rags, whose exact relation to their own white man they could
never understand. Even for those simple minds poor Jim remains
under a cloud.

"Doramin, alone, immense and desolate, sat in his arm-chair with
the pair of flintlock pistols on his knees, faced by an armed throng.
When Jim appeared, at somebody's exclamation, all the heads
turned round together, and then the mass opened right and left,
and he walked up a lane of averted glances. Whispers followed
him; murmurs: 'He has worked all the evil.' 'He hath a charm.'
. . . He heard them—perhaps!

"When he came up into the light of torches the wailing of the
women ceased suddenly. Doramin did not lift his head, and Jim
stood silent before him for a time. Then he looked to the left,
and moved in that direction with measured steps. Dain Waris's
mother crouched at the head of the body, and the grey dishevelled
hair concealed her face. Jim came up slowly, looked at his dead
friend, lifting the sheet, then dropped it without a word. Slowly he
walked back.

" 'He came! He came!' was running from lip to lip, making a
murmur to which he moved. 'He hath taken it upon his own head,'
a voice said aloud. He heard this and turned to the crowd. 'Yes.
Upon my head.' A few people recoiled. Jim waited awhile before
Doramin, and then said gently, 'I am come in sorrow.' He waited
again. 'I am come ready and unarmed,' he repeated.

"The unwieldy old man, lowering his big forehead like an ox
under a yoke, made an effort to rise, clutching at the flintlock pistols on his knees. From his throat came gurgling, choking, inhuman
sounds, and his two attendants helped him from behind. People
remarked that the ring which he had dropped on his lap fell and
rolled against the foot of the white man, and that poor Jim glanced
down at the talisman that had opened for him the door of fame,
love, and success within the wall of forests fringed with white foam,
within the coast that under the western sun looks like the very

stronghold of the night. Doramin, struggling to keep his feet, made with his two supporters a swaying, tottering group; his little eyes stared with an expression of mad pain, of rage, with a ferocious glitter, which the bystanders noticed; and then, while Jim stood stiffened and with bared head in the light of torches, looking him straight in the face, he clung heavily with his left arm round the neck of a bowed youth, and lifting deliberately his right, shot his son's friend through the chest.

"The crowd, which had fallen apart behind Jim as soon as Doramin had raised his hand, rushed tumultuously forward after the shot. They say that the white man sent right and left at all those faces a proud and unflinching glance. Then with his hand over his lips he fell forward, dead.

"And that's the end. He passes away under a cloud, inscrutable at heart, forgotten, unforgiven, and excessively romantic. Not in the wildest days of his boyish visions could he have seen the alluring shape of such an extraordinary success! For it may very well be that in the short moment of his last proud and unflinching glance, he had beheld the face of that opportunity which, like an Eastern bride, had come veiled to his side.

"But we can see him, an obscure conqueror of fame, tearing himself out of the arms of a jealous love at the sign, at the call of his exalted egoism. He goes away from a living woman to celebrate his pitiless wedding with a shadowy ideal of conduct. Is he satisfied—quite, now, I wonder? We ought to know. He is one of us—and have I not stood up once, like an evoked ghost, to answer for his eternal constancy? Was I so very wrong after all? Now he is no more, there are days when the reality of his existence comes to me with an immense, with an overwhelming force; and yet upon my honour there are moments, too, when he passes from my eyes like a disembodied spirit astray amongst the passions of his earth, ready to surrender himself faithfully to the claim of his own world of shades.

"Who knows? He is gone, inscrutable at heart, and the poor girl is leading a sort of soundless, inert life in Stein's house. Stein has aged greatly of late. He feels it himself, and says often that he is 'preparing to leave all this; preparing to leave . . .' while he waves his hand sadly at his butterflies."

September 1899–July 1900.

THE END

The Text

Textual History

The printed version of *Lord Jim* went through some five revisions: from the periodical version (P) in *Blackwood's Magazine* (October 1899—November 1900) to the first English edition (E¹) and the first American edition (A¹), both of 1900; from the first English to the second English edition (E²) in 1917; from the second English to the second American (A²) in 1920; and from the second American to the third English (E³) in 1921.

In terms of symbols, the line appears to be as follows:

$$P \longrightarrow E^1 \longrightarrow E^2 \longrightarrow A^2 \longrightarrow E^3$$
$$\searrow \downarrow$$
$$A^1$$

The present edition represents a full collation of the three principal editions: the periodical, the first English, and the third English. All discrepancies among these have been checked against the second English and the second American editions. I have essentially ignored the first American edition in the light of Conrad's inscription in Richard Curle's copy: "Set up probably from English proofs but neither revised nor in any other way corrected by me. It is probably much nearer the text of *B'wood's Maga.* than the first English Ed. of book form."[1] This is indeed true of the last ten chapters, but the first thirty-five are, in fact, much closer to the first English edition.[2]

The copy-text for the present edition comes from the limited edition of Conrad's works published by Heinemann in 1921, rather than from one of the many editions published by Dent (in England) and Doubleday (in America) beginning in 1923. Some four years after Conrad's death in 1924 Richard Curle wrote ambiguously that Conrad considered his "final text" to be the "collected edition book form."[3] But a letter from Conrad to Reginald Leon in February 1917 makes clearer Conrad's intentions: "The only edition in which I take interest is the Collected Edition (limited to 1,000 sets in England and in the U. S.) which Doubleday, Page in New York and Wm. Heinemann here are going to publish after the war. I've settled the format, the bindings, the fount, and the paper. For the text, it will be exactly the text of the English first editions freed from misprints and with, perhaps, a few (very few) verbal alterations."[4] The two identical limited editions implied in this letter became ultimately the handsome Doubleday "Sun Dial" edition, which first appeared in 1920 and is still

1. Quoted by John Dozier Gordan, *Joseph Conrad: The Making of a Novelist*, Cambridge, 1940, p. 155.
2. I am indebted to Mr. and Mrs. Kenneth Lincoln for the pertinent collating.
3. *The Last Twelve Years of Joseph Conrad*, New York, 1928, p. 64.
4. Quoted by Eloise Knapp Hay, *The Political Novels of Joseph Conrad*, Chicago, 1963, pp. 181–82n.

being reprinted, and the genuinely limited Heinemann edition of 1921. I have chosen the latter for my copy-text because it was later in time and, being set up in England, would have been easier for Conrad to oversee: it incorporates virtually all the new revisions in the "Sun-Dial" and adds many more. Though some subsequent "collected editions" of Doubleday and Dent did appear within Conrad's lifetime, they derive from the "Sun-Dial" and seem not to have been touched by Conrad.

Lord Jim was much revised. Unfortunately the changes from manuscript to periodical version are not available to me. The bulk of the surviving manuscript (about two-thirds of the novel) is housed in the Rosenbach Collection in Philadelphia and may not be copied. However, the reader can get some sense of the manuscript by reading in this volume the brief Harvard fragment, "Tuan Jim: A Sketch."

By far the most interesting and most numerous (nearly four hundred) substantive revisions occur between the periodical version and the first English edition. This is hardly surprising, since Conrad's conception of the novel changed radically while he was writing it, perhaps after it was already appearing in *Blackwood's Magazine*. (From an intended 20,000 words in four installments, the novel swelled to 120,000 words in fourteen installments.) The most sizable revisions occur in the first half of the novel: Conrad made seventeen drastic cuts (passages from five to fifty-seven lines in length) and well over fifty cuts of one to three lines. Of these major cuts, perhaps the most significant are those dealing with Jim's psychology. Apparently he felt that he had been too explicit in the periodical version, that later in the novel he had sufficiently dramatized his conceptions, and that therefore the explicit statements ought to go. But the revisions illuminate every aspect of Conrad's artistry, especially his sensitivity to tone and his ear for rhythm. A few of the alterations simply correct the inevitable minor mistakes of a foreigner. Substantive changes in later editions are rarer and less important, although the interested reader may find some surprising alterations. According to my count, there are twenty-seven substantive changes between the first and second English editions, thirty-one between the second English and the second American, and sixty-eight between the second American and the third English. The textual notes contain, to the best of my knowledge and ability, all these substantive changes.

With each edition of *Lord Jim*, there were changes in punctuation. Although the first edition shows only about 56 changes from the periodical version, the second English has nearly 200 changes from its predecessor, the second American about 175 more, and the third English an amazing 560 changes from the second American. These changes were frequently additions, particularly of commas. Since no editions heretofore derive from the limited one by Heinemann, readers familiar with *Lord Jim* may notice the slightly slower pacing that results from the heavier punctuation. Perhaps the most common revision in the second English edition is to make more correct and consistent the punctuation of quotations. This edition also frequently removes commas before dashes. The second American edition most characteristically and with great frequency sets off "too" with commas. The third English edition habitually links with commas two or more adjectives; it sets off with commas such adverbs as "nevertheless," "still," and "though"; it uses fewer exclamation points and often substitutes for them commas and question marks; it usually puts in commas before quotations; and in it parenthetical clauses and prepositional phrases are also frequently set off by commas. Further, unlike all the other editions, it sets points of suspension within quotation marks (myself . . . .') rather than outside (myself.' . . .), and hyphenates many words that were either compounds or pairs of words in earlier editions ("head-man" for "headman," "back-water" for "backwater," "swish-swish" for "swish swish"). There are, however, exceptions ("by and by" for "by-and-by," "dark blue" for "dark-blue"). It should be said, finally, that the punctuation in this third English edition, our copy-text, is much the most consistent of all the editions. Practically every degree of heaviness in pointing (commas between two or more adjectives, for example) is represented sporadically in previous editions; only the third English enforces an almost complete consistency.

Just how much these changes in punctuation reflect Conrad's own attitude and how much the style of his publishers, is difficult to ascertain. The manuscript of *Lord Jim* is very lightly punctuated, even more lightly than the periodical version.[5] Perhaps Conrad deliberately left such matters to his editor during his early years and took a greater interest later, or perhaps he habitually acquiesced to the prevailing house style. Lacking proofs corrected in his hand, we cannot tell.[6]

The present text attempts to follow as closely as possible Conrad's intentions in the third English edition. Only where the readings of other editions suggest an error in proofreading have I emended the copy-text. I have therefore not tampered with grammatical errors when they persist in all editions. Emendations are indicated by an asterisk.

Lord Jim exists in the following printed states, published during Conrad's lifetime:

P   The periodical text published in fourteen installments in *Blackwood's Magazine*, CLXVI–CLXVIII (October 1899–November 1900).

E¹ The first English edition, published by William Blackwood and Sons, Edinburgh and London, October 15, 1900. It went through many subsequent impressions: December 1900, 1904, 1905, 1914, 1915, 1917, and some ten more, up to 1948.

A¹ The first American edition, published by Doubleday and McClure Co., New York, 1900. The Library of Congress lists impressions of 1916, 1921, and 1922. In other libraries, I have noted impressions of 1910, 1914, 1915, 1920.

E² The second English edition, with the "Author's Note" for the first time, published by J. M. Dent and Sons Ltd., London and Toronto,

5. I am indebted to Mr. Kenneth B. Newell of U.C.L.A. for this information.
6. That Conrad took some interest in punctuation is indicated by his copy-text for the Heinemann edition of *The Nigger of the "Narcissus"* in the Keat-ing Collection at Yale University. On at least nine pages Conrad, in his own hand, changed punctuation. I am indebted to Mr. David F. Thorburn of Yale for this information.

1917. The Heinemann edition lists a second impression in 1918 and a third in 1920.

A² The second American edition, volume four of *The Works of Joseph Conrad*, "The Sun Dial Edition," published by Doubleday, Page and Company, Garden City, New York, 1920. Although the Library of Congress lists this edition as "limited to seven hundred and thirty-five copies," many subsequent impressions have been taken, of which the two most important are listed below.

E³ The third English edition, volume four of *The Works of Joseph Conrad*, "printed from type that has been distributed," and "limited to 780 sets, of which 750 are for sale and 30 for presentation," published by William Heinemann, London, 1921. The Heinemann edition is the copy-text for the present edition.

A²ᵃ Volume five, *The Works of Joseph Conrad*, "The Uniform Edition," J. M. Dent and Sons Ltd., London and Toronto, 1923. Not a new edition, it derives from the Doubleday "Sun Dial," probably, according to Bruce Harkness,⁷ from a duplicate set of plates. It was reprinted in 1926; in 1946, as part of the "Collected Edition," it appeared with five additional pages of biographical and bibliographical material. It is still in print.

A²ᵇ The earliest American reprinting of the "Sun Dial" that I have seen, the "Personal," published by Doubleday, Page and Company, Garden City, New York, 1923. Also in that year appeared the "Concord Edition." The "Canterbury Edition" came out in 1924, the year of Conrad's death; the expensive "Memorial Edition" appeared in 1925 but must have been planned earlier (and hopefully not as a "memorial"), since Conrad signed the leaves of ninety-nine sets; the "Kent Edition" was issued in both 1925 and 1926. Other impressions have since appeared. There is no evidence that Conrad had a hand in any of these. The "Personal" differs from the "Sun Dial" in only about twenty-five instances, all of which could have been printers' sophistications.

Textual Notes

ix (*Subtitle*) **A Tale** *P* A Sketch *A¹*, *A²ᵇ* A Romance
2.8 Lord Jim [*Ital.*] *E²*, *A²* Lord Jim
2.22, 23 he is *E²*, *A²* he's
*2.29 *E²*, *A²* **June 1917** *E³* 1917
*4.34 *P*, *E¹*, *E²*, *A²* **glass** *E³* grass
7.36 has *P*, *E¹*, *E²*, *A²* had
10.39 Strait *P*, *E¹* Straits
13.15 days. From *P* days. What could happen that he was not able to master and subdue? . . . and the end of his

days was very, very far. Nothing prevented him from believing himself as steadfast as the Atlas bearing up a world, and as invulnerable as the stars. He dared the future as though the Unattainable that dwells beyond the retreating line of the horizon had been lying in the hollow of his palm. From
*15.7 *P*, *E¹*, *E²*, *A²* **drink** *E³* drunk
17.16 if *P*, *E¹*, *E²*, *A²* it
18.7 stabbed. The *P* stabbed, and those

7. *Conrad's "Heart of Darkness" and the Critics*, San Francisco, 1960, pp. 161–63.

questions that stretched his soul on the rack. The

18.14, 15 anything! ¶ **"After** P anything—as if facts mattered in the face of terrors! ¶ After

19.21 things. The P things. There had been a peculiar awfulness in the calm of the sea, in the serenity of the sky, in the words pronounced, in the gestures made, in the silence of a passive world, in the sleep of an unconscious crowd. The

20.9 him. He P him. Those men would never know the truth, nobody would ever know the truth; there could be no truth in a simple yes or no. At that moment he was less concerned about himself than at any time since the inquiry began, but he despaired of his power to show the truth, and it was a great despair. He

20.12 damp P hot

20.41 wayfarer P, wanderer

22.41 tragic as well, began P tragic began

24.1 his head P round

24.40 safe. I've P safe! Oh, I've

25.13, 14 sling, and a P sling; a

25.15, 16 who looked P and looking

26.10 face over P face of regret over

27.4 are P get

27.7 condemnations P, E¹, E² condemnation

28.16 has P had

28.19 will P, E¹, E², A² shall

29.21 those P, E¹ these

29.24 a droll and fearsome effect P an effect of fearsome drollery

29.24 those P the

29.25 one P you

29.26 to P would

29.26, 27 the little box on wheels to P that the little box on wheels would

29.35 snorted P snorting

30.38 moustaches P, E¹, E², A² moustache

32.14 the ghost P the uprisen ghost

33.11 get a smoke P smoke it

33.22 down a P down the tube of a

34.11, 12 enabled me to compose my distracted P was sweeter than balm to my lacerated

34.18 Four P Seven

35.29, 30 That's the man. P Didn't you?

35.31, 32 him. He P him, and had the face of a man sitting out of (*sic*) dull farce in a theatre. He

35.34 those P, E¹ these

35.34 know nothing P in the whole of their lives know no moment

36.3 price. I P price. The serenity of his confidence in himself was intolerable. He had the selfish conceit of a clever boy, bound in the thick hide of a rhinoceros. I

36.32 case. The verdict must have been P case, probing his own soft spot—accused, tribunal, judge, and executioner in one. The verdict was

36.34, 35 was no doubt P must have been

36.37, 38 live. I am in a position to know that it P live. It

36.45 in his relations P in relation

37.21 would have P ought to have

37.43 dial to run, and P dial, and

38.32 him once P him do once

39.33 so far gone as P abandoned enough

42.37 an insect P a beetle

44.41 about. 'You P about. I was so taken up in wondering what obscure processes were taking place within him, that I did not even attempt to recall any external event which might have been the cause of his only too clear intention to create a scandalous disturbance in this, of all places in the world. 'You

45.4 nature. I P nature. Some quality exaggerated into a defect was hurrying him into it. He was carried away; he would be blundering all his life. He was a helpless victim of his mental and physical organisation, about to give himself horribly away, and pathetically ignorant of the curse. All these notions were the outcome of sudden impression rather than of reflection. I

45.14 his own eyes P his eyes

45.17 do. But P do or what to say. But

45.18 was blackness P, E¹, E² was a blackness

45.37, 38 given himself away utterly P utterly given himself away

46.24 tears. I P tears. He turned to me, and I thought he would speak, but I

46.28 appeasement? Who P appeasement? The eye of man can't follow nor the mind of man conceive the crooked ways of another man's thoughts; these naïve perversities of reasoning, inspired by the desperation of self-love, kept up by preposterous hopes, arriving at astonishing, at incredible conclusions. Who

46.30, 31 case. He P case. He had humiliated himself only to be baffled. He

47.10 meaning? 'You P meaning? Was he a slave to unparalleled stupidity or master of the most consummate dissimulation? 'You

47.14 view of him P vista, a new horizon

47.19, 20 views he let me have of himself P new vistas he gave me

47.41 over P across

47.42 floor; now P floor, ministering obsequiously to those ravenous appetites from over the sea; now

48.2 wit embroidering P wit, established during the passage, embroidering

48.9 acquaintance. It P acquaintance, without my being able to imagine where he could have found, within himself, a spot isolated enough for the digging of that convenient grave. It

48.21 weather. My P weather. I was

erecting theories as unstable as castles in Spain,—theories which, I instinctively felt, would be each of them found false, the common fate of all generalisations about men who are only partly in nature. Theirs is always a special case. This was a special case. My

48.24 him. He *P* him. We had been conversing as coolly of vital matters as though there had been no sense of morality left on earth, and my remark was made with all the propriety of a dining-room indifference. He

48.44 chair; I *P* chair for fear of snapping the fine-spun thread of his confidence. I

48.45 He would be confident and depressed all in the same breath, *P* His imagination—a rare thing, the last thing I would have suspected him of— was what was wrong with him. Twenty times in the course of his narrative he would give himself away by some word, gesture, or exclamation, and take himself back with a strange unconsciousness that, upon my word, would make my blood run cold. He would be confident and depressed all in the same breath; it was as though the physical wellbeing produced by food and drink, the chance of open talk, the soothing effect of good tobacco, had overlaid the subtle despair in his mind,

50.3 mistake was *P* mistake on the part of any man was

50.42 distinction. As *P* distinction. He astonished me by the suggestiveness of his expressions. He was uncommon; he made you feel this, not by his argumentation—there was not a beggarly two-pennyworth of logic in him—but by the spirit of subtle resentment that pervaded his narrative, changing it into an *ex-parte* presentation of his case against something indefinite, against the world at large, against some universal and disembodied might that had used him ill. As

51.1 imagine. I *P* imagine. The disembodied might had selected him for the object of a scurvy trick; he had given himself away before the menacing posture of the indefinite and got nothing for it—not even the consolation of knowing he had saved his life. ¶ "I

51.39 last! A *P* last! Oh, he got there without question. A

52.10 it. Presently *P* it. He had infinite resources within him to ward off any attack I could deliver. Presently

52.25 bulk-lamp *P, E¹, E²* globe-lamp

52.32, 33 straightway *P, E¹, E², A²* straight away

52.41, 42 ladder. ¶ "He *P* ladder. ¶ "It was very curious to note that he did not understand in the least the deep significance of the incident. It meant that the tension of his brain was al-

ready too great to allow it to take proper care of the balance of his body. He mentioned the fact casually enough but for a shade of uneasy irritation, as if there had been some inherent and terrifying quality in sailcloth which had been put forth unfairly against his fortitude. In this serious emergency his liability to be startled by trifles was coming to the surface. His imagination was plunging, and ready to bolt with him. He had a narrow escape there, he said in an injured tone. He might, he pointed out, have fallen down the hatchway and broken his leg—'and where would I have been then, with the ship sinking?' he added, with odious innocence. ¶ "He

53.30 do. It *P* do. It was too cruel. It

***53.37** *P, E¹, E², A²* **re-forming** *E³* reforming

54.21 arms *P, E¹, E²* arm

54.28 peaceful *P* resigned

54.36 well *P* best

54.41, 42 water to take *P, E¹, E²* water take

56.5 this. The *P* this; it savoured of the impossible and at the same time carried conviction, extorted a wondering assent. The

56.15, 16 whispering *P* screeching

57.1, 2 below? And the timber—the timber! Would *P* below? Would

***59.34** *P, E¹, E², A²* **black** *E³* back

60.1 those *P, E¹* these

60.2 deception *P* lie

60.2 which *P, E¹, E²* where

60.4 bridge, as far *P* bridge, far

60.9 beside *P* besides

60.41 darker *P* dark

62.25 thick *P* fat

62.41 suddenly, *P* then

64.20 self-control *P, E¹* self-command

65.3 events. Twice *P* events. They stood before me indubitably true, but a little distorted, as if seen by the sinister glow of his burning contempt. It fell on the sky, on the earth, on the ship, on the men—on himself too—oh yes! on himself too: only he seemed honestly confident of his erect attitude in the general wreck of decent appearances. Twice

67.16 me all this *P, E¹* me of all this *E²* me all of this

68.2 living *P* live

68.5 could *P* couldn't

68.36, 37 boat. . . . I *P* boat, and—I

69.23 Another *P* A man

***71.31** *P, E¹, E²·oar A², E³* oars

***71.41** *P, E¹* stooped *E², A², E³* stopped

***71.43** *P, E¹, E², A²* **uninterrupted, a little** *E³* uninterrupted, little

72.22 your hand *P, E¹, E², A²* his hand

72.26 make it out *P, E¹, E², A²* make out

72.28 It saved *P, E¹, E², A²* It has saved

73.26, 27 back to his oar. I *P* back. I

73.42, 43 capital. On the vivid stars the

high corner of the Harbour Office stood *P* capital, with vivid stars between, and to the left the high corner of the Harbour Office coming

74.17 that made *P* that had made

74.17 took *P, E¹, E², A²* taken

74.28 hatred *P, E¹, E²* hate

74.36, 37 triumph, are *P* triumph all over the world's surface, are

77.19 couldn't! All *P* couldn't! There is a time in my life when I had forgotten what sleep was made of, what the word meant; that there was a state in which I could be unconscious of myself. All

78.2 passing. 'Do *P* passing,—something swift and full of purpose, like a cast of the hand-lead taken in shoaling water. 'Do

78.19 a second, glowed *P* the last time, gleamed *E¹, E², A²* a moment, gleamed

78.22, 23 was a youngster *P* was a boy, fair, frank, silly if you will. A youngster

78.40–42 such * * * reward! *P* envy of the past, amusement, and infinite pity. Who could resist it? There is such magnificent vagueness in the impulses that had driven each of us to sea, such a glorious indefiniteness of expectations, such a beautiful greed of adventures that are their own and only reward! In other occupations the youngster knows something; he expects—this—that—the other definite thing. In this he only desires, with all his heart, with all his soul—desires—what? He cannot tell. He does not know. What he gets—well, we won't talk of that; but can one of us restrain a smile? In no other kind of life is the illusion more wide of reality—in no other is the beginning *all* illusion—the disenchantment more swift—the subjugation more complete; and no other has the power to extort bitter love for the sake of unfulfilled hopes. Hadn't we all commenced with the same desire, ended with the same knowledge, carried the memory of the same cherished glamour through the sordid days of imprecation? Well may those few of us who can speak, looking from under the black shadows of sails at the bewitching face of the moonlit sea, whisper to themselves 'Odi et amo.' It is the very truth. The intoxication of charm imagined, the desire of the subtle spirit for ever escaping, the hate of reality sobering and cruel, are like the shadow of the passionate visitation of the gods—the devouring rage of tenderness entwined with the hot rage of anger. 'Odi et amo' they can say as if speaking to life itself, that for all of us begins with the same glamour, and runs through the days of execration to the obscurity of a common end.

80.23 meditated *P* was meditative

80.42 those *P, E¹, E², A²* these

81.15 alone—for myself *P, E¹, E²* alone before myself

88.12 dust. 'I *P* dust. He turned away. 'I

88.34 meat. What *P* meat. I don't know what I expected him to reveal. I certainly expected something. What

89.6 His imperturbable and mature calmness was that of *P* In his imperturbable and mature calmness he did look like

90.1 pronounced finally *P* said with finality

90.2 the personal anecdote *P* the anecdote

90.3 disappointed; the more so as it *P* disappointed. It

90.10 it. And *P* it. One has got to live —you cannot get away from that. And

90.24 rings around *P* rings sparkling and still around

90.28, 29 get on knowing very well that one's *P* live with the knowledge that

90.30, 31 truth the more *P* illusion the less

91.42 by looking at *P* near

91.43 must 'ave *P, E¹, E², A²* must've

92.11 bearded to the waist like *P* bearded like

92.28 the deplorable *P* certain

92.32 left, not *P* left me, not

92.42 neck. Our *P* neck. This is metaphoric speech; but at the time our

93.2 of a formal *P* of formal

93.23 will *P, E¹, E², A²* shall

93.41 kind. . . .' 'It *P* kind to swallow. . . .' 'It

94.2 you can expect *P* you expect

94.17 shades. 'Oh, *P* shades. It was startling to have the thought occur to one—as it did, for some reason, occur to me just then—that his flesh and blood were like mine; his brain too, and whatever else goes to the making of a human being—only that I had escaped being played with in just that infernal way. This consideration checked the many wise things I wished to say; but I spoke all the same. 'Oh!

94.25 thing down—I *P* thing—I

94.31 refused this unique *P* refused. Refused a unique

94.39 said, 'that I *P* said, 'I

95.10 four-and-twenty *P* six-and-twenty

95.40 and from *P* whose safety rests on fidelity to ideas expressed in law, and to despotic and unexpressed ideals. From

96.33 neatly *P* carefully

97.1 had all *P, E¹, E²* and

97.2 exile. This *P* exile. Everything would be over for him. Everything but the distress of his thoughts, the mental suffering, the danger, the poignant incertitude of fate, the regret. This

97.19 then they declared *P* then declared

97.37, 38 duty,' it said. The *P* duty.' The

98.2 stillness wafted *P* stillness as if
wafted
102.4 I've got to *P, E¹, E²* I've to
105.27 have kept *P, E¹* had kept
105.35 the *P, E¹, E²* an
106.5 was *P, E¹, E², A²* were
107.12 Nature *P, E¹* nature
108.20 shore *P, E¹, E², A²* shores
109.37 inconsolable *P, E¹, E², A²* un-
consolable
110.5 resenting.' He *P, E¹, E², A²ᵇ* resenting it.' He
110.31 of asking *P, E¹, E², A²* to ask
112.31 had *P, E¹* have
117.15 chief of *P* chief engineer of
***123.16** *P, E¹, E², A²* **carries** *E³* car-
ried
***123.25, 26** *P, E¹, E², A²ᵇ* **on lifeless**
A², E³ of lifeless
124.29 found refuge *P, E¹, E², A²*
found a refuge
125.42 part *P, E¹* past
127.22 ears *P, E¹, E², A²* ear
128.36 sighed and turned *P* sighed, and
with an air of resignation turned
129.13, 14 so generously encouraging
P generously encouraging; so generously
129.16 legs. Sometimes *P* legs and industriously puffing at his pipe. Sometimes
130.21 im [*Ital.*] *P, E¹, E², A²* in
130.31 So you *P, E¹, E², A²* So if you
***131.37** *P, E¹, E²* **a table** *A², E³* the
table
132.42 seemed *P, E¹, E², A²* seems
133.9 have *P, E¹, E², A²* had
133.29 what *P, E¹, E², A²* that
134.32 Patusan; but *P* Patusan. There
they were out of the way, but
134.35 Cornelius, considered *P* Cornelius something—I don't remember—
considered
135.1 forest *P, E¹, E², A²* forests
136.6 consciousness *P, E¹* conscience
136.21 land *P* earth
137.39 floating *P* indecisive
138.15 power of it, are *P* power it
gives, are
138.15 an *P, E¹, E², A²* a
139.1 but as instruments *P* but instruments
139.26 was *P, E¹* were
139.30 and the stealing *P* and stealing
141.11, 12 and refuge *P, E¹, E², A²*
and a refuge
***145.22** *P, E¹* **roadstead** *E², A², E³*
roadster
***145.31** *P, E¹, E², A²* **this** *E³* his
146.3 gig manned at *P* gig at
146.26 the trade *P* that trade
***147.18** *P, E¹, E², A²* **deported** *E³* de-
parted
147.31 speech; I *P* speech and acts.
During that hurried leave-taking I
147.45 misfortunes *P, E¹* misfortune
148.13 coast of Patusan (I *P* coast (I
148.29 about *P* of
151.19 eh *P, E¹* hey
***153.9** *P, E¹, E², A²ᵇ* **impotent** *A², E³*
important
153.31 immediately afterwards we *P*

immediately we
153.39 colic. I *P* colic or other. I
154.4 short. Thought *P* short. Plop!—
to my waist. Thought
154.7 while *P* when
154.8 slime *P* mud
154.22 fifteen *P* twenty odd
***154.26 kriss** *All editions read* kris
here, but normally E³ *has* kriss. (*Ed.*)
155.35 over his eyes, into *P* in his eyes,
in
156.3 the *P* a
**156.4, 5 of awakening. He remained
lying still for a while, and then he
arose** *P* he gave before he uprose
156.7 animal *P* wild beast
156.43, 44 benevolent eyes *P* benevolent old eyes
156.45 troop *P* whole battalion
157.31, 32 of the Rajah's *P, E¹* of
Rajah's
**159.5, 6 They were wonderfully con-
trasted** *P* It was a wonderful contrast
159.24 on our way *P* and coming
160.8 those *P, E¹* these
162.30 souls *P, E¹, A²* soul
163.3 off together *P, E¹, E²* off all together
165.7 had been *P* was
165.15 was inseparable from *P* hovered
silently round
165.27 had been *P* was
166.17 those *P, E¹* these
166.35 had known *P* knew
166.40 Already he could see *P* He saw
**167.1, 2 After Sherif Ali his turn would
come, and who could resist an attack**
P Who could resist men
167.17 His breathing silences *P* His
silences
167.23 me, while *P* me just then, while
167.37 motherly witch *P* motherly,
brown witch
167.41, 42 removing * * * voice *P*
changing the direction of her eyes, in a
pitying voice she asked
168.19 were the ordinary standpoint *P*
if the ordinary standpoint were
168.26 of split *P* of young split
**168.36 conscience. Through her whole
life the** *P* conscience. The
**168.37, 38 other companion, confidante,
and friend but her daughter** *P* one but
her daughter for companion, confidant,
and friend
168.38, 39 awful Malacca *P, E¹* awful
little Malacca
168.39 after the separation from *P* who
was in reality
168.40 that *P* the
168.43 drop in my hearing, I *P* drop, I
169.10 seeks *P* seems
169.12 caution; for it *P* caution. It
169.29 feelings *P, E¹* feeling
**169.29, 30 warnings, no doubt: warnings
that** *P* warnings—that
169.38 effect. I *P* effect. The romance
applied to everyday uses. Oh, he was
set afloat in a sea of romance, dis-
ported himself, darted here and there,
rested immersed in it, with the uncon-

scious ease of a first-rate swimmer. I
169.43 earnestly *P* in a hurry
170.1 anxious whispers were *P* earnest
whispering was
**170.8, 9 schooner, in which I had my
passage, put** *P* schooner put
170.9, 10 and going ashore, I *P* and I
170.10 the wretched locality *P* it
170.11, 12 big, fat, greasy *P* big, greasy
170.12 of mixed *P* of a hopelessly
mixed
170.12 with turned-out *P* with a pro-
truding paunch and turned out
**170.18 now, he remarked negligently,
and** *P* now—and
170.19 E³, A²ᵇ has *P, E¹, E², A²* had
**170.19, 20 there, I hear . . . . Eh?
What you say?** *P* there . . . Eh?
What?
***170.20** *P, E¹, E²* **Friend** *A², E³* Friends
170.21 verdamte [*Ital.*] *P, E¹, E², A²*
vordamte
170.22 rascal. Eh? *P skelm!*
170.24 Almighty! The *P* Almighty!
Oh, the
170.35 yet. See? Why *P* yet. Why
**170.37 had better look out for him-
self** *P* better look out for that
170.40 trouble. Don't interrupt. I *P*
trouble. I
170.41 know some good people *P* know
people
170.42 can *P* will
171.2 composure that *P* composure
under my eyes that
171.18 fabulously large emerald *P*
fabulous emerald
**171.19, 20 and the belief in it is so
persistent that** *P* while
172.12–14 flowing * * * head *P* She
wore cavalierly a small crimson cap,
something like a fez
172.14 assured *P* quick
172.17 charm and *P* charm, youth and
gravity, and
172.21 At times *P* Or
172.21 down with us and *P* down and
172.23 would remain fastened *P* remained fixed intently
172.24 each pronounced word *P* our
words
173.6 lay down his life *P* wait hand
and foot, to lay down his life if need
be
173.7 silent, indistinct *P* dumb vague
173.10, 11 sound; but when *P* sound.
When
173.12 The girl *P* She
173.21 cautiously—and I *P* cautiously; I
173.35–38 space, * * * slinking. *P* space
of beaten earth as hard as asphalt,
was one torrid blaze of sunshine, and
Cornelius was creeping across with
an inexpressible effect of stealthiness,
of secret slinking, though he was
bathed in intense light, and in full
view from the house and every other
building within the enclosure.
174.4 played a very dubious part (to

say the least of it) *P* played, to say
the least of it, a very dubious part
174.12 war. In this he *P* war. He
**174.13, 14 end, with an utter disregard
of his personal safety, he** *P* end he
174.15, 16 managed to exist *P* existed
174.20 line he was forced to take *P*
it might have been
**174.31, 32 is simply seen skulking on
its outskirts, enigmatical and unclean**
P simply hangs on to it
174.34 have been *P* be
175.3 had a mangy look *P* seemed
mangy
**175.4 the corners of broken mats flap-
ping** *P* broken mats flapping about
**175.17 done in a roundabout way, and
with** *P* done with
**175.19 I left the Bugis quarter and
went** *P* I went
175.21, 22 there was *P, E¹* was there
175.33 not to be *P, E¹* not be
175.41 'Your mother *P* 'She
176.1 outburst *P* paroxysm of rage
176.20 earshot, in order to *P* earshot,
to
176.22 face, and then Jim *P* face. Jim
176.35 affirmed; it *P* affirmed; he was
afraid for her. It
176.37 appeared a base *P* been like a
176.42 gathering obscurely *P* thickening
177.17 his *P, E¹, E²* this
177.28 that very night *P* that night
177.35 girl, motionless against *P* girl
standing under
177.40 idea, and so *P* idea, so
177.44, 45 she on her part could *P*
she could
178.19 footsteps. They *P* footsteps outside. They
178.30 have *P, E¹, E², A²* did
178.35 have *P, E¹* had
180.14 emerge with *P, E¹, E², A²*
emerge out with
180.40 unquestioning, devoted readiness
P unquestioning readiness
181.23 pace in the morning across *P*
pace across
183.38 blinded *P* blind
183.43 sooty smoke from the torch,
P smoke from the torch, thickening
like a black fog
185.6 Then *P, E¹, E², A²* There
185.7 can *P, E¹, E², A²* could
185.12 has *P, E¹, E², A²* had
185.36 disbelieve *P, E¹, E²* disbelieved
186.22 cried *P, E¹, E²* said
**187.6 there? you sale yourself. Is it a
blind monster or only** *P* there? A
blind monster or
188.20 leave us *P* go
188.41 affections *P* emotions
188.42 that time *P* this time
189.10 argued *P* whimpered
189.13 was ready *P* meant
**190.18, 19 that, during the last mo-
ments, being** *P* that, being
190.21 desired to get in, and *P* had
190.30 mere *P* any
190.39 still—it *P* no matter. It

190.42, 43 too, very soon, for *P* too, for

191.4 shocked. Why *P* shocked, as if I had detected her tampering wantonly with the established order of emotions. Why

191.30 will *E¹, E², A²* shall

191.36 tell you? *P* know?

192.2 shall *P* will

192.44 reproving the carelessness of some *P* reproving some

193.1 distinct murmur *P* distinct forcible murmur

193.18, 19 hard and still, as a statue might whisper. *P* preserving her statuesque immobility.

193.26 planets. She *P* planets. But no matter. She

194.1 infinite. 'Why?' *P* infinite. 'Is that the truth?' she said slowly. 'It is the truth,' I answered, in the same low tone. 'Why?'

194.4 repeated louder; 'tell *P* repeated; 'tell

194.4 confounded, she *P* confounded, thinking with despair that nothing had been done, she

194.5 stamped with *P* stamped once with

194.5, 6 Speak.' 'You want to know?' I asked in a fury. 'Yes!' she cried. 'Because *P* Speak.' 'Because

194.7 brutally *P* roughly

194.16 began *P* said

195.14, 15 his heavy laced *P* his laced

196.15 movements *P, E¹, E²* movement

196.37 has *P, E¹, E², A²* had

196.40 it. He *P* it. Well, he is part of the experience, he too lives in the memory. He

197.7 kept him back *P* baulked him

197.9, 10 succeeded, nevertheless, had *P* succeeded had

198.13 of the *P, E¹, E², A²* of his

198.37 protested *P* whined

199.43 will *P, E¹, E², A²* shall

200.1 shouted. He would *P* cried, within two feet of me. He did

200.2, 3 still for a time, and then without a trace of humility began very low: *P* still. His voice, without a trace of humility in it, was very low at first.

200.8, 9 me, dropping into a confidential and piteous tone, that *P* me in a confidential and piteous whine that

200.22 ejaculations, mingled with *P* voice, interrupted by

200.24, 25 an inexpressibly grotesque and vile performance, and I hastened away *P* inexpressibly dismal and vile, and I left him ,

201.4 brave, with his faith in Jim, with *P* brave, with

201.5 and his ironic *P* and ironic

201.5, 6 frightened, suspicious adoration *P* frightened adoration

201.12 "Jim, as I've told you, *P* "We did not part till late. He

201.14 very heart of untouched *P* heart of a primeval

201.18, 19 trees. ¶ "The *P* trees. ¶ "We conversed little. The

201.24 till *P* then

201.27 far-off *P* faint

201.41 of *P* that rested upon

202.5 displayed *P* which spread itself

202.9 of flimsy mat *P* of mat

202.9 over *P* above

202.10 a crooked multitude *P* a multitude

202.13 and the canoe *P* it

202.14 This *P* The

202.15, 16 men crossing over were *P* men were

202.19 heads were *P* hair was

202.20, 21 complaint, voluble, stretching *P* complaint, stretching

202.23 had been *P* was

202.23, 24 his people had collected *P* they had been collecting

202.25 over *P* at

202.27, 28 withdrew obediently to *P* withdrew to

202.29, 30 the silvery gleams in their eyes *P* there were silvery gleams in their eyes as they

202.41 " 'Have *P, E¹, E², A²* " 'Had

202.42, 43 sometimes I wish . . . No! I *P* sometimes . . . I

203.12, 13 whom, perhaps, I *P* whom I

204.2 beach. The *P* beach. He followed me. The

204.6, 7 wet oars flashed and dipped *P* oars rose and fell

204.11 wave *P* sign

204.15 its sombre wall that *P* from north and south: its sombre wall

204.16 night; the *P* night; only the

204.17 one *P* a

204.18 dark and still *P* sleepily

204.21 gone *P* left

204.29, 30 foot, and remained persistently *P* foot, persistently

204.34, 35 ebbing fast from *P* ebbing from

204.37 tiny white speck *P* tiny speck

204.41 off the verandah *P* away

205.25 of *P, E¹, E²* for

205.31 He seemed *P* He seemed to listen to it, then sighed

206.15 can't *P, E¹, E², A²* don't

206.20 laws of order and *P* law of an ethical

206.30 frame *P* send

207.16 the ink blot *P* the blot

207.28 treasured *P* preserved

208.24 will *P, E¹, E², A²* shall

208.32 consequence *P* necessity

208.36 put it down here *P* relate it

208.37 fitted *P* put

*209.17 *P, E¹, E², A²* **much** *E³* such

209.32 hear *P, E¹, E²* here

210.12–18 feverishly; * * * learn. *P* feverishly with a gleeful ferocity and a savage unforgiving contempt for poor Jim; but in the middle of a word, perhaps, an invisible hand would take him by the throat, and he would look at me dumbly with a heaving breast and an expression of doubt and anguish. You could see his coarse lips turn blue behind the drooping, wiry hairs. He seemed to fear that I would get tired of waiting for the end of the choking-fit and go away, leaving him with his tale untold, with his exultation unexpressed. Nothing was farther from my thoughts; I was only afraid that death, hovering over him, would swoop down suddenly and baffle my desire to know. He died during the night, I believe, but by that time I had nothing more to learn. ¶ "I knew the story before, of course; he had only cleared up an obscure point, though the profound blackness of the act cannot be dispelled.

212.4 **did not respond** *P* was inert
212.7 **felt that nothing** *P* felt that it would never exhaust itself, and that nothing
212.31 **those** *P*, *E¹* these
213.10 **black** *P* big
213.41 **those** *P*, *E¹* these
214.22 **let you know, too, that** *P* tell you
215.38 **call at** *P* come-to off
216.6, 7 **stood in mortal fear of imprisonment** *P* was mortally afraid of a prison
216.9 **terror** *P* fear
216.14 **little all clink in its** *P* dollars clink in their
216.15 **(the very next evening, I believe) to** *P* the very next evening, to
216.19 **took good care to tow** *P* towed
216.30 **up suddenly and** *P* up and
216.33 **a long knife** *P* a knife
218.3 **their toes** *P* them
218.40 **quickly** *P*, *E¹*, *E²*, *A²* quick
*220.15 *P*, *E¹*, *E²*, *A²* **truth** *E³* youth
220.21, 22 **expecting to find wisdom and courage in the dwelling** *P* to draw strength from the spirit
220.22 **man. The** *P* man. Their temper was unforgiving. The Bugis especially were exasperated. The
220.23 **or** *P* and
221.24 **others with** *P* others savages with
222.2 **cut off the** *P*, *E¹*, *E²*, *A²* cut the
222.5 **ten** *P* fifteen
223.6 **up as** P up the hill as
223.7 **palace** *P*, *E¹* place
223.12, 13 **dark-blue** *P* white
223.22 **defection of the townsfolk was** *P* defection was
224.11 **here** *P*, *E¹* there
224.31, 32 **afternoon, his men, meantime, resting** *P* afternoon while his men rested
224.32 **stole** *P* stealing
*225.2 *P*, *E¹*, *E²*, *A²ᵇ* **became** *A²*, *E³*, *A²ᵃ* become
225.41 **he had really** *P* he really
226.7 **beyond** *P* far over
226.38 **scooted** *P*, *E¹*, *E²*, *A²* scouted
226.40 **blue lips** *P* blue writhing lips
226.43 **skinny fingers** *P* skinny earthy fingers

227.8 **Kassim had** *P* Kassim, indeed, had
228.15 **was** *P*, *E¹*, *E²* is
230.32 **will** *P*, *E¹*, *E²*, *A²* shall
*234.3 *P*, *E¹*, *E²*, *A²* **dot** *E³* lot
234.5 **his spells** *P* the spell of his fame
234.8 **intention** *P* hope
234.19, 20 **livid hand** *P* livid bony hand
235.11 **had** *P*, *E¹*, *E²* has
235.29, 30 **runs. When** *P* runs. Not a gleam of light, not a break in the mischance. When
235.44 **and of their** *P* and their
236.15 **hand** *P* arm
237.8 **above** *P* before
237.26 **And** *P* But
237.34 **regretfully** *P* mournfully
239.15 **Jim insisted** *P* said Jim
239.16 **courtyard could** *P* courtyard there could
239.28 **failings** *P* failing
242.27 **boats** *E²*, *E³*, *A²* boat
242.45 **the fog lasts** *P* it's so thick
243.7 **something—bullock** *P*, *E¹*, *E²* something—a bullock
243.7 **The shadow** *P* The high shadow
244.21 **alongside, and** *P* alongside of his dug-out, and
244.25, 26 **saw, under the now lifting** *P* saw now, under the lifting
244.30 **many knots** *P*, *E¹*, *E²* many little knots
244.31 **subdued** *P* steady
245.33 **ever** *P*, *E¹*, *E²*, *A²* even
245.35, 36 **When he judged the moment come, Brown** *P* Both its entrances were so narrow and overgrown that the very natives passing in canoes had to look for them carefully. Brown
245.45 **last** *P* third
246.27 **them. Brown** *P* them. No matter. Brown
246.39 **staring at** *P* staring hard at
246.42 **kicking. He** *P* kicking. Twice I gave a blow. He
247.15 **fearfully** *P* hesitatingly
247.35, 36 **despairingly** *P* fearfully
248.32 **heart. The** *P* heart. But he was romantic—romantic—and nevertheless true. The
249.13 **she passed** *P*, *E¹*, *E²*, *A²*, *A²ᵇ* she has passed
250.14 **stooping, took** *P* stooping over the body, took
*250.16 *P*, *E¹*, *E²*, *A²* **ran** *E³* rang
250.35 **Tamb' Itam, advancing with** *P* Tamb' Itam with
251.3 **leave me** *P* go away
251.19 **on his shoulder** *P* violently
251.26 **though** *P* but
251.32 **earnestly upon** *P* long at
252.5 **met seemed awestruck, and stood** *P* met stood
253.30 **he passes from my eyes like** *P* I believe him to have been only
253.31, 32 **earth, ready to surrender** *P* earth—surrendering
*253.39, 40 *A²* **September 1899–July 1900. [*Ital.*] THE END** *E¹*, *E²* September 1899–1900. *E³* THE END

A *Lord Jim* Gazetteer and Glossary of Eastern and Nautical Terms[1]

anna A coin of India equal to one-sixteenth of a rupee, or about two cents. Indian currency was in use in Singapore at this time.

Apia A seaport on the island of Upolu in western Samoa.

Aukland (Auckland) A New Zealand port city on northern North Island, formerly the capital of New Zealand.

Bankok (Bangkok) The capital of Thailand (then Siam).

barque (bark) A three-masted vessel with the foremast and mainmast square-rigged and the mizzenmast fore-and-aft-rigged.

Batavia The former Dutch name of Jakarta, a city in Java.

belaying-pin A pin around which ropes on shipboard are secured to make them fast.

betel The nutlike seed of the betel palm. Wrapped with a little lime in the leaves of the betel, it is the chief masticatory of the East Indies; it is a pungent, astringent stimulant, and stains the teeth black.

binnacle A case or box that holds the compass; it is fitted with a lamp for use at night.

boat-chock One of the cradles in which a ship's boat rests when it is on the deck.

boat-stretcher A narrow crosspiece in a boat against which a rower braces his feet.

Bombay The capital of the state of Bombay, in western India, on the Arabian Sea.

breaking-up yard A place where ships are dismantled when they become old and unserviceable.

brigantine A two-masted vessel with the foremast square-rigged and the mainmast rigged fore and aft.

---

1. Although this glossary draws heavily upon many modern, standard dictionaries, gazetteers, and dictionaries of slang and of nautical words, it also relies upon certain works closer in time to Conrad's nineteenth-century maritime world: J. J. Moore, *The British Mariner's Vocabulary* (1801); *A Naval Encyclopedia* (Philadelphia, 1881); Albert Barrère and Charles Leland, *A Dictionary of Slang, Jargon and Cant* (1897); Captain Paasch, *From Keel to Truck: Dictionnaire de Marine* (1908); and the ninth (1875) and eleventh (1910) editions of the *Encyclopedia Britannica*.

brig-rigged   Square-rigged.

Brisbane   The capital of Queensland, Australia, near the mouth of the Brisbane River.

Bugis   A Malayan people of Celebes and adjacent islands.

bulkhead   A partition separating compartments on a ship.

buster   A southerly, Australian wind of great violence.

by the head   Said of a vessel when it is sunk deeper in the water forward than aft.

caboose   A deckhouse where cooking is done.

Calcutta   A seaport in northeastern India.

campong   A native hamlet or village in a Malay-speaking country.

Cape York   A peninsula on the northeastern coast of Australia.

capstan   A vertical drum revolving on a spindle, used for exerting power required in heaving on a rope or an anchor-cable.

casuarina   A genus of chiefly Australian trees, some species of which grow large and yield heavy hard wood.

catspaw   A light breath of air that ripples the surface of a calm sea.

catting   Hoisting an anchor from the water's edge to the cathead, i.e., to the strong timber projecting from the bow of the ship. Cat tackle is the tackle by which the anchor is lifted from the water level.

coir   A stiff elastic fiber extracted from the outer husk of the coconut.

companion   A stairway or companionway.

corvette   A flush-decked sailing vessel carrying one tier of guns.

country ship   A vessel owned in an Eastern port, as opposed to a home ship.

cuddy   A small cabin, formerly the saloon under the poop deck.

cutter   A broad square-stemmed boat for carrying stores and passengers; it is either rowed or sailed.

Dain   A Bugis title of distinction.

dammar   A resin derived from various evergreen trees in Australia, New Zealand, and the East Indies.

davits   A pair of small projecting cranes on the sides or stern of the ship used for suspending, lowering, and hoisting a ship's boats.

donkey-man   An operator of a donkey engine, a small auxiliary steam engine, especially one used to power a windlass on shipboard.

Dubash   An Indian interpreter.

dug-out   A canoe made by hollowing out a log.

Eden   A port in southeastern New South Wales, Australia.

ensign   The flag hoisted to indicate the nationality of a vessel.

fall   The tackle used in lowering a ship's boat from the davits.

fall off   Alter course away from the wind.

Flensborg (Flensburg)   A German city near the Danish border on an islet of the Baltic Sea.

flying moor, running moor   Anchoring by dropping the first anchor while the ship has headway and letting go the second anchor after she has gone farther ahead.

fore-and-aft rig   The general term for all rigs in which sails extend lengthwise of the vessel.

forefoot   The lower extremity of the stern, usually curved, where it joins the keel.

forepeak   That part of the hold in the extreme forward part of the ship.

fore-top   The platform at the top of the forwardmost mast.

fore-topsail   The second sail up on the foremast.

gather headway   Start to move through the water with increasing speed.

gharry   A horse-drawn cab used especially in India but also in Singapore.

gharry-wallah   A gharry driver.

gig   A long, light ship's boat for oars or sail, usually assigned to the captain.

gripes   The canvas bands and fastenings that secure a lifeboat in its cradle.

gunwale   The upper edge of a boat's side.

Hai-phong (Haiphong)   The main port of Tonkin province, French Indo-China (now North Vietnam); it developed rapidly after the French treaty of 1874.

Haji   The name designating a Moslem who has made a pilgrimage, especially to Mecca.

hawser   A rope or cable used for mooring, towing, etc.

Hector Bank   A ledge located off the southwestern coast of Borneo.

Hobart   A city in Australia, the capital of Tasmania, in the southeastern part of the island on the Derwent River.

home   England, as in home service, home ships.

hooker   A sailor's term for a clumsy, old-fashioned vessel.

Inchi   A Malay term of address equivalent to Mr.

jib-sheet   A rope by which the lower corner of a jibsail is controlled.

Kalashee   A native East Indian sailor.

Kalashee watch   A sailing term for general duty performed by all hands, with no regular watches set.

kanakas   Melanesians imported into Australia as laborers.

Koran   The book composed of writings accepted by Moslems as revelations made to Mohammed by Allah.

kriss   A dagger, often with a serpentine blade, used by the Malays.

lanyard   A short piece of rope or line used on a ship for making anything fast.

lascar   An East Indian sailor.

leeward   Situated on the side turned away from the wind, as opposed to windward.

Levuka   A port town which was the site of the first white settlement in Fiji.

Macassar Straits   The wide channel between Borneo and Celebes.

Madagascar   An island in the Indian Ocean off the southeastern coast of Africa.

main-boom   The spar on which one foot of a fore-and-aft mainsail is extended.

main gaff   The spar extending diagonally upward from the afterside of the mainmast near its top.

Malacca   A port on the Strait of Malacca, 125 miles north of Singapore.

Malaita   A volcanic island northeast of Guadalcanal.

Melanesia A group of islands in the Pacific Ocean northeast of Australia.

Menam Thai for "main river," old name for the Chao Phraya River, the most important in Thailand. It runs 750 miles from northern Thailand through Bangkok to the Gulf of Siam.

middle watch A watch on a ship from midnight to 4:00 A.M.

Mindanao The second largest island of the Philippines (after Luzon), at the southern end of the archipelago.

mizzenmast The aftermost mast in all three-masted vessels and the second one from aft in ships having four or five masts.

Moluccas A large group of islands west of Celebes, formerly part of the Dutch East Indies, now part of Indonesia.

mud-pilot The pilot who takes ships between Gravesend and the London docks.

nakhoda The captain or commander of a ship; a master of a native vessel.

Nazarene A Jewish and Mohammedan term for a Christian.

New South Wales A state in southeastern Australia.

Nuka-Hiva The largest of the Marquesas Islands.

out reefs Let out the reefs; expose the full sail area to the wind.

outward-bound Headed away from the home port (London).

pangeran The Malay term for a regent or headman; a prince.

Panglima A Malay chief.

Parsees Members of a Zoroastrian religious sect, descendants of Persians who fled to India in the eighth century to escape Moslem persecution; many are engaged in commercial and clerical pursuits throughout the East.

patent log, taffrail log A mechanical device used for measuring the distance a vessel has sailed. "In this log . . . the registering cog-wheel work, with its dials, is screwed upon a convenient place on the taffrail, and the propeller towed overboard from it by means of a long line, through which it communicates its motion to the register. . . . A small bell was attached to the register, which would ring automatically at every mile passed" (*A Naval Encyclopedia*, Philadelphia, 1881).

Penang A British settlement on the Malay peninsula at the northern end of the Strait of Malacca.

Perim A British island in the strait of Bab el Mandeb, at the entrance to the Red Sea, ninety-six miles from Aden.

poop A raised deck at the stern; on sailing ships the poop contains accommodations for the master and officers.

Poulo Laut An island off the southeast coast of Borneo. *Poulo* means island; *laut* means sea.

prau The Indonesian name for an undecked native boat, dugout, or plank-built craft that is rowed, paddled, or sailed.

punkah An Indian device for fanning a room, usually a frame covered with canvas and suspended from the ceiling.

quay A landing place at which vessels receive or discharge cargo; usually a solid-masonry wall.

quarter The aftermost portion of a vessel's side.

quartermaster A petty officer who attends to a ship's helm, binnacle, and signals under the master or navigator.

Queensland A state of northeastern Australia.

rajah In India, originally a prince or king; also applied to Malay chiefs.

Rangoon The capital of Burma, at the mouth of the Irrawaddy River.

rattan A portion of the stem of the rattan palm that is used for walking sticks, wickerwork, and cordage.

reach A straight portion of a stream or river.

Red Rag Sailors' term for the Red Ensign, the distinctive flag flown by British merchant ships. It has a red field with a Union Jack in the upper left-hand corner.

reef To reduce the area of a sail by rolling or folding a certain portion of it and making it fast with small ropes.

Réunion A French island in the Indian Ocean east of Madagascar.

roads, roadstead An area of water where ships can ride safely at anchor. More or less open anchorage, it affords less protection than a harbor.

running gear, running rigging The ropes used in handling spars, sails, etc., which usually run through blocks or pulleys.

Rushcutters Bay A bay in New South Wales, Australia, on the eastern side of the capital city of Sydney.

Samarang A port in northern Java.

screw-pile lighthouse A lighthouse built on piles sunk by screws on their lower ends, usually on shoals, coral reefs, or sand banks.

serang The boatswain of an East Indian crew; also, the skipper of a small native boat.

Sherif A title of descendants of Mohammed through his grandson Husain.

ship To fix anything in its place; for example, to ship the oars means to place them in their rowlocks.

ship-chandler A dealer in supplies for ships.

ship-keeper A caretaker placed on board in charge of a vessel when it is in harbor without a crew.

shoulder straps Epaulets.

sidiboy A term for a native personal servant of African descent.

solah topi Pith helmet.

Solomon Islands A group of islands in the western Pacific Ocean east of New Guinea. At the time *Lord Jim* was written, the northern islands belonged to Germany, the southern to Great Britain.

Somali coast A portion of the eastern coast of Africa bounded by the Gulf of Aden and the Indian Ocean.

square-rig A general term for all rigs where sails are extended by yards slung athwartship and trimmed with braces. A square-rigged vessel can spread a large amount of canvas, often out sailing a fore-and-after of the same size and type.

stanchion A small pillar of wood or iron used for various purposes in a ship, for example, to support the decks, rails, awnings, etc.

stem A piece of timber or metal, usually curved, to which the sides of a ship are united at the fore end.

stem-head The top of a ship's stem.

steerage-way   A rate of motion sufficient to make a boat capable of being steered.

stern-sheets   That part of a boat between the stern and the aftmost seat of rowers. It is generally furnished with seats to accommodate passengers.

Stettin   A seaport, now Polish but formerly German, on the Oder River not far from the Baltic Sea.

Stewart Island   A part of New Zealand south of South Island.

Succadana   A region of southeast Borneo.

Sunda Strait   The channel between Java and Sumatra.

taffrail   The rail about a vessel's stern.

taffrail-log   Patent log.

Tagal, Tagalog   One of a predominantly Christian Malayan race, chiefly from central Luzon, Philippine Islands.

Talcahuano   One of Chile's major ports.

Tamatave   A seaport in eastern Madagascar.

Tamil   A member of the most enterprising branch of the ancient Dravidian race, which inhabits southern India and northern Ceylon.

thole-pin   A wooden or steel pin which fits in the gunwale of a boat to keep an oar in place when rowing.

thwart   One of the planks that extend crosswise in an open boat for lateral stiffening and which serve as seats for the oarsmen.

tiller   The bar or lever used to turn the rudder in steering.

Tondano   A town in northeastern Celebes.

top-gallant   The third section of the mast (above the topmast, below the royal mast) and its sail, yards, and braces.

trim   The position of a vessel on the water—i.e., on an even keel and neither bow-heavy nor stern-heavy.

Tunku   A Malay term meaning "My Lord."

union down   The reversed or upside-down position of a ship's ensign as displayed for a distress signal.

unreeve   Haul a line or rope out of a block.

Wajo   A small kingdom on the southwestern peninsula of Celebes.

Walpole Reefs, Walpole Island   An uninhabited 310-acre coral island in the southwest Pacific 135 miles east of New Caledonia.

Wapping   A section of London close to the docks.

warp   A rope, attached at one end to a fixed object, and used in hauling or moving a vessel.

water-breaker   A small cask or barrel used in a ship's lifeboat for drinking water.

way   The motion or speed of a ship through the water.

Wellington   The capital of New Zealand.

windlass   A machine used in merchant ships to heave up the anchors from the bottom.

yard   A long spar designed to support and extend the sail.

Zamboanga   A city on the southwestern coast of Mindanao, Philippine Islands.

Backgrounds

Editor's Note on The Composition of *Lord Jim*

Lord Jim is Conrad's masterpiece in terms not only of its moral and psychological complexity but also of its formal excellence. In view of the historical circumstances of its creation, the artistry of *Lord Jim* is little short of miraculous. Conrad's letters between 1898 and 1900 reveal a life in virtual chaos. Whether husband, wife, or son, some member of the Conrad household was almost always ill. The disasters that struck Conrad's two oldest friends disturbed him greatly as well. Adolph P. Krieger, after years of close friendship and business association, quarreled bitterly with Conrad and then, in dire financial straits, showered him with hysterical letters demanding immediate repayment of the sizable debt of £180. G. F. W. Hope's eldest son was found stripped and beaten to death in the Essex marshes in December 1899, and the Conrads rushed to console Hope and his wife. Also during the time of writing *Lord Jim*, Conrad strove to raise money to bring Stephen Crane, ill with tuberculosis, back from Havana, helped get his stories published, and bade him a painful farewell in Dover, a month before Crane's death at a German spa.

Conrad's financial affairs were a shambles. He had spent the Krieger loan plus a £250 advance on a novel (*The Rescue*) he could not finish. Consequently, he found himself writing several works simultaneously in order to pay off old debts and meet current expenses. His letters to William Blackwood and David S. Meldrum, his publisher and editor, drearily and repetitively request advances of £10, £20, and £50, propose schemes to borrow money on life insurance, contain promises to write still more books, and suggest selling outright to Blackwood's copyrights on books already published.

Fortunately, Conrad at this time appears to have been positively vibrating with creative energy. While working on *Lord Jim*, he wrote all of "Youth" (1898) and "Heart of Darkness" (1899) and some of *The Rescue* (1920); he collaborated with Ford Madox Hueffer on *The Inheritors* (1900) and *Romance* (1903); he projected "Equitable Division" (*Typhoon*, 1902), "A Seaman" (probably "The End of the Tether," 1902), "Dynamite" (probably *Chance*, 1913), and "First Command" (*The Shadow-Line*, 1917). For all their troubles, the Conrads later looked nostalgically to those days when Conrad, in "Youth," discovered Marlow, when they moved to Pent Farm, and when he first published in "Maga" (*Blackwood's Magazine*).

Yet magazine publication provided the greatest menace of all to *Lord Jim*'s formal excellence. Difficult as it is to believe, Conrad originally intended the novel to be a story of twenty thousand words, only slightly longer than the thirteen thousand of "Youth" and running to three or four installments in the magazine. Even in November 1899 when Conrad had been planning and working sporadically on "Lord Jim: A Sketch" for eighteen months and when the second installment was already on the newsstands, he envisioned only four or five installments. Instead it took fourteen! Perhaps the crucial moment in the writing occurred shortly after a letter of February 12, 1900, in which Conrad states flatly that, with twenty chapters finished, he will need only two more to complete the story. Since Chapter Twenty concerns Marlow's visit to Stein, Conrad must still, at so late a date, not have decided to develop fully Jim's life in Patusan. It is hard to imagine how there could have been a Gentleman Brown, or even Jim's death. Although Dickens published his novels serially while he was in the process of writing them, he made elaborate plans before he started. More important, and also unlike Conrad, he subscribed to no Flaubertian ideal of highly wrought novelistic form.

The selections below are intended to show how *Lord Jim* came into being.

ALEXANDER JANTA

[Tuan Jim: A Sketch] †

"THE FEW PAGES I HAVE LAID ASIDE. . . ." [1]

[INTRODUCTION]

In July 1925 the Houghton Library at Harvard acquired a little brown leather album, its cover inlaid with metal and mother-of-pearl. It contained twenty-five pages of Polish poetry which, according to a statement received at the time of purchase was "in the handwriting of Conrad's mother." It definitely was not. The opening page carries the title *Zbiór rożnych wierszy* (Collection of Various Poems) in ornate calligraphy. All the poems in the album have been copied by the same hand, that of a Teofila Bobrowska, who wrote her name at the bottom of the title page.

The album belonged to Joseph Conrad, who made ample use of the blank pages left by Teofila and covered twenty-eight pages [2] with the first draft of *Lord Jim*, here called *Tuan Jim: A Sketch*. One additional page contains a few sentences of the *Rescue*, and another lists tentative titles facing the names Lucas, a critic, and Pawling, Conrad's publisher. The following seven pages have been used for a draft of a play, placed in Italy in the time of the Renaissance.

In his painstaking and fundamental study *Joseph Conrad, The*

† From "A Conrad Family Heirloom at Harvard," Ludwik Krzyzanowski, ed., *Joseph Conrad: Centennial Essays*, New York, 1960, pp. 85–109. I have deleted some material, including footnotes, more relevant to Conrad's Polish heritage than to *Lord Jim*. "Tuan Jim: A Sketch" almost surely represents Conrad's first thoughts about the story. Although he could have jotted down these words as early as 1896 (see Eloise Knapp Hay, "*Lord Jim*: From Sketch to Novel," reprinted below), it was probably not until late May 1898 when Conrad wrote the first words of the novel in his grandmother's keepsake book. Despite the

reference in this manuscript to Jim's retreat to a Malay village, Conrad may initially have intended the "Tuan" to be most ironic and Jim to become not a political hero but a nondescript white trader whose career in Patusan would require only the briefest treatment.
1. Joseph Conrad in his "Author's Note" to the 1917 edition of *Lord Jim*.
2. From the back of p. 15 to p. 29; pagination used here in transcript of text is from figures with which each face of a page in the Bobrowska album, starting with her title page, has been numbered.

Making of a Novelist ³ John D. Gordan ascribes the original owner-ship of the album to Conrad's aunt ⁴ Teofila, who died a young girl, and mentions the fact that it contains a poem by Joseph Korzeniowski.⁵

Since the album is undated, its original ownership and the time of its being first used may be established only in the light of what is known about some of the authors, whose names follow certain of the poems, copied by Teofila Bobrowska. This information may also tell us which of the two Teofilas in Conrad's immediate family could have been the owner and the writer in the album. His mother's sis-ter Teofila died as a girl of 18. In the eighteen twenties his ma-ternal grandmother, Teofila Biberstein-Pilchowska married Joseph Bobrowski and lived in Markusz, about twenty-five miles from Terechowa, Pilchowski's country place in the Ukraine, already un-der Russian rule.

Despite Mr. Gordan's contention that the album belonged to Teofila, Conrad's aunt, it seems certain that it was the possession of his grandmother. She has recorded in it poems of friends and con-temporaries of the eighteen twenties, closely linked with Krzemi-eniec and its Lyceum, an educational institution famous in South Eastern Poland at that time.

The names signed to some of the poems which Teofila selected and copied belong to the minor poets of that time.

The verses set down by Teofila were circulated, as was the cus-tom in those romantic times, in many handwritten copies. Their literary value is, at best, insignificant. Historically, however, and be-cause of Conrad's direct association with it, three Polish items in this album call for special attention.

One is a poem, found on both sides of page 2 in the album, which has often been ascribed to Adam Mickiewicz, although most recent findings deny this ascription. It appears among four poems of which only the last one has been signed with the name of Mikolaj Wąż. A member of the Wąż family in the late nineteenth century (quoted in *Pamiętnik Literacki* (Literary Review) in 1887 by F. Konarski) placed the death of Mikolaj Wąż in 1824 or 1825. He is said to have committed suicide with a pair of scissors in a fit of fever produced most probably by his unhappy love for Caroline Rzewuska, a famous beauty and the wife of Hieronim Sobański. Re-cently, however, I was able to establish the date of his death a few years earlier, in June 1820. He died and was buried in Krzemieniec.

This discovery suggests that the album dates from the early

3. John Dozier Gordan, *Joseph Conrad, The Making of a Novelist*, Cambridge, Mass., 1940, Chapter IV, "The Growth of the Text," pp. 151, 157, 158, 160, 162.

4. "The little brown leather book . . . had belonged to Conrad's mother's sister." *Op. cit.*, p. 374 (Notes to Chapter IV, no. 279).
5. *Ibid.*

rather than the late twenties and the presence and the position of the much discussed poem in the Bobrowska album may now at last help to establish its authorship in a definitive manner.

In the group of four poems mentioned above and signed by Wąż, the last two are devoted to the memory of princess Dorothy San- guszko, followed by a French translation of the signed one. The re- lations of Conrad to that family against the background of his childhood recollections and the historical circumstances of that period are the subject of thorough study by Ludwik Krzyżanowski in his "Joseph Conrad's *Prince Roman*: Fact and Fiction" (*Polish Re- view*, Vol. I, No. 4).[6]

On the verso of page 8 of the album a poem signed by Joseph Korzeniowski has been copied by Teofila. John Dozier Gordan men- tioned it in his book, not certain whether the author of this poem was the novelist known in the latter part of the nineteenth century. He certainly was. He, too, had been connected with the Krze- mieniec Lyceum, and was a member of its Writers' Club, together with Karol Sienkiewicz. Like the other poets in this album, his po- etic talent flourished before 1830, ceasing altogether after that year in favor of other interests.

The three stanzas of the Korzeniowski poem are titled "When Would I Be Happy." It says:

> If I would see my parents in old age, their white hair not burdened by any miseries, I would be happy.
> If I would see my beloved one as a good mother and a good wife, I would even be happier.
> But if my visionary forebodings which so often deceive me would bring me back my country, I would be the happiest of men.

The subject of this poem is in line with the teachings and rec- ommendations of * * * uncle Thaddeus Bobrowski and other friends of Conrad's father. Their influence remained a strong factor in the life of Joseph Conrad after he left Poland. It can be judged from at least two of Conrad's rare Polish letters, one written as a sailor, the other as an author in England.[7] The key to Conrad's de-

---

6. In his *Notes* under nr. 34 the follow- ing information regarding the Prince Sanguszko estate, of which Slawuta was the capital, can be found: "In 1822 Prince Eustachy, Roman's father, built in Slawuta St. Dorothea's memorial church, patterned after that of St. Eu- stace's in Paris."

Dorothea, prince Roman's sister, died young and it is her death that is mourned in the three poems contained in Teofila Bobrowska's album. Thus an indirect relationship with a future sub- ject of Conrad's own reminiscences, which he chose to develop in "Prince

Roman," can be located through his grandmother's album.

7. Written from Teplitz on August 14, 1883, and first published in *Kuryer Warszawski* on June 13, 1937, this letter signed Konrad Korzeniowski contains the following passage: "I am leaving for London in a few days: not knowing where from there, wherever my fate will take me. In the last few years, that means from the time of my first exam, I haven't been too lucky in my travels. I was drowning, I have burned—other- wise I am all right, courage does not fail me nor does willingness to work and

velopment into an English writer could certainly have been found in his numerous letters to his uncle Thaddeus, but they were destroyed in the sack of Kazimierówka during the Bolshevik revolution in 1918.

Possibly Conrad's uncle Thaddeus gave him this album, as he was to sail the seven seas "toward Poland," because of the message contained in the poem of another Korzeniowski transcribed by Conrad's own grandmother. Instead of treating it as a family relic, Conrad, having no other pad to write on at a moment of sudden impulse, used the many blank pages as a notebook.

After his first few books were published and favorably received in England, Eliza Orzeszkowa, the *grande dame* of Polish literature of the time, wrote her now embarrassing, but then stinging attack on Conrad,[8] accusing him of betrayal of his own nation's interest by depriving it of his talent in favor "of the Anglosaxonians."[9] The news of this attack reached Conrad and shocked him deeply.

By understandable association, Orzeszkowa used the name of the novelist Korzeniowski, the author of the poem quoted above, to contrast his writing and his position in Polish letters with that of Conrad. An attack so cruel and so unjustified could conceivably color the whole "sentiment of existence" in a character as sensitive and vulnerable to remorse and doubt as Conrad. A feeling of resentment for anything that reminded him of this experience could even have affected his feelings toward his grandmother's album. Another reason why Conrad may not have displayed this album, once it served him as a notebook, was the lack of reverence or respect with which he had used this precious memento of the dear old lady for scribble in a foreign language, not even remotely corresponding to the calligraphic care with which his grandmother had filled page after page with ornate verse. In the hands of an ill-inspired compatriot, ignorant of the English language and literature, such proof of alleged negligence and abuse by the grandson could once again produce accusations of something in the nature of a sacrilege.

Conrad must have been aware of such dangers after Orzeszkowa's outburst hit him and continued to hurt.

A recently published essay, titled "Patriotic Irritability," by Jerzy Peterkiewicz (*The Twentieth Century*, London, December

attachment to my profession: with that I always remember your recommendation at the time of my departure from Cracow: Remember—you have said—wherever you will sail, you sail toward Poland. This I never have forgotten and never will forget." Recently Czeslaw Milosz in his "Joseph Conrad in Polish Eyes" (*The Atlantic*, 100th anniversary issue, November 1957) quoted another Conrad letter dating from 1903, in which Conrad wrote to a Polish acquaintance (Kazimierz Waliszewski, author of the first Polish study on Conrad, published in 1904): "In the course of my navigations around the globe, I have never separated myself either in my thoughts or in my heart from my native country and . . . I hope to be received there as a compatriot, in spite of my anglicisation."

9. Quotation from letter of Orzeszkowa.
8. Published in *Kraj* (St. Petersburg), No. 16 in 1899.

1957) explores this aspect of Conrad's reactions in psychologically convincing detail.

Once the usefulness of the Polish album as a pad for scribbling was ended, he could have discarded it or even made an attempt to destroy it. Jessie Conrad speaks eloquently of his habit of tearing and burning.[1] She could have saved the album and given it away, or Conrad himself could have disposed of it to someone who could not understand its Polish content and Polish significance. It is tempting to speculate about Conrad's attitude toward this family album, until, if ever, we learn its exact story.

It is a matter of additional interest that seven pages following the poem of Joseph Korzeniowski, Conrad began to write the story which was to become a tale about "the acute consciousness of lost honour" as he himself chose to express it in his "Author's Note" to the 1917 edition of *Lord Jim*.

The transcript of Conrad's *Tuan Jim: A Sketch* and other English notes in his grandmother's album tell their own story. Here we have a most interesting illustration for many pertinent observations by John D. Gordan, who made a study of his exacting corrections and found in the many disconnected jottings, which mark Conrad's struggle with the language and with the subject of his tale, the characteristic gropings of his imagination for expression.[2] The most significant suggestion for a new light on the origin of *Lord Jim* comes from the page which faces the opening paragraph of Conrad's text.

It can be found in my transcript from the album in question, on the back of page 14, and is indicative of the fact that Conrad's own statement in the preface to the 1917 edition of *Lord Jim* was not completely accurate. I refer to the passage in which he said:

> . . . the truth of the matter is that my first thought was of a short story concerned *only* with the pilgrim ship episode; *nothing more*. After writing a few pages, however, I became for some reason discontented and I laid them aside *for a time*. I didn't take them out of the drawer till the late Mr. William Blackwood suggested I should give him something again for his magazine.
>
> *It was only then* that I perceived that the Pilgrim ship episode was a good starting point for a free and wandering tale; that it was an event, too, which could conceivably colour the whole "sentiment of existence" in a simple and sensitive character. But all of these preliminary moods and stirrings of spirit were rather obscure *at the time*, and they do not appear clearer to me now after the lapse of so many years.

1. "Passion for burning MSS was shared by his father who burned all his MSS before his son's eyes while he lay on his death bed." Jessie Conrad in an unpublished letter to W. T. H. Howe, now in the Berg Collection, New York Public Library.

2. Gordon, *op. cit.*, p. 150.

The few pages I have laid aside were not without their weight
in the choice of subject.[3]

There can hardly be any question that with the transcript of the
sketch from his grandmother's album we are facing those few pages
which Conrad had "laid aside" and which were not "without their
weight in the choice of the subject." [4] In this light they assume a
very great significance, indeed.

For it can safely be deduced, now that we have this text under
scrutiny, that while he first wrote the title of his intended story
Jim: A Sketch and underlined it with one bold stroke, after jotting
down certain thoughts on the verso of the preceding page, he already had an awareness of the entire scope of the two part story,
comprising both the Patna episode and its consequence—Patusan.
He could have added *Tuan* to the initial version of the title without
turning the page.

Thus, the pages found here were indeed "not without weight in
the choice of the subject." What is not accurate in his own subsequent estimate of that weight is the assertion that his first thought
was of a short story concerned *only* with the pilgrim ship; *nothing
more*.[5] As indicated by the addition of the word *Tuan* to the first
version of the title *Jim: A Sketch*,[6] that "first thought" was immediately expanded into a much broader concept, the full scope of
Lord Jim.

3. Paragraphs 3, 4, and 5 of the "Author's Note" of June 1917, preceding a
new edition of *Lord Jim*.
4. Gordan agrees that the few pages
which Conrad "laid aside for a time"
and which he estimated at 17, are the
28 in the Polish memory book in the
Harvard University Library. *Op. cit.*,
p. 260.
5. We are well aware of Conrad's letter
of 1898 to Edward Garnett announcing
his plans for a collection of short stories
for McClure in America and mentioning
Lord Jim as one of 20,000 words. In a
later letter he explains to Garnett that
"the talk of the short stories has been
commenced by . . . Blackwood and Mc-
Clure" as if wanting to excuse himself
for the idea "of what he would do." The
tentative titles listed against the names
of Lucas and Pawling which we find on
page 30 of the Bobrowska album (in-
cidentally the only entry in it, which
Conrad made in ink) belonged most
probably to the same category of his
planning. These titles, of which one
only, that of the *Outcast*, has been
actually used, although the book was
published not by Pawling of William
Heinemann Ltd., but by Fisher & Unwin
in 1896, could be helpful in the attempt
to establish an approximate date of the

time in which Conrad used to write in
Bobrowska's album.
It has been noticed by Gordan that
Conrad's "dependence upon instinct"
had given him a distrust of notebooks
and preliminary sketches, and in this
respect the album is in a way unique. It
goes without saying that the first draft
of *Lord Jim* precedes the letter to Garnett and also Orzeszkowa's attack on
Conrad, which took place after the publication of his first few books—in 1899.
As far as is known today *Lord Jim* was
mentioned for the first time by Conrad
in connection with a proposed volume
for McClure. How much of the story he
had written before and whether, as a
certain similarity of his writing in the
Bobrowska album and of the first part
(in pencil) of the MS of *Lord Jim* from
the Rosenbach Museum suggests, he
may have made more than one early
attempt to get this story under way, is
difficult to prove.
6. The title in *Blackwood Magazine*
serial of "Lord Jim" retained the original statement "A Sketch." In his letters
he referred to it as "Jim." *A Sketch*
was later changed to read: *A Tale* or
A Romance, as in the first American
edition of *Lord Jim*.

It is noteworthy that the content of the page where this expanded view of Jim's story was recorded, though confused and still groping for a way, leads clearly toward the second part of the future novel and found its place in the ultimate and published version of *Lord Jim*. The third paragraph of the first chapter reads as follows:

> *Afterwards, when his* keen *perception of the Intolerable drove him away* for good from seaports and *white man*, even into the virgin forest, *the Malays of the* jungle *village*, where he had elected to conceal his deplorable faculty, added a word to the monosyllable of his incognito. They called *him Tuan Jim: as one might say—Lord Jim.*
> (All the words of this passage found already in the grandmother's Polish album are printed in italics).

Taking into account that Conrad had the habit of reworking even already published texts, as demonstrated by comparative quotations by J. D. Gordan,[7] the words in question seem to have had considerable importance, surviving, as they did, the evolution of the story from the first scribble in the grandmother's album, through the subsequent rewritings in his manuscript, the typescript, the serial, the corrected serial, until they found a permanent place in the first and all subsequent editions of the completed novel, although he made a number of minor changes, eliminating completely the "provoking and brutal stare" for instance.

While the elements contained in this text recur nowhere else in the first twenty-three chapters of *Lord Jim*, the second paragraph of Chapter 24 shows the elderly headsman of the fishing village at the mouth of the Batu Kring branch of the estuary on the coast of Patusan who, speaking of the first white man he had ever seen, in Conrad's words "called him Tuan Jim."

There is another almost verbatim quotation in the text of the second part of *Lord Jim* from Conrad's notes on the verso of page 14 in Bobrowska's album. Toward the end of the last paragraph but one in Chapter 24 of the forty-five-chapter book, we find Cornelius speaking to Brown, who says: "They call him Tuan Jim here. As you may say Lord Jim."

The transcription [8] of Conrad's writing in the Bobrowska album is made as accurately as it could be read from his penciled, careless, and quick handwriting which looks as if it could not have been written at his desk. It has been copied according to Conrad's own instructions to a typist which can be found on the title page of Chapter 14 (page 308) in the manuscript of *Lord Jim* at the Rosenbach Museum in Philadelphia. It reads: "Where MS illegible leave blank space. Mistakes—repetitions and imperfect sentences to be

7. *Op. cit.*, p. 163 and *passim*.
8. By permission of the Harvard College Library.

typed *exactly* as written." (The word has been underlined by Conrad.)

On page 23 of this draft for *Lord Jim* the word count which Conrad was making, and which I have transcribed, jumped suddenly from 1300 to 3300 and is indicative of a number of pages, which must have been written on separate sheets, until Conrad resumed his narrative in the notebook. He stopped counting words altogether with the figure 3500 on page 24, although he continued to write for another 8 pages.

Parentheses in the transcript indicate that the word or sentence enclosed was crossed out by the author. Parentheses have been left empty when erased words were unreadable. Words unreadable in the proper text have been replaced by dots. Where a whole page or paragraph was crossed out, brackets have been used. All numbers on the margins have been copied as Conrad wrote them.

[THE MANUSCRIPT]

TUAN JIM: A SKETCH

page 15

(*They called him Jim.*)
(*By the*) *All the white men by the waterside and and*
(*board ships*) *the captains of the ships in the ( ) road-*
steads ( ) called him Jim. He was over six feet and stared
downwards at one with an ( ) air of overbearing watch-
fulness. You felt sometimes that (if you happened) were
you to say something (some) the one special thing which
he did not want to hear, he would ( ) knock you down ( )
without more ado. But as a water-clark of a leading ship
chandler in a certain Eastern port, he was popular

back of page 14

Afterwards when his (he disappea—
(*The Malay*) *red from a)*
perception of the intolerable
drove him away from the
haunts of white men, the
Malays of the village where he
(*has fancied himself free from*
the intolerable) without exercising
his perceptive faculty added (called)
him Tuan Jim—as one (would) might
Lord Jim
He had never to my own

knowledge (born his) (had) been ( ) guilty
of an assault. This provoking
and brutal stare (was the) being only the result
of an exquisite sensibility

back of page 15

[*A water-clerk (in the Eastern) need not know anything ( )*
under the sun but he must have ( ) ability in the ab-ct and
apply it practically. His work consists in going on board
arriving ships greeting (them) the Capt cheerily, forcing
upon him a card—the business card of his employer—
and, (piloting him) on his first visit ashore, piloting him
without ostentation to a (store where) vast cool shop
where he is received like a brother by men he never saw
before There is a parlour, (bottles cigars) easy chairs,
bottles, cigars and a warmth of welcome that melts the
salt of an eighty days' passage out of the heart.]

⌈ *(where) which is full of things that are eaten and drunk on* ⌉
| *board ships, where ( ) you can get everything to make her* |
| *seaworthy and beautiful from ( ) chain-hooks for her cable* |
⌊ *to a pot of gold paint for the carving of her stern* [9] ⌋

16

[*Jim then was a water clerk—When a water-clerk (has*
abstract Ability and is also) has been a seaman and pos-
sesses also abstract Ability he is worth good wages and
(some . . .)]

II   Jim.

After two years of training he went to sea and entering
into the regions so well known to his imagination found
them singularly barren of adventures. (It was severe
and monotonous.) The task (of earning his bread) before
him was (severe and monotonous) (prosaic) (with forseen
demands and a limited outlook.) He made m . . . voyages.
He knew the ( ) magic monotony of existence between sky
and water. He knew the criticism of men the exactions
of the sea

back of page 16

and the prosaic severity of the ( ) daily task (where true
men) that gives bread but whose only reward is in the per-
fect love of the work. He did not ( ) have that reward but
there is nothing more enticing disenchanting and enslaving
than the life at sea. His prospects were good. He was
gentlemanly, steady, tractable (and . . .) with a thorough

9. These four lines were written in the margin of the manuscript [Editor].

knowledge of his duty. And in time . . . young he be–
came chief mate of a fine ship without ever having been
tested by those events of the sea that [(. . . .) the inner
worth of a man, the quality of his resistance and the
devotion of . . . . not only to others but even to him-
self.]

17

[(and the secret bustle of his pretences not only to others
but (even) also to himself)]
that brings into the light of day the inner worth of a man,
the edge of his temper and the fibre of his stuff; that
(bring to the light) reveal the quality of his resistance and
the secret truth of his pretences not only to others but
also to himself.
150 *Only once ( ) in that time he (had) (he) had again the*
glimpse of the earnestness in the anger of the sea. There
are many shades in the danger of adventures and gales,
and only now and then there appears on the face of facts a

back of page 17

sinister violence of (purpose) intention (a destination . . .)
a hint of (. . . . certain destruction) mercilessness, that
indefinable something that ( ) enforces upon the mind and
the heart of a man that this complication of accidents or
(or this fury means business) this elemental fury (and is
beyond control malice is there for the purpose of destruc-
tion) is coming at him with a purpose of (destruction)
malice with a strength beyond control and with an
unbridled cruelty that (aims at life,) meaning to tear out
from him his hope and his fear, the pain of his fatigue and
his longing for rest; (equally . . .) to (obliterate from
his) smash to destroy to annihilate what he has

18

known, loved, enjoyed or hated what is (precious) priceless
and (hateful) necessary (our memories and our future)
the sunshine, the memories the future—(and by
300 *taking away his life) to sweep the (world) whole precious*
world utterly from his sight by the simple act of taking
his life.
At the beginning of a week of which his Scotch Captain
used to say afterwards, "M'an! it's a complete meeracle
she lived through it," Jim disabled by a falling spar laid
in his berth ( ) dazed with the dull pain ( ) (and what
seemed an eternity) as if at the bottom of an abyss of
unrest. ( ) He was (glad) secretly glad he had not to go
on deck. (The limited capacity for emotion . . .). He

did not care what the end would be and he overvalued

back of 18

[*his indifference. (The passive) The exhausted courage
is the result of exhausted emotion and (when the body
rest) in the motionless body imagination, this enemy of
man and the father of terror, rests in a slumber that
resembles the peace of conscious resignation.*

seven lines erased

*The struggle went on somewhere near . . .
gets dull . . .
the certitude of . . .
to a call on deck . . .
motionless body . . .
          ( ) imagina-
tion, that enemy of man and the father of all terrors, sank
into a slumber that resembled the peace of resignation.*]

19

[*his indifference. The fact he did not see, he had not to
exert himself and passive courage is easy since it is a sign
that imagination the enemy of man, the father of all
terrors is asleep in a motionless body
As he had not to look menace in the face, as he had not
to exert himself the danger became only a matter of faith,
and imagination the enemy of man the father of all terrors*]

back of 19

*Indifference. The danger when not seen has the vagueness
(of the Impossible) of our imperfect thoughts. Imagination the enemy of man the father of all terrors must have
something to feed upon, otherwise it sinks to rest (from)
(in) in the . . . of exhausted emotions. One admits
(may or may not . . .) the possibility of being struck from
behind, in sleep, or in the dark, but one does not believe in
it till the blow comes. It is otherwise when meeting danger
with brain, eye and hand. Then it is only ( ) a serenity of
temper, (and a) combined with contempt not of death but
for life (. . . . .)* .

20

*than can (face) meet efficiently the aimed blow. Jim
saw nothing but the ( ) (of his) disorder of his tossed
cabin and the certitude of not being liable to a call on deck.
Once or twice he (felt that anguish at the pit of his stomach) felt uncontrolled anguish grip him bodily as he lay*
500 *( ) battened down the only man on board. And the brutal*

*unintelligence of an existence such (an existence) liable
to the agony of such sensations filled him with a despairing
(anger) desire to escape at all costs. The fine weather
returned. He thought no more about it.
His lameness however persisted and when the ship arrived
at an Eastern port, he had to go the hospital. His recovery
was (so slow that he was left behind) slow and when the
ship left*

back of 20

*he had to remain. The hospital stood on a hill above the
town and in the white men's ward there were only two
patients beside Jim: (anoth) the purser of a gunboat, who
had broken his leg, and kind of railway contractor from
a neighboring (province who held the doctor for an ass)
province afflicted with some mysterious tropical disease
who held the doctor for an ass and surreptitiously committed debaucheries of patent medicine which his Tamil
boy used to smuggle in with unwearied devotion- - They
chatted, played cards a little ( ) lounged in easy chairs
before the open windows. And the gentle breeze entered
( ) from the wide windows seemed to bring into the bare
cool room the softness of the sky, the languor of earth the
bewitching breath of the Eastern waters. There were perfumes in it and suggestions of endless dreams—Jim ( )
looked daily above*

21

700 *(the palms) the thickets of gardens above the roofs of the
town, above the fronds of palms or that roadstead that is
a thoroughfare to the East, the roadstead dotted (with)
by garlanded isles, ( ) lighted by (with) festal sunshine,
( ) its ships like toys, ( )*

three lines erased

*its ( ) brilliant activity wearing the air of a holiday pageant,
with the eternal serenity of the Eastern sky overhead, and
and the eternal ( ) peace of the Eastern seas (spread before
750 his eyes as far as the horizon) possessing the space as
far as the horizon.*

*When he could walk without a stick he descended into
the town to look for some chance to get home. Nothing
offered at once and ( ) while waiting he associated naturally
with ( ) the men men of his calling belonging to the*

back of ₋1

port. These were of two kinds. Some [some of these—not
many—( ) (energetic faces . . .)
(energy undefaced by the breath of the East, the temper
of buccaneers and the eyes of dreamers, and their lives went
on] very few and seldom seen led mysterious lives, had
800 an unde . . . energy, the tempers of buccaneers and the
eyes of dreamers. ( ) They lived in a crazy maze of plans,
hopes, enterprises, ahead of civilization in the dark places
of the sea and their death was the only ( ) event of their
900 fantastic and fiery existence that had a reasonable probability of achievement. Others were ( ) men ( ) who like
himself ( ) thrown there by some accident ( ) became
officers of (the) country ships. They had the horror of
the home service ( ) with its hard conditions ( ) heavy
duties ( ) and the hazard of stormy oceans. They were
attuned to the eternal peace of the sky and sea. They
loved (a lazy life), short passages, good deck-chairs,

22

1000 large native crews and other distinction of being white—
They shuddered at the thought of long days at sea ( ). They
led ( ) (precarious) easy and precarious existences always
on the verge of dismissal, (always engaged) serving Chinamen, Arabs, (and) half-castes—would have served the
(devil if he made it easy . . . .) devil had he made it only
easy enough. There was (an air) a suspicion of failure
1100 about them. ( ) They talked (always) everlastingly of
(getting) turns of luck; how So-and-So (had) got charge
of a boat (in the Chin) on the coast of China—a soft
thing; how this one had an easy billet in Japan and that
other one in the Siamese [navy—. . . a soft thing in
China or the billet in Japan, in the Navy of Siam ( ) had
the air of being (. .) of being disguises for an uncon-
querable loafing] navy; and in all their words in all their
acts in their looks in their persons could be detected
(an invincible fidelity)

back of 22

[an ( ) unconditional surrender to the charm of a loafing
existence.]
(1150) [The soft spot, the place of decay, the determination to
loaf through existence.
Jim listened for days to (their) the endless professional
(1150) gossip, (to the jealousies) of these men who as seamen
seemed at first to him (as thin as shadows) unsubstantial
as shadows. Then some responsive chord in his nature was
struck and he let himself go. There was a charm in seeing

1200 *all these men well clothed well fed and knowing so little*
of danger or toil. And after a few days instead of going
home he secured a berth as chief mate of the ( ) 'Patna.']

23

[*The 'Patna' was a steamer (lean (as) like a greyhound),*
as old as the hills, lean like a greyhound and eaten up with
1300 *rust like a kettle on a rubbish heap. She was owned by*
a Chinaman, chartered by an Arab and commanded by a
sort of renegade (of) New South Wales German who on
the strength of Bismarcks achievements brutalised those
he was not afraid of and wore (a) a 'blood and iron' air
combined with a bottle-nose and a red moustache]
3300 *After she had been painted outside and whitewashed inside*
six hundred more or less pilgrims were driven on board of
her (as she lay) with steam up alongside of a wooden quay.

back of 23

240) ( ) *They streamed aboard over three gangways, they*
(14) *streamed in (moved) urged by ( ) faith and the hopes of*
..) *paradise, they streamed in( ) with a great thud and shuffle*
··) *of bare feet without a word, a murmur or a look*
··) *back (. . . . .) and when ( ) clear of the rails spread on all*
.)] *sides over the deck, flowed forward and aft, ( ) overflowed*
down the yawning hatchways filled ( ) the innermost
3400 *recesses of the ship with their bodies like water fills*
a cistern flowing into crevices and crannies. Six hundred
men and women with faiths and hopes with affections
and memories. They had been collected there, coming
from North and South and from the East (coasting in the
water craft in canoes) after treading (the forests) the
forest paths, descending the rivers, coasting in the shallows,
crossing from island to island, passing through suffering

24

meeting strange sights, beset by strange fears, upheld by
one desire. They came (for the) from the jungle, and from
cultivated lands, they came from solitary huts ( ) leaving
( ) the protection of their rulers, their fields, their clearings,
their prosperity, their poverty, the homes they were born
in and the graves of their fathers. They flowed in (with)
3500 *the strong men at the head of parties, the ( ) lean old men*
(who would never return) pressing forward without a hope
of return, the boys looking on fearlessly with serious eyes,
the little girls with . . . long hair hugging a bunch of
bananas or a small bundle of dried fish the muffled women
pressing ( ) to their breast the long headcloths ( ) sleeping

babies, the unconscious pilgrims of the True Faith.—
—"Look at these cattle" said the german skipper to his
new mate.

back of 24

An Arab, the chief of this pious voyage came last. He
walked aboard handsome and grave in his white ( ) gown
and large turban, [a string of beads (rosary) in his hand.]
( ) His servants followed with lots of luggage and the
Patna (left the) backed away from the wharf.
  She ( ) headed between two islands, crossed oblique by
the ( ) anchoring ground of sailing ships, swung through
half a circle in the shadow

25

of a hill and ranged close to a ledge of foaming reefs.
The Arab at the stern recited the prayer of travellers by
sea. He invoked the favour of the Most High. His blessing
on the journey and on the secret purposes of the hearts.
(The sun set) The steamer pounded in the dusk the calm
water of the straits; (The steamer was in clear water) and
far astern (a) of the pilgrim ship

back of 25

a three-legged lighthouse planted by unbelievers on a
[perched on a shoal winked maliciously its eye of flame at
her errand of faith.] treacherous shoal seemed to wink at
her its eye of (fire) flame as if in derision of (at) her
errand of faith.
[She went on heading west across the Bay of Bengal.
There was not a cloud]

26

[on the sky.—And under the cloudless sky the calm sea
stretched its ( ) motionless and smooth surface.
There was not a wave, nor an undulation nor a ripple nor
a splash. And the Patna ploughing through the plain of
lifeless waters left no trace but]

back of 26

She went on (for days heading West) out of the Strait
across the Bay, through the One-degree passage. She went
(on for days) under a ( ) cloudless sky, under (sky a
scorching sky) through dazzling days (of) through an
unbroken (serenity) hot serenity, (through) in a fulgor
of sunshine, killing all thought, oppressing the heart, ( )
destroying all impulses of strength and energy. And under
that scorching sky the great sea blue, and profound (lay)
remained without a stir, without a ripple, without a
wrinkle

(a sea of) viscous, stagnant, dead. The 'Patna' (rolling)   27
with a slight(ly) list passed over that plain luminous and
smooth unrolling a (long) black ribbon of smoke across
the sky, and on the water a white ribbon of foam, that
vanished (together) at once like the phantom of a track
(left by the phantom of a ship.) traced on a sea without life
by the phantom of a ship.
There were only five white men aboard. The

back of 27

Capt, two mates and the engineer; they (lived) had their
berths amidships living, eating, sleeping on the long
(bridge) lower bridge without ever coming down amongst
the live cargo. "(Damn) Dirty rascals. Ferfluchte stink
there" said the Captain.
A crew of Malays with on Old Serang and two tindals
attended to the cleanliness of the ship as best they could.
The awnings covered the (ship) decks from stern to stern
with a white roof. Jim kept his watch. He

28

felt himself lulled, overcome conquered by (a feeling of)
an insidious langour of safety and rest. It was sailoring
reduced to its simplest expression. (Only the engineer)
There was nothing to do, nothing but a little navigating.
(To look out) Watchfulness even seemed unnecessary in
(this) such an empty universe. Only the engineers swore
at the heat and the Chinamen stokers would come up
from (below) their fires wildeyed (with) and streaming
with wet as though they had been overboard.
All went well and the ship neared the entrance of the
Red Sea.

Correspondence Related to Lord Jim †

6/4/98   *Conrad to Meldrum*
Last night I posted you the last pages of *Youth*. Here I send the
first 18 pages of *Jim: A Sketch* just to let you see what it is like. It

---

† These extracts from letters dramatize
how, to Conrad's consternation, the
novel grew and grew and grew; they
also contain hints about some of Conrad's artistic intentions. The bulk of the
letters come from the correspondence between Conrad and his publisher, William
Blackwood, and the Blackwood editor,
David S. Meldrum. These letters appear
in *Joseph Conrad: Letters to William
Blackwood and David S. Meldrum,*
edited by William Blackburn, Durham,
N. C., 1958, pp. 21–156, *passim.* Edward Garnett, publisher's reader for T.
Fisher Unwin, "discovered" Conrad
through the manuscript of *Almayer's
Folly* in 1895 and became a very close
friend. The letters to Garnett come from
Letters From Joseph Conrad, 1895–
1924, edited by Edward Garnett, Indianapolis, 1928, pp. 137–73, *passim.*
In 1893 John Galsworthy met Conrad
on the clipper *Torrens,* where Galsworthy was a passenger and Conrad the
first mate. The portion of the letter to
Galsworthy appears in Jean Aubry, *Joseph Conrad: Life and Letters,* 2 vols.,
Garden City, N. Y., 1927, I, 295.

will give you an idea of the spirit the thing is conceived in. I rather think it ought to be worked out in no less than 20–25 thousand words. Say *two* numbers of "Maga."

6/4/98 [1] *Conrad to Garnett*

I've sold (I think) the sea things to B. for £35 (13,000 words). Meldrum thinks there's no doubt—but still B must see it himself. McClure has been the pink of perfection "We will be glad to get as much as we can for you in America"—and so on. He is anxious to have a book of short tales. I think *Jim* (20,000) Youth (13,000) A seaman (5,000) Dynamite (5,000) and another story of say 15,000 would make a volume for B here and for McC. there. That is after serial publication. I broached the subject and they seem eager. Have made no conditions but said I would like to know what B. would offer. As to McC. I leave it vague for the present.

The Rescue shall not begin till *October* next. That means book form for winter season of 1899. A long time to wait—and to find it after all a dead frost—perhaps.

I don't feel a bit more hopeful about the writing of Rescue than before. It's like a curse. I can't *imagine* anything.

6/27/98 *Meldrum to Blackwood*

Conrad . . . would be delighted if we arranged to publish a book of short stories—all of the sea—next spring, if the stories are ready: if not, then in the following autumn.

8/10/98 *Conrad to Meldrum*

Very many thanks for the cheque for £20 which you have so kindly sent me. It shall be paid back as soon as I get my advance from M^r B'wood.

As to Jim: I think that September *is* safe *quite*. Strictly speaking you have enough for two instalments now in hand. If you divide in that way the story may run into 4no. But even if you distribute the whole into three I am confident of coming to time. This work isn't like the *Rescue* where I aim at purely esthetic (if I dare say so) effects. I am now in tolerable health. There's really nothing to stand in the way of a happy termination <to> of Jim's troubles; and its as likely as not the story will be finished a long time before the second instalment comes out.

If America is in the way of the dates I shall not Write any slower for it. I *never mean* to be slow. The stuff comes out at its own rate. I am always ready to put it down; nothing would induce me to lay down my pen if I *feel* a sentence—or even a word ready to my hand. The trouble is that too often—alas!—I've to Wait for the sentence —for the word.

---

1. This date is supplied by Blackburn, p. 22. Mr. Blackburn encloses words crossed out by Conrad in brackets < > [*Editor*].

What wonder then that during the long blank hours the doubt creeps into the mind and I ask myself whether I am fitted for that work. The worst is that while I am thus powerless to produce my imagination is extremely active: whole paragraphs, whole pages, whole chapters pass through my mind. Everything is there: descriptions, dialogue, <reflection> reflexion—everything—everything but the belief, the conviction, the only thing needed to make me put pen to paper. I've thought out a volume in a day till I felt sick in mind and heart and gone to bed, completely done up, without having written a line. The effort I put out should give birth to Masterpieces as big As Mountains—and it brings forth a ridiculous mouse now and then.

Therefore I must sell my mice as dear as I can since I must live; that's why I beg you very earnestly to arrange matters so as not to give McClure any excuse for losing My Am: Ser: rights of *Jim*. It <seems> looks as if I were very mercenary but God knows, it is not so. I am impatient of material anxieties and they frighten me too because I feel how mysteriously independent of myself is my power of expression. It is there—I believe—and some thought, and a little insight. All this is there; but I am not as the work men who can take up and lay down their tools. I am, so to speak, only the agent of an unreliable master.

1/6/99 *Meldrum to Blackwood*

It surprises me that he can get along at all. His long story costs two years' work. He may get £400 out of it, not more. And we see what he does besides his long story—two or three short ones each year, bringing in at the most £100. That means that his total income from his work doesn't exceed £300. Of course he doesn't attempt the impossible by living in London on that, but even in the country it must be difficult always to put his hand on money, if he hasn't any private capital. And I think it very splendid of him to refuse to do any pot-boiling and hope, for him and for ourselves too, that it will pay him in the long run.

2/14/99 *Conrad to Blackwood*

I have a story *Jim* half-written or one-third written (10.000 words) which is intended for the volume. There are with *Youth* (13.000) and *H of D* (38.000? say 50 to 52 thousand words ready. *Jim* being 20 or 30 thou: would almost make up matter enough for a book. But—are 3 stories only, enough? And supposing even I finished *Jim* in time could it go serially into Maga before the date you contemplate? Besides I thought of two other stories (more in the 'note' of my 'Maga' work) one of them being called *First Command* and the other (a sketch) entitled A *Seaman*. These are not written. They creep about in my head but [have] got to be caught and tortured into some kind of shape. I think—I think they would turn out good as good as (they say) *Youth* is. But the whole thing is complicated by my horrible inability to finish the *Rescue* for which McClure has made arrangements. I must peg away at it.

It seems horribly ungrateful of me to talk about the difficulty of doing what you wish, but I must face the consequences not of my neglect <of> or laziness but of positive ill-health which has caused <this> the shameful delay in writing the R. It is small consolation to think I could *not* help it though I did my best. My best has been so very bad after all.

—Yet: if in your opinion *Youth. H of D* and *Jim* would make a Volume I shall *try* to get *Jim* finished in April (my heart sinks when I think how days pass and how slow my work is). In that case I would forego the serial pub: of *Jim* not to delay the appearance of the volume. I only can say I shall *try*. I dare say no more after my recent experiences as to being punctual. The Vol of the 3 Stories would not be positively bad. Whether you would judge such a publication opportune or not I shall do my best to finish *Jim* in April.

Even in the matter of the title I am unable to answer you decisively. I've not thought of it yet—and it is by no means easy to invent something telling and comprehensive. 'Youth" and Other Tales" would not do? I wish to convey the notion of something lived through and remembered. *Tales from Memory* (.?) you may think a clumsy title. It is so. I don't seem able to think of anything to-night. Why not: "Three Tales" by Joseph Conrad. Flaubert (mutatis mutandis) published Trois contes. The titles of the three tales could be printed on the cover in smaller capitals thus: Youth; A Narrative. Heart of Dark: Jim: A sketch. That is only if the vol: is to be of the three stories. Pardon the lenght of this letter, and the unsatisfactory nature of its contents. I *am* an unsatisfactory person, and to no one more than to myself.

6/99   *Conrad to Garnett*

This is the sort of rot I am writing now. Frankly it is not worth troubling about but still I send you this—the first part of a B'wood story in two parts.

7/6/99   *Conrad to Meldrum*

Herewith 3 chap^{rs} 31 pp. of Lord Jim, or to speak correctly two complete chapters and as much of the third as is ready.

Confiding in your friendly offices I ask you for a typewritten copy of this batch for myself, together with the return of my own type. The text is pretty correct as it stands now and any small changes I may wish to make shall wait till I get the proof from Maga. This is not enough for one instalment but I will be sending you pages (a few at a time) and work at it steadily till the end. I trust the end of the Month will come together with the end of the story. Your good letter has cheered me. The story will improve as it goes on. You will arrange the time for publication <in America> with McClure; I should not like to lose the American serial of this story if it can be avoided.

The story will be fully 40000 words and I shall ask Mr Blackwood for £120 which is a little more than the agreed rate but expect to do more work for Maga before the year is out—that is if you want me—and make it right in that way. We must talk this matter over when we meet next as I have had proposals made for a series of short stories (or rather short serials) and would like to know M^r B'wood's intentions. I may say at once that I would rather work for *maga* at a less rate than those people offer me; but some revision of terms must take place. However there is plenty of time for that discussion. The important thing now for me is to get rid of my deplorable Jim with honour and satisfaction to all concerned.

7/31/99 *Conrad to Meldrum*
Here's the end of Chap^r III. Chap IV whole and the beginning of Chap^r V. pp. of my type 32 *to* 50 which I should like to be doubly copied—one set for me and the other for E'burgh.

I shall be sending you MS almost daily if only a few pages at a time keeping it up till the end which, I pray, may be soon but is not in sight yet by a long way.

*   *   *

These three tales will make a thick vol or I am much mistaken. Jim may turn out longer than *H of D* even. Whether as good?—that's a question. Let us hope.

8/18/99 *Meldrum to Blackwood*
For the story itself—'let's see the end of it' is what I feel myself saying. I think it will come out as well as the 'Heart of Darkness': both, to my mind, want the 'form' of Youth.

8/22/99 *Conrad to Meldrum*
I've dispatched today 12 pp. more of Jim—addressed to the office. More would have been sent but my wife not being very well could not type yesterday. They shall be coming in very soon: I am going straight ahead with Jim and am rather pleased with him so far.

8/22/99 *Conrad to Blackwood*
I am glad you like Jim so far. Your good opinion gives one confidence. From the nature of things treated the story can not be as

dramatic (in a certain sense) as the *H of D*. It is certainly more like *Youth*. It is however longer and more varied. The structure of it is a little loose—this however need not detract from its interest—from the "general reader" point of view. The question of *art* is so endless, so involved and so obscure that one is tempted to turn one's face resolutely away from it. I've certainly an idea—apart from the idea and the subject of the story—which guides me in my writing, but I would be hard put to it if requested to give it out in the shape of a fixed formula. After all in this as in every other human endeavour one is answerable only to one's conscience.

I have this day sent off another 3000 words to your London office. 2000 more are actually written or rather scrawled and awaiting the domestic typewriter. I devote myself exclusively to *Jim*. I find I can't live with more than one story at a time. It's a kind of literary monoganism. You know how desperately slow I work. Scores of notions present themselves—expressions suggest themselves by the dozen, but the inward voice that decides:—this is well—this is right—is not heard sometimes for days together. And meantime one must live!

10/18/99 *Conrad to Meldrum*
Jim is approaching his climax.

10/24/99 *Conrad to Meldrum*
Here's some more Jim. The Jany inst is well advanced if not wholly finished. I've despatched the proofs and additional type for the Dec^{er} Number yesterday, proposing that the inst^t should include Cap^r VIII if possible. I hope they will see their way. In that case Jan and Febr <numbers without> installments without being unduly long will contain the end of the story.

10/26/99 *Conrad to Garnett*
Thanks for your letter. If I don't send proofs or type it is because there is, alas, so little to send and what there is, is not worthy. I *feel* it bad; and, unless I am hopelessly morbid, I can not be altogether wrong. So much I am conceited; I fancy that I know a good thing when I see it.

I am weary of the difficulty of it. The game is not worth the candle; of course there is no question of throwing up the hand. It must be played out to the end but it is the other men who hold the trumps and the prospect is not inspiring.

*　　*　　*

As to Jim, I entreat you: Wait till the 2d inst^{mnt} comes out (in a few days) and I shall send you the two together. The first is too bad to stand alone. The fifth (and last inst) is not written yet—and what it will be God only knows.

10/27/99 *Conrad to Blackwood*

The greater part of the Ja^{ny} inst. is written and practically ready; some of it in London for a fair copy and seventeen pages on the table before me to be pecked at, slashed, turned over, for two days more, and depart for Paternoster Row on Monday. I *am* glad you like it—for tho' the thing were not absolutely bad it might not have been exactly to your mind. The beginning wobbles a good deal; I did cut up shamefully the proofs without being able to put it firmly on its feet; however my little band of faithfuls professes itself (in various letters) to be immensely pleased. You express yourself hopefully about the book. You may be sure that none of your kind of words are wasted. The man here wants them, wants everything he can get of such genuine encouragement.

10/30/99 *Conrad to Meldrum*

My mind is eased by what you say about Jim's lenght. It would be to my interest to cut it short as possible, but I would just as soon think of cutting off my head.

11/8/99 *Conrad to Blackwood*

The Jany number of Jim is practically ready and Feb^r is on the way to completion. The March issue will see the end of the story— and of the vol: * * * Just now it is all for Jim! And no amount of sacrifice seems too much for him.

11/19/99 *Conrad to Garnett*

I also send you the 2^d inst of Jim—which is too wretched for words. It would have been less shocking if it had included another chapter.

11/24/99 *Conrad to Garnett*

You are a dear good old critic—you are! You've a way of saying things that would make an old sign-post take to writing. You put soul and spunk into me—you, so to speak, bamboozle me into going on—and going on and going on. You can detect the shape of a mangled idea and the shadow of an intention in the worst of one's work—and you make the best of it. You would almost persuade me that I exist. Almost!

11/25/99 *Conrad to Meldrum*

I am still at Jim. I've sent 6 more pages yesterday. I shall send 7 more today to end Chap XIII. The Story will be finished of course this year. I trust they will give me as much space as possible in the Jan. Febr. & Mch numbers. I shall want all I can get.

12/3/99 *Conrad to Meldrum*

In the matter of space—if Maga gives room in Jany N^o to all all *nearly all* [*sic*] of the copy I am sending to-morrow the end of the story may be divided between the Febr^y and March numbers.

12/17/99   *Conrad to Meldrum*

I send here a MS lot of Jim which would be most of the Febr^y instalment. My poor wife is too taken up just now with domestic worries to be able to type for me and I do not want to stop the trickle of copy.

The lot published and in proof together as present in Edinburgh amounts to 40,000 words already. I trust I am not making myself objectionable by unduly lenghtening my contribution   *   *   * still think I shall finish the story this year.

12/22/99   *Blackwood to Conrad*

Glad to hear you are within sight of the end. The story I think makes good progress and promises to come out well. It will probably be April before I can publish the last instalment as I was obliged to shorten the January part from what was settled upon, owing to pressure upon my space caused by some long articles which could not be longer delayed.

12/26/99   *Conrad to Blackwood*

The tale progresses and in five more days' time it will be still nearer the end which seems well in view now. I say seems, because I do suffer at times from optical delusions (and others) where my work is concerned.

*   *   *

the forthcoming volume [will] be a fat book—and not, perhaps, well balanced to the eye. Still we are in for it now I fancy. *Lord Jim* would have hardly the lenght and certainly has not the substance to stand alone; and the three tales, each being inspired by a similar moral idea (or is it only one of my optical delusions?) will make (in that sense) a homogeneous book. Of the matter I am not ashamed and the mere size won't, I hope, militate against such commercial success as is within my reach.

1/3/00   *Conrad to Meldrum*

I am sending by this post a batch of MS. Lord Jim to end Ch XVII. Of course the chap.^s are short.

The next batch should be the last, unless I were to forward an instalment before the 15th inst^t.

L.J. is a rather bad business for me on account of its length that is to say. Otherwise I am pleased with it and, I think, with some shadow of a reason.

But the artistic pleasure is neither here nor there. Bread is the thing

1/7/00   *Conrad to Blackwood and Sons*

Herewith further inst^t of Lord Jim p. 376–394. Chap xviii.

I trust you've received all eight previous inst^ts p. 342–375 sent by registered packet.

1/20/00   *Conrad to Garnett*

You make my head whirl when you write like this. What a letter for a poor devil to get! You've knocked my evening's work on the head; I found it impossible to write any copy. You frighten me; because were I to let you take me up on these heights by your appreciation the fall before my own conscience's smile would be so heavy as to break every bone in my body. And yet what, oh! what would become of me if it were not for your brave words that warm like fire and feed like bread and make me drunk like wine!

No. I didn't know anything about Jim; and all I know now is that it pleases you; and I declare as true as there are blind, deaf-mute gods sitting above us (who are so clear-eyed; eloquent and sharp of hearing) I declare it is enough for me; for if you think that because I've not been sending you my MS., your opinion has ceased to be a living factor in my individual and artistic existence, you are lamentably mistaken. I was simply afraid. And I am afraid still. You see the work fragmentarily; and the blessed thing is so defective that even that far within it you cannot possibly (with all your penetration and sympathy) you cannot possibly know where I tend and how I shall conclude this most inconclusive attempt. You don't; and the truth is that it is not my depth but my shallowness which makes me so inscrutable (?). Thus (I go cold to think) the surprize reserved for you will be in the nature of a chair withdrawn from under one; something like a bad joke—it will strike you no doubt. Bad and vile. Now had you taken the whole thing the fall would not have been so heavy, I imagine.

2/12/00   *Conrad to Blackwood*

I've had an exceedingly rough time of it since the 25th of last month when beginning with a severe fit of malaria I continued with bronchities and an attack of gout, giving my wife a variety entertainment. The poor woman can hardly stand, and as to myself I managed yesterday to totter downstairs for the first time

This sorrry news will explain my delay in returning proofs of Maga: and book, and the stoppage of further copy.

To-day (monday) I send off proofs of chap. xvi and xvii and also proofs of book up to page 208 I have yet ch xviii in proof, which I shall forward very soon together with two more chap^rs of copy. After these another two chapters will see the end of Jim.

You have no idea what an anxious time I had. The illness looked much more serious than it has turned out to be and the thought of 'copy' nearly distracted me. All's well that ends well.

2/14/00 *Conrad to Meldrum*

In an hour we shall leave here to go to H. G. Wells for two days. It'll do me good I think and perhaps when I get back I shall be able to grapple with pen ink and paper. I haven't done anything yet tho' my head is full (too full) of Jim's end but when it comes to putting it down black on white the brain wanders. When I start 10 days will be enough to finish the thing.

2/16/00 *Meldrum to Blackwood*

. . . On my return from Edinburgh I got a letter from Conrad that he was ill, and knowing the nervous condition of the man I delayed pressure on him to wind up "Jim". I am sorry that the length of "Jim" doesn't suit *Maga* which I can well understand; but, on the other hand, it makes it a more important story—it is a great story now—and in the annals of *Maga* half a century hence it will be one of the honourable things to record of her that she entertained "Jim". I only wish that "Charlotte" [2] whom you are good enough to honour with permit to follow in "Jim's" steps were at all likely to do the old lady such credit. . . .

2/20/00 *Conrad to Blackwood*

* * * staying with H. G. Wells for a much needed change * * * has done me some good so that yesterday I got hold of Jim again. When I get into the stride a fortnight will see the end of the story, through I shall not hurry myself since the end of a story is a very important and difficult part; the *most* difficult for me, to execute— that is. It is always *thought out* before the story is begun.

3/26/00 *Conrad to Garnett*

I am still at Jim. I've been beastly ill in Feb.^{ry} Jessie is hunting all over the house for the *Feb^{ry}* No to send you. I am old and sick and in debt—but lately I've found I can still write—*it* comes! *it* comes!—and I am young and healthy and rich.

The question is *will* I ever *write* anything?

I've been cutting and slashing whole pars out of Jim. How bad oh! HOW BAD! Why is it that a weary heaven has not pulverised me with a wee little teeny weeny thunderbolt?

4/3/00 *Conrad to Meldrum*

I am sending a fresh inst. of *Jim* and now I start to write the last chap.

* * *

---

2. Meldrum's *The Conquest of Charlotte, Blackwood's,* July 1901–July 1902.

I've been horribly disappointed by the shortness of the inst^t in the Ap N^o the more so that the break just there destroyed an effect. If one could only do without serial publication! Don't think me an ungrateful beast. Jim is very near my heart. I don't apologize now for springing on Mr Blackwood such a long affair and for the unfortunate dragging manner of its production. Apologies butter no parsnips—to adapt the popular saying. It won't happen again.

4/12/00   Conrad to Blackwood

Yesterday I sent off the Edinburgh proofs of Maga and the book, together with an instalment of typewritten matter, and to London a batch of further MS. I feel the need of telling you that I've done something anyway and to assure you that *Lord Jim has* an end, which last I am afraid you may be beginning to doubt. It has though—and I am now trying to write it out. A dog's life! this writing out, this endlessness of effort and this endless discontent; with remorse thrown in, for the massacre of so many good intentions.

This by the way. The real object of this letter is to tell you that should you find Jim unconscionably long (for Maga—I mean) I am ready to shorten (what remains) by excision. I am however in such a state of mind about the story—so inextricably mixed up with it in my daily life—that I feel unequal to doing the cutting myself; so, addressing you in your character of Editor of *Maga*, I declare my readiness to make conscientious joints, if the parts that can be taken out are marked for me and the MS with such indications is returned. I would not keep it for more than a day or two—and, as (I trust) you will have the story complete in a week or so, there would be time to look through it before the copy is required for setting up.

5/15/00   Blackwood and Sons to Conrad

We duly received to-day the revised proof of the Magazine portion of Lord Jim and a further instalment of copy, namely, chapters 28, 29, 30 and the beginning of 31. The story has now exceeded the original estimate of its extent and Mr. Blackwood has had under his consideration the exact publication of Lord Jim and the other two stories "Youth" and Heart of Darkness. The printers started the book form of these stories on a comparatively close page on the understanding the Lord Jim would end with at the latest the June number of Maga. But we now find that even in this close page Lord Jim will run to at least 320 pages and we conclude from the portion you sent today that there is still a further instalment to come which may possibly add 10 pages more to the book. In consultation with Mr. Blackwood to-day he indicates that the proof returned this morning and the new copy will run him into the August number of the magazine at least if not also into September and he suggests that it would be advisable to your interest as well as in his own that Lord Jim should be made a separate volume and be published not later than the middle of September by which time the last instalment will have appeared in Maga or at any rate there will be little more of the serial issue to follow that date.

This suggestion of course somewhat alters the arrangement for the volume "Three tales of Sea and Land" but we presume there will be no difficulty on your part in allowing Youth and Heart of Darkness (which are now set up in type and of which plates have been made) to lie in our hands until you are able to add one or two more stories which would make up a reasonable crown 8vo volume to sell at 6/—or may be 3/6.

5/19/00   *Conrad to Meldrum*

Now the proposal has come from Mr. Blackwood the thing seems unavoidable. Perhaps the story will please. Perhaps! I would like to know what you think. I am too fond of it myself to be very hopeful. It has not been planned to stand alone. H of D was meant in my mind as a foil, and Youth was supposed to give the note. All this is foolishness—no doubt, the public does not care—can not possibly care—for foils and notes. But it cares for stories and Jim is as near a story as I will ever get. The title will have to be altered to Lord Jim. A tale—instead of A sketch. And yet it is a sketch! I would like to put it as A simple tale A plain tale—something of the sort—if possible. No matter.

*   *   *

Lord Jim should be considered separately of course. It will be (it seems incredible) of, apparently, 100,000 words or very little short of that.

7/14/00   *Conrad to Blackwood*

The last word of Lord Jim is written but before I retire to rest I must <as it were> with the same impulse, the same dip of the pen as it were say a word to you.

Whatever satisfaction I have now or shall have out of the book I owe very much to you—not only in the way of material help but in the conditions which you have created for me to work in by your friendly and unwearied indulgence.

I feel I owe you also an apology—many apologies for this long work about which the only thing I am sure of is the good faith I brought to its writing. I can't say much more. I would like to express something that would not be mere banality. But I cant. I've been now for 23 hours at work and feel unable to collect my thoughts.

We should like to leave for Bruges on Wednesday next. The type of the last part of MS will be sent to me here. I must live with the end for a bit. There are many places which a bit [of] judicious cutting would improve and so on. As there is enough copy set up to go on with I suppose I may take a little time. But it will be only a matter of few days at most. In a few hours I start for London with the last pages. I am too tired to feel either glad or sorry just now. But it is a relief of some sort.

7/18/00 *Blackwood to Conrad*

Your very kind letter of thanks for the help I may have afforded you in the writing of this book has gratified me much and I am only carrying out what has been the desire of all those who have gone before me in our connection with our authors.

7/18/00 *Conrad to Blackwood*

It seems to me that *Lord Jim* as title for the book is meagre—perhaps misleading? Could not a sub-title be invented? I am hammering the sorry remnant of my brain without being able to get sound or sense out of it. Perhaps even thus *Lord Jim: A romance* in one line would be better. I feel it's a poor suggestion.

Another matter, if it is not too late already, has occurred to me. Would it not be better seeing the form of the novel (personal narrative from a third party as it were) to dispense with the word *Chapter* throughout the book, leaving only the Roman numerals. After all, these divisions (some of them very short) are not Chapters in the usual sense each carrying the action a step further or embodying a complete episode<s>. I meant them only as pauses—rests for the reader's attention while he is following the development of *one* situation, only *one* really from beginning to end. I fear however that it may be now too late to make the alteration.

7/19/00 *Conrad to Blackwood*

The end of Lord Jim in accordance with a meditated resolve is presented in a bare almost bald relation of matters of fact. The situation—the problem if you will—of that sensitive nature has been already commented upon, illustrated and contrasted. It is my opinion that in the working out of the catastrophe psychologic disquisition should have no place. The reader ought to know enough by that time. I enlarge a little upon the new character which is introduced (that of Brown the desperate adventurer) so as to preserve the sense of verisimilitude and for the sake of final contrast; but all the rest is nothing but a relation of events—<a> strictly, a narrative.

Pardon this egotism. My head is full of this thing yet.

7/20/00 *Conrad to Galsworthy*

The end of *L.J.* has been pulled off with a steady drag of 21 hours. I sent wife and child out of the house (to London) and sat down at 9 A.M. with a desperate resolve to be done with it. Now and then I took a walk round the house, out at one door in at the other. Ten-minute meals. A great hush. Cigarette ends growing into a mound similar to a cairn over a dead hero. Moon rose over the barn, looked in at the window and climbed out of sight. Dawn broke, brightened. I put the lamp out and went on, with the morning breeze blowing the sheets of MS. all over the room. Sun rose. I wrote the last word and went into the dining-room. Six o'clock I shared a piece of cold chicken with Escamillo [3] (who was very miserable and in want of sympathy, having missed the child dreadfully all day). Felt very well, only sleepy: had a bath at seven and at 1.30 was on my way to London.

11/12/00 *Conrad to Garnett*

You are great and good.

Yes! you've put your finger on the plague spot. The division of the book into two parts which is the basis of your criticism demonstrates to me once more your amazing insight; and your analysis of the effect of the book puts into words precisely and suggestively the dumb thoughts of every reader—and my own.

Such is indeed the effect of the book; the effect which you can name and others can only feel. I admit I stood for a great triumph and I have only succeeded in giving myself utterly away. Nobody'll see it, but you have detected me falling back into my lump of clay I had been lugging up from the bottom of the pit, with the idea of breathing big life into it. And all I have done was to let it fall with a silly crash.

For what is fundamentally wrong with the book—the cause and the effect—is want of power. I do not mean the 'power' of reviewers' jargon. I mean the want of illuminating imagination. I wanted to obtain a sort of lurid light out (of) the very events. You know what I have done—alas! I haven't been strong enough to breathe the right sort of life into my clay—the *revealing* life.

I've been satanically ambitious, but there's nothing of a devil in me, worse luck. The *Outcast* is a heap of sand, the *Nigger* a splash of water, *Jim* a lump of clay. A stone, I suppose will be my next gift to the impatient mankind—before I get drowned in mud to which even my supreme struggles won't give a simulacrum of life. Poor mankind! Drop a tear for it—but look how infinitely more pathetic I am! This pathos is a kind of triumph no criticism can

3. Conrad's dog.

touch. Like the philosopher who crowed at the Universe I shall know when I am utterly squashed. This time I am only very bruised, very sore, very humiliated.

This is the effect of the book upon me; the intimate and personal effect. Humiliation. Not extinction. Not yet. All of you stand by me so nobly that I must still exist. There is *You*, always, and never dismayed. I had an amazing note from Lucas. Amazing! This morning a letter came from Henry James. Ah! You rub in the balm till every sore smarts—therefore I exist. The time will come when you shall get tired of tending true and most well-intentioned sham —and then the end'll come too.

But keep up! keep up! Let me exhort you earnestly to keep up! as long as you can.

I send you the H.J. letter. A draught from the Fountain of Eternal Youth. Wouldn't you think a boy had written it? Such enthusiasm! Wonderful old man, with his record of wonderful work! It is, I believe, seriously intended (the latter) as confidential. And to you alone I show it—keep *his* secret for us both. No more now.

Late in his life Conrad wrote in a friend's first English edition of *Lord Jim*:

When I began this story which some people think my best— personally I don't—I formed the resolve to cram as much char– acter and episode into it as it could hold. This explains its great length which the tale itself does not justify.[4]

4. *The Richard Curle Conrad Collection*, New York, 1927, item 35.

The Division, by Chapters, of the Monthly
Installments of *Lord Jim: A Sketch* in
Blackwood's Edinburgh Magazine

Sources

Edited by
NORMAN SHERRY

UNIVERSITY OF LIVERPOOL

The present essay draws upon materials contained in
Norman Sherry's *Conrad's Eastern World*, published
in 1966 by the Cambridge University Press, to whom
grateful acknowledgment is made.

Map of Conrad's Eastern Seas

From Norman Sherry, *Conrad's Eastern World* (Cambridge and New York: Cambridge University Press, 1966), p. xi. Reproduced by permission of the publishers.

Introduction

Lord Jim derives largely from Conrad's experiences as a merchant seaman in those Eastern seas from which, as he wrote, he "carried away into [his] writing life the greatest number of suggestions." Between the years 1883 and 1888, Conrad spent in all only a few months in Eastern waters. He made three visits—March 15 to the beginning of May 1883; September 22 to October 19, 1885; and July 1, 1887, to March 1888. During these visits he came to know only three areas at all well—the port of Singapore; the port of Bangkok, capital of Thailand; and a trading post on the River Berau in Dutch East Borneo. And his knowledge of these areas was further limited by the nature of his calling—that of a mariner, with all it implies of brief contacts with lands and peoples and with that contact further limited, for the most part, to members of the seafaring class.

It is not surprising that his most famous novel of the East should be based on a sea disaster involving a pilgrim ship that was abandoned at sea by her captain and officers. The incident caused a great scandal in London and Singapore, and was the subject of two inquiries, one at Aden and one at Singapore; a debate in the Singapore Legislative Assembly; and a question in the British House of Commons. My first section deals, therefore, with the pilgrim-ship episode and Conrad's contact with it.

For the second part of his novel, Conrad drew on his limited knowledge of conditions at the trading post on the River Berau in Borneo, and the second section here sets out what has been discovered of those conditions. But this knowledge was not sufficient, and Conrad consequently turned to a third source—travel books and accounts of men who had lived most of their lives and often made their fortunes in that part of the world.

Although much of the information that follows is given through documents, it should be remembered that Conrad probably obtained a great deal of his knowledge from what he called "marine shore talk," i.e., the gossip of seamen, and also from his own observation.

The Pilgrim-Ship Episode

The steamship *Jeddah*, owned by the Singapore Steamship Company, was used to carry Muslim pilgrims from Singapore to Jeddah, an Arabian port on the Red Sea. She left Singapore on July 17, 1880, on one of these trips with almost a thousand pilgrims on board, calling at Penang, crossing the strait of Malacca and the Bay of Bengal, and passing Cape Guardafui on her way to Jeddah.

On August 10 she was reported to have foundered off Cape Guardafui with the loss of all those on board except the captain and officers and a few others. The *Globe*, London, reported the loss with these headlines: DREADFUL DISASTER AT SEA. LOSS OF NEARLY 1000 LIVES. But on the following day it was learned that, after a stormy passage during which the *Jeddah*'s boilers had given trouble and she developed a leak, the ship and her passengers had in fact been abandoned on August 8 by her European captain and officers. They had been picked up by the steamship *Scindia* and taken to Aden, where they reported that the *Jeddah* had foundered. The appearance of the *Jeddah* at Aden a day later, towed in by the steamship *Antenor* with her passengers still on board, sparked a scandal and subsequent inquiry.

These cables were received by Syed Muhammad bin Alsagoff, Managing Director of the Singapore Steamship Company, as reported in the *Singapore Daily Times*, August 12, 1880:

Aden, 10th August 8:20 P.M.
Jeddah foundered. Self, wife, Syed Omar, 18 others saved.
Clark[1]

Aden, 11th August 9:15 P.M.
Antenor towed down here *Jeddah* full of water. All life saved, now in charge of Government. Telegraph further particulars tomorrow. Omar gone Jeddah last night.

The next documents are from the *London Times* of August 11 (second edition) and August 12, 1880:

TERRIBLE DISASTER AT SEA.
(REUTER'S TELEGRAM.)

ADEN, AUG. 10.

The steamer Jeddah, of Singapore, bound for Jeddah, with 953 pilgrims on board, foundered off Cape Guardafui on the 8th inst. All on board perished, excepting the captain, his wife, the chief officer, the chief engineer, the assistant engineer, and 16 natives. The survivors were picked up by the steamer Scindia and landed here.

ADEN, AUG. 11, 7.50 P.M.

The Jeddah, which was abandoned at sea with 953 pilgrims on board, did not founder, as reported by the master. She has just arrived here, all safe, in tow of the steamer Antenor.

(FROM LLOYD'S.)

Lloyd's agent at Aden, telegraphing under date August 11, 8.40 p.m., announces that the report of the steamer Jeddah having foundered off Guardafui on the 8th of August, and that up-

1. Joseph Lucas Clark, master of the *Jeddah*.

wards of 1,000 lives had been lost, is erroneous. The Jeddah has been towed into Aden by the steamer Antenor, belonging to the Ocean Steamship Company. Crew and passengers saved.

The Jeddah, a screw steamer of 1,541 tons, was built at Dumbarton in 1872, and owned by the Singapore Steamship Company, and classed 100 Al.

Following are examples of editorial comment in the London newspapers (The *Times, Daily Chronicle, Globe,* and *Daily News*) concerning the *Jeddah* incident, all from the August 12, 1880, issues:

London was startled yesterday by the announcement of a disaster which, if true, would have been the most dreadful of recent times. The news was that a ship named the Jeddah, of Singapore, bound for Jeddah, had foundered last Sunday off Cape Guardafui, the easternmost point of Africa, near the Straits of Bab-el-Mandeb, with 953 Mahomedan pilgrims on board. All, it was stated, had perished, excepting the captain, his wife, the chief engineer, the assistant engineer, and sixteen natives. The survivors had been picked up by the steamer Scindia and landed at Aden. There was something very unpleasant in the facts thus stated; for, to the honour of sailors, nothing is more rare than that, in a disaster at sea, the captain and the principal officers of the vessel should be the chief or the sole survivors. Nothing can be more admirable than the manner in which, as a rule, the commanders of vessels stay by them to the end, and insist on being the last rather than the first to be saved. Apart from this consideration, the reported loss of life was unprecendention in such an accident, and would have amounted to more than the average total loss on British vessels during the year. But before we have had time to realize the extent of the disaster, the still stranger news arrives that it has never occurred. A telegram from Aden states that the vessel arrived there yesterday in tow of another steamer. She had been abandoned at sea, but did not founder, as the master had reported. This statement is an immense relief; but, as need hardly be urged, it suggests inquiries of a very painful character. Was the vessel, with this vast number of passengers on board, actually abandoned by the master and some of his chief officers? If she was towed into Aden, she could not have been in a condition which would justify her officers in leaving her at all; and the abandonment of duty which would be involved in such conduct is so disgraceful that we must regard the whole matter as a mystery until full particulars are furnished. It would have been terrible that more than nine hundred helpless pilgrims should have perished at sea. But that they should have been abandoned by the officers of the ship to which they had intrusted themselves, and saved by the accidental services rendered them by another vessel, is scarcely credible. The facts at present before us imply as much; but it will be but just to suspend all judgment on the subject until all the facts are accurately known. (*The Times*)

. . . That she should thus have been abandoned and her living freight left to their fate is one of the most dastardly circumstances we have ever heard of in connection with the perils of the deep. . . . It is to be feared that pilgrim ships are officered by unprincipled and cowardly men who disgrace the traditions of seamanship. We sincerely trust that no Englishman was amongst the boatload of cowards who left the *Jeddah* and her thousand passengers to shift for themselves. (*Daily Chronicle*)

. . . even if the *Jeddah* had afterwards foundered there would have remained an indelible stain of discredit upon the men who had thus run away at the moment of peril. But the fact that the ship was not in any extremity of peril is clearly proved by her eventual safety and the charge becomes thus one of over-timidity as well as simple *laches*. . . . (Evening issue of the *Globe*)

. . . The relief which is felt at the safety of the pilgrims will be modified by a feeling of indignation and horror at what seems the cowardly desertion of their post and trust by the master and seamen of the ship. (*Daily News*)

A *London Times* correspondent reported a letter received from Captain Henry Carter, relating his experiences with pilgrim-ship traffic in general:[2]

THE ABANDONMENT OF THE JEDDAH.

A Correspondent says that, pending the arrival of the details of the reported abandonment of the steamship Jeddah, with between 900 and 1,000 Moslem pilgrims on board, the following extract from a letter written to a friend in London by Captain Henry Carter, of Obelisk fame, shortly before his death on the 10th of January last seems to suggest that the strange desertion of their ship by the captain and his chief officers may only too possibly have been prompted by a natural instinct urging them to trust themselves to the sea rather than face perils of a more dreadful kind. Captain Carter's last employment was in this pilgrim traffic, which, under date November 30th, 1879, on board the steamship King Arthur, then lying in the port of Jeddah, he thus graphically describes:—

"No one who has not witnessed the pilgrims actually *en route* can form the slightest conception of the unromantic and unpicturesque appearance of these wretched fanatics. It is a pity that some philanthropist will not take the trouble to make the tour, and go on board one of the pilgrim vessels about to start on a voyage to Jeddah. There are horrors on board such a ship which no Christian has ever dreamt of, and none but those who grow rich by such wickedness can form any idea of what goes on in

2. *London Times*, August 14, 1880.

these vessels under the British flag—wickedness worse, by far, than was ever found on board a slaver. Only fancy 1,000 or 1,200 fanatics cooped up on the deck of a small vessel for 18 or 20 days, with no room to move, and little or no fresh air to breathe. There is no medical man to attend their wants when sick, and but a limited stock of medicine on board. I lost seven pilgrims in about 10 days, and I firmly believe that prompt medical treatment by a doctor would have saved them all. Of course, if these wretched beings die *en route* to Mecca, their eternal happiness is assured, so that they generally seem glad to give up the ghost and fly to the realms of joy. I wish you could have seen some of our little scenes of excitement. You must understand that my 'batch' consisted of Turcomans, Arabo-Persians, and Bedouins. They all came on board armed to the teeth, but, of course, I had all their weapons taken charge of by my officers and locked up in safety. I mean all the weapons we saw. They take up their quarters in any part of the ship, and from the moment of embarcation set the captain and officers at defiance. One day I had occasion to give orders for the removal of some luggage, which I found placed on the steering-gear, and which, of course, interfered with the navigation of my vessel. I was informed by my officers that the owners of this luggage refused to shift it, and, on my insisting on obedience to my orders, I found about me 150 cut-throat Arabs, all armed and prepared to resist my authority. Discretion was the better part of valour, for my three officers and myself were the only Englishmen on board, so that the odds were too great, and I quietly gave way. I thus found I had not got possession of all the swords, daggers, and firearms, which grieved me much. We were often alarmed by cries of "Fire!" but on only one occasion was it at all serious. In this instance some of these men had lighted a fire on the bare deck, in order to prepare some tea. Of course, a dry pine deck, with its oakum and pitch, was soon a blaze. Luckily it was the upper deck, so the fire was soon mastered. Had it happened below the result would have been terrible, for the 'tween decks would have filled with smoke, the confusion and panic would have rendered the pumps unworkable, the five boats would have been taken possession of and swamped, and a dense cloud of smoke would have been the quickly vanishing sign of a dreadful disaster. The ship and her living freight would have been among 'the missing.' A shocking scene occurred one very dark night, which convinces me of the utterly savage nature of the men I had to deal with. It was reported to me at 10 P.M. that one of the pilgrims was dead. So I gave orders that the friends of the deceased should take the body to the lee side and prepare it for burial. This was being done, but in carrying the corpse across the deck the bearers happened to disturb some Persians who were asleep. Instantly there was a terrible uproar. Swords, daggers, and bludgeons were brandished; the corpse was nearly torn to pieces; and one of my officers, who attempted to quell the disturbance, was thrown down. An implement, something between a tomahawk and a pickaxe, was aimed at his head, but a friendly hand was near, and his life was saved. I have carefully preserved this formidable weapon as a memento of such happy times. A few years ago a pilgrim vessel was stranded on one of the reefs in the Red Sea, and before any attempt could be made to get the ship off the captain and his officers were tied to the mast, and their throats were cut. When the wreck was discovered their bodies were found in this state, and out of the ship's 500 passengers 450 were drowned."

In a letter to the editor of the *London Times*, George Campbell replied to Captain Carter's statement of two days earlier:[3]

THE ABANDONMENT OF THE JEDDAH.

TO THE EDITOR OF THE TIMES

Sir,—I do not know whether the late Captain Carter, of "Obelisk fame," whose letter appears in *The Times* of to-day, is the man who abandoned or the man who saved the Obelisk, nor can I quite make out whether he most intended to condemn the "wretched fanatics" who sail in pilgrim ships or the avaricious Britishers who make money by sailing ships on board which are "such horrors as no Christian ever dreamt of," but I hope the latter, and certainly the letter of one having the practical experience that he had will have effect in drawing attention to these horrors and to the treatment of the pilgrims illustrated by the shocking, though, happily, not fatal, case of the Jeddah.

I dare say Turcomans and Bedouins, when carried in the dreadful way described by Captain Carter, are a rough and dangerous lot; but I wholly deny that there is any ground for applying such a term as "wretched fanatics" to the ordinary pilgrims from the English and Dutch East Indies. Pilgrimages are not unknown in Europe, and to this day many English and very many Americans flock to Jerusalem. The Indian pilgrims to Mecca and Kerbeleh are generally very decent and quiet Mahomedans with no special fanaticism; but they are very little accustomed to sea-voyaging, and somewhat helpless. There is no reason whatever why they should not be protected against barbarous ill-treatment and horrible arrangements on shipboard such as Captain Carter describes.

Though there was probably never before so pronounced a case as that of the Jeddah, unfortunately this is far from being the first case in which wrecks have been brought before the Indian Government where very large numbers of native passengers have been left to drown while the officers and crew escaped; and on account of many abuses the British-Indian law on the subject has carefully, and, I hope, to some degree effectually, provided for the protection of these poor people. But I know that when I was in office there was not equal protection in the case of vessels sailing

3. *London Times*, August 16, 1880.

from Singapore, and, as the Jeddah came from that colony, I am very anxious to know if the present regulations are sufficient, and if there are the means of insuring a thorough inquiry into and adequate treatment of this case. I have given notice of a question in the House of Commons; but meantime there seems difficulty in ascertaining whether the matter will rest with the British, Indian, or colonial authorities, and whether there is anywhere any central power which has sufficient control in cases of vessels sailing between different jurisdictions. I trust you will do what can be done to draw public attention to this dreadful subject. Remember Captain Carter's statements:—"Wickedness worse by far than was ever found on board a slaver;" "one thousand or 1,200 fanatics cooped up on the deck of a small vessel for 18 or 20 days, with no room to move and little or no fresh air to breathe;" no medical man, very little medicine; great mortality due to these hardships, and occasional desertion by those to whom they are intrusted.

Your obedient servant,
GEORGE CAMPBELL.
[Member of Parliament.]

August 14.

Following is a verbatim reprint of the notice to the British House of Commons to bring the question of the *Jeddah* incident before the members: [4]

House of Commons

Notice given Monday 23rd. August 1880.

Question to be put on Tuesday 24th. August 1880.

By Sir George Campbell—To ask the President of the Board of Trade if he would state where, how, and by whom inquiry will be made into the abandonment of the Steamship "Jeddah" by the Captain and Officers and what is the penal law applicable to any grave dereliction of duty found to have occurred in such a case.

If he will communicate with the India Office regarding the occurrence of several successive cases in past years in which large numbers of native Passengers were drowned while the Officers and Crew escaped and in which a strong suspicion arose that native passengers were not always treated as white Passengers would be and will ascertain whether in consequence of the above mentioned losses the Indian law on the subject was made more stringent *and with what result.*

Whether owing to the neglect of the precautions deemed necessary by the Government of India in the vessels engaged in the Singapore Pilgrim traffic an attempt was made to enforce the Indian Laws on such vessels coming to the port of Aden, but was

---

4. Public Record Office copy of Colonial Office 273/111.

abandoned owing to the remonstrance of the Colonial Authorities.

And if he will lay upon the Table the regulations on this subject now in force at Singapore *and ascertain whether those regulations are bonâ fide carried out or are evaded by taking additional Passengers outside the limits of the port or otherwise.*

Captain Clark's statement was printed in the *Straits Times Overland Journal*, September 8, 1880:

THE S.S. "JEDDAH"

Captain Clark, lately of the S.S. *Jeddah*, has furnished us with the following statement signed by him of the particulars of the abandonment of that vessel.

"I left Penang on 20th July with a crew of 50 men, 5 European officers and 953 adult pilgrims bound to Jeddah. The weather was heavy and threatening, strong head winds and high seas up to the "1½ degree channel," for two days only we had fine weather. After this (29th July) the weather became very heavy the wind increasing almost to hurricane force at times with a very high cross sea, the ship rolling, pitching and straining heavily. The gale continued with unabating fury and the ship labouring and straining heavily caused the boilers to break adrift from their fastenings on the 6th August. Steps were immediately taken to secure the boilers, but the weather was so bad that all the toms put in were broken up and every connection with the boilers broken. The water rose in the ship very rapidly and the steam pumping power was rendered useless. The deck pumps were all at work and the Hadjis and firemen were bailing the water out of the engine room in buckets. Notwithstanding, the water gained about an inch per hour, and on the 7th, the water still increasing, all the boats were ordered to be prepared and provisioned. On the night of the 7th there was a great difference in the demeanour of the pilgrims, they armed themselves with knives and clubs. About 400 men were clustered all around my cabin on deck and I was informed it was their deliberate intention to murder my wife. I satisfied myself assuredly on this point from the various conversations of the Hadjis and their demeanour left no doubt in my mind as to their intention. At midnight they refused to take the pumps, saying that they would sooner die than pump. I passed my wife through the window of my cabin and got one of the officers to put her in one of the boats. Immediately after this, when starting to lower the boat, a general rush was made by the pilgrims and I was pushed into the boat during which I received several serious blows. The boat was manned by the Chief Engineer with a boat's crew. The boat went down with a rush, the Chief Mate who was in the ship, was hurled overboard and every effort was made to sink my boat. The Hadjis cut us away from the ship. There was a heavy sea on. The third Engineer jumped or was thrown into the boat during the excitement and attack. I picked up the first officer and took him into my boat. This is all I know personally. It transpired in evidence at the Court of Inquiry that the second mate and 11 others—Hadjis and Crew—who were in another boat, were similarly attacked and the boat cut away, the boat went down and all were drowned. I kept my boat's head hove to sea during the remainder of the night and in the morning I saw no signs of the *Jeddah*. My boat was picked up about 10 A.M. by the *Scindia* and taken to Aden."

(SD.) J. L. CLARK.

A letter to Syed Muhammad bin Alsagoff from his agent in Aden, followed by a report of the reaction in Singapore to the *Jeddah* affair, from the *Straits Times Overland Journal*, September 13, 1880:

From the Daily Times, 8th September

THE S.S. "JEDDAH."

Mr. Syed Mahomed bin Alsagoff, Managing Director of the Singapore, Steam Ship Company, has kindly placed at our disposal the following letter, which we print *verbatim et literatim*, from his Agents in Aden regarding the abandonment of the S.S. *Jeddah*, and which contains the only information he has received on the subject independent of Captain Clark's statement. The telegrams announcing the circumstance, which were received by Mr. Syed Mahomed, have been, it will be remembered, already published:—

Steamer Point,
Aden, August 20th, 1880.

Syed Mahomed Alsagoff, Esq.,
Managing Director
Singapore S.S. Company,
Singapore

Dear Sir,—With deep regret we have to report you the sad circumstances of your good S.S. *Jeddah*.

Captain Clark came with Mr. Omar to our office at about 9 P.M. on the 18th (*sic*) inst., to our surprise, they reported that the S.S. *Jeddah* is foundered this side of the "Socotra" Island, and he himself and his wife, Syed Omar, 1st Mate, 1st Engineer and 21 others arrived per S.S. *Scindia*, and he, Captain Clark gave the Captain of the S.S. *Scindia* Rs. 700 as a remuneration for bringing them with food, &c., supplied to all people.

On the 11th instant at about 6 P.M. it was reported, and came into anchor about 7 P.M., the S.S. *Jeddah*, in tow of Messrs. Alfred Holt's S.S. *Antenor* which was more surprising when it was reported that she had foundered. Immediately on her arrival the authorities ordered the Police Superintendent and Harbour Pilot to go on board, to see what was to be done, and of course our people as well as others went on board for anxiety of the ship and people reported are foundered; the water was only in the Engine room and nowhere else, the bearers of the Boilers broke down and Boilers shifted and whole cause in consequence of the Boilers on one side and the feed pumps gave way, and rapidly the water filled up the Engine room, with pumping of water day and night by passengers they tired after pumping 4 days and nights, and when Captain Clark found that all people on board are tired, they thought the ship must be foundered. The authority, on arrival of the ship, took charge to land passengers and to keep the ship in safe place, and for about 4 or 5 days they put their own men to pump water out of her and to get clean, &c. When your message came to us of course we guaranteed for expenses and to send the passengers to Jeddah and took charge of her and we have had a survey ourselves and Government had another survey on Engine room and Boilers, and the report we forward herein by which you will see what is wanted and we shall be able to do all work here. The second survey we called on the cargo, and glad to say it is not damaged. Copy of survey is herein enclosed. We shall have a Marine Survey on the ship and see what is deficient. At present we can see the sails are all broken in pieces and more lost, 2 life boats are lost, 2 compasses, 2 chronometers are gone, and we have to place whole of these before she is ready for sea. Capt. Clark has left his one chronometer on board.

The Court has finished the trial, and will give verdict this afternoon, and what we have heard is that Captain Clark will lose his certificate, but no one else be injured in any way.

The 2nd Mate is lost by jumping in boat when Captain Clark left the ship, and 3 Khallasees and passengers, in all 18 lives, are lost.

We telegraphed you to send a Captain and we believe you will find a good Captain in Singapore to engage him and send him by a first steamer; it will be much cheaper in long run than to engage here a stray one.

Regarding Officers and Engineers, we shall report you in our next.

Captain Clark has got leave to proceed on, and he is going to-day to Singapore with his wife per M. M. Co's steamer.

He has Rs. 710 to pay to Captain of the *Scindia* who brought them, which we have debited to the Company.

We shall send you copy of the Court decision on the trial in our next which will give full light on the subject, but it is a bad job done by Captain Clark.

About 300 passengers are already sent away at Rs. 10 each, and we shall send them as the opportunity may offer. The authorities do not like to keep them longer, fearing of sickness breaking out amongst them and may cause an epidemic in the place.

You may rest assured that we shall not fail to do all for the interest of the Company in a most economical way. We have received the credit for $10,000 and will draw as we may require. In meantime we close this in haste as the time of mail is quite near for closing at the Post Office.

We remain, Dear Sir,
Yours faithfully,
Cowasjee Dinshaw & Bros.

From the Daily Times, 10th September

THE S.S. JEDDAH.

The fame of Captain Clark, who, we believe, is realising his property here with the object of leaving for England, has preceded him. The London newspapers publish the details, eagerly, of his desertion of his ship. For our own part we await the receipt of the evidence given at the Court of Inquiry at Aden, in a spirit of fair play, before we make any comments or draw conclusions. Most persons here have formed their opinions as to Captain Clark's conduct but until the whole of the facts are before us, we prefer to keep silent. The London *Standard* contains the following telegrams and general remarks on the subject. Mr. Syed Mahomed hopes to obtain the copy of the evidence given before the Court of Inquiry by the next mail, he has not received any letter from Aden by this mail:—

Aden, 10th August.—The steamer *Jeddah*, of Singapore, bound for Jeddah, with 953 pilgrims on board, foundered off Cape Guardafui, on the 8th inst. All on board perished excepting the captain, his wife, the chief officer, the chief engineer, the assistant engineer, and 16 natives.

The survivors were picked up by the steamer *Scindia* and landed here.

Aden, 11th August, 7.50 p.m.—The *Jeddah*, which was abandoned at sea with nine hundred and fifty-three pilgrims on board, did not founder as reported by the master. She has just arrived here, all safe, in tow of the steamer *Antenor*.

A court of Inquiry was held at Aden into the cause of the abandonment of the Jeddah.[5]

(No. 896.)

"JEDDAH." (S.S.)

REPORT of a Court of Inquiry held at Aden into the cause of the abandonment of the steamship "JEDDAH."

The steamship "Jeddah," of Singapore, official number 67,990, under British colours of $993\frac{44}{101}$ tons register, and owned by the Singapore Steamship Company, Limited, Joseph Lucas

5. No. 896, Indian Office Library, London.

Clark, master, left Singapore on the 17th July 1880, for Penang.

On arrival at Penang she filled up with pilgrims, making a total complement of 953 as adult passengers, and proceeded on her voyage on the 19th idem for Jeddah direct; she had 600 tons of cargo on board, principally sugar, garron-wood, and general merchandise. Her crew consisted of 50 souls all told, which number included the master, first and second mates, and third engineer, who were Europeans, and with the captain's wife, the only Europeans on board.

The "Jeddah" appears to have experienced heavy weather for the most part of her voyage. On the 3rd August 1880, the wind increased almost to a hurricane, with high breaking sea.

On this date the boilers started from their fastenings and began to work, and steps were subsequently taken to secure them with wedges.

The weather increased in severity until the 6th August; on that day, about 9.30 P.M., the feed valve of the port boiler broke, and the ship had to be stopped for repairs, and the vessel then, it was considered, commenced to leak considerably, having shipped much water previously. As soon as repairs were executed, at 1.30 P.M., the vessel again proceeded under steam, when the feed valve on the starboard boiler also broke; and after again stopping for repair, the ship proceeded at 8.30 P.M. with one boiler only. All hands and passengers were then working at the pumps and baling. As the water appeared to increase, the bilge injection was utilized and the leak reduced; but as that became choked, and the vessel stopped to clear it, the leak increased, it is stated, so rapidly as to put out the fires. In consequence of the quantity of water in the stoke-hole, and from the temporary wedges and supports to the boilers having washed away, and the boilers working backwards and forwards owing to the rolling of the ship, every connection pipe was carried away, and the engine-rooms became untenable and a wreck.

Sail was apparently set as soon as the engines became useless, but these were blown away, and other sails subsequently set when the wind moderated.

In the meantime pumping and baling was resorted to, and the passengers appear to have given willing assistance after the evening of the 7th August. On that day the master ordered the boats to be got ready, provisioned, armed, and swung out.

Pumping continued on the part of the passengers up to 12 midnight, then apparently some diminution took place. Certain of the crew were then ordered shortly after to man a boat or boats; the bulk of the crew appear to have manned the boats.

At this time the passengers appear to have become partially disorganized, and to have entertained the idea that the boats were going to leave the ship. The master then appears to have decided to hang the starboard lifeboat astern, and to remain in it with his wife and the first engineer and a boat's crew until daylight, being, he states, afraid of his own and his wife's life being attempted if he remained on board. The starboard lifeboat was then about to be lowered, and the captain and his wife and chief engineer got into it. The captain's wife had to pass some 50 feet from the cabin to the boat. When the boat was lowered, the pilgrims commenced to throw boxes, pots and pans, and anything they could lay hands on, into the boat, and pulled the first officer, who was lowering the boat, off the rails; and seeing they could not prevent the lowering of the boat, they attempted to swamp it. The third engineer had in the meantime got into the boat, and the first officer found himself in the water, and was taken into it, and the boat was then cut adrift, and for about a couple of hours the boat's head was kept to the wind and sea, but after that allowed to drive and partially sail before the wind, until at 10 A.M. on the 8th August, it was sighted by the steamship "Scindia," and the persons in it rescued and brought to Aden, where they arrived on the 10th August. On arrival at Aden, the master and others rescued reported the foundering of the "Jeddah" with all on board, and also reported that the second officer and second engineer had been murdered.

After the master left the "Jeddah" it appears that the passengers tried to prevent the second officer leaving the ship, which he appears to have attempted, by leaving the captain's boats and going over to the port side to the boat to which he was appointed, and which was manned and ready for lowering. Two of the passengers, Lojis, and an Arab, appear also to have got into this boat. On the pilgrims ordering the people to come out of the boats, and on their refusal, some of the pilgrims (it cannot be ascertained who) cut the falls, and it fell into the sea bow first from the fore fall being cut first, and all in it appear to have perished.

Shortly after this, the second engineer, who was awoke out of his sleep a little time before by the second officer, and told to go to his boat, proceeded to his boat, also on the port side. This boat was to have been commanded by the first officer, the Lojis, finding this boat also manned with the second engineer in it, got in, and threw all the men back from her into the ship, and would not allow them to leave. They then appear to have resumed pumping and baling, and continued doing so without intermission, gaining on the leak; and on the following morning, 8th August, finding themselves in smooth water, they sighted land and made for it, having had sail set all night. They hoisted signals of distress, and at 3 P.M., when about 7 or 8 miles from land, the wind died away. At about 4.30 P.M., the steamship "Antenor," seeing the signals, bore down on the disabled ship; and the master, after ascertaining the state of affairs, sent his chief mate on board, and took charge, and brought the "Jeddah" in tow to Aden, where both vessels arrived on the afternoon of the 11th August.

The water in the "Jeddah" was considerably reduced by the

exertions of the passengers, under the direction of the chief officer of the "Antenor," and that officer on first boarding the ship, and seeing the quantity in her, came to the immediate conclusion that the vessel could be saved. Three sailors, one topman, one syrang, eleven firemen, and one clerk, one fireman working his passage, were all the crew on board the "Jeddah" when brought to Aden, together with the second engineer and supercargo, and 992 passengers—778 men, 147 women, and children 67, not counting infants in arms, were on board.

The above appear to the Court to be, as far as can be ascertained, the circumstances connected with this case; and in reviewing them, and after a patient and careful inquiry into all the details, the Court record the following opinion:—

It appears that the fastenings of the boilers, which are placed athwartships in the " Jeddah, " were defective, and in consequence of the rolling of the ship and the heavy sea, these fastenings gave way, and caused a leak by the breaking of the connecting pipes with the ship's bottom. This leak, though serious in itself, was intensified by the vessel shipping large quantities of water, and the boilers having to be blown off or emptied into the ship's bilge on several occasions instead of into the sea, when repairs were being executed. With the rolling of the ship, the quantity of water in the stoke-hole appeared greater than it actually was, and from the engine and donkey-engine being useless, the vessel having water also in the after-hold through the sluice, the actual condition of affairs was thought more serious than was the case; the ship having a leak, and being in a heavy sea. It appears to the Court that sufficient notice was not at once taken of the movement of the boilers, and every available means adopted to secure them as much as possible, immediately it was ascertained that they had shifted and were working.

The chief engineer of the "Jeddah" appears to have treated this matter lightly, and is, in the Court's opinion, primarily responsible for his ignorance in not knowing the extent of the risk and danger run by the boilers moving, and not insisting on all available means being employed at once to stay them.

Had more energetic measures been taken at the outset, it appears just probable to the Court that subsequent events might have been averted. When steam power was no longer available on board the "Jeddah," it appears to the Court that no regular system of reducing the leak was organized by the master. He appears to have come to the conclusion early on the 7th August that the boats would probably be required, and they were prepared and swung out, and the crew engaged in attending to them rather than to the vessel's condition. The firemen, however, appear to have been steadily engaged in working the ash buckets up to midnight of the 7th August.

The master does not appear to have taken his passengers into his confidence or to have endeavoured in the least degree to raise their hopes in any way. On the contrary, it seems he informed them that if they would not pump the vessel would founder, thereby giving no hope. On this point, situated as he was, the Court consider he was wanting in simple judgment, for he had much in his favour to dispel fear and raise the hopes and energies of his passengers, who appeared ready and willing to assist. Land was not far distant, and yet by his act in ordering the boats he led the passengers to believe that the vessel would probably founder, and the boats would be lowered. Although there is conflicting evidence that the master was of this opinion before the Logis had their thoughts averted from the pumping, the master's action after being picked up by the "Scindia," and brought to Aden, and his report of the "Jeddah" having foundered, leads the Court to infer that the master considered the vessel would founder whether pumped and baled out or not. The Court consider he was under the impression from his acts that the "Jeddah" would founder under any circumstances, but, apart from his impressions, his action in ordering the boats to be prepared was an inducement to disturbance, as only about one quarter of the souls on board could have been accommodated in them.

The Court consider that in this the master showed a want of judgment and tact to a most serious extent, and that he caused disorganisation and discontent, not to say despair, at a time when none of these feelings should have been engendered.

The master states that on finding the pilgrims would not work the pumps, shortly after midnight on the 7th and 8th August, and that they appeared altered in demeanour and were some of them armed with knives, he feared that his wife's life and his own would be attempted, as he had been led to infer the same from what he had been told, and consequently very shortly after he found that this was the state of affairs, in place of resorting to measures to restore confidence or to organize any system of defence in case of need, for the protection of the lives of himself and the Europeans on board, which he could easily have done by keeping the bridge with the arms on board, he determined on lowering a boat, in which he intended, he states, first to place his wife and to remain in her himself, to hang astern of the ship until daylight. What the master's intentions were after daylight does not appear. He ordered the boat to be manned, and, after having his wife placed in it, he himself got in and others did also. Up to this time it is evident that no violence or even show of force had been made by the pilgrims to anyone on board; it was only when the boat was being lowered and they became aware of what was taking place, that they appear to have resorted to force, and then not such force as they might have utilized, armed with knives as they were. Failing in preventing the lowering of the boat, the pilgrims proceeded to endeavour to swamp her; two pistol shots were fired in the direction of the pilgrims from the boat by the first officer, and these appear to have prevented any further attempts to swamp the boat, which then was cast off and away from the ship. The passengers, finding other boats were manned, they proceeded to endeavour to prevent their leaving the ship, and, in the case of the second officer's boat, cut it adrift when its inmates would not return on board, and unceremoniously ejected those who had got into the third boat with the second engineer.

The Court consider that the action of the pilgrims tends to prove that they never intended to harm the master and his officers had they remained in the "Jeddah," that their demeanour is accounted for by the evidence that they had made up their minds that they should not be deserted by the only persons capable of protecting and helping them in the circumstances in which they were placed, and consequently they would prevent to the utmost the master or his officers leaving the ship. It is in the Court's opinion more than probable that the master was misled in regard to the real intentions of the pilgrims, but he has himself to blame for not making more certain of these intentions, or waiting for some more clear proof of these intentions than took place. It is to be regretted that the principal witness, Lezed Omar, on this point could not be examined, as he had left Aden for Jeddah the day after his arrival, and before the steamship "Jeddah" was towed in.

There is no evidence before the Court to show that the life of the captain's wife was in danger by reason of any threats made by the pilgrims, and this man, Lezed Omar, alone appears to be the authority of this report, and he is stated to have been in dread himself and much frightened for his own safety.

Doubtless the master on hearing this report, as well as imperfectly understanding the threats actually made by the pilgrims, viz., "that they would not allow any one to leave the ship, and would prevent them to the extent of violence if necessary," the fact of the pilgrims having armed themselves to a certain extent to carry out this threat if need arose, aided by the officious ill-advice of his chief officer, entirely forgot his first duty as a shipmaster, and proceeded to be one of the first instead of the last to leave his disabled vessel to her fate. This last act roused the pilgrims to violence in attempting to swamp his boat, and such the Court consider might naturally have been expected from any body of human beings, even Europeans, situated as the pilgrims were.

With every consideration for the master under the trying circumstances in which he and his crew found themselves placed, the Court is reluctantly compelled to state that they consider that Captain Clark has shown a painful want of nerve as well as the most ordinary judgment, and has allowed his feelings to master the sense of duty it is the pride of every British shipmaster to vaunt, and they consider that in the instances mentioned he has been guilty of gross misconduct in being indirectly the cause of the deaths of the second mate and ten natives, seven crew and three passengers, and in abandoning his disabled ship with nearly 1,000 souls on board to their fate, when by ordinary display of firmness, combined with very little tact in dealing with natives, with whom he is no stranger, he could have ensured their co-operation and gratitude, and saved considerable loss to his owners. The Court must here also remark on the want of anxiety shown by the master for the fate of the "Jeddah," in not doing all in his power to induce the "Scindia" to search for her, as there is little doubt but that a proper statement of facts and little persuasion would have induced the master of the "Scindia" under the circumstances to steam for an hour or so to windward, when the "Jeddah" would certainly have been sighted.

The Court feel compelled to mark their sense of the master, Joseph Lewis Clark's, conduct by ordering, subject to the confirmation of the Bombay Government, that his certificate of competency as master be suspended for a period of three years.

Before concluding, the Court consider it necessary to place on record their disapprobation of the conduct of the first officer of the "Jeddah," Mr. Williams, who may be said to have aided and abetted the master in the abandonment of his vessel. The Court consider it very probable that, but for Mr. Williams's officious behaviour and unseamanlike conduct, the master would (by the first mate's own showing) have done his duty by remaining on the ship.

Had there been any evidence, except the first mate's own statement, on this point, the Court would have felt constrained to have put him on trial also, they cannot therefore refrain from remarking that they consider that in this instance he has shown himself unfitted for his position as first mate on a crowded pilgrim vessel.

The Court have to regret that, owing to the positive report made of the "Jeddah" having foundered, no steps were taken to detain or record the evidence of the master and officers of the steamship "Scindia," as to the reasons and causes for their not searching for the steamship "Jeddah" after picking up her master and others. The examination of these witnesses would have completed the evidence which otherwise is not as complete as it might, and very desirable that it should be in this case—the most extraordinary instance known to the Court of the abandonment of a disabled and leaking ship at sea by the master and Europeans, and almost all the crew, with close to 1,000 souls on board when no immediate danger existed of her foundering. The Court consider that it is due to the master of the "Antenor" to place on record their opinion of the contrast of his conduct to that of Captain Clark, and consider him worthy, with his chief officer, Mr. Campbell, of great commendation for their action, not only for rescuing those on board the "Jeddah" from a perilous position and shipwreck, but also for saving a valuable ship and her cargo from loss.

In conclusion the Court consider it is not out of place to re-mark, that in their estimation nearly 1,000 souls on board a vessel of the tonnage of the "Jeddah" was a greater number than should be allowed by any regulation, especially for a long sea voyage, as taken by the "Jeddah," and at a season when bad weather might naturally have been expected.

(Signed)   G. R. GOODFELLOW

Resident and Sessions Judge.

Aden, 20th August 1880
    I concur.

(Signed)   W. K. THYNNE

Assessor.

Confirmed.

(Signed)   JAMES FERGUSSON,

Governor of Bombay.

The Merchant Shipping Act, in the case of a Board of Trade certificate, only requires the confirmation of the Local Govern-ment with reference to the regularity of the proceedings. Had I been advised that any option rested with it with reference to the details, I should have declined to confirm them, as I think the sentence inadequate to the offence committed by the master of the "Jeddah" as described by the Court.

Assuming that his abandonment of his ship, without necessity, and with the probable loss of an enormous number of helpless people for whose safety he was responsible, was the result rather of cowardice and want of resource than of inhumanity, his subse-quent conduct in not doing his utmost to procure them succour showed that latter quality. But in either point of view, he has, in my judgment, shown himself entirely unfit to be entrusted with the charge of life and property at sea.

(Signed)   J.F.

ASSESSOR'S REPORT on the abandonment of the steamship
"JEDDAH," of Singapore.

I consider the chief engineer of the "Jeddah" very much to blame for not taking the most active measures to secure the boilers when he first saw them move on the 3rd of August, more especially as the vessel was labouring heavily. When the matter was reported to the master is doubtful, but from the chief en-gineer's own statement, my opinion is that the engineer did not report to the master the moving of the boilers until the following day; the reason given by the engineer, viz., that the pipes in con-nection with the boiler were copper and could stand any strain caused by the moving of the boilers, the movement first observed being three-eighths of an inch, but which gradually increased to about two inches, before the boilers became totally useless by all the important pipes breaking, including the donkey engine steam-pipe. Before this happened, the vessel leaked a good deal in the engine-room, and as long as the engines could be worked the leak could be kept down. Had the chief engineer exercised a little judgment, he surely would have known that the movement of the boilers (which was of a jerky nature) was a most dangerous thing, and likely to become more and more dangerous with every heavy roll of the ship, and was a matter which required his most vigilant care from the first. I cannot understand how the engineer could make himself believe that the movement of the boilers (huge masses, each weighing probably not less than 30 tons when filled with water) was a matter of no consequence at first, merely because the movement was only three-eighths of an inch. Common sense might have taught him that the movement was likely to increase with every roll of the ship.

On the 6th August the engines and steam pumps became useless, the ship leaking, but not to any alarming extent. The bilge injection when working being able to keep the leak down; pumps were manned and baling started without any attempt being made to organize the Hadjees into working gangs, with regular reliefs, or replenishing the supply of buckets, by making canvas ones.

At noon of the 7th August, the ship's position was said to be in latitude 11° 55′ north, and longitude 51° 55′ east, "Abdul Kuri" bearing north-east ½ east, true distant about 28 miles. With this position, the bearing of Cape Guardafui would be nearly due west, distant about 35 miles. Shortly after the position of the ship had been ascertained, the order was given to get the boats made ready, which was done before sunset, and crews told off, the engineers and officers were informed what boats they were to go in should the boats leave the ship. Before midnight some of the passengers, it was said, had been heard to say they would kill the captain and his wife. This was reported to the captain. Again it stated that the passengers would use force to prevent the captain from leaving the ship; some of the passengers were observed about midnight to be armed with their knives, stated to be any number from 20 up to 300. The second engineer went to bed at midnight; he did not see any man armed. The captain was warned by the first mate to be careful how he went about the decks, as the passengers might kill him. Up to the time the captain left the ship he was not molested, until he went into the starboard lifeboat at 2:30 A.M. The first and second mates were at the lowering of this boat. The second mate left at once, called the second engineer, and got into his own boat on the port (*i.e.* weather) side, which was all ready for lowering. As the boat was being lowered the falls were cut by the Hadjees, which caused one end of the boat to fall first, and it is supposed threw the crew out, who were drowned.

Nothing was ever seen of this boat. The Hadjees did what they could to destroy her, they also did what they could to destroy the starboard lifeboat, and I believe knocked the first mate overboard. The distance from the captain's cabin to the starboard lifeboat is stated to be about 40 feet; the captain's wife was passed through one of the windows of the cabin, and either walked along or was carried and put into the boat without being molested, the first mate taking a prominent part in this proceeding.

The first mate of the "Jeddah," according to his own statement, is greatly to blame in doing what he could to demoralize the master, by advising him to leave the ship, telling him his life was in danger, also his wife's life; that he, the master, was sure to be killed if he remained on board; and that he, the first mate, did thrust the master into the boat. The mate worked on the fears of the master for the safety of his wife, and by so doing hurried the master into leaving the ship.

From noon of the 7th until the "Jeddah" was picked up by the "Antenor" she was on the port tack under short canvass, blowing hard from the south, steering west, every hour bringing the vessel nearer to a weather shore, where smooth water might be expected. When the master left the ship at 2:30 A.M. on the 8th August, he must have been distant from Cape Guardafui about 10 miles, judging from the position of the vessel at noon of the 7th of August, viz., latitude 11° 55' north, and longitude 51° 55' east; and her approximate position at 4:30 P.M. of the 8th August, viz., latitude 12° north, and longitude 51° 6' east, when the "Antenor" steered for her and picked her up.

When the "Scindia" picked up the starboard lifeboat the "Jeddah" would be distant about 22 miles, bearing from the "Scindia" about south-south-west.

The "Jeddah" having been towed into Aden harbour on the 11th instant, with the water reduced nearly two feet in the afterhold, proved there was nothing hopeless in the state of the ship when abandoned.

1. I am of the opinion the master was not compelled to leave the "Jeddah."

2. That the master left the "Jeddah" against the will of his passengers.

3. That no disturbance took place until it became known that the master was leaving the ship, and that such disturbance was confined to damaging the boats and occupants when lowering and when lowered by throwing at and into the boats anything which first came to hand, and by cutting the boats' falls.

4. That by leaving the ship the master was the means of causing the loss of 11 [*sic*] lives, and the ship to be abandoned by the major portion of her crew, thereby greatly increasing the danger of the vessel being lost with all on board had she been leaking very badly. The master concluded she had foundered about three hours after he left her, as he was unable to see her at daylight.

5. The master of the "Jeddah," when picked up by the "Scindia," was guilty of great cruelty in not representing matters in such a way to the master of the "Scindia" as would have induced him to steam dead to windward, or in such a direction as might have been considered best to look for the "Jeddah," more especially as the master before leaving had no expectation of her foundering soon.

6. A vessel with upwards of 1,000 souls on board is a charge of great responsibility, and makes it more binding if possible on the master to remain on board to the very last, and by so doing tend to inspire his crew and passengers with courage and determination to save the ship if possible, and by so doing, their lives and property.

I am of opinion had the master's wife not been on board the master would not have deserted his ship.

I am of opinion had the master received proper assistance and advice from his first mate, he, the master, would not have left the ship.

I am of opinion had the master not left the "Jeddah" no lives would have been lost.

I am further of opinion that the first mate should not be permitted to go in the ship again.

The master of the "Antenor" states he passed Cape Guardafui about 3:30 P.M., 3' distant, and steered N. 62° W., true, until he sighted the "Jeddah" at 4.30, Cape Guardafui being distant about 14 miles, bearing S. 60° west. This bearing is wrong, and should be, according to the course steered, about south 46° east.

> Given under my hand at Aden, on this the 20th day of August 1880.
>
> (Signed) W. K. THYNNE, Assessor,
> Port Officer, Aden.

These findings of the Court of Inquiry of August 20 were published in full in the *Straits Times Overland Journal* the following month, on September 13. In the same issue of the paper was the comment:

Public excitement has risen to fever heat here in surveying the conduct of Captain Clark, who is well known here, and his officers and engineers in deserting the S.S. *Jeddah*.

There is no doubt that if the Governor or the Secretary of State could have taken criminal action against Captain Clark and Chief Officer Williams they would have done so. In a *Straits Settlement Dispatch* from Governor Weld on September 20, 1880, there is a reference to the indignation felt in Singapore at "the dastardly conduct of the Captain and the greater part at least of his officers," but Weld admits that for want of witnesses they are unable to prosecute. The Board of Trade held the same view, and the sentence—suspension of certificate for three years for Captain Clark and a reprimand for Chief Officer Williams—seemed to them to be totally inadequate, as is evident in the following letter the Board sent to the Under Secretary of State, India Office: [6]

> The misconduct of the Master in deserting his ship with 1,000 lives on board, and not only taking no step to send them assistance, but, on the contrary, reporting falsely that she "had foundered, and that the second officer and the second engineer had been murdered," deserves the severest punishment which could be inflicted by law, and even if the Authorities at Aden had no power to take steps for the criminal prosecution of Mr. Joseph Lucas Clark, there can be no doubt that the Court should by cancelling his Certificate, have done all in their power to prevent him from again having command of a British Ship.

Apart from Captain Clark, only one other member of the *Jeddah's* crew returned to Singapore: Chief Officer Augustine Podmore Williams, whose conduct had been criticized so severely at the Aden inquiry; he arrived on Wednesday, September 15, 1880, on the S. S. *Naples* from Aden. Only the day before his arrival, the Singapore Legislative Council had debated a motion to have the master of the *Jeddah* arrested and retried, and an account of the debate appeared in the *Singapore Daily Times* on September 16. A. P. Williams was to be the only member of the *Jeddah's* European crew to remain in Singapore. The attitude of the others is suggested by a letter from Charles Baldwin, the chief engineer of the *Jeddah*, to a resident of Singapore, which was published in the *Straits Times Overland Journal* on October 2, 1880.

THE S. S. "JEDDAH."

The following is a copy of a private letter, dated Jeddah 16th September, received by a resident here from Mr. Baldwin, who was Chief Engineer of the vessel when she was abandoned:—

I little thought when the *Jeddah* left Singapore, that the run would terminate so unfortunately. In fact everything went so well for the three weeks we were under steam that I had begun to congratulate myself on the evident decrease in the consumption, and the continued easy working of the engines. But pride goeth before a fall. And it was a considerable shock my pride got one morning when we were within eighty miles of the African coast, the feed check valve chests gave way one after the other. The cast iron brackets supporting the port boiler broke in pieces allowing the boiler to come down two inches on to the fore and after beams, breaking the pipe communicating from the donkey and main boilers to the donkey engine and breaking the bolts holding

6. Register of Letters written for 1881   M. T. 4/300 no. 2777.

the main blow down cock to the ship's bottom, causing a leak which in the course of the next twenty four hours let in water enough to lift the plates and bearers in stoke hole and engine-room, and which water with every roll of the ship surged into the furnaces, and returned in streams from the tube doors of the boiler to leeward. I kept the bilge injection open as long as we could get a turn out of the engines, but when the last valve chest gave way, and no means remained for pumping water into the boilers, and our store room flooded, and all but knocked to pieces, and six feet of water to navigate about in and the three of us half drowned, and knocked up for want of sleep, I was at last compelled to own we could do no more and set the firemen to draw water in ashbuckets up the ventilator. I had had the carpenter down trying to stay the boilers from shifting, but the weight of the boilers and superheater and water, combined with the impetus of the rolling of the ship, crushed the wooden blocks like so much dry tinder, and allowed the boilers a travel of about one and a half inches. For myself and the other engineers, I believe we were perfectly justified in acting as we did. Poor Scott in the hurry had got in the wrong boat, from which he was hauled by the Hadjis and I believe would have been knocked under but for the interposition of Ali the supercargo. Had there been more Europeans left on board when the Captain and Syed Omar left the ship, there would have been more scrimages, and but one Ali. However the whole affair was bad enough to make me decide to have no more to do with the *Jeddah,* and so I told the Agent in Aden, who telegraphed for another Chief, and last Tuesday Mr. J. C. Anderson arrived here with Capt. Craig and the mates. The Agent offered to continue my pay if I would give a hand for a few days which I have done fixing new angle iron brackets under the boilers, and assisting generally. I leave this to-morrow or next day for home. The *Jeddah* is also going to London, and the Agent has offered me a free passage, but I prefer paying my way in another steamer. And so will finish other two years of seagoing, the one dark feature in which is the drowning of our second mate and fourteen others while attempting to lower their boat.

The following are extracts from the report on the action for salvage brought by Alfred Holt, managing partner of the Ocean Steam Ship Company of Liverpool, owners of the British steamship *Antenor*, against the steamship *Jeddah*, her cargo and freight, in the Vice Admiralty Court of the Straits Settlement on October 17, 1881, before Sir Thomas Sidgreaves, Kt., Chief Justice.[7]

7. Printed in *Cases Heard and Determined in Her Majesty's Supreme Court of the Straits Settlements 1808–1884,* edited and reported by James William Norton Kyshe, Esq., Acting Registrar of the said court in Malacca, 3 vols., Singapore, 1886, II, 37–42.

On the 8th August, at 5 P.M., the *Antenor*, an iron screw steam-ship of 1,644 tons, bound on a voyage from Shanghai to London, and with a full complement of 680 passengers, sighted a vessel which subsequently proved to be the *Jeddah*, flying signals of distress. The signals of distress were, on one mast, "We are sinking;" on another, "Send immediate assistance." The flying of the first signal was denied by the defendants' reply, but was clearly proved not only by the witnesses called on behalf of the plaintiffs, but by one of the witnesses, Mahomed Khan, clerk on board the *Jeddah*, called by the defendants. A boat containing the first mate, the boatswain, and four of the crew of the *Antenor*, was sent, and on boarding her they found the *Jeddah* in a very disabled condition. According to the Act on Petition framed upon the affidavits of the Captain and Chief Officer of the *Antenor*, "the Engines were totally disabled, and the Engine fires put out; there were 7 or 8 feet of water in the vessel, and everything on board was in confusion, and all persons on board were panic stricken until the arrival on board of the First Mate and Boatswain of the *Antenor*. The boilers on board were adrift and had broken from their fastenings, and all the pipe connections with the boilers were broken, and no steam-power on board could be used. The steam-pipes on board could not be used, and all fires were out. The position was about 13 miles to the westward of Cape Guardafui and about 9 miles from the African coast. She was under foretopsail jib, and fore and main topsails, and was heading for some bluffs 1,300 feet high on the Coast of Africa. There was an East wind blowing, with a heavy ground swell, and the vessel was being driven through the water in a quasi derelict condition at the rate of 2½ to 3 knots an hour towards the coast. A heavy surf was breaking on the coast, and it was becoming rapidly dark as the sun set at 6 P.M." After the Chief Mate had ascertained by personal observation the state of things on board the *Jeddah*, he returned to the *Antenor* and reported to the Captain. It must be admitted that the Captain found himself confronted with a task of no ordinary difficulty. In command of a ship with a valuable cargo and a full complement of passengers on board, whose interests and those of his owners he was first bound to consider, and with darkness fast coming on, he had to choose between jeopardizing his own ship, cargo and passengers, or leaving a ship abandoned by the Captain and officers, and with nearly 1,000 souls on board, to the inevitable fate that seemed to await her of foundering at sea or being dashed to pieces on the coast. After a short consultation between the Captain and the Chief Officer, it was decided to make an attempt to save the *Jeddah*. They considered it impossible to take the *Jeddah's* passengers on board the *Antenor*, as the *Antenor* was already full, but they thought that it might be possible to tow her into Aden if they could manage to keep her afloat by inducing the pilgrims to work at the pumps. The Chief Officer returned to the *Jeddah* with the Boatswain and 4 of the crew, after arranging signals with the Captain to be used in case of the *Jeddah* sinking, so as to take them off in time. The boatswain and crew returned to the *Antenor* at 10 P.M., but from that time until the *Jeddah* was successfully towed into Aden, the Chief Officer never left her. Though taking the *Jeddah* in tow was accomplished after considerable difficulty, and with the exercise of much patience, skill, and ingenuity, the Chief Officer steered the *Jeddah* himself until he had taught two of the crew of the *Jeddah* to steer; and he induced the passengers to exert themselves in pumping and baling. The conclusion he had come to at first was, that the ship was sinking when the *Antenor* fell in with her, and that without great exertion in baling and pumping, she must sink.

He says: "I called the headmen amongst the pilgrims together and organised gangs amongst the pilgims to pump and bale the vessel. This was done, the men constantly relieving one another, and by the evening of the 9th of August, we had gained 6 inches on the water, and during the following night we gained a foot on the water and continued to gain on the water thenceforward until the water was reduced to 3½ feet in the engine room and 5 feet in the after hold."

Upon this point Captain Bragg in his evidence, says:—"On the 9th, as the sun went half way down from the horizon, the Chief Officer telegraphed 'gained 4 inches,' and I called all hands aft to give him a cheer to encourage him—we were corresponding all the time. The question was, whether we could overpower the water, or the water overpower us."

An incident of this sort, slight in itself, yet tends to shew the hearty good-will with which the salvors were conducting their operations and how likely it would be that they would reanimate, by their coolness and determination, the failing spirits and flagging energies of the pilgrims.

* * *

Captain Worsley, Master of the Telegraph ship *Sherard Osborne*, says:—"I have been Master Mariner, twenty years;—have commanded sailing ships and steam-ships in all parts of the world. I know the waters about Cape Guardafui. Under the circumstances described in the 5th & 6th paragraphs of J. T. Bragg's affidavit, I should say the *Jeddah* was in great danger. If the *Antenor* had not come up to her, I believe she would have become a total wreck. It would not have been practicable to put her about unless they got the propeller to revolve, *i.e.*, disconnected the propeller; it is not usual to have special disconnecting gear on such ships. She was heading right on to shore, I don't think she could have been steered so as to land on any particular spot on the beach. I should have considered her a hopeless derelict, —worse than a derelict with all those people on board. I don't think she could have been, under the circumstances, brought up under her anchor, if they had let the anchor go. If she had a steam windlass on board I think she would have run an awful risk for fear of the chain carrying away the bows. If it were blowing a gale outside, there would be a heavy ground swell off Cape Guardafui—there would be surf on the shore. I don't think boats would have lived through the surf. I don't know the nature of the bottom—if coral it would be very bad holding. I think that when a ship was left as she was described to be, she was in a helpless state. Second Engineers in ships of this class do not know about the navigation of a ship. The Carpenter is the important man under the Chief Officer as regards anchoring. After hearing the accounts read on the affidavits of Bragg and Campbell of how the *Antenor* got the *Jeddah* off in that night, I think the *Antenor* ran considerable risk; even in smooth water there is a risk of collision in a large steamer going alongside another near enough to take a hawser on board, more particularly when there is a strong current running, as there is there. The darkness would enhance the risk. There was very serious risk to the *Antenor's* screw, so great that unless there was imminent danger I should not attempt it until daylight. If the *Antenor* had snapped her rope and fouled her screw she would have been in danger."

Charles Powell, in his evidence, stated: "Last year I was in command of the *Lusitania,* one of the Orient line, of nearly 4,000 tons. I passed Cape Guardafui on August 7th at noon. We had very stiff weather from Ras Hafun to Guardafui; after we got round Guardafui there was a stiff breeze to the next point to East, I know this coast pretty well. Having heard the position and circumstances of the *Jeddah,* with the native crew and great part of them gone, and with 900 and odd pilgrims on board, I consider she was in great danger. If the *Antenor* had not come up to the *Jeddah,* I certainly think at night-time she would have gone on shore. She was heading for the bluffs. If I had been on board as a passenger I should have considered her case as a very hopeless one. I consider she was in great danger when first sighted, having so much water in her hold; she could not be steered at all. From Mr. Campbell's description, I should say it was blowing a strong breeze; it corresponds with my experience of the day: this was at the height of the monsoon when a strong breeze is generally blowing. If she made any speed at all, it must have been with the help of her canvas; when she was picked up I think she was waterlogged. I think she would have gone ashore before daylight. If they had succeeded in getting the anchor down, it was just a chance if they held on: there was danger to the *Antenor* of colliding, and also of getting the hawser foul of her screw—a real danger. If I had been in command of the *Antenor,* I should have considered the position a dangerous one as regards the *Antenor,* and a very risky thing to do."

There can be no doubt, I think, that the *Jeddah* was in imminent danger when she was sighted by the *Antenor,* and that but for the services rendered her by the *Antenor* she would in all probability have foundered or been dashed to pieces, with the loss of every life on board. Taking into consideration the number of the lives thus rescued from the probability of impending death, this is, I believe, a case of life-salvage of a totally unprecedented character.

Conrad's contact with the pilgrim-ship episode stretched over a period of years, and the story probably came to him in varied and vivid forms. No doubt he read most of the details—though not the report of the inquiry at Aden—in the London papers in August 1880. At that time he was staying in London prior to embarking on the *Loch Etive* for Sydney on August 21. His seafaring acquaintances must also have discussed the incident.

His next contact with the tale must have been more vivid. On March 22, 1883, he arrived in Singapore in the S.S. *Sissie*, having been picked up by her after the *Palestine*, on which he was serving as second mate, had been abandoned on a journey from England to Bangkok when her cargo caught fire. The *Palestine* was an extremely old ship, and she sank quickly in calm weather. There was no negligence or cowardice on the part of her captain and crew, as the subsequent Court of Inquiry proved, but it must have seemed significant to Conrad that on his first trip to the East he was involved in an inquiry into the abandonment of a ship, just as the *Jeddah* crew had been involved in Aden. Furthermore, the day before he arrived in Singapore the *Jeddah* had arrived there, and the story of her desertion was no doubt a legend among the seamen. Conrad surely heard of it again, and of the sensation it caused in Singapore, in the very port from which the *Jeddah* had sailed and in which she was then docked.

During his second visit to Singapore, in 1885, he was able to observe something of her later history. The following advertisement appeared in the *Straits Times* of September 8:

For Sale—The A. I. Steamer "Diamond" of 1,035 nett register carrying about 27,000 piculs dead weight. Engine of 200 horse power, speed 10 knots, with a consumption of 14 tons Cardiff. Built by Wm. Denny & Bros. of Dumbarton. For further particulars apply to M. Alsagoff, Manager, Singapore.

The *Diamond* was the *Jeddah* in disguise. She had not returned to Singapore after the desertion in 1880 until July 25, 1881—a year later. As the *Jeddah* she had then continued on the pilgrim run to Jeddah, but it would seem that her reputation still clung to her, for during 1884 and 1885 she was almost entirely disengaged. Returning from Jeddah on November 7, 1884, she was put up for sale. At this point the owners apparently employed a ruse to get rid of the ship's bad reputation. Her name dropped out of the "Shipping in Harbour" column of the *Straits Times* on February 28, 1885, although she was not listed as having been cleared from the harbor. Significantly, however, the S.S. *Diamond*, with the same tonnage and the same commander—a Captain Geary—was cleared for Palalangan. The Register of Shipping, Harbour Office, Singapore, shows that the *Diamond* was indeed the *Jeddah*, for the date and place of her origin and all other particulars were the same.

Inevitably, Conrad changed the name of the pilgrim ship when he wrote *Lord Jim*, calling it the *Patna*. On January 17, 1888, a 1,149-ton steamer called the *Patna* came into Singapore harbour.[8] At this time Conrad was staying at the Sailors' Home in Singapore (January 4 to January 19, 1888) before leaving on the S. S. *Melita* for Bangkok to take over the command of the bark *Otago*.

There was a particular reason for Conrad's interest in the master of the *Jeddah*, Captain Joseph Lucas Clark. As early as 1872 Clark was carrying pilgrims to Jeddah in the *Sumfoo*. The *Straits Times* of March 7, 1874, reported that Clark took the *Sumfoo* through the Torres Straits. As the first master of a steamer to make this dangerous journey, he was highly praised. Conrad was later to set the same course as commander of the sailing ship *Otago*, and it is extremely likely that he knew of Clark both in this connection and in connection with the *Jeddah*.

The first mate of the *Jeddah* at the time of the desertion was a man called Augustine Podmore Williams. Everything I have been able to discover about him from his descendants and from official and unofficial documents suggests that he was Conrad's inspiration for the whole of the first part of the novel.

Williams' background is, in fact, identical with that of Lord Jim. A. P. Williams came from a parsonage and was one of five sons. His daughter, Mrs. Norah Thornett of Sussex, confirms in a letter (July 13, 1962) that her "father was from a parsonage as mentioned in *Lord Jim* & was one of five sons. He was born at Porthleven, Cornwall on May 22, 1852."

The parsonage at Porthleven was centuries old, and Conrad has given a fairly accurate description of it. The present vicar of Porthleven had this to say about the parsonage in a letter of September 7, 1962:

> I should say that, allowing for a certain amount of "writer's licence," the description of the rectory in *Lord Jim* is of Porthleven Vicarage, as one can see from the garden through the trees, Breage Church (very ancient) standing out on a hill about 2 miles away. The Vicarage here is a mixture of brick and stone/

or granite—mostly granite blocks. The lawn slopes steeply in the front and there is a belt of fir trees, with a small stable and orchard at the back. Of course, the garden is much altered now and there are no greenhouses; but the description, on the whole, tallies with Porthleven Vicarage.

According to Miss Nancy Williams of Penzance, the fir trees were planted by her grandfather, A. P. Williams' father. So far as I know he was the first of the Williams family to hold the living. "The old parson" at the time of the *Jeddah* disaster was fifty-seven.

Though A. P. Williams' daughters knew nothing of his early life, it seems likely that he went to a "training ship for officers of the mercantile marine," as did Lord Jim. I have a photograph dated 1868 that was sent to me by his niece, Mrs. Neill. "This antique," she writes, "shows my grandfather and his family." The photograph appears to have been taken at the back of the rectory, probably in the orchard. A. P. Williams, who was then sixteen, is on the extreme left of the family group. He is wearing a uniform of some kind that, with its brass buttons and cap, could be the uniform of a cadet officer of a training ship.

On July 2, 1880, when he was twenty-eight years old, A. P. Williams was taken on at Singapore as first mate of the *Jeddah*. It was not his first appointment as an officer of a ship in the East; prior to this time he had been first mate on the S.S. *Dale* from April 4, 1879, although only for four months. His first chance as chief officer was on the S.S. *Washi* (registered at Hong Kong) for one year, from July 1877 until August 3, 1878. The earliest date I have been able to trace for his arrival in the East is October 3, 1876, when he served on the S.S. *Thales* as second mate.

What must have struck Conrad most forcibly if he met Williams in Singapore was that here was no ordinary coward. Williams returned to Singapore, after leaving the *Jeddah*, on the S.S. *Naples*, and the return of one "whose name has been so frequently mentioned in the findings of the Court of Inquiry at Aden" was announced in the *Straits Times Overland Journal* on September 20, 1880. He did not return home as he might have done, for his certificate, unlike that of the master of the *Jeddah*, was not suspended. In spite of the severe censuring he had received both in the report of the inquiry and in the Singapore Legislative Council, William chose to return to a Singapore that was buzzing with news of the desertion—"Public excitement has risen to fever heat" (*Straits Times*, September 13, 1880). In those days the mercantile society in Singapore was so small that there would have been no

9. This information is from Williams' application for a copy of his first mate's certificate, dated 1915. The application is held by the Registry of Shipping and Seamen, Cardiff.

chance for Williams to lose himself in anonymity, even if he had wished to.

This determination to face it out is also reflected in the letter he wrote to the *Daily Times* in Singapore, printed on September 20, 1880, and reprinted in the *Straits Times* on his return to Singapore:

> To the Editor of the Daily Times.
>
> Sir,—In reading your journal of yesterday's date giving a report of the debate in the Legislative Council regarding the *Jeddah*, I find in Mr. Campbell's speech the following remarks:—"From the evidence adduced at the Court of Inquiry it would seem that his (Captain Clark's) fears were utterly unfounded. However he orders a boat to be lowered, in which he puts his wife, and into which he, with his Chief Officer and the Chief Engineer manage to get."
>
> I am the Chief Officer of the *Jeddah* referred to, and I beg to inform you Mr. Campbell's statement, so far as it refers to me, is untrue. The evidence given before the Court of Inquiry will show that I was thrown overboard by the Hadjis after a severe wound was inflicted on my hand, and that I was afterwards picked up out of the water by Captain Clark and taken into his boat. In official discussions it would be advisable to keep to facts.
>
> I wish to say no more.
>
> Yours obediently,
A. P. Williams,
Late S.S.*Jeddah*.

Linked with Williams' attitude is the ideal of the English gentleman. Mrs. Thornett writes in a letter of September 30, 1962, that her "father was conscious of being a gentleman and in some ways a snob. . . . I have the seal of gold with the crest and coat of arms which belonged to my father and I remember he always had this on his watch chain which hung on his waistcoat." What Mrs. Thornett says about the seal is verified by three photographs of Williams I have in my possession. The "seal of gold with the crest and coat of arms" on his watchchain are clearly apparent. The Williams family crest was of a lion passant (walking in profile) bearing a broken chain and the motto *Vinctus Sed Non Victus* (chained but not conquered).

The conception of what is appropriate to a gentleman probably accounts for the kind of language used by Jim on occasions and particularly in chapters *xvii* and *xxiii*. I have not been able to discover whether this language was typical of A. P. Williams, although an old Singaporean who knew him says he was "very polished in speech—very good mannered." Certainly Jim is given preparatory-school language and enthusiasms that do not at all suit the man we have met earlier narrating the story of his disaster to Captain Marlow. It may have been Conrad's intention to offer a submerged criticism of Lord Jim, indicating his fundamental immaturity, but there is no doubt that Conrad was trying to reproduce the language of a young gentleman. English was not Conrad's native tongue, and preparatory-school slang may have sounded less absurd then than it does now.

Physical likeness between a fictional character and his source is not an easy thing to prove, but Williams had certain outstanding physical features. His height, powerful build, and neat dress are confirmed by Mrs. Thornett. I asked her to compare the description in *Lord Jim* with her memories of her father, and she wrote to me on July 13, 1962 that she had "read *Lord Jim* and it certainly does seem that reference is made to my Father & the description in Chapter 1 seems typical. From my recollection of him as a child, he was powerfully built, very tall and had a deep voice, though gentle at heart." Later, on September 30, 1962, she added: "My father did dress carefully, very neat, all in white, I believe they were called 'tutop' . . . the jackets were buttoned up the front to the neck." A local inhabitant in Singapore has told me that A. P. Williams was a big man, certainly not under six feet—taller, in fact—and broad, while another old Singaporean said he was "bluff, handsome, head up in the air"; my photographs of Williams confirm all this. Mrs. P. Ward of Perth, Australia, stated in a letter August 21, 1962 that her father, A. P. Williams, "had beautiful china-blue eyes."

If Conrad met him in Singapore, Williams must then have been about thirty-one, and twenty-eight at the time of the *Jeddah* incident. The four photographs I have obtained of Williams show him at various stages of his life and certainly in the first two it is possible to trace those less-easy-to-define aspects of manner and stance that were typical of Jim. The first is dated 1868, when Williams was sixteen. He is leaning against a chair, legs crossed and hands in pockets, looking firmly and a little suspiciously into the camera. He is certainly "upstanding, broad-shouldered, with his hands in his pockets" and "clean-limbed, clean-faced, firm on his feet"; given a few years more in age, he might well be the Lord Jim who turned away from the other deserters, looking "unconcerned and unapproachable as only the young can look."

In the second photograph he is probably in his thirties and is photographed in a sitting position, with his wife beside him. The features most noticeable here are his size, powerful build, and direct stare, which could certainly be described as a "kind of dogged self-assertion." He looks out of the photograph with a determined, aggressive pride that is lacking in the younger Williams but that recalls the attitude of Lord Jim when, in his determination not to be called names by any man, he "bullies" Marlow.

Although Williams did not spend years attempting to run away from his past, his later life does have certain similarities with that of Jim. Mrs. Thornett could tell me only that "he was sea-faring to start with and then joined McAlister & Co., as a ship's chandler." On returning to Singapore Williams had obviously tried to continue as a seaman. He was taken on as first officer in the S.S. *Cleator*, a much smaller ship than the *Jeddah*, in January, 1881. He left this ship after two months, and seems to have been unemployed until he joined an even smaller vessel, the S.S. *Vidar*, as first officer in May 1882. This is a most interesting fact, for Conrad himself was first officer on the *Vidar* from August 1887 to January 1888. Williams served on this ship for about the same length of time as Conrad did (May to October 1882) and made the same journeys from Singapore to Berau, the settlement in eastern Borneo on the Berau River that was to become Conrad's source for Patusan. At Berau Williams must have met, as Conrad was to do later, Olmeijer (the original of Almayer), Captain William Lingard (Conrad's Rajah Laut), and Jim Lingard, whose Malay title "Tuan Jim" provided Conrad with the title of his novel. One of Jim Lingard's daughters, who is now living in Singapore, has told me that the Lingard children who were educated in Singapore played with the Williams children, and this suggests a friendship between the two men. The first and second engineers of the *Vidar*, James Allen and John Niven, who appear in *The Shadow-Line*, had been with the *Vidar* at least as early as 1883,[1] and I strongly believe that they joined the *Vidar* earlier than this. Conrad must also have heard of Williams from these two men while he served on the *Vidar*, and then probably have met him as a water-clerk in the port of Singapore.

The first reference to him as a ship chandler's water-clerk is in *Singapore and Straits Directory* of 1884. He was then working for McAlisters, a small but well-known firm in those days and certainly well known today in Singapore. Mrs. Thornett says that her father "was . . . the first man out as the ships came into harbour."

A. P. Williams married in the East, an indication perhaps of his determination to settle here and also of the fact that he had given up the idea of returning home. Mrs. Neill writes that he "shocked and horrified his father—also mine, by marrying a Eurasian! Aunt Jane I believe was clever—cultured, of high caste and attractive, and it was apparently a very happy marraige. They had a large family— some black—some white." The record of Williams' marriage is in the registry at St. Andrews Cathedral, Singapore. It records that

1. *Singapore and Straits Directory*, 1883, p. 96.

George Augustine Podmore Williams, aged 30, Master Mariner, married E. Jane Robinson, aged sixteen years, on January 22, 1883.

Williams was still in business in 1915, according to the *Directory*, but in 1916 he died. An obituary appeared in the *Singapore Free Press* on April 20, 1916:

> There passed away yesterday morning, at his residence, Shamrock, Barker Road, Mr. Austin Podmore Williams, who for 27 years was employed at Messrs McAlister & Co., as their chief outside superintendent in the Dubash and Shipchandlery Department. . . . The late Mr. Williams was chief officer of the Singapore Steamship Co.'s *Jeddah*, a pilgrim ship which met with an accident in the Red Sea and was abandoned with about a 1,000 coolies aboard.

In his will are the words: "I desire that my funeral should be quiet, cheap and simple and no fuss made about it." His grave is in the Bidadari Cemetery, Upper Serangoon Road, Singapore. Williams, clearly, regarded himself to the last as a master mariner, in spite of his long years on land, for his headstone was engraved with an anchor.

Although not referred to by name, Singapore is the port that provides the background to the inquiry in *Lord Jim*. It should be remembered that Conrad himself was involved in an inquiry in that port into the loss of the *Palestine* in 1883.

When he reached Singapore for the third time, in the summer of 1887, Conrad spent six weeks in the hospital for treatment of a back injury he had suffered in an accident on board the *Highland Forest*. The European Hospital in Singapore was situated just behind and slightly to the right of the present General Hospital, on a slope some distance from the harbor. Ships at anchor in the harbor can still be seen from the site. Two years before Conrad was in the hospital, convent sisters had been allowed to nurse the sick there. In *The Mirror of the Sea* (1906) Conrad tells how he lay on his back "looking at the fronds of the palm-trees tossing and rustling at the height of the window."

The Harbour Office in Singapore was then a white-fronted building beside the quay, with a pillared portico; the Esplanade, with grass plots facing the sea, is close by; and the bandstand, although no longer in existence, used to be directly opposite Coleman Street, which terminated in the long stretch of the Hotel de l'Europe.

An account of an open-air concert is recorded by Braddell: "The bands used to play . . . twice a week; the chains were taken down opposite Coleman Street and the carriages were driven in and stood in a circle around the bandstand." [2]

2. R. St. J. Braddell, "The Merry Past," *One Hundred Years of Singapore*, 2 vols., London, 1921, II, 495.

There has never been a Malabar Hotel in Singapore—although there was and is a Malabar Street—but Conrad's description of this hotel in *Lord Jim* corresponds closely to the appearance of the Hotel de l'Europe. Although this hotel is no longer in existence, a photograph in my possession shows that it had a "big dining-room," that its long "front gallery" was used "for coffee and cigars," and that the view from it would be the same as that from the Malabar Hotel: "the riding lights of ships." Indeed the Hotel de l'Europe (described also, although not named, in *The Shadow-Line*), was the only hotel in Singapore that faced the sea; it could be clearly seen from the Harbour Office.

The Sailors' Home, also quite close to the seafront, stood just behind the Hotel de l'Europe. A mercantile marine officer could pay one Malayan dollar per day to stay there, and no doubt this is the sum Conrad himself paid when he stayed at the home (January 4 to January 19, 1877) after he left the S.S. *Vidar*.

The master-attendant who gives a dressing down to the captain of the *Patna* is based on Captain Ellis, the master-attendant in Singapore at that time, a man whom Conrad introduced as a character in "The End of the Tether" and *The Shadow-Line* as well as in *Lord Jim*. Henry Ellis was the man who appointed Conrad to the command of the *Otago*. On July 5, 1963, his grandson, the Reverend Henry Ellis Briscow, wrote to me:

> Captain Henry Ellis was my grandfather. . . . He was a big broad shouldered man with a powerful voice that stuck terror into all his subordinates, whether oriental or occidental; his word was law and he always spoke with the authority of a man who was not accustomed to having his opinions controverted. He ruled with a rod of iron. He had a horror of red tape and did not take kindly to interference from government officials. Henry Ellis had a very violent temper and shouted and roared when things did not go his way. . . . He died of a broken leg because he would not let the doctor put it in splints. He was offered a very good appointment in Venezuela after his retirement in Singapore but was advised not to take it because of his violent temper. This would have eventually led to his being knifed.

Articles about Ellis published in the *Singapore Free Press* (December 5, 1907, and February 20, 1908) confirm some of the aspects of Conrad's fictional portrait:

> He was an Irishman of intensity, a real good man and kindly, but with a quickness of temper that almost set the river on fire. One minute he would be a stately and dignified official, courteous and gentlemanly; the next he was boiling over with temper and hardly knew what he was doing. Next morning he was all right

again and never omitted to make amends for the havoc he had wrought in his haste.

* * *

Captain Ellis was a strong official, blunt and straightforward, standing no nonsense, with a good deal of Irish humor about him and some national touchiness as well. He was by virtue of his office, one of the best known men in Singapore, although in private life he mixed little in Society. . . .

The suicide of the master of the clipper *Cutty Sark* in 1880 was another source for the pilgrim-ship episode of *Lord Jim*.

Conrad may well have heard or read the story of the *Jeddah* and the story of the *Cutty Sark* at the same time. In the *Singapore Straits Times* editorial column on September 20, 1880, there was a report of the motion "touching the abandonment of the S.S *Jeddah* in open sea by her master and officers when she had over 1,000 souls on board" which was discussed in the Singapore Legislative Assembly. In the same column is the report of the arrival in Singapore of the chief officer of the *Jeddah*, A. P. Williams, just above the following paragraph:

Another painful story from the sea. The British barque *Cutty Sark*, formerly a tea clipper, arrived here on Saturday morning from Anjer, and the second officer, in whose charge she arrived, reports that while at Anjer the chief officer struck a seaman who died from the effects of the blow. The Chief officer, alarmed at the consequences of his act, made his escape. . . .

The only full account of the *Cutty Sark* incident I have been able to obtain is that written by Basil Lubbock, who drew his information from the ship's log and from the narratives of sailors on board at the time. It is likely that he was, in this last instance, drawing upon the kind of hearsay Conrad would have had access to.

The incident on the *Cutty Sark* was as follows. Sydney Smith, the chief mate, gave an order to John Francis, a Negro seaman, which Francis did not obey. Because of the man's insolence and the fact that he threatened Smith with a capstan bar, there was a struggle during which the mate got possession of the capstan bar and brought it down on Francis' head, knocking him unconscious. Francis never regained consciousness and died three days later. According to Lubbock's account of the incident, the mate retired to his cabin for the rest of the passage. When the *Cutty Sark* arrived at Anjer, the mate persuaded his skipper, Captain Wallace, to help him escape, and he was eventually smuggled aboard an American ship, the *Colorado*. The mate was not heard of for two years, but then was found, arrested, tried in London, and sentenced to seven years' imprisonment for manslaughter. Soon after he had helped the mate to escape, Captain Wallace committed suicide.

Lubbock gives an account of Wallace's suicide. Wallace was very upset by the mate's escape:

> Ever since the escape of the mate he had been unable to sleep. . . . Night and day he stood gazing out to sea or walked with bowed head up and down the poop. . . . On the fourth day after leaving Anjer, the watch had just been called at 4 A.M., when the captain, who was standing at the break of the poop with the carpenter, turned to his faithful petty officer and asked if the second mate was on deck.
>
> "Chips" replied that he was just coming up. Whereupon Captain Wallace left the carpenter and walked aft: called the helmsman's attention to the course; then deliberately stepped on to the taffrail and jumped overboard.[3]

A report in the *Singapore Daily Times* of September 18, 1880, on the *Cutty Sark* incident suggests reasons for Wallace's suicide:

> The Captain appears to have assisted the chief officer to escape on board an American ship bound for Saigon and afterwards whether from pangs of conscience or fear of future trouble he threw himself overboard and was drowned.

Wallace was a young and successful skipper. He took his second mate's certificate when he was 21, his first mate's when he was 23, and his master's when he was 24. At twenty-seven he was commander of the famous clipper *Cutty Sark*, and in the same year he committed suicide by walking over the side of the ship. The death of this famous skipper at such an early age, when he was at the height of his career and when there was no strong reason for such an act, must have caused a great deal of speculation.

The Bornean River and Its People

The second part of *Lord Jim* moves from the *Patna* disaster and the sophisticated Eastern port to the primitive, remote area of the Bornean river, with its two lonely traders and its political intrigue among the native rulers. Conrad himself made such a transition when, on August 22, 1887, during his last visit to Singapore, he signed on as mate of a trading ship called the *Vidar*. The *Vidar* sailed among the islands of the Southeast Archipelago, calling at ports and making her way up rivers to trading settlements, in particular the post on the River Berau in Dutch East Borneo. This is the settlement called Tandjong Redeb, although it is also referred to in

---

3. Basil Lubbock, *The Log of the Cutty Sark*, London, 1925, p. 196.

accounts by the names of the two villages on either side of the Berau River, Gunung Tabur and Sambaliung.

Conrad uses the same setting in *Almayer's Folly* (1895) and *An Outcast of the Islands* (1896), but calls the place Sambir; and he also draws upon his knowledge of Berau for "The Lagoon" and "Karain" (1897), "The End of the Tether" (1902), "Freya of the Seven Isles" (1912), and *The Rescue* (1920).

Conrad made only four trips on the *Vidar*, probably spending no more than three days at Tandjong Redeb on each occasion. He could not, therefore, have gained any intimate knowledge of the area and its people, and he must have relied primarily upon observation and hearsay. As might be expected, those aspects of the fictional Patusan which can be shown most conclusively to be based on Berau are ones that would catch the attention of any seaman involved in the navigation of a river and the trading carried on by his vessel. But for specific incidents, personalities, and situations, Conrad appears to have consulted written accounts not only of this area but of other places in the Archipelago, such as the following, from the *Eastern Archipelago Pilot*.[4]

The KURAN or BERAU RIVER, one of the five principal streams on the east coast of Borneo, is formed by the junction of the rivers Segah and Kalai, which unite opposite the towns of Tabur and Sambaliung, at a distance of 34 miles from the sea. There is an extensive delta at the mouth, the principal channels through which are the Pantai, Garura, Manussur, and Tidung. The first named, which is in fact the mouth of the river of the same name, is one of the most frequented by ships, and its entrance is well defined by several isolated hill tops, which rise from the otherwise low and marshy shore. At Gunong Santul, 26 miles from the sea, the left bank of the river becomes hilly, while on the right bank, and at a distance of about 3 miles, lies a chain of hills from 100 to 160 feet in height, which forms the watershed between the Berau and Pantai rivers. Below Gunong Tabur, the Berau river has a breadth of from 660 to 1,310 yards, its mean depth at ordinary low water being 18 feet, with a minimum depth of 12½ feet at a spot on the west side of Sandang-besar island, known as "Lingard's Cross";[5] in flood the river rises 9 feet.

Trade.—The principal articles of export are rattan, gutta-percha, and dammar (gum copal), in quantities of about 250

4. First edition, London, 1893, p. 340.
5. Named after Captain William Lingard, who apparently discovered it. He is the Captain "Tom" Lingard of *Almayer's Folly, An Outcast of the Islands*, and *The Rescue*. William Lingard set up a trading post on the river at Tandjong Redeb about 1870 and established Olmeijer (the Almayer of *Al-* *mayer's Folly*) there, and later, about 1880, his nephew, Jim Lingard. Lingard used only sailing ships and appears eventually to have lost his monopoly of the Berau trade, probably through the intervention of the steamship *Vidar*, owned by Syed Masin Bin Salleh Al Joofree, an Arab in Singapore.

tons, 120 tons, and 300 tons respectively, a year. The principal trade is with Singapore, chiefly in the vessels of Messrs. Lingard & Co., and only a small portion goes to Java or Dutch East India ports. The forests in the Berau lands could furnish an inexhaustable supply of good and fine timber.

Communications.—A tolerably regular steam service between Singapore, Pasir, Berau river, and Bulungan, is maintained by a vessel belonging to an Arab at Singapore, but running under the British flag. There is also irregular steam communication with Makasser, and occasionally with Pontianak.

Another description of the area appeared in the *Straits Times Overland Journal* on March 26, 1883:

Gunong Thabor and Sambaliung, formerly forming together the State of Berouw [Berau] are situated right and left on the Berouw river. The villages therein are insignificant; even the Sultan's house appears miserable. In 1879 only one European resided there, he being a storekeeper from Macassar. There is very little trade, though the soil is very rich and fruitful. Rattans, gutta percha, and coals are the principal products. The inhabitants are lazy and unenterprising. Labour is for women and slaves only. Slaves are met with in almost every house. On the lower river, there is even a large village wholly inhabited by slaves. The authorities allow this, in spite of Art.115 of the Government reg. whereby slavery in Netherlands India has been abolished. Most of the slaves are fairly well off excepting those who have to work in the mines. The number of these unfortunates yearly sold at Gunong Thabor is estimated at 300. These people are brought or kidnapped from the islands of Sooloo and the other Philippines' and then bartered for gunpowder, muskets, revolvers, lillas cloths, calico, opium, Dutch candles etc.

In 1869, the commandant of H.N.M's steamer *Salak* intercepted a shipment of slaves concealed in four prahus and packed like herrings. This living cargo consisted of young and charming children, a few older beauties (destined for the harem of the Sultan of Gunong Thabor) and several young men, amounting altogether to 34 persons. . . .

Captain Sir Edward Belcher made an excursion up the River Berau in 1845 in search of some British seamen—a Captain Brownrigg and his crew—who had wrecked their ship at the mouth of the Berau and had been taken prisoners by the sultan of Gunung Tabur. Belcher wrote an account of his search for the men in his *Voyage of "H.M.S. Samarang."* The following extracts suggest the kind of topographical and historical detail available to Conrad, and should also be read with the incident of Gentleman Brown in mind.[6]

8. Sir Edward Belcher, *Narrative of the Voyage of "H.M.S. Samarang,"* 2 vols., London, 1848, I: 212–13, 214– 15, 218, 219, 239, 241–42, 279; II: 167–68.

About 9, A.M., on the 30th of December, we noticed what at first sight appeared to be a Malay battery, or stockade, constructed upon the summit of a hill which completely commanded the whole reach of the river below this place. * * * we soon discovered that the place was not only without inhabitants, but that the town which had been near it, had been lately burned * * * and the plantain and other fruit trees lately cut down, exhibit-[ing] indubitable symptoms of recent war.

* * *

In the morning we again moved forward, still without any signs of human beings, although every mile that we advanced the cleared condition of the land, and other objects, satisfied us that we could not be far distant from their dwellings. Shortly before eight, we discovered the first inhabited house, and immediately afterwards the outskirts of the town of Gunung Taboor.

The boats being in a condition for work, with all useless lumber stowed below, we advanced towards the town; it was found to be closely stockaded. * * * On the range of stockade, numbers of small Dutch flags were displayed. On our approach, an ambassador was sent to convey the welcome of the Sultan. * * * as I saw nothing but Dutch colours I was at a loss how to act, until I knew what power held the place; he immediately rejoined, that there were no Dutch here. * * * "the colours you see are Bugis, from Celebes, excepting that large Dutch flag, which was a present from the Governor of Macassar."

* * *

He informed me that all the Europeans had been taken away from Sambiliong, the fortified position on the heights, on the opposite side of the river, distant three miles, on the 26th of October last, by a Dutch schooner-of-war, and he produced a Dutch document to that effect.

* * *

He further stated, that the English became very troublesome, and although better fed than themselves, were sullen and discontented; that they leagued with the Rajah Muda, his cousin, who had rebelled, and, as he required their aid to work his guns, had seduced them to escape to him, under the promise of sending them safely to Kotai.

* * *

The Rajah Muda, who has established himself, in defiance of the Sultan's authority, at Sambiliong, and assumed the title of *Sultan Muda*, (or young Sultan,) is a cousin of Si Atap, but, as before noticed, having quarrelled about the Europeans, has been closely shut up in his fortress, and will probably be destroyed.

* * *

In proof of his anxiety to befriend the English, the Sultan [of Gunung Tabur] offers to give them a separate place within his town to live in, to protect them, to give them a preference in trade, and as a further exhibition of his sincerity to open trading connexions, he gave me a letter under his official seal, containing the list of goods which he would engage as certain cargo, to any vessel which I would send in the May following.

* * *

"The next river is a very large one, sometimes called *Barow*, and sometimes *Curan*, from different places near it; the first is an independent state, in alliance with Sooloo, the other is subject to Sooloo. The river has three fathoms at the mouth, but there are several shoals which require a pilot."

This river has been already noticed. It is the Pantai, one of the branches, or properly the main stream, which takes the name of *Brraou*, and gives its name to people of the district, the city being Gunung Taboor. * * *

"There is a considerable trade in Cocoa-nuts carried on from *Tuallee*, or *Celebes*, to *Barow*, which they call *Barong*; according to their accounts, the river is very deep within, and the country yields much Bird's nests, and other valuable commodities. But, although the Sooloos agree in the magnitude of the river, they deny that their country is of much consequence with respect to its produce. This river is in the bottom of a deep bay, the land running from thence to the eastward, terminating in a point of red land, called on account of its peculiar colour, *Tanna Mera*, (Red land,) off which are many islands." [7]

* * *

I not only used every effort to open trade direct with Gunung Taboor, Tambisan, and Kabatuan; but at my persuasion, two persons have made the attempt; others met me with the observation: "All which you state is very true, and the prices are favourable in the highest degree, *but you cannot warrant half a cargo, even for a small schooner.*" At Gunung Taboor the Sultan bound himself to supply a cargo for one vessel filling up with rattans, Cassia bark, &c., but more he could not promise, as the collection of *one year*. * * * until the colony is firmly settled, and piracy annihilated on the range of coast by which trade must pass, this state of affairs will be slow of arriving; and when it does, still, until the habits of the inland tribes become settled, and they plant for, and send to your market, the same scantiness of tonnage must prevail.

In 1869 the naturalist Alfred Russel Wallace first published an account of his wanderings and discoveries in the Southeast Asian Archipelago during the 1850's and 1860's.[8] Reissued frequently, the work was, according to Richard Curle, Conrad's "intimate friend for many years." [9]

7. Here Belcher is quoting from "Oriental Repertory" by Dalrymple, the explorer.
8. Alfred Russel Wallace, *The Malay Archipelago*, London, 1894, pp. 127–29, 167–68, 173, 236–37, 257–58, 419.
9. Richard Curle, *The Last Twelve Years of Joseph Conrad*, New York, 1928, p. 109.

At length, about an hour after noon, we reached our destination—the village of Coupang, situated nearly in the centre of the island—and entered the outer court of a house belonging to one of the chiefs with whom my friend Mr. Ross had a slight acquaintance. Here we were requested to seat ourselves under an open shed with a raised floor of bamboo, a place used to receive visitors and hold audiences. Turning our horses to graze on the luxuriant grass of the courtyard, we waited till the great man's Malay interpreter appeared, who inquired our business and informed us that the Pumbuckle (chief) was at the Rajah's house, but would soon be back. As we had not yet breakfasted, we begged he would get us something to eat, which he promised to do as soon as possible. It was however about two hours before anything appeared, when a small tray was brought containing two saucers of rice, four small fried fish, and a few vegetables. * * *

At length about four o'clock the Pumbuckle made his appearance, and we informed him of our desire to stay with him a few days, to shoot birds and see the country. At this he seemed somewhat disturbed, and asked if we had brought a letter from the Anak Agong (Son of Heaven), which is the title of the Rajah of Lombock. This we had not done, thinking it quite unnecessary; and he then abruptly told us that he must go and speak to his Rajah, to see if we could stay. Hours passed away. The sun set, and it soon became dark, and we got rather hungry as we sat wearily under the shed and no one came. Still hour after hour we waited, till about nine o'clock, the Pumbuckle, the Rajah, some priests, and a number of their followers arrived and took their seats around us. We shook hands, and for some minutes there was a dead silence. Then the Rajah asked what we wanted. * * * questions were asked about my guns, and what powder I had, and whether I used shot or bullets; also what the birds were for, and how I preserved them, and what was done with them in England. Each of my answers and explanations was followed by a low and serious conversation which we could not understand, but the purport of which we could guess. They were evidently quite puzzled, and did not believe a word we had told them. They then inquired if we were really English, and not Dutch; and although we strongly asserted our nationality, they did not seem to believe us. * * * At length, about one in the morning, the whole party rose to depart, and, after conversing some time at the gate, all went away. We now begged the interpreter, who with a few boys and men remained about us, to show us a place to sleep in, at which he seemed very much surprised, saying he thought we were very well accommodated where we were. It was quite chilly, and we were very thinly clad and had brought no blankets, but all we could get after another hour's talk was a native mat and pillow, and a few old curtains to hang round three sides of the open shed and protect us a little from the cold breeze.

* * *

As soon as I was well, I again went to Goa, accompanied by Mr. Mesman, to beg the Rajah's assistance in getting a small house built for me near the forest. We found him at a cock-fight in a shed near his palace, which however he immediately left to receive us, and walked with us up an inclined plane of boards which serves for stairs to his house. This was large, well built, and lofty, with bamboo floor and glass windows. The greater part of it seemed to be one large hall divided by the supporting posts. Near a window sat the Queen squatting on a rough wooden arm-chair, chewing the everlasting sirih and betel-nut, while a brass spittoon by her side and a sirih-box in front were ready to administer to her wants. The Rajah seated himself opposite to her in a similar chair, and a similar spittoon and sirih-box were held by a little boy squatting at his side. Two other chairs were brought for us. Several young women, some the Rajah's daughters, others slaves, were standing about; a few were working at frames making sarongs, but most of them were idle. * * * Everything had a dingy and faded appearance, very disagreeable and unroyal to a European eye. The only thing that excited some degree of admiration was the quiet and dignified manner of the Rajah, and the great respect always paid to him.

* * *

Close to my house was an inclosed mudhole where three buffaloes were shut up every night, and the effluvia from which freely entered through the open bamboo floor.

* * *

About the centre of it is the palace of the Sultan, now a large, untidy, half-ruinous building of stone. This chief is pensioned by the Dutch Government, but retains the sovereignty over the native population of the island, and of the northern part of Gilolo. The sultans of Ternate and Tidore were once celebrated through the East for their power and regal magnificence. When Drake visited Ternate in 1579, the Portuguese had been driven out of the island, although they still had a settlement at Tidore. He gives a glowing account of the Sultan. * * *

All this glitter of barbaric gold was the produce of the spice trade, of which the Sultans kept the monopoly, and by which they became wealthy. Ternate, with the small islands in a line south of it, as far as Batchian, constitute the ancient Moluccas, the native country of the clove, as well as the only part in which it was cultivated. Nutmegs and mace were procured from the natives of New Guinea and the adjacent islands, where they grew wild; and the profits on spice cargoes were so enormous, that the European traders were glad to give gold and jewels, and the finest manufacturers of Europe or of India, in exchange.

The character of Stein appears to have been built up from a number of sources, including Wallace himself and other people (for example, a German naturalist named Bernstein) mentioned in his book. Following are a description from Wallace of Mr. Mesman, a Macassar-born Dutchman living in Celebes; an account of Wallace's own emotion on finding a rare butterfly; and a reference to Wallace's young assistant, Charles Allen.

[Mr. Mesman] lived in a spacious house near the town, situated in the midst of a grove of fruit trees, and surrounded by a pefect labyrinth of offices, stables, and native cottages occupied by his numerous servants, slaves, or dependants. He usually rose before the sun, and after a cup of coffee looked after his servants, horses, and dogs, till seven, when a substantial breakfast of rice and meat was ready in a cool verandah. Putting on a clean white linen suit, he then drove to town in his buggy, where he had an office, with two or three Chinese clerks who looked after his affairs. His business was that of a coffee and opium merchant. He had a coffee estate at Bontyne, and a small prau which traded to the Eastern islands near New Guinea, for mother-of-pearl and tortoiseshell.

* * *

During my very first walk into the forest at Batchian, I had seen sitting on a leaf out of reach, an immense butterfly of a dark colour marked with white and yellow spots. I could not capture it as it flew away high up into the forest, but I at once saw that it was a female of a new species of Ornithoptera or "bird-winged butterfly," the pride of the Eastern tropics. * * * The next day I went again to the same shrub and succeeded in catching a female, and the day after a fine male. I found it to be as I had expected, a perfectly new and most magnificent species and the most gorgeously coloured butterflies in the world. Fine specimens of the male are more than seven inches across the wings, which are velvety black and fiery orange, the latter colour replacing the green of the allied species. The beauty and brilliancy of this insect are indescribable, and none but a naturalist can understand the intense excitement I experienced when I at length captured it. On taking it out of my net and opening the glorious wings, my heart began to beat violently, the blood rushed to my head, and I felt much more like fainting than I have done when in apprehension of immediate death. I had a headache the rest of the day, so great was the excitement produced by what will appear to most people a very inadequate cause.

* * *

Charles Allen made a voyage to New Guinea * * * . On his return he went to the Sula Islands, and made a very interesting collection, which served to determine the limits of the zoological group of Celebes * * * . His next journey was to Flores and Solor, where he obtained some valuable materials * * *. He afterwards went to Coti on the east coast of Borneo, from which place I was very anxious to obtain collections * * * . On his return thence to Sourabaya in Java, he was to have gone to the entirely unknown Sumba or Sandal-wood Island. Most unfortunately, however, he was seized with a terrible fever on his arrival at Coti, and, after lying there some weeks, was taken to Singapore in a very bad condition, where he arrived after I had left for England. When he recovered he obtained employment in Singapore, and I lost his services as a collector.

Wallace returned home, but Allen remained and prospered in the East. In the *Singapore and Straits Directory* for 1883 he is listed as the manager of the Perseverance Estate, which' was owned by a Mr. J. Fisher and extended over a thousand acres. In 1888, Conrad's last year in the East, the *Directory* shows that Allen was by then the owner of the estate. There is a photograph of the estate, said to be about three miles out of Singapore, in *British Malaya: Twentieth Century Impressions.*[1]

Major Fred McNair's book *Perak and the Malays*, from which the following extracts are taken,[2] provided Conrad with accounts of piracy and warfare in the area. In 1873 McNair was one of two British commissioners who, after a pirate attack on a Malay boat, watched the proceedings of the court that tried and punished the pirates, a court "composed of the Viceroy of Salangore, with three Native Commissioners appointed by the Sultan. * * * The sitting of the court took place at a stockade," behind which seven of the eight pirates were executed by the Sultan's kris the next day. Before the trial and execution, a British admiral

> had an interview with the Sultan, who was surrounded by his chiefs and people, and in as much state as he was capable of showing. The Admiral, in referring to the barbarity of the Jugra piracy, advised and urged upon the Sultan to caution his people against being guilty of such acts in future, pointing out how it was impossible that they could be left unpunished. * * *
> The Sultan listened very attentively, and then turning quickly round to his people, he exclaimed: *Dungar lah, jangan kitah main main lagi!*—"Hear now, my people! Don't let us have any more of this little game!"

McNair also describes the murder, on November 2, 1875, of the Resident of Perak, J. W. W. Birch, who had fallen out of favor with the Sultan, and tells of the subsequent fighting.

> * * * the infuriated Malays, armed with spears and krises, made a rush in a body down to the river-bank, where Mr. Birch was ashore at the bathing-house, his orderly being on guard with a revolver. He let his leader, however, be taken completely by surprise. * * * [Mr. Birch] was savagely attacked, some of the Malays driving their keen limbings through the rattan mat that

1. Ed. Arnold Wright, London, 1908, p. 664.
2. Major Fred McNair, *Perak and the*   *Malays: "Sarong" and "Kris,"* London, 1878, pp. 289, 369–70, 380, 392–93, 400–401, 130–31, 169.

formed a screen, while others went to the end of the bath, and, as the wounded Resident struggled up out of the water, one man cut at him with a sword, when he sank.

* * *

[The Malay Stockade] was a strong place, with deep ditch, earth-work, wattled fence, and pointed bamboos, while it was armed with a large iron gun and a small pivot "lelah."

* * *

Consequent upon the difficulties of the task, and the weight of the guns [two seven-pounders] which had to be dragged [by the British] over and through a variety of serious obstacles, only four miles were advanced in two hours and a half, and at the end of this time the first symptom of the presence of the enemy was found in the shape of several trees felled across the track. * * * Nothing further occurred for a couple of hours, when the advance was again checked by trees felled across the path.

* * *

Captain Channer, with whom was Lieutenant North, R.E., pushed on—his route having been along the bed of a torrent till the way was blocked by felled trees. A rearguard was left to cut through these obstructions; and nothing daunted by the rough nature of the country, Captain Channer threw out men right and left, himself leading the left body of twenty-five men. He had given up his guides, for they evidently knew nothing of the position of the enemy; and trusting to himself, he went on working cautiously through the jungle, till he saw the enemy's smoke and fires, and soon after came upon one of the stockades, and reconnoitered the Malay defences. This jungle fort was composed of logs surrounded by a palisade, and sharp spiked bamboos were everywhere about the ground.

This was an important moment; for if the Malays had caught sight of the attacking force the alarm would have been given at once; but by using precautions, and watching the enemy, Captain Channer was able to learn the easiest way into the stockade. Then, supported by two Ghoorkhas, he leaped over the palisade, where he could hear the Malays talking inside—no look-out being kept, as the enemy was cooking; and then dashing forward, followed by his two men, he boldly attacked the twenty or thirty who constituted the garrison, shot down one man with his revolver, while the two Ghoorkhas each shot down theirs. Five Malays in all were killed in the first instance, and the remainder of the little flanking party coming up, the enemy, believing themselves to be surrounded, took to flight.

From his limited experience of Borneo, Conrad would hardly have been able to distinguish between Malayan races such as the Malays and the Bugis. The physical characteristics of the two races, from the foreigner's point of view, are very much the same, and other differences relating to character and way of life must have been quite beyond Conrad's knowledge. Yet in his novels he makes distinctions between Malay, Bugis, and Arab. *Perak and the Malays* may well have contributed to this knowledge as well as to the specific characters of Doramin and his wife.

The Bugis are evidently a distinct race from the Malays, and come originally from the southern part of the island of Celebes. They compare most favourably with the Malays proper, being intelligent, courageous, and enterprising; and though very similar to them in appearance, they speak a different language. The Malays fear and respect them above all the other races of the Archipelago; and among them are to be found the principal native traders and merchants. * * * The character given to the Bugis is not always of the best, for he has been termed a beggar, treacherous, given to stealing, braver than a Malay, but not possessing the other's good points, being one who will lay his plans to obtain revenge on the offending party.

The Bugis race has kept itself very distinct from the people amongst whom it dwells, but occasionally inter-marriages take place. One of the most important of late has been that of the well-known Bugis chief of Perak, Nakoda Trong, who led to the hymeneal altar one of the Perak ladies of distinction, Inche Maida, or Princess Maida.

* * *

The house to the left is really the kitchen, while that on the right is, as far as its principal apartment is concerned, fitted up with a bed which occupies about two-thirds of the room. * * * Upon the introduction taking place between [the British] general and princess [Maida], the lady claimed the former as her guest, and with all the pride of an English country dame of the last century over her well-filled ticks, drew his attention to the bed.

Conrad's source for the character of Lord Jim changed once his hero moved to Patusan. It has been suggested that he derived much material at this point from reading about Rajah James Brooke of Sarawak, who was mentioned in all the travelers' tales already cited, as well as others.[3] Conrad could have found accounts in a number of books of how the Englishman James Brooke came to Sarawak on the west coast of Borneo, helped the local governor, Muda Hassim,

3. Other contemporary writings referring to Brooke are: Captain the Hon. Henry Keppel, *Expedition to Borneo of H.M.S. Dido for the Suppression of Piracy; with Extracts from the Journal of James Brooke, Esq. of Sarawak*, London, 1846; and *Visit to the Indian Archipelago, in H.M. Ship Maeander: with Portions of the Private Journal of Sir James Brooke, K.C.B.*, London, 1853; Hugh Low, *Sarawak: Inhabitants and Productions*, London, 1848; and Captain Rodney Mundy, *Narrative of Events in Borneo and Celebes down to the Occupation of Labuan: from the Journals of James Brooke, Esq. Rajah of Sarawak and Governor of Labuan; together with a Narrative of the Operations of H.M.S. Iris*, London, 1848. For a full discussion, see John Dozier Gordan, *Joseph Conrad: the Making of a Novelist*, Cambridge, Mass., pp. 64–73, and "The Rajah Brooke and Joseph Conrad," *Studies in Philology*, XXXV, 1938, 613–34.

put down a rebellion, and, in 1841, became the Rajah of Sarawak. The following extract from *The Malay Archipelago* [4] is but one suggestion of the kind of inspiration Brooke might have provided.

A few words in conclusion, about the government of Saráwak. Sir James Brooke found the Dyaks oppressed and ground down by the most cruel tyranny. They were cheated by the Malay traders, and robbed by the Malay chiefs. Their wives and children were often captured and sold into slavery, and hostile tribes purchased permission from their cruel rulers to plunder, enslave, and murder them. Anything like justice or redress for those injuries was utterly unattainable. From the time Sir James obtained possession of the country, all this was stopped. Equal justice was awarded to Malay, Chinaman, and Dyak. The remorseless pirates from the rivers farther east were punished, and finally shut up within their own territories, and the Dyak, for the first time, could sleep in peace. His wife and children were now safe from slavery; his house was no longer burnt over his head; his crops and his fruits were now his own, to sell or consume as he pleased. And the unknown stranger who had done all this for them, and asked for nothing in return, what could he be? How was it possible for them to realize his motives? Was it not natural that they should refuse to believe he was a man? for of pure benevolence combined with great power, they had had no experience among men. They naturally concluded that he was a superior being, come down upon earth to confer blessings on the afflicted. In many villages where he had not been seen, I was asked strange questions about him. Was he not as old as the mountains? Could he not bring the dead to life? And they firmly believe that he can give them good harvests, and make their fruit-trees bear an abundant crop.

In forming a proper estimate of Sir James Brooke's government, it must ever be remembered that he held Saráwak solely by the goodwill of the native inhabitants. He had to deal with two races, one of whom, the Mahometan Malays, looked upon the other race, the Dyaks, as savages and slaves, only fit to be robbed and plundered. He has effectually protected the Dyaks, and has invariably treated them as, in his sight, equal to the Malays; and yet he has secured the affection and goodwill of both. Notwithstanding the religious prejudices of Mahometans, he has induced them to modify many of their worst laws and customs, and to assimilate their criminal code to that of the civilized world. That his government still continues, after twenty-seven years—notwithstanding his frequent absences from ill-health, notwithstanding conspiracies of Malay chiefs, and insurrections of Chinese gold-diggers, all of which have been overcome by the support of the native population, and notwithstanding financial, political, and domestic troubles—is due, I believe, solely to the many admirable qualities which Sir James Brooke possessed, and espe-

4. Wallace, *op. cit.*, pp. 71–72.

cially to his having convinced the native population, by every action of his life, that he ruled them, not for his own advantage, but for their good.

Since these lines were written, his noble spirit has passed away. But though, by those who knew him not, he may be sneered at as an enthusiastic adventurer, or abused as a hard-hearted despot, the universal testimony of every one who came in contact with him in his adopted country, whether European, Malay, or Dyak, will be, that Rajah Brooke was a great, a wise, and a good ruler—a true and faithful friend—a man to be admired for his talents, respected for his honesty and courage, and loved for his genuine hospitality, his kindness of disposition, and his tenderness of heart.

But surely Conrad observed, at first hand, another James—Captain Lingard's nephew, a young man living in the jungle, isolated, yet with some local standing. At the time Conrad visited Berau, there were certainly two traders there—Charles Olmeijer (a Eurasian), and Jim Lingard. Both appear to have been protégés of Captain William Lingard (who was himself a partial source for Stein in that he was a trader and explorer), who had established the trading post, and both were related to him. It is possible that jealousy existed between them and that Olmeijer saw Jim as a rival.

Traditionally it is believed that Conrad took the name of his hero—Lord Jim—from the Malay title given to young Lingard—Tuan Jim. But there were other characteristics in Jim Lingard that might have contributed to Lord Jim. As far as I can gather, Jim Lingard was in love with a native girl, a sea-Dyak. He had as well a remarkable manservant called Lias. His daughter, Mrs. Oehlers of Singapore, has told me that when her father went upriver into the interior Lias always accompanied him, and she recalled that Lias always slept on the verandah of her father's home.

Although Jim Lingard has previously been looked upon as a person of little importance, a letter has survived that shows him as a man of some influence.[5] Mr. Alex Cook, at that time Treasurer General of British North Borneo, describes a visit to the area in 1887:

I arrived at Balangan (*sic*) per S.S. *Royalist* on 31st August: next morning I sent my letter of introduction accompanied by a small present to the Sultan. * * * Wm. James Lingard who is on very friendly terms with the Sultan agreed to go with me.[6]

Finally, it seems to me likely that Conrad was impressed that a man five years younger than himself should be prepared to spend the rest of his life—and he did just that—in such an isolated place. His daughter told me that her father used to say: "I am the only white man on the East Coast."

5. My attention was drawn to this letter by Professor Nicholas Tarling, University of Auckland.

6. Public Record Office, London, F. O. 12/86.

Essays in Criticism

TWO EARLY REVIEWS

From the *New York Tribune* †

If Mr. Conrad's new story excited admiration as it appeared serially in the pages of "Blackwood's Magazine," it exacts a double tribute from the reader now that it is published in book form. Though originally projected on a small scale, its unpremeditated expansion to the form of a full fledged novel has done nothing to spoil the simplicity and balance of the design. It is a long narrative, but it should be read, if possible, at a sitting. Not alone because one idea is dwelt upon with almost painful persistency, but because Mr. Conrad's mode of composition demands it. He makes the whole story fall from the lips of one man, who either states facts as he knew them himself or quotes them from the conversation of others, and despite the amount of material packed into this book one apprehends it best by taking it as an uninterrupted stream of spoken tragedy and eloquence. What the author has to say is absorbing, but even more so is the way in which he says it. Miss Gwendoline Keats, better known as "Zack," has shown in the book called "On Trial" what can be made of an analysis of a coward's nature when the bitter story is expressed in terms of ordinary speech, accented by borrowings from peasant dialect. Mr. Conrad deals with a coward, and he is mercilessly direct in his exposition of the man's most fugitive emotions, but over every page there is flung the indescribable romance of the immemorial East.

Marlow, the suppositious narrator of Jim's half prosaic, half tragic, history, is a student of human nature whose years of traffic on the sea have moulded him to meditative, wistful ways of thinking. The leading points he has to set forth are simple enough. In his boyhood Jim leaves the commonplace English parsonage in which he has been born and brought up. He goes to sea because his imagination has persuaded him that life may thus be made more romantic than he has ever found it at home. After some years fate sends him aboard the steamer Patna, in Oriental waters, as chief mate. The ship leaves port carrying eight hundred native pilgrims. On a night of tropic calm the rotten craft goes to the bottom like a shot, with all hands save a few members of the crew. For Jim there is a choice. He might stay, rouse the sleeping pilgrims and help save some of them. Or he can jump into the single boat that is lowered and escape with the scoundrels who are foully deserting the unconscious people

† November 3, 1900, p. 10. Unsigned.

360 · *From the* Spectator

under their charge. Jim jumps, and pays for his bodily salvation by
years of remorse, in which regret for a specific act of cowardice can
never lose the added pang of his infidelity to the ideal of which he
has long dreamed. Somewhere in his heart is the germ of strength;
somehow, he feels, he can some day atone for his sin. How he
atones, how he buries himself in the primeval jungle among natives
to whom he becomes a providence and a demi-god, how the life of
steadfast truth to which he attains culminates in an episode of almost intolerable bitterness, it were easy to tell in a few words. But
Mr. Conrad gives most of his volume to the telling, and justifies
himself in making every word magical and precious.

The man Marlow muses like an oracle. He seems to stand immobile before us; there is a gesture now and then; occasionally he shifts
his position; often he pauses, relapses into silence, then picks up
the narrative again as though it were an effort to detach himself
from the myriad memories that come swarming back upon him. He
describes Lord Jim—so called by the natives with whom he finds
asylum—he gives you Jim's version of this or that moment in the
Patna's last hours; he portrays the young native woman who gives
her love to the refugee from his own conscience; he lets down at
short intervals, like curtains in a theatre, wonderfully painted pic-
tures of luxuriant scenery or of the unmarked sea. It is all a record of
little truths; it is a mosaic, formed with zealous solicitude for justice,
of the thousand and one facts, emotions, shares of emotion, which
in the long run go to make Jim comprehensible, explain his conduct,
and make him intensely interesting. It is as accurate as a legal document; Jim's secrets are laid bare as though with the knife of a
surgeon. But always it is an oracle that speaks, always the truth
comes wrapped about with the awe inspiring atmosphere of a mysterious land and a dark problem of human will and destiny. Sorrow
broods over the story. "Lord Jim" is a hard book to read, for it communicates to the reader a grievous sense of man's weakness and of
the woe that he can bring down upon his own head. But it is a book
of great originality, and it exerts a spell such as is rarely encountered
in modern fiction.

From the *Spectator* †

It may be that amongst the hundred and twenty-five novels still
awaiting notice on our shelves some work of uncommon talent may
reveal itself to gladden the heart of the reviewer; in the meantime,
we have no hesitation in pronouncing Mr. Conrad's *Lord Jim* to be
the most original, remarkable, and engrossing novel of a season by

no means unfruitful of excellent fiction. That it may not strike all
readers in this light we readily concede. Mr. Conrad's matter is too
detached from "actuality" to please the great and influential section of readers who like their fiction to be spiced with topical allusions, political personalities, or the mundanities of Mayfair,—just
now the swing of the pendulum is entirely away from the slums,
and almost altogether in the direction of sumptuous interiors. Mr.
Conrad, in a word, takes no heed of the vagaries of fashion or of
pseudo-culture—he only once mentions an author and only once
makes a quotation—he eschews epigrams, avoids politics, and keeps
aloof from great cities. His scenes are laid in unfamiliar regions,
amid outlandish surroundings. But if you once succumb to the
sombre fascination of his narrative—as the present writer did years
ago on reading *An Outcast of the Islands*—your thraldom is complete. Several writers have derived literary inspiration from their so-
journ in the Malay Archipelago; but Mr. Conrad, beyond all others,
has identified himself with the standpoint of the natives, has interpreted their aspirations, illumined their motives, and translated
into glowing words the strange glamour of their landscape. Such an
achievement, though remarkable in itself, seems to indicate a de-
nationalisation that might inspire a certain amount of distrust. But
in the volume before us, though the "noble savage" is once more
prominent, the story is half finished before we reach Malaya, and
the central figure who rivets our interest throughout, though intensely romantic by temperament, is the son of an English country
parson, and throughout all his long exile never loses touch with the
sentiment, the ideals, the essential *ethos*, of his race. Jim—"Lord
Jim" is merely the translation of the title "Tuan Jim," by which he
is known amongst the Malays—is a mate in the merchant service, an
engaging, handsome lad, full of confidence in his ability to cope
with any emergency, whose career is wrecked at the outset by a sudden act of futile cowardice, unless, indeed, we are to regard it as the
result of a temporary mental paralysis. Along with his skipper and
the engineers, he deserts what he imagines to be a sinking ship with
a freight of eight hundred pilgrims; the derelict is subsequently
brought into port, and as a result of the inquiry Jim's certificate is
cancelled. A kindly ship's captain at Aden—the narrator of the
story—attracted by Jim's frank and engaging personality, bestirs himself in his behalf and procures him a fresh start. But wherever he
goes Jim is dogged by the rumour of his past, and he throws up post
after post until at last Captain Marlow introduces him to Stein, a
trader in the Archipelago, who appoints him his agent at Patusan,
an inland village in one of the native States. Here, beyond the ken
of civilisation, Jim at last finds the occasion for rehabilitating himself in his own self-esteem. Here, bearing a charmed life, he baffles

the plots of the Rajah, overthrows a raiding Arab chieftain, the terror of the neighbourhood, and wins fame by his valour and sagacity. Here also he wins the devoted love of the only white woman in Patusan, the stepdaughter of a Portuguese half-caste, and here, in the words of the narrator, "an obscure conqueror of fame, tearing himself out of the arms of a jealous love at the sign, at the call of his exalted egoism, he passes away under a cloud, inscrutable at heart, forgotten, unforgiven, and excessively romantic." We despair within the limited space at our disposal of conveying any adequate notion of the poignant interest of this strange narrative, the restrained yet fervid eloquence of the style, the vividness of the portraiture, the subtlety of psychological analysis, which are united in Mr. Conrad's latest and greatest work. The wizardry of the Orient is over it all. We can only congratulate him on an achievement at once superlatively artistic in treatment and entirely original in its subject.

HUGH CLIFFORD

From *The Genius of Mr. Joseph Conrad* †

* * * "The Nigger" marks an epoch in Mr. Conrad's literary career, because it proved him to possess, in addition to his other qualities, extraordinary psychological insight of a peculiar kind, and showed that his mind—the mind of the Sclav, more delicate and more subtle than the mind of the Englishman,—was able to analyze human nature in a fashion distinctively its own. Since 1898, three more books have come from Mr. Conrad's pen—"Lord Jim," "Youth," and "Typhoon,"—the first an elaborate psychological study, the others collections of short stories. Space forbids a detailed examination of these volumes, any one of which would suffice to make the reputation of an author. Of the three, "Lord Jim" is the most important, and, indeed, is in some respects the greatest of Mr. Conrad's books. On the other hand, it suffers because we are asked to believe that the story as written was told by the seaman Marlow to his friends after dinner, an illusion which it is impossible to sustain. "Lord Jim" resembles nothing more nearly than some delicate piece of mosaic, of which each of the myriad tiny fragments that compose it is essential to the whole. It is built up, sentence by sentence, paragraph by paragraph, almost word by word, and lacking any phrase it would be marred and incomplete. In a word it is *written*, as in this age of speed and hurry few books are written; but, putting aside all question of its length, the very subtlety of this

---

† *North American Review*, CLXXVIII (June, 1904), 851.

study of a man's soul makes its delivery by word of mouth in the circumstances described a sheer impossibility. * * *

GUSTAV MORF

Lord Jim †

Faust to Mephisto: Thou call'st thyself a part, yet seem'st a whole to be?
                                                                    Goethe

Je crois que ce que j'aimais le plus en lui, c'était une sorte de native noblesse, âpre, dédaigneuse, et quelque peu désespérée, celle, meme qu'il prête à Lord Jim.
                                                        André Gide on Conrad

Lord Jim is more than a novel, it is a confession. As a confession of a man tortured by doubts and nightmarish fears it must be understood, if it is to be understood at all. Such is, at least, my strong conviction, sprung from a psychological analysis of the novel.

Among the works of Joseph Conrad, *Lord Jim*, in many respects, stands apart. This is so evident that people frequently asked Conrad if it were not the one he preferred most of all. Those who asked the question received (in his "Author's Note") but an evasive answer.

The method that I am going to employ in the analysis of the novel is based on the psychology of Freud and Jung. For this is a case where no other method would do. If we are ever to solve the riddle which surrounds *Lord Jim*, we must succeed in tracing the unconscious forces guiding Conrad in the choice of his subject and in the development of its theme.

It would take a whole book to give the complete theory (and practice) of what I call the "biology of artistic creation," let it suffice here to explain its general principles.

If we want to understand fully any given artistic creation (especially if it belong to the "mystic" kind), we must admit that besides the intention to please, there is always, in very variable a degree, the tendency to move, to persuade, to teach, to give to the reader's thoughts a new direction. In other words, besides the æsthetic element which is static, there is a "dynamic" intention. A book, the publication of which did not change just the least bit the face of the world, would be meaningless. The proportion between the two opposites, beauty and force, is not invariable. Sometimes one of them is so strong that the other merely appears to be its servant.

† From Gustav Morf, *The Polish Heritage of Joseph Conrad*, Haskell House, New York, 1965, pp. 149–66. First published by Sampson Low, Marston and Company, Ltd., London, 1930. Reprinted by permission. Mr. Morf's references, which appeared originally in parentheses in the text, have been converted into footnotes by the editor.

This "dynamic" intention of artistic work can express itself unconsciously or half-consciously. In both cases, the process can be described as follows:

Whatever repressed conflicts, fear, wishes, hopes, or joys there happen to be in the artist's soul will be exteriorised (or *sublimated*) in his work. These unconscious elements constitute so many forces guiding him in the choice of his subject, in the invention of the plots, in the treatment of his characters, and in a hundred small details, thus leading him to treat those problems which he cannot solve in his conscious life. The solution will be symbolical, as in dreams and fairy tales. This is the only possible way, since the conscious mind cannot solve problems to which it attributes insolubility. On the other hand, repressed conflicts must be solved, if they are not to endanger the mental well-being of the person concerned.

The exteriorization (or *sublimation*) of conflicts takes place through the medium that responds most easily. Artistic creation, religious fervour, dreams, a sudden enthusiasm for some ideal or some hobby are the most common of mediums. Goethe explained the secret of his inspiration by the fact that *he was able to express what he suffered.* Beethoven's superhuman greatness is ultimately due to titanic conflicts, the sublimation of which, in a man like him, was only possible in music. The writing of a book or of a piece of music often means, therefore, a relief to the artist, just as churchgoing ought to be a relief to us who sing: "*Lift up* your hearts. . . ."

It may sound improbable that the repressed part of ourselves, our savage or shameful or childish or insane complexes, the very refuse of our personality, should go into the making of the highest art. Nevertheless it is so. Just as even the finest flowers live on dirty matter, on refuse, so artistic creation draws its force and its inspiration from the otherwise useless or dangerous by-products of our conscious life.

In the whole of modern fiction I could not wish for a better example to illustrate this than *Lord Jim.*

The plot of the novel may be recalled here: A young man ("not yet four-and-twenty"), Jim by name, is suddenly confronted with the temptation of his life while serving as chief mate on board an old steamer. On her way across the Indian Ocean, the ship has touched some floating derelict, and when the engines have been stopped, her condition seems so precarious that the disreputable gang who serve as officers decide to clear out as quickly and noiselessly as possible, under the cover of a dark night, leaving the eight hundred Moslem pilgrims on board to their fate. Jim does not mean to accompany them, but, in a moment of excitement, and urged by a voice in the darkness calling insistently: "Jump! Jump!"

he deserts the *Patna* in the firm belief that she is already sinking under his feet. They are picked up by a ship, and as to the abandoned vessel, it is sighted and towed to Aden by a French gunboat. A court of inquiry is held, and the officers of the ship, Jim included, have their certificates cancelled. From this moment, in spite of the sympathetic support of friends, Jim finds it impossible to "live it down." Wandering from port to port, and chased everywhere by the echoes of a past which he dares not face, he is finally sent to Patusan. In that forlorn corner of the East, his arrival means the beginning of a New Era. He soon exercises a great authority over the natives. He lives for some time in the illusion of having mastered his fate, of having forgotten his past.

Jim's illusions are shattered by the arrival of a white outcast, "Gentleman Brown." It would be easy for Jim to disarm him and to send him away, or, in case of resistance, to let him die of starvation. But Jim does nothing. Overcome by a curious weakness, he remains passive. When making off, Brown shoots some volleys into a camp of Jim's Malays, and Jim, feeling that his attitude is responsible for the tragedy, delivers himself up to the relatives of the victims, who kill him.

Lord Jim has often been called a psychological novel, because the source of the conflict resides within the tortured soul of the hero, but those who bestowed this epithet upon the book expressed only very vaguely the nature of Conrad's psychology, and seemed to ignore altogether the important fact that *Lord Jim* is eminently autobiographical and symbolical, that it is built up of the same elements as a dream.

Before discussing the symbolical bearing of the novel, a preliminary point must be made clear. It is the influence of Brown upon Jim which brings about the final tragedy. Before Brown's arrival, Jim was living in an atmosphere of faith and trust. His past was forgotten. Nothing reminded him of what he had done. He was the undisputed king of Patusan. But then, as if to prove that such an ideal state of affairs could not last long, Brown appeared. In the eyes of the natives, he is Jim's rival. The more they fear Brown, the less they will respect Jim. Brown's apparition is Jim's supreme test. A duel fought with spiritual weapons must ensue. If Jim wins, he is forever the master of hearts and arms in Patusan, but if he loses, it will be a proof that he did not deserve the high situation he had acquired.

And Jim loses. To him, Brown is the embodiment of that unforgettable and unforgiving past which stands up against him in the very moment when he expected it least. Brown, on the other hand, realizes Jim's situation with a remarkable intuition. He understands at once that Jim's past is the weapon that will give him the final victory over his adversary.

Already, at the first of his meetings with Brown, Jim is disarmed by an allusion to his past:

"Who are you?" asked Jim at last, speaking in his usual voice. "My name's Brown," answered the other, loudly; "Captain Brown. What's yours?" and Jim after a little pause went on quietly, as if he had not heard: *"What made you come here?"* "You want to know," said Brown, bitterly. "It's easy to tell. Hunger. *And what made you?"*

"The fellow started at this," said Brown . . . *"The fellow started at this and got very red in the face. Too big to be questioned, I suppose."*

In their second meeting, Brown pushes his point much farther. The following is his own account:

"We aren't going into the forest to wander like a string of living skeletons dropping one after another for ants to go to work upon us before we are fairly dead. Oh! no!——" "You don't deserve a better fate," he said. *"And what do you deserve,"* I shouted at him, "you that I find skulking here with your mouth full *of your responsibility, of innocent lives, of your infernal duty? What do you know more of me than I know of you?* I came here for food. D'ye hear?—food to fill our bellies. *And what did YOU come for? What did you ask for when you came here?* We don't ask you for anything but to give us a fight or a clear road to go back whence we came——" "I would fight with you now," says he, pulling at his little moustache. "And I would let you shoot me and welcome," I said. *"This is as good a jumping-off place for me as another.* I am sick of my infernal luck. *But it would be too easy. There are my men in the same boat—and, by God, I am not the sort to jump out of trouble and leave them in a d——d lurch,"* I said. He stood thinking for a while and then wanted to know what I had done ("out there," he says, tossing his head downstream) to be hazed about so. *"Have we met to teach each other the story of our lives?" I asked him. "Suppose you begin. No? Well, I am sure I don't want to hear. Keep it to yourself. I know it is no better than mine. I've lived—and so did you, though you talk as if you were one of those people that should have wings so as to go about without touching the dirty earth. Well—it is dirty. I haven't got any wings. I am here because I was afraid once in my life.*[1] Want to know what of? Of a prison. That scares me, and you may know it, if it's any good to you. *I won't ask what scared you into this infernal hole,* where you seem to have found pretty pickings. That's your luck and this is mine. . . ."

1. This is exactly the case of Jim. Compare the conversation between the French officer and Marlow: "And after all, one does not die of it." "Die of what?" I asked swiftly. *"Of being afraid."*

Brown is obviously feeling his way better and better. By an extraordinary piece of luck (it is just his "infernal luck"), he hits upon the very words which will paralyse Jim's will-power. His allusion to "a jumping-off place," to the "men in the same boat," whom he is not going to "leave in a d——d lurch," his well-assumed indifference to the story of Jim's life, bring back to Jim a past which had to remain buried if he were to live. Jim falls silent with the silence of guilt.

It may seem unnatural that Jim should at first want to know what Brown had done "out there," for to touch Brown's past is to touch his own. It seems that the initiative to speak of the past ought to come from Brown alone. I think that what makes Jim really ask this last question is fear, and what may be called "the fascination of fear." There are things which attract because they are dangerous.

When Brown started to talk with Jim, he did so without much hope, just to gain time. To his great surprise, he was to find an adversary whom he could easily impress and even frighten. Just like his "infernal luck!" Feeling that he is becoming the master of the situation, Brown goes straight ahead, *alluding only to what is* common to them both, and leaving out whatever enormous differences exist between them.

> When he [Brown] asked Jim, with a sort of brusque despairing frankness, whether he himself—straight now—didn't understand that *when "it came to saving one's life in the dark, one didn't care who else went—three, thirty, three hundred people"* —it was as if a demon had been whispering advice in his ear. "I made him wince," boasted Brown to me. *"He very soon left off coming the righteous over me—*. He just stood there *with nothing to say*, and looking as black as thunder—not at me—*on the ground."* He asked Jim *whether he had nothing fishy in his life to remember that he was so damnedly hard upon a man trying to get out of a deadly hole by the first means that came to hand*— and so on, and so on. And there ran through the rough talk *a vein of subtle reference to their common blood, an assumption of common experience; a sickening suggestion of common guilt, of secret knowledge that was like a bond of their minds and of their hearts.*

Jim's final and deadly mistake, the permission to let Brown and his men go away *in possession of their arms*, is due to the paralysing influence of this identification. Jim's attitude reminds us of that of Hamlet who cannot bring himself to avenge the murder of his father, and who does not know "why yet I live to say 'This thing's to do,' sith I have cause, and will, and strength, and means, to do't."

After this mistake, Jim's fate is settled. His past has proved stronger than his will to live. "Henceforth events moved fast without a check, flowing from the very hearts of men like a stream from a dark source."

When identification becomes as complete as in the case of Jim and Brown, there is neither choice nor free will. We find an illustration of this not only in *Lord Jim*, but in the tale *The Secret Sharer*, which is one of Conrad's best psychological tales. It is really the story of the identification between the "captain" (he is obviously Conrad himself) and a murderer, Leggatt, whom the captain gives the hospitality of his cabin for some time. There is another example of an identification in Shakespeare's *Hamlet*, if we make Sir Ernest Jones' view (which is not necessarily opposed to Bradley's) our own. Hamlet's will-power is completely paralysed by his identification with his uncle, who appears to him as a sort of lower self. Their "common bond" is their common love for the queen. In all cases of identification, the unconscious wish becomes the master of men's lives and deeds. Jim's unconscious wish is to see Brown (i.e. himself) go off free and powerful, the captain's is to see the murderer Leggatt escape, Hamlet's to see his uncle live and enjoy the fruit of his crime. Brown is Jim's other self as certainly as Leggatt is the captain's "secret self" or "own reflection" or "double." It might be Jim speaking of Brown when the captain says of Leggatt: "He appealed to me as if our experiences had been as identical as our clothes," and "a mysterious communication was established already between us two."

Identification is characterized always by an extraordinary indulgence for the second self, an indulgence which must of necessity remain incomprehensible to any other person. When we feel a profound sympathy with or pity for somebody, we identify ourselves always *more or less* with the person who inspires us with these feelings, but the identification hardly ever becomes so complete that the subject loses himself in the object. Jim is an extreme case, a neurotic, while the captain in *The Secret Sharer* is a more normal character.

Jim's indulgence for Brown is typical. He simply cannot resist the evil *because the evil is within himself*. Being acutely aware of his own sins, he cannot throw stones at Brown. To a question of Jewel, if Brown was a very bad man, he gives, "after some hesitation," the answer: "Men act badly sometimes without being much worse than others," a definition which is evidently so formulated as to fit himself as well as Brown. Of necessity, he cannot think of Brown's past without thinking of his own, nor judge Brown without judging himself. To condemn the outcast would be to condemn himself. His effort in excusing Brown is a last desperate attempt to save his own moral integrity, one of those fifth-act attempts that are doomed to fail. And so Jim dies ultimately of this identification with Brown, that is, he dies of the mistake of his life, for that mistake alone explains why the first outcast coming along and greeting him as a brother on grounds of their common experience, appears to him fatally as his own hideous self.

A person acting under the influence of a strong identification is incapable of giving the true reasons for his or her behaviour. To themselves, their acts seem inexplicable but absolutely compelling and obeying a logic of their own; to their environment they seem inadequate and foolish, if not downright mad. Everybody thinks that Hamlet is mad, the crew in *The Secret Sharer* suspect their captain of drunkenness, and wonder at his violent temper. In *Lord Jim*, the natives cannot understand Jim's sudden partiality for a handful of common robbers. The reasons which Jim gives for his decisions are strangely inadequate. His declaration (that the robbers are not to be disarmed) naturally produces an "immense sensation." Tamb' Itam, Jim's most faithful servant, is "thunderstruck" at his master's folly. Had Jim been at all capable of listening to common sense then, these unmistakable signs of dissent would have enlightened him. But he did not want to know better. Following a dark and compelling impulse, he did not care, just as Hamlet did not care. "His fate, revolted, was forcing his hand."

It is not without interest to discuss the resemblance between the young man who served as a model to Jim and the hero of the novel. Conrad states himself (in his "Author's Note"): "one sunny morning in the common-place surroundings of an Eastern roadstead, I saw his form pass by—appealing—significant—under a cloud—perfectly silent." But this statement, made in reply to critics who had called Jim "a figure of the Northern mists," proves or disproves singularly little. Aubry has identified the young man as a certain Jim Lingard (the same who served as a model to Tom Lingard in Conrad's Malay novels) and has come to the conclusion that "the real Jim Lingard and the Lord Jim of Conrad's novel have nothing in common except their name and physique."

What was Lord Jim's physique then? He was tall ("an inch, perhaps two, under six feet"); powerfully built; had a youthful ("boyish") face, and enjoyed marvellous good health. All these qualities, Jim Lingard may have possessed, but that is not as interesting as the fact that these very qualities Conrad *had not*. Joseph Conrad was rather little, he looked in his youth considerably older than his age (this may be seen by the photograph taken of him when 26 years old, and reproduced in Aubry), and his health, after the Congo adventure, was always rather precarious. As far as his figure, his youthfulness, and his health were concerned he must have often experienced a feeling of inferiority, and the fact that he chose as a

2. G. Jean-Aubry, *Joseph Conrad: Life and Letters*, London, 1927, I, 97.

model for Jim a fellow who had in a remarkable degree those qualities in which he was lacking, may be put down to his unconscious wishes for compensation. Men with youthful faces are exceedingly frequent in Conrad's books.

(That Conrad experienced a feeling of inferiority with regard to tall men is shown in the following anecdote reported by F. M. Hueffer:

> Over and over again he related how overwhelming, *with his small stature*, he found negotiations with heavy spars, stubborn cordage and black weather. He used to say, half raising his arms: "Look at me. . . . How was I made for such imbecilities?" [3]

A man with Jim's physique is, moreover, not unfit to undergo a psychological tragedy. Hamlet is also a strong and healthy young man. It is a fact of everyday experience that tall, well-built men have often a character curiously delicate and introvert.

Using the psychoanalytical terminology, it may be said that *physically* Jim is the projection of Conrad's unconscious wishes for compensation. Mentally or morally, he is, on the other hand, the projection of Conrad's repressed fears.

The novel *Lord Jim* is eminently symbolical. The circumstances leading up to Jim's "jump" are modelled on those leading to Conrad's naturalization as a British subject. Jim's father is a parson. We know that in Conrad's writings a clergyman easily stands for a man believing too blindly in Providence. Apollo Korzeniowski belonged to that very type. He was * * * a great religious idealist. Of Jim we read that "after a course of light holiday literature his vocation for the sea had declared itself." We recognize in this sentence the slightly ironical tone Conrad uses when speaking of himself. Jim's youth is but a humorous version of his own. In fact, his readings, and not the sight of the sea nor the call of any family or national tradition, awoke in him the desire to become a sailor. Jim is sent to a training ship. Conrad's relations wanted first to send him to the Austrian Naval School at Pola,[4] but they finally decided to let him go to Marseilles.

Jim's first voyage to the East takes place in very much the same circumstances as surrounded Conrad's early voyages. Jim was "not yet four-and-twenty," Conrad's age was respectively twenty-one and twenty-three when he made his first two voyages to Australia. Jim is disabled by a falling spar and has to lie for weeks in an Eastern hospital: it is Conrad's accident on board the *Highland Forest*.[5] Jim's library, like that of Joseph Conrad, consists mainly in a green one-volume set of Shakespeare's works. And similar to Conrad, Jim is reckless, without fear, and sometimes "a regular devil for sailing a

3. Ford Madox Ford (Hueffer), *Joseph Conrad: A Personal Remembrance,* London, 1924, p. 109.

4. Aubry, I, 28.
5. *Ibid.,* I, 93.

boat." The smuggling adventures of Dominic and Conrad, the dangerous manœuvres of the Captain in *The Secret Sharer* and Conrad's Torres Straits episode, as related in *Geography and Some Explorers*, belong to the same order. F. M. Hueffer says that he knows from several officers who sailed with Conrad that he "would indulge in extremely dangerous manœuvres, going about within knife-blades of deadly shores." [6] The natives of Patusan called Conrad's hero *Tuan Jim*, "as one might say—Lord Jim," just as the Polish peasants and servants must have called the young Conrad *Pan Józef*, an expression meaning literally *Lord Joseph*! Jim had particular reasons to use only his Christian name and to drop his surname. The same was true of Joseph Conrad Korzeniowski. One may or may not admit the significance of these facts, [but] it is interesting to note the extreme shyness with which Conrad mentioned his real name. When about to arrange the journey to Poland in 1914, according to Mrs. Conrad "he had forgotten some important formality as to the date of his naturalisation, and he had omitted to put his full name, Korzeniowski." [7] It is true that Conrad signed his *Polish* letters always with his full name; only, in these, he appears distinctly as a Pole, not as an Englishman.

Finally, when Jim asks himself so anxiously whether public opinion will back him up, whether the sanction of his foreign friends will be absolute enough to absolve him in his own eyes, we again recognize in Jim Conrad himself. Jim's authority over the "natives" stands really for Conrad's success in the English-speaking world.

In spite of his origin and of his careful education, Jim "jumps." In all probability, he would not have done it, had not his very superiors urged him to go, and had not the ship been sure to sink the next moment. This is exactly what happened to Joseph Conrad. *The sinking ship is Poland.* The very names are similar. *Patna* is the name of the ship, and *Polska* the (Polish) name of Poland. *Poland* (i.e. polonity) is doomed to disappear in a short time. There is, rationally speaking, no hope whatever for her. Such was at least the opinion of Jim's superiors, i.e. of Conrad's uncle and guardian, T. Bobrowski. The machines have been stopped, i.e. the independent Polish Government has ceased to exist. At this moment, Jim's superiors advise him to "jump," but Jim did not want to for a long moment. As a matter of fact, Conrad's uncle *urged him during more than seven years* to become a British subject.[8] And finally, Jim yielded and jumped, i.e. Conrad became a British subject.

6. Ford, p. 107.
7. Jessie Conrad, *Joseph Conrad as I Knew Him*, New York, 1926, p. 63.
8. Joseph Conrad was not at all in a hurry to become a British subject, as this passage from a Bobrowski letter shows: "One cannot be 'Vogel Frey' one's whole life, one must belong to some nation or other. Sooner or later you will have to take a decision, but in any case it is always better to do it when one is free, instead of waiting till the circumstances force a decision upon one." These lines were written on the 30th of May, 1880, five years before Conrad's naturalisation!

But then, the ship is successfully towed to Aden by a French gunboat. This is the expression of the repressed hope that every genuine Pole ever cherished at the bottom of his heart (Nicholas B. for instance, who prophesied that Conrad would see "better times"), the hope that the day would come when Poland would be saved. That is why of all things it is a *French gunboat* that rescues the *Patna*. Ever since the rise of Napoleon, the Poles have expected their help to come from France. The Polish national anthem "Poland is not yet lost" is a song which originated in the Polish legions serving under Napoleon.

These are the facts of Conrad's life, and his wishes and fears which underlie the first part of *Lord Jim*. The second part of the book (from Chapter 19 onwards) is not less symbolic than the first. But while the first part is the representation of a real state of affairs, the second part is the expression of Conrad's fear that the desertion of his native country might ultimately prove a fault by which he had forfeited his honour. The final destruction of Jim consecrates the author's triumph over the guilt-complex. Tuan Jim's defeat is Joseph Conrad's victory. A man who, like Jim, has suffered so much, and who has paid off his debt with his death, is no longer guilty. His death adds much to the poignancy of his fate, it really makes him *a hero*. If we did not regret Jim's fate (though feeling its inevitability), the novel would have missed the mark. This is the reason why *Lord Jim* must of necessity have what is called "an unhappy ending." In fact, Jim's death is the only satisfactory closing note. Now we can obsolve Jim entirely. His memory will be that of a man of unstained honour. This ending is also logical, since Conrad assumes from the very beginning that the conflict is insoluble.

R. Curle made a remark which is strangely inadequate, when he wrote that Jim is "not an Englishman at all, but a passionate and melancholy Pole." [9] Jim, like Hamlet, is the personification of that brooding part which every introvert possesses, and which will govern him if he does not govern *it*. All the difference between a normal person and a neurotic is that the former can keep that part in its proper place, that, unlike Jim (but very much like Conrad), he masters his fate. That is why Jim is not a Pole, but simply a neurotic and, as such, a perfectly true and convincing character. There are thousands of English men and women like him, thousands whose lives are obscured and sometimes destroyed by guilt-complexes. They do not, as a rule, die in such romantic circumstances as Jim or Hamlet, but end by suicide or in a lunatic asylum. Their fate may be less pathetic because it is not grasped and expressed by the mind of an artist, but it is just as real.

---

9. Richard Curle, *Joseph Conrad: A Study,* London, 1914, p.123.

Lord Jim is unique amongst Conrad's books. It is perhaps not his best, but his most intimate. It is a book in which he tells us more about the darker sides of his personality than in *A Personal Record* and the *Mirror of the Sea* put together, for in these two books Conrad has taken great care that no "Conrad en pantoufles" (to use his own expression) should appear before the public. In *Lord Jim*, Joseph Conrad exteriorized, in a symbolic form, the deepest conflicts that arose from the dualism Polish-English within himself.

Lord Jim is more than a psychological novel, it is a psychoanalytical novel written before psycholanalysis was founded. It appeared in 1900, the very year when Freud published his first book, *Interpretation of Dreams*, which indirectly helps us to explain the novel. Both books, one in a subjective, the other in an objective form, threw light upon "that side of us which, like the other hemisphere of the moon, exists stealthily in perpetual darkness, with only a fearful ashy light falling at times on the edge."

It was only in the nature of things that Conrad should dislike Freud intensely, as he disliked Dostoievski. Freud was in possession of the same truths as himself, but he appeared to him as a too crude, a too explicit double of himself.[1]

EDWARD CRANKSHAW

[Art vs. Didacticism in *Lord Jim*] †

Not only is there no *ad hoc* manipulation of events to favour a didactic purpose—there is very frequently a manipulation obscuring the clarity of the general moral bias and springing from æsthetic requirements. It is manifest in "Lord Jim," in "Nostromo," and in "The Rescue," amongst other novels, and more than anything else it seems to me a demonstration of how, despite the extremely positive nature of Conrad's bias, the artist in him completely overwhelms the preacher.

Of all Conrad's novels the most didactic is supposed to be "Lord Jim." Through the points of conduct involved in it something of a stir arose at its first appearance, and the interest has remained ever since a moral one. The novel certainly has to do with the problem of honour, but it is not so much a thesis on the theme of honour as a fantasia. And this fact kills it as a didactic essay while making it as

1. In the *Nouvelle Revue Française*, December 1924, M. Lenormand relates how he started once to speak to Conrad of Freud, but Conrad changed the conversation at once. M. Lenormand attributes this very rightly to the fact that Conrad did not want to know the

objective truth about his own work.
† From *Joseph Conrad: Some Aspects of the Art of the Novel*, by Edward Crankshaw, New York, Russell and Russell, 1963, pp. 50–54. First published by John Lane, London, 1936. Reprinted by permission.

a work of art. To the casual glance the issue may seem unambiguously simple, but really it is so infinitely complex that it can hardly be called an issue at all—not, at any rate, a moral one. That unsatisfactory hero, one may take it, was chosen by Conrad because his problem had to do with the problem of honour which to Conrad was important; but more than that one really cannot say. Certainly Jim is used to illustrate no thesis: the only thesis of the book is Jim himself, preoccupation with whom necessitates the taking into account in an inconclusive manner of certain issues of a moral nature.

"It is a story," says Mr. Curle, "of remorse and the effort to regain self-respect," and that is probably a widespread notion. Surely, though, that is precisely what it is not. The whole trouble about Jim is that he never does lose his self-respect. He is unshakeably convinced of his own worth. He has been unfairly got at, for in all those countless situations in which he saw himself heroically in action there was not one which exactly fitted the actual situation in which he suddenly found himself on board the leaking *Patna*. He was simply taken unawares, but given another chance he will prove himself. Like the English, he does not know when he is beaten. Very like the English. His very wretchedness springs not from loss of self-respect but from public disgrace. His flight ever farther eastwards takes him not from himself but from public contempt. In saying that "he is a slave to the idea of rehabilitation," Mr. Curle is perfectly accurate; but that statement is at odds with the earlier one taken from the preceding page. And Conrad himself leaves us in no doubt.

At first, knowing Conrad, knowing the importance he attached to the few simple virtues, imagining that here he is giving way to temptation to the extent of preaching, we do wonder about Jim. But it is troubling to find so much being made of the *Patna's* unsinkability. To fit a straightforward moral purpose Jim's forlorn odessey should have begun at the moment of his jump, *with* that jump, and no later. If the argument is to run as it seems to be running, the whole business of the *Patna's* unforeseen seaworthiness is question-begging and misleading. Compared with the fact of that jump the public disgrace from which Jim's pilgrimage actually starts is nothing. Had the *Patna* foundered according to schedule there would have been no public disgrace, but Jim's guilt would have been no less. . . .

What then? One does wonder a little, imagining that Conrad is indulging himself in a little didactic essay; but the doubt is soon eased away. With the entry of Marlow it becomes increasingly apparent that this is no obvious tale of right and wrong, even a complex right and wrong, but a study of infinite subtlety a thousand leagues removed above the plane of didactic purpose. And soon

Conrad himself gives the word which finally proves that in spite of the golden opportunity at hand for improving the hour with an allegorical exposition of his moral views he is here, as usual, engaged in rendering, not in preaching. Marlow is speaking of Jim as he saw him lording it in Patusan:

> That was my last view of him—in a strong light, dominating, and yet in complete accord with his surroundings—with the life of the forests and the life of men. I own that I was impressed, but I must admit to myself that after all this is not the lasting impression. He was protected by his isolation, alone of his superior kind, in close touch with nature, that keeps faith on such easy terms with her lovers. But I cannot fix before my eye the image of his safety. I shall always remember him as seen through the open door of my room, taking, perhaps, too much to heart the mere consequences of his failure. . . .
>
> . . . I don't mean to say that I regret my action, nor will I pretend that I can't sleep o' nights in consequence; still, the idea obtrudes itself that he made so much of his disgrace while it is the guilt alone that matters. He was not, if I may say so, clear to me. He was not clear. And there is a suspicion that he was not clear to himself either. There were his fine sensibilities, his fine feelings, his fine longings—a sort of sublimated idealized selfishness.

After that there can be no doubt at all. Conrad is not concerned with driving home a clear-cut issue, but with rendering a complete personality in relation to his environment—a borderline position if ever there was one. Through Marlow Conrad manages to get in a handful of his own reflections on destiny and life, of which that passage is a fair sample. But such comments are by the way, arising out of the subject; the subject most emphatically does not arise out of them. They can, moreover, hardly be regarded even in their smallness as *ad hoc* reflections; they are there primarily as a means of illumination, as an aid to the complete rendering of the subject, which is Jim himself in all his aspects, and in accordance with Conrad's usual methods, methods dictated by psychological limitations, the detailed working of which we shall have to examine later.

The crux of it all is that at the end we ask what precisely Conrad's intentions were—did he approve of Jim or did he not? And there is no answer to that question—none but the simple, all-sufficing one, that he strove "to make us see." We do see Jim as Conrad, a man of vision, saw him, and we are left with that spectacle to make what we can of it for ourselves.

And this, knowing how positive, how definite, was Conrad's moral outlook, argues a fine personal restraint. It is the restraint of the artist, whose only reward is an uncomprehending stare, and the injured question—"but what does it *mean?*"

It is plain enough that Jim has fallen. The task of the artist is to show you the man and his fall, not to measure heights and depths.

DOROTHY VAN GHENT

On *Lord Jim* †

Marlow's last view of Jim, on the coast of Patusan, is of a white figure "at the heart of a vast enigma." Jim himself is not enigmatic. The wonder and doubt that he stirs, both in Marlow and in us, are not wonder and doubt as to what *he* is: he is as recognizable as we are to ourselves; he is "one of us." Furthermore, he is not a very complex character, and he is examined by his creator with the most exhaustive conscientiousness; he is placed in every possible perspective that might help to define him. The enigma, then, is not what Jim is but what we are, and not only what we are, but "how to be" what we are.

Jim's shocking encounter with himself at the moment of his jump from the *Patna* is a model of those moments when the destiny each person carries within him, the destiny fully molded in the unconscious will, lifts its blind head from the dark, drinks blood, and speaks. There is no unclarity in the shape that Jim saw at that moment: he had jumped—it is as simple as that. But because the event is a paradigm of the encounters of the conscious personality with the stranger within, the stranger who is the very self of the self, the significance of Jim's story is *our own* significance, contained in the enigmatic relationship between the conscious will and the fatality of our acts. Jim's discovery of himself was a frightful one, and his solution of the problem of "how to be" was to exorcise the stranger in a fierce, long, concentrated effort to be his opposite. The oracle spoke early to Oedipus, too, in his youth in Corinth, telling him who he was—the man destined to transgress most horribly the saving code of kinship relations—and Oedipus' solution of the problem of "how to be" was the same as Jim's: he fled in the opposite direction from his destiny and ran straight into it.

Jim is one of the most living characters in fiction, although his presentation is by indirection, through Marlow's narrative; that indirection is itself uniquely humanizing, for we see him only as people can see each other, ambivalently and speculatively. He is nevertheless an extraordinarily simplified *type*, obsessed with a single idea, divested of all psychological attributes but the very few

† From *The English Novel: Form and Function*, Rinehart and Co., New York, 1953, pp. 229–44. Copyright by Doro- thy Van Ghent. Reprinted by permission.

that concretize his relationship with his idea. The simplification is classical; it is a simplification like that of Aeschylus' Orestes, possessed by the divine command, and like that of Sophocles' Oedipus, possessed by his responsibility for finding out the truth. Conrad is able thus to imply a clear-cut formal distinction between the man and his destiny (his acts), even though he conceives destiny as immanent in the man's nature and in this sense identical with him. Here is Jim, "clean-limbed, clean-faced, firm on his feet, as promising a boy as the sun ever shone on," and there are his acts—the destruction of his best friend, the destruction of himself, the abandonment of the Patusan village to leaderlessness and depredation. Similarly Orestes and Oedipus, human agents simplified to a commanding ethical idea, are analytically separable from their destinies, the *anankē* or compelling principle fatally inherent in their acts. This subtle but tangible distinction between the human agent and his destiny allows the classical dramatists to orient clearly what we may call the metaphysical significance of the hero's career, the universal problem and the law of life which that career illustrates .We see the hero as an ideal human type (literally "idealized" through his devotion to an idea of ethical action); but his fate is pitiful and terrible —a fate that, if a man's deserts were to be suited to his conscious intentions, should fall only on malicious, unjust, and treasonable men; and the problem, the "enigma," thus raised is the religious problem of the awful incongruity between human intention and its consequences in action, between ethical effort and the guilt acquired through such effort; and the law—if a law appears—will be the law that justifies, to man's reason and feeling, that appearance of awful incongruity. Conrad's treatment of Jim's story is classical in this sense, in that he sees in it the same problem and orients the problem in the same manner.

"In the destructive element immerse," Stein says, voicing his own solution of the problem of "how to be." There is no way "to be," according to Stein, but through the ideal, the truth as it appears, what he calls "the dream," although it is itself "the destructive element." "Very funny this terrible thing is," Stein says,

> "A man that is born falls into a dream like a man who falls into the sea. If he tries to climb out into the air as inexperienced people endeavour to do, he drowns—*nicht wahr?* . . . No! I tell you! The way is to the destructive element submit yourself, and with the exertions of your hands and feet in the water make the deep, deep sea keep you up. So if you ask me—how to be? . . . I will tell you! . . . In the destructive element immerse."

Stein's words are but one outlook on the universal problem that is Jim's, but it is the outlook dramatized in Jim's own actions. It is that dramatized by Sophocles also. Oedipus "submitted" himself to his ideal of the responsible king and citizen, self-sworn to the discovery of the truth. It was the "destructive element," bringing about the terrible revelation of his guilt. So also Jim submits himself to his dream of heroic responsibility and truth to men, fleeing from port to port, and finally to Patusan, to realize it. And, again, the ideal is the "destructive element," bringing about the compact with Brown (a compact made in the profoundest spirit of the dream) and inevitably, along with the compact, destruction. The irony is that Jim, in his destructiveness, was "true." This is the classical tragic irony: the incongruity and yet the effective identity between the constructive will and the destructive act.

Whether Conrad goes beyond that particular tragic incongruity to the other ancient tragic perception, of ennoblement through suffering, is doubtful. The "enigma" that Marlow finds in Jim's career has this other dark and doubtful aspect. When, at the end, after receiving Doramin's bullet, "the white man sent right and left at all those faces a proud and unflinching glance," is he really fulfilled in nobility in our sight? Has his suffering, entailed in his long and strenuous exile and his guilt and his final great loss, given him the knowledge, and with the knowledge the nobility, which is the mysterious and sublime gift of suffering? The answer is doubtful. We need to bring to bear on it the fairly inescapable impression that the only character in the book in whom we can read the stamp of the author's own practical "approval" is the French lieutenant who remained on board the *Patna* while it was being towed into port. The French lieutenant would not have acted as Jim did in the last events on Patusan—indeed is inconceivable in the Patusan circumstances. If, in Conrad's implicit evaluation of his material, the French lieutenant represents the ethically "approved" manner of action and the only one, Jim can scarcely support the complete role of the tragic hero of the classical type, the hero who achieves unique greatness through suffering. (The French lieutenant suffers only for lack of wine.) For our notion of what constitutes a "hero" is thus surely divided: if the French lieutenant's heroism is the true heroism, Jim's is not, and conversely. No doubt the division—and it seems to be real in our response to the book—is associated with a division of allegiance on Conrad's part,[1] between emotional allegiance to Jim's suffering and struggling humanity, in all its hybristic aspiration, and intellectual allegiance to the code represented by the lieutenant, in all its severe limitation and calm obscurity. With this division in mind, it is impossible to identify the "view of life" in the book as a whole with Stein's view of life, impressive as Stein is in his broad and enlightened sensitivity: for the French lieutenant knows

1. Albert Guerard discusses this division of allegiance in his *Joseph Conrad*, New York, 1947.

nothing of a "destructive element," and if he did—which he could not—would doubtless think that to talk of "submitting" oneself to it was sheer twaddle.

What intervenes between Conrad's ambivalent attitude toward Jim's story and the attitudes of Aeschylus and Sophocles toward their subjects is modern man's spiritual isolation from his fellows. Jim's isolation is profound, most profound and complete at that last moment when he "sent right and left at all those faces a proud and unflinching glance": here his aloneness in his dream—his illusion—of faith to men is unqualified, for the material fact is that he has allowed a brigand to slaughter Dain Waris and his party, and that he has left the village open to ravage. Moral isolation provides a new inflection of tragedy. Orestes freed Argos from a tyranny, and Oedipus freed Thebes from a plague. Their guilt and suffering had a constructive social meaning; they had acted for the positive welfare of the citizens; and that social version of their heroism, internal to the dramas in which they appear, is the immediate, literal basis of our (because it is the citizen-chorus's) appraisal of their heroism. But Jim—to use parallel terms—destroys his city. Thus there is nothing structurally internal to Jim's story that matches the positive moral relationship, in the ancient dramas, between the social destiny and the hero's destiny, the relationship that is presented concretely in the fact that the hero's agony is a saving social measure. There is nothing to mediate, practically and concretely, between Jim's "truth" and real social life, as a benefit to and confirmation of the social context. Jim is alone.

And yet one asks, is his last act, when he "takes upon his head" the blood-guilt, an atonement? If it were so, it would be atonement not in quite the same sense that the madness and exile of Orestes and the blinding and banishment of Oedipus were atonements, for these involved the restoration of community health, whereas Jim's final act brings about (projectively) the destruction of the community—but in the necessary modern sense, necessitated by the fact of the disintegration of moral bonds between men: an atonement for that social sterility, a sacrifice offered in the name of moral community. If it were so, Jim would still be, metaphorically speaking, the savior of the city. No doubt Sophocles, civic-minded gentleman, did not "approve" of Oedipus: when parricide and incest occur in the leading families, what are the rest of us to do? how is the world's business to be kept up decently? what model shall we look to? But the Greek cities were said to have carried on quarrels over the burial place of Oedipus, for his presence brought fertility to the land. So also the story of Lord Jim is a spiritually fertilizing experience, enlightening the soul as to its own meaning in a time of disorganization and drought; and Conrad's imagination of Jim's story has the seminal virtue of the ancient classics.

In James's *The Portrait of a Lady* we watched the creation of a self. In Conrad's austerely pessimistic work, the self stands already created, the possibilities are closed. Again and again, and finally on Patusan, a "clean slate" is what Jim thinks he has found, a chance to "climb out," to begin over, to perform the deed which will be congruent with his ideal of himself. "A clean slate, did he say?" Marlow comments; "as if the initial word of each our destiny were not graven in imperishable characters upon the face of a rock." The tension, the spiritual drama in Conrad, lie in a person's relation with his destiny. The captain in "The Secret Sharer" acknowledges his profound kinship with a man who has violently transgressed the captain's professional code (the man has murdered another seaman during a voyage, and murder at sea is, in Conrad, something worse than murder; whatever its excuses, it is an inexcusable breach of faith with a community bound together by common hazard); but by the acknowledgment he masters his own identity, integrates, as it were, his unconscious impulses within consciousness, and thereby realizes self-command and command of his ship. In contrast with the captain of "The Secret Sharer," Jim repudiates the other-self that has been revealed to him; at no time does he consciously acknowledge that it *was* himself who jumped from the *Patna*—it was only his body that had jumped; and his career thenceforth is an attempt to prove before men that the gross fact of the jump belied his identity.

James works through recognitions; the self-creating character in James develops by taking into consciousness more and more subtle relations—"seeing" more in a world of virtually infinite possibilities for recognition, and thus molding himself. Conrad works through epiphanies, that is, through dramatic manifestations of elements hidden or implicit in the already constructed character. The difference of method is suggestive of the difference of world view: in James, the world ("reality" as a whole) being, as it were, an open and fluid system, essentially creative; in Conrad, a closed and static system, incapable of origination though intensely dramatic in its revelations. (Paradoxically, the environments in James's open world are closed environments of city and house, while those in Conrad's closed world are those of the open, the mobile sea.) The word "epiphany" implies manifestation of divinity, and this meaning of the term can serve us also in analyzing Conrad's method and his vision, if we think of the "dark powers" of the psyche as having the mysterious absoluteness that we associate with the daemonic, and if we think mythologically of a man's destiny both as being carried within him, and, *in effect*—since his acts externalize his destiny—

as confronting him from without.

The sunken wreck that strikes the *Patna* is one such epiphany in *Lord Jim*, and this manifestation of "dark power" is coincident with and symbolically identifiable with the impulse that makes Jim jump, an impulse submerged like the wreck, riding in wait, striking from under. Outer nature seems, here, to act in collusion with the hidden portion of the soul. But Conrad's supreme mastery is his ability to make the circumstance of "plot" the inevitable point of discharge of the potentiality of "character." [2] The accident that happens to the *Patna* is not merely a parallel and a metaphor of what happens to Jim at that time, but it is the objective circumstance that discovers Jim to himself. The apparent "collusion" between external nature and the soul, that gives to Conrad's work its quality of the marvelous and its religious temper, is thus, really, only the inevitable working out of character through circumstance.

Another major epiphany is the appearance of Brown on Patusan. The appearance of Brown is, in effect, an externalization of the complex of Jim's guilt and his excuses for his guilt, for he judges Brown as he judged himself, as a *victim of circumstances* (the distinction is radical) rather than as a character exposed by circumstances, at least to be given that benefit of doubt which would discriminate intention from deed, ethos from the objective ethical traits to be seen in a man's actions. Therefore he gives Brown a "clean slate," a chance to "climb out"—from himself! But Jim's compact with Brown is more than a compact with his own unacknowledged guilt; it is at the same time, and paradoxically, a lonely act of faith with the white men "out there," the men of Jim's race and traditions, the men upon the sea whose code he had once betrayed, the "home" from which a single impulse of nerves had forever exiled him. Brown is the only white man who has appeared on Patusan to put to test Jim's ethical community with his race and his profession, and in "taking upon his head" responsibility for Brown's honor, he is superbly "true" to that community. But his truth is, effectively, betrayal; it is "the destructive element." Since only a chance in thousands brings Brown to Patusan, again outer nature seems to have acted in collusion with the "dark power" within Jim's own psyche, in order to face him once more with his unacknowledged identity when he is in the full hybris of his truth and his courage. But again the apparent collusion is only the working out of character through circumstance.

The impossibility of escape from the dark companion within leaves a man more perfectly alone in this world because he has that

2. Morton Dauwen Zabel points this out in his Introduction to *The Portable Conrad*, New York, 1947.

companion—who is always and only himself. The physical settings of Jim's career concretize his isolation. In constant flight from the self that he reads on men's lips but that he refuses to acknowledge except as a freakish injustice of circumstances, and, as he flees, pursuing the heroic ideal which would reconstitute him in the ranks of men where his salvation lies (for, as Conrad says, "in our own hearts we trust for our salvation in the men that surround us"), he comes finally to Patusan, ascends the river to the heart of the island, unarmed (why carry a loaded revolver when it is only oneself that one must face?)—ascends, that is, the dark paths of his own being back to its source: [3] "thirty miles of forest shut it off."

The first description that Marlow gives of the interior of the island is of a conical hill that is "split in two, and with the two halves leaning slightly apart," and in his reminiscences he returns frequently to the image of the hill (it is, indeed, the hill up which Jim hauled the cannon, in his first great exploit when he won the faith of the natives and became their protector), particularly to a scene of moonlight when the moon is rising behind the fissured mass.

> On the third day after the full, the moon, as seen from the open space in front of Jim's house . . . rose exactly behind these hills, its diffused light at first throwing the two masses into intensely black relief, and then the nearly perfect disc, glowing ruddily, appeared, gliding upwards between the sides of the chasm, till it floated away above the summits, as if escaping from a yawning grave in gentle triumph. "Wonderful effect," said Jim by my side. "Worth seeing. Is it not?"
>
> And this question was put with a note of personal pride that made me smile, as though he had had a hand in regulating that unique spectacle. He had regulated so many things in Patusan! Things that would have appeared as much beyond his control as the motions of the moon and the stars.

On Marlow's last night on the island he sees the same spectacle again, but the mood is different, oppressive.

> I saw part of the moon glittering through the bushes at the bottom of the chasm. For a moment it looked as though the smooth disc, falling from its place in the sky upon the earth, had rolled to the bottom of that precipice: its ascending movement was like a leisurely rebound; it disengaged itself from the tangle of twigs; the bare contorted limb of some tree, growing on the slope, made a black crack right across its face. It threw its level rays afar as if from a cavern, and in this mournful eclipse-like light the stumps of felled trees uprose very dark, the heavy shadows fell at my feet on all sides . . .

3. The observation is made by Mr. Guerard in *Joseph Conrad,* cited above.

Together Jim and Marlow watch "the moon float away above the chasm between the hills like an ascending spirit out of a grave; its sheen descended, cold and pale, like the ghost of dead sunlight." Carried to the mind by the image of the fissured hill, with the suspiciously ghostlike moon floating out of the chasm, is the relentless solitude of Jim's fate. He is not only an outcast from his kind but he is also an outcast from himself, cloven spiritually, unable to recognize his own identity, separated from himself as the two halves of the hill are separated. And the rebounding moon, in which he has so much pride, "as though he had had a hand in regulating that unique spectacle," remains in the mind as a figure of the ego-ideal, even that ideal of truth by which, Marlow says, Jim approached "greatness as genuine as any man ever achieved": its illusionariness, and the solitude implied by illusion. At the end, after all—when the silver ring that is the token of moral community falls to the floor, and through Jim's "truth" his best friend has been killed and the village under his protection betrayed—Jim is only what he has been; he is of the measure of his acts. To be only what one has been is the sentence of solitary confinement that is passed on everyman. It is in this sense, finally, that Jim is "one of us."

Since Jim is "one of us," the truth about Jim will be—within the scope of the expressiveness of Jim's story—a truth about life; and in view of this responsibility, Conrad's task of evaluation demands that *all* the accessible evidence be presented and that it be submitted to mutually corrective hypotheses of its meaning. There are Jim's actions, which are concrete enough and simple as the concrete is simple. But the significance of action is significance in the judgments of men, which are various; and as soon as judgment is brought to the act, the act becomes not simple but protean. *What*, then, *is* the act? The question defines Conrad's method in this book, his use of reflector within reflector, point of view within point of view, cross-chronological juxtapositions of events and impressions. Conrad's technical "devices," in this case, represent much more than the word "device" suggests: they represent extreme ethical scrupulosity, even anxiety; for the truth about a man is at once too immense and too delicate to sustain any failure of carefulness in the examiner.

The omniscient early chapters give briefly the conditions of Jim's upbringing, his heroic dreams, two incidents in his sea training, the *Patna* voyage up to the moment when the submerged wreck strikes, and the courtroom scene with Jim in the dock: that is, the first chapters take us up to the point where the accused is placed before us and the processes of judgment have to begin. From here, Marlow takes over. Marlow is unofficial attorn y both for the defense and the prosecution. He selects, objectifies, and humanizes the evidence on both sides, but he lets it—intensified and set in perspective through his intelligent, freely roaming curiosity—speak for itself. Marlow is the most familiar narrative mechanism in Conrad's work; and in this particular book *Marlow has to exist*. For Jim's "case" is not an absolute but a relative; it has a being only in relation to what men's minds can make of it. And Marlow provides the necessary medium of an intelligent consciousness, at once a symbol of that relativity, a concretization of the processes by which just judgment may be evoked, and—through his doubt and reverence—an acknowledgment of the irony of judgment of the relative.

The few particulars that are given of Jim's home environment are all we need to give the word "home" potency for this chronicle: there is the parsonage, its decency, its naïveté, its faith, its sterling morality, its representativeness of "the sheltering conception of light and order which is our refuge." In the thirty-fifth chapter, where Marlow takes final farewell of Jim, and Jim says,

> "I must stick to their belief in me to feel safe and to—to" . . .
> He cast about for a word, seemed to look for it on the sea . . .
> "to keep in touch with" . . . His voice sank suddenly to a murmur . . . "with those whom, perhaps, I shall never see any more. With—with—you, for instance."

the parsonage home, as well as the community of men upon the sea, contains the "those" with whom Jim must keep in touch through faithfulness in word and act. "Home" is the ethical code which enables men to live together through trust of each other, and which, in so binding them, gives them self-respect. The exclusiveness and naïveté of the parsonage background interpret the symbol of "home" in all its own relativity, its merely provisional status in the jungle of the universe. When we close the book, the symbol of "home" is as ghostlike as the moon over Patusan. But it is the only provision for salvation, in the sense in which Conrad uses the word salvation when he says, "In our own hearts we trust for our salvation in the men that surround us."

The two incidents in Jim's early sea training, the storm in Chapter 1, when he was "too late," and, in Chapter 2, his disablement at the beginning of a hurricane week, when he "felt secretly glad he had not to go on deck," counterpoint his belief in himself with actualities of frustration. A certain distinct polarity is already established, between his dreams and the "facts"; and when, in Chapter 2, Jim suddenly decides to ship as mate on the *Patna*, it is as if we saw a bar magnet curved into a horseshoe and bent until its poles closed, sealing personal will and fatality of circumstances in a mysterious identity that is the man himself; for his unexplained choice of the *Patna* is in more than one sense a choice of exile. He could have gone back to the home service, after his convalescence; but he throws in his lot with the men he has seen in that Eastern port (and disdained) who "appeared to live in a crazy maze of plans, hopes, dangers, enterprises . . . in the dark places of the sea," and with those others who had been seduced by "the eternal peace of Eastern sky and sea," who talked "everlastingly of turns of luck . . . and in all they said—in their actions, in their looks, in their persons—could be detected the soft spot, the place of decay . . ." Moreover, on the *Patna* he is in a special sense a man alone, alone with a dream that is unsharable because he is among inferiors: the third chapter presents "the *Patna* gang" from Jim's point of view—"those men did not belong to the world of heroic adventure . . . he rubbed shoulders with them, but they could not touch him; he shared the air they breathed, but he was different . . ." Is his choice of the *Patna* a measure taken to protect his dream from reality? Is it thus significant of his "soft spot"? There is no choice but reality, and actually none but the single, circumscribed, only possible choice that is one's own reality —witnessed by Jim's jump from the *Patna*, as by his shipping on the *Patna* in the first place.

When Sophocles, in his old age, wrote of Oedipus again, he had Oedipus assert his innocence and curse those who had banished him; for Oedipus had acted in ignorance of the circumstances, and therefore could not be held guilty for them. Jim puts up a fight as Oedipus did, and the causes involved are the same: is the self deducible from circumstances? is one guilty for circumstances? is one guilty for oneself when one has no choice but to be oneself? is one guilty for oneself when one is in ignorance of what oneself is? if, with lifelong strife, one refuses to acquiesce in the self, is one guilty for the self? who has a right to pronounce this judgment?

Obviously from this point another device of presentation must be used, other than either objective presentation by the author or subjective presentation through Jim, for Jim is too youthful, idealistic, and ingenuous to throw light on himself, and "objectivity"— the objectivity of the camera and the sound recorder—is hopelessly inadequate to the solution of these questions. Marlow has to take up the case, and Marlow—intelligent professional man of the sea, and insatiably curious psychological observer—brings to bear on it not only Jim's own evidence (and his friendship with Jim draws from Jim much more than he could ever say for himself—brings out gestures and tones, situations and impulses, that only sympathy could bring out), and not only the reactions of the judges (and the judges are more in number than those in the courtroom), but also a marvelously sensitive registration of the concrete detail of life, bits of color and form and movement, a chin, a hand, a shuffle, a vase of dry flowers, a striped pajama suit, that could not be admitted as "evidence" in a formal inquiry, but that are nevertheless essential psychological evidence to the sensitive investigator.

The *Patna* gang has to be presented over again, not now from Jim's point of view but from Marlow's. So far as the *Patna* gang is concerned, the question is, is Jim one of them or "one of us"? Marlow has only to see the group on a street corner to know that Jim is not one of them; but he pushes further—he is around when the fat captain, in his nightsuit, squeezes into the ramshackle gharry and disappears, "departed, disappeared, vanished, absconded; and absurdly enough it looked as though he had taken that gharry with him." It is Marlow's impression of the obscenely ridiculous captain that conveys to us the captain's sur-reality: he is, through Marlow's view, not simply stupid and inferior as he appeared to Jim, but a frightful manifestation of underground evil, as mysterious and unaccountable in its apparition as the captain's vanishing with the gharry is complete; that the captain wears a sleeping suit (like the murderer in "The Secret Sharer") emphasizes the psychological, that is to say spiritual, symbolism of his evil; he is another epiphany, a "showing" from the daemonic underground of the psyche—but he is only that, and the psyche, Jim's psyche, is more than the obscene man in the sleeping suit.

Then Marlow interviews the chief engineer in the hospital, the man with the noble head and the pink toads under his bed. The effort is an effort again to test his perception that Jim is not one of them, but "one of us"; for the initial perception alone is scarcely to be trusted, since Jim, whatever his excuses, had identified himself with the *Patna* gang by jumping from the ship. The pink toads under the chief engineer's bed are a fearful inversion of Jim's own dream: they too are a dream—and the dreamer has a noble head. The pink toads are a horrible degeneration of the dream. They serve as a commentary on the dream that cannot be evaded (no more than can the captain in the sleeping suit). But Jim had stayed for the trial, while the captain had disappeared, the chief engineer had cultivated the d.t.'s, and the second engineer wasn't around (the little man will reappear later, for the act is immortal). It is Jim's dream that makes him stay for the trial, and therefore Jim's dream cannot be identified with the chief engineer's, however identifiable they are in illusionary quality and spiritual potency. Marlow's visit with the chief engineer fixes this judgment of a difference, as well as of a similarity.

These two observations of Marlow's project the question of identity (the question "Who am I?" that is Oedipus' as well as

Jim's), that can only be decided by comparison of like things and different things, discrimination of congruences and incongruences. Two identifications of Jim with other persons have been rejected—although even the impulse to distinguish suggests subtle similarities between the objects compared, and we can never forget that Jim was in the lifeboat with the *Patna* gang, though at the other end. The rest of the narrative moves through a devious course of identifications and distinctions. Brierly, the unimpeachable professional seaman, in some astounding way identifies himself with the accused man, Jim, and commits suicide. Is this another version of Jim's "jump"? If so, in avoiding by suicide the possibility of being Jim, Brierly succeeds merely in being what he was trying to avoid; this is Jim's "case" all over again. The loathsome Chester also identifies himself with Jim; Chester instantly spots him as the man for his job—fantastic exile on a guano island; "He is no earthly good for anything," Chester says, "he would just have done for me"; the man has a "soft spot," and for men with a soft spot, as Jim himself had observed, "death was the only event of their fantastic existence that seemed to have a reasonable certitude of achievement"; for Chester, Jim is "one of us" in a sense that disgusts Marlow, and Marlow's disgust with Chester and therefore with Chester's appraisal of the man helps us to measure Jim: but the fact that Marlow, during those grueling hours in the hotel room when he is writing factitious letters in order to give Jim a chance for privacy with his ordeal, can hesitate between recommending Jim for a decent job and turning him over to Chester still suggests a doubt as to what "one of us" means, whether it has Chester's meaning or Marlow's.

The French lieutenant whom Marlow encounters, though he is a sympathetic man, does *not* identify himself with Jim; and curiously, while the French lieutenant represents the approved ethos of the profession (and not only of the profession of the sea, but of the profession of being human, as the author evaluates his material; for, in that evaluation, being human, as humans ought to be, *is* a profession, with an austere Spartan-like discipline [4]), he is the only person in the book who does not, in some way, identify himself with Jim except for Cornelius and Brown, who hate him as an opposite and as an indictment of their evil (perhaps the captain of the *Patna* and the chief engineer could be included here, but their presentation is more objective and their attitudes less determinable; although the same point would hold): that is to say that the only cases in which subjective identification with Jim does not take place are those of a man—the French lieutenant—who is above Jim's failings by virtue of his mediocrity, and of men who are below

4. In his *Joseph Conrad*, Mr. Guerard thoroughly clarifies this issue.

Jim's problem by virtue of their psychotic maliciousness. The portrait of the French lieutenant is extremely careful, as all the portraits in the book are done with extreme care, for on the nature of the man who judges depends the validity of the judgment.

> He clasped his hands on his stomach again. "I remained on board that—that—my memory is going (*s'en va*). Ah! *Patt-ná. C'est bien ça. Patt-nà. Merci.* It is droll how one forgets. I stayed on that ship thirty hours . . ."

And just a moment before, we have learned that "all the time of towing we had two quartermasters stationed with axes by the hawsers, to cut us clear of our tow in case she . . ." The French lieutenant's failure to remember even the name of the ship, on which he had stayed for thirty hours *after* Jim had jumped, and the laconic tone of the information about the quartermasters' assignment, are a judgment of Jim in terms of Jim's own dream. The French lieutenant's unconscious heroism is the heroism that Jim had made a conscious ideal; and his witness measures Jim's failure by the painful difference of fact. And yet this damning commentary appears as inconclusive as that of the pink toads under the chief engineer's bed; it is as far from and as near to "the case."

The distinguished naturalist Stein offers another approach. Stein has been a hero of action like the French lieutenant, but he is also a hero of the intellect, and, in his way, a psychologist, a philosopher, and an artist. Stein is able to identify himself with Jim through his own profound idealism (as Marlow does through doubt). But Stein's idealism, so far as we know, has never differentiated itself from his actions; he has the gift of nature which is itself ideal; he had known, Marlow says, how "to follow his destiny with unfaltering footsteps." Stein "diagnoses the case" of Jim, making it quite simple "and altogether hopeless" by framing it in the question: "how to be." "I tell you, my friend," he says,

> "it is not good for you to find you cannot make your dream come true, for the reason that you not strong enough are, or not clever enough. *Ja!* . . . And all the time you are such a fine fellow, too! *wie?* . . . How can that be? . . ."
> The shadow prowling amongst the graves of butterflies laughed boisterously.

Stein gives Jim his great chance to make his dream come true, by sending him to Patusan. This journey is ambiguous: "once before Patusan had been used as a grave," Marlow reflects; while Stein prowls "amongst the graves of butterflies," Brierly's remark about Jim recurs to Marlow's mind: "Let him creep twenty feet underground and stay there"; and there is the fissured hill at the heart of Patusan, whose chasm is like a "yawning grave," from which the moon (the dream) rises "like an ascending spirit out of a grave . . . like the ghost of dead sunlight." The ancient mythical heroes, Odysseus and Aeneas, made the "journey underground" to Hades in search of wisdom, and brought it back to daylight—the wisdom which was knowledge of their own destinies. And shadowily behind them is the barbarous ritual that made a king by burying him and disinterring him, a surrogate perhaps, or a "story" (mythos), to stand for the killing of an old king and his "resurrection" in a new one. In the grave of Patusan—"the secular gloom and the old mankind" —Jim's dream does come true. But the doubt remains as to whether, like the ancient heroes, he brought back to daylight the wisdom of his destiny—or, in other terms, whether in that grave an old self was really buried and from it a new one congruent with his dream was resurrected.

The test of daylight, of the bright sea beyond the dark island, offers itself only through Brown. Jim identifies himself with Brown in two ways, through his guilt, and through his honor: Brown is at once the "dark power" in Jim's psyche and his only effective bond with the brightness outside himself, the community of tradition to which "we trust for our salvation." Brown's ambivalence for Jim is Jim's own ambivalence, and it is, in its most extensive sense, the ambivalence that exists in all historical and personal stages of experience where law (the "code") and the self question each other—as well in the Athens of Thucydides and Euripides as in our own time, and as well, we must surmise, in Conrad as in Jim. The tale Conrad prepared to narrate was a tale in the manner of the older classical dramatists, wherein law—whether divine, as with Aeschylus, or natural, as with Sophocles—is justified to the self, whatever its agonies of discovery. But he managed to do a tale that put both the law and the self to question, and left them there. At the end (dated July 1900), Stein does not help:

> Stein has aged greatly of late. He feels it himself, and says often that he is "preparing to leave all this; preparing to leave . . ." while he waves his hand sadly at his butterflies.

ALBERT J. GUERARD

Lord Jim †

I

Lord Jim is * * * Conrad's first great impressionist novel. We may recognize various anticipations: the involutions of Our

† From Conrad the Novelist, Harvard University Press, Cambridge, Mass., 1958, pp. 126–34, 145–74. Reprinted by permission.

Mutual Friend and *The Possessed*, the narrator-witnesses and atmospheres of *Wuthering Heights* and *Bleak House*, the minute control of the reader's responses to ambiguity in *Benito Cereno*, even (after all) *Madame Bovary's* ambivalence. Yet *Lord Jim* is not really like any of these novels, though it is most like *Benito Cereno*. It appears at the turn of the century as the first novel in a new form: a form bent on involving and implicating the reader in a psycho-moral drama which has no easy solution, and bent on engaging his sensibilities more strenuously and even more uncomfortably than ever before. An essential novelty, though borrowed perhaps from the mystery or "police" tale, is to force upon the reader an active, exploratory, organizing role; compel him, almost, to collaborate in the writing of the novel. Ford Madox Ford liked to define the impressionist aim as a higher realism: to come closer to actual life by presenting experience as a sensitive witness would receive it— casually, digressively, without logical order. But the game is a more sinister one than that. We certainly do not receive the facts of Lord Jim's life in the order that a citizen and observer of 1880, say Marlow himself, would have received them. The digressive method does indeed convey the "feel" of life. But the impressionist aim is to achieve a fuller truth than realism can, if necessary by "cheating"; and to create in the reader an intricate play of emotion and a rich conflict of sympathy and judgment, a provisional bafflement in the face of experience which turns out to be more complicated than we ever would have dreamed. This aim is present even in the spare and unintellectual *The Great Gatsby*, certainly in the endless *Remembrance of Things Past*, even (since everything is present there) in *Ulysses*. But the culminating triumph of Conradian impressionism is *Absalom, Absalom!* This austere masterpiece, by complicating each of Conrad's complications, helps us define the earlier experiment. We see the novel developing a musical form. But the main instruments are the reader's mind, feelings, nerves.

"If he keeps on writing the same sort," an early reviewer of *Lord Jim* remarked, "[Conrad] may arrive at the unique distinction of having few readers in his own generation, and a fair chance of several in the next." [1] The impressionist novel, obscuring story, requires a certain magnitude and universality if it is to survive its own difficulty; requires these as a novel say by Trollope does not. *Absalom, Absalom!* is strengthened by its myths of a doomed family and land under a curse, and by the violence of Thomas Sutpen's destructive "innocence." Also: who has not been turned away from a door? And who has not, briefly at least, harbored an obsessive design? The universality of *Lord Jim* is even

---

1. *The Critic*, XXXVIII (1901), 138, quoted by John D. Gordan, *Joseph Conrad: The Making of a Novelist*, Cambridge, Mass., 1941, p. 297.

more obvious, since nearly everyone has jumped off some *Patna* and most of us have been compelled to live on, desperately or quietly engaged in reconciling what we are with what we would like to be. It may be that Jim should have required no more than that thickness of paper between the right and wrong of the affair. Yet he faces "boundary stituations" both on board the *Patna* and in Patusan, and these necessarily involve us. Dorothy Van Ghent argues that the derelict which strikes the *Patna* is an epiphany and manifestation of "dark power" . . . coincident with and symbolically identifiable with the impulse that makes Jim jump, an impulse submerged like the wreck, riding in wait, striking from under."

Even more persuasively, she compares Jim with Oedipus, that other man of good intentions. The impulse to discriminate between what we are and what we do, or to dissociate our*selves* from what exists in our unconscious, is a form ancient enough of making excuses. And the experience in Patusan, which to some critics seems irrelevant, corresponds to the fairly common dream of a second chance and total break with the guilty past. "A clean slate, did he say? As if the initial word of each our destiny were not graven in imperishable characters upon the face of a rock." Jim can only go to meet that destiny or await it, since it exists in his temperament; his failure is tragically certain. But he is one of those great fictional characters whose crime, like Michael Henchard's, makes as well as breaks him. A Henchard who did not sell his wife would have been a haytrusser to the end of his days; would have had neither the strength to become mayor of Casterbridge nor the strength to destroy himself so completely. So too Jim, had the *Patna* not struck a derelict, would presumably have drifted through life seeking ever softer and more suspect berths. The first four chapters show him clearly headed down that path, and content to substitute revery for action. It is discomforting but true to say that involuntary crime brings him into the moral universe. At least this: a reader cannot fail to care about a man of good intentions who deserts a supposedly sinking ship, leaving eight hundred persons to die.

A further obvious remark on the humanity of great fictions is worth making, since critics rarely pause to make it: that the Lord Jims and Thomas Sutpens are more interesting and more attractive to us than they would have been had we met them in "real life." In real life (unaware of Sutpen's childhood or of his grand design) we might have shared all Miss Rosa's distaste for the "demon." Certainly we would have been disgusted by the surface personality of this somber and rude man. And in real life we might have felt toward Jim what Marlow professes to feel only once so strongly: "I perceived myself unexpectedly to be thoroughly sick of him. Why these vapourings?" We might dismiss as intolerable this aggressive yet overly sensitive man in his vanity and his clean white shoes, perpetually thrusting on us his introspections and excuses. We would probably not accept him as "one of us." And would we not, in real life, also turn away from the gross vulgarity of Jay Gatsby and his mass of silk shirts, or from the rugged brutality of Michael Henchard, or from the violent tirades of Ahab, or from the posturings of Emma Bovary, or from the lank ugliness and mad loquacity of Don Quixote? Or from Lear, Macbeth, perhaps even Hamlet? Art induces greater sympathies (but also sterner judgments) than most of us are capable of in the daily conduct of our lives; it compels us to live less indifferently, and frees us from the irrelevant. This does not mean that art, cheating us, is untrue to life, but that it asks for an intensified response to something "like life." In fiction we may, for one thing, be more than once spectators of the same event! The spectator in real life of Jim's death would indeed be inhuman who blamed him for his last "proud and unflinching glance," sent right and left after Doramin's shot. But the novel, especially on a rereading, legitimately asks us to decide whether Jim, still "at the call of his exalted egoism," is really in the clear at this moment; whether he is truly redeemed.

Lord Jim rests, then, on the bedrock of a great story and an important human situation; it has some appeal even for the casual reader who moves through a novel as clumsily as he moves through life. And yet it is, of course, an art novel, a novelist's novel, a critic's novel—perhaps the first important one in England after *Tristram Shandy*. This means that it becomes a different novel if read very attentively; or, becomes a different novel when read a second or third time. The usual Victorian novel surrenders most of its drama and meaning at a first rapid reading and thereafter becomes inert. If we return to *David Copperfield* after a year or twenty years and find it a different book from the one we remembered, this is not because the book has changed. It is we who have changed. But certain novels—*Benito Cereno* as a mild example, *Absalom, Absalom!* as an extreme one, *Lord Jim* somewhere between the two—do change. They do become different novels at a second attentive reading. The mere factual mysteries are solved, and no longer preoccupy us. We now know that Don Benito is not a villain, that Thomas Sutpen is the father of Charles Bon, that the *Patna* did not sink; we cannot twice be made dupes of deceptive appearance to the same degree. But now by the same token we can watch the drama of moral ambiguity as such, and the mechanisms of deception; and we can watch the observers or narrators of the action, their mistakes, their withheld or grudging commitments. The human situation becomes more rather than less complex. Yet we are at the same time somewhat freer to observe art as art: the game of management and grouping and perspective. And matters that merely baffled or exasperated at first, notably the "irrelevant" digressions, assume an ironic or clarifying force. Only at a second reading—only, specifically, when we have come to share most of Marlow's knowledge—can we begin fully to share or imagine his feelings: the horror he would have felt, for instance, during his interview with the dying Gentleman Brown. For we know now, as Marlow knew then, that Brown was responsible for the death of Jim, this "younger brother."

The difference is important and even generic: between the complex art novel and the novel that is, rather, a clear orderly imitation of life; between *Lord Jim* and *Middlemarch* or *Barchester Towers*. A great deal of confusion may be traced to the critic's refusal to recognize this difference as generic, and to his tacit assumption that all novels ought to accomplish whatever they are going to accomplish on a first reading. Normally, I should think, the critic ought to be concerned with the impression *Middlemarch* or *Barchester Towers* might make on an ideally alert first reading; neither novel intends a subtle or deceptive relationship with the reader. But the critic of *Lord Jim* and of most impressionist novels ought to be concerned, and ought to admit this frankly, with both first and subsequent readings, and especially with the latter. For the novel of psycho-moral ambiguity can never, reread, be quite the same book.

No amount of casual rereading, to be sure, will discover *Lord Jim*'s full complexity. Isn't this one secret purpose or at least value of Conrad's difficulty, as of Joyce's and Faulkner's: that it makes casual reading less likely? Anyone who truly cares for fiction cares for story, experiences sympathies and repulsions, is interested in places and lives different from his own. We may define a casual reader (and many professional critics are casual readers) as one who cares for little else. And who, above all, identifies very quickly with one of the characters on the basis of the most obvious appeal and thereafter refuses all other appeals. In a word, the reader becomes one of the characters himself; climbs into the book, and, having done so, turns all complex situations into simple ones. It is easy enough to separate the critical from the casual reader of *Lord Jim*, and not merely from that casual reader for the New York Tribune who remarked that "on a night of tropic calm the rotten craft goes to the bottom like a shot, with all hands save a few members of the crew." [2] For the casual reader usually

2. November 3, 1900, quoted by Gordan, pp. 294–95.

ignores or minimizes the important evidence *against* Lord Jim, is insensitive to ironic overtone and illustrative digression, assumes that Conrad wholly approved of his hero, and is quite certain that Jim "redeemed himself" in Patusan. Thus this casual reader, identifying with Jim so completely, is incapable of responding to the novel's suspended judgments and withheld' sympathies; he has committed himself, simply and unequivocally, to a highly equivocal personage. (Very rarely a casual reader is found who goes to the opposite extreme, and develops no sympathy for Jim at all.) So too, since his whole concern is with Jim, the casual reader regards Marlow as no more than an irritating technical device. And he responds not at all to structure and style, to the beauty and meaning inherent in the elaborate ironic play of recurrence and reflexive reference.

But even for a more alert reader, that first reading of *Lord Jim* is very different from a second. Can we remember a genuine first impression, unaffected by our later knowledge of what happened to the *Patna*? The conflict of judgment and sympathy would already exist, but in much simpler terms. Through four chapters, we would listen to an omniscient narrator, who gives us a distinctly ironic portrait of Jim: a man of "exquisite sensibility" who has "elected to conceal" some "deplorable faculty"; who as a boy in training dreamed of rescues but did not act when action was demanded, who could yet return at once to his self-deceptive dreams. And presently we see him on board the *Patna*, the chief mate of a steamer, still dreaming of heroic rescues. We then move to the court of inquiry: see Jim's shame and assume there is some reason for this shame. The officers must have deserted a sinking ship. At what point does our hypothetical first reader realize that the ship didn't sink? On page 32 the crazed chief engineer's remark that he saw her go down is referred to as a "stupid lie"; on page 50 Marlow speaks of an "unforeseen conclusion of the tale" and on the next page interjects, casually: "So that bulkhead held out after all." On page 60: "These sleeping pilgrims were destined to accomplish their whole pilgrimage to the bitterness of some other end." Conceivably our reader might not know what happened until page 82 ("towed successfully to Aden") or even until the French lieutenant refers very specifically to his own role in the salvage. But meanwhile he has come to sympathize with Jim as a conscientious man on a rack, who stayed to face the inquiry. He is hardly prepared to recognize how damaging it is—the evidence of this French lieutenant who stayed on board the *Patna* thirty hours and who recalls that the unloading of the pilgrims at Aden was accomplished in twenty-five minutes. The sympathetic reader is not likely to remember that Jim stayed on board twenty-seven minutes before jumping. These figures (rather deceptive, since the situations were not comparable and lifeboats were lacking) may have a sharply devaluing effect on later readings.

As with large conceptions, so with fine details of texture: a first valid and interesting effect may, on rereading, be replaced by a very different one. Consider, for instance, the elaborate description of the pilgrims steaming onto the *Patna*:

> They streamed aboard over three gangways, they streamed in urged by faith and the hope of paradise, they streamed in with a continuous tramp and shuffle of bare feet, without a word, a murmur, or a look back; and when clear of confining rails spread on all sides over the deck, flowed forward and aft, overflowed down the yawning hatchways, filled the inner recesses of the ship—like water filling a cistern, like water flowing into crevices and crannies, like water rising silently even with the rim.

At a first reading we watch these ghostly pilgrims with some detachment, though they and the rising water are secretly preparing us for disaster at sea; the tenor is "drowned" by the vehicle. In any event this seems to be a matter concerning only the reader and the narrator, who strikes us as rather literary. We are not particularly conscious of Jim as a possible watcher of the scene. But on a second reading we may see these flowing silent pilgrims and this drowning ship only through his eyes. And now the scene reminds us of something we have come to know fairly well: Jim's faculty of "swift and forestalling vision." It prepares us to accept more fully than before the fact that he will be immobilized by his power to imagine these same pilgrims in panic. Thus what had seemed a rather literary comment by a detached narrator is now, intimately, in character with Jim. He, not the author or narrator, is the dangerously "imaginative beggar."

One further example of reflexive reference will indicate how a second reading differs from a first. In Chapter 26, after a brief introduction of the chief Doramin and his son Dain Waris, Marlow summarizes Jim's account of his already legendary exploit: the capture of Sherif Ali's camp. "He has made himself responsible for success on his own head." Not a very disturbing remark, since we know that he was successful. And the portrait of Doramin may seem merely amusing. He is carried up the hill in his armchair, then sits with a pair of flintlock pistols on his knees. "Magnificent things, ebony, silver-mounted, with beautiful locks and a calibre like an old blunderbuss." They were, Jim adds, a present from Stein, in exchange for the talisman ring. All this may seem unimportant and digressive, no more than the small vivid details that confirm a novel's authority and actualize its scenes. But in fact the passage is dropping its associations—"Upon my head" . . . flintlock pistols . . . talisman ring—into the fringes of our consciousness; it is preparing us to respond to the full significance, a hundred and fifty pages later,[3] of Jim's words, "Upon my head." And above all preparing us to recognize and believe the Doramin of the last pages and those pistols on his knees: the deliberateness of the shooting, and the ironic closing of a circle as the ring rolls against Jim's foot. Thus the first reading. On a second reading of Chapter 26 those pistols reflect a light thrown backward; we respond very strongly to the scene itself and its tragic irony. For it reminds us—at the very moment that we hear about the greatest active success of Jim's life, in fact almost his only active success to reach us dramatically—of how the story will end: with Jim immobilized once more by a dream, and then immobile in death.

* * *

Lord Jim, then, is an intricate novel about possible emotional and moral responses to a relatively simple man, even to a "type" of man. However, it would be a mistake to dwell too much on Jim's simplicity, or to say that there's "nothing there." For this man repeatedly taken "unawares," and who is possessed by what he thinks he possesses, offers a major dramatic image of the will and the personality in conflict, of the conscious mind betrayed by the unconscious, of the intent rendered absurd by the deed. The conscious mind discovers, belatedly, what the betraying dark powers have accomplished: "I had jumped, it seems . . ." Just so Jim makes his more successful jump over the palisade in Patusan: "at once, without any mental process as it were, without any stir of emotion, he set about his escape as if executing a plan matured for a month." A little more addicted than most men to deliberate revery, Jim is a little more than most subject to the undeliberate unconscious mind and its sympathetic or hostile acts. This is best dramatized in the major scene of crippling identification with Gentleman Brown. But it also appears very interestingly in his compulsion to make others reënact his sudden jump from the *Patna*. This may be too elaborate a construction to put on Jim's act of throwing the crosseyed Dane, now of the Royal Siamese Navy, into the Menam river. But it does seem to account for his curious behavior in making the would-be assassins jump into the river in Patusan. There is a link with the *Patna* incident, in Conrad's imagination if not in Jim's unconscious, between the torch flung in the river and the *Patna*'s masthead light, which had seemed to drop "like a lighted match you throw down."

3. In this edition, ninety-one pages later (pp. 161 to 252) [*Editor*].

"Jump!" he thundered. The three splashes made one splash, a shower flew up, black heads bobbed convulsively, and disappeared . . . His heart seemed suddenly to grow too big for his breast and choke him in the hollow of his thoat. This probably made him speechless for so long, and after returning his gaze she flung the burning torch with a wide sweep of the arm into the river. The ruddy fiery glare, taking a long flight through the night, sank with a vicious hiss, and the calm soft starlight descended upon them, unchecked.

A novelistic portrait may show psychological intuition through its accurate dramatization of mental processes and significant notation of behavior. But it may also show it through the efficiency of its often unconscious symbolizing imagination. Significantly enough, if a hat does truly symbolize the personality, Jim turns up on board Marlow's ship without a hat, after throwing the Dane into the river. He has been stripped once again of his disguise, or stripped of his illusion of self. So it is at his most critical hours. He lost his cap, jumping from the *Patna*, and the next day the "sun crept all the way from east to west over my bare head." And when the time comes, at the end, to meet the fatal destiny, he is "fully dressed as for every day, but without a hat." Is it or is it not the *real* Jim who, hatless, takes the disaster "upon his own head" in pride and/or atonement?

Simple Jim may be. But there is nothing simple about Conrad's own understanding of him. We must, as always, except Dostoevsky: the first Freudian novelist and still the greatest dramatist of half-conscious and unconscious processes. And we have seen how *The Nigger of the "Narcissus,"* a symbolist study of identification, prepared the way. Otherwise, *Lord Jim* is perhaps the first major novel solidly built on a true intuitive understanding of sympathetic identification as a psychic process, and as a process which may operate both consciously and less than consciously. The fact that *Lord Jim* takes this process as its center long eluded its readers. But this does not mean that the subject and interest were not unequivocally "there," or that Conrad left matters unreasonably obscure. The fault was ours not his. We may put the case as we must often put it for Dostoevsky: that Conrad dramatized relationships which we could recognize as interesting and perhaps feel to be true, but which we could not accept or explain conceptually.

Dramatically as well as theoretically, *Lord Jim* is a story of sympathies, projections, empathies . . . and loyalties. The central relationship is that of Marlow and Jim. We can see why Jim needs Marlow, as an "ally, a helper, an accomplice." He cannot believe in himself unless he has found another to do so. And he needs a judge, witness, and advocate in the solitude of his battle with himself. All this is evident. But why does Marlow go so far out of his way, very far really, to help Jim? Why does Marlow need Jim? He speaks of the fellowship of the craft, of being his very young brother's keeper, of loyalty to "one of us," of mere curiosity, of a moral need to explore and test a standard of conduct. And we may say with much truth that this is a novel of a moving and enduring friendship between an older and a younger man. But Marlow—in several passages recalling *The Nigger of the "Narcissus"*'s central comment on identification—acknowledges a more intimate or more selfish alliance. He is loyal to Jim as one must be to another or potential self, to the criminally weak self that may still exist.

> Was it for my own sake that I wished to find some shadow of an excuse for that young fellow whom I had never seen before, but whose appearance alone added a touch of personal concern to the thoughts suggested by the knowledge of his weakness—made it a thing of mystery and terror—like a hint of a destructive fate ready for us all whose youth—in its day—had resembled his youth? I fear that such was the secret motive of my prying.

> He appealed to all sides at once—to the side turned perpetually to the light of day, and to that side of us which, like the other hemisphere of the moon, exists stealthily in perpetual darkness, with only a fearful ashy light falling at times on the edge.

> If he had not enlisted my sympathies he had done better for himself—he had gone to the very fount and origin of that sentiment, he had reached the secret sensibility of my egoism.

Marlow is not fatally paralyzed or immobilized by this young "double." But Big Brierly is. Brierly is successful, and seems to know nothing of indecision and self-mistrust:

> The sting of life could do no more to his complacent soul than the scratch of a pin to the smooth face of a rock. This was enviable. As I looked at him flanking on one side the unassuming pale-faced magistrate who presided at the inquiry, his self-satisfaction presented to me and to the world a surface as hard as granite. He committed suicide very soon after.
> No wonder Jim's case bored him, and while I thought with something akin to fear of the immensity of his contempt for the young man under examination, he was probably holding silent inquiry into his own case. The verdict must have been of unmitigated guilt, and he took the secret of the evidence with him in that leap into the sea.

Insofar as Brierly can explain matters to himself (or to Marlow) he feels humiliated, a white man and seaman, by Jim's evidence given in the presence of natives—"enough to burn a man to ashes with shame." He wants Jim to run away, and offers two hundred rupees to finance the evasion. But professional and racial pride are scarcely sufficient motives for suicide. Marlow sees, in retrospect, that "at bottom poor Brierly must have been thinking of himself" when he wanted Jim to clear out. He had recognized in Jim an unsuspected potential self; he had looked into himself for the first time. "If I understand anything of men, the matter was no doubt of the gravest import, one of those trifles that awaken ideas —start into life some thought with which a man unused to such a companionship finds it impossible to live."

Doubtless Conrad was interested in the case of Brierly (presumably based on the suicide of Captain Wallace of the *Cutty Sark*) in its own right. And for some readers it may exist as one of the many sources of a light thrown obliquely on Jim: possibly (by the very fact of the suicide) to magnify him and give his case importance; possibly (by the integrity of Brierly's last moments as a seaman) to devalue Jim the poor officer. But the episode's chief function is to prepare us to understand (or at least accept) Jim's paralyzed identification with Gentleman Brown and suicidal refusal to fight him; and to prepare us, also, for the deliberateness of Jim's march up to Doramin. The aesthetic principle may be obvious, but the execution of it is seldom easy—to prepare the reader to accept a "strangeness" of major importance and concern by first dramatizing that strangeness in a setting seemingly minor, anecdotal, neutral. And we will need to believe, dramatically if not conceptually, that interview with Gentleman Brown, since it is the direct cause of Jim's death.

The immediate preparation for the interview (Chapters 37–40) shows Conrad's impressionism at its most successful, dramatically speaking. We have an inkling from Brown, on his unclean deathbed, that Jim himself may be dead; we learn from the benumbed Tamb' Itam that Jim "would not fight," and from Jewel that "he had been driven away from her by a dream." Thus in Brown and his cutthroat crew, but also in what we know and recall of Jim's character, we see his destiny approach. It became probable from the moment Brown heard of Jim's power, and started upriver to seek his share of the loot. And thus we are conditioned, during Jim's absence, to see the chief menace of Brown as ruthless and cynical intelligence at the service of pure love of destruction; we expect a combat of wills. And such it turns out to be. "They faced each other across the creek, and with steady eyes tried to understand each other before they opened their lips. Their antagonism must have been expressed in their glances," Marlow suggests. "I know that Brown hated Jim at first sight."

The crafty Brown capitalizes at once on Jim's obvious reluctance to answer questions. He finds a way "as broad as a turnpike, to get in and shake his two penny soul around and inside out and up-side down—by God!" He asks Jim what had made him come to Patusan, what had scared him into this infernal hole, and even says something that would inevitably remind Jim of the *Patna*. It is one of the great dramatic scenes in Conrad: the cynical Brown's unerring discovery of his antagonist's weakness. "And there ran through the rough talk a vein of suble reference to their common blood, an assumption of common experience; a sickening sugges-tion of common guilt, of secret knowledge that was like a bond of their minds and of their hearts." It is a paralyzing, an immobilizing bond; and Jim refuses to fight. According to Morf, Jim immediately identifies himself with Brown, and identification "is characterized always by an extraordinary indulgence for the second self, an in-dulgence which must of necessity remain incomprehensible to any other person . . . Jim's indulgence for Brown is typical. He sim-ply cannot resist the evil *because the evil is within himself*." And his "unconscious wish is to see Brown (i.e., himself) go off free and powerful . . ."

It could be argued that Morf's phrasing is too blunt; it leaves little room for exceptions. And identification may lead to hostility rather than sympathy, as in a condemnation of self by proxy. Still Morf's analysis (which in 1947 struck me as largely mis-taken) now seems more accurate than my own rationalist explana-tion: that Jim's hard-won assurance was destroyed by the fact that the first visitor from the outside world brought a reminder of the *Patna*, and that Jim was unwilling to shed white men's blood. These are indeed possible related or additional motives for Jim's refusal to fight. But the emphasis Morf gives to half-conscious and unconscious identification is, I am now persuaded, correct. It is at the center of Conrad's psychology—as it was, almost con-temporaneously, at the center of André Gide's.

II

Not only the characters of a fiction experience such sympathies. The related central preoccupation of Conrad's technique, the heart of the impressionist aim, is to invite and control the reader's identifications and so subject him to an intense rather than passive experience. Marlow's human task is also the reader's: to achieve a right human relationship with this questionable younger brother. Marlow must resist an excessive identification (which would mean abandoning his traditional ethic); he must maintain a satisfactory balance of sympathy and judgment. No easy task, since Jim demands total sympathy. "He wanted an ally, a helper, an accomplice. I felt

the risk I ran of being circumvented, blinded, decoyed, bullied, perhaps, into taking part in a dispute impossible of decision if one had
to be fair to all the phantoms in possession—to the reputable that
had its claims and to the disreputable that had its exigencies." And
this is, far more than in most novels, the reader's moral drama and
situation: to be subjected to all the phantoms in possession, to be
exposed to a continuous subtle and flowing interplay of intellectual
appeals to his judgment and poignant appeals to his sympathy.

The reader must survive this experience and go through this
labyrinth of evidence without the usual guide of an omniscient
author or trustworthy author-surrogate. The reader (looking incor-
rigibly for the author's convictions and final decisions) is likely
to put his trust in Marlow, including the Marlow who speaks of
Jim's "greatness," "truth," and "constancy." But he does so at
his peril. Or he may put his trust, even more dangerously, in Stein,
Jim's fellow-romantic. Stein's wise and assured tones and his central position in the novel, geographically speaking, have led many
readers to assume that he conveys the author's judgment. It would
be much more accurate to say that Conrad's moral judgment is
isolated, if anywhere, in the austere nameless "privileged man" of
Chapter 36, and that his uncorrected sympathy is isolated in Stein.
(The "privileged man" would not admit that Jim had mastered his
fate, and maintained "that we must fight in the ranks or our lives
don't count.") Then to whom and to what should the reader
attend, if not to his professed guides? The answer of course is
that he should attend, eagerly yet skeptically, to everything: to
the moralizing of the guides, yes, but even more to every scrap of
evidence they offer by way of anecdote, disgression, example. The
reading of this novel is a combat: within the reader, between
reader and narrators, between reader and that watching and con-
trolling mind ultimately responsible for the distortions.

Doubtless the common impression left by a first reading is
that the formal rational evidence is preponderantly favorable to
Jim, and that the novel finally reaches a lenient verdict, even a
judgment of "approval." Jim emerges as, simply, a hero and a
redeemed man. But the evidence (as we discover on rereading) is
by no means preponderantly favorable; and Lord Jim is as much
a novel about a man who makes excuses as a novel that makes
excuses. Our first impression that the novel "approves" Jim turns
out to derive not from the area of rational evidence and judgment
but from the area of novelistic sympathy; we discover, as we look
a little more closely, that Marlow has repeatedly taken us in. He is
a considerably more lenient witness than his austere moralizing
tone suggests. On various occasions he brings in the damaging evi-

dence (he is, after all, obliged to bring it in) very casually and digressively, as though inviting us to overlook it. So too, when we are inclined to judge harshly, Marlow diverts our attention from the suffering, "burning" Jim to those who merely rot in the background, or who live safely in a world of untested rectitude. "You've been tried." Jim has, at least, been tested and tried. Therefore he exists. Marlow evokes both sympathy and a more lenient judgment whenever he reminds us of those who are safe: Marlow's listeners, or Jim's father sending his four-page letter of "easy morality and family news," or the tourists in the Malabar Hotel where Jim begins his story. Their irrelevance colors our response to Jim's very questionable denial that he was afraid of death: "They were exchanging jocular reminiscences of the donkeys in Cairo. A pale anxious youth stepping softly on long legs was being chaffed by a strutting and rubicund globe-trotter about his purchases in the bazaar. 'No, really—do you think I've been done to that extent?' he inquired very earnest and deliberate." When we return to Jim a moment later, we listen to him more attentively: " 'Some of the crew were sleeping on the number one hatch within reach of my arm,' began Jim again."

Such sudden corrective juxtaposition is at once the novel's characteristic way of redressing a balance of meaning and its chief way of moving us emotionally. It may operate in both directions, of course: correcting an excessive austerity of judgment or correcting an excessive sympathy. The matter is not easy to sum up, and my conclusion is perhaps debatable. But here it is: that on a first reading we are inclined to think Marlow's own judgment of Jim too harsh (since we have missed some of the evidence that led him to that judgment); that on a second reading (because we are discovering that evidence with a force of delayed impact) we may think Marlow's judgment too lenient. In other words, the unfavorable evidence that Marlow had half-concealed through deceptive casualness of manner grows upon us at a second or third reading, and becomes more difficult to discount. But meanwhile our natural sympathy for Jim—the center of attention, the man on the rack, the conscientious sinner, the man who has been "tried"—has correspondingly diminished. We have, in other words, the very reverse of the situation that pertains in *Absalom, Absalom!*, where the favorable evidence has been more than half-concealed. Hence, at a second reading, we think more not less of Thomas Sutpen. But the aesthetic principle, and the implicit assumption that a serious novel like a serious poem is meant to be read more than once, is the same.

The delicate interplay of sympathy and judgment, managed

with such ease in the novel itself, is difficult to describe. We may take, as an example of crucial evidence within deceptively unemphasized digression, the testimony of the Malay helmsman in Chapter 8. For some pages we have listened to Jim's own vivid account of his emotions after looking at the bulging bulkhead, and to Marlow's slightly more distant and meditative retelling; together they have taken us as close as we ever come to the original experience of quite understandable fear. We are *there* as Jim, thinking the ship may go at any moment, struggles with the pilgrim importuning him for water to drink; as back on the bridge he finds the officers trying to get one of the boats off the chocks. And at the moment of Jim's most urgent appeal for both sympathy and understanding—"Where was the kindness in making crazy with fright all those people I could not save single-handed—that nothing could save?"—Marlow characteristically withdraws to comment on Jim's longing for ally, helper, accomplice.

In the next paragraphs Marlow holds a very fine balance: reminding us of Jim's self-deceptions and weakness but also of his conscientious shame, magnifying the struggle through allusion and analogy, admitting his own allegiance. The effect at a first reading is to transfer our attention from Jim's dubious acts on board the *Patna* to the magnitude of his present "dispute with an invisible personality." When at last we get back to the *Patna*, Marlow not Jim does the telling, and we can see Jim, a not wholly ignoble figure, standing apart from the other officers and the boat. "The two Malays had meantime remained holding to the wheel"—only thoughtless, immobile figures, not even part of our moral universe. We are quickly diverted from them by the stunning retrospective information that the ship didn't sink. "And still she floated! These sleeping pilgrims were destined to accomplish their whole pilgrimage to the bitterness of some other end." Marlow remarks, casually, that the behavior of the two helmsmen was not "the least wonder of these twenty minutes."

We then move away from the *Patna* to the inquiry, where the two helmsmen were questioned, as for relief from dramatic and moral intensity. It is a moment for attention to flag. The first helmsman, when asked what he thought of matters at the time, says he thought nothing. The second "explained that he had a knowledge of some evil thing befalling the ship, but there had been no order; he could not remember an order; why should he leave the helm?" And the evidence he gives—if we attend to it, as we do on later readings—pricks Jim's balloon. Not the man on the rack and tortured sinner but the old Malayan helmsman devoted to and formed by the honest traditions of the sea is heroic. He defines himself when he pours out the names of skippers and ships. We are reminded of Conrad's pride in "these few bits of paper, headed by the names of a few Scots and English shipmasters."

To some further questions he jerked back his spare shoulders, and declared it never came into his mind then that the white men were about to leave the ship through fear of death. He did not believe it now. There might have been secret reasons. He wagged his old chin knowingly. Aha! secret reasons. He was a man of great experience, and he wanted *that* white Tuan to know —he turned toward Brierly, who didn't raise his head—that he had acquired a knowledge of many things by serving white men on the sea for a great number of years—and, suddenly, with shaky excitement he poured upon our spell-bound attention a lot of queer-sounding names, names of dead-and-gone skippers, names of forgotten country ships, names of familiar and distorted sound, as if the hand of dumb time had been at work on them for ages. They stopped him at last.

Marlow refers to the helmsman rightly as an "extraordinary and damning witness." But he is silenced, in the novel, very quickly indeed. And we are taken back to the ship. There follow thirty-five pages [4] of a detailed and tormented account of Jim's last minutes on board, of his jump "into an everlasting deep hole," of his harrowing time in the lifeboat with the "three dirty owls" and his day spent apart from them under a burning sun, deliberating whether to die. The reader cannot fail to take Jim's part against theirs, and is more and more tempted to take seriously his assertion that it was not *he* who had jumped. "I told you I jumped; but I tell you they were too much for any man. It was their doing as plainly as if they had reached up with a boathook and pulled me over." By the end of Chapter 11, recollecting his debates on suicide, Jim has again threatened to convert the *Patna* episode into an entirely interior affair.

Hence it is high time we return to material matters, to physical things and acts: to what might and might not have been done. And Marlow sweeps us ahead more than three years to his meeting with the French lieutenant of Chapters 12 and 13, who is perhaps the most damning witness and reflector of all. He too appears very casually, within a nominal digression, and I understand he is discounted by some readers as a stuffy and uninteresting figure. Marlow, who in these chapters clearly diverges from Conrad, would have liked so to dismiss him. But his role in the novel may be as crucial as Stein's; the scenes are in a way pendant. For Stein, the intellectual and dreamer who is also a successful man of action, Jim is "romantic"—which is very bad and "also very good." His

4. In this edition, twenty-one pages (pp. 61 to 82) [*Editor*].

dream and his anguish are what make him exist. But the French lieutenant, a moving figure of professional competence and integrity, and a man certainly capable of sympathy, at once calls attention to something else: Jim "ran away along with the others." Marlow the observer professes to be irritated by his stolid assurance. But Conrad obviously finds him both likable and admirable, and he has (like a Hemingway figure) the esoteric wound betokening virtue:

> This was absolutely the first gesture I saw him make. It gave me the opportunity to "note" a starred scar on the back of his hand—effect of a gunshot clearly; and, as if my sight had been made more acute by this discovery, I perceived also the seam of an old wound, beginning a little below the temple and going out of sight under the short grey hair at the side of the head—the graze of a spear or the cut of a sabre. He clasped his hands on his stomach again. "I remained on board that—that—my memory is going (s'en va). Ah! Patt-nà. C'est bien ça. Patt-nà. Merci. It is droll how one forgets. I stayed on board that ship thirty hours." [5]

Time "had left him hopelessly behind with a few poor gifts . . ." But, unlike Jim, he had done what had to be done. And of the thirty hours during which he remained on board the *Patna*, with two quartermasters stationed with axes to cut her clear of the tow if she sank, he chiefly remembers with irritation having had no wine to go with his food. He too was aware of the chief sources of danger, panic among the pilgrims and the "villainous" bulkhead. But he saw them as matters to be taken care of. The way to behave in crisis is to act efficiently. His words are distantly echoed, from one language to another, by Stein's account of an ambush:

> . . . this manoeuvre eased the strain on the bulkhead, whose state, he expounded with stolid glibness, demanded the greatest care (éxigeait les plus grands ménagements).

> "It was a little intrigue, you understand. They got my poor Mohammed to send for me and then laid that ambush. I see it all in a minute, and I think—this wants a little management. My pony snort, jump, and stand, and I fall slowly forward with my head on his mane."

At the end of the interview with the French lieutenant, Marlow is "discouraged about Jim's case." Earlier—noting the lieutenant's admission that everyone experiences fear, and his acknowledgment that Jim "might have had the best dispositions"—Marlow was glad to see him take "a lenient view." A suspicious reader

---

5. For instance, the arrow wound of the count in *The Sun Also Rises*.

might even suppose the lieutenant had begun to confess, on the preceding page, to an act of cowardice similar to Jim's. But the lieutenant means to do no such thing, and he does not take a lenient view. For he has "no opinion" as to what life is like when honor is gone. Hence he has not *acted* in cowardice. "I was confronted," Marlow says,

> by two narrow grey circlets, like two tiny steel rings around the profound blackness of the pupils. The sharp glance, coming from that massive body, gave a notion of extreme efficiency, like a razor-edge on a battle-axe. "Pardon," he said, punctiliously. His right hand went up, and he swayed forward. "Allow me . . . I contended that one may get on knowing very well that one's courage does not come of itself (*ne vient pas tout seul*). There's nothing much in that to get upset about. One truth the more ought not to make life impossible . . . But the honour—the honour, monsieur! . . ."

We do not, even after this second damning witness has spoken, get back to the Malabar House and Jim's narrative at once. Another reflector and witness appears, by way of a digressive development of a modifying clause: Bob Stanton. Marlow has been speaking of Jim's unglamorous mode of life as a water-clerk for De Jongh. Or is the business of an insurance canvasser, which "Little Bob Stanton" had been, even less glamorous? As with the French lieutenant, the introduction is casual and faintly ironic. And then we are told, as though it had no bearing on Jim's case, the story of Stanton's drowning while trying to save a lady's maid in the *Sephora* disaster. He too had done what had to be done. As chief mate he would leave no one on board a sinking ship; Jim had left eight hundred. Stanton reminds us of what the officer is expected to do, irrespective of temptation or mitigating circumstance. And at this point (after seventeen pages [6] of damaging evidence in the guise of digression) we return to Jim and his heroic introspections. "Clear out! Couldn't think of it," he replies, when Marlow offers Brierly's plan of escape. But we are less impressed than we would have been before listening to the French lieutenant and before hearing of Stanton's death.

The natural unreflective heroism of the French lieutenant and Stanton thus help to put Jim's reveries of heroism, and his actual failures and excuses, into a clearer perspective. We must remember that in every chapter and on every page the double appeal to sympathy and judgment is made, though one or the other may dominate; we are not being subjected to the blunt regular swings of a pendulum. Still, this is perhaps the point in the first part of

6. In this edition, ten pages (pp. 82 to 92) [*Editor*].

the novel where our view of Jim is most severe. The following chapter sets in a strong returning flow of sympathy. We see Jim's formal punishment delivered in a "chill and mean atmosphere. The real significance of crime is in its being a breach of faith with the community of mankind, and from that point of view he was no mean traitor, but his execution was a hole-and-corner affair." In a sense a proper judgment has been passed on Jim's romantic ego and his vulnerable idealism: *certificate canceled*. Then, and almost at once, we see Jim's version of "how to be" in the very different perspective of Chester's gross cynicism: Chester who wants someone "no good" for his guano island, and who regards Jim as "no good" because he takes his downfall to heart. "You must see things exactly as they are"—as Chester's partner Robinson did, who ate his comrades rather than starve, and afterward showed no remorse.[7] Marlow does not accept Chester's proposal. But he vivifies it sufficiently to make us more sympathetic with Jim's plight. And again, though in Marlow's imagination only, we have the "secret sharer" image of the guilty man alone under a burning sun: "I had a rapid vision of Jim perched on a shadowless rock, up to his knees in guano, with the screams of sea-birds in his ears, the incandescent ball of the sun above his head; the empty sky and the empty ocean all a-quiver, shimmering together in the heat as far as the eye could reach." The classic Promethean image of unending punishment magnifies Jim's suffering; it reminds us too of the moral isolation into which he will now enter more deeply than before. And the section ends (Chapters 15, 16, 17) with the not unsympathetic picture of Jim's long silent struggle with himself, while Marlow writes letter after letter. "He was rooted to the spot, but convulsive shudders ran down his back; his shoulders would heave suddenly. He was fighting, he was fighting—mostly for his breath, as it seemed." The "idea obtrudes itself that he made so much of his disgrace while it is the guilt alone that matters." Nevertheless the impression left, at the end

7. *Lord Jim* explores the fine distinctions between guilt and sense of disgrace yet remains ambivalent toward the character who—accepting what he has done as done—lives without remorse. Stein is such a man. But so too is Robinson, who three weeks after his rescue "was as well as ever. He didn't allow any fuss that was made on shore to upset him; he just shut his lips tight, and let people screech. It was bad enough to have lost his ship, and all he was worth besides, without paying attention to the hard names they called him."

In this connection, and though it may reflect only one of several moods, an 1891 letter from Conrad to Marguerite Poradowska is of interest: "Each act of life is final and inevitably produces its consequences in spite of all the weeping and gnashing of teeth and the sorrow of weak souls who suffer as fright grips them when confronted with the results of their own actions. As for myself, I shall never need to be consoled for any act of my life, and this because I am strong enough to judge my conscience rather than be its slave, as the orthodox would like to persuade us to be" (*Letters of Joseph Conrad to Marguerite Poradowska, 1890–1920*, translated and edited by John A. Gee and Paul J. Sturm, New Haven, 1940, p. 36).

of this part, is of a kind of stubborn courage.

This then is *Lord Jim's* chief way of provoking in its readers a strong human response and meaningful conflict: to interweave or suddenly juxtapose (rather than group logically and chronologically) the appeals to judgment and sympathy, to criticism and compassion. A man is what he does, which in Jim's case is very little that is not equivocal. But also he "exists" for us by the quality of his feeling and the poignant intensity of his dream. He is not "good enough" (as Marlow tells Jewel, as the Malay helmsman and other witnesses verify) yet his childish romanticism may be preferable to a cynical realism. In any event, as Marlow goes on to say, "nobody is good enough." This is not a relativistic conclusion. It reminds us rather how strong Marlow's moral and community engagement was, against which his brotherly and outlaw sympathy contended.

These peculiar groupings—of incident and witness and evidence, of intellectual and emotional appeal—distinguish *Lord Jim* from most earlier fiction. But imagery also leaves us in provisional and perhaps lasting uncertainty. Is Jim "in the clear"? The novel's chief recurrent image is of substance and reality obscured, often attractively so, by mist or by deceptive light. *Fog, mist, cloud,* and *veil* form a cluster with *moonlight*, and with *dream*, to dramatize certain essential distinctions: between the conscious mind and the unconscious, illusion and reality, the "ego-ideal" and the self's destiny as revealed by its acts. Imagery is supposed to reveal an author's ultimate and perhaps unconscious bias. But much of the imagery here is grouped fairly consciously as part of a multiple appeal to the reader. These images—if they do form a cluster, if we do properly take them together—should help determine the delicate relationship of idealism and self-deception. And hence they should help us to evaluate Stein's advice ("follow the dream") and Jim's ultimate conduct in Patusan, when opportunity comes to his side, veiled like an Eastern bride.

At a first reading all this imagery of nebulosity may magnify and glamorize Jim (as fog magnifies Wordsworth's sheep), and also may be partly responsible for our first impression that Jim is an exceedingly mysterious person. But its later effect may be to persuade us that Stein is not, unequivocally, a spokesman for the author, and to throw still further doubt on Jim's "redemption" in Patusan. "I ask myself whether his rush had really carried him out of that mist in which he loomed interesting if not very big, with floating outlines—a straggler yearning inconsolably for his humble place in the ranks."

The meaning of *mist*, as we look at its various appearances, is clearer than we might have expected. It can refer generally to am-

biguity but more centrally refers to the aura of deception and
self-deception that surrounds Jim's reality. Now and then Marlow has a "glimpse through a rent in the mist in which he moved
and had his being," as Jim says something truly revealing: as he
tells of his impulse to go back to the spot of the *Patna*'s abandonment, or as he recognizes the good Marlow does him by listening.
But the mists close again at once when Jim refers to his plights
as "unfair." Thus we may call the mist his illusion of self
or ego-ideal, which is in turn responsible for the deceptions; it
may impose the "mask" of a "usual expression." Reality can then
appear in an "unconscious grimace," or through rifts caused by
the inward struggles. He stumblingly reveals the truth; or, we
stumble upon it. "The muscles round his lips contracted into an
unconscious grimace that tore through the mask of his usual expression—something violent, short-lived, and illuminating like a
twist of lightning that admits the eye for an instant into the
secret convolutions of a cloud." The provocative reality in this
instance was a fact normally evaded: that he was in the lifeboat with
the others. Or, "The mist of his feelings shifted between us, as if
disturbed by his struggles, and in the rifts of the immaterial veil
he would appear to my staring eyes distinct of form and pregnant
with vague appeal like a symbolic figure in a picture." This questionable sentence would suggest that the "real" Jim behind the
apparent one has the vague symbolic appeal. Very possibly this
dubious phrasing simply came to Conrad, who refused to examine it
closely.

Still, we can say that mist, fog, and veil conceal or blur reality.
So too does moonlight, whose "occult power" can rob things of
their reality: "It is to our sunshine, which—say what you like—is
all we have to live by, what the echo is to the sound: misleading
and confusing whether the note be mocking or sad. It robs all
forms of matter—which, after all, is our domain—of their substance, and gives a sinister reality to shadows alone." Dorothy
Van Ghent advances an interesting argument: that the split conical
hill on Patusan suggests Jim's spiritual cleavage, and the moon rising between the two halves suggests a "figure of the ego-ideal"
with its "illusionariness, and the solitude implied by illusion." [8]
The moonlight of Patusan is certainly associated with immobility
and isolation, and with times when Jim is seriously entranced by
his pride and illusions of success. This moonlight comments on
the unreality of his aspirations. So too (when Jim still confuses
guilt with disgrace, and thus comes "no nearer to the root of the
matter") Marlow notes the "irresistible slow work of the night

8. This may be true, though the split
hill exists in the "source" of Brooke's
memoirs. The imagination makes its
significant selections from reality.

settling on all the visible forms, effacing the outlines . . ." But if the light of the moon is associated with illusion and a blurring of reality, the dark of the moon can be a very important reality, and one largely responsible for our acts: the unconscious itself. "He appealed to all sides at once—to the side turned perpetually to the light of day, and to that side of us which, like the other hemisphere of the moon, exists stealthily in perpetual darkness, with only a fearful ashy light falling at times on the edge." Whatever their sympathies in the matter, Marlow and Conrad clearly believe that we shall be saved by the sunlight of action and that deceptive half-lights are menacing.

All this (if we are to trust Marlow at all) has an important bearing on Stein's ambiguous advice: to submit yourself to the "destructive element" of the ego-ideal; to attempt through action to realize (or live with?) that illusion of self; to "follow the dream." Jewel remarks, very accurately, that Jim "had been driven away from her by a dream." Marlow's introduction ("one of the most trustworthy men I had ever known") together with Stein's grave tones and the memorably cryptic quality of his utterance create an initial confidence. At a first reading we naturally identify Stein's judgment and Conrad's. But the imagery which occurs to Marlow, immediately after Stein gives his advice, seems to say something very different. It associates Stein and his "conviction" with the half-lights of deception and menacing illusion; it brings Stein down to Jim's level rather than raises Jim to his. We cannot be sure what Conrad thought about Stein. Neither, possibly, could Conrad himself. This is Marlow's comment:

> The whisper of his conviction seemed to open before me a vast and uncertain expanse, as of a crepuscular horizon on a plain at dawn—or was it, perchance, at the coming of the night? One had not the courage to decide; but it was a charming and deceptive light, throwing the impalpable poesy of its dimness over pitfalls —over graves. His life had begun in sacrifice, in enthusiasm for generous ideas; he had travelled very far, on various ways, on strange paths, and whatever he followed it had been without faltering, and therefore without shame and without regret. In so far he was right. That was the way, no doubt. Yet for all that the great plain on which men wander amongst graves and pitfalls remained very desolate under the impalpable poesy of its crepuscular light, overshadowed in the center, circled with a bright edge as if surrounded by an abyss full of flames. When at last I broke the silence it was to express the opinion that no one could be more romantic than himself.

"One had not the courage to decide . . ." The passage, which sounds perilously close to deliberate double talk, probably owes some of its ambiguity to Conrad's inner conflicts discussed in the first chapter. For here the idealist, the skeptic, and the outlaw ("strange paths . . . without regret") all have their say. The ambiguity of Stein's remarks on the "destructive element" (which have regrettably come to mean anything any casual reader wants them to mean) may derive from the same conflicts. Conrad wants both the dreamer and the man who acts to survive: ". . . with the exertions of your hands and feet in the water make the deep, deep sea keep you up." But there is also a rhetorical ambiguity in the famous passage, which derives from our habit of thinking of the ideal or the illusory as "higher," and of air as higher than water. This is no doubt one reason why readers are tempted to equate the "destructive element" with life, action, and so on, and the air with ideal illusion. But the passage, which is prefaced by a reference to the "dream" as the dream of what we would like to be, doesn't say that. The dream is equated with the ideal of self or ego-ideal *and* with the sea *and* with the destructive element:

> "A man that is born falls into a dream like a man who falls into the sea. If he tries to climb out into the air as inexperienced people endeavour to do, he drowns—*nicht wahr?* . . . No! I tell you! The way is to the destructive element submit yourself, and with the exertions of your hands and feet in the water make the deep, deep sea keep you up."

Or: *A man is born ready to create an idealized conception of self, an ego-ideal. If he tries to escape or transcend this conception of self, he collapses. He should accept this ideal and try through action to make it "viable."* (Which is very far from the frequent reading: *man must learn to live with his unideal limitations.*)

But this has become a very dark saying—not only because we think of the ideal as something that transcends, of the ideal as higher, of air as more illusory than water, but also because we think of those who submit to the ego-ideal as "inexperienced" and of those who try to correct it as "experienced." The passage turns out to say something very different from what it appeared to say. There are several possibilities here, including one seldom considered in discussions of famous passages: that Conrad produced without much effort a logically imperfect multiple metaphor, liked the sound of it, and let matters go at that. There is also the possibility that Conrad wanted to show Stein giving confused advice. And there is the very real possibility that Conrad made less distinction between "ego" and "ego-ideal" than we are now accustomed to make. (If the "dream" is equated with "ego" we have less trouble with the climbing into air.) But whether we begin with the ego or with the ideal which, having originated in the ego, carries its own destruction within it, we can probably ascribe to Conrad the pessimism he ascribes to Anatole France:

> He knows that our best hopes are irrealisable; that it is the almost incredible misfortune of mankind, but also its highest privilege, to aspire towards the impossible; that men have never failed to defeat their highest aims by the very strength of their hsmanity which can conceive the most gigantic tasks but leaves them disarmed before their irremediable littleness.[9]

Lord Jim has its great structural innovations and successes. What shall we say of its alleged formal weakness: its apparent break into two separate novels, with the second one inferior to the first? A division into two parts certainly exists: the first concerned with Jim's introspective response to the *Patna* incident, the second with his adventurous "second chance" in Patusan. "You've put your finger on the plague spot," Conrad wrote to Garnett concerning this division. A story of continuing distress or slow deterioration might have been more symmetrical. But the very echoing of the crucial names—*Patna, Patusan*—suggests why we must have that second part. The most remote place and unrelated circumstance discovers, in us, the character with which we set out. "A clean slate, did he say? As if the initial word of each our destiny were not graven in imperishable characters upon the face of a rock." There is an aesthetic reason for the Patusan chapters fully as compelling: that by Chapter 17 a story of passive suffering (though the subject was by no means exhausted) threatened to exhaust the reader. Some outlet in action, or at least the illusion of such an outlet, had become necessary. And it is in fact astonishing to see, as we look back, how little has happened in those seventeen chapters in a fictional present time. We have had Jim's gestures as he talks; Marlow and Jim have had their misunderstanding over "cur"; Marlow has had his conversations with Chester and Brierly and Jim has refused Brierly's offer; Marlow has pressed upon him a letter of recommendation. And that is about all.

At the end of Chapter 17 Jim sets out with renewed confidence; his last words are "clean slate." Chapters 18–20 may be regarded as transitional: the first two on Jim's retreat "in good order towards the rising sun," as he throws up various jobs; the third on the famous interview with Stein, who sends Jim to Patusan. The second part of the novel would then begin with Chapter 21, or at the latest with Chapter 22 and Marlow's forestatement of Jim's initial success in Patusan. And its surface material is that of military and political adventure in a remote exotic setting. We may further divide this "second part" in two. Chapters 22–35 deal

9. *Notes on Life and Letters*, New York, 1926, p. 33.

with the period of Jim's success and carry us to the end of Marlow's original narrative. Chapters 36–45 deal with the Gentleman Brown incident and Jim's ruin.

It would be pedantic to attach much importance to the fact that *Lord Jim* divides into parts (most novels of its length do) or to be seriously concerned about the shocks of transition. For these shocks are slight, and are not to be blamed on Patusan. The major break comes not with the introduction of the Patusan material (Chapters 21, 22) but with the end of Marlow's oral narrative (Chapter 35). The important question is whether the novel and its reader are violated in a serious way: either because the material of the second half contradicts the material of the first and devalues it, or because Conrad imagined this material less well, or because it is intrinsically less interesting, or because it demands from us an entirely different kind of attention. Is there, that is, any damaging change in the delicate relationship of author-material-reader?

These questions must be asked, more specifically, of Chapters 22–35. For this section of the novel, exciting enough at a first reading, does not bear much rereading. The later chapters (36–45), though "adventurous" and "romantic," are very moving; they recover the *authenticity in depth* of the first part. There, once again we are watching character in action; not luck but destiny. And I think this points to the serious weakness of Chapters 22–35: that the adventures—the wearisome matter of getting the guns up the hill, for instance—have nothing to do with the essential Jim. Hence Conrad (who is less interested in or less convinced by this other Jim) gives a disproportionate attention to the Patusan background. Or can we say—following upon Gordan's demonstration that this successful Jim was based to some degree on James Brooke of Sarawak—that Conrad was here too bemused by his sources? For a while the appalling success of the historic Brooke must have made Jim's introspections seem unimpotant; the physical perils are emphasized, not the perils of soul. Marlow now and then steps in to remind us that all this fed Jim's romantic egoism, these successes and physical dangers overcome. But for pages on end the reader is allowed to forget this moral problem and theme. We may add that a characteristic mediocrity sets in with the introduction of Jewel in Chapter 28: with women and their frightening "extra-terrestrial touch," the second standard ingredient of exotic romance. But Chapters 25–27 (on the defeat of Sherif Ali) seem the weakest of all on later readings.

The technical problem for Conrad, at this point in the novel, was a grave one. Only a continuation of the impressionistic method, he must have reasoned, could bridge the gap between the two parts: cover not only the separation of Marlow from Jim and the passage of time, but also the sharp change from passive suffering to adventurous action. Perhaps the reader, caught in the old familiar web and involuted structure, would not try to escape? The reasoning was sound enough, so far as it went. Yet the impressionistic method is one real source of our irritation with Chapters 25–27, since it has no intrinsic justification. For the method is designed to evoke complex, wavering, suspended responses to infinitely debatable psycho-moral questions; the intricacies and evasions are justified by the fullness of human involvement. But 'here is little in the three chapters to warrant such reader involvement. They deal with nothing more ambiguous than practical maneuvers: a military action that did or did not succeed.

But this must not be exaggerated. In a novel of great and subtle artistry this structural flaw is one of the few aesthetic facts easy to detect and isolate, hence easy to overemphasize. There is, for instance, no collapse in style as we move into the Patusan material, only a very slight change to suggest that Conrad's creative relationship to the story has changed. With Chapter 37 Marlow begins to *write*, though nominally for only one reader: the "privileged man." But a slight significant change to a more written style had already occurred in Chapters 21 and 22. It suggests that (as Marlow loses his intimate touch with *listeners*) Conrad's own attitude becomes more detached. The style in Chapter 21 now and then approaches that of *The Mirror of the Sea:* "We wander in our thousands over the face of the earth, the illustrious and the obscure, earning beyond the seas our fame, our money, or only a crust of bread; but it seems to me that for each of us going home must be like going to render an account." The distinction between one style and another is a rather delicate one, especially since the speaking Marlow possesses the richness and variety of a written style and the writing Marlow preserves the best qualities of voice. The first of the following passages, though elaborate, keeps the illusion of a man speaking aloud to men; the second, though it has a quality of voice, is essentially "written." The difference comes, among other things, from a higher degree of abstraction in the second passage. There is more of a "novelistic" impulse in the first, no doubt, but both are well done:

> But she turned her back on them as if in disdain of their fate: she had swung round, burdened, to glare stubbornly at the new danger of the open sea which she so strangely survived to end her days in a breaking-up yard, as if it had been her recorded fate to die obscurely under the blows of many hammers. What were the various ends their destiny provided for the pilgrims I am unable

to say; but the immediate future brought, at about nine o'clock next morning, a French gunboat homeward bound from Réunion.

It seems impossible to believe that mere greed could hold men to such a steadfastness of purpose, to such a blind persistence in endeavour and sacrifice. And indeed those who adventured their persons and lives risked all they had for a slender reward. They left their bones to lie bleaching on distant shores, so that wealth might flow to the living at home. To us, their less tried successors, they appear magnified, not as agents of trade but as instruments of a recorded destiny, pushing out into the unknown in obedience to an inward voice, to an impulse beating in the blood, to a dream of the future.

The second passage, frankly expository and transitional, is not of course typical of the later chapters. But it does suggest the greater distance or at least altered angle from which Conrad now looked at his story. The solitary white man adventuring into the interior, there to traffic with the natives and become their virtual ruler, and who is presently possessed by what he possesses—such a figure had fascinated Conrad from the first. At the two extremes of fortune might be the Georges Antoine Klein, or Kurtz, who died on board the *Roi des Belges* and the James Brooke who became Rajah of Sarawak, founding a dynasty which lasted until very recently, and one of the world's great fortunes. Both—together with an officer of the *Jeddah* who was not fast enough to get away with the others and so stumbled into undeserved heroism, and together with the braggart Jim Lingard whom Conrad had met—may have gone into the dreaming of *Lord Jim*.[1] But Conrad could dream failure more easily than he could dream success. He could imagine magnificently the failure of Kurtz (when he broke away from *Lord Jim* to write "Heart of Darkness"). And he could imagine magnificently Jim's failure and death. What he could not imagine, at the same level of intensity and belief, was Jim's period of success.

Discussions of *Lord Jim*, concerned as they are with interpretative and structural problems, regularly neglect the purely novelistic side of vivid particular creation. Mine has been no exception. Yet without the particulars of place and person, without the finely evoked atmospheres and brilliant minor vignettes, the novel's amount of brooding debate might have become intolerable. Its pleasures in any event would have been different ones. Page by page, *Lord Jim*'s consistent great appeal largely depends on its changing of the lens, on its sudden shifts from a distant and often

1. Gordan, pp. 57–73.

nebulous moral perspective to a grossly and superbly material foreground. Marlow's tendency to make such shifts is his most personal
and most useful mannerism. It lends reality to the unsubstantial
reveries, as gross substance is bound to do, yet invites us to look at
them more critically. But most of all it offers the pleasure of a
creative surprise. Thus (to take a fine example of sudden rescue
from the vague and vast) Cornelius interrupts Marlow's revery,
which once again has indulged its fondness for the old problem of
"illusion":

> . . . I have that feeling about me now; perhaps it is that feeling
> which has incited me to tell you the story, to try to hand over to
> you, as it were, its very existence, its reality—the truth disclosed
> in a moment of illusion.
>
> Cornelius broke upon it. He bolted out, vermin-like, from the
> long grass growing in a depression of the ground. I believe his
> house was rotting somewhere near by, though I've never seen it,
> not having been far enough in that direction. He ran towards me
> upon the path; his feet, shod in dirty white shoes, twinkled on
> the dark earth: he pulled himself up, and began to whine and
> cringe under a tall stovepipe hat. His dried-up little carcass was
> swallowed up, totally lost, in a suit of black broadcloth.

Conrad's success with such minor figures is (as we look back on
the earlier work and forward to *Nostromo*) one of the substantial
advances registered by *Lord Jim*. Cornelius, Marlow remarks, merely
skulks on the "outskirts" of the story. But the account of his trembling attempt to get rid of Jim is fine dramatic writing. Through a
slight narrative distance (we are never told in so many words what
Cornelius intends) we watch him try to sell Jim protection for
eighty dollars, then hover outside the house in the darkness, apparently waiting to see him killed. We know his intentions by his behavior when Jim appears unexpectedly: the way he ducks sideways
as though shot at, his panic as he clings to the rail of the verandah,
his "faint shriek" when Jim appears again.

Criticism, it may be, pays too little attention to the vivid minor
figure, and to the pleasure and actualizing effect of the surprise. *Lord
Jim* obviously depends very heavily on intellectual surprise, as the
reader is compelled to make large and sudden adjustments and resolve conflicting demands. But the lesser surprises are important
too. The German captain of the *Patna*, for instance, reaches us
through a series of surprises. He is created by them. He is dramatically introduced, after a long elevated passage on the pilgrims coming aboard the *Patna*, by his brief remark: "Look at dese cattle
. . ." And a surprise may be most effective when it proves to be
true in an unexpected way. The fanciful metaphor to convey his
voice has its exactness: "From the thick throat of the commander of

the *Patna* came a low rumble, on which the sound of the word *schwein* fluttered high and low like a capricious feather in a faint stir of air." Presently we see him (who also is being taken "unawares") slide into the harbor office and Archie Ruthvel's presence: "something round and enormous, resembling a sixteen-hundred-weight sugar-hogshead wrapped in striped flannelette, up-ended in the middle of the large floor space." And finally we see him drive off in the gharry to the astonishment of his subordinates, the monstrous fatness somehow squeezed into that "little box on wheels":

> . . . but it only sank with a click of flattened springs, and suddenly one venetian blind rattled down. His shoulders reappeared, jammed in the small opening; his head hung out, distended and tossing like a captive balloon, perspiring, furious, spluttering. He reached for the gharry-wallah with vicious flourishes of a fist as dumpy and red as a lump of raw meat. He roared at him to be off, to go on. Where? Into the Pacific, perhaps. The driver lashed; the pony snorted, reared once, and darted off at a gallop. Where? To Apia? to Honolulu? He had 6,000 miles of tropical belt to disport himself in, and I did not hear the precise address. A snorting pony snatched him into "ewigkeit" in the twinkling of an eye, and I never saw him again . . .

A connected account of *Lord Jim* (unless it is to rival the novel in length) is bound to neglect such fine particulars. Thus a discussion of Chapter 14 must mention Jim's loss of his certificate and the cynicism of Chester's offer. But our living experience of the chapter is no little affected by the plaintiff in the assault case: "an obese chocolate-coloured man with shaved head, one fat breast bare and a bright yellow caste-mark above the bridge of his nose, sat in pompous immobility: only his eyes glittered, rolling in the gloom, and the nostrils dilated and collapsed violently as he breathed." It is affected infinitely more, of course, by the brief portrait of Captain Robinson, who had once been reduced to cannibalism. Chester's story is made vivid in classical fictional ways:

> ". . . a boat of Her Majesty's ship *Wolverine* found [Robinson] kneeling on the kelp, naked as the day he was born, and chanting some psalm-tune or other; light snow was falling at the time. He waited till the boat was an oar's length from the shore, and then up and away. They chased him for an hour up and down the boulders, till a marine flung a stone that took him behind the ear providentially and knocked him senseless. Alone? Of course . . ."

This is fine enough, and credible enough. But the great fictional stroke was to interrupt Chester's talk with the appearance of Captain Robinson himself, a doddering and "amiable" old man:

An emaciated patriarch in a suit of white drill, a solah topi with a green-lined rim on a head trembling with age, joined us after crossing the street in a trotting shuffle, and stood propped with both hands on the handle of an umbrella. A white beard with amber streaks hung lumpily down to his waist. He blinked his creased eyelids at me in a bewildered way. "How do you do? how do you do?" he piped, amiably, and tottered. "A little deaf," said Chester aside.

The naked chanting Robinson and the Robinson with amber-streaked white beard, the plaintiff with his one fat breast bare and eyes rolling in the gloom, the monstrously fat captain of the *Patna* and the monstrously fat Doramin, the slinking Cornelius and his twinkling white shoes, Gentleman Brown and the "sunken glare of his fierce crow-footed eyes"—all alike remind us of the old paradox: that the successfully achieved grotesque has a kind of fictional reality that the flat and commonplace seldom attains. Conrad will show even more of this novelistic creativity, this intense visual and dramatic surprise, in *Nostromo*.

ELOISE KNAPP HAY

Lord Jim: From Sketch to Novel †

"Tuan Jim: A Sketch," Conrad's original version of the first two chapters of *Lord Jim*, has rested in Harvard's manuscript collection for almost forty-three years—since the year following Conrad's death, when Jessie Conrad, his widow, harassed by a long sequence of unhappy events in her family and nearly incapacitated by lameness and diabetes, felt compelled to let it go.

I call it a version, for it is certainly more than a draft of the opening chapters we know. The penciled manuscript fills twenty-eight pages (fourteen recto and fourteen verso) in a small notebook. It presents a fully suggestive account of Lord Jim's self-exile "from the haunts of white men," a flashback to his years in the English merchant service, the shipboard accident that landed him in the hospital of an Eastern port, and his decision while convalescing to leave the "harder conditions" of the home service for an easy berth aboard the *Patna*. The manuscript Chapter Two ends roughly at the close of Chapter Two in the finished novel, with Jim on watch on the rusty old ship, sailing monotonously toward the entrance of the Red Sea.

This beginning, which Conrad dropped completely although he

† *Comparative Literature,* XII (Fall 1960), 289–309. Reprinted by permis-   sion with revisions by the author.

used much of its thought and even many of its sentences in the novel he finally published in 1900, is apparently the start he referred to when he wrote:

> my first thought was of a short story, concerned only with the pilgrim ship episode; nothing more. And that was a legitimate conception. After writing a few pages, however, I became for some reason discontented and I laid them aside for a time.

Although the "Tuan Jim" version of the novel's beginning has been available in print for several years,[1] there has been no published comment on the differences between this first draft and the final opening of the novel, and on what these differences might suggest concerning Conrad's original idea for the novel. Without indulging here in a word-by-word comparison of the two versions, we may note one important addition Conrad made while writing for the serial publication that began in October 1899.[2] The Harvard manuscript gives us nothing of Jim's tendency to cast himself in the role of a hero—a tendency which, in the serial version as in all editions of the book, was already fully developed in the first chapter, when Jim, as a boy aboard a training ship, met his first emergency situation, and failed in it.

The beginning of the Harvard manuscript is similar to the later version in that it opens with a visual impression of Jim after "the Intolerable drove him away from the haunts of white men." At this point Jim is serving as water clerk to a ship's chandler in an Eastern port—or various Eastern ports, to be exact. In the published version, but not in the Harvard manuscript, the first chapter then gives us a four-page flashback to Jim's boyhood, telling of his decision to go to sea "after a course of light holiday literature," his apprenticeship aboard a "training-ship for officers of the mercantile marine," and his habit aboard ship of dreaming that he was "a man destined to shine in the midst of dangers." The published first chapter alone concludes with the account of a collision near the training ship during a gale, the boys scrambling into a cutter, and one of the boys heroically rescuing a man from the water. But Jim "stood still," paralyzed by the confusion of the emergency, his imagination lost in his dreams, unable to adjust to the immediate requirements of

1. *Conrad Zywy*, ed. Wit Tarnawski, London, 1957. The manuscript, transcribed by Alexander Janta, is of course published in English, though the text of the book is Polish. A helpful English summary of the essays is appended. [The manuscript is reprinted above, pp. 283–91. Editor.]

2. *Blackwood's Magazine*, CLXVI (1899), 441–59. The serial ran for fourteen numbers, ending in November 1900. Many minor changes were made

after the serialization for the book. For a discussion of these and the difference between the English and American editions, see John D. Gordan, *The Making of a Novelist*, Cambridge, 1940, pp. 150–73; and George Whiting, "Conrad's Revision of *Lord Jim*," *English Journal* (College ed.), XXIII (1934), 824. In my essay I am concerned only with the major changes between sketch and novel, which would hold true for all published forms of the novel.

the situation. Then he wakes up and feels cheated, also contemptuous of the hero of the occasion: "The gale had ministered to a heroism as spurious as its own pretence of terror."

Eight chapters later in the novel we learn that the same paralysis, "a strange illusion of passiveness," came over him when the *Patna* struck the submerged derelict. According to Marlow, who visualizes the catastrophe of the *Patna* with sympathetic insight, Jim's paralysis was the result not of an inert mentality but of an overactive imagination: "you must remember he was a finished artist in that peculiar way, he was a gifted poor devil with the faculty of swift and forestalling vision. The sights it showed him had turned him into cold stone . . ." Coleridge's diagnosis of Hamlet's disability fits Jim very well. Jim's mind is afflicted by the "morbid excess" of one faculty, which leads him in critical moments to lose the "*equilibrium* between the real and the imaginary worlds," as a result of which "the images of his fancy are far more vivid than his actual perceptions." [3]

The effect of adding the training ship episode in the novel is more than incidental. It gives us a quick insight into the nature of Jim's "tragic flaw," which is then further revealed in Chapter Two. It illuminates, moreover, an aspect of Jim's fatal imagination that apparently had not occurred to Conrad when he was writing the sketch. Originally he had left the discussion of Jim's imagination until Chapter Two. Another of Jim's attributes—his ability—was more or less the subject of the original Chapter One. (It is perhaps significant that in the original manuscript Conrad capitalized "Ability" in Chapter One and did not capitalize "imagination" in Chapter Two. In the book "Ability" is capitalized in the first chapter and "Imagination" is also capitalized in the second.) Conrad's discussion of Jim's imagination in Chapter Two of the sketch is very similar to his revised discussion of it in the same chapter of the novel, but in the original sketch we must rely on what we learn in Chapter Two alone for our knowledge of Jim's early temperament.

In both "Tuan Jim" and the published novel we are told that, after Jim finished his training and went to sea, before he joined the *Patna*, there was only one occasion on which the "magic monotony . . . the prosaic severity" of the seaman's life had been interrupted

3. Samuel Taylor Coleridge, "Hamlet," *Complete Works*, ed. W. G. Shedd, New York, 1884, IV, 145. A sense of impending disaster, probably founded in childhood memories, seems to have been as ingrained in Conrad's temperament as it was in Lord Jim, who had had no such childhood experience. (Hence, perhaps, Conrad's inability to understand why Jim's sensitivities puzzled many of his English readers.) Conrad's early life, as seen through his uncle Tadeusz Bobrowski's letters particularly, makes us wonder to what extent his chronic drift toward reverie may have caused his fear of emergency situations—his fear aboard the *Vidar* that he would go blind like Captain Whalley, for instance—and to what extent his tendency to dreaming was itself caused by early experiences of disaster.

for him by an emergency situation. In a storm so violent that his ship nearly foundered, a storm in which there appeared "on the face of facts a sinister violence of intention," he had been struck by a falling spar and consigned to his cabin for the rest of the voyage. When inactivity was thus forced upon him, his "faculty of swift and forestalling vision" atrophied. "Imagination, the enemy of men, the father of all terrors, unstimulated, sinks to rest in the dulness of exhausted emotion." This is the crucial psychological "event" of Chapter Two in both versions.

At this point in the finished book, however, we realize that for Jim "imagination" has two striking features, has in fact a dual nature. On one side, so to speak, it carries him away from "reality" with images of his own possible heroic actions. On the other, when an emergency strikes, his imagination magnifies the horror beyond all grasp. Both aspects of this faculty working together rob him of the motor responses he needs in order to deal with experience. Because of the paralysis such an imagination forces upon him, he fails both aboard the *Patna* and later in Patusan, when the villainous Brown accidentally touches upon his old failure, reminding him of its tyrannous power over him and challenging him in effect to prove his mastery over it. Of course Jim remains its victim. Having pursued his dream of heroism and rehabilitation to a new land where he could begin anew, he has indeed driven his rival self to bay and won an illusory victory over it through action and the earned love of men who depend on him. But Brown revives the tyrannous faculty to its full force. If at this point Jim had another sinking ship to protect, he could have remained firm. He has conquered the part of his imagination that produces paralysis through fear, but he cannot learn how to keep it from distorting the objective requirements of the situation. Fidelity is now partly a matter of admitting the truth of Brown's insinuations, and he is so passionately conscious of his old guilt that he loses the power to judge Brown objectively.[4]

This time he does not desert the men whose lives depend on him, but he cannot take arms against the enemy. And this time no favoring fortune turns to save his dependents in his delinquency. They are massacred, and all Jim's work of years is obliterated in a bloody sacrifice. As he was man enough to accept the judgment due him while his fellow officers fled the trial of the *Patna* case, he now accepts the ultimate sentence for his ultimate crime. Weary of failure and yet disdainful of men who never shared his exalted vision, he goes out to meet his executioner. "He was overwhelmed by the inexplicable; he was overwhelmed by his own personality—the gift

4. For a different, or at least a deeper, analysis of this passage, see Gustav Morf; Thomas Moser, *Joseph Conrad: Achievement and Decline*, Cambridge, Mass., 1957, *passim*; and Albert J. Guerard.

of that destiny which he had done his best to master."

Such is the history of Jim's *psychomachia* in the finished novel. In the original sketch, imagination of a kind was obviously to be the fatal "gift" that would force Jim to desert the *Patna*. The sketch gives us, furthermore, the clue that, after leaving the sea for good, Jim would make his way to a Malayan village where he would be known as Tuan Jim. Knowing how Conrad worked in his first two novels and the unfinished *Rescue*, which must have been outlined in his mind at the time, we could safely predict that "Tuan Jim" already foreshadows that Jim's fatal flaw will be active to the end of the story, perhaps leading to his death (like Willems' failings in *An Outcast of the Islands*); or at least leading to the failure of his hopes (as the illusions of Almayer and of Tom Lingard had led to failure in *Almayer's Folly* and *The Rescue*).

What is missing from "Tuan Jim" is any mention of the dual nature of Jim's imagination. Here we are told, to be sure, that he is a youth of "exquisite sensibility," who has developed a "provoking and brutal stare" as a shield against all possible mention of the intolerable—his desertion of the *Patna*. But there is no reference to or suggestion of the quality of self-idealization which plays so prominent a part in the finished novel. Already in the sketch we learn that he will come to be called "Lord Jim," which in the finished novel is so appropriate to one who has from boyhood fancied himself destined to be a savior of men. But almost any white man in Malaya, as we know from Conrad's other novels, could be known as "Tuan." In the sketch we find one key sentence that could be interpreted to reflect Jim's inflated egoism: "he became chief mate of a fine ship without ever having been tested by those events of the sea that . . . reveal the quality of [a man's] resistance and the secret truth of his pretences, not only to others but also to himself." Again, however, this is not necessarily a suggestion of Jim's pretensions to heroism. We can recall that most of the main characters of the first two novels and *The Rescue* had "pretences," illusions about themselves that could not stand the test of events. They did not, however, like the fully developed Jim, indulge in grandiose visions.

The manuscript sketch carries the reader in twenty-eight pages up to the *Patna's* smooth voyage toward the entry of the Red Sea. (pp. 10-11 of the novel). Nothing significant is left out of the novel that was in the sketch, and nothing significant is added to the sketch to make the novel—except the incident aboard the training ship that reveals the duality of Jim's imagination, particularly with respect to his illusions of grandeur.

We do not need this episode to foresee, in the sketch, that Jim's imaginative faculty will be the determining force in his life. Although Chapter One of the sketch gives no idea of Jim's motives in going to sea, the beginning of Chapter Two tells us that, after two years of training, "he went to sea, and entering into the regions so well known to his imagination, found them singularly barren of adventure." It appears that Jim went to sea very much as Conrad tells us in A *Personal Record* he went himself, in response to a mysterious appeal of "innocent adventure," [5] or at worst of "romantic folly." [6] Like Jim, Conrad had found the sea less glamorous in reality than in books, but, like Jim too, he had learned his lesson manfully and passed all examinations with distinction. No less autobiographical, in a way, is Jim's "air of overbearing watchfulness." It is quite in keeping with the typical, "unforgettable Englishman" in A *Personal Record* whose face revealed a "headlong exalted satisfaction." [7] Disabled by a falling spar, Jim "was secretly glad he had not to go on deck." But in the sketch Conrad immediately explains: "exhausted courage is the result of exhausted emotion, and in the motionless body imagination, this enemy of man and the father of all terror, rests in a slumber that resembles the peace of conscious resignation." And this, too, was straight from Conrad's life, as he later described the results of his own disablement after the same kind of accident:

> inexplicable periods of powerlessness, sudden accesses of mysterious pain; and the patient agreed fully with the regretful murmurs of his very attentive captain wishing that it had been a straightforward broken leg. Even the Dutch doctor . . . offered no scientific explanation. All he said was: "Ah, friend, you are young yet; it may be very serious for your whole life." [8]

In the manuscript Conrad struggled for over three pages to clarify his conception of Jim's imagination at the start. Apparently the state of Jim's courage bothered him especially, for he crossed out "exhausted courage is the result of exhausted emotion" and put "passive courage is easy since it is a sign that imagination . . . is asleep in a motionless body." Finally he crossed out the question of courage altogether, or perhaps deferred it, reducing the three pages to one sentence for the published novel: "The fear grows shadowy; and Imagination, the enemy of men, the father of all terrors, unstimulated sinks to rest in the dulness of exhausted emotion."

In the manuscript, curiously, Conrad seems as eager to excuse Jim's moral lapse in joining the *Patna*, rather than a home ship, as if the problem were his own. (The steamship *Vidar*, which Conrad joined after his hospitalization in Singapore,was indeed an "Eastern

5. *A Personal Record,* London, 1946, p. xiv.
6. *Ibid.,* p. 43.
7. *Ibid.,* p. 40.
8. *The Mirror of the Sea,* London, 1946, pp. 54–55.

ship," principally owned by an Arab.) [9] This would make sense if he did in fact begin by identifying the romantic youth with himself emotionally [1] while giving him the physical traits of a typical Englishman, according to his early idealized notion. The story originally contemplated was evidently a sort of *Hamlet* of the sea, with the difference that Jim's imaginative faculty would have forced him to two failures, one aboard the *Patna* and one in Patusan. As in *Hamlet*, the hero's imagination would have been the mark of his superiority as well as the cause of his undoing. Hamlet was no egoist, and neither was the original Jim. Jim was no less and no more than what we find him to be in Chapter Two of both sketch and novel.

In both versions of this chapter the imagination that made Jim go to sea deserted him after he was crippled by a falling spar, during his first bad storm at sea. This is Jim's first emergency situation in the sketch, his second in the novel. And because this catastrophe, in the sketch, merely cripples him without testing his moral stamina, the atrophy of his imagination leads quite simply and logically to his decision to join the *Patna*. In the novel, when the element of self-idealization is added in the training-ship episode, the reader should feel Jim's surrender to the easy life of the Eastern seas as a second and more serious moral lapse. At this point in the sketch, one's attention is drawn rather to Jim's gradual, almost imperceptible regression from the weeks of his hospital life, through the period of his unsuccessful search for a home ship, to the easy job he takes aboard the *Patna*. And, in the sketch, Conrad had already provided Jim with a strong alibi immediately after the accident, making the failure of his mental powers a perfectly normal reaction of his physical disability:

> Imagination . . . must have something to feed upon, otherwise it sinks to rest. One admits the possibility of being struck from behind in sleep or in the dark, but one does not believe in it till

9. G. Jean-Aubry gives an account of the circumstances in which Conrad joined the *Vidar* in *La Vie de Conrad*, translated by Helen Sebba as *The Sea Dreamer*, New York, 1957, pp. 119–20. 1. That Conrad was often arrested by accounts of actual villainies, which "sprang to life" for him when his mind sought extenuating circumstances for renegades who had committed them, is now commonly recognized. Lord Jim was based on one of the officers who abandoned an actual ship named the *Jeddah*. Nostromo has recently been traced by John Halverson and Ian Watt (*RES*, n.s., X, 1959, 45–52) to another unregenerate criminal. The originals of Gasper Ruiz and Razumov are other

examples among Conrad's characters, to mention only two. The question of why Conrad manipulated characters in this way, however, is far more complex than has been fully explained. That he was sympathetic with anarchistic types is one suggestion, but this does not adequately explain why he made villains more villainous than the life, rather than heroes out of certain anarchistic figures. Kurtz in *Heart of Darkness* and Peter Ivanovitch in *Under Western Eyes* are good examples. Clearly Conrad had a more discerning consciousness of law and lawbreaking than would be indicated if his leaning were consistently toward lawlessness.

the blow comes. It is otherwise when meeting the danger with brain, eye and hand.

The second and third sentences of this passage, and the imperative "must" of the first—Conrad's valid justification for Jim's apostasy—are missing in the finished novel, so that only a hint of the apology is allowed to remain. In the sketch, however, because of this justification, Jim's defense seems to grow stronger as his resolve weakens. While already in a state of mental flaccidity, he "had to go to the hospital. His recovery was slow and when the ship left he had to remain." Life in the hospital is langorous and makes a subtle appeal to his slumbering imagination, to his tendency to indulge in dreams without reference to mundane experience: "The gentle breeze entered from the wide windows" carrying "suggestions of endless dreams." Unaware of his condition, he is released from the hospital.

> When he could walk without a stick he descended into the town to look for some chance to get home. Nothing offered at once and while waiting he associated naturally with the men of his calling belonging to the port. These were of two kinds. Some . . . had an undefaced energy. . . . Others were men who like himself [2] thrown there by some accident, became officers of country ships. They had the horror of the home service with its hard conditions. . . . would have served the devil had he made it only easy enough . . . and in their persons could be detected . . . the soft spot, the place of decay.

Because of the mental lassitude that has come over Jim in convalescence, he surrenders to the moral lassitude of the second sort. In the novel at this point we are less certain than we are in the sketch that Jim, in his right mind, would have resisted "an unconditional surrender to the charm of a loafing existence." But after he had "listened for days to the endless professional gossip of these men . . . some responsive chord in his nature was struck and he let himself go."

Thus in both sketch and novel, as to some extent in Conrad's life, a crippling accident forces Jim's fatal imagination to become detached from the objective necessities of life and, as a result, he falls prey to the seductions of an irresponsible crowd of men. In the finished novel, however, we are made to understand that the moral lapse leading to betrayal of a trust was all the more tragic because it

---

2. The sentence beginning "Others were men who like himself," etc. is less ambiguous in the final book than in the sketch, for in the book the tense of the final verb is "had become officers," making it clear that "like himself" applies only to Jim's being thrown by accident into the port. There is no suggestion that Jim is like them at the start in any other way, though he too did later become an officer of a country ship. He was not like the first type because he had not deliberately broken his ties with England to go East.

occurred in a man who desperately wanted to prove himself heroic.

If it is true that Conrad changed his original conception of Jim's psychology, adding the heroic "thrust" later on, there may have been two very good reasons. First, he may have been troubled by a weakness in his original conception and therefore, as he says, put it aside for a time. Second, something may have occurred to him—a new and more ominous disability that could affect Jim's mind—sending him back to the manuscript with fresh interest. Some such change in thought seems implied when Conrad writes in the Author's Note to *Lord Jim* that he suddenly "perceived that the pilgrim ship episode was a good starting point for a free and wandering tale; that it was an event, too, which could conceivably color the whole 'sentiment of existence' in a simple and sensitive character." He goes on to say that the original few pages "were not without their weight," but that "the whole was rewritten deliberately," and that he knew the revised version would be a long book, though not so long as it in fact became.

All this appears quite appropriate to the differences we have noted between the first two chapters in the sketch and in the book, particularly when Conrad says that "the whole was deliberately rewritten," which is true only in the matter of conceptualizing Jim's imagination. What is not so apparent and can only be a matter of guesswork is why Conrad came only later to see the pilgrim episode as an event "which could conceivably color the whole 'sentiment of existence' in a simple and sensitive character."

In suggesting a possible answer, I must point out that it has long been assumed without sufficient evidence that Conrad wrote the Harvard manuscript in the spring of 1898, when he first mentioned to Garnett the stories he was planning to write for William Blackwood.[3] Conrad tells us in the Author's Note just mentioned, however, that the first pages of *Jim* had already been put aside in a drawer when Blackwood "suggested I should give him something again."

A stronger argument against the notion that Conrad began "Tuan Jim" in 1898 might be made from consideration of the notebook in which he set down these two chapters. I have found myself looking at the little leather notebook with its water-stained cover and imagining that it was among the keepsakes Conrad had among his possessions, along with the half-finished manuscript of *Almayer's Folly*, when his boat nearly capsized in the Congo rapids between Kinchassa and Leopoldville in 1890.[4] It would be possible, even, to think that it was in the trunk carrying things he had on the

3. Undated letter to Edward Garnett, which Garnett places in May 1898. *Letters from Joseph Conrad,* Indian-apolis, 1928, pp. 137–38.
4. *A Personal Record,* p. 14.

Congo trip which Jessie Conrad says turned up unexpectedly in France on their honeymoon.[5] If so, possibly he took out the little book as early as that, in the summer of 1896, and wrote in it the first two chapters of "Tuan Jim," based on an actual sea disaster that had occurred in 1880. It is difficult to think why, if not then, Conrad would have used that heirloom, a commonplace book in which his maternal grandmother, Teofila Bobrowska,[6] had copied a number of Polish poems that took her fancy and made a landscape sketch in brown ink, as a present for her husband in 1819.

The book had undoubtedly been passed on to Conrad by his uncle Tadeusz Bobrowski, either in 1890 when Conrad visited him before going to the Congo or at Bobrowski's death in 1894. Conrad was in the habit of using full, standard or legal-size, sheets of paper for his manuscripts. The only sewn notebooks among his manuscripts are the two Congo diaries (also at Harvard and also written in pencil, but showing a handwriting decidedly more angular than "Tuan Jim") and the Polish commonplace book. All three notebooks were later scrupulously guarded by Jessie Conrad, apparently because of Conrad's penchant for destroying his manuscripts as soon as he was done with them.

Besides using the book for his first sketch of *Lord Jim*, Conrad made a brief note in it for a scene of *The Rescue*. It may be significant that this bit of *The Rescue* was penciled on the back of the last page of the "Tuan Jim" sketch. *The Rescue* fragment appears to be a note for Part III, Chapter V, of the novel, on which Conrad was working in June 1898,[7] and possibly later. As early as July 1896, however, and in France, he wrote to Garnett that he was "setting Beatrix [originally the name of Edith Travers], her husband and Linares (the Spanish gent) on their feet." [8] And, in the novel as conceived from the beginning, Part III was to be the section where these people would be first fully introduced.[9]

There are other notes on other pages of the little notebook following the "Tuan Jim" sketch which may be of interest to other scholars. What interests me here is only the possibility that Conrad carried the idea for *Lord Jim* in his head for at least two years before June 1898, when he sent Blackwood's eighteen typescript pages of it—possibly more or less a copy of the notebook sketch. That the rest of the "story" did not come easily to him even then is apparent from the fact that over a year later he had written only three chapters in all, and these not even finished, when he informed

5. Jessie Conrad, *Joseph Conrad and His Circle,* New York, 1934, pp. 32–4.
6. G. Jean-Aubry, *The Sea Dreamer,* pp. 17, 47.
7. Garnett, p. 139.
8. *Ibid.,* p. 61.

9. For a discussion of the original manuscript of *The Rescue,* see Thomas Moser, "The 'Rescuer' Manuscript: A Key to Conrad's Development—and Decline," *Harvard Library Bulletin,* X (1956), 325–55.

Blackwood's in July 1899 that he was sending thirty-one pages of
Jim.[1]

This was by no means the first time that Blackwood had asked
him "again" for a story, but Conrad was under particular pressure
in July 1899 to complete the volume of which the finished "Youth"
and *Heart of Darkness* were to be a part. In February 1899 Conrad
was not yet sure that *Jim* would be long enough to complete such
a volume. He was still thinking, apparently, only of the pilgrim-ship
episode. By June, however, it seems evident, he had begun to see
the story as a long tale, falling into two parts—probably he had by
then decided to make Jim's life in Patusan as important as the
events leading up to his desertion of the *Patna* and his trial. Patusan
would balance *Patna* not only in length but in the very sounds of
the names. Conrad was delighted with the new plan, though he
later had misgivings about it when he wrote Garnett, "You've put
your finger on the plague spot. The division of the book into two
parts . . ."

Whatever changed his mind about the tale between his writing
of the two chapters in "Tuan Jim" and his revision of these chapters as they stand in the novel in all likelihood occurred between
February 1899—when he wrote Blackwood he was not sure *Jim*
would be long enough to make a volume with "Youth" and *Heart
of Darkness*—and July 1899, when he knew the story would be
novel length, "fully 40,000 words," presumably tracing "the 'sentiment of existence' in a simple and sensitive character."

We know of at least one circumstance occurring in these five
months that affected Conrad strongly and may have left its mark
upon the work that engaged him most during the period. In March
1899 a Polish critic and philosopher named Vincent Lutoslawski,
who had been living in Boston and had visited Conrad in England,
published an article mentioning Conrad in *Kraj* (The Country),
a Polish journal published in St. Petersburg. The article, titled "The
Emigration of Talents," defended the thesis that Poles, either living abroad or naturalized in foreign countries, were able to serve
the cause of Poland as loyally as people who remained at home.
"The work produced is Polish," Lutoslawski wrote, "even though it
is published in a foreign language, for it is the fruit of the Polish
spirit, differing from that of other nations." Lutoslawski said he
could not "bring a charge of disaffection for their native country
against those who could not remain in a suffocating atmosphere,
who courageously went forth to take part in the universal struggle
for the conquest of material or moral riches, a large part of which

1. It is unfortunate that neither this
typescript of the first two chapters nor
the eighteen pages Conrad sent Blackwood's a year earlier seem to have survived. The fragmentary typescript in
the Rosenbach collection begins much
later.

would be returned to their homeland." [2] Naming Conrad as an example of such émigrés, he quoted Conrad's words spoken during their visit together in 1896: "I should never have dared to foist my attempts upon the beautiful literature of Poland." [3]

Lutoslawski's article brought forth an impassioned protest in the next issue of *Kraj* by a famous Polish woman, Eliza Orzeszkowa, who singled out Conrad's name among the émigrés Lutoslawski had mentioned because Conrad, like herself, was a novelist. Emotion carried her to assumptions far from true concerning Conrad's literary success in England at the time. She referred to him as "this gentleman, author of novels written in English which are all the rage and lucrative as one could wish." [4] With female precision she found her way to one of Conrad's most sensitive nerves. His inability to support his family by his pen was an embarrassment all the more acute because of his ingrained prejudice against money-making—a prejudice common among Polish nobles, who traditionally supported themselves from their lands, in professions, or by services to the state. Behind Orzeszkowa's words rang a clarion call to heroism, familiar to all Poles.

Is this the way creative artists should associate in the exodus? Till now it was a question only of engineers, attorneys, and opera singers. And now they are ready to absolve writers! If it were a matter of chemistry or even philosophy [a jab at Lutoslawski], I might see certain reasons for editing them in foreign languages; but if it is a question of the novel, a fragment of creative effort, then I am involved. I know our commitments to the corps, *fort comme la mort*, and with all my strength I protest. Creative gifts are the floral crown, the crest of the tower, the very heart of the nation. And this flower, this crest, this heart, to see it torn from our nation and surrendered to the Anglo-Saxons, who lack nothing among the goods of this world, and for the lovely reason that they pay better! . . . And to top everything, this gentleman has to bear what name? That of his direct ancestor, perhaps, that Joseph Korzeniowski [5] whose novels made me shed my first tears and feel the first flames of noble ardor and virtuous resolutions. No little Polish girl will weep a generous tear or form a magnanimous resolution on the novels of Mr. Konrad Korzeniowski . . . but on reflection, this incident brings me only a moderate sadness, for I have faith in real creative genius and I do not suppose that ours ever wanted to respond to the call of a canteen woman or a salesgirl of the marketplace. [6]

2. Joseph Ujejski, *Joseph Conrad*, tr. Pierre Duméril, Paris, 1939. I have translated from the French where this work is quoted. The original is in Polish.
3. Jean-Aubry, p. 237.
4. Ujejski, p. 16.
5. This novelist and dramatist, who lived from 1791 to 1863, was not directly related to Conrad, according to his own account. He mentions this to Garnett the following year, as if the subject were fresh in his mind. Garnett, p. 165.
6. Ujejski, pp. 16–17.

We do not know that Conrad read the issues of *Kraj* in which his case was argued, though it would have been natural for Lutoslawski to send him a copy of at least the first. But it appears that Orzeszkowa wrote him a letter. He harbored the memory of it fifteen years later when in 1914 his cousin Angela Zagórska unwittingly suggested that he read one of Orzeszkowa's novels. "Don't bring me anything from that shrew. . . . She wrote me a letter once," he replied cryptically.[7]

His most direct answer to this woman was in Chapter Two of *A Personal Record*. Most interesting for our consideration of the revisions of "Tuan Jim" are his words there concerning his own peculiar loyalty: "The inner voice may remain true enough in its secret counsel. The fidelity to a special tradition may last through the events of an unrelated existence, following faithfully too the traced way of an inexplicable impulse." Jim's apparent disloyalty to the special tradition of the English merchant service was no measure of the truth of his "inner voice." But only after Orzeszkowa's tirade did Conrad see that Jim's desertion of the *Patna* "could conceivably color [his] whole sentiment of existence"—for Jim, too, an "unrelated existence," unrelated not to Poland, but to England and the sea.

Since Conrad began *Lord Jim* before Orzeszkowa's attack, the novel certainly could not have been first conceived as an answer to her, as Jean-Aubry and Ujejski imply it was. Furthermore, a careful reading of the novel shows that Conrad's view of Jim was less, not more, sympathetic with Jim after Orzeszkowa's outburst than before it. As we have seen, the original "Tuan Jim" traced Jim's moral lapse aboard the *Patna* to nothing more reprehensible than an overactive imagination and the effects of immobilization after an accident. If Conrad had begun the novel by identifying Jim with himself, even to the extent of questioning how a sensitive and highly responsible man could desert a position of public trust, it is possible to suppose that the argument in *Kraj*, with its emotional references to "the Polish spirit," revived in Conrad a memory of his past that suggested another dimension for Jim's dilemma.

Lutoslawski's earnest concern with "the Polish spirit, differing from that of other nations," and how this spirit could be served even by those who had left Poland for good, struck a note that shook the nerves of many among the Polish intelligentsia, who had been nurtured on the idea that every Pole was an integral part of a sacred number, of a sacred body that must not be desecrated. This latter analogy had been carried to mystical heights by Poland's

7. *Ibid.*, p. 18.

romantic poets, particularly Mickiewicz,[8] who likened the body of Poland and her members to the figure of Christ, the suffering servant. Even the more worldly Polish patriots kept the faith that Poland was undergoing a period of privation in the nineteenth century which would end in a glorious resurrection, but which must, for the present, be borne heroically as a continuing proof of Poland's moral superiority among the nations. The living members must be content to be momentarily forgotten, must not seek personal happiness, but must live only for the resurrection of the whole. This idea and faith had become the ruling passion of Conrad's father, especially after the death of his wife, during his exile in Russia when he wrote an essay called *Poland and Russia* and had it smuggled abroad for publication.[9]

Conrad's attitude toward this generative myth was evidently very complex. "The spirit of the land, as becomes the ruler of great enterprises, is careless of innumerable lives. Woe to the stragglers! We exist only in so far as we hang together." These words, in the mouth of the English Marlow as he begins the story of Jim's life in Patusan (Chapter Twenty-One), remind us that Marlow's pervading uncertainty about Jim's very existence is certainly more Polish than English. But there is a critical irony in Marlow's image of "the spirit of the land," a suggestion of resistance to this spirit.

We see something of Conrad's own resistance to his political heritage in the ambivalent description he gave Garnett of the fanatic patriot who was his own father, "a man of great sensibilities; of exalted and dreamy temperament; with a terrible gift of irony and of gloomy disposition; withal of strong religious feeling degenerating after the loss of his wife into mysticism touched with despair." [1] Something of this man's character seems to have gone into the remodeling of Jim when Conrad began his story again in 1899.

Apollo Korzeniowski, Conrad's father, was a complex man—a poet, a satirical dramatist, and a translator of Shakespeare and French romantic poetry. Not a man of simple character like Jim, he was yet, like Jim of the novel, a man who dreamed of saving people, the people of Poland. And like the fully developed Jim, his actions had the opposite effect from what he hoped. Korzeniowski and his wife gave up their lives to free Poland, pinning their faith on the rebellion of 1863, which Korzeniowski helped to foment, but which failed and tore down with it many of the painful gains

8. For a discussion of Adam Mickiewicz's messianic revelation, derived from the mystic Towianski, see Wiktor Weintraub, *The Poetry of Adam Mickiewicz*, The Hague, 1954.
9. Czeslaw Milosz, "Apollo Nalecz Korzeniowski," *Kultura* (Paris), Feb. 1956, p. 76. This article was translated for me from the Polish by Mrs. Walter Drzewieniecki.
1. Garnett, p. 167.

won by Poland in the previous decades. Conrad's uncle Tadeusz
Bobrowski commented dryly on Korzeniowski's heroic sacrifice after
his death, remarking that his dreams had betrayed him: "I assert
only that in general poets, men of imagination and ideals, are
not capable of clearly formulating the concrete postulates of
existence." [2]

Korzeniowski was far from unique among Poles. The poet rebel
was a revered figure among a people deprived of representative
statesmen, who had a political voice only under fictive disguises.
Like the more famous political exile and poet Adam Mickiewicz,
Korzeniowski borrowed from religion and poetry romantic myths
prognosticating the rebirth of Poland. Warning Conrad against any
such fantasies, Bobrowski wrote:

> Our country, as Slowacki well says (although he himself was not
> free from the reproach), is the "peacock of the nations," which,
> in plain prose, means that we are a nation who consider ourselves
> great and misunderstood, the possessors of a greatness which
> others do not recognize and will never recognize. If individuals
> and nations would set duty before themselves as an aim, instead
> of grandiose ideals, the world would be a happier place. . . . I
> have taken the motto *"usque ad finem"* as my guide, the love
> of the duty which circumstances define.[3]

Bobrowski and other Polish historians, brooding on the fiasco of
1863, probed into the motives of its leaders, distrustful of their
heroic devotion. Bobrowski wrote that, although Korzeniowski

> considered himself a sincere democrat (and others considered
> him as a "fanatic" and "red"), he had in him, as I often tried to
> persuade him, a hundred more times the aristocratic instinct than
> I had myself—I who never passed for a democrat.[4]

Recently Czeslaw Milosz has returned to the question of Korzeniowski's interest in "the people," apart from his own dream of
their use. "It wasn't that Korzeniowski scorned the people, but he
sought in it essentially a capacity for national élan." [5]

Under Bobrowski's careful schooling, Conrad resisted the powerful influence of his father's personality and ideas. There is every
evidence that Korzeniowski, while deprecating his own qualities,
sought to make Conrad in his image: "a good Pole," that is, a man
(such as Orzeszkowa might have respected) who would sacrifice
everything for a heroic dream, the dream of national liberation.

Korzeniowski died when Conrad was eleven years old. Bobrowski became Conrad's guardian and systematically set about curing
him of his father's influence. He strove to make sure that Conrad's
"inexplicable impulse" to go to sea should not turn into a "roman-

2. Milosz, p. 70.

tic folly." Perhaps aware that Conrad's overpowering urge to free himself of what even Orzeszkowa allowed might be "suffocating" associations, in a land representing nothing so much as a coffin where his loved ones were buried alive, Bobrowski was concerned that he should not transfer his father's self-idealizing fantasies to the life at sea, expansive as the plains of Poland but free, and possibly also a symbol of irresponsibility. As late as 1891, when Conrad was thirty-three, Bobrowski was warning him to be on his guard against the idealization of self and of Poland that he called "the defects of the House of Nalecz." And the following year again: "Your weakness comes from the Nalecz Korzeniowski. Your grandfather and uncle were always entertaining projects which had no validity except in their imaginations. . . . Your father was an idealistic dreamer." [6]

Bobrowski died in 1894. How deeply his words affected Conrad we know, not only from the reverence in which he held the memory of his uncle, to whom he dedicated his first novel, but also in the impression of Bobrowski's wisdom traceable in Conrad's life and work. The motto *usque ad finem* might be that of every Conrad hero, from his unimaginative men of duty like the captains Allistoun and MacWhirr to tragic dreamers like Charles Gould and the Russian Razumov. But here is the wonder: through the alchemy of his genius Conrad breathed fire into the ashes of old wisdom and found the romance and tragedy inherent in the dry cautions of his lawyer uncle's confirmed stoicism. *Usque ad finem* becomes in *Lord Jim* the blazon not of the "realists" who scorn Jim's dream but of the romantic Stein, who sanctifies Jim's fidelity to his ego's ideal. "That was the way. To follow the dream, and again to follow the dream." Marlow, Jim's father confessor, finds relief in Stein's diagnosis. Jim's self-frustrating drive to serve heroically "in the ranks" [6a] gives him the knowledge of his own humanity that few men can bear to have. Jim is able to "stick" to the end of his duty, even facing up to the worst and most unimaginable trick his own personality finally plays upon him. Brierly's "sham" was his inability to face this knowledge, which for him (though not for Jim) invalidated the code that held his life together. By implicit contrast, Marlow learns from Stein that the pain of Jim's self-knowledge is what gives him—and the code he longed to serve—an "imperishable reality."

3. Jean-Aubry, *Joseph Conrad: Life and Letters*, New York, 1927, I, 148. Wiktor Weintraub has called my attention to Jean-Aubry's mistranslation of "peacock of the nations," a quotation from Slowacki which Jean-Aubry's translator recorded as " 'pan' of the nations." Cf. the Polish original of Bobrowski's letter, published by Jablkowska, "Listy Tadeuza Bobrowskiego do Conrada,"

Kwartalnik Neofilologiczny, III, 110–11.
4. Milosz, p. 69.
5. *Ibid.*, p. 70.
6. Jean-Aubry, *Life and Letters*, I, 146.
6a. A major point the novel makes is that Jim's "yearning . . . for his humble place in the ranks" does square with the last discovery that "of all mankind Jim had no dealings but with himself."

When Conrad added to the sketch of "Tuan Jim" the halo and curse of Jim's romantic egoism, he introduced a theme which was, though few of his English readers recognized it, a matter of concern to all Poland, and perhaps through Poland to all Europe. Conrad knew that the Polish heroic idea was potentially deceptive though irresistibly seductive. Even Bobrowski, an admirable public servant who had spent his life resisting the Polish tendency to quixotic idealism, was not perfectly immune. While exhorting Conrad to take citizenship in any land where he could make a useful life for himself, Bobrowski had reminded him never to forget what he owed "to the nobility of the race"—meaning nation—to which he belonged and would always belong wherever else he placed his allegiance.[7] Clearly Conrad remembered. But the study of nobility became for him more than a question of how he represented Poland. It became an inquiry into man's power for loyalty and sacrifice to causes which are likely to shift deceptively between public and private goals.

One cannot measure, one can only suggest the extent to which Conrad's efforts to control illusions about himself and his "race" became in his fiction a voice struggling to censure sympathetic dreamers, the greatest of whom was Jim. We must not forget, at the same time, that this same struggle may have armed Conrad with his unambivalent insights into culture heroes like Kurtz in *Heart of Darkness*.

If the argument in *Kraj* about his own exemplification of the Polish spirit, recalling his father's ghost and the ghost of Polish romanticism, brought to his mind a new way of regarding Jim's fatal imagination, it is obvious that Conrad did not turn to defending Jim and indirectly himself. Jim plainly failed, and failed more disastrously as his motives became more heroic. But, between the early sketch and the finished novel, the simple Jim also grew into a superb and unforgettably tragic figure. Into the new draft came a new tension, a straining to express to uncomprehending readers, English perhaps more than Polish, the power and glory of Jim's self-defeating ideal. The narrator Marlow cannot resist him, but paradoxically identifies his own yearning for proof of the seaman's code (for belief in the power of an absolute and unchangeable standard of conduct) with Jim's determination to redeem his failure under the code. It was as if Jim "had been an individual in the forefront of his kind, as if the obscure truth involved were momentous enough to affect mankind's conception of itself." While half-despising his own liking for Jim, Marlow can find no one, even among seamen true to the code, who is true as Jim is true—in full knowledge of his capacity for un-

7. Jean-Aubry, *Life and Letters*, I, 59.

witting betrayal. Jim's dream of heroism, egotistical as it may be, may also be—like the Polish "spirit"—the burning energy without which any fixed standard of conduct is a cold shell, or "a bit of ass's skin," as the realist Chester calls the English officer's certificate in *Lord Jim.*

There is good reason to suppose that Marlow rescued Conrad at a critical moment in the writing of *Lord Jim,* at the point where Conrad decided to shape Jim's character more rigorously by introducing the heroic obsession. At this point he would have wanted, perhaps needed, another character in whom he could pour the full measure of his ambivalence toward men who consider themselves larger than life size. Marlow is nowhere in evidence in the two chapters of "Tuan Jim." Of course, even in the novel he does not enter the picture until Chapter Four, which seems not to have been written until the summer of 1899. We may recall too that Conrad, in February 1899, was thinking of *Jim* as a story to finish the *Youth* volume, that he wrote *Heart of Darkness* as well as "Youth" with Marlow as narrator, and may have decided as early as the summer of 1898 (when he told Garnett the Congo story he had in mind to write) that Marlow could serve as a connecting link between "Youth," *Heart of Darkness,* and the story of Jim. In any case, when Jim's tale became so much more involved than it started out to be, Marlow was there to argue Jim's brief as both prosecutor and defense attorney.

The power of Conrad's feeling for Jim, as well as the force of his judgment against him, are the responses of a man mightily involved on two planes, one personal and one public, with the dynamics of good and evil. The evil in *Lord Jim* is one thing on the surface and another beneath our grasp. It is of course the evil of men who have no sense of loyalty to anything, like the villanious *Patna* officers and like Cornelius and Brown. Less recognizably perhaps, it is the evil of "realists" like Chester and Brierly (as opposed to romanticists like Jim and Stein, characterized by their ability to persevere in spite of, possibly even *because of,* their knowledge of human frailty and suffering), who think there is nothing to life but external facts. But there is evil also in the impulses we uncritically call "good," generous yearnings like Jim's heroic ideal, that may give life its whole meaning but may also destroy the very things it hopes to save. Insofar as one can take a moral stand on this hidden Lucifer, Conrad strove to take one in *Lord Jim* and achieved, I think a remarkable if precarious balance.

The probable influence on the finished novel of Eliza Orzeszkowa's attack, and the general argument about the Polish spirit that was published in St. Petersburg, has been hardly mentioned by English-speaking critics. Conrad's devoted biographer Jean-Aubry (*La*

Vie de Conrad, 1947) was the first writer in a Western language to refer to it, probably taking his lead from the French translation in 1939 of Joseph Ujejski's *Joseph Conrad,* where the subject is treated in some detail. Both Ujejski and Jean-Aubry assumed that the novel was conceived as an answer to Orzeszkowa's charge of disloyalty, perhaps giving more weight than it deserved to Gustav Morf's "strong conviction, sprung from a psychological analysis of the novel" (and published in 1930) that *Lord Jim* "is more than a novel, it is a confession. As a confession of a man tortured by doubts and nightmarish fears it must be understood, if it is to be understood at all."

My own reading of *Lord Jim* has long disagreed with Morf's contention that the novel should be read as a confession, the expression of a guilt complex. Certainly I disagree with Morf's view that Jim is "not a Pole but simply a neurotic." Without seeing Jim as a Pole, I would argue that he personifies a spirit very like the Polish spirit in something like the way epic heroes personify their nations. Because Conrad's attitude toward his nation was more ambivalent and also more intensely personal than were the attitudes of Homer, Virgil, or even Mickiewicz toward their nations, we would expect his epic hero to be at once more vulnerable and less single-minded than theirs.

I think Conrad did feel the need to explain why he left Poland, but to feel the need to explain is not tantamount to feeling a conscious or unconscious conviction of guilt. If Conrad felt guilty about anything, it was, at least as much and perhaps more, about his congenital and chronic drift toward reverie, a curious compound of inner vision with outward inertia, that made him fear he could not fulfill his obligations wherever they happened to lie—aboard ship while he was at sea, at his desk when ashore. He was in fact, we know, guilty of delinquencies (though unintentional, like Jim's) through this failing. In *The Mirror of the Sea* he confesses delinquencies at sea. And later ashore, in August 1898, while "Tuan Jim" was on his desk, he wrote his publisher: "The worst of it is that while I am thus powerless to produce, my imagination is extremely active."

This was the tragic flaw he first conceived as the center of Jim's story. When Orzeszkowa published her attack, he was undoubtedly wounded to the core, but she unlocked his word hoard. Our wonder must be at the mysterious way in which he then transmuted the stuff of romanticism into the material he needed to make Jim's story a masterpiece. Jim started out to be a sort of English Conrad. He ended resembling an epic hero, as Marlow saw him: "like a figure set up on a pedestal to represent . . . the virtues of races that never grow old, that have emerged from the gloom. I don't know why he should always have appeared to me symbolic." The only "race" likely to claim Jim as its symbol in 1900 was the great lost Polish nation, which Conrad held in both love and fear—a nation Tadeusz Bobrowski had called "great and misunderstood, the possessors of a greatness which others do not recognize and will never recognize."

MURRAY KRIEGER

The Varieties of Extremity: *Lord Jim* †

"Very funny this terrible thing is. A man that is born falls into a dream like a man who falls into the sea. If he tries to climb out into the air as inexperienced people endeavour to do, he drowns —*nicht wahr?* . . . No! I tell you! The way is to the destructive element submit yourself, and with the exertions of your hands and feet in the water make the deep, deep sea keep you up."

But the call to willful triumph in the last of these words of Stein is soon muted. The victorious "shadow," speaking with confidence from the unreality of the "shapeless dusk"—existing outside "this concrete and perplexed world"—returns to the light and can pursue his fervor no longer: ". . . his twitching lips uttered no word, and the austere exaltation of a certitude seen in the dusk vanished from his face. . . . The light had destroyed the assurance which had inspired him in the distant shadows." Ironically, taking the symbolic form of light, the reality proves itself as the destructive element by destroying the shadowy dream that claimed to have found the way to overcome it. And Stein senses his ultimate defeat, despite the heroic resilience seen in his biography. It is his romantic self-assertion, his ability to "follow the dream" in the face of failure, that he bequeathes to Jim, but his self-delusion—perhaps recognized in this scene—will be Jim's also, and Jim will also come to a recognition of it, a far more costly one.

Yet the sea in Stein's metaphor appears to represent the dream rather than reality, so that the dream rather than reality would appear to be the destructive element. However, to the romantic—as Stein conceives him and as Jim realizes him even more completely than Stein did—the dream *is* the reality, the existence into which he has been capriciously hurled. As, for the modern existentialist, man suddenly wakes up to find himself catapulted into existence and proves his humanity by the strength of his response to the

† From *The Tragic Vision: Variations on a Theme in Literary Interpretation,* Holt, Rinehart and Winston, Inc., New York, 1960, pp. 165–79. Copyright by Murray Krieger. Reprinted by permission.

meaninglessness of the challenge, so Conrad—through Stein—sees as the critical moment of man's existence his awakening to the sealike, dreamlike quality of the life into which he has fallen and which now claims him. And we must remember the dreamlike, indeed the nightmarish, atmosphere which pervaded "the night of the first ages," the irrational unconscious symbolized by Conrad as the *Heart of Darkness*. There, we were told, it is the nightmare which is the terrifying reality that, as we have seen, must be purposefully ignored in the interest of sanity: "When you have to attend to things of that sort, to the mere incidents of the surface, the reality—the reality, I tell you—fades. The inner truth is hidden—luckily, luckily." And Marlow has earlier acknowledged the Kafka-esque quality of this inner truth and of the invulnerable solitude with which one is overcome by it as a reality-principle as well as a dream:

> It seems to me I am trying to tell you a dream—making a vain attempt, because no relation of a dream can convey the dream-sensation, that commingling of absurdity, surprise, and bewilderment in a tremor of struggling revolt, that notion of being captured by the incredible which is of the very essence of dreams. . . .
>
> . . . No, it is impossible; it is impossible to convey the life-sensation of any given epoch of one's existence,—that which makes its truth, its meaning—its subtle and penetrating essence. It is impossible. We live, as we dream—alone. . . .

As a visionary Lord Jim may hardly seem to be enough like Kurtz to justify my using *Heart of Darkness* to shed light on the longer novel. For Jim may seem to have found his salvation—within the total resolution that allows tragedy—by sacrificing himself to what society may demand of the hero, while Kurtz has sacrificed society to his own satanic appetites. But the stories have more in common than the presence of Marlow * * * . It is rather that his very presence and the similarity of his role suggest something in common between the two men he tries to save and fears to judge.

Quite clearly *Lord Jim* revolves about what Stein calls the "romantic" attitude, which tells us that our protagonist is one of that uncompromising tribe that seeks and finds extreme situations.[1] At the beginning Jim is filled with schoolboy notions of honor and sees himself as uniquely chosen for the courageous and the sacrificial deed: "always an example of devotion to duty, and as unflinching as a hero in a book." But the trials of exacting necessity find him

---

1. For a discussion of an earlier, a related but weaker—if more optimistic—attempt by Conrad to deal with this sort of protagonist, see my "Conrad's *Youth*: A Naive Opening to Art and Life," *College English*, XX (1959), 275–80.

wanting. He has two seemingly insignificant failures before that major catastrophe on the *Patna*. Each time the world, suddenly transformed, presents him with its terrifying aspect. It is this that paralyzes him into inaction. In his first failure at training school the gale blows

> with the strength of a hurricane in fitful bursts that boomed like salvoes of great guns firing over the ocean. . . . Jim had threatening glimpses of the tumbling tide. . . . There was a fierce purpose in the gale, a furious earnestness in the screech of the wind, in the brutal tumult of earth and sky, that seemed directed at him . . .

Before he fails again, Conrad tells us:

> There are many shades in the danger of adventures and gales, and it is only now and then that there appears on the face of facts a sinister violence of intention—that indefinable something which forces it upon the mind and the heart of a man, that this complication of accidents or these elemental furies are coming at him with a purpose of malice, with a strength beyond control, with an unbridled cruelty that means to tear out of him his hope and his fear, the pain of his fatigue and his longing for rest: which means to smash, to destroy, to annihilate all he has seen, known, loved, enjoyed, or hated . . .

Despite the openness of nature's challenge—its frank revelation that it will not cooperate with his dream of glory—the lad complains that he has been caught "unawares." That night on the *Patna*, however, he is not given so open a view of universal malevolence. Instead, nature shows only a pleasant and tranquil face and so beguiles him into a false security. That fateful night Jim "was penetrated by the great certitude of unbounded safety and peace that could be read on the silent aspect of nature like the certitude of fostering love upon the placid tenderness of a mother's face." Marlow later comments, "and all the time it was only a clouded sky, a sea that did not break, the air that did not stir. Only a night; only a silence." As Jim returns to his high heroic dreams, he feels "something like gratitude for this high peace of sea and sky," unaware that he is to be repaid at once and not in kind. The nightmare reality that Stein later sees as the "destructive element" has engulfed Jim, and only out of a kind of stubborness does he resist his complete destruction.

After the inquiry he persists, not quite "shirking his ghost" or "facing him out," although something of each. The opportunity Stein finds for him in Patusan (a name which is obviously meant to echo the *Patna*) Jim answers brilliantly. He never allows himself to be caught unawares here, so that heroic act follows heroic act in a faithful service that surely seems more than atonement enough for his faithlessness to those other non-Europeans who staked all on the white man's loyalty. He seems indeed to have immersed himself in the destructive element without succumbing to it: precisely Stein's formula for the "romantic" who would yet manage life. Instead of the alienation forced upon him by his earlier failure, he not only has integrated himself into the Patusan world but has reconstructed that world about him.

Why is it, then, that Marlow still has his doubts, that he fears that the "opportunity which, like an Eastern bride, had come veiled to [Jim's] side," may still be veiled? What is there about Jim's situation in Patusan that is still so profoundly unsatisfying? Now that he has reversed his earlier incapabilities and has surely realized everything that a hero of schoolboy romance could ask, what nagging thing mars it all?

To begin with, about the entire affair of the *Patna* lurks an intangible mystery, a circle of moral ambiguities, in light of which no answer like the simple about-face in Patusan can satisfy Marlow—or us. Referring to the elusiveness of the *Patna* episode, Jim says:

> "It was not a lie—but it wasn't truth all the same. It was something. . . . There was not the thickness of a sheet of paper between the right and wrong of this affair. . . . Suppose I had stuck to the ship? . . . In thirty seconds, as it seemed certain then, I would have been overboard; and do you think I would not have laid hold of the first thing that came in my way? . . . I would have meant to be [saved]. . . . And that's more than I meant when I . . . jumped . . ."

This impalpability helps draw Marlow into the situation. As he witnessed the questioning of Jim at the inquiry, he saw Jim's helplessness as he tried to unmask the true reality of what happened that night. Nor can the mere facts help. Those least of all: "They demanded facts from him, as if facts could explain anything!"

> The facts those men were so eager to know had been visible, tangible, open to the senses, occupying their place in space and time, requiring for their existence a fourteen-hundred-ton steamer and twenty-seven minutes by the watch; they made a whole that had features, shades of expression, a complicated aspect that could be remembered by the eye, and something else besides, something invisible, a directing spirit of perdition that dwelt within, like a malevolent soul in a detestable body. . . . his mind positively flew round and round the serried circle of facts that had surged up all about him to cut him off from the rest of his kind . . .

Perhaps Marlow recalls his own words out of another of his tales. For Jim, thrust into a dream that constitutes his reality, echoes the full sense of what we have already heard Marlow, in Stein-like tones, tell his listeners in *Heart of Darkness*:

> . . . it is impossible to convey the life-sensation of any given epoch of one's existence,—that which makes its truth, its meaning—its subtle and penetrating essence. It is impossible. We live, as we dream—alone. . . .

Conrad distrusts facts since they deceive us: the utter intimacy of personal experience is incommunicable, and this insulation belies the smug and pretentious claims of facts to tell us about the human history of each of us. The effect Conrad achieves may remind us of that other weaver of sea stories who cultivated the mystic, unsharable sanctity of personal experience—the Herman Melville of *Benito Cereno*. Here we—with Captain Delano—are presented with an obvious, and often obviously misleading, mystery. Suddenly it seems to have cleared, the facts have been straightened out. And then, just to be certain there are no misunderstandings, Melville gives us endless excerpts from Don Benito's deposition in the court records. The facts are laid out again and again, in inexhaustible and repetitious detail. But ironically, the real mystery has not been solved; it has only deepened. For the more Delano knows, the farther he is from capturing the heart of that darkness which fills Don Benito's soul and sends him to his death. Indeed is this not much of what Melville is about when, in *Moby Dick*, he burdens his narrative with the often puzzlesome cetological intrusions? Does not the multiplication of exposition's facts, drawn from many descriptive studies, still leave us infinitely removed from the whale's fullest significance? Hence Ishmael's weariness with his data even as he dare not give up these only contacts with the reality of the whale that obsesses his pages. And we are perhaps reminded finally of Shakespeare's impatience, in his Sonnet 116, with the finitude of fact as he seeks to define love as the star

> Whose worth's unknown, although his highth be taken.

Indeed, the complex manipulation of Conrad's point of view and time sequence is not a mere virtuoso display. Rather, it is yet another attempt to indicate how unreachable Jim's problem is. The course of events is gone over again and again, in all varieties of chronological order and from all varieties of points of view. Seemingly crucial bits of information are added here and there as revelation always seems beyond the next turning. But the heart of the matter still remains just beyond grasp. Thus the enumeration of Jim's heroic actions is something less than immediately convincing.

The haunting theme of common guilt also serves to cloud Jim's success in Patusan. It is a theme that has been with us from the beginning. It helps explain, for example, why Marlow becomes so obsessed by Jim's case that he manages to get to all the sources of information and of different attitudes that he needs to tell his story. For Jim is "one of us," as Marlow often says, so that Marlow is profoundly troubled that as "one of us" Jim should be involved in the ugly business of the *Patna*.

> Why I longed to go grubbing into the deplorable details of an occurrence which, after all, concerned me no more than as a member of an obscure body of men held together by a community of inglorious toil and by fidelity to a certain standard of conduct, I can't explain. You may call it an unhealthy curiosity if you like; but I have a distinct notion I wished to find something. Perhaps, unconsciously, I hoped I would find that something, some profound and redeeming cause, some merciful explanation, some convincing shadow of an excuse. I see well enough now that I hoped for the impossible—for the laying of what is the most obstinate ghost of man's creation, of the uneasy doubt uprising like a mist, secret and gnawing like a worm, and more chilling than the certitude of death—the doubt of the sovereign power enthroned in a fixed standard of conduct. It is the hardest thing to stumble against; it is the thing that breeds yelling panics and good little quiet villainies; it's the true shadow of calamity. Did I believe in a miracle? and why did I desire it so ardently? Was it for my own sake that I wished to find some shadow of an excuse for that young fellow whom I had never seen before, but whose appearance alone added a touch of personal concern to the thoughts suggested by the knowledge of his weakness—made it a thing of mystery and terror—like a hint of a destructive fate ready for us all whose youth—in its day—had resembled his youth? I fear that such was the secret motive of my prying. I was, and no mistake, looking for a miracle. The only thing that at this distance of time strikes me as miraculous is the extent of my imbecility. I positively hoped to obtain from that battered and shady invalid some exorcism against the ghost of doubt.

Somewhat later Chester, Conrad's version in this novel of the insensitive "aesthetic" fool, says of Jim:

> "Takes it to heart? . . . Then he's no good. . . . You must see things exactly as they are—if you don't, you may just as well give in at once. You will never do anything in this world. Look at me. I made it a practice never to take anything to heart."

And he offers to bury Jim on a guano-filled island. Marlow's reaction, as he rejects the proposal, is significant:

> To bury him would have been such an easy kindness! It would have been so much in accordance with the wisdom of life, which

consists in putting out of sight all the reminders of our folly, of our weaknesses, of our mortality; all that makes against our efficiency—the memory of our failures, the hints of our undying fears, the bodies of our dead friends.

With Brierly, ironically one of the judges at the inquiry, this awareness of common guilt is fatal. Temperamentally much like Jim, in his romanticism at least, Brierly has been an unequaled and continual success. Jim's trial so unnerves him, so persuades him to identify himself with the culprit, that he tries desperately to send Jim away before its conclusion—a reminder of Marlow's remarks about burying him to keep him out of our way and out of our awareness. About Brierly's subsequent suicide Marlow has few questions. During the inquiry, he tells us, Brierly "was probably holding silent inquiry into his own case. The verdict must have been of unmitigated guilt, and he took the secret of the evidence with him in that leap into the sea."

In view of these universal fears, we can hardly expect Marlow to be utterly convinced—as convinced as Jim wants him to be—by what he sees on his last visit to Lord Jim's domain. In answer to Jewel's fears, Marlow is forced to admit to her, whose admiration for Jim will not allow her to believe it, that Jim will never leave her for the outside world that drove him there "because he is not good enough." But his moral sensitivity leads him to add, "Nobody, nobody is good enough."

"Is it not strange . . . that all these people, all these people who would do anything for me, can never be made to understand? . . . What more can I want? If you ask them who is brave—who is true—who is just—who is it they would trust with their lives?—they would say, Tuan Jim. And yet they can never know the real, real truth . . ."

And then he confronts Marlow with the key question, on which he never does get Marlow's reassurance: "But all the same, you wouldn't like to have me aboard your own ship—hey? . . . Only . . . you just try to tell this to any of them here. They would think you a fool, a liar, or worse." Nobody is good enough, Jim no more so than the rest, and his growing awareness of this truth gives him a maturity which demands more than the schoolboy heroism he can now turn on at will.

When at the end Marlow visits Stein and there sees Tamb' Itam and Jewel, the disappointed, even disgusted report of Jim's last actions ("He would not fight") is meant to delude us into believing that the *Patna* episode has occurred again, that Jim's hard-won heroism has crumbled. He seems superficially to have come full circle to a paralysis that destroys a sacred trust. Yet he promised Marlow,

that last time, to be "faithful"; and although Jewel bitterly charges
him with being "false," Stein's assurance is unquestionable as he tells
Jewel, "No! no! Not false! True! true! true!" Of course, "true" here
can only mean faithful in the appropriately chivalric context of
knighthood. Marlow himself, finally the unromantic ethical man
with a worldly commitment—a commitment to "a fixed standard
of conduct"—but not one exclusive enough to mar the all-embrac-
ing sympathy he requires as narrator, is almost persuaded despite
some lingering doubts that he dare not give up. After describing
the "proud and unflinching glance" with which Jim accepts his
death, Marlow suggests this to have been Jim's moment of vision in
which the veil was raised and the face of the Eastern bride, his opportunity, finally revealed. And why not? We remember that after
the *Patna* episode Jim insisted on rejecting the temptation of death:

> "Sick of life—to tell you the truth; but what would have been
> the good to shirk it—in—in—that way? That was not the way. I
> believe—I believe it would have—it would have ended—noth-
> ing. . . . No! the proper thing was to face it out—alone for my-
> self—wait for another chance—find out . . ."

When he allows himself to decide in favor of death in Patusan, we
realize that this last act is no failure and that he *has* found out. He
now can accept the punishment he earlier wanted and sought but
had to resist, because the act which now brings it about is one of
profound courage, however similar it may seem to that earlier act
of cowardice.

There are two interlocking justifications for this final action. One
of them relates to Jim's new-found and fully exploited capacity for
action. Having reversed his initial inability to act so that he has
fullfilled all that bravery could demand, he must now commit the
supremely brave act of choosing not to act. The redemption Jim so
long sought and finally thought he found in Patusan was based only
upon the deed, and the deed was proved by the respect it engendered from the society it served. But we have seen that the satisfactions it provided Jim were but superficial. He has discovered as only
relative that which he must have as absolute, since he has lost so
much in its name. This painful relativism Jim had to be aware of as
he witnessed himself worshiped in Patusan and despised as unworthy of trust in the world beyond. It would seem, then, that the
deed, the applause, and social service cannot be final moral criteria
for him. He must reject the simple schoolboy code and the conform-
ing obligations under which it placed the would-be hero in order to
meet a wider obligation. And whatever the final cost, this final action is a victory over relativism in that he has consciously chosen the
inaction that lets down his people and even forces them to execute

him in a death he rushes to accept.

But of course this is no willful anti-social perversity. There is reason enough why he should have let them down precisely this way—which leads us to the second justification for this action, based on yet another modulation of that ubiquitous theme of common guilt. The criminal Brown, who in talking Jim out of destroying him talks him into his own destruction, seems instinctively to touch Jim's sore spot. Turning upon Jim's moral pretensions as defender of Patusan, Brown challenges him in just the right way:

> "And what do you deserve . . . you that I find skulking here with your mouth full of responsibility, of innocent lives, of your infernal duty? . . . I came here for food. . . . And what did *you* come for? . . . I won't ask you what scared you into this infernal hole. . . ."

Brown seems to make their fellowship more intimate with every word he speaks:

> When he asked Jim, with a sort of brusque despairing frankness, whether he himself—straight now—didn't understand that when "it came to saving one's life in the dark, one didn't care who else went—three, thirty, three hundred people"—it was as if a demon had been whispering advice in his ear. "I made him wince," boasted Brown to me. "He very soon left off coming the righteous over me. He just stood there with nothing to say, and looking as black as thunder—not at me—on the ground." He asked Jim whether he had nothing fishy in his life to remember that he was so damnedly hard upon a man trying to get out of a deadly hole by the first means that came to hand—and so on, and so on. And there ran through the rough talk a vein of subtle reference to their common blood, an assumption of common experience; a sickening suggestion of common guilt, of secret knowledge that was like a bond of their minds and of their hearts.

And who is this Brown with whom Jim identifies himself? He is not only an indiscriminate murderer, but one who has chosen his profession out of utter misanthropy, out of purely diabolical spite. Yet Brown for Jim is also "one of us": "These were the emissaries with whom the world he had renounced was pursuing him in his retreat. White men from 'out there' where he did not think himself good enough to live."

Jim as romantic must still insist on extremity: he cannot close the circle and so limit those who are one of us, not even to exclude one such as Brown. He cannot stop with surface similarities as can Marlow or even the ill-fated Brierly, or the daring captain in the more optimistic *The Secret Sharer.* As extremist Jim must now embrace the dream as his element in a final, full awareness of its destructive quality. And Stein's recognition, with which we began, is now Jim's too. So Brown comes to be the case for common guilt a fortiori, as a gratuitous murderer the very worst possible of his kind. But, ironically, Jim must disdain moral hierarchy and see likeness rather than difference. As Brierly saw himself in Jim—and not utterly without reason—Jim goes the full length and beyond all reason and sees himself in Brown. Mere ethical judgment becomes impossible when the judge sees himself in the accused, finds the same dirt on his hands. When Jewel asks Jim if these men are very evil, Jim answers significantly, "Men act badly sometimes without being much worse than others."

Only paralysis, the refusal to act, can follow from this seemingly Christian insight. And yet he is being faithful in the way he promised Marlow on his last visit; not in any merely racial way though it may seem—as it must have to Doramin—that he has chosen the worst of his kind over the best of Doramin's. But such a view stems only from the reasonable ethical judgment which equates men (as Kyo would put it) with what they do; and Jim has moved willfully beyond. In a more profound sense he is being faithful to the world outside, the world which has judged him and before which he must still prove himself in a way beyond the possibilities for action afforded by his Patusan domain. It is a world of more subtle moral awarenesses than the self-enclosed, ruthless, and finally vengeful demand for self-preservation of Doramin's people, a demand that the still embattled Jim was earlier too young and too ethically eager to question. The faithfulness for which—out of an act of ethical and social treachery—he turns his back on all is, then, a faithfulness, what Marlow at the end calls an "eternal constancy," to "a shadowy ideal of conduct" surely Western and very likely Christian.

We must note finally that this ideal of conduct, while formed in the very shadows from which we heard Stein's formula for victory with which we began, finds itself—like Stein's formula—tested in the light. Here at the end, "within the coast that under the western sun looks like the very stronghold of the night," we find that we have not really left the *Heart of Darkness* after all. But we saw Stein reduced to twitching uncertainty as he moved from the shadows to "the ring of faint light" and into "the bright circle of the lamp." Emerging from the dark "into the light of torches," Jim carries his "shadowy ideal of conduct" with him still, and just as firmly. In surrendering "himself faithfully to the claim of his own world of shades," Jim—more than the successful Stein ever could—has earned his right to the "proud and unflinching glance" "sent right and left at all those faces" whom he has so fearlessly and irrevocably betrayed.

But as a solution to the moral dilemma Jim's tentative alternative proves to be a delusion: as Doramin's rage reveals, the Christian refusal to act is also, alas, a form of action and doomed with the others. Thus closes another door on the existential trap, confirming the claims of Axel Heyst, the protagonist of *Victory*, that all action—Jim's as well as Kurtz's—is the devil's work but adding what Heyst's career, in flying from action, attests: that inaction is as deadly as the rest and with fewer satisfactions. It opens no door out of the dilemma but only one that leads in again to the tragic.

TONY TANNER

Butterflies and Beetles—Conrad's Two Truths †

In *Lord Jim* when the sagacious and tentative Marlow recalls taking Jim's case to the wise merchant Stein he tells his patient listeners that he considered Stein "an eminently suitable person to receive my confidences about Jim's difficulties"; he also tells them, in almost the same breath, of Stein's curious private interest in beetles and butterflies. For Stein is a "learned collector." "His collection of Buprestidae and Longicorns—beetles all—horrible miniature monsters, looking malevolent in death and immobility, and his cabinet of butterflies, beautiful and hovering under the glass of cases of lifeless wings, had spread his fame far over the earth."

We feel, from the start of that crucial interview, a connection between Stein's distinction as a collector and his suitability to appraise Jim, to help him. And of course what we learn is that Stein seems to have an uncanny knowledge of the qualitative extremes of humanity: man as butterfly, man as beetle, he knows them both. Considering that this is an early book the suggestive hints that Conrad weaves into the scene work with an unusually silent and effective tact Consider, for instance, the way the insects are differently housed. "Narrow shelves filled with dark boxes of uniform shape and colour ran round the walls, not from floor to ceiling, but in a sombre belt about four feet broad. Catacombs of beetles." Not a hierarchy of beetles but a great thick belt of them: and that last short sentence makes just the right sinister impact. "The glass cases containing the collection of butterflies were ranged in three long rows upon slender-legged little tables." It is those slender legs we see—clean, fragile, graceful, and artistic: the appropriate furniture to set off a display of butterflies. The analogy between Jim and the butterflies is pressed still firmer before Marlow has even broached the subject. "I was very anxious, but I respected the intense, almost

† *Chicago Review*, XVI (Winter-Spring 1963), 123–40. Reprinted by permission.

passionate, absorption with which he looked at a butterfly, as though on the bronze sheen of these frail wings, in the white tracings, in the gorgeous markings, he could see other things, an image of something as perishable and defying destruction as these delicate and lifeless tissues displaying a splendour unmarred by death." While Marlow is *thinking* about Jim, Stein is *examining* a butterfly with great care: we feel that the very quality of reverent attention with which Stein studies his insects somehow qualifies him to make a key assessment of Jim. For the whole inquiry of the book is directed at ascertaining whether there is contained within the perishable "gorgeous markings" of Jim something, some quality, some essence, which will defy destruction, some "splendour" which will remain "unmarred by death." But Conrad is not so simple as to offer a one-to-one correlation between Jim and the butterfly: just as the analogy threatens to become obvious Conrad breaks it:

> "To tell you the truth, Stein," I said with an effort that surprised me, "I came here to describe a specimen . . ."
> "Butterfly?" he asked, with an unbelieving and humourous eagerness.
> "Nothing so perfect," I answered, feeling suddenly dispirited with all sorts of doubts. "A man."

Leaving the rest of that discussion let us re-examine Jim—bearing in mind the possible metaphor of the butterfly, a creature of beauty, a creature with wings which can carry it above the mere dead level of an earth which beetles crudely hug. Straight away we recall Jim's aversion to dirt. When we first meet him he is "spotlessly neat" and "apparelled in immaculate white from shoes to hat" and this fastidious, scrupulous dazzling whiteness is invested with a slightly mystical quality. For instance when Jim is received by the treacherous Rajah Allang in Patusan, Conrad first of all establishes the fact that the people who have gathered to witness his first appearance among them are "dirty with ashes and mud-stains." By contrast Jim glows with an almost supernatural brightness:

> In the midst of these dark-faced men, his stalwart figure in white apparel, the gleaming clusters of his fair hair, seemed to catch all the sunshine that trickled through the cracks in the closed shutters of that dim hall, with its walls of mats and a roof of thatch. He appeared like a creature not only of another kind but of another essence.

This is not racism, not a belief in white-supremacy peeping through. Jim shows up against the world. Thus when Marlow sees him for the last time:

He was white from head to foot, and remained persistently visible with the stronghold of the night at his back. . . . For me that white figure in the stillness of coast and sea seemed to stand at the heart of a vast enigma. The twilight was ebbing fast from the sky above his head, the strip of sand had sunk already under his feet, he himself appeared no bigger than a child—then only a speck, a tiny white speck that seemed to catch all the light left in a darkened world. . . . And, suddenly, I lost him. . . .

It is perhaps too easily portentous: the enigma could be anything and the encroaching darkness which finally seems to snuff him out is a touch of cosmic melodrama in the Manichean vein— but the intention is clear. Jim is a creature of "light" threatened by the forces of darkness; he is the creature of purity who stands above the dirty crowd. Throughout the book his characteristic stance is a superior contemplation of a life which goes about its muddled business far below him. As a boy at the marine school he was "very smart aloft. His station was in the fore-top, and often from there he looked down, with the contempt of a man destined to shine in the midst of dangers, at the peaceful multitude of roofs cut in two by the brown tide of the stream." When Marlow visits him in Patusan they stand talking on the top of a hill. "He was like a figure set up on a pedestal, to represent in his persistent youth the power, and perhaps the virtues, of races that never grow old, that have emerged from the gloom." Even at his ignominious trial "he stood elevated in the witness-box" and dark faces stare up at him from below. So much is obvious, perhaps too obvious. So perhaps are Conrad's pointers to the vulnerabilities and limitations inherent in Jim's characteristic heroic pose. His incurable taste for romantic daydreams nourished on fictional situations, his incapacity for self-knowledge, even the physical fact of his being "an inch, perhaps two under six feet" with which the book all too significantly begins, make "the subtle unsoundness of the man" a somewhat less subtle thing than Conrad probably thought. Jim is all too obviously flawed. But his most crucial shortcoming is more interesting. It is hinted at in his first failure to take the opportunity for heroic action which offered itself while he was still a boy at the marine school. While he is indulging in heroic daydreams a real distress signal goes up and the young trainee-sailors have to effect a rescue. But active as he is in his dreams, when confronted by the real thing Jim is paralysed. "He stood still," Conrad uses the phrase twice, "as if confounded." This inability to act is more glaringly revealed on board the refugee ship *Patna*. The nature of the captain and other men who desperately work to lower one lifeboat for themselves with no thought for the hundreds of sleeping refugees is made very clear: they are base, cowardly animals (the skipper particularly is described in the most bestial terms) who, with no thought for dignity or duty, are galvanised into frantic efforts to save their skins. To Jim they are contemptible, loathsome fools involved in scenes of grotesque "low comedy." But Jim himself?—he simply doesn't move. "He wanted me to know he had kept his distance; that there was nothing in common between him and these men—who had the hammer. Nothing whatever. It is more probable he thought himself cut off from them by a space that could not be traversed." He does not do anything to alert the sleeping passengers, but he does not take part in the almost farcically crude attempts to lower that one shameful lifeboat. He does nothing. He is the passive hero who is faced by scenes of macabre low comedy and doesn't even know how or where to begin. He feels a shuddering contemptuous disdain for the men shamelessly acting on their basest motives—he wouldn't even touch a hammer. (But that hammer betokens action—and the procuring of the hammer was in fact an heroic act even if done for the basest motives.) And yet as Jim tells his story to Marlow it becomes a terrible case of *"qui s'excuse s'accuse."* He protests too much—that he has nothing in common with these men; yet when the pinch comes, when it seems as though he is really faced by the alternative of life and death, albeit an ignoble life and an heroic death, he suddenly finds that he has jumped, that he is down among those most contemptible of men. The space separating the butterfly and beetle—in men, in one man—can in fact be "traversed"—traversed in an instant. The physical descent is wonderfully apt for this is indeed a classic "fall." The heroic heights are abandoned: the butterfly is suddenly seen sprawling ingloriously among the beetles and an awful question arises. Has Jim at this moment found his true "level"?

We must leave Jim for a moment and consider the other objects of Stein's study—the beetles. Let us regard beetles as ugly earthbound creatures, devoid of dignity and aspiration, intent merely on self-preservation at all costs: but gifted with a hard shell which serves them well in their unscrupulous will to live—to live on any terms, and capable of great malevolence when that life is threatened. There are hordes of such insects in *Lord Jim.* In fact one could describe the logic of Jim's continual flight as an attempt to escape from the beetles of mankind: and the drama of his travels is generated by the beetles who are continually crossing his path. Apart from the skipper of the *Patna,* who is in some ways the grossest beetle of them all, the most important are Chester, Cornelius, and Brown.

Chester is waiting for Jim after his trial like a morality-play tempter. Jim's dishonour is symbolized by the cancelling of his certificate, and the punishment literally staggers him: he walks weakly away from the court. Immediately Chester appears to talk to Marlow—robust, healthy, tough, and contemptuous of all man-made standards.

> He looked knowingly after Jim. "Takes it to heart?" he asked scornfully. "Very much," I said. "Then he's no good," he opined. "What's all the to-do about? A bit of ass's skin. That never yet made a man. You must see things exactly as they are—if you don't, you may just as well give in at once. You will never do any-thing in this world. Look at me. I made it a practice never to take anything to heart." "Yes," I said, "you see things as they are."

From his conversation it is clear that Chester is a figure of vigour, resourcefulness, and endless energy of action: he is never enfeebled or immobilized by a sickly conscience. "The Lord knows the right and wrong of that story" is his typical comment on the rumour that his accomplice Robinson once indulged in cannibalism. As far as he is concerned, if Robinson ate human flesh to keep himself alive, then that does credit to his realistic turn of mind—he, too, saw things as they were. Chester offers Jim a job of dubious morality and Marlow refuses on Jim's account. Chester shrugs and leaves Mar-low with this comment on Jim: "He is no earthly good for any-thing." Or as we might re-phrase it—he is no good for any earth-bound activity. And so it appears. Jim takes job after job and performs with great efficiency until a beetle turns up, usually with the story of the *Patna* and his own acrid comments on it. At various times Jim is explicitly or unconsciously called a cur, a skunk, a rat —all those repulsive animals with which the butterfly part of his nature least wishes to have anything to do. Cornelius turns up in more unusual circumstances. He is the lazy, sluggish, dilapidated father of the girl Jim loves in Patusan. He wretchedly mistreated his wife so that she died crying, and now he continues his indolent tyranny over the girl. He is a man who has gone morally to seed. But when Jim and the girl fall in love he asserts his odious presence. His base nature is wonderfully intimated in kinaesthetic terms by Conrad. Just to watch the man walk is to know him for what he is:

> Cornelius was creeping across in full view with an inexpressible effect of stealthiness, of dark and secret slinking. He reminded one of everything that is unsavoury. His slow laborious walk re-sembled the creeping of a repulsive beetle, the legs alone moving with horrid industry while the body glided evenly. I suppose he made straight for the place where he wanted to get to, but his progress with one shoulder carried forward seemed oblique. He was often seen circling slowly amongst the sheds, as if following a scent; passing before the veranda with upward stealthy glances; disappearing without haste round the corner of some hut.

He soils the air in which Jim is trying to work out his salvation, and seems to embody a repulsive but ineradicable presence. "He has his place neither in the background nor in the foreground of the story; he is simply seen skulking on its outskirts, enigmatical and unclean, tainting the fragrance of its youth and of its naiveness." But this man has a certain momentum of hate. And from his base perspective he sees the weakness of Jim. He tells his opinion to Marlow. "He is a big fool, honourable sir. . . . He's no more than a little child here—like a little child—a little child." With this insight (and the animus generated by Jim's refusal to give him money for his daughter) he knows enough to set about betraying and destroying Jim. In his own miserable way he *acts*. And Cornelius too has the lineaments of a figure in a morality play. "Somehow the shadowy Cornelius far off there seemed to be the hateful embodiment of all the annoyances and difficulties he [Jim] had found in his path." It is no use Jim's crying out "nothing can touch me" (they are almost his dying words), for somehow such foul presences as Cornelius always loom up to finger with soiled hands the weak spots in his honour. The most notable beetle however is Brown, the man who turns up unexpectedly and is directly responsible for Jim's downfall. As Marlow talks to him on his death bed it becomes clear that Brown feels a profoundly instinctual antipathy towards Jim, a hatred of him which is not accounted for by the narrative facts.

> "I could see directly I set my eyes on him what sort of a fool he was," gasped the dying Brown. "He a man! Hell! He was a hollow sham. As if he couldn't have said, 'Hands off my plunder!' blast him! That would have been like a man. Rot his superior soul! He had me there—but he hadn't devil enough in him to make an end of me."

The revulsion is mixed: Jim's air of moral superiority maddens Brown, as evidence of a superior ethic will always infuriate a man who lives by a baser one, for what Jim sees as a moral mission, his sacred obligation to the natives, Brown can only see as potential "plunder." On the other hand Jim's refusal to fight like a man, his incapacity for diabolical *action*, revolts the man of devilish energy. For Brown, Jim is repulsive because he pretends to be more than a man, and yet in his hollow inactivity he reveals himself to be devoid of all those attributes which make a man man-like. He is, thus, a "fraud." Brown's description of his crucial encounter with Jim brings the issues of the book to a head. Marlow paraphrases Brown's account:

> I know that Brown hated Jim at first sight. . . . he cursed in his heart the other's youth and assurance, his clear eyes and untroubled bearing. . . . And there was something in the very

neatness of Jim's clothes, from the white helmet to the canvas leggings and the pipeclayed shoes, which in Brown's sombre, ir-ritated eyes seemed to belong to things he had in the very shap-ing of his life contemned and flouted.

Brown then recalls the exchange in his own words, an exchange, it should be remembered, which means life or death to Brown. " 'We are all equal before death,' I said. I admitted I was there like a rat in a trap, but we had been driven to it, and even a trapped rat can give a bite. He caught me up in a moment. 'Not if you don't go near the trap till the rat is dead.' " It is a typical answer—Jim still has an incurable distaste for any action which means involving him-self with base, dirty people. He doesn't want to take a part in any low comedy, although we may recall that on one occasion Jim him-self was described as a rat. But even as a rat he has no bite to him. Brown pursues his case with an amoral anarchic gusto which has a curious sort of unscrupulous heroism all its own ("a virile sincerity in accepting the morality and consequences of his acts"), and as he makes his points we seem to see Jim withering before our eyes.

> "And I would let you shoot me and welcome," I said. "This is as good a jumping-off place for me as another. I am sick of my in-fernal luck. But it would be too easy. There are my men in the same boat—and, by God, I am not the sort to jump out of trouble and leave them in a d—d lurch," I said. . . . "I've lived —and so did you though you talk as if you were one of those people that should have wings so as to go about without touching the dirty earth. Well—it is dirty. I haven't got any wings. I am here because I was afraid once in my life. Want to know what of? Of a prison."

Brown is strong because he can admit to fear without letting it undermine his mainsprings of action; he is strong because his ele-ment is the dirt of the world; he is strong because he lives by action (he only fears the arresting walls of a prison), and being a man of action he would never do the one thing which has soured Jim's life, leave his mates, abandon his ship. And Jim finally takes what is to Brown the easy way out and lets himself be shot. On his own terms Brown is "right"—he "sees things as they are" and therefore al-ways acts with a prompt and savage confidence (he feels the "lust of battle," an emotion foreign to Jim). And because of this he can get through Jim's faulty heroic armature and "shake his twopenny soul around and inside out and upside down." Perhaps Conrad makes the opposition between the two men too clear, but Brown is a con-vincing figure, the man of dirt who wishes to soil the disdainful immaculateness of Jim, the man of action who wishes to grab hold of that "don't-you-touch-me sort of fellow," the man without wings who yearns to drag down into his element those superior souls who think they can live without touching the earth. He has an Iago streak in him—the basic diabolical compulsion to bring everything to chaos, to reduce fine things to a mess: he has both the irresistible impulse and the requisite satanic insight to puncture the Othellos and Jims of this world. He is the anti-heroic, anti-idealistic supreme: and he is supremely successful because he has an uncanny instinct for attacking just those faults of self-deception and inaction and shame which mar Jim's armour of idealism. The moral to be drawn from Brown's unforeseeable and disastrous appearance in Jim's moral hide-out is not that a bad penny always turns up but that you can never get away from the beetles of this world, their amoral ferocity, and their murderous truth.

Before returning to Jim I want to draw attention to one of Conrad's most notable creations of the beetles of this world. I refer to Donkin in *The Nigger of the "Narcissus."* Once Conrad starts on his description of Donkin he can scarcely control himself. The torrential abuse certainly mars the texture of the book but it clearly reveals the author's preoccupation with this kind of man. I quote only certain key extracts.

> He looked as if he had known all the degradations and all the furies. He looked as if he had been cuffed, kicked, rolled in the mud; he looked as if he had been scratched, spat upon, pelted with unmentionable filth . . . and he smiled with a sense of security at the faces around.

> His neck was long and thin; his eyelids were red; rare hairs hung about his jaws; his shoulders were peaked and drooped like the broken wings of a bird; all his left side was caked with mud which showed that he had lately slept in a wet ditch.

A broken-winged creature at home in the mud—Donkin is related to Brown.

> They all knew him. Is there a spot on earth where such a man is unknown. . . . He was the man who cannot steer, that cannot splice, that dodges the work on dark nights; that, aloft, holds on frantically with both arms and legs, and swears at the wind, the sleet, the darkness; the man who curses the sea while others work. . . . The independent offspring of the ignoble freedom of the slums full of disdain and hate for the austere servitude of the sea.

Donkin subsumes in his one person all the basest instincts and inclinations of man. He too has a devil of destruction in him, a rancorous feral hate for all the illusions which sustain and dignify mankind.

He had a desire to assert his importance, to break, to crush; to be even with everybody for everything; to tear the veil, unmask, expose, leave no refuge—a perfidious desire of truthfulness!

That last word comes as something of a surprise, but Conrad means it. This emerges more clearly when Donkin starts trying to sow dissent among the sailors when the voyage gets rough: he complains about everything—discipline, work, pay; he denies the point of all effort. "His picturesque and filthy loquacity flowed like a troubled stream from a poisoned source." But the men listen: his "filthy loquacity" appeals to and elicits a response from all of them. "We abominated the creature and could not deny the truth of his contentions. It was all so obvious." Donkin is in complete command of one kind of truth, the beetle's truth, the truth that asserts that a certificate of duty is a mere piece of ass's skin, that ideals of conduct are "no earthly use," that honour is a fraud. For Conrad this was the abominable truth of the ditch. But it was a truth.

If this is the only kind of truth then Jim is a deluded fool indeed; but for Conrad Jim is something more complex and interesting. In a letter to Edward Garnett written in 1908 Conrad complains of his critics: ". . . there is even one abandoned creature who says I am a neo-platonist. What on earth is that?" Conrad disliked all facile classification, but against that outburst of astonishment we can put an extract from a letter to Sir Sidney Colvin written in 1917.

I have been called a writer of the sea, of the tropics, a descriptive writer, a romantic writer—and also a realist. But as a matter of fact all my concern has been with the "ideal" value of things, events and people. That and nothing else. The humorous, the pathetic, the passionate, the sentimental *aspects* came in of themselves—*mais en vérité c'est les valeurs idéales des faits et gestes humains qui se sont imposés à mon activité artistique.* Whatever dramatic and narrative gifts I may have are always, instinctively, used with that object—to get at, to bring forth *les valeurs idéales.* Of course this is a very general statement but roughly I believe it to be true.

It is also a letter and must not be taken as a pondered creed—but the reiteration of the notion of "ideal value" is surely significant. Of course Conrad was not a systematic Platonist of any kind, but undoubtedly he had felt an urge to locate and identify a value which lay under the surface of certain people, actions, or things, a value inaccessible to the beetles with their relentlessly accurate eye for the surface facts, their diabolical gift for seeing things "as they are." Jim is made a crucial focus of this inquiry, this question of the other truth. Is he just a child, a fool, a coward, a fraud? Or does he embody some sort of ideal value, no matter how debased that ideal may be by an involvement with the mud of the world? This takes us back to Marlow's interview with Stein. Stein habitually talks in ellipses and paradoxes and his speech is full of cryptic lacunae. Thus he mutters: "To follow the dream, and again to follow the dream— and so—*ewig*—*usque ad finem* . . ." And more specifically on Jim: " 'He is romantic—romantic,' he repeated. 'And that is very bad—very bad, . . . Very good, too,' he added." Then he throws at Marlow the question of why Jim exists so strongly for him. Marlow searches his mind. "At that moment it was difficult to believe in Jim's existence . . . but his imperishable reality came to me with a convincing, with an irresistible force! I saw it vividly, as though . . . we had approached nearer to absolute Truth, which like Beauty itself, floats elusive, obscure, half submerged, in the silent waters of mystery."

We have been taught to shy at capitalised abstractions in the novel and perhaps rightly—the passage is easily faulted. But it does reveal Conrad's intention, or perhaps we should say Conrad's problem. Jim stands for our best illusions, those exercises of the imagination which we allow to guide our conduct in order to give it purpose, dignity, and, in Conrad's word, glamour. It is our illusions, our ideals, which give us "gorgeous markings" and aspiring wings. Is there anything that can be called truth in them, do these "pure exercises of imagination" contain any of "the deep hidden truthfulness of works of art"? Such seems to be Marlow's line of questioning. Of course to have employed the persona of Marlow is a gesture of detachment, of possibly ironic disengagement on Conrad's part —the narrator examines his character, the author scrutinizes both; but in this early work it is hard to feel that Marlow's tenative Platonic musings are not in fact Conrad's own. When Marlow offers such remarks as: "the truth disclosed in a moment of illusion" or "our illusions, which I suspect only to be visions of remote unattainable truth, seen dimly," we inevitably feel that the author is backing him up to the hilt. Jim reminds Marlow—and, we feel, Conrad—"of those illusions you had thought gone out, extinct, cold": not everybody lives by illusions of course—"it is respectable to have no illusions—and safe—and profitable," but it is also "dull." Illusions redeem life momentarily from its dullness or dirtiness: they are responsible for "that light of glamour created in the shock of trifles, as amazing as the glow of sparks struck from a cold stone—and as short-lived, alas!" Are the illusions true? Marlow is vague—memorably vague: "he [Jim] felt . . . the demand of some such truth or some such illusion—I don't care how you call it, there is no little difference, and the difference means so little." From an author that would be unacceptable—from a genial after-dinner raconteur we let it pass. And we let it pass because a better sentence follows. "The thing is that in virtue of his feelings, he matered." The horizons Jim dreamed of are unattainable, the heroic deeds he imagined to himself he cannot realize in action, life consecrated to an ideal of conduct cannot be lived, not only because of the ungovernable hostility of baser men but also because of the inexpugnable weaknesses in the ideal itself. But the feelings that lie at the root of all these aspirations and ideals—you cannot give the lie to those. Such would seem to be Marlow's point.

And it is because of the unflagging persistence of those feelings, their determination to operate at the highest attainable level, that both Marlow and Stein are inclined to speak of the "truth" of Jim's later life. When Jim's widow complains to Stein that Jim at the end was false, Stein answers with unusual emotion. "No! no! True! true! true!" and Marlow speaks, rather curiously, of "the sheer truthfulness of his last three years of life" as though, like the Great Gatsby, Jim had lived up to "his Platonic conception of himself." As Marlow says early in the book, he was aware of "an obscure truth" in Jim's attitude to life which seemed "momentous enough to affect mankind's conception of itself." Jim's conception of himself is vulnerable and romantic in the extreme and is responsible for culpable failures to act in the right way at the right time. But Conrad is obviously allowing him a poetic gloss, as though there is something he cannot, dare not, bring himself to utterly condemn. For this reason Marlow's account of Jim tries, at the end, to convince us that "his spirit seemed to rise above the ruins of his existence." But it is a weak gesture, and the last line of the novel has a melancholy ring to it. "Stein has aged greatly of late. He feels it himself, and says often that he is 'preparing to leave all this; preparing to leave. . . .' While he waves his hand sadly at his butterflies."

One can see *Lord Jim* as Conrad's regretful farewell to the butterflies. Like the actual butterfly which Stein shows Marlow in their first interview, Jim was the last of a dying species as far as Conrad was concerned. "Only one specimen like this they have in *your* London, and then—no more." For the terrible unavoidable truth about Jim is that "he is not good enough"—the worst truth to Conrad is that "nobody, nobody is good enough." Jim cannot triumph over the ugly *facts* (a key word in the novel) though he spends his time trying to: he cannot "lay the ghost" of the ugly fact that he himself embodies and must carry with him wherever he goes. And these ugly facts are beetle facts and together with the brute facts of an indifferent Nature they seem to have the malvolent desire "to annihilate all that is priceless and necessary." But these facts are true—which is why truth is always referred to as "painful" or "sinister" in the later Conrad. Jim, despite the Platonic halo and the author's efforts to shore him up poetically, is not finally true. Or not true enough for the relentlessly penetrating eye of Conrad. The realists have no ideals—thus their lives are ugly. But the idealist has no grip on reality: he cannot live properly at all. *Lord Jim* is a prelude to profound pessimism. Like Winnie Verloc in *The Secret Agent* Conrad came to feel "profoundly that things do not stand much looking into." Unlike Winnie he cannot help continuing to look. And what he comes to see is an abysmal absence of meaning and value in the world. If E. M. Forster is right in saying that "the secret casket of his genius contains a vapour rather than a jewel," that is because Conrad felt that at the center of existence there was only a vapour, and not the much desiderated jewel. There is an arresting passage in a letter to Cunninghame Graham which refers to the last sentence of that writer's preface to *Mogreb-al-Acksa*. The sentence enigmatically implies that there is a safe and meaningful destiny at the end of the road somewhere just to the right of a lone tree on the horizon. Conrad comments:

> Ah! the lone tree on the horizon and then bear a little (a very little) to the right. Haven't we all ridden with direction to find no house but many curs barking at the heels. Can't miss it? Well, perhaps we can't. And we don't ride with a stouter heart for that. Indeed, my friend, there is a joy in being lost, but a sorrow in being weary. . . . But what business have you, O Man! coming with your uncomprehended truth,—a thing less than mist but black, to make me sniff at—the stink of the lamp? Ride to the tree and to the right,—for verily there is a devil at the end of every road. Let us pray to the poor bellied gods, to gods with more legs than a centipede and more arms than a dozen windmills: let us pray to them to guard us from the mischance of arriving somewhere.

Arriving, that is, at the final truth which is "less than mist but black." It seems to me that Conrad reached that last stage of pessimism which very few other writers—Melville is one—have experienced. The stage at which the greatest fear is not that the meaning of life might be evil but that there might be absolutely no meaning at all to be found. It is easy to state it thus glibly: but to have that conviction gnawing at you for the better part of a lifetime must be a rare and unenviable experience. Which is perhaps why Conrad's letters are among the most anguished any writer has left to us. Such a man may well pray for the grace of non-arrival.

There is no time here for a full study of Conrad's pessimism but the conclusions which it seems to me that Conrad reached, however unwittingly and unwillingly, in *Lord Jim* throw an interesting light on two recurring themes of his work, namely, the experience of total darkness, and the more than nautical significance of "steering." It is commonly agreed that in many of his early works Conrad exhibits a rather facile predilection for melodramatic atmospherics: there is too much ineffable, ineluctable darkness, too much of the "tenebrous immensity" style of writing. But at certain key moments in his books the experience of utter darkness carries a profound moral and psychological significance. Jim really discovers the difficulty of living according to a preconceived ideal not when he makes the fatal jump—he does that in a mood of almost paralysed passivity—but when he is alone with the other base cowards in the complete darkness of the sea. The way he describes the experience is revealing. "After the ship's lights had gone, anything might have happened in that boat—anything in the world—and the world no wiser. . . . We were like men walled up in a roomy grave. No concern with anything on earth. Nobody to pass an opinion. Nothing mattered." And later: "But the lights. The lights did go! We did not see them. They were not there. If they had been, I would have swum back—I would have gone back and shouted alongside—I would have begged them to take me on board. . . ." He is referring to the lights of the abandoned ship, which would have told him that the ship was not sinking after all. But they mean more than that. They are clues to ethical conduct which the external world gives us, the signs which we have to interpret and then act upon, irresistible reminders from the world of men. Conrad is interested in those crucial moments when we are utterly "alone with ourselves," when to all intents and purposes nothing matters, when all the guidance must come from within, when all the lights have gone out. Jim claims that in such circumstances "there was not the thickness of a sheet of paper between the right and wrong of this affair" and "not the breadth of a hair between this and that." Marlow answers, rather mordantly, "It is difficult to see a hair at midnight." Impossible, we might concede. And it is exactly *then* that Conrad wants to know how a man behaves, how a man should behave, how he can find sanctions and supports to resist the insidious gravitational pull towards the base, beetle-like, irresistible argument that "nothing matters." The narrator of *The Shadow Line* goes through a similar experience. During the storm: "I was alone, every man was alone where he stood. And every form was gone, top, spar, sail, fittings, rails; everything was blotted out in the dreadful smoothness of that absolute night" and then: "both binnacle lamps were out. . . . The last gleam of light in the universe had gone." In such circumstances "the eye lost itself in inconceivable depths," or as we might more crudely put it, the moral eye has nothing to focus on. *That* is the testing time. Darkness is an all too easy shortcut to portentous effects but at certain moments Conrad manages to invest it with a compelling elemental terror and he does so, I think, because it symbolised for him a passionately felt philosophical darkness. At times it as palpable and convincing as "The Cloud of Unknowing" and for similar reasons. Conrad also had an intimate acquaintance with the experience of "the lacking of knowing." This subterranean doubt and scepticism comes very near the surface of some of his letters:

> I have often suffered in connection with my work from a sense of unreality, from intellectual doubt of the ground I stand on.
> Everyone must walk in the light of his own heart's gospel. No man's light is good to any of his fellows. That's my creed from the beginning to end. That's my view of life—a view that rejects all formulas, dogmas and principles of other people's making. These are only a web of illusions.
> My task appears to me as sensible as lifting the world without that fulcrum which even that conceited ass, Archimedes, admitted to be necesssary.

The fulcrum he lacks is the fulcrum of faith, the fulcrum of immovable and clarified convictions: "There is no morality, no knowledge and no hope: there is only the consciousness of ourselves which drives us about a world that, whether seen in a convex or concave mirror, is always but a vain and floating appearance." Given this view of the world then any idealism seems as pointless "as though one were anxious about the cut of one's clothes in a community of blind men." And yet Conrad was deeply concerned about a man's moral dress even when he was invisible to the rest of the world. The behaviour of the crowd held no interest for Conrad. And to the question, how should one behave in the dark, he had one firm answer—you steer.

Thus extrapolated the idea is vague in the extreme, but let us return to *The Nigger of the "Narcissus"* for a concrete image of this one positive which Conrad fervently believed in. I refer to Old Singleton's behaviour in the storm during which Donkin whines, complains, and incites the men to abandon a pointless and exacting duty.

> Apart, far aft, and alone by the helm, old Singleton had deliberately tucked his white beard under the top button of his glistening coat. Swaying upon the din and tumult of the seas, with the whole battered length of the ship launched forward in a rolling rush before his steady old eyes, he stood rigidly still, forgotten by all, and with an attentive face. In front of his erect figure only the two arms moved crosswise with a swift and sudden readiness, to check or urge again the rapid stir of circling spokes. He steered with care.

The last telling short sentence (short sentences are rare in Conrad and always used for special emphasis) underlines the simple unquestioning dedication with which Old Singleton does what, in the circumstances, most needs to be done. It makes it seem as though he were acting in unflinching compliance with a categorical imperative. The particularly Conradian aspect of this conception of duty is the fact that he can no longer produce the sanctions and proofs which would justify and enforce the standards of conduct which he nevertheless feels to be "imperative." Singleton steers but without being able to see the final destination. Some people would say that such persistence was futile. Conrad had been in such a situation.

> Sufficient moral tenacity is all I pray for, not to save me from taking to drink, because I couldn't even if I wanted to, but from the temptation to throw away the oar. And I have known good men do that too, saying: "It's no use." Then was my turn to keep the boat head to sea for fourteen solid hours.

Singleton steers (Donkin, we recall, cannot steer): but this is not the kind of steering which Shaw meant when he made Don Juan in hell say: "To be in hell is to drift: to be in heaven is to steer." For Shaw, a social meliorist, meant that men and society should allow themselves to be guided by their best intelligence, the brain, "the organ by which Nature strives to understand itself." Shaw could see, or thought he could, the destination and wanted us to use our heads and hurry up getting there. But for Conrad the mind could be a curse, an inhibitor or interrupter of proper conduct. Cunninghame Graham once wrote to Conrad suggesting he create a Singleton figure with an education added. Conrad's reply is much to our point.

> But first of all—what education? If it is the knowledge of how to live, my man essentially possessed it. He was in perfect accord with life. If by education you mean scientific knowledge then the question arises—what knowledge? How much of it—in what direction? Is it to stop at plane trigonometry or at conic sections? Or is he to study Platonism or Pyrrhonism, or the philosophy of the gentle Emerson? Or do you mean the kind of knowledge which would enable him to scheme, and lie, and intrigue his way to the forefront of a crowd no better than himself? Would you seriously of malice prepense, cultivate in that unconscious man the power to think? Then he would become conscious,—and much smaller,—and very unhappy. Now he is simple and great like an elemental force. Nothing can touch him but the curse of decay,—the eternal decree that will extinguish the sun, the stars, one by one, and in another instant shall spread a frozen darkness over the whole universe. Nothing else can touch him— he does not think.

There is a good deal of the essential Conrad in that paragraph. As he wrote elsewhere: "It is impossible to know anything, tho' it is possible to believe a thing or two." Haunted by the impossibility of knowledge, Conrad could not accept the beetle—Donkin's view of things—and he renounced the fallible, if beautiful, butterfly-Jim conception of life: but he believed in Singleton and the value and necessity of keeping the hands to the wheel, the dignity of standing erect and uncomplaining in the storms of a hostile nature and the darkness of encircling doubt.

BRUCE M. JOHNSON

Conrad's "Karain" and *Lord Jim* †

More than a year before beginning what he thought would be a short piece called "Tuan Jim: A Sketch," Joseph Conrad had written an awkwardly complex short story which seems to have cleared some of the intellectual and emotional ground for *Lord Jim*. In "Karain, a Memory," published in *Tales of Unrest* and begun sometime early in 1897, Conrad produces characters and a motif which anticipate some of the more basic involutions of the later novel.

Albert J. Guerard has shown that Conrad's use of the engaged "I" represents a modest but important step toward the Marlow technique. Guerard goes on to develop the idea at length, mentioning in his discussion some close thematic similarities between the story and the novel:

> The man of good intentions and his impulsive crime and long remorse; his need to communicate guilt and so acquire further witnesses; the desperate attempt to leave in space what always travels with him in time; the sympathetic yet detached listener —these foreshadowings of *Lord Jim* are obvious.[1]

But Guerard slights the engagingly ironic end of the story, in which a young English sailor gives a Jubilee sixpence to the native lord, Karain, convincing him that the Queen's image will ward off evil spirits and one spirit in particular. Guerard concludes that Karain is in Conrad's eyes ultimately "only a superstitious native," even though the young sailor sounds the typically Marlovian note of involvement with Karain's sense of guilt and loss: " 'Every one of us,'

† *Modern Language Quarterly*, XXIV (March 1963), 13–20. Reprinted by permission.
1. Albert J. Guerard, *Conrad the Novelist*, Cambridge, Mass., 1958, p. 91. I am also indebted to Walter F. Wright's fine explanation of the story as romance in his *Romance and Tragedy in Joseph Conrad*, Lincoln, Neb., 1949, pp. 25–36.

he said, with pauses that somehow were more offensive than his words—'every one of us, you'll admit, has been haunted by some woman . . . and . . . as to friends . . . dropped by the way. . . . Well . . . ask yourselves.' " [2]

It would appear, however, that Conrad is far from thinking Karain merely a superstitious native and that there are many details in the story designed to bring Karain and the Englishmen together in the same illusion-haunted human predicament. The story needs to be read much more sympathetically than it has been lest it seem an entirely unsophisticated, faltering step toward *Lord Jim.* Even Guerard's sensitive appreciation disparages its arrangement of illusion as a major theme.

Karain has joined his friend Pata Matara in a search for Matara's sister, who has broken her marriage contract by running off with a redheaded Dutchman. Thus disgraced, she is pursued by these two young Malays in a prolonged odyssey during which Karain falls in love with the thought of the girl, with her vision. So enchanted is he that when she and the Dutchman are discovered, Karain involuntarily shoots Pata Matara rather than let him kill his sister. As in "The Lagoon," a masculine bond is betrayed for the sake of passion.

Having killed his friend, Karain is haunted by his apparition until he meets an old shaman who becomes his exorcist and sword-bearer. As long as this old man is behind him (Karain continually turns around to make certain he is there), the apparition does not appear. Finally the shaman dies, and Karain, distraught, swims out to the boat of the Englishmen who have been selling him guns and who are his good friends. He asks sanctuary and, eventually, to go with them

to your people, who live in unbelief; to whom day is day, and night is night—nothing more, because you understand all things seen, and despise all else! To your land of unbelief, where the dead do not speak, where every man is wise, and alone—and at peace!

Clearly, Karain believes he can leave this ghost far behind by traveling to the land of hardheaded English pragmatists.

In wandering with his shaman sword-bearer, Karain has assembled a band of hardy natives and has created a nice little kingdom for himself. He rules here as Jim does in Patusan: both men have great guilt hanging over their heads but seem able to put it off by the sheer success of their governing enterprise. They are revered by their subjects and appear "clothed in the illusion of unavoidable success." Yet, like Jim, Karain seems to wear a mask: "He was ornate and disturbing, for one could not imagine what depth of horrible void such an elaborate front could be worthy to hide." And

2. *Tales of Unrest,* Dent Collected Edition, London, 1947, p. 47.

there is some hint that his contemplated war on tribes over the hills is simply a drug for that same guilt.

Conrad continually reminds us that Karain is on a stage: "He was treated with a solemn respect accorded in the irreverent West only to monarchs of the stage, and he accepted the profound homage with a sustained dignity seen nowhere else but behind the footlights and in the condensed falseness of some grossly tragic situation." He acts as Jim does, as though his native state were a stage on which must be enacted that "illusion of unavoidable success." The state actually is, Conrad tells us, shaped like a stage, "like a young moon," with hills behind. "Day after day he appeared before us incomparably faithful to the illusions of the stage, and at sunset the night descended upon him quickly, like a falling curtain." All this is much like Jim's theatrical performance in Patusan, especially in the way that Jim too, despite his burden of guilt, exudes confidence in his "unavoidable success."

Even in the normal course of trading, Karain likes to return to the English boat after dark for long conversations, at which times he displays another aspect of Jim, "simplicity itself . . . all in white." Karain, as I have indicated, feels he can allay his guilty apparition by being among these "unbelievers." Jim, of course, seeks to redeem himself by governing Patusan: the native flees to the white man, the white man to the native. It is as though both expect the guilt to become manageable at some sort of cultural barrier. Conrad's point in *Lord Jim*, though not in "Karain," is that this kind of purgation is illusory, that all men are in the same uncomfortable position when guilt and expiation are concerned.

It is nevertheless true that throughout the Patusan episode Jewel talks as though white men were peculiarly susceptible to illusion. When Marlow tries to set her mind at rest, to assure her that Jim has no intention of leaving Patusan, she replies: "You all remember something! You all go back to it. What is it? You tell me! What is this thing? Is it alive?—is it dead? I hate it. It is cruel. Has it got a face and a voice—this calamity?" She is, of course, speaking of illusion, and especially of the ego ideal which impels Jim almost as though it were love for another woman. Jewel has been taught by her disappointed mother to expect that white men will follow the dream away from their native women.

Although Karain's flight to his pragmatic saviors is treated ironically, Karain is not, as Guerard suggests, a simple native whom Conrad is not yet willing to call "one of us." Conrad insists that Karain's illusion has its potent counterpart in the West, where ghosts are perhaps less bizarre, but no less dogged in their haunting. The final scene in the ship's cabin, when Karain asks for a charm, brings this out. The first things we notice about the "unbelieving" narrator here are his remarkably spooky similes and metaphors: "A vivid flash of lightning made the two round sternports facing him glimmer like a pair of cruel and phosphorescent eyes." And then, as though a seance were about to begin, "The flame of the lamp seemed to wither into brown dust for an instant, and the looking-glass over the little sideboard leaped out behind his back in a smooth sheet of livid light." Although the image reveals mainly Conrad's own brilliant visual sense (the flash of lightning causes the flame to pale in contrast), the description is also there to point out a surprisingly occult bent in this Western mind.

Karain talks against a background of "two chronometers . . . ticking along with unflagging speed against one another." It is blatantly incongruous that this tale of Eastern revenge and guilt should play against an especially Western background of Greenwich standard time. Later, after Karain has unleashed his story, the narrator says, "The silence was profound; but it seemed full of noiseless phantoms, of things sorrowful, shadowy, and mute, in whose invisible presence the firm, pulsating beat of the two ship's chronometers ticking off steadily the seconds of Greenwich Time seemed to me a protection and a relief." The Englishmen, however, cannot really take refuge in Western "unbelief," if such exists, and the chronometers simply add to the irony of the entire scene.

It is as though Karain is described by Marlow when he arrives on the fateful night. The sense that he is "one of us" is strong at this point, and the narrator is almost literal in saying so. He remembers that those who say a native will not speak to a white man are mistaken: "No man will speak to his master"; but when the two men are equals, "One heart speaks—another one listens," and the whole universe hears "the futile tale of the burden of life." At this point one could wish that Conrad would begin to see some important differences between East and West, for if there are none, the utility of the exotic frame is called into question. Does it really make any difference that Karain wears a sarong rather than a business suit? In this story the answer is probably "yes." Without the apparent differences between native and white man, their actual affinity could not be so effectively rendered. But the question of the exotic frame still exists for all the other Malayan stories and has never been satisfactorily answered.

In a very real sense, both Karain and Jim have gone to unbelievers for help. Jewel, it will be remembered, believes Marlow is lying to her when he suggests that Jim is not wanted back in the world because he is "not good enough." Indeed, most of the disgrace Jim brings with him is simply disbelieved in Patusan. There seems almost to be a cultural inability on the part of the natives to read the peculiar kind of ego failure which marks Jim. It takes Gentleman

Brown, another Westerner, to see through Jim, despite his obvious success in the state (that same success, by the way, quite understandably blinds the natives to the possibility that Jim is anything but a nearly supernatural Lord). Marlow himself makes a useful distinction in explaining why Dain Waris could not immediately have led an attack against Brown: "He was not the visible, tangible incarnation of unfailing truth and of unfailing victory. Beloved, trusted, and admired as he was, he was still one of *them*, while Jim was one of *us*." Here Conrad intimates some psychological differences between the illusion generated by East and by West, but he seems never to have resolved the question.

There is, then, in both characters the intuition that guilt (if we may say that it is guilt Jim feels) can be overcome by passing a cultural or racial barrier. I do not mean to oversimplify things by implying that Conrad denies this, tying all men into a painful brotherhood of illusion. The natives in *Almayer's Folly* and *An Outcast of the Islands* are not prey for the same sort of ego ideal that impels the Westerners. Often it is the natives who are arch pragmatists, veritable Renaissance men in their political scheming (I am thinking mainly of Babalatchi). When they are haunted, and they often are, it is not by some ideal of truth or conduct Platonic in its white inaccessibility.[3]

It is remarkable the number of times that Jim's self-image is likened to the peculiarly Western search for some Platonic ideal of truth which is also the good. In *Lord Jim*, Marlow says (and he seems to be speaking of Westerners), "It was a strange and melancholy illusion, evolved half-consciously like all our illusions, which I suspect only to be visions of remote unattainable truth, seen dimly." The difference between these two states of mind apparently corresponds to the difference between "old mankind" and "races that never grow old, that have emerged from the gloom." To Conrad and Marlow, Jim is symbolic of something ineffably Western, something tragically and yet profitably adolescent.

However this may be, Karain seeks the same sort of cross-cultural purgation. The regularly measured Greenwich standard time ticks in the background, and the three sailors—one young and recently returned from a trip home; another a blond giant who strums love songs on a guitar and sings them in bad Spanish; the third our Mar-

---

3. Even the sense of honor and fidelity shown by a few natives is exaggerated and possibly destroyed when Westerners interfere. Lingard, in *The Rescue*, presses the honorable cause of his native prince and princess beyond their fondest hopes, as though they had turned over the ideal to a specialist. Finally (and typically), he is lured away by a phantom in the person of Edith Travers, and having allowed the whole native ideality to escalate, he abandons it. The compulsive honor which drives Karain and his friend is always seen as the practical minimum for saving face and really bears little resemblance to Jim's fantasy.

low prototype—are lost for a reply to Karain's amazing request. He has come to them because they are unlike him, and Conrad's point is that they both are and are not. Conrad, despite his ironic stance, is puzzled by Karain's and Jim's attempts to leave behind or metamorphose their guilt via some cultural barrier. The story is ambiguous about this point.

The narrator allows that there are beneficial as well as destructive illusions: "I thought . . . of all the men that wander amongst illusions . . . of the illusions that give joy, that give sorrow, that give pain, that give peace . . ." But he is surprised to discover that the relative peace Karain's shaman had given him was as real to Karain as other more respectable illusions would be to a "saint, philosopher, or fool of us all." He is, in short, just beginning to see the community and parity of illusion, although he has earlier given lip service to both. The young sailor mutters to him, after he has rather awkwardly tried to quiet Karain's anxiety, "You won't soothe him with your platitudes."

Discounting the point of view, it almost seems, as Guerard says, that it is "as though Conrad did not yet want to admit that Lord Jim [here, Karain] with his crime was 'one of us.'" But Conrad makes it appear that it is the narrator of "Karain" who is not really prepared to admit that this native with his exotic guilt has much to do with the West. Conrad himself is usually so prepared, and he arranges an ironic distance between himself and the narrator. Despite a rather wordy declaration to the contrary, the narrator cannot comprehend that Karain's story is more than a Gothic tale meant to be entertainingly shocking. And this is true even at the end of the story.

The young sailor, Hollis, however, is the instrument of Conrad's irony. He is the one who punctures the narrator's saccharine attempt to quiet Karain ("And there is forgetfulness in life," the narrator tastelessly observes). And he is the one who provides the ironic comment on Karain's description of the West as a place where "the dead do not speak, where every man is wise, and alone —and at peace!" "'Capital description,' murmured Hollis, with the flicker of a smile."

Of the three, it is young Hollis who catches the spirit of the game. The others are helpless and begin to resent the knowledge that they must somehow get rid of Karain. Hollis leaves for a moment and reappears with a small leather box containing personal talismans, souvenirs of love and apparently of disappointed love:

> There were there a couple of reels of cotton, a packet of needles, a bit of silk ribbon, dark blue; a cabinet photograph, at which Hollis stole a glance before laying it on the table face downwards.

A girl's portrait, I could see. There were, amongst a lot of various small objects, a bunch of flowers, a narrow white glove with many buttons, a slim packet of letters carefully tied up.

The narrator concludes, as we must, "Amulets of white men! Charms and talismans!" Jackson, the blond giant, thinks Hollis cynical in his apparent desire to fish some charm out of the box; but Hollis replies that his accuser has no "guile."

Of the three men, Jackson doubtless takes Karain's problem most to heart—so much so that he is reluctant to go along with Hollis' plan. But Jackson is ponderously serious and not the sort of man needed in this situation. Hollis, with his racial bias ("Those Malays are easily impressed—all nerves you know . . ."), actually helps Karain, while the other two are incapacitated by their Western sincerity. Hollis sews the Jubilee sixpence (carrying the Queen's image) into a small leather pouch made from the white glove; he is afraid the image will anger Karain's Mohammedan people, and so produces a kind of covered charm after the fashion of "those Italian peasants." The pouch hangs from a piece of ribbon which has sentimental value for Hollis, who says, "I'll give him something that I shall really miss." He smiles at the ribbon "scornfully," apparently feeling some disdain for his own susceptibility rather than for Karain's artlessness. Then, too, there can be no doubt that all of Hollis' charms, i.e., illusions, are incommensurate with Karain's enormous guilt. But that is not the point.

The charm works beautifully; Karain seems immediately "to step into the glorious splendor of his stage, to wrap himself in the illusion of unavoidable success." One cannot miss the resemblance to Jim, who, when given the ring by Stein, seems at once to wrap himself in a similar illusion. In both cases a charm lays certain ghosts to rest, and in both the gratuitous evil of illusions—dreams —is salved by their equally gratuitous benevolence. There is not really much difference between the two talismans, although it would appear that Stein's is a genuine sign of fidelity earned back in Patusan, while the sixpence is a joke. This is not the case, however, for the coin, despite its origin in guile, is ceremoniously given significance by the sheer will of Hollis and, finally, of the others.

The potency of both charms derives from the weight of human intention behind them; both are in themselves meaningless. The one may be slightly comic (the puffy old Queen setting this passionate heart at ease); but then there is a scene in *Lord Jim*, after Stein has tendered the ring, when even that charm becomes absurd.

[Jim] dropped his knife and fork (he had begun eating, or rather swallowing food, as it were, unconsciously), and began a search all round his plate. The ring! The ring! Where the devil . . .

Ah! Here it was. . . . He closed his big hand on it, and tried all his pockets one after another. Jove! wouldn't do to lose the thing. . . . Would hang the bally affair round his neck! And he proceeded to do this immediately, producing a string (which looked like a bit of cotton shoe-lace) for the purpose.

And so both Karain and Jim sally forth like a pair of Italian peasants, with slightly absurd (shoestring, piece of blue ribbon—it is all the same) yet potent charms hanging around their necks. Finally, Karain appears alone on shore, detached from the group of delighted natives as the schooner puts out to sea. This last resemblance to Jim (who stood alone as Marlow went out to sea, leaving Patusan) is perhaps enough to convince us that at least in certain mundane physical details Karain is one of Jim's literary relatives.

But the resemblance between the short story and the later novel is not, after all, based on such superficial matters. The deep-seated affinity of the two principal characters lies in the way each contributes to the main theme of illusion. Both are aided by a man who recognizes that dreams are "cured" with dreams. Stein and Hollis, despite apparently vast differences in age and attitude, are spiritual brothers, romantics (remember Hollis' box of charms, not unlike Stein's collection of butterflies) who unashamedly repair dreams with like dreams. Both are willing, in a way that the narrator of either story is not, to immerse themselves in the idiom of charms and amulets.

Hollis is a proto-Stein, an anticipation of the theme which is full-blown in the later character. He accepts the dream on its own terms, while both narrators instinctively measure it against some ideal of self-knowledge, against some sort of French Lieutenant. The last remark the narrator contributes in "Karain" is directed to Jackson, that blond fellow who has been too sympathetic to help. Jackson, just returned to England, says that somehow Karain and his story seem more real to him than the crush of prosaic life that surrounds both men as they stand talking in the street.

> "Yes; I see it," said Jackson slowly. "It is there; it pants, it runs, it rolls; it is strong and alive; it would smash you if you didn't look out; but I'll be hanged if it is yet as real to me as . . . as the other thing [illusion] . . . say, Karain's story".

The narrator replies, "I think that, decidedly, he had been too long away from home," meaning not necessarily that Jackson is wrong, but that it is dangerous to think as he does. The narrator, like Marlow, has a great fear of encountering the dream without measuring it. He cannot, like Hollis, adopt a purely empirical attitude, and so can never really help such people as Karain or Jim. Even Marlow, despite his efforts in Jim's behalf, can never offer the talismanic gesture (within the power of Stein) which will seem to Jim to be a real "opportunity." He and Jim are simply not vibrating on the same frequency.

In truth, the narrator of "Karain" and Marlow must continually separate illusion from "reality" because they are afraid of the consequences of not doing so. They cannot, even for a moment, play the game engaged in by Stein or Hollis—cannot, that is, therapeutically manipulate illusion. To them it is a continual life-and-death struggle; or, better, it is a matter of sanity. Hollis can acknowledge the potency of illusion, yet manipulate it without any qualms, not because he is immune but because, in Stein's famous image, he is "immersed," letting the "deep, deep sea keep [him] up." The Marlow-type duplicates Hollis' act only once, when Marlow lies at the end of *Heart of Darkness*. Otherwise, the Marlows of this world must always badger the truth lest through manipulating illusion they defile it and be consumed by it. In suggesting this important but by no means final step in Conrad's analysis of illusion, "Karain" ultimately resembles *Lord Jim* and thus finds its appropriate relation to the better stories and novels.

DONALD C. YELTON

Symbolic Imagery in *Lord Jim* †

Whether *Lord Jim*, as many Conradians have held from the time the author's work was completed, is Conrad's supreme achievement in the novel form, the fitting counterpart among his longer fictions to "Heart of Darkness," need not be argued here. The book has had its detractors, among them F R. Leavis, who consigned it to the second rank of the Conrad canon; and the writer has recently heard a critic and teacher of repute characterize the second half of the book as "all a muddle," the work of an author who had lost control of his material. This is a rather different thing from Arthur Symons' judgment, pronounced in the year of publication of the novel: "a model of intelligent disarray," [1] but both judgments suggest that *Lord Jim* is a work in the composition of which the author risked much—even to the final bafflement of sophisticated readers.

But whatever its rank among Conrad's other major novels (and it must, *pace* Leavis, be ranked among the greatest, which is to say that it constitutes one of the towering achievements of the modern

† This essay, composed especially for the Norton critical edition of *Lord Jim*, is derived in large part from the writer's *Mimesis and Metaphor: An Inquiry into the Genesis and Scope of Conrad's* *Symbolic Imagery*, Mouton & Co., The Hague, 1967, pp. 160–72; 223–36; 264–69.

1. Arthur Symons, *Dramatis Personae*, Indianapolis, 1923, p. 20.

English novel) it must always figure for originality of method as the most irreplaceable of the novels, a work the loss of which would most impair our view of Conrad as artistic pioneer and as liberator from traditional narrative conventions and formal constraints.

The structural involutions, the inversions of time sequence, the frequent effect of cinematic montage, the multiplication of posts of observation, and the immense development of the traditional device of the engaged narrator in which the formal originality of the book may be said largely to inhere have been widely noted and defined, and will not be examined in this essay. What Conrad's method in *Lord Jim* achieved, more conspicuously perhaps than in any of the other novels, was a fictional work of which, as an early critic (Edward Crankshaw) aptly put it, the parts are "bathed suggestively in the light of the whole." [2] Apart from the structural involutions themselves, and the inversions of time, this effect of saturation is in large degree the product of a density of figurative language, a proliferation of recurrent symbolic or thematic metaphor unexampled among Conrad's more extended writings, and exceeded only by the shorter fictions of the *Youth* volume, notably "Heart of Darkness." In Marlow Conrad found, among other valuable assets, the ideal vehicle for an image-making faculty of exceptionally great richness and diversity, with a scope that ranges from picturesque colloquialisms to metaphoric set-pieces rivaling those of Proust or Flaubert in extension and elaboration. From the time of the invention of Marlow at the turn of the century and throughout the period of his richest productivity, thematic imagery—simile and verbal metaphor in constant reciprocity of suggestive power with the objective images produced by the narrative episodes and the natural environment —remained one of Conrad's most characteristic and effective methods of communicating his imaginative vision. Grounded in an unfailing grasp of objective reality, in a sensory apparatus exceptionally well equipped to record the impressions of an objective world, that metaphoric vision, that image-making faculty, collaborates in *Lord Jim* with Marlow's unexampled colloquial and dialectic gifts to bring into constantly shifting focus the themes that obsessed Conrad when he imagined Jim's career and fate. What this study undertakes is a summary examination of the major strains of verbal metaphor in *Lord Jim* and the major natural images allied with them, in their implied relation to the psychological and moral issues dramatized in the novel.

In the zoological imagery and the animal references in *Lord Jim* we may see with peculiar clarity the sort of metaphoric saturation that characterized Conrad's imaginative processes. If we include the

2. Edward Crankshaw, *Joseph Conrad: Some Aspects of the Art of the Novel*, London, 1936, p. 173.

frank colloquialisms largely deprived by usage of their imaging function (but not for that reason shorn of their suggestive power, where the implicit suggestions are reinforced by the context) we find no fewer than eighty animal similes and metaphors; and these are augmented by a vocabulary that comprises several score of epithets and predicates originally, or characteristically, applied to animals, but in the novel applied—in many instances repeatedly—to human subjects or agents. The pervasive impression conveyed by metaphor is enforced by such epithets as "game," "prey," "spawn," "ass," "cattle," "cur," "hound, "hyaena," "insect," "owls," "puppy"; such modifiers as "fishy," "mulish," "shrewish," "wolfish"; such verbs as "bark," "bellow," "bleat," "cackle," "crow," "screech," "yap"—most of them to be found in the passages dealing with the crew of the *Patna*, but many recurring throughout the novel.

Indeed, having regard only to the figurative texture of the language, the succession of similes and the related vocabulary of epithet that clusters around them, one may confidently say that *Lord Jim* contains the most significant ensemble of animal images in Conrad's fiction, constituting as it were a sort of evoked bestiary of great range and diversity, in which as so often in Shakespeare are mirrored the acts and gestures of the human characters. Without attempting to catalogue the animal imagery in all its variety, I note an instance in which an animal simile serves, discreetly but unmistakably, as a *ficelle*, harkening back from Jim's final crisis, the encounter with Gentleman Brown, to the crisis that dominates the first half of the book, the leap from the *Patna*, enforcing at the level of suggestion the dramatic and psychological nexus between the two. In the forty-first chapter Brown identifies himself with "a rat in a trap"—a simile developed in dialogue with Jim and emerging finally in Brown's plea (as reported to Marlow): "I would have thought him too white to serve even a rat so." And the reader (if his imagination is engaged to the degree which, for a full response, the novel demands) recalls the formula with which, in Chapter Eighteen, Egström had expressed his bafflement at Jim's abrupt throwing up of his job as water-clerk:

> "What is it you're running away from?" I asks. "Who has been getting at you? What scared you? You haven't as much sense as a rat; they don't clear out from a good ship. . . . This business ain't going to sink," says I. He gave a big jump.

The implicit reference back to the abandonment of the *Patna*, to Jim's first leap, via the exchange with Egström, is unmistakable. It is a telling example of the seriousness of Conrad's engagement with the vocabulary and the imagery of his adopted language, his in-

stinct for "revitalizing clichés" (as Raymond Las Vergnas put it [3])
and reanimating the congealed metaphors of vulgar speech. For it is
largely through such verbal echoes that Jim's susceptibility to the
"sickening suggestion of common guilt" is made actual to the
reader.

Woven into the narrative tissue are episodes involving objective
animal life—the "yellow-dog" incident following the *Patna* inquiry, which occasions the first verbal communication between Marlow and Jim (Chapter Six); the devotion of Brierly's retriever; and
above all Stein's preserved specimens, his butterflies and beetles,
and the marvelously suggestive account (in the great central chapter
of the novel) of his capture of the most prized specimen of his
collection. To these episodes one may find in the texture of dialogue and descriptive prose correspondent figurative locutions pro-
longing and amplifying, as in an echo chamber, the suggestions
implicit in them, and receiving, in turn, an increment of energy
from the narrative episodes. Our recollection of Stein's butterflies
and beetles, our imaginative engagement with the literally inexhaustible imagery of that great twentieth chapter, lends intensity
to the later evocations of Jewel and her "tenderness" under the aspect of unfolding and fluttering wings; and it supplies a prospective
context for the insectile epithets to be applied to Jewel's father,
Cornelius, whom Marlow first introduces to his auditors under his
emblematic sign, with "slow laborious walk resembling the creeping of a repulsive beetle, the legs alone moving with horrid industry
while the body glided evenly." The yellow-dog episode, though we
may see it as one of Conrad's strokes of purely novelistic resourcefulness, admirably contrived to open communication between the
two central characters in circumstances revelatory of Jim's temperament and the defensive-aggressive stance it dictates ("Who's a cur
now—hey?") lends resonance to Jim's later evocation of the captain
and chief engineer in the boat, "yapping before me like a couple of
mean mongrels at a tree'd thief."

The Stein of Chapter Twenty, who serves the plot as a sort of
deus, or demi-deus, ex machina, and in whom, with his oracular utterance and his talisman ring, Elliott Gose has seen a faithful
presentment of Jung's archetype of the "wise old man," [4] is the
most complicated of those prismatic human "lenses" which make
of *Lord Jim*, more markedly than any other of Conrad's fictions, a
sort of great composite eye through the facets of which Marlow,
and after him Conrad's readers, successively focus upon the aspects
of Jim and his clouded "case." But if Stein is a lens, it is not

3. Raymond Las Vergnas, *Joseph Conrad: Romancier de l'exil*, Lyon, 1959,
pp. 15f.
4. Elliott B. Gose, Jr., "Pure Exercise
of Imagination: Archetypal Symbolism
in *Lord Jim*," *PMLA*, LXXIX (March
1964), 137–47. The passage referred to
is found on p. 143.

through his words only that our vision is refracted. We make what we can of his diagnosis of Jim's case and of his prescription for it. His words—apart from the directness of his assertion that Jim is "romantic" (a condition at once rendered ambiguous by Stein's characterization of it as "very bad"—and "very good, too")—are elliptical, metaphoric, designedly allusive in the way they enshrine in that famous image of the human condition ("A man that is born falls into a dream like a man who falls into the sea") an oblique reference to the particularity of Jim's destiny, designedly elusive in the equally celebrated prescription for Jim's case, the answer to the question "How to be?": "In the destructive element immerse." The passage containing that image is one of the great passages in all of Conrad's fiction; but its appeal, which is ineluctable, is largely to the imagination rather than to the discursive understanding. And behind the imaginative appeal of Stein's pronouncements on man's destiny and conduct are the images of Stein himself in colloquy with Marlow on their candlelighted passage through the shifting half lights of his chambers, of Stein with his legendary history and his collector's passion and of the creatures to which his passion attaches—a passion that furnishes the substance of the final sentence of the novel.

Admitted to Stein's house, Marlow finds his friend rapt in contemplation of a butterfly of exceptional splendor and rarity; in the intensity of his absorption we recognize (it is, I think, the first thing we see) the model of Marlow's absorption in his human specimen. So far, indeed, Conrad takes us by the hand as though solicitous that sluggish imaginations shall not fail to make the connection:

> "The work," he began, suddenly, pointing to the scattered slips, and in his usual gentle and cheery tone, "is making great progress. I have been this rare specimen describing . . . Na! And what is your good news?"
>
> "To tell you the truth, Stein," I said with an effort that surprised me, "I came here to describe a specimen . . ."
>
> "Butterfly?" he asked, with an unbelieving and humorous eagerness.
>
> "Nothing so perfect," I answered, feeling suddenly dispirited with all sorts of doubts. "A man!"

Possession of the butterfly is for Stein the fulfillment of an ideal aspiration, a thing dreamed of at the very height of prosperity and good fortune. His own long-delayed success is commentary upon his prescription for Jim: "That was the way. To follow the dream, and again to follow the dream—and so—*ewig—usque ad finem.* . . ." And we feel too, in his account of the events surrounding his discovery and capture of the butterfly (following an ambush foiled by his instinctive resourcefulness and intrepidity), a hint of the exigencies that surround Jim's own pursuit of the dream, even a "foreshadowing"—in a peculiarly literal sense, since Stein's first awareness of the creature's presence is his glimpse of its shadow crossing the face of one of his dead assailants—of the fatal outcome of Jim's quest.

Praising Conrad's psychological acumen (which he likened to Dostoevsky's), Edwin Muir distinguished between the two by declaring of Conrad that "the soul he has not tried to know at all." [5] In speaking of Jim's pursuit of "the dream" we remain safely within the limits of Stein's (and Conrad's) vocabulary and run no risk of fetching too far the metaphor of Stein's pursuit and capture of his butterfly. The "dream" we are free to construe as whatever mode of self-realization we choose—self-knowledge, or self-fulfillment, or at a lower level mere self-vindication. We need not move outside the universe of Stein's and Conrad's discourse, or ask whether we are to see in Stein's gorgeous quarry, winged and radiant as Psyche was imaged by the Greeks, with its color and markings enduring in death, a latent image of the human soul; but if we follow the indications of the text, taking Stein's butterfly (captured, as we recall, on a "heap of dirt") as figuring the object of "the dream," that object, whether we call it self or soul, is seen *sub specie aeternitatis.* This, at any rate, is what I derive from Marlow's account of how, in his colloquy with Stein, he contained his impatience to broach the subject of Jim out of respect for

> the intense, almost passionate, absorption with which he looked at a butterfly, as though on the bronze sheen of these frail wings, in the white tracings, in the gorgeous markings, he could see other things, an image of something as perishable and defying destruction as these delicate and lifeless tissues displaying a splendour unmarred by death.

Did Conrad recall when he conceived this scene that Psyche of the butterfly wings was, in some versions of her legend, imaged as the butterfly itself? It would, after all, make the imagery neither more nor less evocative if we knew the answer; nor if we knew whether, in contraposing to the butterflies the beetles that complement them in Stein's collection—"horrible miniature monsters, looking malevolent in death and immobility"—he intended an image of another and darker aspect of the soul, the "shadow" side, the aspect Plato imaged in the dark steed of the *Phaedrus,* which Marlow hinted at when he spoke of "the infernal alloy in [Jim's] metal" and which he identified in another image when he remarked of Jim that

5. Edwin Muir, *Latitudes,* New York, 1924, p. 48.

he appealed to all sides at once—to the side turned perpetually to the light of day, and to that side of us which, like the other hemisphere of the moon, exists stealthily in perpetual darkness, with only a fearful ashy light falling at times on the edge.

The imagery is there, with its freight of inexhaustible suggestion; and we are not obliged, as in Yeats's dialogue, to discriminate between self and soul, setting them over against one another. Whether Jim did or did not fulfill himself or attain to self-knowledge (as some critics pose the question of his destiny), and whether in doing or failing to do these things he saved or lost his "soul" (if we postulate such an entity as an object of Conrad's concern), are questions for our value judgment. The imagery cannot answer them for us or even define with semantic precision the terms of the questions; it can only help to make them momentous. "In virtue of his feeling he mattered," Marlow says of Jim; and by virtue of the total feeling-response that Jim's fictive destiny aroused in his creator, and that he communicates to his reader in large part through the ramifying suggestions of his symbolic imagery, Jim's destiny matters so intensely to us.

Animal imagery is, then, one of the dominant rhetorical and symbolic modes of the novel, and this imagery (though in the case of Stein's preserved specimens not wanting in metaphysical suggestions) serves—together with the wealth of sensory imagery ("to make you *see*") that from first to last characterizes Conradian impressionism—to anchor in a palpable element a system of metaphor that is, in the ensemble, one of the most disquieting in any major work of English fiction. For it is with the figure of Marlow—adventurer in the realm of shades, voyager to the interior of continents, of islands, of the human psyche, his own or another's—that Conrad's imagery assumes, in *Lord Jim* and the slightly earlier "Heart of Darkness," that definitive inward-looking bent, that preoccupation with what I should call *expressionistic* metaphor—with the spectral, with the themes of enchantment, of haunting and exorcism, with the abyss, and with cosmic and meteorological manifestations, with their constant interplay of light and dark—which constitutes one of the most characteristic Conradian perspectives on the human situation.

The motif of spectral haunting is first sounded impersonally in an image that suggests an amplified echo of a familiar Coleridgean line: the glimpse of the *Patna*'s wake "like the phantom of a track drawn upon a lifeless sea by the phantom of a steamer." It is sustained by the evocation of the audience at the inquiry as "staring shadows" and the "court peons" flitting "as noiseless as ghosts," of the chief engineer in flight from the inquiry haunted by his "spectral alarms," of Jim, after judgment has been pronounced, as one who "lived surrounded by deceitful ghosts, by austere shades." It achieves a sinister intensity in Marlow's suggestion that the *Patna* had been crippled by "a kind of maritime ghoul on the prowl to kill ships in the dark." As Dorothy Van Ghent first noted, the Marlovian elaboration of this metaphor, with references to "wandering corpses," sinister gales like "vampires," and "aimless . . . devilry," bringing home the implication of possession by "dark powers" latent in the motif of haunting by specter or shade, suggests unmistakably a symbolic identification between the "maritime ghoul" and some dangerous unassimilated portion of Jim's psyche. The mortuary imagery itself (one of the most persistent strains of Conradian metaphor) is ordinarily assimilated to this dominant theme of spectral haunting or malevolent enchantment, as in Marlow's assertion that he "listened [to Jim's account of the abandonment of the *Patna*] as if to a tale of black magic at work upon a corpse," or his statement that "the corpse of his [Brown's] mad self-love uprose from rags and destitution as from the dark horrors of a tomb," or (toward the beginning of the book) his first formulation of his reaction to "the facts" of the *Patna* affair, following Jim's first appearance before the board of inquiry, when he tells his audience that "they made a whole that had features, shades of expression, a complicated aspect that could be remembered by the eye, and something else besides, something invisible, a directing spirit of perdition that dwelt within, like a malevolent soul in a detestable body."

Recurrently applied to Jim—in metaphors that identify him with the specter or apparition or, alternatively, that show him as accompanied by, or grappling with, the specters of imagination and introspection—this vein of imagery culminates in Marlow's account of his interview with Jewel (when he "stood up, like an evoked ghost, to answer for Jim's eternal constancy") in which Marlow conjures up a tableau of two Vergilian shades beside a river "as black as Styx," in colloquy concerning an absent brother shade ("my brother from the realm of forgetful shades"). It links with the cosmic imagery in the repeated presentment of the moon floating up from between the twin peaks of Patusan (Jim's lunar "spectacle") "like an ascending spirit out of a grave." And the vein emerges at the end, in company with the related images of Jim's enveloping cloud and his opportunity "veiled like an Eastern bride," in that final recapitulation of metaphoric themes with which Marlow wraps up his narrative:

> and yet upon my honour there are moments, too, when he passes from my eyes like a disembodied spirit astray amongst the passions of this earth, ready to surrender himself faithfully to the claim of his own world of shades.

There is a continuous vein of imagery, evidenced rarely in extended simile, more often in concise metaphor and a sort of recurrent saturation of the diction, which sounds the tonic metaphoric chord of "the abyss," as though preluding or echoing the basic trope supplied to Marlow by Jim's own tormented eloquence when he defines the terminus of his jump from the *Patna* as "an everlasting deep hole." Around this as node Marlow's evocations of the abyss vibrate. The word "abyss" itself is the nuclear term in no fewer than six similes and metaphors dispersed throughout the *Patna* and into the Patusan chapters, of which the first two belong to the preliminaries of the novel, prior to the *Patna*'s collision: "an abyss of unrest" (defining Jim's state after his injury by a falling spar on an eastward passage), "the days . . . as if falling into an abyss forever open in the wake of the ship." The others follow: the squall over the crippled *Patna* "confounds sea and sky into one abyss of obscurity"; the crew of a ship that fails you is like "the souls of men floating on an abyss"; the world of the living is as if "surrounded by an abyss full of flames"; light falls on the forested landscape of Patusan "as if into an abyss." Throughout his recital Marlow finds other formulas to evoke the image: "the brow of yawning destruction," "the brink of annihilation," "a chasm without bottom," "the depths of a crystalline void," "a jump into the unknown," "the bottom of an immensely deep well." One might continue, citing "indefinite immensities," "indefinite open spaces," "the dread of the unknown depths," but the examples cited are sufficient to suggest that in this vein of imagery we have what may be taken as a series of overtones on a tonic chord, or metaphoric elaborations of a central theme—the theme of a man who, having jumped into "an everlasting deep hole," tries to get out, refuses the abyss.

The close relation between cosmic and meteorological imagery in the novel is typified by the final sentence in the paragraph of description devoted to the dining room of Malabar House, scene of Marlow's first extended colloquy with Jim (Chapter Seven):

> The riding lights of ships winked afar like setting stars, and the hills across the roadstead resembled rounded black masses of arrested thunder-clouds.

This, no doubt, is a fragment of pure impressionism; but elsewhere imagery of cloud and related meteorological phenomena, invoked to register the succession of Jim's moods, his inner weather ("You know," Marlow remarks, "that sailor habit of referring to the weather in every connection"), is employed with unmistakably symbolic intent. Marlow's phrase, "under a cloud," repeated throughout the second half of the book with characteristic Marlovian iteration and recurring at the very end, is the emblematic image here; it is in the *Patna* chapters, however, that we find this imagery most arrestingly employed for purposes of characterization—or perhaps one had better say for the purpose of evoking an interior landscape. Of the more imposing of these images, the first registers Marlow's impression of Jim on their first encounter (the "yellow-dog" episode):

> to watch his face was like watching a darkening sky before a clap of thunder, shade upon shade imperceptibly coming on, the gloom growing mysteriously intense in the calm of maturing violence.

The second records Jim's expression as he recalls the moments in the boat following his jump:

> The muscle round his lips contracted into an unconscious grimace that tore through the mask of his usual expression—something violent, short-lived, and illuminating like a twist of lightning that admits the eye for an instant into the secret convolutions of a cloud.

The third expresses Marlow's intuition of Jim at a later point of his recital:

> He heard me out with his head on one side, and I had another glimpse through a rent in the mist in which he moved and had his being.

The "cosmic image"—understood as a variant of a basic trope in which a fragment of human reality is suddenly envisaged within a framework of cosmic events—is recurrent in Conrad, not so much a device of style as an ineluctable modality of his vision of the human, as it was with the Elizabethan dramatists. The image of ship as planet, first evoked in the early pages of *The Nigger of the "Narcissus"* ("The ship, a fragment detached from the earth, went on lonely and swift like a small planet") and re-evoked twenty years later in *The Shadow-Line* ("My command might have been a planet flying vertiginously on its appointed path in a space of infinite silence"), may be taken as the type-image, symbolizing the cosmic perspectives evoked in related metaphors in perhaps a dozen novels and stories. It is in *Lord Jim*, however, that such imagery is most insistent and most unmistakably symbolic. The planetary image applied to the *Patna* sounds the first note of this metaphoric *sostenuto* which, in a sort of canonic relation to the meteorological imagery, will continue to sound throughout the novel:

The ship moved so smoothly that her onward motion was imperceptible to the senses of men, as though she had been a crowded planet speeding through the dark spaces of ether behind the swarms of suns, in the appalling and calm solitudes awaiting the breath of future creations.

Cosmic imagery, closely allied to the abyssal imagery, is most insistent and impressive in those pages of Chapter Ten in which Marlow distills Jim's recital of the night in the boat following the abandonment of the *Patna*—notably in Jim's final apocalyptic glimpse of the ship's yellow masthead light, "high up and blurred like a last star ready to dissolve," and in the counterimage of the sunrise on the following morning: "the tremble of a vast ripple running over all the visible expanse of the sea, as if the waters had shuddered, giving birth to the globe of light"—an image that, upon successive readings of the novel, figures also as a counterpart to that dominant image of the Patusan chapters of the moon floating up from the cleft peak "like an ascending spirit out of a grave."

This image of the ascending moon, repeatedly rebounding from the cleft of the two-headed mountain, constitutes one of the most imposing natural symbols in Conrad's entire work and one of the most inexhaustible in its implications. Conrad, doubtful of the novel's unity of conception, of the cohesion between the two halves (since *Lord Jim*, like others among his major novels, had grown to its final proportions from an original conception that was much more modest, a short story only), lamented in a characteristically desperate letter to Garnett the "want of illuminating imagination" in the book, adding that he had "wanted to obtain a sort of lurid light out [of] the very events." But in the image of that rebounding moon his imagination kindled a light that, as the criticism of the past decade or so amply testifies, has not failed to enlist the responsive imaginations of his readers.

The unnamed mountain that furnishes the setting for the repeated spectacle is one of a number of topographic features in Conrad's work—one thinks especially of Higuerota in *Nostromo*, of Koh-Ring in "The Secret Sharer" and the later *Shadow-Line*—which, with varying practical significance, suggest a symbolic function, more or less definable. The cleft peak (or twin peaks; Conrad's equivocation is perhaps deliberate) is the scene of a significant action in the campaign of pacification that marks Jim's rise to predominancy in the affairs of Patusan; symbolically it seems to figure the split in Jim's consciousness between dream and reality, the ideal and the actual—perhaps also the corresponding cleavage effected in his life by his leap from the *Patna* and his subsequent jump from the stockade into the affairs of Patusan.

But the mountain—of which John Dozier Gordan found an exemplar in the Rajah Brooke literature,[6] and Miss Jerry Allen in a piece of the Bornean hinterland visited by Conrad the mariner [7] —is chiefly memorable for providing the setting for the recurrent spectacular rising of the moon, a phenomenon in which Jim takes pride "as though he had had a hand in regulating that unique spectacle."

The spectacle is first described by Marlow at the time of our first introduction to Jim's realm (Chapter Twenty-One) :

> On the third day after the full, the moon, as seen from the open space in front of Jim's house (he had a very fine house in the native style when I visited him), rose exactly behind these hills, its diffused light at first throwing the two masses into intensely black relief, and then the nearly perfect disc, glowing ruddily, floated away above the summits. "Wonderful effect," said Jim by my side. "Worth seeing. Is it not?"
>
> And this question was put with a note of personal pride that made me smile, as though he had had a hand in regulating that unique spectacle. He had regulated so many things in Patusan! Things that would have appeared as much beyond his control as the motions of the moon and the stars.

The reprise of the spectacle occurs in Chapter Thirty-Four, on the last night of Marlow's final visit to Patusan, and it has, by virtue of its different context, a different emotional tonality. It coincides with Marlow's reflection that "nothing on earth seemed less real now than [Jim's] plans, his energy, and his enthusiasm."

> It threw its level rays afar as if from a cavern, and in this mournful eclipse-like light the stumps of felled trees uprose very dark, the heavy shadows fell at my feet on all sides, my own moving shadow, and across my path the shadow of the solitary grave perpetually garlanded with flowers.

The two following sentences, which close the paragraph—the first evoking a realm of the dead, the second likening the lumps of white coral that shine around the dark mound of the grave (it is the grave of Jewel's mother) to "a chaplet of bleached skulls"—compound the disquieting impression, reflexively modifying our impression of the earlier image.

Dorothy Van Ghent, in her admirable chapter on *Lord Jim* in *The English Novel: Form and Function*, proposed that we see in the recurrent image of moonlight "a figure of the ego-ideal," with "its illusionariness, and the solitude implied by illusion"; and Albert Guerard in his *Conrad the Novelist* has developed this view,

6. John Dozier Gordan, *Joseph Conrad: The Making of a Novelist*, Cambridge, Mass., 1940, p. 66

7. Jerry Allen, "Conrad's River," *Columbia University Forum*, V (Winter 1962), 29–35.

persuasively and at length, citing Marlow's characterization of moonlight as "the ghost of dead sunlight," related to the sunshine ("which—say what you like—is all we have to live by") as the echo to the sound, misleading and confusing, giving "a sinister reality to shadows alone." "The moonlight of Patusan," Mr. Guerard has written, "is certainly associated with immobility and isolation, and with times when Jim is seriously entranced by his pride and illusions of success."

That this view accounts, in part, for Conrad's intention, or at any rate describes his achievement, in mounting his lunar spectacle would seem to be irrefragable. Marlow's reflections on the opposed qualities of moonlight and sunlight must be assumed to be relevant to his creator's intention. Certainly "isolation" and "pride" define to a degree Jim's posture throughout the book; moreover the passage illuminated by the second of the moonrises is portentous of Jim's final immobility in the face of catastrophe. But suggestive and valuable though these formulas are, when we turn back to the texts in question and their surrounding contexts we find, I think (as always in dealing with works of the order of symbolic complexity that Conrad achieved in *Lord Jim*), that some of the suggestive power of the symbol escapes from between the meshes of the finest-drawn critical formula. In an analytical vein, we might ask, for example, whether at the time of Marlow's first visit and of his first account of the moonrise we can—unless we are to think of Jim as an "unmoved mover"—properly refer the entranced immobility of the scene to the ascendant warrior and administrator of this period; or whether, if Jim is indeed entranced by pride and by illusions of success, he is more conspicuously so—or more isolated—under that first moonrise than in the closing paragraph of Chapter Twenty-One, following his account of the reduction of Sherif Ali's "impregnable" camp, when he stands with Marlow "high in the sunshine on the top of that historic hill of his," a "symbolic" figure dominating "the forest, the secular gloom, the old mankind" as though "set up on a pedestal, to represent in his persistent youth the power, and perhaps the virtues, of races that never grow old, that have emerged from the gloom." More importantly, however, we must ask whether the view of Jim's lunar spectacle briefly identified above does, in fact, account for all aspects of the phenomenon as Conrad presents it.

In the end, one can, in such matters, do no more than testify to one's own response, and other than stating the foregoing reservations with respect to the views just cited, I want only to point to an aspect of Jim's lunar spectacle not emphasized by Mrs. Van Ghent or Mr. Guerard—what I should call the kinesthetics of the image

—which for me constitutes an inescapable part of its suggestive power, enforcing a modification of views which concentrate solely upon the metaphysical essence of moon as opposed to sun.

If we identify the moonlight of Patusan with Jim's illusion, his commitment to an illusory "dream," an illusory ideal of self, we still do not remove the imagery from the nexus of "psycho-moral ambiguity" (Mr. Guerard's term) in which the entire novel is involved—it cannot resolve for us the Nietzschean question of the value and necessity of life-illusions which the novel may be said, in one of its aspects, to pose, or the Steinian paradox of a romanticism that is "very bad" and yet "very good, too." To take it in this sense as implying, unqualifiedly, an adverse judgment upon Jim and his destiny would require that we abstract out of the total impression conveyed by the image the repeated notation of a triumphant rise from depths: "as if escaping from a yawning grave in gentle triumph"; "like an ascending spirit out of a grave"; "its ascending movement was like a leisurely rebound." These indications are, or should be, inextricably implicated in our response to the images in question: the kinesthetics of the scene are part of the "wonderful effect," no less relevant than any symbolic properties with which we invest the moon and its spectral light, and more relevant than any associated chaplets of bleached skulls or other images of death, in which we may see simply a foreshadowing. I do not want to insist unduly on what seems to me obvious; but it may be useful to the reader to evoke for himself Jim's spectacle in reverse, and to dwell on the different affective response elicited by a recurrent setting or dropping of the moon into that yawning gravelike chasm. No doubt a resourceful criticism might discover a symbolic fitness in a spectacle so arranged, but it is not the spectacle arranged for Jim by his creator—and I think we may take it that in this instance Conrad (as he liked to declare to his correspondents) "knew what he wanted to do," even though the intention may only have been consciously formulated subsequent to the conception. That soaring flight from chasm or yawning grave appears to me to be an unmistakable countersymbolism to the repeated imagery of the abyss in the earlier part of the book, as resumed in Jim's phrase, "an everlasting deep hole," and in Brierly's prescription, "Let him creep twenty feet underground and stay there."

Jim's lunar spectacle is then, a true "insight symbol," unmistakably involved with the "psycho-moral" issues of the novel, inciting to perspectives on them, but to diverse perspectives as we view it from diverse angles of vision—endlessly suggestive, but finally unamenable to any univocal interpretative device. The symbol, as Ernst Cassirer remarked, "harbors the curse of mediacy; it is bound to obscure what it seeks to reveal"; [8] and if we believe with Coleridge and Goethe that it is characteristically produced in partial unconsciousness, or with only a tardy awareness, of its symbolic function, we might add that it sometimes, in compensation, reveals more than it actively seeks to reveal. Its "curse," however, is the secret of its fascination, and something is always risked when we attempt to render it immediately available to the discursive understanding. The moon of Patusan is a questionable shape, ascending in triumph, but shedding a questionable light and casting questionable shadows. In questioning it we need not look for unambiguous answers; indeed, we may well conclude that its peculiar fitness within its narrative context is precisely its final and irreducible ambiguity.

8. Ernst Cassirer, *Language and Myth,* New York, n.d., p. 7.

SELECTED BIBLIOGRAPHY

A great deal has been written about Joseph Conrad and *Lord Jim*, particularly in the last twenty years. Maurice Beebe's usefully organized "Criticism of Joseph Conrad: A Selected Checklist," *Modern Fiction Studies*, X (Spring 1964), 81–106, contains toward two hundred general titles and one hundred having to do with *Lord Jim*. An earlier bibliography includes reviews, unpublished dissertations, and books and articles not in English: Kenneth A. Lohf and Eugene P. Sheehy, *Joseph Conrad at Mid-Century: Editions and Studies, 1896–1955*, Minneapolis, 1957.

The works listed below, except for a few biographical and general studies, deal directly with *Lord Jim* and should be of special interest to students of the novel.

Allen, Jerry. *The Sea Years of Joseph Conrad*, Garden City, New York, 1965.

Aubry, G. Jean. *The Life and Letters of Joseph Conrad*, 2 vols., Garden City, New York, 1927.

Baines, Jocelyn. *Joseph Conrad: A Critical Biography*, New York, 1960. Reprinted 1967.

Bradbrook, M. C. *Joseph Conrad: Poland's English Genius*, Cambridge, 1942.

Crews, Frederick. "The Power of Darkness," *Partisan Review*, XXXIV (Fall 1967), 507–525.

Flamm, Dudley, "The Ambiguous Nazarene in *Lord Jim*." *English Literature in Transition*, XI, No. 1 (1968), 35–37.

Fleishman, Avrom. *Conrad's Politics*, Baltimore, 1967.

Ford, Ford Madox. *Joseph Conrad: A Personal Remembrance*, Boston, 1924.

Fraser, G. S. "*Lord Jim*: The Romance of Irony," *Critical Quarterly*, VIII (Autumn 1966), 231–241.

Gordan, John D. *Joseph Conrad: The Making of a Novelist*, Cambridge, Mass., 1940. Reprinted 1966.

Gose, Elliott B., Jr. "Pure Exercise of Imagination: Archetypal Symbolism in *Lord Jim*," *PMLA*, LXXIX (March 1964), 137–147.

Guerard, Albert J. *Joseph Conrad*, New York, 1947.

Haugh, Robert F. "The Structure of *Lord Jim*," *College English*, XIII (Dec. 1951), 137–141.

Hay, Eloise Knapp. *The Political Novels of Joseph Conrad*, Chicago, 1963.

Heilman, Robert B. "Introduction," Rinehart edition of *Lord Jim*, New York, 1957.

Hewitt, Douglas. *Conrad: A Reassessment*, Cambridge, 1952.

Hodges, Robert. *The Dual Heritage of Joseph Conrad*, The Hague, 1967.

Leavis, F. R. *The Great Tradition*, London, 1948. Reprinted 1954.

Meyer, Bernard C. *Joseph Conrad: A Psychoanalytic Biography*, Princeton, 1967.

Moore, Carlisle. "Conrad and the Novel as Ordeal," *Philological Quarterly*, XLII (Jan. 1963), 55–74.

Moser, Thomas. *Joseph Conrad: Achievement and Decline*, Cambridge, Mass., 1957. Reprinted 1967.

Najder, Zladislaw. *Conrad's Polish Background*, London, 1964.

Rosenfield, Claire. *Paradise of Snakes: An Archetypal Analysis of Conrad's Political Novels*, Chicago, 1967.

Sherry, Norman. *Conrad's Eastern World*, Cambridge, 1966.

Stallman, Robert W., ed., *Joseph Conrad: A Critical Symposium*, East Lansing, 1960.

Stegner, Wallace. "Variations on a Theme by Conrad," *Yale Review*, XXXIX (March 1950), 512–523.

Tanner, Tony. *Conrad: Lord Jim*, Great Neck, N.Y., 1963.

Watt, Ian. "Joseph Conrad: Alienation and Commitment," in *The English Mind*, ed. Hugh Sykes Davies and George Watson, Cambridge, 1964, pp. 257–278.

Whiting, George W. "Conrad's Revision of Lord Jim," *English Journal,* XXIII (Dec. 1934), 824–832.
Wiley, Paul L. *Conrad's Measure of Man,* Madison, 1954.
Wright, Walter F., ed., *Joseph Conrad on Fiction,* Lincoln, 1964.
Zabel, Morton D. "Introduction," Riverside Edition of *Lord Jim,* Boston, 1958.